SET THIS
HOUSE
IN ORDER

SET THIS HOUSE IN ORDER

A Romance of Souls

MATT RUFF

HarperCollins*Publishers*

HarperCollins books may be purchased for educational, business, or sales pro-motional use. For information, please write: Special Markets Department, HarperCollins Publishers Inc., 10 East 53rd Street, New York, NY 10022.

FIRST EDITION

Designed by Joseph Rutt

Printed on acid-free paper

Library of Congress Cataloging-in-Publication Data is available upon request.

ISBN 0-06-019562-2

03 04 05 06 07 ❖/RRD 10 9 8 7 6 5 4 3 2 1

For Michael, Daniel, J.D., Scooter, and the rest of the gang

I am all the daughters of my father's house, and all the brothers too . . .

—*William Shakespeare,* Twelfth Night

SET THIS
HOUSE
IN ORDER

My father called me out.

I was twenty-six years old when I first came out of the lake, which puzzles some people, who wonder how I could have an age without having a past. But I get puzzled, too: most people I know can't remember being born, and what's more, it doesn't bother them that they can't remember. My good friend Julie Sivik once told me that her earliest memory was a scene from her second-birthday party, when she stood on a chair to blow out the candles on her cake. It's all a blank before that, she said, but she didn't seem upset by it, as if it were the most natural thing in the world to be missing two years of her life.

I remember everything, from the first moment: the sound of my name in the dark; the shock of the water; the tangle of the weeds at the bottom of the lake where I opened my eyes. The water is black down there, but I could see sunlight on the surface far above me, and I floated towards it, drawn up by my father's voice.

My father waited for me on the lakebank with Adam and Jake and Aunt Sam. Behind them stood the house, with Seferis up in the pulpit keeping an eye on the body; and from the windows overlooking the lake, and from the edges of the forest, I could feel the others watching me, too shy to show themselves. Gideon must have been watching too, from Coventry, but I didn't know about him then.

I suppose I should explain about the house. Aunt Sam says that a good storyteller only reveals important information a little at a time, to keep the audience interested, but I'm afraid if I don't explain it all now you'll get confused, which is worse than not being interested. So just bear with me, and I promise to try not to bore you later.

The house, along with the lake, the forest, and Coventry, are all in Andy

Gage's head, or what would have been Andy Gage's head if he had lived. Andy Gage was born in 1965 and murdered not long after by his stepfather, a very evil man named Horace Rollins. It was no ordinary murder: though the torture and abuse that killed him were real, Andy Gage's death wasn't. Only his soul actually died, and when it died, it broke in pieces. Then the pieces became souls in their own right, coinheritors of Andy Gage's life.

There was no house back then, just a dark room in Andy Gage's head where the souls all lived. In the center of the room was a column of bright light, and any soul that entered or was pulled into the light found itself outside, in Andy Gage's body, with no memory of how it had gotten there or what had happened since the last time it was out. As you can imagine, this was a frightening and terrible existence, made more terrible by the continuing depredations of the stepfather. Of the seven original souls who descended from Andy Gage, five were later murdered themselves, broken into still more pieces, and even the two survivors were forced to splinter in order to cope. By the time they got free of Horace Rollins, there were over a hundred souls in Andy Gage's head.

That was when the real struggle began. Over many years, the two surviving original souls—Aaron, who is my father, and Gideon, my father's brother—pieced together enough of a sense of continuity to figure out what had happened to them. With the help of a good doctor named Danielle Grey, my father worked to establish order. In place of the dark room, he constructed a geography in Andy Gage's head, a sunlit countryside where the souls could see and talk to one another. He created the house, so they'd have a place to live; the forest, so they'd have somewhere to be alone; and the pumpkin field, so the dead could be decently buried. Gideon, who was selfish, wanted no part of any of this, and did everything he could to wreck the geography, until my father was forced to exile him to Coventry.

The effort required to complete the house exhausted my father, and left him with little enthusiasm for dealing with the outside world. But somebody had to run the body; and so, on the day the last shingle was nailed in place, my father went down to the lake and called my name.

Something else that puzzles me about other people is that a lot of them don't know their purpose in life. This usually does bother them—more than not being able to remember being born, anyway—but I can't even imagine it. Part of knowing who I am is knowing why I am, and I've always known who I am, from the first moment.

My name is Andrew Gage. I was twenty-six years old when I first came out of the lake. I was born with my father's strength, but not his weariness; his persistence, but not his pain. I was called to finish the job that my father had begun: a job that he had chosen, but that I was made for.

I

EQUILIBRIUM

FIRST BOOK:
ANDREW

1

I met Penny Driver two months after my twenty-eighth birthday—or two months after my second birthday, depending on how you want to count it.

Jake was up first that morning, as he is most mornings, barreling out of his room around sunrise, thundering down the stairs to the common room, the clamor of his progress setting off a chain reaction of wakings among the other souls in the house. Jake is five years old, and has been since 1973, when he was born from the wreckage of a dead soul named Jacob; he is a *mature* five, but still basically a little kid, and not very good about respecting other people's need for quiet.

Jake's stomping roused Aunt Sam, who started up cursing; and Aunt Sam's cursing woke Adam, who has the room next to hers; and Adam, who *is* old enough to respect other people's need for quiet, but often chooses not to, let out a series of war whoops until my father banged on the wall and told him to knock it off. By then, everyone was awake.

I might have tried to ignore it. Unlike the others, I don't sleep in the house, I sleep in the body, and when you're in the body, even the loudest house-noises are just echoes in Andy Gage's head that can be tuned out at will—unless they come from the pulpit. But Adam knows this, of course, and whenever I do try to oversleep, he's out on the pulpit in no time, crowing like a rooster until I take the hint. Some days I make him crow himself hoarse, just to remind him who's boss; but on this particular morning, my eyes were open as soon as Jake hit the stairs.

The room where I slept—where the body slept—was in a renovated Victorian in Autumn Creek, Washington, twenty-five miles east of Seattle. The Victorian belonged to Mrs. Alice Winslow, who had first taken my father on as a boarder back in 1992, before I even existed.

We rented part of the first floor. The space was large but cluttered, clut-

ter being an inevitable side effect of multiplicity, even if you make an effort
to keep real-world possessions to a minimum. Just lying there in bed, and
without even turning my head, I could see: Aunt Sam's easel, brushes, and
paints, and two blank canvases; Adam's skateboard; Jake's stuffed panda;
Seferis's kendo sword; my books; my father's books; Jake's little shelf of
books; Adam's *Playboy* collection; Aunt Sam's stack of art prints; a color television with remote that used to be my father's but now belonged to me; a
VCR that was three-fifths mine, three-tenths Adam's, and one-tenth Jake's
(long story); a CD player that was one-half mine, one-quarter my father's,
one-eighth Aunt Sam's, and one-sixteenth apiece Adam's and Jake's (longer
story); a rack of CDs and videotapes of various ownerships; and a wheeled
hamper of dirty clothes that no one wanted to lay claim to, but was mostly
mine.

That's what I could see without even looking around; and besides the
bedroom, there was a sitting room, a big walk-in closet, a full bathroom that
was full in more ways than one, and the kitchen that we shared with Mrs.
Winslow. The kitchen wasn't so cluttered, though; Mrs. Winslow cooked
most of our meals for us, and strictly limited our personal food storage to
one shelf in the refrigerator and two shelves in the pantry.

I got us out of bed and into the bathroom to start the morning ritual.
Teeth came first. Jake really enjoys brushing for some reason, so I let him do
it, stepping back into the pulpit and giving him the body. I stayed alert. Jake,
as I've mentioned, is a child; but Andy Gage's body is adult and five-foot-
seven, and hangs on Jake's soul like a suit of clothes many sizes too big. He
moves clumsily in it, and often misjudges the distance between his extremi-
ties and the rest of the world; and as we've only got the one skull between us,
if he bends over to get a dropped toothpaste cap and bashes his head on the
corner of the sink, it is a group tragedy. So I kept a close eye on him.

This morning there were no accidents. He did his usual thorough job of
brushing: side to side, up and down, getting every tooth, even the tricky
ones in back. I wish he could handle the flossing as well, but that's a little
too dexterous for him.

I took the body back and had a quick squat on the toilet. This is my job
most mornings, though my father occasionally asks to do it—the pleasure of
a good shit, he says, being one of the few things he misses from outside.
Adam also volunteers sometimes, usually just after the latest *Playboy* has
arrived; but I generally don't indulge him more than once or twice a month,
as it upsets the others.

After the toilet came exercise. I stretched out on the bath mat beside the tub and let Seferis run through his routine: two hundred sit-ups followed by two hundred push-ups, the last hundred evenly divided between the right and left arms. I came back from the pulpit to muscle burn and a lather of sweat, but I didn't complain. The body's stomach is as flat as a washboard, and I can lift heavy things.

Next I gave Adam and Aunt Sam two minutes each under the shower, starting with Aunt Sam. They used to alternate who went first, but Aunt Sam likes the water a lot warmer than Adam does, and Adam was always "forgetting" to adjust the temperature control before handing off the body, so now every day it's Aunt Sam, then Adam, then me—and Adam knows if he gives me ice water or an eyeful of soap suds, he'll lose his shower privileges for a week.

When my turn came I washed up quickly (the others rarely bother to do any real scrubbing), rinsed and toweled off, and went back into the bedroom to get dressed. My father came out on the pulpit to help me pick clothes. Away from home I have control of the body full-time, so daytime wardrobe really ought to be my responsibility alone, but Aunt Sam says I was born with no fashion sense, and I think my father feels guilty about that.

"Not that shirt," he suggested, after I'd laid my initial selection on the bed.

"Does it clash with the pants?" I asked him, trying to remember the rule. "I thought blue jeans went with everything."

"They do go with everything," my father said. "But some clothes clash with everything, even blue jeans."

"You think it's ugly?" I held up the shirt and examined it more critically. It was a bright yellow plaid, with red and green checks. I'd gotten it along with a bunch of other bargains at a spring clearance sale, and I thought it looked cheerful.

"I *know* it's ugly," my father said. "If you really like it, you can wear it around here, but I wouldn't recommend it for public viewing."

I hesitated. I did like the shirt, and I hate having to give things up just because of what other people might think. But I also really want other people to think well of me.

"It's your choice," my father said patiently.

"All right," I said, still reluctant. "I'll wear something else."

We finished dressing. I put my watch on last, and checked it against the clock on the nightstand beside my bed. 7:07 A.M., the clock said, MON APR 21. My watch agreed about the day and date, but not about the time.

"Two minutes off," my father observed.

I gave a little shrug. "The watch runs slow," I reminded him.

"You should get it repaired, then."

"I don't need to get it repaired. It's fine the way it is."

"You should fix the VCR clock, too."

This was a longstanding bone of contention between us. My father used to own dozens of clocks, as protection against missing time; but I was less concerned with that, never having lost so much as a second as far as I knew, and had cut back to one clock per room. We'd fought about that decision, and about my failure to keep the remaining clocks perfectly synchronized. My casual attitude towards the VCR clock in particular drove my father crazy: after a power outage or an accidental unplugging, it might flash 12:00:00 for days before I bothered to reset it.

"It's really not that important," I said, more harshly than I intended to. I was still disappointed about the shirt. "I'll get around to it."

My father didn't answer, but I could tell he was frustrated: when I wouldn't look directly at the VCR, I could feel him trying to use the body's peripheral vision.

"I *will* get around to it," I insisted, and left the bedroom. I passed through the sitting room—whose own clock was a scandalous minute ahead of the one on the nightstand—and went down the side hallway to the kitchen, where Mrs. Winslow had breakfast waiting.

"Good morning, Andrew," Mrs. Winslow said, before I'd spoken a word. She always knew. Most mornings it was me at first, but even if I'd given the body to someone else, Mrs. Winslow would have known, without being told. She was like Adam in that sense, an almost magical reader of persons. "Did you sleep well?"

"I did, thank you." Ordinarily it's polite to repeat the question back, but Mrs. Winslow was a chronic insomniac. She slept less well than anyone I knew, except for Seferis, who doesn't sleep at all.

She'd been up since five at least, and had started cooking when she'd heard the shower. It was a measure of both her kindness and her affection for us that she was willing to do this; like everything else in the morning, breakfast is a shared activity, and no small effort to prepare. I sat down not to one meal but to a hybrid of several, each serving carefully proportioned, starting with half a plate of scrambled eggs and a mug of coffee for me. I ate my fill, then let the others take the body, each soul greeting Mrs. Winslow in turn.

"Good morning, my dear," Aunt Sam said grandly. Aunt Sam's breakfast portion consisted of a cup of herbal tea and a slice of wheat toast with mint jelly; she used to smoke half a cigarette, too, but my father made her give it up in exchange for a little extra time outside. She sipped at the tea and nibbled daintily at her toast until Adam got impatient and started clearing his throat from the pulpit.

"Good morning, gorgeous," said Adam with mock flirtatiousness. Adam likes to pretend he is a great ladies' man. In reality, women between the ages of twelve and sixty make him nervous, and if Mrs. Winslow's hair hadn't been gray, I doubt he'd have had the courage to be so fresh with her. As he devoured his breakfast—half an English muffin and a bacon strip—he gave her his idea of a seductive wink; but when Mrs. Winslow winked back, Adam startled, sucked bacon down the wrong pipe, and ended in a fit of coughing.

"Good morning, Mrs. Winslow," Jake said, his high voice raspy from Adam's choking fit. He dug awkwardly into the little bowl of Cheerios she set out for him. She poured him a tiny glass of orange juice, too, and he reached too quickly for it. The glass (which was really made of plastic; this had happened before) went flying.

Jake froze. If he'd been with anyone but Mrs. Winslow, he would have fled the body altogether. As it was, he hunched up, fists clenched and muscles tense, bracing for a smash across the knuckles or a punch in the face. Mrs. Winslow was careful not to react too suddenly; she pretended not to even notice at first, then said, very casually: "Oh dear, I must have put that too close to the edge of the table." She got up slowly, crossed to the sink, and wet a rag to mop up the spill.

"I'm sorry, Mrs. Winslow!" Jake blurted. "I—"

"Jake dear," Mrs. Winslow said, wiping the tabletop, "you do know that Florida is a *huge* state, don't you? They have *lots* of orange juice there; plenty more where this came from." She refilled his glass, handing it directly to him this time; he took it gingerly in both hands. "There," Mrs. Winslow said. "No harm done. It only *looks* like gold." Jake giggled, but he didn't really relax until he was back inside the house.

Seferis only nodded good morning. His breakfast was the simplest of all: a small plate of salted radishes, which he popped into his mouth one at a time and crunched like candy. Mrs. Winslow had started in on her own breakfast by then, warmed-over biscuits with marmalade. When the lid stuck on the marmalade jar, she offered it to Seferis.

Seferis's size ratio to the body is the inverse of Jake's: his soul is nine feet tall, and crammed into Andy Gage's modest frame he radiates energy and strength. He got the jar lid off with a simple twist of thumb and forefinger, a trick I couldn't have managed even using the same muscles.

"*Efcharisto,*" Mrs. Winslow said, as Seferis handed the jar back to her with a flourish.

"*Parakalo,*" Seferis replied, and crunched another radish.

When the last of the food had been consumed, Mrs. Winslow switched on the little black-and-white TV on the kitchen counter, and poured a fresh mug of coffee for my father, who came out to visit with her for a while. They liked to watch the news together. Mrs. Winslow used to watch with her husband, and I guess my father's company brought that back for her in some way; likewise, sitting with Mrs. Winslow gave my father a sense of the normal family life he'd always wished for. But this morning was less pleasant than most. The lead news item at the bottom of the hour was an update on the Lodge camping tragedy; it upset my father even more than the VCR clock, and blackened Mrs. Winslow's mood as well.

Maybe you remember the Lodge story; it never received as much national coverage as it might have, because of another similar case in the news at the same time, but people did hear about it. Warren Lodge was a groundskeeper from Tacoma who'd gone camping in Olympic National Park with his two daughters. Two days after the start of the camping trip, the state police spotted Mr. Lodge's jeep weaving between the lanes on Route 101 and pulled him over. Mr. Lodge, who appeared delirious and had a deep scratch across his scalp, claimed that a cougar had invaded the campsite and attacked him, knocking him unconscious. When he came to, he found his daughters' tent slashed to ribbons, their sleeping bags torn and bloody; the girls themselves—Amy, twelve, and Elizabeth, ten—were nowhere to be found, although he'd searched for many hours.

It could have been true. Cougar attacks are not uncommon in the Pacific Northwest, and Mr. Lodge looked strong enough to survive a wrestling match with a big cat, if he got lucky. But watching him on TV—the day after the police pulled him over, he called a press conference to plead for volunteers to help search for his girls—I felt a growing sense of unease. Mr. Lodge's story *could* have been true, but something about the way he told it was wrong. It was Adam, looking out from the pulpit into Mr. Lodge's tear-stained face, who first put my intuition into words: "*He's* the cougar."

Ever since then—almost a full week, now—we'd been waiting for the police to reach the same conclusion. So far there hadn't been a whisper of a suspicion in public, although Adam said the cops had to be thinking about it, unless they were totally incompetent. My father, meanwhile, had pledged that if Mr. Lodge weren't arrested soon, he was going to call the Mason County DA's office himself, or have me do it.

"Do you really think he killed them?" Mrs. Winslow asked now, as the newscast replayed Mr. Lodge's plea for volunteers; the update was just a rehash of previous reports, with an added note that the searchers had all but abandoned hope of finding the girls alive.

My father nodded. "He killed them, all right. And that's not all he did to them."

Mrs. Winslow was quiet for a moment. Then she said: "Do you think he's insane? To kill his own children?"

"Crazy people don't try to hide their crimes," my father said. "He knows what he did was wrong, but he doesn't want to face the consequences. That's not insane. That's selfish."

Selfish: my father's worst epithet. Mrs. Winslow didn't ask the obvious next question, the one I always wondered about, which was Why? Even granting a total disregard for the welfare of others, what would make someone *want* to do to another human being what Mr. Lodge had done to his own daughters? Mrs. Winslow didn't ask that question, because she knew my father didn't have an answer, though he'd spent most of his life searching for one. She didn't ask any other questions, either, only sat there in angry silence as my father finished his coffee and the newscast turned to other matters. Soon it was time for us to leave for work; my father kissed Mrs. Winslow on the cheek and gave me back the body.

There was a family portrait that hung in the Victorian's entrance foyer: a younger, darker-haired Mrs. Winslow with her late husband and her two sons, all of them standing on the front lawn of the Victorian back before it was renovated. I always slowed down a little going past that photo, ever since my father had told me the story of what happened; today I actually stopped, until Mrs. Winslow came up behind me and steered me forward out the front door.

Outside, the sky was unseasonably clear, the only visible clouds huddled in a group around Mount Winter to the east. Mrs. Winslow handed me a bag lunch (one complete meal; lunch isn't shared). She wished me a good day, then took a seat in the swing chair on the porch to wait for the morning mail. The postman wasn't due for another few hours yet, but she'd wait just the same, just as she always waited, bundling up in an old quilt if it got too cold.

"Will you be all right, Mrs. Winslow?" I asked before leaving. "Do you need anything?"

"I'll be fine, Andrew. Just come home safe, that's all I need."

"Don't worry," I told her. "If anyone tries anything, I'll have them out-numbered." This is an old multiple's joke, usually good for a polite smile at least, but today Mrs. Winslow only patted my arm and said: "Go on, then. Don't make yourselves late."

I started down the front walk. At the sidewalk I turned back to look; Mrs. Winslow had picked up a magazine and was reading, or pretending to read. She looked very small against the side of the Victorian, very small and very alone—*really* alone, in a way I could only imagine. I wondered what that must be like, and whether it was easier or harder than always having other souls for company.

"Don't worry about her," Adam said from the pulpit. "She'll be fine."

"I think the newscast really bothered her."

"It didn't *bother* her," Adam mocked me. "It pissed her off. And it should. You want to worry, worry about people who don't get mad, hearing about a thing like that."

I waved to Mrs. Winslow one last time and made myself start walking. When we were down the block and the Victorian was out of sight behind us, I said: "Do you think they'll catch him? Warren Lodge, I mean."

"I hope so," said Adam. "I hope he gets punished, whether they catch him or not."

"What do you mean?"

"It's just a thing that happens sometimes. Sometimes people think they've gotten away with something, think they've fooled everybody, only it turns out they haven't. They get punished after all."

"How?" I asked. "By who?"

But Adam didn't want to talk about it anymore. "We'll just hope a police-man gets him," he said. Then he went back in the house, and didn't come out again until we were almost at the Factory.

2

I worked at the Reality Factory on East Bridge Street. My boss there, Julie Sivik, was also the first real friend I ever made on my own.

When my father first called me out, he was working as a restocker for Bit Warehouse, a big computer outlet store just off Interstate 90 between Autumn Creek and Seattle. The original plan was that I would take over for him there, just as I took over all the other aspects of running the body, but it didn't work out. Being an effective restocker means knowing where things go, knowing where to find them again after they've gone, and—because of Bit Warehouse's "Ask Anybody" customer service policy—knowing what they're actually used for once they're found. After three years on the job, my father had all that knowledge, but I didn't.

This is one of those metaphysical issues that people who aren't multiple have a hard time grasping. Obviously, in creating me, my father had given me a great deal of practical knowledge. I came out of the lake knowing how to speak. I had a concept of the world and at least some of what was in it. I knew what dogs, snowflakes, and ferryboats were before I ever saw a real dog, snowflake, or ferryboat. So it may seem natural to ask, if my father could give me all that, why couldn't he also give me the know-how to be a champion restocker? For that matter, why couldn't he give me Aunt Sam's understanding of French, Seferis's martial-arts prowess, and Adam's knack for lie-detecting?

I wish I knew, because there are times when all of those skills would come in handy. Of course I can always have Aunt Sam translate for me, Seferis stands ready to defend the body at a moment's notice, and Adam hangs out in the pulpit calling bullshit on people whether I ask him to or not, but none of that is quite as good as having the abilities myself. For one thing, help from other souls isn't free—they expect favors in return, and not all of their wishes are easy to grant. It would be much simpler, and cheaper, if I could just borrow their talents somehow.

The reason why such borrowing isn't possible, my father thinks, has to do with the difference between information and experience. If you'd asked me on the day I was born to tell you what rain is, I'd have given you the dictionary definition. Ask me today and I'll still give you the dictionary definition—but as I'm giving it, I'll think of that moment on overcast mornings when you have to decide whether an umbrella is worth taking with you (the answer, in these parts, usually being yes). Or I'll think of the upside-down world reflected in puddles, or the awful tacky feeling of a drenched wool sweater, or the smell of wet leaves in Lake Sammamish State Park. Experience hasn't changed the form of my answer much, but the *meaning* of my answer has been utterly transformed.

Memory makes the difference. There are facts that everyone knows, but memories, and the feelings they evoke, are unique to individual souls. Memories can be described, but can never truly be shared; and knowledge that is bound up in especially strong memories can't be shared either. Like Aunt Sam's knowledge of French: it's more than just grammar and vocabulary, it's the memory of her high school teacher Mr. Canivet, the first adult she ever knew who didn't betray her in some way, who always treated her kindly and never hurt her. I never met Mr. Canivet, and can't love him the way Aunt Sam does. Any feelings I have about him are purely secondhand, and the things Aunt Sam learned from him will always be secondhand to me too.

My father's job experience had the same sort of proprietary quality. It couldn't be shared; it had to be acquired personally. We tried coaching for a few weeks—my father guiding me step by step from the pulpit, answering a thousand questions about RAM chips and SCSI ports and null-modem cables—but there was just too much to learn in too short a time. Given six months we might have managed it, but by the end of the third week my father's work-performance rating—*my* work-performance rating—had deteriorated to the point where we were in danger of being fired.

Of course it didn't help that my father hadn't told his coworkers about me; I still think he would have done better to be open about the fact that he was training a replacement. But two involuntary commitments had left him reluctant to reveal his multiplicity to people, and while he'd risked trusting Mrs. Winslow, nobody at Bit Warehouse knew. Not knowing, they were mystified when Andy Gage started acting like a whole other person—one who was constantly distracted and had trouble with even the simplest tasks.

Mr. Weeks, my supervisor, was especially concerned; after I accidentally reformatted the hard drive on the Warehouse's main inventory computer, he wondered aloud whether I'd been using drugs.

"We could try telling him the truth," I suggested. "We could tell everybody the truth."

"Not everybody would understand," my father replied. "It's a complicated truth, and people don't like complications. Especially people in authority. You'll learn."

You'll learn. That was my father's stock response whenever I asked a question that only experience could answer. I heard it a lot in those days, and it was frustrating, for him as well as for me. He'd thought that the hard part was over once he got the house built; turning things over to me was supposed to be easy. But he was still learning from experience, too.

One thing we'd both learned was that I couldn't just step into my father's old life. I had to create my own: find my own job, choose my own friends—and make my own decisions about who to trust.

I went to Mr. Weeks's office and told him I was quitting. He nodded, as if he'd been expecting this, and said that he hoped I'd consider getting professional substance-abuse counseling. I told him I would think about it—another stock response I'd picked up from my father—and went back out on the Warehouse floor to finish out the day. That was when I met Julie Sivik.

When she found me I was up on a ladder in Aisle 7, rearranging boxes on the overstock shelf. Even though I'd given my notice I was still interested in learning about computers, and my father and I were having a pretty involved discussion about graphical user interfaces, so Julie had to say "Excuse me" several times to get my attention.

"Hello," I said, when I finally noticed her. I slid down the ladder and brushed my hands on my shirt. "Can I help you?"

At first glance she was a little intimidating. She was a couple of inches taller than I was, with broader shoulders. She wore a brown leather jacket over a black T-shirt and dark jeans; her hair was dark too, very straight and severe, collar-length. And she had an annoyed look on her face, like she'd already decided I must be dense. I'd seen that look on other customers' faces, but Julie was better at expressing annoyance than most people, as if something in her features allowed for clearer transmission of impatience.

"I'm looking for some tax-preparation software," she said, holding up a short stack of shrink-wrapped boxes. "I was wondering which of these you'd recommend."

"Ask her what she wants to use it for," my father said, and I relayed the question: "What do you want to use it for?"

Julie looked at me as if I were very, *very* dense. "For preparing my taxes," she said. "Obviously."

"Personal income tax or small business?" my father said.

"Personal income tax or small business?" I asked.

"Oh . . ." Julie's expression softened. "That makes a difference?"

"Well . . ." I began, and then paused while my father filled me in. "Well," I continued, "if all you're looking for is a program that can fill out a 1040, then I'd probably suggest that one." I pointed to the box at the top of the stack. "Because . . . because it's the least expensive, very basic but with a good tutorial, as long as you don't need any specialized forms . . . On the other hand, if you're self-employed or running a small business, you'll probably need something more sophisticated . . . You're not a farmer, are you?" Even as I asked this question, following my father's prompting, I wondered what was so special about farmers' taxes. But Julie wasn't in agriculture, so I never got a chance to find out.

"But I *am* starting my own business," she said. "And I've also got to fill out a personal 1040 for last year, so I guess what I need is—"

"Wait," I interrupted her, holding up a finger. My father was saying something else now.

"Wait?" said Julie.

"Just a second . . ."

The annoyed look resurfaced on Julie's face. "What the hell am I waiting on?" she demanded.

"My father," I told her.

"Your father?"

"Oh great," said Adam, who'd joined my father in the pulpit. "This should be entertaining."

"Your father?" Julie repeated.

"Yes, my father."

She made a show of checking to see if there was someone standing behind me, first leaning sideways, then going up on tiptoe to peer over the top of my head. "Where?" she finally said.

"In the pulpit," I told her, after a quick backward glance of my own.

"Pulpit?"

"It's a sort of balcony, on the front of the house. In my head."

"What are you, schizophrenic?" Julie said.

"No, I'm a multiple personality. Schizophrenia is different."

"A multiple personality. You have other personalities sharing your body."

"Other souls." Remembering what my father had told me, I added: "It's a complicated truth."

"I'll just bet it is." It was at this moment, Julie later confided in me, that she decided I must be sincere or one of the best liars she'd ever met—either of which was interesting. "What was that you said about a house?"

She ended up asking me out for a drink after I got off work, and I was so excited I said yes without checking with my father first. But he was glad to see me taking some initiative, and Adam officially pronounced Julie safe: "She's not an ax murderer, anyway . . . although she's probably wondering if you're one."

So at quarter past eight that evening I met Julie in the parking lot outside the Warehouse. Usually I depended on public buses to get around, but Julie had her own car and offered to pick me up. When she found out I lived in Autumn Creek, she suggested a bar on Bridge Street that was only a few blocks from Mrs. Winslow's. "My own place is right around the corner," Julie added.

The car was a 1957 Cadillac Sedan de Ville, "a minor classic," Julie said, which she'd bought from her uncle and was planning to sell for a profit once she got it fixed up.

"What's wrong with it?"

"Pretty much everything." Julie recited a list of the car's defects and Adam pointed out a few more that she didn't mention; as we drove out of the parking lot, something hanging off the undercarriage banged against the pavement, leaving a trail of sparks in the Cadillac's wake. "It needs some serious work."

"Won't that cost a lot of money?"

"Some of the replacement parts will. But I figure I can handle most of the labor myself . . . Can you roll down your window a second? We need to make a right-turn signal here."

Maybe to get away from the subject of car repairs, Julie started telling me about herself. She was twenty-four, and came originally from Rhode Island, though she'd lived in a lot of different places since leaving home at sixteen. She'd attended Boston University for a couple of years, and had majored successively in physics, engineering, and computer science before dropping out without completing a degree; since then, she'd worked as a lab technician, a machinist, a gas-station attendant, a museum tour guide, a set designer for a low-budget horror film, a fire spotter, a short-order cook, a blackjack dealer, a sign painter for the Eugene, Oregon, Department of

Public Works, and, most recently, an assistant to a physical therapist in Seattle. "Never a farmer, though," she said, and grinned.

Anyway, she continued, since things had gone sour with the physical therapy job she'd decided it was time to stop screwing around and put her life in order, get serious about a career. With the help of the same uncle who'd sold her the Cadillac, she'd secured a small business loan and taken out a lease on a building in Autumn Creek, where she planned to set up a computer software design company.

"What kind of software are you going to design?"

"Virtual-reality software," Julie said. She looked at me as if I was supposed to know what that meant, but I'd never heard the expression before.

"What's virtual reality?"

"You work at Bit Warehouse and you don't know what virtual reality is?"

"I haven't worked there very long."

"Gee, I guess not."

"So what is it?"

Instead of answering, she changed the subject again—or at least I thought she did: "Tell me about the house in your head."

We were at the Bridge Street bar by then, sitting in a booth near the juke-box. Julie had ordered us a Saturday Night Special, which I found out too late was a gallon-sized pitcher of dark beer. Drinking alcohol was against my father's rules, and I'd meant to ask for a soda, but rather than admit the mistake I let Julie fill my glass and then left it untouched as we went on talking.

I told her about the house: about the dark room in Andy Gage's head, and my father's struggle to create a geography there. I wasn't as clear as I would have liked; it was my first time telling a story to someone, and I was nervous, unsure which details to include or what order to put them in. It also didn't help that I had a critic. My father had left the pulpit to give me some privacy, but Adam was still up there. He thought I was being far too candid with this stranger.

"But why shouldn't I be? You said yourself she's not dangerous."

"I said she's not an ax murderer. That doesn't mean it's OK to tell her everything about us."

"I'm not—"

"So Horace Rollins is your father?" Julie asked, not realizing she was interrupting.

The question startled me. "Not *my* father," I told her. "Andy Gage's father. Andy Gage's *step*father. He's no relation to me at all. No relation to Andy Gage either, really."

"Your real father died?"

"Andy Gage's father," I corrected her. "Silas Gage. He drowned."

"Andy Gage's father . . . So when you talk about *your* father, you don't mean Silas Gage, and you don't mean Horace Rollins, you mean another personality. Another 'soul.'"

"Aaron," I said, nodding. "My father."

"The one who called you out of the lake . . . who created you."

"Right."

"And when exactly was that?" Julie wanted to know. "That you were called out?"

I'd been hoping she wouldn't ask that. Contrary to Adam's accusation, there were a number of things I'd consciously avoided telling Julie. In most cases these omissions were instinctive, and I couldn't have explained the reasoning behind them at the time. But I knew perfectly well why I'd been vague about my birthdate: I was embarrassed. Julie had so much life experience, and I had so little, I was afraid she wouldn't want to be friends once she found out how immature I really was. But there was no helping it now.

"A month ago," I admitted. "I came out of the lake a month ago. I know I probably seem really naive—"

"Wait," Julie said. "You're a *month* old?"

"No," I said, confused. "I'm twenty-six years old. I was *born* a month ago."

Julie shook her head. "How can both of those things be true?"

"They just are," I told her. "What's the problem?"

"So it's your physical body that's twenty-six?"

"No, the body is twenty-nine."

"Then what part of you is twenty-six?"

"My soul."

Julie shook her head again. I went to Adam for help.

"All right . . . Adam says, because your body and your soul have always been joined together, they're basically reflections of each other. They're like twins."

"You mean they look the same? Souls have an appearance?"

"Of course."

Julie laughed. "So my soul has crooked teeth?"

"I guess," I said, glancing at her mouth. "If your body does. And it's got the same-color eyes, and the same build, and the same voice—and the same age. But for us, it's not like that. None of us is in the body all the time, so there's not that same connection. Adam says—"

"Who's Adam?"

"My cousin."

"This is another soul? Like your father?"

"Yes."

"And how old is Adam?"

"Adam is fifteen."

"Has he always been fifteen, or has he gotten older?"

"He's gotten a little older," I said.

"How much is a little?"

"Well, it's hard to say exactly. It depends on how much time he's spent outside. Adam used to steal time in the body, the same as the others; if you added up all that stolen time, plus the time he's been allowed out since my father took over and started building the house, that would tell you how much older he's gotten. My father thinks it's about a year, but Adam won't say."

"He doesn't want your father to know how much time he really stole," Julie guessed.

"He doesn't want to have to explain what he did with it," I told her.

"Souls only age when they're in control of the body?"

"Of course."

"Why?"

"I don't know. That's just the way it works."

"What does Adam say about it?"

"Adam says . . . Adam says it's the same reason you don't get better at poker unless you play for real money. I'm sorry, I don't know what that means."

"That's OK," said Julie. "I think I do."

She picked up the pitcher to pour herself some more beer, and noticed that my glass was still full. "What's wrong?" she said. "You don't like stout?"

"I don't drink, actually," I confessed, feeling caught out. "House rule."

"You sure?" She held up the pitcher, which still had more than half the gallon in it. "If I finish this myself, you may have to carry me out of here."

"I'm sorry. I should have said something."

"No, it's all right. I should have asked." Julie gestured in the direction of the bar. "Do you want something else?"

"No, really, I'm fine."

"Suit yourself . . ." She refilled her own glass, then said: "So tell me something about *your* soul."

"What do you want to know?"

"Well, what do you really look like? If I could see your soul and compare it to what I see now, what would be different?"

"Oh," I said. "Not that much, actually. I look a lot like my father, and my father looks more like Andy Gage than any other soul except . . . well, it's a very close resemblance."

"But there are differences?"

"A few. My hair's darker, and my face is thinner—it's put together a little differently, too."

"What else?"

"Well, scars." I pointed to a jagged line above Andy Gage's right eye. "Jake—he's another one of my cousins—Jake did this one time when he had the body. He tripped and fell against the edge of a glass table. Jake's soul has the same scar, but mine doesn't, because—"

"Because it didn't happen to you."

"Right."

"What about this one?" Julie touched a spot on the body's left palm, just above the ball of the thumb. Her fingers were cool and damp from the beer glass, and felt good in a way I hadn't experienced before. But when I realized what she was talking about, I pulled the hand away from her.

"That's just something my father did once," I said. "He stuck himself on a bill spike." I think Julie could tell there was more to the story than that, but she didn't press me on it.

"Any other differences?" she asked.

"Just some little things. Nothing major."

In the pulpit, Adam let out a snort. "Sure, nothing major. Nothing except—"

"Adam!" I warned.

"What?" said Julie.

"It's nothing," I told her. "Adam just said something very rude, is all."

She leaned forward, curious. "What did he say?"

"It's nothing, really. Just Adam being a pest."

"Has he been listening to us this whole time?"

I nodded. "Listening and commenting. It's what he does."

"Can I talk to him?"

It was an innocent request, and, as I eventually learned, a common one. Like a lot of Julie's other questions, though, it caught me by surprise; instead of recognizing that she was simply curious about Adam, my first thought was that she didn't want to talk to *me* anymore.

"What did I do wrong?" I asked Adam.

"You didn't do anything wrong. She's not mad—she just wants to see a trick."

"A trick?"

"A magic trick."

"You want to see a magic trick?" I asked Julie, confused again.

"What?" said Julie.

"Here," Adam offered, "I'll show you what I mean. Just let me have the body for a second . . ."

I should have refused; even a month out of the lake, I knew better than to trust Adam's generosity. But he sounded so self-assured, and I was so at a loss, that I stepped back into the pulpit and let him take over.

Now it was Julie's turn to be startled. People who have never seen a switch before often expect some dramatic physical transformation, like a werewolf sprouting hair and fangs under a full moon. In reality it's much more subtle—the body doesn't change, just the body language, which can actually be a lot more unsettling. I'm naturally a little shy, and though I try to keep eye contact for courtesy's sake, I have what Aunt Sam calls "a politely unintrusive gaze." Adam, of course, is the opposite of unintrusive. The first thing he did when he took the body from me was flash Julie his crudest adolescent leer. I could tell by the way she reacted: she stopped smiling and shifted back defensively in her seat. It was my first hint that I'd just made a big mistake.

"Hello, Julie," said Adam, in a silky voice that even spooked me a little. "Watch closely." He lifted up his right arm and waggled it in the air. "Nothing up this sleeve . . ." He did the same with his left arm. ". . . and nothing up this one." He lowered his arms and brought them together, hands clasping around the sides of the beer pitcher. "Watch . . ."

"Oh no," I said. "Adam! No!"

The beer: of course: it was the beer that he wanted. Alcohol is against the rules of the house, but Adam doesn't care about the rules—he is Gideon's son, after all. And he loves drinking, even more than he loves *Playboy*.

As he brought the pitcher to his lips I tried to wrest the body back from him, but he was determined to hang on until he finished. He didn't need to hold me off for long. Blitz-drinking is one of Adam's most refined "talents": he just threw his head back, and the stout in the pitcher slid out of sight like rainwater washing down a drainpipe, with no pause for swallowing.

"Aaaaaaahhhh—" Adam slammed the empty pitcher down on the table. He drained the glasses next, grabbing Julie's in one fist and mine in the other, tossing them back as if they were no more than thimble-sized, and ending with a flourish: *"TA-DAAAA!!!"* Then he leaned forward across the table, opened his mouth and belched explosively, right in Julie's face.

And that was all. Cackling hysterically at his joke, Adam fled the body and ran back into the house, leaving me to deal with the aftermath.

Julie looked as though she'd been slapped: she sat bolt upright, palms flat and rigid against the edge of the table as if frozen in the act of pushing away. From inside the house I could hear my father roaring in fury, and beneath the roar a door slam as Adam, still cackling, barricaded himself in his room, but that was all very distant. The immediate universe was made up of Julie and her wide-eyed expression of shock.

I jerked back in my own seat and my hands flew up to my mouth, as if I could somehow cram Adam's belch back inside. I would have given a lot to be able to abandon the body myself just then, to push it and the whole situation off on another soul; but that wasn't allowed. I could call on Seferis to handle physical threats, but coping with embarrassment was my own responsibility—even when it wasn't my fault. House rule.

"I'm so sorry . . ." The words came rushing out, muffled by the hands still pressed to my mouth. "I'm *so* sorry, Julie—"

Julie blinked and came back to life. "That was Adam?" she asked me.

I nodded. "That was Adam."

"You were right," she said. "He *is* a teenager."

The evening ended pretty soon after that. I kept apologizing, even as Julie insisted that she hadn't been offended. "I'm just a little stunned, is all." But she seemed more than stunned; she seemed wary and withdrawn. She didn't ask me any more questions, and the conversation fumbled to a standstill.

I started to feel strange, light-headed and nauseous. Adam had taken as much of the drunk with him as he could, to savor it in private, but there's enough alcohol in a half gallon of stout to make two souls woozy. Julie saw my eyes glazing over and said: "I think it's time for you to go home."

"No," I said, head weaving side to side, "I'm fine, really, I just—" But Julie had already slipped out of the booth and gone to settle the tab. I stared at a bit of foam on the lip of the beer pitcher until she came back. "Come on," she said, prodding me in the shoulder. "I'll take you home."

Her fingers didn't feel so nice this time; when I looked up, her expression was unsmiling and cold. "I can walk home," I suggested.

"I wouldn't count on it."

"Are you sure you can drive?"

Julie let out a terse bark of a laugh. "Yeah, I think so," she said. "I only had the one glass, remember?"

It was a very short ride, but by the time we reached Mrs. Winslow's I was starting to nod out. "Is this it?" Julie asked, nudging me awake. "You said 39 Temple Street, right?"

I swung my head up. We were parked in front of a Victorian, but it took a moment to be sure it was the right Victorian. "I think this is it," I said. "But it looks funny. *Everything* looks funny . . ."

"Go inside," Julie commanded. "Go to bed."

"All right . . ." But before getting out of the car, I tried to apologize one more time. Julie cut me off: "Go to bed, Andrew."

"All right," I said. "All right." I tugged at the door handle; the latch seemed stuck, so I shoved hard and the door swung open with a screech, scuffing off paint in a broad streak against the curb.

Julie let out a hiss. Then I started to apologize again, and she said: "Just get out of the car. Just get out, and let *me* shut the door."

I got out. With my weight out of the front seat, the right side of the Cadillac bounded up a little, lifting the edge of the door from the curb; but when Julie slid over to pull the door closed it sank down again. Cursing, she tried to scoot her butt as far to the left as possible without letting go of the door handle.

"Maybe I should do this," I said.

"I've got it!" Julie snapped. With a last curse, she gave up the delicate approach and yanked the door shut, scraping off another layer of paint. There was a loud click as she slapped the door button down.

"Good night!" I called to her. "Thanks for inviting me out!" If she said good night back I didn't hear it; as I bent down to the passenger window to wave good-bye, Julie revved the Cadillac's engine and pulled away. Just up the street she hit a pothole, generating another huge shower of sparks; this time it sounded like something had actually fallen off the car's undercarriage, but Julie never even slowed down.

I woke up the next morning with a splitting headache. A present from Adam: though he'd taken half the drunk, he left me the whole hangover. It felt like the house was on fire.

To make things worse, my father was angry with me: "You shouldn't have given Adam the body."

"Well I wouldn't have," I said, "if I'd known he was going to behave that way."

"How he behaved is beside the point. Running the body is supposed to be *your* job."

"But Julie asked to speak to Adam!"

"And that's why you gave up control? Because Julie asked you to?"

"Well . . ."

"Well?" my father demanded.

"I was confused . . . I didn't really understand what Julie wanted, and Adam said he did, so—"

"No," my father said. "That's no good, Andrew. You're in charge of the body—but you won't *stay* in charge if you give Adam the idea he can come out whenever you're confused. From now on, when we're out in public, I don't want you giving up the body for *any* reason other than a life-and-death emergency. Understood?"

"Understood," I said. "But . . ."

"Andrew—"

"But what if somebody asks to speak to Adam, and I'm not confused about it, but I just don't want to be rude? What do I do then?"

"If somebody *needs* to speak to Adam, you come talk to me about it first. And then *I'll* make sure Adam behaves."

He decided not to punish me, figuring the hangover was punishment enough. The hangover, and also the consequences of my mistake—once my head started to clear, it dawned on me that Julie and I hadn't exchanged phone numbers, so I had no way of getting in touch with her. She did know my address, and for a few days I held out hope that she might drop by, but after a week with no visit I reluctantly concluded that Adam had scared her off.

Then about a week after that I was walking on Bridge Street when some tourists stopped to ask me for directions. They were French Canadians who didn't speak English very well, and I ended up calling Aunt Sam out to the pulpit to help translate. It was a laborious process—Aunt Sam would tell me what the tourists had said, and I would tell her what I wanted to say back, and she would give me the French, and I would try to repeat it out loud. After the tourists finally drove off, I turned and found Julie Sivik standing beside me, smiling and shaking her head.

"Amazing," she said. "Like watching someone receive a satellite transmission. So who's the French-speaker in the family? Your cousin Adam again?"

"No," I said, "my Aunt Samantha—really she's my cousin too, but we call her Aunt Sam because she's older." I went on: "Adam's still being punished for what he did in the bar."

"Punished? How?"

"Well, for a while after he drank the beer he wouldn't come out of his room, so my father locked him in for three days. He's got the run of the house again now, but he still can't come out on the pulpit for another week."

"Sounds pretty harsh," Julie said, but there was an undertone of approval in her voice.

"What Adam did to you was very rude," I said. "And I was wrong too, to just let him out without warning you."

"Yeah, well, I was kind of freaked out by that," Julie admitted. "I was also pissed about the car . . ."

"I'd be happy to pay for repainting the door," I offered.

"Nah, it's no big deal . . . The paint job wasn't so great to begin with, to be honest."

"No, really, let me pay for it . . . Or at least, let me pay you back, once I start my new job."

"New job?" Julie said. "That's right, I heard you were looking for work."

"Heard from who?"

"Your old boss. I was out at Bit Warehouse the other day and I asked for you, but the manager told me you'd quit."

"You asked for me? Really?"

"Yeah, well . . . once I calmed down, I felt kind of bad about just dumping you in front of your place that night. I had to pick up some things at the Warehouse anyway, so I thought I'd see how you were. But you were gone. So what's the new job?"

"I haven't actually found one yet," I said. "I'm having a little problem with references."

Julie nodded. "Yeah, the guy I talked to at the Warehouse mentioned something about a drug problem." She raised an eyebrow. "Adam again?"

"Not exactly . . . It's kind of a long story."

"Another 'complicated truth'?" Julie grinned. "What kind of work are you looking for?"

I shrugged. "Anything, really. As long as it's something I can learn on the job."

"Any objections to working with computers again?"

"No . . . except that I still don't know that much about them. Why?"

"Just a thought," Julie said. "My lease starts today—my commercial lease, the one for the business I'm starting?—and I was actually just on my way down to check the place out. I could use an extra pair of hands while I'm setting things up . . . and who knows, there might even be a long-term position in it for you."

"I don't see how," I said. "I mean, I'll be happy to help you get your office set up, but I honestly don't know anything about virtual reality."

"Oh, but you do, though. You know more about it than anyone I've ever met."

"I don't know anything about it!" I protested. "I don't even know what it is. You never told me."

"Put it this way: it's a lot like what you've got in your head."

"You mean it's like the house? But that can't be right. The house isn't real."

"Well, neither is virtual reality."

"I don't understand."

"That's OK," Julie said, smiling at my confusion. "You'll learn." And then she surprised me again, by linking her arm in mine as if we were old friends and the incident in the bar had never happened. "Walk with me. I'll explain my master plan along the way."

3

There are actually two bridges on Bridge Street. The west bridge, which passes over the creek that gives Autumn Creek its name, is the main route out of town. The east bridge is used mostly by timber trucks. It spans a gully called Thaw Canal, a springtime tributary of Autumn Creek. Beyond the canal, East Bridge Street is only paved for the first quarter mile, after which it turns into a gravel-top service road.

On the morning I met Penny Driver, I hiked to work across the canal bridge, following the same path I'd first taken with Julie Sivik two years before. The Reality Factory was located on a half-acre lot alongside East Bridge Street's last stretch of asphalt. My father thought the lot had originally been a truck depot—there was an old fuel island with rusted-out diesel pumps at one end of the property—but for several years before Julie took out her lease it had been a storage facility. The main building, the one that became the Factory, was a long, concrete-walled shed. Shed anyway is what Julie called it, although it was huge, as big as Bit Warehouse inside, with nothing but a double row of support columns to break up the space.

I got to the Factory a little after eight. Julie had arrived ahead of me; her car was parked on the lot, under an awning by the diesel pumps. It was the same '57 Cadillac sedan she'd been driving two years ago, still in the process of being fixed up. You might be thinking she can't have worked very hard at repairing it, but in fact she had, at least off and on—but for every problem she fixed, another seemed to develop, so that the overall condition of the car never really improved. Julie still insisted she was going to sell it one day, though she no longer talked about making a profit.

I went around to the side door of the Factory and let myself in. Inside, Julie's voice echoed from the shed's rafters—she was back in the maze of army tents somewhere, having an argument with one of the Manciple brothers. Probably Irwin, the soft-spoken younger Manciple; only Julie's half of the argument was audible, and that wouldn't have been true if she'd been fighting with Dennis. Humming to myself so as not to overhear what didn't concern me, I made my way to the captain's tent that served me as an office and sat down to check my e-mail.

I should explain about the tents.

The first time I saw the shed, it was a mess. The power was off, and the building had no windows, so Julie shined a flashlight around to give me some idea of how spacious the interior was. It was spacious, all right, but it was also full of junk: the flashlight beam swept over long heaps of broken metal pipe. Old scaffolding, Julie explained, that had once held racks of storage lockers. When the storage facility shut down, the lockers had been removed and the scaffolding cut up for scrap; only somehow the scrap got left behind. Our first order of business would be to rent a dump truck and haul all the scrap away. "I know it looks like a disaster area right now, but I think it's got a lot of potential once we get all this crap cleared out."

"Oh sure . . . and I can definitely help with that, the clearing-out part. I can lift heavy things."

"Shouldn't take more than a week or so, I figure, once we get into it. And after the junk's all gone, we can start setting up the tents, and—"

"Tents?"

"One minor problem with this building." Julie tilted her flashlight upwards, illuminating a peaked ceiling of stained wooden planks. "The roof leaks. Not *terribly*, I mean we're not talking deluge, but still I wouldn't feel safe leaving computer equipment exposed underneath it."

"So you're going to set up tents in here? To keep the computers dry when it rains?"

Julie nodded. "Surplus army tents. My uncle knows a quartermaster at Fort Lewis who can get them for me practically free—all sizes, as many as I want."

"Wouldn't it make more sense to just replace the roof?"

"I can't afford to, at least not right away. Once the Factory's up and running and I get some venture capital, or maybe some grant money—"

"But why should you have to pay for it? If you're leasing this place . . ."

"It's part of the deal I made. One of the reasons the rent on this place is so low, I agreed to make certain improvements to the property at my own expense."

"You promised to fix the roof yourself?"

"Among other things, yes."

"But if you can't afford to fix it . . ."

"I can't afford it *right now*," Julie said. "But that's OK, it doesn't have to be done now, just sometime before the lease ends. But in the meantime there's other stuff that's more pressing, like getting this junk cleared away, and making sure the electrical system can handle all the gear I'm going to bring in . . . replacing the roof, that's more of a long-term project. A project for you, maybe," she added, "seeing as you're architecturally inclined."

"It was my father who built the house," I reminded her. "And the carpentry was all imaginary."

But she wasn't listening. Caught up in her own imaginings, she had turned away and was sweeping the flashlight around again, measuring the space. Watching her, I had a sudden realization: Julie was not a practical person. I know you probably figured that out already, but it was a new thought for me. It was also the first character judgment I ever made entirely on my own, with no help from Adam or my father, and it gave me a weird sense of accomplishment, almost as if I'd discovered something positive about her. And maybe it was good that I felt that way—Julie's inability to do things simply drove a lot of people crazy, but I was always able to be patient with her, and even find her impracticality endearing, because it confirmed my own perceptiveness.

Besides which, her ideas weren't always as impractical as they first appeared. Like Julie's car, the Factory roof was never fully repaired—though I was up on it many times to patch leaks that had gotten too big to ignore—so the tents became a permanent fixture. But even if they hadn't been necessary, we probably would have kept them anyway, because of a surprising side-benefit: in addition to keeping the equipment dry, the tents also made the Factory a lot cozier by dividing up the shed's one big room into many smaller rooms. They created privacy, and while something similar might have been accomplished using standard office-cubicle partitions, the tents, in hindsight, were a more effective solution, not to mention more fun. Working at the Reality Factory was like working in a gypsy camp, especially after Julie got creative and had us paint the outsides of the tents different colors.

My tent was sky-blue, with spray-painted clouds that Aunt Sam had shown me how to make stencils for. It was furnished with a big oak desk that Julie and I had salvaged from the same junkyard where we'd dumped the scaffolding, and equipped with a reconditioned Pentium computer. With Julie's help, I'd set up my own Web site to exchange information with other multiples online. Julie had offered to get me a second computer to keep at Mrs. Winslow's, but my father and I had jointly vetoed that idea—the last thing we needed was to have Adam and Jake fighting over Internet access.

This morning as I tried to dial in to our Internet provider, I kept getting error messages. This happened sometimes; after two years of troubleshooting, the Factory's electrical grid was fairly reliable, but our connection to U.S. West was still chancy.

I called out: "Dennis?"

From the tent next door, Dennis Manciple called back: "It's down."

"Is it the switchboard again?" I asked.

"Irwin says no," Dennis replied. "We've still got voice phone, you just can't get online. Probably trouble at the other end. Give it a few minutes."

"Yeah," Adam snickered. "Give it a few minutes, and the regular phone will go dead, too."

"Be quiet." I left my computer idling and went over to Dennis's tent, which was blood-red and riddled with fake bullet-holes, and had spray-paint portraits of Lara Croft and Duke Nukem guarding the entrance flap. As usual, Dennis was busy writing software code, but he was also fully dressed, which surprised me.

The Manciple brothers were originally from Alaska. Their parents were homesteaders; Dennis and Irwin grew up in a bush settlement on the Yukon River, and were in their teens before they visited a town with more than a hundred people in it. The isolation of their formative years—they went to grade school by radio—had left its mark on them. It wasn't so much that the brothers had no social graces, Julie Sivik once said, as that they had a different set of social graces than most of the rest of the world. (When I suggested that something similar could be said about me, Julie made a distinction that I'm still not sure I understand: "You're just strange," she told me. "The Manciples are *odd*.")

Dennis had a thing about clothes. Partly due to the climate where he grew up, and partly because he was fifty pounds overweight, he was always too hot, even in temperatures that would have most people wishing for a parka. He went around underdressed as a matter of course, and whenever he settled someplace for more than a few minutes, he started loosening and then removing the few clothes he had on. It was normal to find him in his tent wearing nothing but underpants and a back brace, but today he had on an actual shirt with buttons and a pair of short pants. And shoes.

"Dennis," I said, "you're dressed." I sniffed the air in the tent, which seemed fresher than usual. "And you bathed." You could say things like that to Dennis, who never took offense at anything; Irwin you had to be a lot more delicate with.

"Commodore's orders," Dennis said, meaning Julie. He called Julie made-up titles like "Commodore," and "the General," and occasionally "Bitch Empress," though that last one didn't sit well with her. "We have a new employee coming in today. A girl. I'm not supposed to let her see my chest hair for at least the first week."

"A new employee? Who is she?"

Dennis shrugged. "Just somebody the Jewel met in Seattle last month."

"Julie didn't say anything to me about it."

"Why should she? Are you married or something?"

"No, but . . . what does this new person do? What's Julie hiring her for?"

"Beats me," said Dennis. "I'm still not sure what she hired *you* for."

Not only did Dennis never take offense, he never worried about giving it, either. But I didn't blame him for teasing me about my job description. Officially Julie had hired me as a "creative consultant" to the Reality Factory. It was a position I was uniquely suited for, she said, because I had firsthand experience with what virtual reality was ultimately meant to be: an imaginary universe where different people could meet, interact, and be creative together.

Once I got past the obvious objection—my father had built the house as a means of crowd control, not to express his creativity—I had to admit it sounded intriguing. But it's hard to be a consultant to a project that is years ahead of its time.

My first virtual experience was particularly disappointing. It was a really awful home video-game called *Metropolis of Doom* that used a set of cheap stereoscopic goggles and a handheld trigger button. The goggles showed you a bright red 3-D line drawing of what was supposed to be a city. As you inched forward along the city's main street, riding on an invisible conveyor belt, little flying pyramids meant to be attack jets would zip out from between the "buildings" and fire rockets at you. The object of the game was to shoot the jets down; the goggles could sense movement, and by turning your head you could aim a crosshairs that hung in the center of your field of vision. But the motion sensor was sluggish—you'd turn your head, wait a beat, and *then* the crosshairs would move—and by the time I shot down my first jet, I had a headache. Then the goggles fogged up.

"I'm sorry," I told Julie, wiping sweat from my eyebrows as I handed the goggles back to her. "I don't think I can help you with this."

"Don't be so hasty," Julie said. "This isn't my prototype. It's just to give you an idea—"

"It isn't like what you described—like what I *thought* you described. And it isn't anything like the house. The house isn't real, but it *seems* real. This, though . . . it's not even a good toy."

"I know it's not. But the VR system my partners are working on is *much better*, much more state-of-the-art . . ." She grew thoughtful: "Seems real, you said. How real?"

"Hmm?"

"You said the house seems real, even though it isn't. I want to know more about the quality of the experience. When you're in the house, you still have all five senses, right?"

"Sure. Of course."

"So it's like a perfect hallucination."

I frowned. "Hallucination is the wrong word for it, I think."

"What's the right word?"

"I don't know. I don't know if there is one."

"What about a dream?" Julie asked. "Is it like dreaming?"

"No. It's like what I thought you said virtual reality was like: like being wide awake in an imaginary place, with other people. But"—I pointed at the goggles—"it's *nothing* like that, so now I'm not sure how to describe it."

But Julie, not the least bit discouraged, said: "You should let me introduce you to my partners."

Despite growing up in the bush, the Manciple brothers were no strangers to high technology. Their parents' homestead was powered by a solar array during the summer months, and there had been a computer in the house as far back as 1975, when Dennis and Irwin's father had ordered a build-it-yourself Altair kit through the mail. The brothers grew up with the Altair and the series of ever more sophisticated personal computers that came after it, and passed a lot of long winter nights programming—or sometimes, in Irwin's case, tinkering with the innards of the older machines. Then in 1993, a shareware adventure game called *The Stone Ship* that the brothers had coauthored (Irwin came up with the story, while Dennis wrote most of the actual code) earned enough money to convince them to turn professional. They left Alaska and came south to seek their fortunes in the software industry, choosing Seattle over Silicon Valley out of fear that California would be too warm.

Julie met them through her job at the physical therapist's, where Dennis came for help with his back problems. By that point, late 1994, the brothers had been in Seattle for over a year with nothing to show for it. In spite of *The Stone Ship*'s success, they'd been unable to interest any of the established software houses in their ambitious follow-up project, and having spent most of their money, they were starting to think about quitting and going home. But Julie, who was having her own career difficulties (she and the physical therapist had been dating for a while, and now they weren't, and she was about to be fired and evicted in the bargain), talked them into founding the Reality Factory instead, taking her on as business manager, chief fund-raiser, and unofficial CEO.

The brothers' virtual-reality system was called Eidolon. Like *Metropolis of Doom*, it used a set of 3-D goggles, although, having been custom-designed by Irwin, the Eidolon goggles were more comfortable to wear and didn't fog up so quickly. There was also a "data glove" that told the Eidolon software what your right hand was doing, whether you were pointing or waving or grabbing.

It *was* better than *Metropolis of Doom*. The graphics were full-color, with solid, textured shapes rather than wireframe outlines. Instead of riding on a conveyor belt, you had complete freedom of movement—you could spin around, float up and down, slide backwards and forwards and sideways, all by gesturing with the data glove. And nobody was shooting at you: instead of a war-torn city, the world in the Eidolon goggles was a sort of playroom with toys, like a bouncing ball you could toss or bat around, and a magic mushroom that, if you poked at it, made violets and dandelions sprout up out of the floor.

It still wasn't anything like the house, though. The graphics were better but still more cartoon-like than real, and though you could see things, you couldn't really touch them: poking the magic mushroom was like poking air. You couldn't smell the flowers, or taste the water in the rubber-duck pond. The first time I tried Eidolon, you couldn't even hear the ball bouncing—the goggles had stereo earphones built in, but Irwin hadn't got them working yet. And the "free" movement could still be annoyingly sluggish or jerky, especially if you tired out the computer by making it draw too many dandelions.

Also, I wasn't exactly sure what the point of the whole thing was.

"The point is whatever the end-user wants the point to be," Julie told me. "That's the point."

"Well, but . . . not that it isn't neat, and all, but do you really think people will pay money just to play an imaginary game of catch?"

"You don't get it, Andrew," Julie said. "Eidolon isn't the playroom."

"It isn't?"

"No. Eidolon is what *built* the playroom." She went on to explain that

Eidolon was actually a "software engine," a sort of programming language and interpreter. "The playroom is just a sample application. A demo. But you can use the engine to design any sort of geography you want, for any reason you want. So maybe you're a real-estate developer who wants to take someone on a walk through a building that only exists as a blueprint; Eidolon will let you do that. Or maybe you *do* want to play an imaginary game of catch, but using your own laws of physics; Eidolon will let you do that, too."

"Hmm." I didn't say so out loud, but these examples still didn't sound very interesting. But Julie sensed my lack of enthusiasm, and quickly came up with an application that did interest me.

"Or," she said, "maybe you've been hurt."

"Hurt? Hurt how?"

"In an accident, say. Let's suppose you've had a spinal injury that leaves you partially paralyzed, with no feeling in your legs. You might be stuck in a wheelchair for the rest of your life. But with this"—she tapped the back of the data glove—"you can still get up and dance any time you want to."

"The engine would let you do that?"

"Sure." She smiled. "So you see, it's not just an expensive toy. With the right application, it can be a tool for living a fuller life."

A tool for living a fuller life . . . I liked that phrase. "It *sounds* good," I said. "But who would actually program that application? I mean—"

"The end-user," Julie said.

"The person in the wheelchair?"

Julie nodded. "The finished version of the programming interface will be very intuitive, very easy to use. You'll be able to define and create whole new geographies using just the headset and the glove."

That got my attention. Inside Andy Gage's head, only my father was allowed to make changes to the house and the grounds; but here was an opportunity to wield a similar power myself.

"Can you show me how that works?" I went to pick up the goggles and the data glove again, but Julie stopped me: "The *finished* version, I said. It's not finished yet."

"Oh . . . you mean there's not even a test version I could try?"

"Nope. Sorry. Dennis is still working on the core Eidolon engine, so for now, applications have to be coded individually. The simplified geography editor—we call it Landscaper—is still a ways down the road yet."

"How far down the road?" I had a sudden nagging suspicion. "When is Eidolon supposed to be finished?"

"When it's done," said Julie.

Every few months Dennis would cobble together a new demo program, showcasing the latest version of the still-unfinished Eidolon engine, as a lure for potential investors. These demos were the closest thing the Reality Factory had to an actual product. They were also my only real chance to play consultant: before Dennis started coding, Julie would sit me down with him and have me offer suggestions about what the demo should include. But these brainstorming sessions never lasted very long, and most of my suggestions were things that Dennis couldn't possibly implement. "This is not the holodeck on the starship *Enterprise!*" he would end up shouting at me, his patience exhausted. "I can't program it to let you *smell* things!"

So I ended up spending most of my time doing nonconsulting work: helping Irwin assemble and disassemble hardware, entering data strings for Dennis, running errands for Julie, patching the shed roof, and handling other maintenance chores around the Factory—like emptying the Honey Bucket— that Julie and the Manciples couldn't be bothered with. Generally I kept busy enough to feel I was earning my six-dollar-an-hour salary. But there weren't *that* many spare chores, and I couldn't see what a fifth employee would do.

"Supposedly she knows something about interface design," Dennis said now, as I continued to question him.

"Interface design? You mean she's a programmer?"

"The High Commander seems to think so."

"So she'll be working with you?"

"Or with you," said Dennis. "It depends on whether *I* think she's a programmer."

"Does this mean you're finally going to implement Landscaper?"

"Could be." Then he thought the question over a little more seriously, and added: "Better be. It's not like I need help with the engine itself."

"No, of course not," Adam chimed in from the pulpit. "He's only been working on the thing for four years, why would anyone think he needed help?"

"Be quiet."

Dennis swiveled his chair around to face me. "What?"

"Nothing," I said.

"Comments from the peanut gallery?"

"Just Adam mouthing off."

"Uh-huh." Dennis knew about the house, but I'm not sure he ever completely believed in it; whenever he overheard me talking to Adam or my father, he reacted as if I were displaying signs of mental illness.

Penny Driver arrived at the Factory about fifteen minutes later. I'd gone back to my own tent and made a few more unsuccessful attempts to connect to the Internet; I was coming back out to look for Irwin when I saw her.

Penny had let herself in through the shed's side door. (The shed had a front door, too, a garage-style door big enough to drive a Mack truck through, but the one time we got it open it took us two days to close it again, so now we pretended it was a wall.) She stood just inside the doorway, one hand behind her still holding onto the knob, looking ready to duck out again in a hurry. I guess Julie hadn't told her what to expect.

"You're in the right place," I called to her.

She literally jumped at the sound of my voice: took a little hop off the floor, and let out a sharp squeak. Her free hand came up and pressed itself against her chest in the heart-attack gesture.

"Sorry," I said. I walked up to her slowly, as if she were Jake. "Sorry, I didn't mean to startle you. But this *is* the Reality Factory, if that's what you're looking for."

I held out my hand, but she didn't take it. All at once she didn't seem startled anymore, just puzzled; she stared at me the way you'd stare at a can of beans that you didn't remember putting in your grocery cart. Not sure what else to do, I stared back.

She was physically a very small person, just over five feet tall, and slight. She wore a faded gray sweater that hung almost to her knees, and a wrinkled pair of blue jeans. Her close-cropped hair was mussed, as if she'd just rolled out of bed after a long sleep, but her eyes were bloodshot and there were dark circles under them.

Suddenly she let go of the doorknob and crossed her arms in front of her. She took three quick strides forward, moving so swiftly that I had to jump aside to get out of her way. Ignoring me, she panned her head around, surveying the length of the shed: taking in the tents, the stained roof planks, the drip buckets, the rusting bits of leftover scrap piled in the far corners, the snaking cables wrapped in waterproof insulation. Her lip curled.

"Jesus fucking Christ," she said. "What a motherfucking shithole."

"Excuse me?" I said.

"You heard her," said Adam, sounding amused. "What word is giving you trouble, 'shithole' or 'motherfucking'?"

Penny uncrossed her arms. She blinked and turned to me again, seeming freshly alarmed to find me standing right next to her. This time she didn't jump or squeak; but she stepped back as abruptly as she had come forward. Her back once more to the door, she raised her hand in a timid wave hello.

"Hi," she said.

"Hi," I said back.

"Hello," said Adam. "Did anybody just see a parade go by?"

Julie appeared from between two tents, with a glum-faced Irwin trailing after her. "Hi, Penny!" she called, adding, with a nod to me: "I see you two have met."

"Kind of," I said. It was a morning for peculiar behavior, apparently: as Julie approached us, I could have sworn I saw something funny in her expression—a hint of smugness in her smile, some private amusement in her eyes—but then I shrugged it off, thinking it must have something to do with the fight she'd had with Irwin. Adam might have told me differently, but he was still focused on Penny.

"So," said Julie, coming to stand beside us, "I guess formal introductions are in order. Andrew Gage, this is Penny Driver. Penny, this is Andrew."

"Pleased to meet you, Penny," I said, and once again offered my hand. This time she shook it, though I could see she didn't want to. I pumped her arm once, gently, and let it go.

"Actually," said Julie, "she likes to be called Mouse."

"No she doesn't," observed Adam from the pulpit. "Did you see the way she flinched just then? She *hates* being called Mouse."

"Adam," I asked, being careful not to speak the words aloud, "does Julie seem weird to you this morning? She's got this look on her face, like—"

"Hi, Mouse!" Dennis Manciple's voice boomed out. He came out of his tent with his top three shirt buttons unbuttoned, drawing an instant scowl from Julie. "Dennis!" she snapped, pinching the lapels of her own blouse together.

Dennis ignored the signal. His chest hair exposed to the world, he marched up to Penny and grabbed her hand so roughly he nearly yanked her off her feet. "Nice to meet you, Mouse!"

"He likes her," Adam snickered. "He thinks she's *sexy* . . . but she thinks he's a big fat disgusting pig boy."

I thought that last bit might be a projection on Adam's part—although it's true that as Dennis shook her hand, Penny looked as though she'd stuck her fingers in something nasty. "But what about Julie, Adam?"

"I don't know," Adam said. "She's always a little weird anyway, so it could be nothing. Or maybe she's got some half-assed idea about getting the two of you together."

"The two of us—you mean me and Penny? Like boyfriend and girlfriend?"

"Yeah." More snickering. "'Like boyfriend and girlfriend.' That could be it . . . or maybe *she's* seen the parade, too."

"What parade? What are you talking about?"

"Just pay attention," said Adam. "You'll see it."

Dennis was still shaking Penny's hand; he seemed prepared to go on shaking it all day. "Enough, already!" Julie said. She stepped between them and flicked her hand impatiently at Dennis's open shirtfront. "What did I tell you about this?"

"A thousand pardons, O Great One," said Dennis. He rebuttoned himself, but he took his time doing it.

"Asshole." Julie turned and flashed an apologetic smile at Penny. "Sorry," Julie said. "As you can see, we're pretty informal here—a little *too* informal, sometimes. This nudist is Dennis Manciple. And Mr. Pouty over there is his brother Irwin."

Irwin, still standing a good ten paces back from the rest of us, didn't try to shake Penny's hand or even nod hello. He was sulking.

"Now that you've met everybody," Julie continued, "why don't we all go back to the Big Tent and show you the system? You can try out one of our demos to get a better idea of what you'll be working on."

"OK," Penny agreed. She said it like it was actually the last thing in the world she wanted to do, but she let Julie take her elbow and lead her just the same, with only one last wistful glance back at the door she'd come in by.

The Big Tent, as its name suggested, was the largest tent in the Factory. It was set up in the shed's south end, oriented diagonally to the shed walls— the only way it would fit between the support pillars. Originally it was an army mess tent, but we had painted it to look like a circus big top (or actually, *I* had painted it, after Julie and Irwin made a halfhearted start; red and white stripes get boring pretty quickly). It housed the majority of the Factory's equipment, including a bank of networked computer-graphics workstations that Julie's uncle had picked up off the street after they'd fallen from the back of a truck.

The Big Tent was as cluttered as my bedroom and as messy as the shed itself had once been. But there were levels of disorder, and as we came in I thought I saw the reason for Julie's spat with Irwin: overnight, one of the workstations had been gutted, its parts spread out across a worktable. This happened all the time—Irwin was constantly taking one or another of the computers offline, taking it apart and reconfiguring it to squeeze out an extra ounce of performance—but having one of the machines down could cause problems with the rest of the network, especially when we were running a demo. So either Julie had forgotten to tell Irwin she'd be needing the full system today, or, more likely, he hadn't listened.

The sight of all the hardware in the tent triggered another odd reaction from Penny. She pulled her arm loose from Julie's grasp, went over to the worktable, and made a very authoritative-sounding observation about the collection of computer parts. I couldn't really understand what she said—she used the techno-dialect that ex-employees of Bit Warehouse are supposed to be fluent in, but which I'd never learned—but it impressed Irwin enough to bring him partway out of his sulk.

"That's right," he told her. "Have you worked with one of these before?"

Instead of answering, Penny examined the other two workstations, the ones that hadn't been taken apart. She ran her thumb over a rough spot on one computer's plastic-and-metal shell. "Did you sand off the brand names?" she asked.

"They came that way," Julie spoke up. "Part of a special deal."

"Yeah," Adam said. "Ninety percent off, with no serial numbers . . ."

"Be quiet."

Penny was staring at me.

"Oops," I said. "Sorry, I didn't mean you."

"Andrew hears voices in his head," Dennis explained, smirking. "He's got family up there."

"Family . . . ?"

"It's complicated," said Julie. She shot a warning glance at Dennis. "Andrew will explain it to you himself, *if* he feels like it."

I definitely didn't feel like it, not just then. "So," I said, hoping to change the subject, "what demo are we going to run?"

Dennis sat down at a computer terminal and punched a few keys. "What about Dancing Cripples?" he suggested. "You like that one."

Dancing Cripples was a demo version of the application Julie had dreamed up to pique my interest back when I'd first tried Eidolon—the application that a paraplegic was supposed to be able to program himself, using the headset-and-glove Landscaper interface. Though the interface had not yet materialized, I'd asked Julie about the application itself so many times that she'd finally had Dennis code a demo the hard way—and a representative from the Veterans Administration (we were careful not to call it "Dancing Cripples" in front of *him*) had liked it enough to give us a five-thousand-dollar research grant.

"All right," I said. "Let's do that one."

"Good," said Julie. "Andrew, why don't you be the guy in the wheelchair? We'll let Penny wear the data suit."

A data suit was a full-body version of a data glove. The Reality Factory had three data suits, each in a different size: one for large adults, one for small adults, and one for kids. Julie grabbed the kid-sized one for Penny.

"You'll have to take this off, Mouse," Julie said, tugging at one of the sleeves of Penny's oversize sweater. Penny looked startled again, and made no move to do as she was told. "Here," said Julie, "let me help you . . ." She stepped behind Penny, grabbed the sweater at the waist with both hands and started tugging it upwards.

For just a moment Penny went rigid, resisting. There was an incredibly fast flickering of expressions on her face, as if she couldn't make up her mind whether to be frightened or outraged or cooperative. I even saw—or thought I saw—a flash of anger so intense that it seemed Penny might turn around and hit Julie for presuming to undress her. But the anger vanished as quickly as it had appeared, and Penny became passive; she let her arms be lifted into the air and let the sweater be lifted over them, and off.

She wasn't wearing much, underneath. In fact the only article of clothing beneath the sweater was a very skimpy tank top that bared Penny's shoulders and collarbone, and left no doubt that she didn't have a bra on. The tank top was bright pink, and had the words FUCK DOLL printed across the front. I must have blushed when I read that—and Penny, seeing me blush, hearing Dennis whistle, crossed her arms over her chest as if we'd caught her naked. Meanwhile Julie, crouched behind Penny and unable to see any of this, tried to get her to step into the legs of the data suit: "I need you to lift your right foot, Mouse . . . Mouse?"

I went to get the wheelchair I'd be using for my part in the demo. The wheelchair itself was totally ordinary—more army surplus—but the data glove that went with it had been specially programmed to interpret individual finger movements as the movement of whole limbs. After I'd seated myself in the chair and, with Irwin's help, got the data glove plugged into the network, Dennis punched another key at his terminal that caused a computer-generated mannequin figure to appear on the monitor in front of him. I curled my index finger in the glove, and the mannequin figure raised its left leg, kicking back; I curled my middle finger, and the figure raised its right leg; I tapped my index and middle fingers together against a sensor pad on the wheelchair armrest, and the figure clicked its heels and jumped in the air; I wiggled my thumb and pinky, and the figure waved its arms.

"Looks good," said Dennis. Next he turned his attention to Penny, who, with much coaxing, had finally let Julie zip her up inside the data suit. This part of the systems check took longer, because checking out the data suit requires that the person wearing it actually stand on one foot, jump up and down, wave his or her arms, etc., and Penny had become extremely self-conscious—but eventually, with still more nudging from Julie, the check was completed successfully.

Now it was time to put on the headsets. As I've already mentioned, Irwin had designed these to be comfortable, but they can still be a bit claustrophobic at first, before the power is switched on—like heavy blindfolds with cables attached. As Irwin adjusted the strap on the back of my headset, I could hear Julie crooning, "Relax, Mouse. It'll only be dark for a second."

Irwin plugged my headset into the network and turned it on. A 3-D test pattern appeared in front of my eyes. Dennis ran a sound check: an invisible locomotive rumbled past my left ear, then past my right ear, then past both ears at once. I gave Dennis a thumbs-up.

"All right," said Dennis. "Here we go . . ." As he tapped out a last sequence on his keyboard, I crooked my index and middle fingers in the data glove, bending them like the legs of a sitting man.

The test pattern dissolved into a first-person view of the Eidolon universe, which in this demo consisted of a giant ballroom with a white-and-black checkerboard floor, ringed by blue marble pillars. The ballroom had no walls or ceiling; the checkerboard floated in a void that started out dull red but would grow brighter, shifting color like a sunrise, as the demo progressed.

I panned my head down and examined my "self": not my real self but my Eidolon self, a mannequin figure in a cartoon wheelchair. The illusion was surprisingly convincing, and would have been even more so if I hadn't felt my real legs to be in a slightly different position than those of the mannequin. I made a flicking motion with my index finger; while my real leg stayed put, Eidolon Andrew swung his left foot forward, proving that he wasn't such a cripple after all.

I looked up and saw Eidolon Penny facing me across the dance floor. Eidolon Penny was taller than real-world Penny: she had thicker arms and legs, a larger frame, and much bigger breasts; her face was a texture-map of some swimsuit model's face that Dennis had scanned into the computer, with an expression that never changed. But while she might not look like the real Penny, she moved like her: shifting uncomfortably from foot to foot, crossing and uncrossing her arms, glancing back over her shoulder as if she expected a monster to materialize behind her at any moment.

The music started. The song was Lyle Lovett's "The Waltzing Fool," a slow piano-and-guitar ballad that I really liked even if it was a little sad. As the first strains sounded, I straightened out my index and middle fingers; in the real world I remained seated in the wheelchair, but in the Eidolon universe, Eidolon Andrew stood tall on two good legs. I twisted my hand counterclockwise and swung my index finger to the side; Eidolon Andrew turned halfway around and kicked out at his wheelchair, which shattered, morphing into a flock of doves that flew up into the air and began circling the ballroom, weaving between the marble pillars. I twisted my hand clockwise, curled my thumb in front of my index finger, and dipped my hand forward; Eidolon Andrew turned back towards Eidolon Penny, crossed his left arm in front of his waist, and bowed.

Eidolon Andrew was careful to keep his distance from Eidolon Penny. If I had approached her, there was a subroutine in the demo that would have allowed our two eidolons to actually join hands and dance together, but unless we simultaneously touched in the real world, we wouldn't have felt any contact—and embracing someone you can see but not feel is a very disorienting experience, one that I thought would probably freak Penny out completely. So I stayed back, and just air-danced with her: Eidolon Andrew stretched his right arm out to the side, kept his left arm curled in front of him, and swayed in time to the music. Eidolon Penny swayed too, but she wouldn't raise her arms, and she kept looking up nervously to see what the doves were doing.

Then Dennis's voice cut in over the headset speakers, saying, "This song is bo-o-oring!" and Lyle Lovett's soft ballad was replaced in mid-stanza by the Rolling Stones' "Brown Sugar." I jerked my head involuntarily, and something in my headset came unplugged. The goggles went dark, even as the earphones kept blasting away.

"Damn it, Dennis!" I said, reaching up to yank my headset off.

Dennis paid no mind to my complaint. He was gaping at Penny, who still had her headset on and was still dancing. Only it wasn't the same dance anymore.

The self-conscious sway had disappeared. Now Penny's whole body was in motion, hips, arms, legs, hands, feet, all gyrating to the beat, without a hint of shyness. And the *way* she moved . . . well, as Adam later observed, all of a sudden the slogan on her tank top didn't seem so inappropriate.

Dennis stared, transfixed. Irwin stared too. *I* stared. The only one of us who didn't stare at Penny was Julie—and that was because she was staring at me, instead, with that same funny smile on her face. Eventually I noticed this, and when Julie saw that I noticed, she inclined her head in Penny's direction and raised her eyebrows as if to say: *So, what do you think?*

"Adam," I said, "what the hell is going on?"

"Well gee, Andrew, I don't know," said Adam, his voice dripping with sarcasm, "but if I didn't have my head up my ass, I might think Penny was acting like a different person . . . or maybe like a whole *bunch* of different people." Then he broke up laughing, and added: "I just love a parade, don't you?"

SECOND BOOK: MOUSE

4

Mouse is lying in a strange bed, in a strange house, with her hand pressed between the thighs of a man she has never seen before. She doesn't know what day it is, or what city; she has no idea how she got here.

A moment ago it was Sunday evening, April 20th, and she was sitting in the kitchen of her apartment, checking the movie listings in the *Seattle Times*. She was drinking a glass of red wine—never a good idea, but she had an overwhelming craving for it, and someone had left an open bottle in the cupboard above her sink. So she poured herself a glass, took a sip, and traced her finger down the column of showtimes, trying to decide between *The English Patient* and the new Jim Carrey movie.

—and now she is *not* there. There's no sense of having lost consciousness; all she did was blink, and suddenly everything is different. Where she was clothed and seated, she is now naked and lying on her side. The fresh taste of wine has become the stale aftertaste of vodka and cigarettes—she doesn't drink hard liquor or smoke, but she recognizes that aftertaste as if she does both, a lot. The cool roughness of the newsprint under her finger has become the warm clasp of flesh around her hand. And the face of a stranger has materialized, just inches from her own, snoring gin fumes.

She doesn't scream. She wants to, but a lifetime of losing time—and covering up the fact—has left her skilled at controlling her reactions. She screams inside; outside she only squeaks, a short sharp note like a hiccup. Even this is muted, as her lips clamp together to bottle the sound before it can grow.

It's a bad one. Losing time is never good—it is a symptom of insanity, which in turn is evidence of what a worthless and terrible person she is—but there are degrees of badness, and finding herself in bed with a stranger ranks near the bottom of the scale. Not that this is as bad as it could be: this stranger is asleep, at least, and only her hand is touching him. Mouse has come back from missing time into tight embraces, into the middle of intimate conversations; once she found a man on top of her, pushing her legs apart, and that time she did scream out loud.

This isn't that bad, but it is bad enough. And yet even as she thinks that, thinks what a horrible insane person she must be to find herself in these situations, another part of her mind she thinks of as the Navigator detaches itself, rises above her fright and self-loathing and becomes coolly analytical, seeking to reorient her in place and time. It feels like morning; dim gray light seeps through the window of this tiny bedroom, suggesting dawn. Just which morning is harder to figure. Monday morning, she hopes; that would mean she's only lost a night. But subjectively, there's no difference between losing a single night and losing a whole week—and she has lost whole weeks before, even whole months. Once, when she was younger, she lost an entire year. No matter the duration, all missing time feels exactly the same: like no time at all.

There are ways to tell, though. With her free hand she touches her scalp to see if her hair has grown. Mouse likes to keep her hair short and as plain as possible, but during her blackout periods she forgets this; the sudden development of a hairstyle is often her first clue that she has lost significant time. This time her hair length doesn't seem to have changed. Then she remembers that she bit the inside of her cheek during lunch on Sunday. Her tongue probes the spot and finds the wound still there, still fresh.

Monday morning, then. Most likely. And if it has only been one night, and if she spent most of that night . . . *being with* . . . the stranger beside her, she can't have traveled far. She must still be in the Seattle area, close to home. That's both good and bad: good, because finding her way back shouldn't be too difficult; bad, because she might have told *him* where she lives.

She tugs at her captive hand. It pulls loose easily, but as she withdraws it her forearm brushes the cold rubbery lump of a used condom lying on the bed sheet. A cry of disgust passes her lips before she can stop it.

The stranger's eyes move beneath still-closed lids; his own hand comes up, pawing at his mouth and nose. He snorts. And then, as Mouse holds her breath, he rolls over, turns his back to her. He settles again into sleep; but the sound of his snoring has changed now, becoming shallower, closer to true waking.

The Navigator gets her moving before fear can paralyze her. She's light;

the bedsprings hardly notice as she slips off the edge of the mattress. She ends up in a crouch on the floor beside the bed and freezes there, listening, but this time the stranger doesn't react.

Her clothes are over by the bedroom door. Her shoes and jeans are, anyway; she doesn't actually recognize the black lace panties or the pink tank top, but as they are part of the same pile it seems reasonable to assume they belong to her too. She notes with passing annoyance that there's no bra. Though she's small enough that she doesn't actually need to wear one, she thinks it looks slutty not to. Not that she's in a position to complain about looking slutty.

She dresses as quickly and quietly as possible. As she does so, she scans the room for other possessions. When you don't know what you brought with you, you can't be sure you aren't forgetting something, but she finally concludes that there is nothing else—and if there is, she can only hope that it's not irreplaceable.

Dressed and ready to leave, she checks herself in the mirror that hangs on the back of the bedroom door, and notices for the first time the obscene phrase printed across the front of the tank top. At first she thinks it's a trick—the words must be written on the mirror somehow, as a curse or an admonition to the kind of woman who would find herself sneaking out of this room at dawn. But no—she looks down—the words are on her clothing, on *her*.

She cannot go outside like this. Her anxiety rising in a tight spiral, she turns and scans the room again. A carelessly discarded sweater lies draped over the top of a dresser beside the bed. It's not her sweater—it's too big—but it will serve to cover her until she gets home. She snatches it up, dislodging several small articles from the dresser top; they clatter noisily to the floor. The stranger stirs, and Mouse, clutching the sweater, bolts from the room.

The cramped passageway outside the bedroom reminds her of the side-corridor of a train sleeper car, with windows along one wall and doors along the other. This triggers a fresh wave of alarm as she wonders if she might really be on a train. But no, the Navigator points out, real train corridors aren't this messy; passengers aren't allowed to store their personal effects in the halls. And besides, it's not moving.

What kind of house looks like a train car, but isn't one? A trailer-house, she realizes. She's in a trailer. This simplifies finding a way out: if the bedroom is at one end of the trailer, the exit must be somewhere towards the other end.

She follows the corridor. Halfway down the trailer's length, it opens out into a living-room/dining-area furnished in classic trailer-trash style: there is a sagging couch, a battered TV set, a fake plug-in fireplace, a splintery dining table piled high with beer cans and dirty plates. A counter with a peeling linoleum top separates the living room from a tiny kitchenette, where more beer cans are stored.

Trailer trash. It is ridiculous, but Mouse is shamed by the tawdriness of the place, shamed far more deeply by that than by the simple fact of being here at all. For all the times this sort of thing has happened to her, she has never once woken up in a *nice* house. It is as if the mad spirit that constantly disrupts her life meant to impress upon her that this is what she deserves, that gutter is the best she can aspire to. Never mind that she strives to keep her own home tasteful, orderly, and neat—she will always come back to this.

She has to get out of here. The trailer's outside door is in the far corner of the living room, by the entrance to the kitchenette; Mouse hurries to it. She puts on the sweater—it fits her more like a poncho, and reeks of beer and cigarettes—and opens the door. A chilly dawn wind blows in past her, rattling the beer cans on the table.

And Mouse thinks: *What about a coat?*

It was cold last night; wouldn't she have worn a coat? On the verge of escaping, she turns back again, and spies two coats on the floor in front of the phony fireplace. One of them, a scuffed leather jacket, looks like it might fit her, although, like the panties and the tank top, she doesn't actually recognize it.

She hesitates. If it is her jacket, she should take it; she wants to leave nothing of hers behind, nothing that might allow *him* to trace her. On the other hand, she is already stealing the sweater; if the jacket is not hers either, and she steals it too, *he* might call the police. What to do?

The sound of movement from the direction of the bedroom ends her indecision. She leaves the leather jacket behind and scoots out the door, even as a man's voice calls sleepily: "Hello?"

Outside, on the trailer's wooden stoop, Mouse finds a copy of the *Seattle Post-Intelligencer,* still wrapped in its plastic delivery bag. She checks the date, and learns that she was right: today is Monday, April 21st, 1997. She has only lost a night. It would be difficult to overstate her relief at this confirmation.

Mouse's car is parked in the street right in front of the trailer. No question that it's hers; it is a Buick Centurion, an unmistakable big black hulk of an automobile. She bought it used for $1,000 down and forty-eight additional monthly payments of $150, which she is still making. It is not the car she wanted. The car she *thought* she was buying was a Honda Civic, much smaller and much more economical, but somehow she ended up signing a sales contract for the Buick instead.

Whoever was driving the car last night has a thing or two to learn about parallel parking. Not only does it have one wheel up on the curb, it is facing the wrong way. But the driver was not totally careless: the Centurion's doors are all locked, and Mouse can see looking through the window that the keys are not in the ignition. She checks the pockets of her jeans and discovers that the keys are not there, either.

"No," Mouse whispers. "No, no, *no*—" She was so close to getting away! She begins to go through her pockets a second time, turning them inside out.

"Hey," a voice calls to her.

Mouse squeaks. A handful of pocket change goes flying; nickels and pennies patter across the roof of the Centurion like flat hailstones.

The stranger is standing at the top of the stoop. Ignoring the chill, he has come outside wearing only a T-shirt and a dingy pair of boxer shorts. The leather jacket is slung over his arm, and with his left hand he is jangling a set of keys. "You won't get far without these," he tells her.

Mouse swallows hard. Is he taunting her? The Navigator doesn't think so; his tone is not malicious, and he seems preoccupied with blinking the sleep out of his eyes. But he does not come down off the stoop or make any move to offer her the keys.

"Listen," the stranger continues, stifling a yawn. He gestures lazily at the trailer behind him. "You want to come back in for some breakfast? Or if you wait a few minutes, we can go out somewhere . . ."

Mouse shakes her head, trying not to look scared. But the stranger sees something in her expression; his own expression sharpens with concern.

"Hey," he says. "You're not bugging out on me about last night, are you? I mean, I know we were both pretty fucked up, but . . . you do remember, right? I asked you, I asked you *twice*, if you were sure you wanted to come back here with me. And you said you did. You said sure."

Yes, his expression is full of concern. But it is not concern *for* her, she realizes; it is concern *about* her. "You remember that, right?"

"I have to go," Mouse tells him.

"You said *sure*," the stranger insists. "I mean, you want to regret it now, light of day and all, that's your fucking prerogative, but what you said last night . . ."

"I have to go," Mouse repeats, louder this time.

"Sure, in a minute. I just want to be clear we both understand what happened. I want to be clear—"

Maledicta the Foul-Speaker, tiring of this bullshit, shoves Mouse aside and stalks forward, screaming: "Shut up and give her the fucking keys, cocksucker!"

Mouse blinks. She has teleported from the curb to the bottom of the stoop. Her hands are balled into fists, and her throat is tight, as if she'd just been shouting. The stranger is staring at her.

"All right," he tells her, his voice placating. "All right, Jesus, calm down! I'm not trying to keep you here, I just—"

"—fucking *bitch!*" Mouse is back at the curb, holding the leather jacket and turning a key in the Centurion's driver's door. Over her shoulder she sees the stranger, now at the foot of the stoop, staggering in a circle with one hand cupping his groin and the other pressed to the side of his face, which appears to be bleeding. "You fucking *bitch*, what did you—"

Silence. Mouse is sitting in her car in the parking lot of a bank. The car's engine is off but the keys are in the ignition; the leather jacket lies on the passenger seat beside her. Outside, the sky is brighter than it was.

Mouse just sits with her hands gripping the steering wheel, waiting to see if the scene will shift again. She watches a digital clock-thermometer on the side of the bank-building cycle from time to date to temperature; the time slowly increments, and the temperature rises by a degree, but there are no sudden jumps and the date remains constant.

Mouse begins to relax, and as she does, it occurs to her that she knows where she is now. The bank building is new, but across the street from it are a number of older storefronts that she recognizes. She is in Seattle's University District, not five blocks from the basement flat where she lived when she was a student at the U. of Washington.

She can get home from here. She is eager to do so, to change out of the obscene tank top and get rid of it, along with the foul-smelling sweater. But first, at the Navigator's insistence, Mouse checks around the inside of the car for a list.

Today's list is stuffed in the Centurion's glove compartment, along with a half-empty pack of Winston cigarettes and a vodka flask that Mouse pretends not to see. Hastily jotted on a crumpled bar napkin, the list enumerates half a dozen chores and appointments, with space to check off each one after it is completed. Item number one, in letters twice as high as the rest, reads: REALITY FACTORY—8:30 A.M. DRESS NICE! BE ON TIME!!!

In one sense, Mouse does not need to be reminded about her new job. She has thought of little else since Friday evening, when she first found out about it. In fact it was mainly to stop herself worrying—to get it out of her mind for a few hours—that she hit on the idea of going to see a movie last night, and took down the bottle of wine from her cupboard.

But *last night* feels like it was less than an hour ago, and Mouse still has it in her head to think that her new job starts tomorrow. The list drives home the fact that tomorrow has become today. Mouse looks at the bank clock again and realizes with dismay that she does not have time to go home. If she still lived in her old U. District flat she might make it, she might even manage a quick shower, but her current apartment on Queen Anne Hill is a fifteen-minute drive in the wrong direction. If she wants to get to Autumn Creek by 8:30, she needs to get on the freeway in the next ten minutes.

"Oh God . . ." Mouse tugs at the hem of the sweater she is wearing, feels how filthy it is. She looks at the bank clock. "Oh God." DRESS NICE, says the list, BE ON TIME, but there is no way now that she can do both. She hasn't even started her new job yet and already she has screwed up.

"You worthless piece of shit," Mouse says, catching sight of herself in the Centurion's rearview mirror. She slams her fist down into her thigh, pounding rhythmically, hard enough to bruise: "Worthless piece of *shit*, worthless piece of *shit*, worthless piece of *shit*—"

The bank clock marks another minute gone by. Mouse stops hitting herself; she switches on the Centurion's engine and guns it, drives screeching out of the lot. Two blocks down, stopped at a traffic light, she feels indecision tearing at her again. Which is worse: to come to work late but well-groomed, or to come to work on time but looking like trash?

A loud bang interrupts her reverie. A big man in a U.W. Huskies sweatshirt, crossing the street in front of her, has just bounced a basketball off the Centurion's hood. It wasn't an accident; the man noticed that Mouse was talking to herself and decided to scare her. Catching the ball on the rebound, he laughs, happy to have made her jump.

It is too much. Mouse disappears. Malefica comes, Malefica the Evil-Doer, who is Maledicta's twin sister. She taps the accelerator pedal; the Centurion lurches forward into the crosswalk, catching the Huskies fan in the shins. It's just a nudge, just enough to make him drop the ball and fall face forward onto the hood. Just enough to scare him.

It *does* scare him, for a moment. Malefica sees the fear in his eyes. But then he makes a bad mistake: he thinks to himself that Malefica is just a little girl, that she does not really know what she is doing here, who she is messing with. His fear turns to anger; he starts pushing himself up off the hood, meaning to come around and rip open the driver's door.

Malefica depresses the accelerator pedal again, holding it down. The Centurion rolls forward at five, then ten miles per hour, pushing the Huskies fan backwards. Fear recaptures him. "Hey!" he shouts, the soles of his shoes skidding over the pavement, his palms slapping at the car's hood. "Hey! *Hey! HEY!*" Fear becomes terror as he locks gazes with Malefica through the windshield and reads her intention; he throws himself to the side even as she floors the accelerator.

Still gathering speed out the far side of the intersection, Malefica checks the rear view: back at the crosswalk, the Huskies fan is picking himself up off the ground. He is shouting something after her, waving his fist, but it's hard to look threatening when you've just pissed yourself.

Malefica laughs. She is a little girl, yes, but a little girl with a *big fucking car*, and no one had better try to fuck with her. At the next corner she rolls right past a stop sign, scattering another three pedestrians with a blast of the Centurion's horn.

—and Mouse is driving east on Interstate 90 towards Autumn Creek, her decision made, though she does not recall making it. The air in the Buick is dense with cigarette smoke; Mouse takes a hand off the wheel to slap at a dribbling of ash on the front of the stolen sweater and nearly loses control of the car.

"Oh God . . ." Mouse steadies the Centurion and pulls it over into the slow lane. She rolls her window down; the smoke clears, but the rush of cold air does nothing for the sweater, which still reeks. *She* still reeks.

Maybe she can say she was sick last night. Sick to her stomach: she ate something bad for dinner, and was up half the night with cramps . . . and too late, she realized that she'd forgotten to do her laundry . . .

Yes, Mouse thinks, with a thrill of elation. It is short-lived. Yes, they might believe that—they might even be proud of her, coming in on time for her first day, despite having been sick. But Mouse knows full well that there will be other mistakes, other screw-ups requiring excuses, and there are only so many lies she can hope to get away with. Eventually, they will see through her. Eventually, inevitably, they will know her for what she truly is.

Worthless piece of shit . . .

5

Mouse isn't exactly sure how she lost her last job. It ended without warning three days ago, but whether she quit or was fired is something she really can't say; all she knows is that Julie Sivik was somehow involved.

The repair shop where she worked, Rudy's Quick Fix, is tucked into a narrow storefront just off Pioneer Square in downtown Seattle. Rudy Krenzel, the shopowner, has been in the same location for forty-five years. For the first thirty of those years, he fixed mainly typewriters, stereos, and television sets, but since the 1980s, his business has focused more and more exclusively on the repair of computer equipment, with college-age "apprentices" doing most of the work.

Mouse applied for the apprentice position last August, after Rudy's previous assistant left to attend graduate school in Boston. The job interview started out badly, with Mouse fumbling her answer to Rudy's question about how much experience she had fixing PCs. The truth was she had a lot of experience; she must have. She'd held other jobs that required her to maintain and repair computers, and had been complimented on her work—she'd been told she had a real gift for it, in fact. But because she couldn't remember a single instance of actually fixing a machine, her description of her talents came out sounding disingenuous, as if she doubted her own résumé. Rudy picked up on this, and became suspicious. "If you're such a hot shot," he asked her, "how come you want to work for *me*?" And Mouse blurted out: "It was on the list."

After that she was sure he wouldn't hire her. But Rudy decided to test her before kicking her out of his store. He led her back into a crowded workroom, where four broken PCs were lined up on a table. "Show me what you can do with those," Rudy said. For a moment Mouse just stood there, without the slightest idea of how to begin. Then Rudy cleared his throat impatiently, and Mouse took a step towards the nearest PC, and the next thing she knew she and Rudy were back in the front of the shop, shaking hands.

"—see you tomorrow morning," Rudy was saying. "I've got a big backlog piled up since Larry quit, so you can start first thing."

"OK," Mouse said. Rudy held the door open for her; she walked out, dimly aware that she had gotten the job after all. But she didn't really believe it until she saw the next day's list.

She'd been at the Quick Fix nearly eight months by the time Julie Sivik showed up. Eight months at the same job was a record for Mouse; her average was closer to three months, and her previous job, at the Cybertemps temp agency, had lasted only three weeks. Three *good* weeks, it had seemed like, until it suddenly all fell apart. Right up until the end her supervisors had been telling her what a valuable employee she was, what a hard worker, the companies she'd been hired out to all said so; and then one day she'd come in to the Cybertemps main office for a new assignment only to have the receptionist demand of her: "What the hell are *you* doing back here?"

"Getting a new placement . . ." Mouse said.

"Not here you're not," the receptionist told her. And before Mouse could learn what had happened, a security guard arrived to escort her from the premises.

Why had Cybertemps fired her? Mouse tried to pretend she didn't know, but it was obvious: because she was a bad person, that's why. The fact that she was also a good worker—or at least capable of faking it—had disguised her basic rottenness at first, but in the end she'd slipped up somehow, shown her true colors, and her employers had turned on her. It was the only rational explanation.

So she was surprised as month after month went by, and Rudy Krenzel showed no signs of starting to dislike her. It must have had something to do with the nature of her new work environment; Mouse had noticed in the past that she seemed to last longest in jobs where she had little contact with other people. Though the Quick Fix shop was small, she and Rudy didn't talk much. They said hello in the morning, and good-bye in the evening, but for most of the day, Mouse was back in the workroom while Rudy stayed up front. She fixed computers; he dealt with customers. When business was slow, Mouse worked on the daily crossword puzzle in the *Seattle Post-Intelligencer* and listened to the radio; Rudy read from a stack of James Michener books he kept stashed under the front counter. They sat less than ten feet apart, but might as well have been in separate buildings.

About the only time Mouse was really aware of Rudy's presence was when one of his old army buddies dropped by the Quick Fix. Around these men—big, heavyset guys in gray crewcuts—the normally soft-spoken Rudy Krenzel became boisterous, cracking dirty jokes and laughing so loud it hurt Mouse's ears. Sometimes, if the visitor hadn't been by before, Rudy would call Mouse up front and introduce her. She would say hi and shake hands, and as soon as possible would excuse herself and go back into the workroom, shutting the door and turning up the radio.

One afternoon in April, Mouse heard a new voice in the front room, a woman's voice. That was unusual; women in the area who needed computers repaired usually went to the PC Doctor up on Third Avenue, which charged twice as much as the Quick Fix but didn't look so much like a pawn shop. But this woman sounded more like one of Rudy's army buddies than a customer. Curious, Mouse opened the workroom door a crack and peeked out.

The woman was leaning across the counter to brush away a crumb that had gotten caught in Rudy's beard stubble. It was a flirty gesture—the woman's bosom pressed against Rudy's arm as she was grooming him—and Rudy blushed and said something about his ex-wife that made the woman laugh.

Mouse opened the door a little wider so she could hear better. She told herself she wasn't really eavesdropping, just waiting for Rudy to call her out and introduce her, but she stayed so quiet that neither Rudy nor the woman noticed she was there. They went on talking, and from their conversation Mouse learned that the woman's name was Julie Sivik, that she was the niece of a Corporal Arnold Sivik who'd served in Rudy's outfit in Korea, and that she'd come to the Quick Fix to pick up a package that "Uncle Arnie" had left for her. Mouse wasn't sure what the package contained, but she gathered that Rudy was uncomfortable having it in his shop; in fact he might even have gotten angry about it, if he hadn't been so disarmed by Julie's flirting.

"I've got no problem doing Arnie a legitimate favor," Rudy said at one point, "but I'm not running a warehouse for hot property here. I don't need that kind of heartache."

"Hey," Julie Sivik said, putting her hand on Rudy's arm. "That stuff is not stolen. Not *really* stolen, anyway . . ."

"Uh-huh," said Rudy. "That's not the impression I got from Arnie." Pulling his arm away, he got up off his stool and turned towards the workroom. Mouse ducked back out of the doorway.

"It's down in the basement," Rudy said, entering the workroom and making for a set of stairs in the back. "Arnie told me to keep it out of sight, which is a funny request for something that's not *really* stolen."

"Rudy . . ." Julie Sivik said. She tried to follow him, but he stopped her at the head of the stairs.

"Just wait up here," he said. "I'll bring it to you."

Mouse bent over the worktable, pretending to focus on the PC in front of her. She grabbed a tool at random—a tiny screwdriver with a red plastic handle—and used it to poke at the inside of the open case.

"Hi," Julie Sivik said, from two feet away. Mouse squeaked and threw the screwdriver in the air.

"Whoah!" said Julie. "Whoah, hey, don't be so jumpy! . . ."

Mouse pressed a hand to her chest. "I . . . I thought you were over there," she said, gesturing towards the stairs.

"I was," Julie said. She offered her hand to shake. "I'm Julie Sivik. And you are . . . ?"

"Penny. Penny Driver."

"Mouse," Julie said, hand back at her side. "That's a cute nickname. Kind of suits you. So, what's wrong with it?"

"With my nickname?"

"With the computer you're fixing."

"Oh," Mouse said. "It . . . it's broken."

"I see," said Julie. "I guess that would explain why you're fixing it, huh? But *how* is it broken?"

"I . . . don't really know yet. I just started on it."

"Uh-huh," Julie said. She glanced inside the PC's open case. "So tell me something, Mouse: do you always pull the power supply out of a computer before you know what's wrong with it?"

"Tell *me* something, you nosy cunt," Maledicta snapped. "Do you always fucking interrogate people when they've got work to do?"

"The power supply," Mouse stammered. "The power supply is . . . it's *part* of the problem, but I had to take it out to, to see what else is wrong. So it's still, I'm not really sure yet . . ." She paused, noticing how the color had drained from Julie's face. "Is something the matter?"

Rudy came back up the stairs, lugging a cardboard box with u.s. army surplus stenciled on its side. "Here," he said, thrusting the box at Julie. She moved quickly to take it from him.

"Thanks, Rudy. I *really* appreciate this . . ."

"Yeah, yeah . . . you two introduce yourselves?" Rudy asked, with a nod to Mouse.

"Uh, yeah," Julie said. "We were just getting acquainted . . . Mouse says you keep her pretty busy."

Rudy chuckled. "She keeps *herself* pretty busy. Hardest worker I ever hired."

"Really . . . Does she just do hardware, or can she debug code, too?"

"Why?"

"No reason. Just curious . . ."

"Don't get any ideas," Rudy warned. "I have a hard enough time replacing mediocre assistants."

"Ideas?" Julie beamed an innocent smile at him; but Rudy, past flirting now, answered her with a scowl. "All right," he said, "I think it's time you and your not-stolen property hit the road."

"On my way," said Julie. "See you around, Mouse . . ." She walked out, and Rudy followed her, pulling the door shut behind him. Mouse turned up the radio and got back to work.

The rest of the afternoon passed in no time.

Mouse didn't go home after work that day; instead, as instructed by her list, she went over to the Elliott Bay Book Company. She found an empty table in the bookstore's basement café and got a cup of Earl Grey tea. While the teabag steeped, she set up a laptop computer on the table. The laptop had been in Mouse's possession for some time, though she couldn't have said exactly how long, or where it had come from in the first place. But she didn't worry about that now—just switched it on and started up Microsoft Word.

As the program was loading, Mouse glanced at the clock on the café wall; it was 6:25. The next time she looked up, the clock read 7:13, and Julie Sivik was standing beside her again.

"—anybody home?" Julie passed a hand in front of Mouse's eyes. "Mouse?"

Mouse reached out hurriedly to fold down the laptop's screen. She got a brief glimpse of the file she'd been working on—the title bar said "Thread.doc"—before it dropped out of view. Only after the laptop's latch clicked did she look directly at Julie.

"Hello," Mouse said.

"Hello," said Julie, eyeing the laptop. "I'm interrupting again, aren't I?"

Mouse didn't answer, just stared, waiting for Julie to state her business. After a moment, Julie said: "Well listen, first off, I wanted to apologize for being so nosy today at the shop . . ."

"Nosy?"

"Yeah . . . you seemed kind of upset by my questions."

Mouse shook her head. She remembered being uncomfortable, but not upset.

"Well," said Julie. "Well anyway, I *did* want to apologize, and also—"

"How did you find me here?"

"My car broke down," Julie explained. "Triple A's got it at a garage right now, a few blocks from here. Supposed to be ready by eight o'clock. I came in here to kill some time; finding you was just good luck." She smiled.

"*Any*way," Julie continued, "I really don't want to be a pest, but seeing as I have run into you, I'm still wondering about that last question I asked at Rudy's."

"About the power supply?" Mouse chewed her lip nervously; though she knew she'd finished repairing the broken PC sometime after Julie's visit— the machine's owner had picked it up just before closing—she still had no idea what had been wrong with it.

"Power supply . . . ?" Julie said, then shook her head. "No. No, not that. The question I asked Rudy, about whether you did any work debugging code." To Mouse's blank stare: "You know, *code*? Software code?"

"Oh," said Mouse. "I—"

"See, here's the thing," Julie said. She reached for Mouse's laptop; Mouse started to protest, but Julie was only moving it aside, making room on the table for a laptop of her own. She grabbed a chair and sat down, sliding in so close that her knee and Mouse's were touching. "The thing is," Julie continued, "I've got this software company, and we've been working on this virtual-reality project for a couple years now. And my lead programmer, Dennis, he's a really sharp guy, but lately he's just not getting things done fast enough. So the past few months I've been thinking about bringing in somebody new, to sort of light a fire under Dennis's ass."

Julie tapped on her laptop's keyboard, opening a window on the screen that filled with a scroll of letters, numbers, and symbols. Software code, Mouse guessed, though it might as well have been Chinese. "This is part of the source code for one of our program modules," Julie explained. "Or rather, it *was* part of the source code—this version of the software turned out to have a bug in it. Nothing complicated; it only took Dennis a few minutes to track down and fix, once he got around to it. But I kept this copy of the original code to use as a sort of test for potential employees . . ." She looked expectantly at Mouse.

Mouse shook her head. She opened her mouth, intending to say that she was sorry if she had somehow given Julie the wrong impression, but she wasn't looking for a second job, and besides—

Her chair slid back abruptly from the table. Julie didn't seem to notice: she was leaning forward now, studying the laptop's screen.

"Huh," Julie said, rubbing her chin. "I don't think this is the same fix Dennis came up with . . ." She dug through a sheaf of papers that lay on the table, pulling out one page and comparing it with what was on the screen. "No, it isn't the same." She extracted a second page from the pile. "Shit . . . I think your solution might be better . . . It's *simpler*, anyway . . ." Julie put the pages back down, and turned to Mouse with a look of new respect. "So how happy are you, working for Rudy?"

Mouse shrugged, not sure how to answer that question. She worked for Rudy so she could pay her bills, and because it was on the list; what did being happy have to do with it?

"It can't be a very interesting job," Julie suggested. "Sitting in that back room all day, replacing bad circuit cards . . ."

"I don't mind it."

"You should let me tell you more about my company," Julie said. She waved a hand at Mouse's empty cup. "Why don't I get you some more tea, and we'll chat?"

"I don't really like tea," said Mouse.

"Oh-*kay* . . . something else to drink, then? A beer, maybe, or a glass of wine?"

"Wine," said Mouse. "Some red wine would be OK."

—and she was home, in her apartment kitchen, the clock above the stove reading 11:55. She had a bad headache and she was starving. After a quick stop at the refrigerator—she found a slab of turkey roast and a brick of cheddar cheese and devoured them both standing up, chasing them with half a carton of milk—Mouse staggered into bed, too tired even to check her list to make sure she'd completed all her chores.

The next day at work, Rudy started treating her differently. Not right away; when Mouse first came into the shop he said good morning the same as he always did. But after she came back from lunch (she didn't remember going out), Rudy seemed tense, and that evening he didn't reply when she wished him good night.

That was Tuesday; and every day after that, Rudy's mood seemed to get worse. On Wednesday morning he yelled at her for the first time ever, complaining that the workroom was "a complete mess" and that "I'll never be able to find anything back here, the way you've let it go."

"What are you looking for?" asked Mouse, alarmed. "I'll help you find it." But this offer of assistance only seemed to anger Rudy further; he told her to have the workroom straightened out by closing time Friday and stalked out.

On Friday, the moment she'd been dreading for eight months finally arrived. It happened as Mouse was preparing to leave. As ordered, she'd straightened up the workroom; she'd also finished the last two pending repair jobs. "All done," she announced, coming out front shortly before six.

Rudy, who sat reading a copy of *The Drifters* with a sullen expression on his face, wouldn't acknowledge her.

"OK, then," Mouse said. "If there's nothing else you need me to do today . . ."

No response.

"OK," Mouse said. "I'll be going, then. I'll see you on Monday, Rudy."

Her hand was on the door when Rudy said: "No you won't."

Mouse turned around. Rudy was glaring at her over the top of his book. "I won't?" Mouse said.

"No," said Rudy. "Don't you remember?" He snorted. "Hell, maybe you don't. Maybe the 'numbing boredom' of working for me numbed your memory, too." He set down his book and took a deep breath. "I've got something to say to you before you go. If you don't like your job, whatever the reason, that's fine—I don't want anybody working here against their will. But you've got no right to shit on me personally. Maybe this place *is* just 'a hole in the wall,' but I've got pride in it just the same—I worked for it, I built it up, I kept it going for years without any help from anybody, and you've got *no right* to shit on that. It may not be much, but it's more than *you've* got, as far as I can tell . . ."

Mouse felt her lower lip quivering. She wanted to cry; she wanted to beg Rudy's forgiveness for whatever she'd done. But she was terrified that if she did either of those things, made any sound or interrupted Rudy in any way, he'd come out from behind the counter and start hitting her. So she stayed mute and still by the door, while Rudy continued to berate her. He went on for a long time.

". . . so that's it," he concluded, when his rage was finally spent. By this point his eyes were rimmed with red, as if he too were on the verge of crying. "That's all I've got to say to you. Now get the hell out of my shop."

"Rudy . . ." Mouse tried to say, but the word came out as a meaningless twitter. Then Rudy stood up, shoving his stool back with a loud screech, and Mouse bolted.

She ran from the Quick Fix so swiftly that she was all the way to her car before the tears started. She slid into the driver's seat, slapped down the door locks, and then hunched over the steering wheel blubbering for almost twenty minutes. She kept hoping she would lose time, lose this moment, this day, and so find herself beyond it. But time stayed with her, and eventually the crying fit tapered off. She drove home.

A red light blinked in the darkness of her apartment as she let herself in: there was a message on her answering machine. After switching on the living-room lights, Mouse hit the playback button, and heard Julie Sivik's voice: "Hey Mouse! It's Friday afternoon, around four, and I'm calling to confirm that we're all set for Monday . . ."

The top of the stand on which the answering machine rested was glass-inlaid wood; as the message continued—with Julie expressing concern about how Rudy had "taken the news"—Mouse caught sight of her reflection in the glass. Holding her own gaze, Mouse wondered: *What have you done?*

But even though she already knew she was crazy, she didn't dare ask that question aloud.

6

Today's list includes a set of directions for finding the Reality Factory, but even so, and even going there directly without stopping off home, Mouse arrives several minutes late. Distracted by a tailgating semi-truck, she misses the turnoff for Autumn Creek and is forced to backtrack from the next exit; and having found her way into the town, she doesn't recognize the Factory at first. *Across 2nd bridge, quarter mile beyond on left side,* the directions read, but during a phone conversation over the weekend, Julie Sivik described the Factory as being "just a little rundown," so Mouse is not expecting a ruin. She drives right past it, and goes another mile down the road before realizing her mistake.

"Oh God," Mouse exclaims as she drives in the Factory gate, having backtracked once more. The property isn't just rundown; it looks abandoned. But there is an old Cadillac with new bodywork parked on the lot, and Mouse remembers Julie mentioning on the phone that her car was a fixed-up Caddy. So this really must be it: this is where she works now. Mouse parks her Buick just inside the gate, pointed outward, ready for a quick getaway. And even though she is late, she sits for a moment after shutting off the engine, gathering her courage before stepping out.

Enter main building through side door, the directions read. The main building must be the long, low warehouse-like structure at the center of the lot. Mouse walks around it to the left (a mountain of old tires enclosed by a chain-link fence blocks passage on the right), turning frequently to check that nothing is creeping towards her out of the thickets of weeds and bushes that encircle the property. At the door she pauses to adjust her sweater; she tugs at both the collar and the hem, making sure it covers the tank top completely.

The wording of the directions implies that she should let herself in, but

Mouse knocks anyway. No one answers. Reluctantly she tries the doorknob, which turns easily. She opens the door and steps inside.

Oh God. The building is just a shell, concrete walls and a patchwork roof sheltering a collection of . . . *tents?*

"This is the place," a woman's voice calls to her. Mouse squeaks. "Sorry, sorry," the voice apologizes, and Mouse sees that it isn't a woman after all: the voice belongs to a boyish-looking man with a tousle of sandy hair. He darts towards her with startling swiftness, and Mouse, frightened, backs up against the door.

Mouse is relieved when Julie Sivik appears. But her relief is short-lived: Julie tells the boyish man to call Mouse by her nickname, and another man—a fat, ugly man, like a chubby troll—pops out of a nearby tent shouting "Hi, Mouse!" He too darts towards her, his speed belying his size, and engulfs her hand in a damp doughy two-fisted grip.

Mouse is overwhelmed. The morning starts to fragment, bits of time dropping out, shuddering the smooth flow of events. "Let's go try out the system," Julie says, and they walk towards a big tent at one end of the building: Julie and Mouse, the boyish man, the fat man, and a third man, a skinny glum guy who doesn't talk. Mouse feels as though she ought to know the men's names by now, but she doesn't.

Julie holds open the tent flap for her, elbowing aside the troll, who is attempting to perform the same service. Mouse enters; she has a brief impression of the tent's interior, a musty, mildewy smelling space filled with all sorts of electronic equipment.

—and then she is standing in the middle of the tent with the three nameless men staring at her while Julie tries to pull her sweater off—

—and something heavy is being forced down over her head, covering her eyes—

—and she is caught up in a hallucination of a giant checkerboard floating in space. A fluorescent ghost glides towards her over the surface of black and white squares, and the voice of the troll speaks in her ear, commanding her to dance.

Too much. Too much. Mouse disappears. Drone comes, Drone who does what she is told and feels nothing. "Dance, Mouse," the troll says, and Drone rocks obediently from side to side. Then the music changes—Drone is not even aware of the music until it changes, but it changes—and Loins takes over, recognizing a song she loves. Loins actually *enjoys* dancing; it was she who went out last night to the Rain Dancers roadhouse, she who met up with George Lamb, the stranger, and agreed to follow him home. She would have fucked him, too, but by the time they got to George's trailer, she'd realized it wasn't going to be any fun, so she pushed *that* chore off on Drone.

Loins dances until the music stops, until the dream-world is switched off and the virtual-reality headset is lifted from her brow. Then she gives way to the Brain, who fixes PCs and writes code . . .

By the time Mouse comes back, the morning is over. She returns to find herself inside another, smaller tent. She sits in a wooden folding chair, while Julie speaks to her from behind a beat-up desk. A digital clock on the desktop informs her that it is now 12:12. Mouse has a headache but is not tired, and the Navigator surmises that it is 12:12 P.M., not A.M.

"—have a sit-down with Dennis after lunch and hash out exactly what you'll be working on," Julie is saying. Mouse doesn't really pay attention to the words. Instead, as discreetly as she can, she checks herself: she looks down and sees that she is wearing the sweater, that her tank top is once again covered, if in fact it was ever uncovered. That brief flash she had of Julie trying to strip the sweater off her—maybe *that* was a hallucination too, like the floating checkerboard.

But if she did hallucinate, if she had some kind of psychotic episode, what did she actually *do* while it was happening? Did anybody else notice? Mouse observes Julie for a moment, and decides that the way Julie is talking to her—calm, relaxed—is not the way she would talk to someone she had seen acting crazy a little while ago. Still, Mouse thinks, 12:12—that's three and a half hours since she got here. What *happened?*

"—hungry?" Julie asks.

"What?" says Mouse. Julie smiles indulgently at her. "I'm sorry," Mouse says. "I . . . I drifted off for a second . . ."

"It's all right," says Julie. "I asked whether you were hungry. I was thinking, maybe I'll dip into petty cash, round up the guys, and take everybody out to lunch on the company. How's that sound?"

"OK," Mouse says. What Mouse would really like to do is go home, call up Rudy Krenzel, and plead for her old job back. But that doesn't appear to be an option—it's not on her list.

Mouse stays close as Julie goes to get the others. By paying careful attention, she is finally able to put names to two of the men. The boyish man is called Andrew; the troll—whose shirt is hanging wide open when they find him, earning him a sharp rebuke from Julie—is Dennis. Mouse still can't catch the name of the third man, but he is so quiet that she decides it doesn't matter; you don't need to know what to call someone if they don't talk to you.

They go outside, where Julie expresses concern that they will not all fit comfortably in her car, due to unspecified problems with the backseat cushions. "That's OK," Mouse tells her, not unhappy with this development. "I can follow you in my car."

"I volunteer to ride with Mouse!" Dennis shouts, and Mouse cringes. But Julie comes to her rescue: "No, Dennis," she says, "you ride with me. I need to talk to you about something."

"What, right now? We can talk at the diner."

"No, Dennis," repeats Julie. "Andrew, why don't *you* ride with Mouse? Make sure she doesn't get lost."

"Get *lost?*" Dennis exclaims. "What the fuck, Commodore? The diner is on Bridge Street. All she's got to do is turn right out the gate and drive straight."

"Just get in the damn car, Dennis." Grumbling, Dennis stomps around to the passenger side of the Cadillac, where the quiet man is already waiting for Julie to unlock the doors. "You ride in back!" Dennis bellows, shoving the quiet man aside.

As soon as they are seated in the Caddy, Julie and Dennis start arguing with each other again, but the car's windows are rolled up and Mouse can't make out the words. She turns to Andrew, who is mumbling to himself and seems lost in thought. After a moment he snaps out of it, looks at Mouse and shrugs apologetically. "When Julie makes up her mind to do something in a certain way," he says, "there's not much point in fighting it." He nods his head in the direction of Mouse's Centurion. "Want to go?"

Andrew makes polite small talk on the way to the diner. It's a good effort, but not good enough to hide the fact that he is uncomfortable being alone with her. Mouse wonders if he saw something that Julie missed. *What was I doing this morning between nine and twelve?* she thinks of asking him, but of course she doesn't say that. Wounded by his apprehension, Mouse decides that she doesn't like Andrew.

Soon enough they are at the Harvest Moon, a Fifties-style malt shop with lots of chrome and neon. Mouse follows Julie's Cadillac into the lot behind the diner. She barely has time to set the parking brake before Andrew exits the car. "Cocksucker," Maledicta grumbles at his back.

Inside the diner, Dennis tries to sit next to Mouse, but once again Julie Sivik intervenes; she takes the seat to Mouse's left for herself and insists that Andrew, not Dennis, sit on Mouse's right.

"What the hell is this, Dial-a-Date?" Dennis complains loudly. "What do you keep putting *him* next to her for?"

"Here Dennis," says Julie, handing him a menu. "You'll feel better once you've got food in front of you."

A waitress takes their orders, and while they wait for their lunches to arrive, Julie tries unsuccessfully to get a conversation going. More specifically, she tries to get Andrew and Mouse to have a conversation; she does this by asking Andrew a series of set-up questions, like "So Andrew, did you know that Mouse once worked at Bit Warehouse, same as you did?" But Andrew won't follow her lead, and between his obvious discomfort, and Dennis's jibes about Dial-a-Date, Julie is soon forced to give up. No one says anything else until the food comes.

It is while they are eating that the thing happens that changes Mouse's mind about disliking Andrew. Within sight of their table is a booth in which a man sits with a young girl of four or five. The man saws mechanically at a large T-bone steak, forking one piece of meat after another into his mouth. The girl isn't hungry; there is a plateful of peas and mashed potatoes in front of her, but rather than eat any of it, she just uses a spoon to push the peas around and trace patterns in the gravy. Eventually she grows bored with this; as an experiment, she taps the rim of the plate with the bowl of her spoon. Pleased with the sound it makes, she begins striking it repeatedly, like a gong.

The man sets his fork down. He grabs the girl's spoon hand, stilling it; he doesn't speak, but his eyes flash a warning. The girl, momentarily chastened, goes back to pushing peas. The man returns to his steak. Then the girl, growing bored again, clinks her spoon against the side of a water glass.

This time the man doesn't bother to put his fork down; he just hauls off and backhands her across the face. It is a powerful blow: the girl is knocked sideways in her seat and nearly falls out of the booth. Her face turns purple and she begins to cry, softly. A few of the other diner patrons look around at the sound, and look away again.

Then Andrew stands up. ("Oh Jesus," says Dennis, "here we go," but Andrew ignores him.) He walks over to the booth, positioning himself on the girl's side of the table, and stares at the man, who has gone back to sawing at his steak.

"Excuse me," Andrew says.

The man in the booth takes a moment to finish chewing a bit of gristle. "What do *you* want?" he finally asks.

"Is this your daughter?" asks Andrew.

"Yes, it's my daughter," the man in the booth says. "What do you *want*?"

"You could have broken her eardrum, hitting her like that," Andrew informs him. "Or her jaw. Or"—he points to the fork clutched in the man's fist—"you could have put her eye out."

The man drops the fork into his plate and brushes his hands together. He sighs impatiently. "Get out of my face, asshole."

"Don't call me an asshole," Andrew says.

The man in the booth seems amazed to hear these words coming out of Andrew's mouth. He is bigger than Andrew by a fair margin, and much meaner-looking; he wears a suit, but it is rumpled and worn, as if he spends a lot of time engaged in hard physical labor . . . or administering beatings to people who annoy him. "Would you like me to poke *your* eye out?" he says. "Or rip out your fucking—"

"Don't threaten me," says Andrew, his own voice not threatening but firm, the voice a father—a *good* father—might use to dissuade a child from pursuing a dangerous course of action: *Don't play with those matches, honey!*

And the man in the booth hesitates, confused by Andrew's lack of fear. He studies Andrew's face for a moment, then looks down—checking Andrew's hands, Mouse realizes, to see if he is holding a weapon. He isn't. And though Andrew is physically fit, he doesn't carry himself like a fighter. It is a conundrum.

"What are you, crazy?" the man in the booth asks. Andrew lets the question hang there, and the man in the booth continues, wary now: "How I treat my kid is none of your business, pal."

"A grown man beating up a little girl is everybody's business," Andrew tells him; he says this in a loud voice, and once more heads begin to turn. "You should be ashamed of yourself."

"*Ashamed* of myself!" the man guffaws. He looks out of the booth, seeking a confederate among the diner patrons who are staring at him. His gaze settles on Julie. "Do you believe this guy?" he asks her. "He thinks he's my goddamn conscience!"

"Maybe you need one," Julie says.

The man bobs his head. "Well," he says, turning back to Andrew, "well, there you go. That's one vote for you."

"I don't need votes," Andrew says.

"No, of course not," says the man. "You *know* you're right, right? You're an *expert* on childcare. But let me tell you something: if *you* had to put up with this fucking kid—"

"If she were my daughter, I wouldn't call her 'this fucking kid.' And she wouldn't be crying while I stuffed my face."

For an instant it looks as though the man is going to take a swing at

Andrew after all. But Andrew doesn't blink or flinch, just goes right on looking him in the eye, and in the end the man in the booth decides not to risk finding out why Andrew isn't afraid. "Fine," he says. He twists in his seat, digs frantically in one of his pants pockets. "Fine, tell you what: you go *get* yourself a kid, OK? You get yourself a kid, live with it for a couple years, then you come back and lecture me on how it's done." He slaps a twenty-dollar bill down on the table next to his plate. "Come on, Rebecca!" he barks, sliding out of the booth. He shoves Andrew aside and scoops up the little girl, who has been watching the confrontation with great interest, her tears forgotten. The man starts to carry the girl away; halfway to the door he stops, turns back, and points a finger at Andrew. "You'd better hope I never see you again. *Asshole.*"

"If I hear you've been beating up little kids," says Andrew, "you will see me again. And not just me."

"Crazy." The man lowers his arm, shakes his head. Catching a waitress's eye, he says: "You've got crazy people eating here, you know that?"

He walks out, taking the girl with him. Andrew watches until they are gone, then returns to the table.

"I wish to *Christ* you wouldn't do that," Dennis says.

Andrew nods, and replies sadly: "I know you do, Dennis."

"That guy could've killed you. He could've pulled out a gun and shot you dead. It happens."

"I don't think he had a gun, Dennis."

"He had a *steak knife.* He had fists . . ."

Andrew shakes his head. "Adam didn't think he'd hit me."

"Adam . . ." Dennis rolls his eyes. Putting audible quotes around the name, he says: "And what if 'Adam' was wrong?"

"Then Seferis would have protected me."

"Seferis . . . you really are a mental case, you know that? That guy was right. And you know what the worst part of it is? It's not going to make any difference. Do you really think that guy is going to stop hitting his kid just because you said 'Shame on you'?"

"It's more likely than if I'd said nothing," Andrew argues. But he looks unhappy, as if he fears Dennis may be right.

"Nah," says Dennis. "Nah, he's not going to change."

"That doesn't matter!" Andrew insists. "I mean . . . I mean it *does* matter, but you can't just do nothing. You can't just sit by while somebody does something wrong, and not call them on it."

"Why not? If calling them on it doesn't make any difference . . . the next time that guy feels like slapping his daughter around, do you think he's even going to remember you?"

"No," Mouse says, surprising herself by speaking up, "but the girl will remember." Andrew and Dennis both look at her, and Julie smiles.

After lunch they go back to the Reality Factory, where Mouse starts losing time again. It's not unexpected; it happens just as Julie announces that it is time for Mouse to get to work. "OK," Julie says, "let's you and Dennis and I go sit down and start—"

—and the next thing Mouse knows she is alone, crouching in the space between two close-set tents. Uncertain what she is doing there, she starts to get up, but pauses when she hears two voices coming from the tent to her left. One voice is Julie's; the other is Andrew's.

"—textbook MPD," Julie says. "I talked to three, maybe four different people."

"The parade," says Andrew. "That's what Adam calls it."

"The funny thing is, I might not have recognized it if I didn't know you. I might have just thought, 'Wow, she's *really* moody!' But once you know what to look for . . . I got an inkling right away, when she snapped at me at Rudy's. But it wasn't until I bumped into her again at the bookstore that I was sure. After she got a couple drinks in her it was really obvious."

"You got her drunk?"

"I didn't *mean* to," Julie says, sounding defensive. "I offered to buy her a glass of wine, and then she asked for a second. And then she went and bought three more glasses on her own."

"Julie!"

"Well what was I supposed to do? I didn't even know who was ordering those last three drinks."

"I hope you drove her home afterwards."

"I tried, Andrew. Really I did. She wasn't *acting* drunk, but she's so little, and after five glasses . . . but she wouldn't let me give her a ride. When I pressed her on it, this new person came out who I hadn't met yet, and he said—he was male, definitely male, and his voice was stone-sober—he said, 'No, she's going to need her car to get to work in the morning.' And I said, 'Are you sure she should be driving after all that wine?' And he said, 'Don't worry, I'll drive her home. I've done it before.' Even then I didn't just let her—him—go. I said good night, pretended to walk the other way, and then turned around and followed them. I figured I'd at least see that they got to their car all right. But they didn't go straight to the car, they went into a coffee shop. So I hung around outside for as long as I could, until I had to go get my car, and they never came out, so I thought, OK, they'll be fine, they're waiting to sober up . . . I felt bad about it, Andrew, but what else could I do? It wasn't—it wasn't like that time *you* got drunk."

Andrew makes a sound that Mouse, listening through the tent fabric, cannot interpret. There is a silence. Then Andrew says: "So you offered her a job."

"*Before* she had the second glass of wine, yeah. And she said yes."

"Who said yes?"

Julie laughs. "Yeah, that question occurred to me, too. She gave me her home number, so I called up early the next morning, partly to double-check that she really had made it home OK, partly to see if she remembered accepting the job offer."

"And did she?"

"Somebody did. Whoever answered the phone. But when I talked to her again on Saturday she seemed kind of clueless, like all of a sudden she didn't remember but was trying hard not to show it. To tell you the truth, I wasn't a hundred percent sure she'd show up this morning."

Andrew asks: "Why did you offer her the job, Julie?"

"Why?" Julie exclaims. She says it as if she is astonished that there could be any question about the reason, but even listening through the tent wall, Mouse can tell that her surprise is faked. "Because she's a natural programmer, that's why. At least, *one* of her souls is. You should have seen after lunch today, even Dennis was impressed once he saw her in action." A pause. "What, you don't believe me?"

"I believe she's a good programmer," Andrew says, "but Adam thinks there's another reason why you hired her, and I think he's right."

Another pause.

"Well . . ." Julie says.

"Well?"

"OK," says Julie, "OK, OK, here's the thing. Her programming skills really are the *main* reason I hired her—I'd been thinking about bringing somebody new in, at least part-time, for a while now, so it really was in my head to sound her out about a job, even before I made the connection about the MPD. That's the God's honest truth, Andrew. But when I *did* make the connection, I thought . . ."

"What?"

"See, the thing is, *she doesn't know*. I mean, some of her people know, obviously, like the one who told me he'd drive her home, but she—the woman you met this morning—she doesn't know. I'm sure of it. So I thought, maybe you, you could—"

"Oh, Julie . . . this is a *bad* idea."

"I remember you telling me what it was like for your father, back before he built the house. Before *he* knew. Like living in chaos, you said. Well . . . that must be what it's like for her too, right? Like living in chaos."

"Probably. But Julie—"

"So I would think, having lived through that experience yourself, you would want to help—"

"I didn't live through that experience myself," Andrew says. "My father did. And neither one of us is a psychiatrist, which is what she needs."

"OK, fine, but how's she going to *get* what she needs, if she doesn't even know—"

"If she doesn't know, it's probably because she's not ready to know. And trying to force the knowledge on her could do more harm than good."

"You're saying she's better off being ignorant of her condition?"

"I'm saying that if you upset her by trying to tell her something about herself that she doesn't want to hear, she won't hear it—she'll call out another soul to protect her from the information. And if you keep upsetting her, the protector may decide you're a threat, and try to get her away from you. Only *she* won't know what's going on—she'll just wake up one day with a new job, maybe even living in a new city, and she'll have to cope with that change without understanding why it happened."

"Well," Julie says, sounding reproached. "I wasn't . . . I'm not suggesting you should just *drop* it on her. My idea was that you'd get to know her first, make friends, then maybe share your own history with her. Tell her what things were like for your father and the others before the house got built—"

"Describe the symptoms?"

"Well . . . yes, actually. You could talk about how your father used to lose time, tell her about those lists he used to keep . . . and I mean, don't *push*, but if she says to you, 'Hey, that sounds like *my* life,' then—"

"I still don't think it's a very good idea, Julie. And I really wish you would have asked me about this before you hired her. I mean, speaking of dropping things on people . . . you've known about this for a week already, but the first I heard about it was this morning, from Dennis."

"I know, I know . . . I should have told you. I almost did, but then I thought, I didn't want to prejudice your thinking."

"'Prejudice my thinking'? What does that mean?"

"It means . . . I wanted to see what would happen if you met her without being told about the MPD in advance. If you'd pick up on it without me pointing it out."

"But you said it was obvious. Were you worried that maybe you were wrong, that she wasn't multiple after all?"

"No, I was sure about that, I just thought—"

"What? That it would be fun to surprise me?"

"Andrew!"

"I'm sorry, Julie," Andrew says, "but I'm really . . . it bothers me a lot that you would do this. This isn't a game. It's not a, not a virtual-reality simulation."

"Andrew . . ."

"It isn't fair," Andrew insists. "Not to me, and especially not to her. I really don't know what you were thinking, Julie. I really don't."

"Andrew! . . . Andrew, wait!"

He is leaving the tent. Hugging the canvas wall for concealment, Mouse slides forward and peers around the tent's front corner in time to catch his exit. She sees right away that the walkout is mostly theater; instead of storming off, Andrew stops just outside and waits for Julie to catch up to him. When Julie does, she is contrite, though Mouse wonders if the contrition isn't theater, too.

"All right, Andrew," Julie says, and lays a hand on his forearm—the same flirting, conciliatory gesture Mouse saw her use on Rudy Krenzel. "All right, I fucked up, I admit it, and I'm sorry. Really. But she *is* working here now. I can't take that back. And I hope you aren't going to punish her for my mistake."

"Of course I won't *punish* her. But Julie—"

Julie tugs lightly on his arm, brushing it against the front of her bosom. "Just work with her," she pleads. "If the MPD never comes up, that's fine. If you two don't hit it off, that's fine too—I won't push anymore, I promise. But if—just *if*—it turns out that she does want help, that she's *ready* for help, I hope that—"

"I'm not going to make any promises, Julie."

"And I won't ask you to. We'll just, we'll see what happens, OK?" She smiles at him and bats her eyelashes, and when he doesn't respond she answers the question herself: "OK. So . . ." She gives his arm a last tug and releases it. "I'd better go see how she's doing. I told Dennis to set her up in the spare tent with another test project, but she's probably finished by now."

Julie kisses Andrew on the cheek, which seems to startle him, then turns and walks away, leaving him standing there, looking exasperated and more than a little confused. He watches her go; Mouse watches him watching.

Mouse is fascinated by the conversation she has just overheard, even though there is much of it that she doesn't understand. For the second time today, she considers letting down her guard; she imagines stepping out of her hiding place, tapping Andrew on the shoulder, and asking: *What was that all about? Were you talking about* me *just now?*

This time it is more than an idle thought, but she still doesn't do it. She hangs back, lurking, and a moment later she witnesses something else interesting.

As Julie passes out of earshot, Andrew's face changes. His *expression* changes, she should say, but the transformation seems more fundamental than that. Andrew's confusion evaporates; his look of mild annoyance becomes something much more severe, and much darker: contempt bordering on loathing.

"Cunt," Andrew says. "You meddling cunt."

Then he blinks, and he is once again his boyish, befuddled, lightly exasperated self. "Oh Julie," he mutters. He cocks his head, as if listening, and adds: "Be quiet."

"Mouse?" Julie calls, from elsewhere in the Factory. "Mouse, where are you?"

Mouse, gone again, doesn't answer. Instead Maledicta and Malefica retreat, by turns, to a hiding place they scoped out earlier: a storage-and-supply tent filled with stacks of boxes, boxes that are easily rearranged into a makeshift fortress of solitude. They go in there and wall themselves away. Malefica pulls up a particularly sturdy box to sit on; Maledicta lights a cigarette.

They stay in the fortress of solitude for a long time, thinking.

THIRD BOOK: ANDREW

7

The first two e-mails were waiting for me when I came to work on Tuesday morning.

I'd already been expecting it to be an emotionally trying week, because of my confrontation with Julie the afternoon before. This wasn't the first time Julie had tried to complicate my life without checking to see if I'd mind. She liked volunteering people for things; she liked surprises, too. She didn't like asking permission, or at least didn't always seem to recognize when permission was necessary. And whenever she was called to account for it—whenever someone objected to being involved in some scheme or intrigue against their will—her reaction was consistent, so consistent that Adam had made up a name for it. He called it the Julie Sivik Patented Three-Phase Response to a Good Ass-Chewing.

Phase one, which lasted approximately twenty-four hours, was Contrition. Upon being informed that she'd overstepped the bounds of friendship, Julie would turn meek and conciliatory, so wounded by her own transgression that the friend she'd presumed upon might actually start to feel guilty, as if he were the one who'd gone too far. But even as the first doubts set in, Julie would shift abruptly to phase two, which Adam called Balancing the Scales. During this phase, which lasted anywhere from two to five days, Julie would herself become hypercritical, losing her temper over minor slights and mistakes that she ordinarily wouldn't even have noticed. The worst thing about phase two was that there was no way to get Julie to see the connection between it and phase one. If, a couple days from now, Julie were to yell at me for tying my shoelaces the wrong way, and I said to her, "You know, Julie, the real reason you're angry is because you feel guilty," she not only wouldn't agree, she wouldn't even understand what I was talking about. I knew, because I'd tried it before.

Phase three, Reconciliation, was a milder version of phase one. At some point Julie would turn nice again, and spend a day or two making up, without ever admitting in any way that there was anything to make up *for*. And then it would be over, at least until next time—although if Penny kept working at the Reality Factory, next time might not be that long in coming.

Yesterday afternoon, when Julie had pleaded with me to at least think about helping Penny, I'd told her I wouldn't make any promises. I hadn't actually said no, though, and I knew that Julie was likely to interpret that—the lack of a flat refusal—as if I *had* promised. So of course I had spent some time thinking about helping Penny—most of last night, in fact—and the more I thought about it, the more sure I was that I couldn't do it.

I'd already told Julie some of the reasons: I wasn't a psychotherapist; even if I had been, it wouldn't have done any good unless Penny was ready to be helped. But the biggest reason was one that I hadn't mentioned, because it sounded too mean to say out loud: I didn't *like* Penny.

I don't mean that I disliked her. I mean that my feelings towards her were neutral: neither good nor bad, positive or negative. She was just someone who, if I'd met her by chance, I wouldn't have been especially interested in. Of course that very disinterest was somewhat negative, coming from me: usually I am interested in new people. That I was neutral about Penny was kind of a strike against her—at least that's how Julie would likely see it. But it was how I felt; I couldn't help it.

And because it was how I felt, I couldn't help her. I hadn't been born yet when my father started building the house, but I'd heard enough stories about it to know that it was a difficult, painful process—and not just for him. I love my father, but Aunt Sam says he was hell to be around in those early days, and that's not even counting the times he fought Gideon for control of the body. To stick by him through that rough period, you had to be either a true friend, or family, or a saint like Mrs. Winslow, or a professional like Dr. Grey. A just-met acquaintance with neutral feelings could never have hacked it.

"So fuck it, then," said Adam, as I came in the Factory gates and crossed the lot to the shed. "Penny's not your problem. You didn't bring her here, and you didn't promise to help her."

"I know, but Julie—"

"Oh, *Julie*," Adam sneered. "That's right, I forgot, we can't ever disappoint Julie."

"She's been very kind to us."

"Kind to us. Right. And that's why you're still thinking about this—because Julie's so *kind.*"

Inside the shed I made a beeline to my tent and switched on my computer. I had two e-mail messages, both from someone named Thread. They'd been posted late last night, after midnight; the subject heading of the first was Dear Mr. Gage, and the second was untitled. Thinking that this was probably junk mail, I clicked on the first message, and read:

```
Subject: Dear Mr. Gage,
Date: Tue, 22 Apr 1997 00:33:58
From: Thread <thread@cybernrthwest.net>
To: housekeeper@pacbell.net


Dear Mr. Gage,
I am writing to ask if you would please help Penny find
herself. I know it is a lot to ask -- you don't know us
at all -- but she has been afraid for such a very long
time and it would really help if she understood what was
going on. Please help us.
t.
```

The follow-up message, sent less than three minutes later, read:

```
Subject:
Date: Tue, 22 Apr 1997 00:36:22
From: Thread <thread@cybernrthwest.net>
To: housekeeper@pacbell net


one more thing asshole if you hurt her we will fuck you
up like you wouldt believe
```

This may sound strange, but it was the first message that disturbed me the most, probably because it was more personal, addressed to me by name. "How did they get our e-mail address?" I wondered.

"Guess," said Adam, and when I didn't, he went on: "Thank you, Julie, for being so kind to us . . ."

"Adam!" I said. "Adam, don't, I'm sure Julie didn't—"

"There's someone outside the tent," Adam said.

I sat up in my chair, listening; there might have been a noise, a faint shuffling of feet. "Hello?" I called out. No one answered. I got up, tiptoed towards the front of the tent, put my ear to the entrance flap for a moment, then shrugged and stepped outside.

There was nobody there, at least not where I could see them. "Hello?" I called again. From the tent next door, Dennis hollered: "What?" "Nothing," I hollered back. I circled the outside of my tent, checking carefully around each corner, finding no one. I came back around to the front and started to go back inside, and that was when Julie said "Hey."

"Julie!" I spun around; somehow she had appeared right behind me. "How . . . how are you doing?"

"Good," Julie said, smiling. She laid a soft hand on my arm. "And you?"

"I'm . . . OK, I guess. But—"

"Good," said Julie. "Listen, Andrew, if you're not busy right now, I'd really like to talk some more about—"

The words were out of my mouth before I had a chance to think about them: "I can't do it, Julie."

She paused in midsentence. I felt a twitch go through the hand on my arm.

"What you asked me about Penny," I explained, though I'm sure Julie knew exactly what I was referring to. "I can't do it. I know you asked me to think about it, and I have, but what I'm thinking is that I just can't. So . . . so I wanted to tell you straight out, so we're both clear on it. I hope you understand."

Julie took her hand off my arm. Her lips were pursed. "She understands, all right," said Adam.

"So anyway," I went on, babbling now, "anyway, I've got something important I've got to take care of, so . . . so I'll talk to you later, OK?" Even as Julie opened her mouth to reply, I turned and ducked back into my tent.

I stopped just inside and waited. Julie didn't try to follow me in, but she didn't leave right away either—I could hear her just beyond the tent flap, breathing loud through her mouth. Finally she said, softly but distinctly, "Fuck," and stalked off, the soles of her shoes slapping hard against the Factory's concrete floor.

"Phase two," said Adam, "will be starting early this time."

I went back to my desk, and reread the words on the computer screen:

```
one more thing asshole if you hurt her we will fuck you
up like you wouldt believe
```

"What should I do about this, Adam?"

"Well, you could tell them not to call you an asshole. That worked pretty well yesterday."

"I'm serious. Should I be worried?"

Inside, I felt Adam shrug. "Probably not—not yet," he said. "It sounds like a protector, probably just fronting, talking tough so you'll be careful with her . . . I mean, if they don't take no for an answer, that's different, but for now—"

I had a mental image, not of Penny, but of Julie, stomping away angrily. "Maybe we should try to help them," I said.

"Don't be stupid. It's a bad idea; you said so yourself. Besides, you don't really want to."

I didn't argue the point. Instead I transferred the two Thread messages, unanswered, into my "Saved" folder.

I decided it would be a good day to check on the condition of the shed roof. I got an extension ladder and spent the next hour making a very thorough search for loose shingles, gaps, and rotten planking.

Around ten-thirty I heard Julie calling up to me. She sounded anxious: "Andrew! Andrew!"

"What happened?" I hurried to the edge of the roof, nearly losing my balance. "What happened? Did somebody get hurt?"

Nobody had gotten hurt. Julie sounded anxious because she was mad. "What the hell are you doing up there?" she demanded.

"What the hell do you *think* I'm doing up here?" said Adam. He said it in the same casual tone that he uses when he's feeding me lines, and I had to bite my tongue to keep from repeating the words aloud.

"Checking for leaks," I told Julie. Inwardly, I warned Adam to knock it off.

"Did I tell you to check for leaks today?" asked Julie.

"Well, no," I said, "but . . ." But that was irrelevant, since she almost never told me what to do. "Did you need me for something?"

"Yes! That's why I've been looking for you everywhere!"

"Oh . . . OK, I'll be right down . . . Where do you want me to meet you?" But she had already gone back inside, slamming the door behind her.

"'She's been very kind to us,'" said Adam.

"Be quiet."

I found Julie and the others in the Big Tent. Julie was conferring with Dennis, while Irwin, cross-legged on the floor, replaced some bad wiring on one of the data suits. Penny sat off in a corner, typing away on a laptop. I felt a weird flutter in my stomach at the sight of her, but when she happened to glance over at me, there was no special anticipation or acknowledgment in her eyes; whatever soul was in charge of her body right now, it wasn't the author of either of the e-mails.

I went over to Julie and stood patiently by her side waiting for her to notice me. "Oh," she said mildly, several minutes later. "We don't need you after all. Never mind."

"Oh-*kay* . . ." I said.

"Since you're down here, though," Julie added, before I could walk away, "why don't you give Irwin a hand?"

Irwin looked up at the sound of his name, and I could tell from the baffled expression on his face that he didn't need my help and didn't understand why Julie had said that he did. But I went and sat down with him anyway, and tried to make myself useful.

At some point I felt myself being watched. I turned my head; Penny was staring straight at me now, a new soul looking out through her eyes. *Thread,* I thought.

"Thread," Adam confirmed. "She doesn't look pissy enough to be the other one."

Then Dennis hollered "Hey Mouse!" and Thread, or whoever it was, blinked and disappeared.

Adam and I both kept a lookout, but Thread didn't return for the rest of the morning. After lunch, I went back up on the roof.

```
Subject: Dear Mr. Gage,
Date: Wed, 23 Apr 1997 01:04:17
From: Thread <thread@cybernrthwest.net>
To: housekeeper@pacbell.net


Dear Mr. Gage,
I hope my request was not an imposition. Perhaps I should
have contacted you in person, but I am somewhat shy, and
sensed that you might be too . . . is there some time and
place we could meet, face to face? If it is convenient for
you . . .
t.
```

"I guess I can't put this off any longer," I said. Adam didn't respond. I tried again: "I probably should have written back yesterday, huh?"

Still nothing. It was Wednesday morning, and Adam was giving me the silent treatment, paying me back for taking Aunt Sam's side in an argument last night.

"Fine," I said. "I can handle this myself."

There was the briefest snicker from the pulpit, then silence again. I opened up an e-mail reply window in my Web browser, and poised my fingers over the keyboard.

Dear Thread, I thought, but didn't type, *I'm sorry, but I can't help you,* or *Penny . . .*

Dear Thread, though of course I'd like to help you, I'm afraid I'm not the right person . . .

Dear Thread, if Penny is really ready to "find herself," then what she needs is a good doctor, not—

"Dear Thread," Adam offered, unable to resist, "the truth is I don't give a rat's asshole about you or Penny. But since I'd probably *kiss* a rat's asshole if Julie Sivik asked me to, I've decided to dick around about this—"

"Be quiet," I said.

"What? I thought you wanted my advice."

"I do. But if you're not going to be helpful . . ."

I heard the rustle of someone entering the tent and looked up from the computer. "Julie . . . ?"

It wasn't Julie. It was Penny, or rather, Penny's body. The soul was Thread's. I could see the difference in body language right away: where Penny hunched her shoulders as though expecting at any moment to be snatched up by a predator, Thread stood and moved with greater confidence—even when, as now, she was clearly very nervous.

"Mr. Gage?" she said.

"Hah," I said softly. I took a deep breath: "Hi."

"Hello." She stuck out her hand. I took it, and shook it, my emotions suddenly in an uproar. A moment ago, by e-mail, I'd been ready to put her off, but now that we were face to face, I started remembering my father's stories about when he'd first sought help—how scared he'd been, and how much courage he'd had to muster. All at once, my reluctance to help seemed selfish and mean.

But before that thought could go anywhere, Julie burst into the tent, well into phase two. "Andrew!" she barked at me. "Andrew, I need you to—" She saw Penny's body, and stopped short.

"Oh," Julie said. She looked from me, to Thread, to our two hands clasped over the desktop, back to me again. "Oh, I'm sorry . . . I'll come back later . . ."

"No!" I jumped up and let go of Thread's hand (actually, I didn't just let it go—I kind of shoved it away). "No, you don't have to—"

"Didn't mean to interrupt," said Julie. She was smiling now, the same self-satisfied smile she'd smiled two days ago, when Penny and I had first met. "You two keep on, I'll just . . ." She started to back out of the tent.

"You aren't interrupting *anything!*" I didn't mean to shout, but that's how it came out—as if Julie had accused me of something awful, and I was denying it with all my might.

"All right," said Julie. "Take it easy."

"What . . . what did you want?"

"The Honey Bucket," Julie said. She wasn't smiling anymore. "It's . . . fouled. Courtesy of Dennis, I think. I need you to clean it up, but if you're—"

"I'm not," I said, my voice still too loud. "I'll get right on it."

I glanced at Thread, who seemed stunned by my outburst but was still waiting to continue, or begin, our conversation. I knew that I ought to say something to her, that it would be rude to just leave her hanging, but I couldn't think of anything, especially not with Julie standing right there, so I just nodded and muttered something incoherent. Then I walked out, trying hard not to look like I was running away.

"Very smooth," said Adam, as I broke into a jog outside the tent. "You were right, you're handling this just fine on your own."

"No thanks to you," I said angrily.

"Don't worry. If you keep freaking out every time she tries to talk to you, I'm sure she'll get the message."

"I'm not freaking out. I was just surprised, that's all."

But a few moments later back in the latrine area, as I was preparing to decontaminate the Honey Bucket, I felt eyes on me, and turned to find Thread standing a short distance away, staring at me. My brain locked up again. I looked down at my feet and tried to think of something to say; I asked Adam for help, but he'd once more fallen silent. Finally, thinking that if I just forced out one word, others might magically follow, I looked up and said "Listen . . ."

She was gone, vanished back among the tents. I didn't go after her. When I next saw her—about an hour later, coming out of the Big Tent—she wasn't Thread anymore.

I went back to my own tent then, thinking I'd take another crack at responding by e-mail. My computer was still on, as I'd left it, but the Web browser was closed, and when I reopened it I found that Thread's last message to me had been deleted. I checked the "Saved" folder; the two earlier messages were gone, too.

Subject: Dear Mr. Gage,
Date: Thur, 24 Apr 1997 06:01:03
From: Thread <thread@cybernrthwest.net>
To: housekeeper@pacbell.net

Dear Mr. Gage,
I'm very sorry to have bothered you. I won'twHat the
fuck is your problem asshole ? someone comes to you for
help and you wont even takl to them what is that I ought
to kick your fucking ass you cocksucking cunt

Shortly before noon on Thursday, Julie came looking for me again. I was back in the woods behind the Factory, shoveling fresh lime into the pit where we dumped the Honey Bucket waste. As I saw Julie coming I braced myself for a rebuke—she hadn't told me to lime the pit today—but when she spoke, her voice was concerned, not angry: "Have you seen Penny?"

"Me?" I said. "No, I—"

"Nobody else has seen her either. Her car's not here, and when I called her house just now there was no answer. I hope she's all right."

The last sentence sounded like a question, but I pretended not to notice. "I hope so too," I said.

"So you haven't heard from her at all? She didn't say anything about not coming in today?"

"I haven't . . . spoken to her since yesterday. And no, she didn't say anything about not coming in."

Julie nodded, and I felt a flush of shame for having deceived her. I wanted to tell her about the e-mail messages I'd been getting, but I knew if I did she'd want to get involved, and I was having enough trouble deciding what to do on my own.

"All right," said Julie. "I've got to go into Seattle anyway, so I think I'll stop by Penny's apartment. If she shows up here while I'm gone, will you tell her I'm worried about her?"

"Sure, Julie."

"Thanks." She started to turn away. I bent to pick up the shovel, and Julie said: "Oh. By the way . . ."

"Hmm?"

"What was that all about, yesterday?"

"What was what all about?"

"When I walked in on you and Penny, and you flipped out. What was that about?"

"Flipped out?" I said, trying, and failing, to sound confused. I really am a terrible liar. "I didn't flip out."

Julie said nothing, calling bullshit on me with a lift of her eyebrows.

"I didn't flip out," I repeated. "She, Penny, just came in to say good morning. That's all."

"Uh-huh," said Julie. Then she shrugged, and let it go. "Well, just be sure and tell her I went looking for her . . ."

After I got done with the waste pit I decided to hike into town to pick up some roofing materials. I got some petty cash, grabbed an army backpack from one of the storage tents, and set off down the road.

It was a beautiful day, clear and warm, like summer. At the Autumn Creek Café (a vegetarian restaurant across the street from the Harvest Moon Diner), the waiters had moved some tables out on the sidewalk, so I sat in the sun and had a leisurely meal. There was a radio on inside the café, tuned to an all-news station; as I was finishing up my spinach lasagna, the newscaster announced that Warren Lodge was being sought for questioning by police, who now suspected that he, and not a cougar, was responsible for his daughters' disappearance. That was such good news that I stayed at my table another twenty minutes until the story was repeated, just so my father could come out on the pulpit and hear it for himself. Then I went to the hardware store on Mill Street and bought shingles.

I was crossing the east bridge on my way back to the Factory when I heard a car approaching. I thought it must be Julie returning early from Seattle, or maybe a lost tourist, but when I looked over my shoulder I saw Penny's Buick coming up behind me. I was still so happy about the Warren Lodge news that I forgot to get flustered—I raised my hand to wave, and if it had been Thread driving the car I would probably have flagged her down, climbed in, and finally had a chat with her.

But it wasn't Thread driving, or Penny either. The soul behind the wheel of the Centurion was one I hadn't met before, at least not in person: the foul-mouthed protector. As the car drew close enough for me to clearly make out the protector's expression, I could see that she (or he) was enraged—not just annoyed, or angry, but *enraged.*

"Oh shit," said Adam, and then I knew I was in trouble.

I stopped waving, dropped my arm to my side, and turned my back on the car. My first instinct was to run, but something told me that would be a bad idea, so I quick-stepped the rest of the way across the bridge, then got over on the soft shoulder of the road and slowed up again, hoping that the Buick would pass me by. It didn't; it pulled alongside me, and paced me. I could feel the protector staring at me but just kept walking, my own gaze fixed straight ahead.

Then the protector laid on the Centurion's horn, and I fell back on my first instinct. I broke into a sprint, which turned out to be not so much a bad idea as a useless gesture. With a squeal of tires the Buick sped up, got ahead of me, and swerved onto the shoulder, cutting me off.

The protector leaned out the window and screamed at me: "Get your motherfucking ass in this fucking car right now, cocksucker, or I'll rip your goddamn fucking head off and—"

Adam yelled something at me too—probably "Don't get in the car!"— but I was already racing back towards the bridge. The protector tried to cut me off again, but the Centurion didn't handle as well in reverse, and I managed to get to the bridge ahead of it—and then, instead of going across, I ducked to the side.

There's no path or walkway to the bottom of Thaw Canal, just a steep rocky slope that I equal parts slid, scrambled, and fell down, the pack full of shingles pounding hard against the back of my head and neck. There's no path or walkway along the banks of Thaw Canal either, so instead of trying to escape upstream, I hid underneath the arch of the bridge. Standing knee-deep in freezing water, I listened to the idling of the Buick almost directly above me, and the ranting and raving of the protector as she—it was a she, I was sure now—paced the bridge's span, promising to do me all sorts of harm if I didn't come out and show myself. I pressed a hand over my mouth to keep my teeth from chattering, and tried not to sneeze.

Eventually all the noisemaking frightened some squirrel or woodchuck up along the rim of the gully, and as it crashed through the underbrush, the protector mistook it for me. She ordered it to come back, *right fucking now!*, but it didn't, and shortly after that she gave up. She spat out a few more curses, stalked the length of the bridge two or three more times, then jumped into the Buick and drove off with a furious squeal of tires.

The silence that fell then was broken by the voice of my father, speaking from the pulpit: "We need to have a meeting about this."

Mrs. Winslow opened the Victorian's front door just as I was coming up the porch steps. "Andrew!" she said. "What happened to you?"

"It's complicated," I said.

"Well, come inside then."

I followed her back to the kitchen and had a seat at the breakfast table. Mrs. Winslow brewed coffee; I peeled off my shoes and socks, and, at Mrs. Winslow's insistence, my jeans as well.

Even before Adam warned me not to, I recognized that I couldn't tell Mrs. Winslow the full story of what had happened. Much as I wanted to be completely honest with her, and much as I wanted to discuss this matter with someone outside my own head, I knew that there were elements of what had taken place, like the threatening e-mails, that would upset her beyond all proportion. So I was deliberately vague, saying only: "I'm having some trouble with one of the people at work."

"One of the people . . ." Mrs. Winslow frowned. "Does that mean Julie?"

"No," I said, "it's a new girl, a new programmer. Penny."

"And what did she do, roll you down an embankment?"

I laughed nervously, although I suppose, given my wet and muddy condition, that it wasn't that astounding a guess. "You know I trust you, Mrs. Winslow," I said. "More than anyone. But I think this is something I, we, need to deal with on our own. My father's called a house meeting about it, and I'm sure he'll know what to do. So you mustn't worry."

"I'll respect your privacy, of course," she told me, her tone suggesting she'd make her own decision about whether to worry. "But . . . I know I don't have to tell you this, Andrew, but if you ever do need my help—if you should decide to quit your job, for instance—"

"Quit my job! Why would I do that?"

Mrs. Winslow glanced at my jeans, drying on the back of a chair. "If you need to put some distance between yourself and this Penny person, for instance. If your father thinks that would be a good idea."

"Oh . . ."

"Don't worry about the rent, is all I'm saying."

"Well thank you, Mrs. Winslow. I'm sure it won't come to that, but I, I appreciate it. My father appreciates it. And speaking of my father . . ." I set my coffee mug on the table. "I should probably get to that meeting now."

Mrs. Winslow nodded. "I'll see to it you're not disturbed."

We both stood up. Mrs. Winslow took my mug, and, on her way to the sink, switched on the TV. The sound of a newscaster's voice reminded me of something. "Mrs. Winslow?" I said. "Did you hear about Warren Lodge?"

"I've heard," Mrs. Winslow replied, not sounding nearly as happy about it as I would have expected. Then she explained: "The latest report is that the police can't find him. He's run off."

"Oh," I said. "Well, I'm sure it's only a matter of time—"

"We'll see," said Mrs. Winslow, understandably skeptical. "You go have your meeting now, Andrew. I'll call you for dinner in a few hours."

"All right, Mrs. Winslow."

Somebody has to run the body: that is a truism in many ways, but it's not literally true; it is possible, though generally not a good idea, to leave the body unattended. The trick is to make sure the body is in a safe place, a place where, if bad stuff starts to happen, it will happen slowly and with lots of warning. With this in mind, I prepared for the house meeting by checking my bedroom carefully for open flames, frayed electrical cords, teetering bookshelves, escaped circus tigers, and other potential sources of sudden catastrophe. Though I joke about it, it is serious business: after one memorable early meeting held back before the house was built, my father returned to the body to find a crow pecking at his chest.

When I'd verified to my own and my father's satisfaction that the bedroom was safe (with the windows all shut tight, and latched) I lay down on the bed, arranging myself comfortably on the mattress.

Julie once asked me what it feels like to leave the body. "Do you contract into yourself, or float away, or what?" After several mangled attempts at a description, I came up with the following exercise, which, while not perfect, at least conveys the general idea: Tilt your head back as far as you can. You will feel a tension in the muscles at the back of your neck that quickly becomes painful. Imagine that tension spreading outwards, wrapping around the front of your face and shooting down into your torso, arms, and legs, turning your whole skin into a rigid shell like a suit of armor. Now imagine stepping backwards out of that suit of armor and finding yourself, not behind your body, but somewhere else entirely. Imagine all of this happening in the space between two heartbeats.

That's what it's like, more or less. Or at least that's what it's like for me; from exchanges I've had over the Internet, I know that some multiples experience it a bit differently—and of course, what happens to you after you've left the body depends on what your internal geography is like, something that is different for every multiple.

The map of the geography inside Andy Gage's head looks like this:

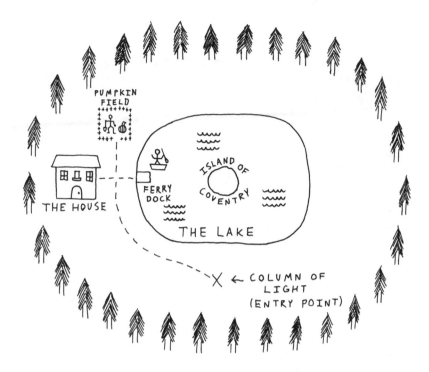

The X at the bottom of the map marks the spot where I appeared, beside the column of light that is the conduit between inside and outside. The column of light touches down on the crest of a hill above the south shore of the lake; from it, a path curves west and north around the lake's perimeter, eventually splitting into three branches. The rightmost branch leads down to a boat dock on the western lakebank; the middle branch runs straight and level to the pumpkin field; and the left branch goes up another, broader hill to the house. The question of distances gets kind of metaphysical, and I will return to it presently, but let's just say for the moment that the length of the path from the column of light to the front door of the house appears to be about a mile.

Colors, sounds, smells, tastes, and tactile sensations are all exactly the same inside as they are outside. The house looks and feels just like a real house; the hills, rocks, and trees just like real hills, rocks, and trees. The only obvious difference is you, since when you're inside, you're not wearing the body—so depending on how tall your soul is, for instance, your eye level may be shifted up or down.

The geography has a sky above it just like the real sky, with a sun, moon, and stars. The motions of these heavenly bodies are all controlled by my father, who for the most part keeps them synchronized with their real-world counterparts: generally, when it's day outside, it's day inside, and ditto for night. The geography also has weather—this, too, controlled by my father—which is definitely *not* in sync with real-world weather, or at least not real-world Pacific Northwest weather: day or night, the sky in Andy Gage's head is almost always clear, and it never rains. Sometimes, around Christmas, my father will stage a brief snowstorm for Jake and the other kids.

As for the laws of physics that apply to the geography . . . well, it's complicated. Because the geography doesn't really exist, certain things are possible inside that are not possible outside—but because I am used to these impossibilities and consider them normal, it's hard for me to list them on demand. One impossibility that I've already alluded to, though, has to do with distances inside: they're optional. Inside, when you want to get from point A to point B, it isn't strictly necessary to pass through all the points in between, the way it is when traveling from A to B in the real world. For instance, if you're on the hilltop beside the column of light, and you want to go to the house, you *can* get there by following the path, but you don't have to—if you're in a hurry, or don't feel like walking, you can just decide to be in the house, and quick as thought, there you are.

Today I wasn't in that much of a hurry, even though I knew that the others were all waiting for me. I stood on the hilltop for a while, staring out across the lake. Inevitably, my gaze was drawn towards Coventry, the lake island where Gideon was imprisoned. There wasn't much to see: a mist had risen from the deep waters in the middle of the lake, reducing the island to a vague outline.

I said that my father controlled the weather inside the geography. He did not control the mist—he didn't summon it, and he couldn't make it go away. In hindsight, it's clear that this should have been cause for concern, but because it was associated with the lake, rather than, say, the forest or the pumpkin field, my father chose to regard it as a harmless anomaly rather than a potential danger sign.

Like the column of light, the lake predates the geography. Originally it was a kind of void, a darker area in the dark room in Andy Gage's head that occasionally vomited out new souls. In the course of constructing the geography, my father tamed the void somewhat—he made it resemble a body of water, which was better than having a gaping black hole in the landscape, and he also learned how to call new souls, like me, out of it at will. But he never fully mastered it. Since the lake was still technically its own entity, it was not completely outrageous that it should act of its own accord, and so my father chose not to worry about it when it did. And since he didn't worry about it, neither did I—but I was curious.

"Andrew," my father said, appearing beside me on the hilltop.

I nodded hello, but kept on staring out across the water, trying to catch a clear glimpse of Coventry in the whiteness. "Does the mist come more often now than it used to?" I asked. My father didn't answer, and I could tell he was growing impatient. Still, I went on: "I think it does come more often. Back when I first came out of the lake, it hardly ever—"

"Andrew."

"Right, I know: the meeting."

"Yes," my father said, "the meeting. Let's go."

We went: thought about being at the house, and were there.

The floor plan of the house in Andy Gage's head looks like this:

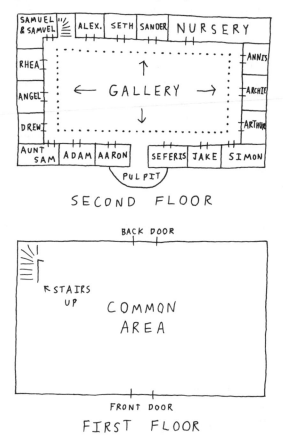

As you can see, it is a fairly simple structure. The first floor is one big common room. A staircase in the southwest corner goes up to a gallery that overlooks the common room on all four sides and gives access to the bedrooms and the nursery. A short hallway off the gallery's east end leads out to the pulpit.

In preparation for the meeting, a long table had been set up in the middle of the common room. The table was wider at one end than at the other, and my father, as head of the household, took his place at the wider end. I sat to my father's right; Adam to his left. The next two seats on my side of the table were occupied by Aunt Sam and Jake; Seferis sat next to Adam. Farther down the table were Simon, Drew, and Alexander; Angel, Annis, Arthur, and Rhea; Sander, Archie, Seth, and the two Samuels; Silent Joe the Gravedigger; and Captain Marco. Many of these were souls who, like my father, had grown weary of dealing with the outside world, and only rarely occupied the body anymore. Silent Joe and the Captain had never been outside; they were helper souls, called out of the lake by my father to perform specific functions within the geography.

There were still more souls up in the gallery, scores of them: the Witnesses. The Witnesses were what impolite psychiatrists like to call "fragments"—fragmentary souls created by a single traumatic event or act of abuse. Living embodiments of painful memory, they resembled small children; more than a few of them were dead ringers for Jake. But they lacked Jake's depth of personality, most having been outside only the one time, in the awful moment that made them. They had sad eyes, and rarely spoke. It was unlikely that they would have anything to add to the proceedings, but because they were members of the household, they were allowed to attend the meeting; they lined the gallery banister, some sitting, some standing. Three adult helper souls circulated behind them, ready to whisk them back into the nursery if they became bored or upset.

My father called the meeting to order.

"We're here," my father said, "because a series of threats has been made against Andrew by one of his coworkers at the Reality Factory. And since some of these were physical threats against the body, they potentially affect all of us . . ." He went on to describe what had been happening with Penny. By the time he finished, more than half of the Witnesses had vanished from the gallery, and a couple of souls at the table had become hysterical. When he got to the part about the protector chasing me in the Buick, Annis clapped her hands over her ears and ran upstairs to her room, and a moment after that Arthur bolted out the back door of the house in the direction of the forest, probably intending to work off stress by chopping down a few stands of trees. My father took all of this in stride; such reactions were perfectly normal for a house meeting. ". . . so that is what has been going on," he concluded, "and now we need to discuss what should be done about it."

Simon raised a hand. "How dangerous is this Penny Driver?" he asked. "Would she really hurt the body?"

My father turned to Adam. "The soul we saw today is capable of real violence," Adam said. "Seferis and I are sure about that. We don't think it actually wants to hurt us, but it might, if it got mad enough."

"Well then," said Simon, looking directly at me, "*somebody* ought to call the police. There's no reason why we should have to tolerate even the possibility of violence." Several other souls around the table murmured agreement.

"Andrew?" my father prompted me.

"I don't think we need to get the police involved," I said, startled by the suggestion. "I mean yes, what happened today was upsetting, but I think Adam's right, the intention wasn't to hurt us. It's just . . . they want help. This isn't about harming us, or making us feel bad. Penny's souls want help, and for better or worse they're convinced that we can give it to them, and I guess they're a little desperate about it."

"That doesn't justify threats!" exclaimed Simon. "Or chasing people in cars!"

"*We* needed help," I reminded him. "Are you going to tell me we were never so demanding that it scared somebody?"

"What are you suggesting, Andrew?" my father asked. "Are you saying we should overlook Penny's . . . desperation . . . and try to help her?"

"Well . . ."

"Because that isn't how you've been acting. You've been acting like you don't want anything to do with her."

"I know," I said. "But maybe . . . maybe the fair thing, if we could just *get* her some help, at least point her in the right direction—"

"LIAR!" Adam's shout spooked another dozen Witnesses into flight. "'Maybe the *fair* thing,'" he mocked. "This isn't about what's fair, or nice— the truth is you don't give a damn about Penny. This is about *Julie.*"

"Oh good grief," said Simon, "not *her* again . . ."

"It isn't just about Julie!" I protested. "I honestly think that—"

"Oh, not *just* about Julie! So you admit—"

"Adam! Andrew!" my father shouted. "Both of you stop—"

"I have a suggestion," Aunt Sam said. Her level voice cut through the ruckus, quieting all of us at once. "I think," said Aunt Sam, "that we should go see Dr. Grey."

Jake, who'd been fidgeting uncomfortably in his seat throughout most of the preceding discussion, now perked up and said: "Oh, *yes!* Let's go see Dr. Grey!"

But my father wasn't so pleased with the idea. "Dr. Grey is retired," he reminded Aunt Sam. "She's not well."

"She's not *dead*," Aunt Sam retorted. "It's high time we paid her a visit anyway, just for courtesy's sake—it's been over a year since we've seen her. And I'm sure she wouldn't mind giving us some advice. Maybe she'd even be willing to meet with Penny personally."

"That's not appropriate. You don't show up at someone's house asking them to—"

"I think it's a great idea," I said. "The part about going to visit her, I mean. Aunt Sam's right, she could advise us what to do. I mean, who better?"

"Andrew—"

"We could go see her tomorrow. We could call her tonight, and see if she's free."

"Tomorrow is Friday," my father said. "You're supposed to be at work."

"But there's no point in my going to the Factory if I'm just going to play hide-and-seek with Penny. Julie won't mind me taking the day off—at least, not after she finds out we're trying to get Penny some help."

"I don't like this idea," my father said. "I—"

Down at the far end of the table, Drew suddenly piped up: "If we do go to see Dr. Grey tomorrow, could we stop at the aquarium on the way back?"

"Ooh!" Jake exclaimed, bouncing in his chair. "And what about the Magic Mouse toy store? That's practically on the way!"

That opened the floodgates. Whatever reservations my father had about visiting Dr. Grey had to be put on hold as half the souls at the table weighed in with suggestions for possible side-excursions. My father rejected all of them, but by the time he was finished, the visit itself had somehow become an established fact.

"All right," my father relented. "All right. We'll go see Dr. Grey."

"And *maybe* the Magic Mouse toy store," Jake added, unwilling to give up.

The meeting ended soon after that. When I returned to the body, Mrs. Winslow was knocking on my bedroom door. "Andrew?"

"Yes, Mrs. Winslow?" I sat up stiffly, checking the clock on the night-stand: it was almost five.

"You have a telephone call," Mrs. Winslow said.

"Is it Julie?"

"No—Julie called earlier, but I told her you weren't available. This person won't give her name, but she's very insistent about speaking to you."

Uh-oh.

"Andrew? Do you want me to put her off?"

"No," I said, swinging my legs out of bed. "No, I'll take care of it . . ." I came out into the sitting room. "I'm sorry about this. I hope she didn't say anything nasty to you . . ."

"She has a colorful vocabulary," Mrs. Winslow allowed, "but nothing I haven't heard before."

The phone was on a stand in the side hallway. Posted prominently on the wall above it was a list of emergency numbers: poison control, hospital, fire department, police department, and FBI.

I picked up the phone. "Hello?" I said.

No answer. But the line wasn't dead.

"Hello? . . ."

I could hear breathing, now. I started to get mad.

"Who is this? What's your name?"

"*Cocksucker,*" the caller hissed, and hung up.

I set the phone handset back in its cradle. Mrs. Winslow, who'd been listening from the kitchen doorway, came forward and stood beside me.

"Andrew?" she said, indicating the list of emergency numbers. "Do we need to call somebody?"

"Yes," I said. "But not the police. Dr. Grey."

"Oh . . . well wait a moment, I think I've got her number in my address book upstairs."

"It's all right," I told her, picking up the phone again. "I'm sure my father still remembers it."

8

A fine drizzle was falling the next morning as I walked up Olympic Avenue to Julie's apartment, but I didn't mind it. I had my umbrella, and the cold damp air blowing past my cheeks helped keep me awake. It was 5:45 A.M., give or take a couple minutes.

It wasn't just the early hour that had me yawning. Penny's souls had called two more times the night before, once at around nine, and then again after midnight. The nine-o'clock call was from Thread, initially; Mrs. Winslow picked it up, and came back to my bedroom to ask "Do you know someone named 'T'?" But once I got on the line, Thread only managed a brief utterance—"Mr. Gage?"—before the foul-mouthed protector took over, blistering my ear with a stream of curses and threats and hanging up before I could get a word in edgewise.

The after-midnight call was Foul Mouth from the first syllable. By sheer luck I answered it instead of Mrs. Winslow. I was having trouble falling asleep, and was walking back to the kitchen to fix myself a glass of warm milk; the call came in just as I was passing the phone in the side hall, and I grabbed it in the middle of the first ring. I lifted the handset to my ear, heard the words "cocksucking cunt," and immediately hung up again. I counted to fifteen to make sure the connection was broken, then left the phone off the hook for the rest of the night. But after that, the warm milk didn't help much.

At least my one outgoing call of the evening had gone well. I'd reached Dr. Grey with no trouble, and she'd said she'd be happy to see me. She sounded good on the phone: her voice was strong, with only a trace of slurring.

I'd thought about phoning Julie as well, to let her know that I wouldn't be coming into work, but realized that that would probably involve more explanation than I was really in the mood for. So I decided instead to get up a little early and leave her a note on my way out of town. Of course, this also served as an excuse to go by Julie's apartment, which, Adam argued, was the real reason I was doing it.

During the first year I knew her—the first year of my life—I was a frequent visitor at Julie's, often following her home from work to hang out, sometimes for hours. At one point these visits became daily, so that it was almost like I was living there—I even had my own key—and in fact, Julie and I had talked about becoming roommates for real. Then things changed; for a long while, Julie's apartment was off-limits to me, though I still saw her every day at work. Even after the no-visits restriction was lifted and I was allowed to come around again, it wasn't the same as before. Having worn out my welcome once, I was afraid of wearing it out a second time, and could never really relax, even when Julie specifically invited me over.

And so a funny thing happened. You'd think that the whole purpose of visiting someone's home was to spend time with them, wouldn't you? Certainly that's what I would have thought. But now, as much as I still liked coming by Julie's apartment, I only got comfortable enough to really enjoy it when she wasn't there. Like the time three months ago, when Julie had gone out of town for a week and asked me to water her plants while she was away: every day, after seeing to the plants, I would go sit in Julie's bedroom for a while, feeling happy. Which made no sense, since without her in it, Julie's bedroom is just a space. But it made me happy anyway, being there, because it reminded me of what it was like back when Julie and I had almost been roommates. Back when my visits were still casual, and I didn't have to worry about overstaying my welcome.

So maybe Adam was right: maybe the real reason I decided to leave Julie a note was so that I could go by her apartment while she was still asleep, and "visit" her without feeling I was imposing on her.

Julie's apartment was the converted attic of a three-story private house. To get to it you had to take your life in your hands and climb an outside staircase, a sort of enclosed wooden fire escape, that had been attached none too securely to the side of the building. The door at the bottom of this covered stairway was missing its knob. The knob had been missing for at least six months now, and though Julie kept talking about getting it replaced, so far the closest she'd come was to thread a rope through the hole and knot it at both ends. A tin letterbox was nailed to the inside of the door. I could have just dropped my note in there, but I told myself that Julie might not see it—after all, there was no reason for her to check the letterbox first thing in the morning. Better to slip it under her apartment door.

I climbed the stairs, which creaked and groaned ominously with every step. Reaching the top was only a partial relief. There was a two-inch gap between the landing and the attic doorway, so that if you looked down as you entered Julie's apartment, you could see the tops of her landlord's garbage cans three stories below.

It was all right; I'm not that afraid of heights. Mainly I was worried that the stairway's groaning would wake Julie. But standing on the landing, I didn't hear any sound of movement from inside the apartment. I decided to stand and listen a while longer, and while I did, I flashed back pleasantly on a winter day in that first year we'd known each other, when Julie and I had hauled a Christmas tree up these very steps, and—

"Oooh," Adam moaned, from the pulpit. "Oooh, baby . . . oh, yes . . . oh, right there! . . . ooooohh . . ."

"Adam!" I whispered sharply. "Adam, cut it out!"

"Oooh, baby . . . oh, oh, oh, *oh* . . . yes . . . *yes* . . . *YES!*"

"Stop it, Adam!"

"I'll stop when *you* stop," Adam said. "Quit mooning around out here and leave the goddamn note already."

"All right, all right . . ." I crouched down, and reached across the gap to slide the note under the apartment door. Then, instead of getting up, I bent lower, placing my hands flat on the landing and dipping my head until my right eye was on a level with the crack under the door. I could see my note, safely on the other side, and the furry edge of a welcome mat, and a pair of Julie's boots, and—

My father's voice: *"Andrew."*

"All right," I said, "all right." I stood up, and got out of there.

I caught the 6:05 Metro bus to Seattle; with intermediate stops and rush-hour traffic, it took about an hour to reach the city. I was pretty bus-sick by then, so I opened my umbrella and took a stroll around Pioneer Square before heading to the waterfront. With what felt like half the souls in the house crowding into the pulpit to sightsee, I had no shortage of window-shopping suggestions.

At 7:50 I boarded the Washington State Ferry to Bainbridge Island. The crossing takes thirty-five minutes; and since this was an unusual day, and since there's only so much trouble you can get into on a boat, my father suspended the normal house rules and agreed to let Seferis, Aunt Sam, Simon, Drew, and Alexander each have a few minutes in the body. Drew and

Alexander were content to just walk around and stare out the windows at the Sound. Seferis, who'd missed his regular morning workout, dropped to the deck to do push-ups. Aunt Sam went to the ferry's snack bar and tried to bum a cigarette off the attendant—she might have gotten away with it, too, if my father hadn't been watching her from the pulpit. Finally Simon took his turn. We were almost at the island by then, and despite the fact that it was still drizzling outside, Simon decided to go out on the open foredeck— without the umbrella—and watch the docking.

Damp and shivering, I disembarked. I hiked a few blocks to the Streamliner Diner, where we took breakfast. It was a lot less efficient, and a lot more expensive, than one of Mrs. Winslow's meals: I ordered two entrees, four side dishes, and three beverages. Most of the food remained on the plates, of course, but even so, by the time we were done, I was stuffed.

It was about twenty after nine now. I went up the street to an arcade, and let Adam and Jake play a dollar's worth of video games apiece. While Adam was engaged in Mortal Kombat, the sun came out, so after he decapitated his last opponent we did some more window-shopping.

Finally, at ten o'clock, I caught another bus to Poulsbo, the town at the head of Liberty Bay where Dr. Grey lived, and where, back before she had her stroke, she used to see patients. I made a quick stop at a florist's to buy a bouquet of daisies, and by five of eleven was at Dr. Grey's house.

This might seem like a long way to come for therapy. But my father used to make the journey regularly, at least once a week, sometimes twice a week when he could square it with his work schedule. He had to.

Statistically, the average multiple goes through something like eight psychiatrists before being correctly diagnosed. And that's only half the story; even after you get the right diagnosis, you may have to go through *another* eight psychiatrists before you find one who knows how to treat it properly.

The classic therapeutic metaphor for a patient with multiple personality disorder (or "dissociative identity disorder," as they're calling it now) is that of a broken vase. The metaphor suggests an obvious remedy: pick up the pieces, grab some glue, and stick the vase back together. Or in human terms: identify all the shards and fragments of the original personality, and, using a "glue" of talk therapy, hypnosis, and drugs, reintegrate them into a single, unified whole. You know, like in *Sybil*.

The only problem with this scenario is that the metaphor is faulty. You can smash a vase, bury it in the ground for twenty years, dig it up again, and piece it back together just fine. You can do that because a vase is dead to begin with, and its pieces are inert. But human souls aren't made of porcelain. They're alive, and, in the nature of living things, they change; and they keep on changing even after they get smashed to bits.

So forget about the vase; think instead of a rosebush, torn apart by a storm. The branches get scattered all over the garden, but they don't just lie there; they take root again, and try to grow, which isn't as easy now that they are competing with one another for space and light. Still, they manage— most of them manage—and what you end up with, ten or twenty years after the storm, is not one rosebush but a multitude of rosebushes. Some of them are badly stunted; maybe all of them are smaller than they would have been if they'd each had a garden of their own. But they are more, much more, than a simple collection of puzzle pieces.

The remedy suggested by the broken-vase metaphor doesn't work with the rosebush metaphor. To turn a whole rose garden back into a single rose-bush takes more than just fitting and gluing; it requires pruning and uproot-ing and discarding as well, and what you end up with when you're done isn't the original rosebush, but a Frankenstein parody of it. And you may not even get that far: little rosebushes don't always react well to being cannibal-ized for parts.

My father learned this the hard way. Dr. Kroft, the Ann Arbor, Michi-gan, psychiatrist who first diagnosed him with MPD in 1987, was a firm believer in the broken-vase metaphor. Together they spent four years trying to merge my father with the other souls in Andy Gage's head. The only reintegrations that were even partially successful were those involving Wit-nesses; by abreacting—mentally reliving—the incident of abuse that had created a particular Witness, my father could sometimes make that Wit-ness's memories his own, and so absorb it. But the process was extremely traumatic, and it didn't always take. As for attempts to absorb more complex souls like Simon or Drew, not only were they completely unsuccessful, they usually triggered periods of chaos and lost time.

It was in the aftermath of one of these chaotic periods, when my father woke to find himself in a locked observation-ward at the Ann Arbor Psychi-atric Center, that he began to consider the possibility that Dr. Kroft's meth-ods were misguided. Following his release from the ward, my father had a long argument with Dr. Kroft about alternative treatment options. Dr. Kroft insisted that there were no other options: reintegration was the only way to go, period. My father, losing his temper, suggested that Dr. Kroft's "fixation" on reintegration was really a form of projection.

It was a terrible thing to say. Dr. Kroft was an amputee, a former college-football star who'd lost a leg in a drunk-driving accident; my father was insinuating that his MPD treatment strategy was a way of compensating for the fact that he couldn't put *himself* back together. As my father later admitted, this accusation was inexcusably rude, no matter how frustrated he might have felt at the time. Dr. Kroft thought so, too: he retaliated by sending my father back to the locked ward.

After my father got out of the ward the second time, he decided to leave Michigan. He'd heard that the West Coast was the place to go for cutting-edge mental health care, so he relocated to Seattle, where, sure enough, he found plenty of "innovative" psychiatrists. He got to know quite a few of them.

There was Dr. Minor, who believed that most MPD cases were the result, not of ordinary child abuse, but of *ritual* abuse perpetrated by a nationwide conspiracy of Satanic cults. There was Dr. Bruno, who was into past-life regression. There was Dr. Whitney, who as a sideline to his regular practice ran a support group for people who had been sexually assaulted by extraterrestrials. And then there was Dr. Leopold, who recommended litigation as an adjunct to psychotherapy. "Sue your parents," he advised my father during their first session. "You'll never reclaim your sense of self until you strike back at the bastards who did this to you."

The one thing all these innovators had in common was that, like Dr. Kroft, they were proponents of the broken-vase metaphor. Whether they believed that multiplicity was the fault of Satan-worshippers or a side-effect of being drawn and quartered in a previous lifetime, they all agreed that Andy Gage would never be healed until he was one soul again. As Dr. Whitney, the interplanetary-rape counselor, put it: "Of *course* you've got to reintegrate! Don't you want to be *normal?*"

My father was nearing his wits' end when, one day in the spring of 1992, he stopped in the Seattle Public Library and discovered a self-help manual called *The Practical Guide to Living with Multiple Personality Disorder*. The *Guide*, by Dr. Danielle Grey (a local author, according to the sticker on the front cover), approached multiplicity as a condition to be managed, rather than as a pathology to be cured. "The primary difficulty faced by multiple personalities," Dr. Grey wrote in her preface, "is not that they are abnormal; it is that they are dysfunctional. Multiplicity, of itself, is no more problematic than left-handedness. Losing time, being unable to keep a steady job or maintain a residence, requiring detailed lists just to get through the day—*these* things are problems. But they are problems that a well-organized multiple household, acting cooperatively, can learn to overcome."

While Dr. Grey stopped short of saying that reintegration was never an appropriate goal in the treatment of MPD, she made it clear that she considered it, at best, a low priority. The important thing was to eliminate the confusion that resulted from uncontrolled switching: to impose order. Whether you ended up with one soul, or ten, or a hundred—that was a side issue.

It would be an understatement to say that Dr. Grey's views had been poorly received by her peers. But to my father, the *Guide* was a godsend, and he would have traveled a lot farther than Poulsbo to meet Dr. Grey in person.

Dr. Grey's house was a two-story Craftsman that she had designed and built herself, appropriately enough. I knocked on the door and Dr. Grey's partner, Meredith, came to let me in. She complimented me on my choice of flowers, and invited me to wait in the front parlor. "Danny's still getting herself together upstairs," she explained. "It'll be a few minutes."

Meredith took the daisies to put them in water; I went into the parlor. This was the room where Dr. Grey used to meet with her patients, and where she had first spoken to my father about the idea of constructing a geography in Andy Gage's head. The parlor was big and bright, with antique lamps and a working gas-fireplace, and tall windows that could be opened wide, lightly curtained, or tightly shuttered, according to the patient's mood.

An oak coffee table sat on a rug at the center of the parlor, surrounded unevenly by an overstuffed chair with a footstool, a straight-back chair, a padded rocker, and a comfortable sofa that was wide enough to lie down on. Two books had been laid out on the coffee table. One of the books was Dr. Grey's *Guide*. The other, which I didn't recognize, had an illustration of a broken mirror on the cover. The pieces of the mirror were made of some shiny material that was actually reflective, so that when you picked up the book and looked at it you saw your own face, in slivers. The title of the book was *Through Shattered Minds*, by Dr. Thomas Minor.

"God," my father said from the pulpit. "Not that piece of shit." I couldn't tell whether he was referring to the book or its author.

"Is this the same Dr. Minor you used to see?" I asked him.

"Yes. That book's out of print, thank God."

"It looks new," I observed. I flipped it open to the first chapter, and read a paragraph at random:

My initial diagnosis of Theo was that she was a classic neurotic—a spoiled little rich girl, who after squandering several thousand dollars of her parents'

money on therapy would become bored with psychoanalysis and decide, belat-
edly, to grow up and face life, as we all must do. That was my prediction for
the future; but for the time being she was proving to be an enormous pain in
the ass.

I was stunned. "This man is a professional psychiatrist?"

"It gets worse," my father assured me. "And that's only his first book, the one he wrote before he discovered the Satanic conspiracy."

From outside the parlor, I heard a motor whirring: a wheelchair lift, carrying Dr. Grey downstairs. The lift clunked to a halt a moment later; there was a brief silence, a prolonged grunt, a clank, and then I heard Dr. Grey say, "Ah, damn it!" Footsteps came running from the back of the house; Meredith said, "Is that gate stuck again?" Then they were both talking—"I can do this on my—" "Just let me—" "*Damn it*, Meredith!" "Danny, let go of—" "All right, all *right!*" "—roll back two inches while I—" "Hurry *up*"— until finally there was a second clank, and Dr. Grey said, "OK, that's fine, back off!"

Another, smaller motor started humming, and Dr. Grey's wheelchair cruised gracefully into the parlor. "Andrew!" Dr. Grey greeted me, and I tried to act surprised, as if I hadn't heard her coming.

Actually, it wasn't that hard to look surprised; her appearance was a shock. Her voice was strong and clear, as I've said, and her eyes were as bright as ever, but she'd lost a lot of weight—when I bent down to hug her, her body was all loose skin and hard angles. And she'd aged; in the year since I'd seen her last, she'd put on what looked to be ten years' worth of wrinkles, and her hair, once brown, had gone the way of her surname.

"Ah," Dr. Grey said, as I straightened up from the hug, "I see you found Minor's scribble."

"Oh, yes," I said, glancing down at the book in my hand. "My father thought they'd stopped printing it."

"They had; it's being reissued. That's a review copy that Minor had sent to me. His way of gloating."

"Oh. Well that's rude."

"Mmph," Dr. Grey grunted in the affirmative. "Anyway, sit!" She gestured at the sofa. "Sit, get comfortable. Let me say hi to the family."

"Sure." I sat on the sofa, and stepped back into the pulpit so that the others could say hello. This was expected, and only polite, but suddenly I wished, very selfishly, that I could skip it. I was anxious to talk to Dr. Grey about Penny, and worried that the others would tire her out before I got a chance. Our last visit had had to be cut short after Dr. Grey suddenly became exhausted.

She'd had her stroke in January of 1995, just as my father was putting the finishing touches on the geography and the house—potentially disastrous timing. I still wasn't entirely sure how my father had withstood the shock, though I knew Dr. Grey's own foresight had a lot to do with it: the day after she was taken to the emergency room, my father was visited in person by Dr. Eddington—a sympathetic associate of Dr. Grey's, from Fremont— who broke the bad news and offered his services as a trauma counselor. Dr. Eddington also brought a postdated letter from Dr. Grey which said, in so many words: if you are reading this, something terrible must have happened to me; but I don't want anything terrible to happen to you, so please, try to be strong, and accept Dr. Eddington's help.

My father was strong; he finished the house on his own, and called me out of the lake, exactly as planned; that was the official story, anyway. Dr. Grey, meanwhile, remained bedridden for some months; when I first met her, about a week after I was born, she was still struggling to string whole sentences together, and though she improved markedly after that, it became clear early on that she would never fully recover.

The saddest thing about the stroke, other than the damage it had done to Dr. Grey's mind and body, was the effect it had had on Dr. Grey's relationship with my father. This was something I didn't really understand, and my father refused to discuss it with me. At first I'd thought it must just be too painful for him, seeing his good friend so debilitated, but later I decided that couldn't be it. My father had never shown any qualms about visiting Dr. Grey in the hospital, when she was at her worst. It was only after she got out that he became reluctant to visit her or call her—increasingly reluctant, even as she regained her ability to have real conversations. My current theory was that this reluctance stemmed from a combination of guilt and fear: guilt that as Dr. Grey's patient he had contributed to the overwork that had caused her stroke; and fear that as her ex-patient he might, even with a strictly friendly visit, somehow cause her to have another.

Even now he hung back: instead of rushing forward to be the first to say hello, my father let all the other souls go ahead of him. When his turn finally came, he kept his greeting brief and—it hurt to see it—almost emotionlessly polite. When Dr. Grey suggested that he clear the pulpit so that they could have a private chat, my father begged off, saying he didn't want to tax her strength. I should have been happy about this, but it actually disappointed me. Dr. Grey was disappointed, too: she pursed her lips, and looked as if she was about to insist on a private chat, but before she could, Meredith entered the parlor, carrying a tray full of snacks, and my father took advantage of the distraction to pass the body back to me.

"Look, Aaron—" Dr. Grey said, as Meredith cleared a space for the tray on the coffee table.

"Nope, sorry, it's me," I told her. "He's gone back inside."

"Damn it! Tell him I—"

"Aren't these nice?" Meredith said, lifting a vase from the tray.

"Hm!?" Dr. Grey snapped. Then she saw the daisies, and softened. "Yes," she said. "Yes, they are nice." She looked at me. "You brought them?" I nodded. "Very nice," she said. "Very thoughtful, Andrew." Her gaze wandered to the tray. "Would you care for a macaroon?"

"No thank you," I told her, "I'm actually kind of full right now. Maybe I'll have something later."

"As you like." She looked pointedly at Meredith, who took an espresso cup from the tray and filled it from a special pot. Dr. Grey drank the espresso black, gulping it down like medicine. "Another," she said, and Meredith poured her a second dose; Dr. Grey gulped that one down too. Then she grunted "Enough," and waved off Meredith's offer of another refill. Meredith retrieved the cup and left the parlor.

"So, Andrew," said Dr. Grey, "you mentioned on the phone that you were having problems with a woman. Is it . . ." She paused, concentrating. ". . . Julie? That's the name, right, Julie?"

"Yes, Julie Sivik," I said. "She's my boss. She's not the one I'm having a problem with, though."

"But you were, weren't you?" Her eyes became distant, recollecting. "The last time you were here? You were obsessing over her . . ."

"Well, yes, sort of, but—"

"She'd led you on somehow, romantically, then changed her mind about it, and you were having real trouble coming to terms with that."

"Yes, but . . . but that was a while ago. I got over it."

"Ah!" Dr. Grey snapped out of her reverie, brightening. "Well, good! So who's the new girl?"

"Her name is Penny Driver," I said. "But she's not . . . it's not a romantic relationship. We just work together." I paused, for some reason wanting Dr. Grey to acknowledge this point, but she just stared at me expectantly, so after a moment I continued: "She started working at the Reality Factory last Monday—Julie hired her. And it turns out that . . ."

I told her the story. Dr. Grey was attentive but very unresponsive at first, so much so that I started wondering, half-seriously, whether she'd fallen asleep with her eyes open. But when I described how I'd confronted Julie about her ulterior motives for hiring Penny, Dr. Grey came back to life, nodding vigorously. "Good," she said, "I'm glad you called her on it. You were right, it *was* a bad idea, especially springing it on you that way."

"Well," I said, encouraged, "I'm sure Julie meant well—"

"Good intentions are overrated," said Dr. Grey. "Probably you know this, but I'm not a big fan of good intentions."

"Um . . ."

"But that's a tangent. I'm sorry. Continue."

"Um, well, anyway, the very next day . . ."

During the second half of the story, as I described Thread's attempts to get me to "help Penny find herself," Dr. Grey interrupted frequently, quizzing me about the exact wording of the e-mails, and about Penny's, Thread's, and Foul Mouth's demeanors when they'd said and done certain things. She also wanted to know everything *I* had done, and after her comment about good intentions, I was worried that my own actions would be found wanting. But Dr. Grey's judgment, when it came, was positive.

"It sounds like you handled yourself pretty well, under the circumstances," she said.

"Well . . . except for the freaking-out part."

"A certain amount of skittishness is understandable, especially given the threats. But you are going to have to talk to this girl—"

"I know. I just—"

"You're also going to have to tell Julie what's been happening—I know you don't want to involve her, but if Penny's behavior starts affecting your work, your boss needs to know about it. Particularly since it's her responsibility for hiring Penny in the first place."

I didn't say anything to that, but Dr. Grey reacted as if I had. She must have seen something in my face—and whatever else the stroke had done to her, her instincts were as sharp as ever.

"If the situation with Penny were to go from bad to worse," she asked, "do you think Julie would try to hold *you* responsible?"

"Well," I said, carefully, "I don't think she'd blame me directly . . . but she might *act* as if it were my fault."

"Let me ask you something else, then. You told me before that you'd gotten over your obsession with Julie. How, exactly?"

"How?"

"How did you get over it? As I recall, you were pretty hard up for her the last time you were here. And God knows I can't have been much help, zonking out in the middle of our conversation . . ."

"Oh, no!" I said. "You were helpful . . . or at least, as helpful as you could be."

"In other words, not very," said Dr. Grey. "So how did you manage your feelings? Did you and Julie talk it out some more, or—"

"No. No, Julie was pretty sick of talking about my feelings by that point. I can't blame her, really . . . I mean, I know love isn't rational, and there doesn't have to be a logical explanation for why two people can't be together, even if it *seems* like they might be right for each other . . . but I kept on wanting a logical explanation anyway. And Julie did the best she could, trying to make sense of it for me, but eventually she got fed up with me asking the same questions over and over . . ."

"So you couldn't talk to her anymore. How did you resolve it, then?"

"I . . . I overheard something."

"Overheard what?"

I stared at my hands.

"Overheard what?" Dr. Grey repeated, patiently.

"It's kind of embarrassing."

Dr. Grey regarded me soberly. "I promise not to make fun," she said.

I sighed, and forced myself to tell it: "It happened about a week after I visited you. Julie started dating this other guy, a mechanic she met at Triple A, and I went a little crazy over it. One of the things she'd told me when she was trying to explain why we couldn't go out was that she wasn't interested in seeing *anyone* just then—but then she turned right around and started seeing someone after all. So that weekend, even though I knew she was tired of talking, I went by her apartment to try and get her to explain it to me one more time."

"What happened?"

"Well, I was outside the door to Julie's apartment, working up the nerve to knock, and that was when I heard them. Julie and the mechanic."

"Heard them . . . ?"

"Together. You know . . ."

"Ah," said Dr. Grey.

"Julie's bedroom is the farthest room from the outside door, but it's a small apartment, and, well, they were being pretty noisy."

"So you heard them together in the bedroom. Then what?"

"Well, I should have turned away and left."

"Yes, you should have," Dr. Grey agreed. "But what *did* you do? Stay to listen?"

My cheeks were burning, and for a moment I was so ashamed I couldn't look at her. I nodded. "I couldn't help myself," I said, and then, remembering that my father might be listening, I quickly amended: "I mean, I *could* help myself, of course I could, but I chose not to."

"And how did it feel, eavesdropping on that?"

"Awful. Awful, and wrong, but also . . . you know what a cathartic experience is, right?"

"Yes, I do," said Dr. Grey, "but I think you mean a *vicarious* experience."

"No, cathartic. I mean yes, there was a vicarious part to it too, at first . . . Julie sounded like she was *really* enjoying herself, and of course I wished it could have been me who was, who was making her happy that way. Maybe I even imagined that it was me, for a little bit. But then, as it went on, I started to feel . . . *wrenched.* It was like that feeling you have when you're crying so hard that your whole body shakes—only I wasn't crying, or shaking. And when it was over, when they finally finished and I snuck away, I felt washed out: fuzzy, and tired, and a little feverish—but also *better,* somehow.

"I remember thinking to myself: 'Maybe *that's* the reason we couldn't be together.' Maybe, as much as I wanted to make Julie . . . happy . . . that way, maybe I just didn't have it in me, and maybe Julie knew that, and that's why she picked the mechanic instead of me. So I went home, thinking about that, and I went to bed early that night, and slept deep, and when I got up the next day I'd accepted it: accepted that Julie and I could never be a couple. All the obsessive feeling, the need for an explanation, that was all gone."

"Purged," Dr. Grey said.

"Yes."

"Or repressed," she added. "Or split off."

"Split—. . . no!" I objected; this was a serious accusation. "I've never split off *anything!* I've never lost time, not even a second!"

"You did say you slept deep that night . . ."

"That was *sleep,* not a blackout! Besides, if I had lost time, somebody else in the house would have noticed!"

"All right then, that's good," Dr. Grey said. "No blackout. But I still think your feelings about Julie might not be quite as settled as you'd like to believe. And that's worth keeping in mind, if only so that you can keep those feelings separate from your feelings about Penny. Because dealing with a disordered multiple is difficult enough even when your motivations are crystal-clear."

"So what about Penny?" I asked, anxious to change the subject. "What do I do?"

"The first thing you've got to do is talk to her," Dr. Grey said. "To the facilitator, what's her name—"

"Thread."

"Thread, right. Set ground rules. You'll probably have to deal with the protector first, so make it clear, up front, that you won't tolerate abuse. No more threats, no more late-night phone calls, none of that. And this is very important, Andrew." She raised a finger in warning. "If the threats *do* continue, if she escalates the violence in any way, you need to be willing to call the police."

I frowned.

"This is *serious*, Andrew."

"I know it's serious," I said. "But I . . . I don't want to make trouble for her. I don't want to get her committed, for goodness' sake."

"I don't want to get her committed either," said Dr. Grey, "but I also don't want to see you get your head handed to you by a berserk alter. So promise me—"

"All right, I promise. Cross my heart."

"Good . . . good. Now the next step, after you make contact and lay down the law, is to see if they'd be willing to come out here, to meet with me."

"Oh no!" I said. "Dr. Grey, I can't ask you to—"

"I'm not offering to treat them," Dr. Grey assured me. "I can't, I just don't have the energy. But before I make a referral, I do want to meet this woman for myself. Confirm the diagnosis."

"All right. I guess I can bring Penny here. I can try."

"At some point," Dr. Grey added, "I'd also like to discuss a referral for you."

"For me? What for? I'm not—"

"I just think it might be helpful for you to have someone to talk to, a professional I mean. Someone to counsel you on whatever issues come up in your life. It wouldn't have to be weekly sessions—just once a month, or whenever you needed a sympathetic ear. I'd offer to do it myself, but I couldn't guarantee that I'd always be . . . well, as I say, I just don't have the energy." Even as she said this, she seemed to sag a little in the wheelchair, the alertness that had animated her for the past hour draining away.

"Dr. Grey," I said, suddenly afraid, "you are all right, aren't you?"

"That's . . . an essay question, Andrew." She laughed, but it was forced.

"Should I not have come today? My father thought it might be a bad idea, that you were too—"

"No, no, Andrew, please," Dr. Grey said, struggling to rouse herself. "I . . . you know it's odd, having treated your father and the others, I see you as someone familiar. But the truth is . . . the truth is we barely know each other. You've never seen me . . . at my best." She sighed. "It's been a difficult adjustment." Her strong hand thumped the armrest of her wheelchair. "I *miss* seeing patients. Miss . . . miss working as hard as I used to. So don't be sorry you came to me with a problem—I'm *glad* to help, glad to have a chance to help. I just wish I could have helped more when you . . . when you were starting out."

"There's nothing to be sorry about there," I said. "You did enough, just helping my father build the house. It's worked out fine, really."

"Well, good," said Dr. Grey, and then closed her eyes for a moment. "Could you get Meredith in here? I think I need to go back upstairs for a bit, now, and rest."

"Oh sure," I said, getting up. "Should I—"

"I'd like you to stay for lunch, if you can." Dr. Grey opened her eyes again. "I just need a little nap first. You can skim through Minor's book while you're waiting. Let me know what you think of it."

"I've already read one paragraph," I told her, "and I think it's terrible."

"Excellent! Read more paragraphs, then. Over lunch, you can tell me why it's terrible, in detail." She smiled tiredly. "Make my day."

I would have been happy to make Dr. Grey's day. But she never came back down from her nap, and eventually Meredith suggested that we eat lunch without her. We had sandwiches out on the porch, and in between nibbles (I still wasn't very hungry) I asked about Dr. Grey's condition. "Danny has good days and bad days," Meredith said vaguely. "Today is about average—although I know she was glad to see you."

After we finished eating I waited around a little longer, hoping to at least say good-bye, but Dr. Grey went on sleeping. So I wrote her a note, thanking her for seeing me and telling her I would call once I'd made contact with Thread. Then I headed for the bus stop to begin the long trip back to Autumn Creek.

On the way home, I thought about Julie.

9

I guess it's not all that surprising that I would be confused about sex. Unlike many of the other souls in the house, I was never raped or molested; but my practical knowledge of the world had to come from somewhere, and a multiple household's collective understanding of human sexuality is inevitably somewhat warped.

It wasn't the mechanics of the act that confounded me—I figured I had that part pretty much straight, although the thought of actually doing it scared the hell out of me. What puzzled me was the *approach* to sex. How, exactly, did two people decide they wanted to get together, and how did they communicate that fact to each other? I knew about flirting, but wasn't sure how to distinguish it from ordinary friendliness. Suppose you thought somebody wanted you to kiss them: was there a way to find out for certain that they did, without making a fool of yourself? Was it OK to just ask, or did having to ask mean that the answer was probably no? What if you *were* kissing somebody: how did you know when they wanted to go further? What were the signs?

My father's answer to all of the above was a frustrating "You'll learn." I couldn't really blame him for not being more helpful: not counting involuntary acts, my father was (and is) a virgin. As far as I know, he never even dated anyone, nor did he ever express any desire to.

There were other souls in the house who had had sexual or romantic relationships, or pieces of relationships, but as a rule they guarded those memories closely. I knew, for instance, that Aunt Sam had had a "sweetheart" sometime during Andy Gage's adolescence; knew too (from Adam, telling tales out of school) that she and the sweetheart had done a lot of intimate things together. But Aunt Sam would never talk about that; she wouldn't even confirm the sweetheart's existence. "A lady never tells," was all she had to say about the matter. Even if she hadn't been so ladylike, she might not have had anything useful to share with me: after all, just because she had a lot of experience *being in* a relationship didn't mean she knew anything about *starting* one.

So I was more or less on my own when, towards the end of 1995, I began to wonder whether Julie might be attracted to me. Oh, the other souls still kibitzed, of course—they always did that—but it was, to borrow a phrase from Mrs. Winslow, like having elephants give advice about ice-skating.

Or almost like that. In retrospect, I'm forced to admit that Adam (another virgin) had a pretty good read on the situation. But his observations were so crude—and so contrary to what I wanted to hear—that I refused to take them seriously.

"Julie's not interested in fucking you," he told me bluntly.

"And you know this how?" I asked him. "Something you read in *Playboy*?"

I'd meant to insult him, but Adam found this hilarious. "Yeah," he said, cackling. "In the Women With Car Trouble issue . . . Seriously, Julie's a lot of things, but she's not shy. When she really wants something, she lets you know. She might pick the most inconvenient way imaginable to do it, but she lets you know."

"Well maybe this is different," I suggested. "Maybe she's still making up her mind."

"Nah," said Adam. "She just doesn't want to fuck you."

"Adam—"

"I'm not saying she never thought about it. Maybe she has. Maybe she daydreams about it sometimes, when she's bored—maybe that's what you picked up on. But it's not serious. If she *really* wanted to fuck you, she would have by now."

I didn't want to believe him, although my "evidence" that Julie might be interested in me was pretty insubstantial. True, she was very physically affectionate towards me, but as Adam never tired of pointing out, she was like that with almost everyone—even Dennis, on the rare occasions when they weren't fighting. On the other hand, Julie and I had started spending an awful lot of time alone together outside of work, and that was something she didn't do with anybody else. Our private talks were often extremely personal, touching on subjects you wouldn't discuss with just anyone. We shared secrets; Julie called me her "confidant."

And there *were* incidents, things that happened that suggested we were more than just close friends, or could become more. Things that gave me hope.

Like the night before Thanksgiving, when the two of us went out to celebrate the holiday at the same Bridge Street bar we'd gone to the day we first met. Julie ordered a kamikaze; I had a strawberry margarita with no alcohol in it. The waiter who brought our drinks made a comment about how he dreaded going home to see his family tomorrow, and that got Julie talking about her family, in particular about her father. Without going into details that aren't mine to share, let's just say that Julie's relationship with her dad, while nowhere near as bad as Andy Gage's relationship with his stepfather, was still pretty terrible—it's not for nothing that she left home at sixteen.

Julie talked about her father for almost two hours. I did my best to commiserate, although, as I reminded her at one point, I had no personal experience with abusive parents. But Julie didn't seem to care about that; so I listened, and she poured out her heart. She was still talking as I walked her home, holding her hand the whole way.

Then we were on Olympic Avenue, outside Julie's apartment, and she seemed to run out of words. She stood there silently for a moment and then leaned in to me, put her arms around my neck, and asked me if I'd come upstairs and tuck her in. We went up, Julie leaning on me heavily now. In the apartment, she didn't turn any lights on, just guided me back into her bedroom. She scrabbled around in the dark for a box of matches, and lit a candle on the steamer trunk beside her futon. And then, as I stood dumbly by, Julie got undressed right in front of me. *Completely* undressed. Naked, she rummaged through her clothes closet for what seemed like forever; finally she drew out a gauzy white nightgown and slipped it over her shoulders. She came back over to me, put her arms around my neck again, and kissed me full on the mouth.

"Yeah, she kissed you," Adam said later. "But she didn't kiss you and ask you to stay; she kissed you and told you to be careful walking home. Notice the difference?"

Yes, I noticed. But after that night I started noticing other things, too, things that Julie did or said that seemed to have hidden meanings. Like the week after Thanksgiving, when she had a huge fight with her landlord, and came and told me she was thinking about breaking her lease, and then said, kind of offhand, "You know, *we* ought to get a place together"—and when I hedged, saying that it sounded like a nice idea, but that I wasn't sure if I was ready to move out of Mrs. Winslow's, Julie replied, "Oh, I think you'd have a *lot* more fun living with me than with Mrs. Winslow . . ." Or the week after that, the morning Julie's car wouldn't start, and she had to walk to the

Factory through freezing sleet, and she came into my tent stripped down to her underwear, trying to dry herself with a hand towel, and said to me, "Andrew, will you run away with me to Hawaii?" and I said "Um . . ." and she sat in my lap and laid her head on my shoulder, so that her damp hair pressed into the hollow of my neck, and said, *"Please, Andrew? Please* take me away from here?" Or a few days later, when Dennis was teasing me about an idea I'd had for a demo, saying, "One thing you're always good for is a ridiculous suggestion," and Julie remarked in passing, "I bet that's not the *only* thing Andrew's good for . . ."

I know, I know—probably I was reading way too much into all this. But at the time . . . at the time I was sure Julie was sending me signals, Adam's skepticism be damned.

Then it was Christmastime, my first Christmas ever, and Julie insisted on going in with me on a tree. Mrs. Winslow already had a tree for the Victorian, an eight-foot plastic perennial that she'd owned since before she got married, but Julie argued that that wasn't a *real* Christmas tree. "You've got to go out and cut down a live one," she said. "It's tradition."

"You do that every year?" I asked her.

"Well no, actually, I've never done that. But it's still tradition. It could be *our* tradition . . ." Naturally, the thought of establishing a tradition with Julie sold me on the idea immediately.

She got her uncle to drive us to a tree farm in Snoqualmie. He picked us up in his truck one evening after work. Julie, who'd been in a bubbly mood all day, introduced me as her "soul mate." Her uncle, a grizzled older man with one of the raspiest voices I'd ever heard, stuck out a hand and said, "Thrilled." It was the last thing he said for a while; Julie talked pretty much nonstop on the ride out. During the course of her monologue, which concerned the latest goings-on at the Reality Factory, I noticed that she was saying a *lot* of complimentary things about me—how creative I was, how hardworking I was, what a good person I was—which should have been flattering, but mostly just unsettled me. Many of the compliments seemed exaggerated, and a couple were flat-out lies (I'm *not* "musically gifted"; the only soul in the house with any musical talent to speak of is Aunt Sam, and even she's not that good). Once again I found myself wondering whether there was a hidden message here: was Julie telling her uncle something, or was she trying to tell *me* something?

The Snoqualmie tree farm offered precut pine trees in all sizes, but Julie, set on following "tradition," insisted that we borrow a saw and go into the fields. Having selected a tree as far from the farm's parking lot as possible,

Julie assumed a purely supervisory role during the actual felling. While her uncle and I took turns with the saw, she alternated between cheering us on, teasing us for our slow progress, and throwing snowballs. The snowballs were all aimed at me.

When we got back to Autumn Creek, Julie thanked her uncle profusely—"You're the best, Arnie, just the best"—and invited him up to her apartment for a drink; but he declined, saying that he had another errand to run. Climbing into the back of the truck, he uncovered a mound of cardboard cases that had been concealed beneath a pile of furniture pads. He opened one of the cases and pulled out a bottle of scotch for each of us. "Happy holidays," he rasped, and Adam up in the pulpit crowed cheerfully: "Look ma, no tax stamps!"

Julie in turn gave her uncle a tightly rolled-up brown-paper bag. I don't know what was in it, but it made him very happy. "All right, then!" he said, zipping his gift into an inside pocket of his coat. He chucked Julie under the chin and clapped me on the shoulder. "You two stay out of trouble!" With a last wink at Julie, he climbed into the truck cab and drove away.

After the truck was out of sight, I offered Julie my bottle of scotch. "Merry Christmas," I said. "I've got another present for you too, but—"

"Yeah, I've got one for you, too," Julie said. "But let's get this tree inside first."

We hauled the tree up the stairs and into Julie's bedroom. Then she took the scotch and went into the kitchen to make eggnog, leaving me to set up the tree in a stand she'd bought. This was trickier than I expected, but I had it pretty well balanced by the time Julie came back, carrying a mug in each hand. "Cheers," she said, handing one to me.

"Cheers." I took an experimental sip . . . and frowned, tasting liquor in with the eggs and cream. "Uh, Julie . . . I think you forgot, I don't—"

"Shh," Julie said, pressing a finger to my lips. "I won't tell if you won't."

It wasn't a question of telling or not telling, of course; hiding a drink from my father would be like hiding a manicure from my fingernails. But I took another small sip, just to be polite, and then discreetly set the mug aside. "So, do we exchange gifts now?"

Julie shook her head. "Not yet—we've got to finish decorating the tree first." She hauled a big box of Christmas ornaments out of her closet and took out two gnarled strands of Christmas-tree lights, handing one to me. "Start by untangling this."

We set to work, chatting idly as we picked at the knots in the cords. I asked Julie where she'd bought the eggnog mix.

"Mix!" Julie scoffed. "That's homemade, thank you very much."

"Really?" I glanced over at my mug. "I thought the basic eggnog stuff—you know, except for the scotch—I thought that just came in a carton."

"Actually, it comes from eggs," Julie teased, "which come out of a chicken. Also from cream, which comes out of a cow."

"You milked your own cow?"

"No, Andrew . . ." Julie started to look annoyed, then realized I was teasing, too. "All right, all right," she admitted, "so the cream *does* come out of a carton—but I mixed it and the other ingredients together myself." She beamed proudly. "One of the many useful skills I picked up at Lulu's Mexican Kitchen in Phoenix, Arizona."

"You served eggnog at a Mexican restaurant?"

"Around Christmastime we did. The guy I worked the grill with taught me his secret recipe."

The guy I worked the grill with . . . Something about the way Julie said that made me ask: "Was he your boyfriend?"

Julie's brow furrowed; she seemed to concentrate a little more intently on the strand of lights she was holding. "Yes," she said, and Adam up in the pulpit warned: "Don't do it."

But I did, asking haltingly: "Did you . . . do you ever think of *me* that way? As a boyfriend, I mean."

The furrow in Julie's brow deepened, but she went on untangling the lights as if she hadn't heard me. She didn't reply for so long that I began to wonder if I'd forgotten to ask the question aloud. But finally she looked over at me and said: "You remember me telling you about that physical therapist I used to live with?"

"Sure," I said. "The one you worked for before you started the Reality Factory, right?"

She nodded. "Worked for, lived with, everything . . . Since we broke up, I haven't seen him or spoken to him once. I don't even know if he's still in Seattle. And it's the same story with the guy in Phoenix . . . and the guy in Eugene, and the guy in Las Vegas, and the guy in Yellowstone, and the guy in New York, and the four guys in Boston. It's always been that way with me: when I'm lovers with somebody, and it ends, they disappear from my life. And I wouldn't ever want that to happen with you, Andrew—I want you *in* my life, not a stranger."

"Oh," I said, both flattered and disappointed. But the disappointment was greater, and after a moment I suggested hesitantly: "What if . . . what if it didn't end, though? What if—"

Julie smiled sadly at me. "Love affairs always end," she said. "Don't you know that?"

No, I didn't know that—I didn't believe it, either, though I was in a very poor position to argue. Stumped for a rebuttal, I went back to untangling Christmas lights; after a brief uncomfortable silence, Julie announced, with forced cheerfulness, "I'm going to the kitchen to freshen up my eggnog." This time the hidden message was clear: *When I come back, we'll talk about something else.* Which we did; and it wasn't until later, after Julie and I had said our good nights and I was walking home alone, that it occurred to me that she'd never actually said whether she was attracted to me.

"Does it matter?" Adam asked. *"She doesn't want to fuck you.* Get that through your head already."

I tried. I tried very hard, and I might have succeeded, too, if not for what happened the day of the Wednesday After Christmas Party.

Because Christmas Eve and New Year's Eve were both on Sunday that year, Julie had decided that we ought to split the difference and hold a combined holiday office party on Wednesday the 27th. Julie and I handled the refreshments for the party: Julie made punch, using up the second bottle of her uncle's scotch; I baked cookies and a chocolate cake. The Manciple brothers, meanwhile, were put in charge of the entertainment.

At five o'clock on Wednesday afternoon we gathered in the Big Tent for the festivities. Julie ladled out punch for everyone but me; Dennis booted up the Eidolon system. The Reality Factory only had two data suits at that point, so we took turns putting them on and playing Virtual Ping-Pong, Virtual Skee-Ball, and Virtual Bash-the-Piñata (in which you aren't blindfolded, but the piñata can duck). Finally, Dennis announced the "ultimate" virtual party game: Virtual Twister.

"What's that?" I asked.

Julie's eyebrows shot up. "You've never played Twister?"

She described the real-world version of the game, which sounded very strange to me at first. And the VR version was even stranger: in Virtual Twister, the colored circles weren't just on the "floor" but all around you, hanging in space.

"So you reach for these circles," I said, "and you get all twisted up . . ."

"Right," said Julie.

". . . and the first person to fall over loses?"

"Yes, technically. But winning and losing aren't really the point of the game . . ."

What was the point? Part of it, as with virtual piñata-bashing, was to provide comic relief for the spectators. But the main point of Twister, Julie hinted, was to give the players an excuse to roll around with each other. I could understand the appeal of that, given the right playmate—but that aspect of the game didn't translate well into cyberspace. When Irwin and I played our first game of Virtual Twister, our real bodies were in separate corners of the Big Tent, and of course virtual body contact that is unaccompanied by actual body contact doesn't feel like anything. Also, the version of the software engine we were using had a few bugs in its collision-handling subroutines. When the computer gamesmaster told me "Left hand—red," and Irwin's eidolon was blocking the most convenient red circle, instead of reaching around I was able to put my hand right through him.

Julie caught this on one of the monitors and cried foul. "You guys aren't playing it right!" she complained tipsily. "Here, Irwin—let me get that suit for a minute, I'll show you how it's done."

Irwin gave his data suit to Julie. She put it on and had Irwin position us so that our real bodies were the same distance apart as our virtual bodies. "Right hand—blue," the computer commanded me. I saw a blue circle peeking over Julie's shoulder, started to put my hand through her chest . . . and met resistance.

From there on out, the game made a lot more sense to me. It also got more dangerous, as Julie's and my virtual bodies still weren't perfectly synchronized with our real bodies. Not all of the accidents that this caused were unpleasant—I didn't mind so much when Julie reached for a green circle behind my back and grabbed my butt by mistake—but most of them were: Julie probably could have done without me kneeing her in the rib cage, and I know I would rather have skipped the elbow in the stomach. The game ended with Julie going for an overly ambitious "Left foot—yellow" that knocked both my legs out from under me and flipped me hard onto my back.

"Ow," I said.

"Andrew!?" Julie ripped off her headset in a panic, but when she saw that I wasn't badly hurt, she burst out laughing . . . and collapsed, gently, on top of me.

I decided that I liked Virtual Twister, even with the bruises.

We took a break from the games after that and went back to the refreshments. Julie and Dennis got drunk, and Irwin got really drunk. Then around six-thirty—it was amazing that it had taken him that long—Dennis took his shirt off. Julie, helping herself to the last of the punch, said: "You know, Dennis, that is just *so* attractive, you exposing yourself that way."

Dennis, unoffendable as always, raised his arms above his head. "Gotta air myself out," he explained. Then, after his armpits had had a moment to cool, he said to Julie: "So how about it, Fearless Leader? Since I'm *so* attractive, you wanna play a round of Twister with me?"

I think he was kidding; even without his back brace on, Dennis had a hard time fitting into a data suit. But Julie got this look in her eye like she was actually considering it, just to prove she wasn't afraid to take a dare, any dare, and I knew if she called Dennis's bluff he'd do it. It made me feel funny; I didn't want Julie playing Twister with Dennis, or anyone else besides me. Before it could come to that, though, Irwin bent over and vomited on one of the Eidolon headsets, putting a definite end to the games.

"Time to go home," I suggested.

Questions of sobriety aside, Julie's Cadillac was in the shop again, so we all walked back to town. A light snow was falling, and Julie and Dennis, full of crazy energy, kept running ahead, catching snowflakes on their tongues and bursting into choruses of "Auld Lang Syne" (I'm not very familiar with the song, but I'm pretty sure they were making up their own lyrics). Irwin plodded along zombie-like, stopping every now and then to throw up some more. I followed quietly, keeping an eye on Irwin and trying to stay out of Julie and Dennis's way.

We crossed the east bridge and came to the intersection where Julie had to turn off to get to her apartment. I hesitated, uncertain whether to follow her or continue down Bridge Street with the Manciples. But Julie decided for me, slinging an arm around my waist and raising a hand to wave good-bye to the brothers. "See you two tomorrow," she said.

"G'night," Irwin muttered as he plodded on, not even bothering to turn around. Dennis, far more alert, watched curiously as Julie led me away up the side street.

"Hey, Grand Poobah," he called after us, "what are *you* going to do now?"

"You only wish you knew, Dennis," Julie called back.

"Oh yeah?" Dennis said, swaying a little on his feet. "Does that mean you changed your mind about him?"

"Shhhh!" Julie shushed him, laughing.

"What?" Dennis shouted. He cupped a hand behind his ear, as if he were hard of hearing. "I didn't catch that, Commodore. *What?*"

"Good *night*, Dennis!" Julie shouted back, still laughing (but at what?). Then, tugging at my hand: "Come on, Andrew."

"Um, Julie—"

"Let's run!" she said, giving my hand another tug.

So we ran, Dennis behind us hollering something that I couldn't make out. Then we were out of earshot, racing up the street in the dark, Julie leading the way, still laughing, pulling me along.

We reached Julie's building. Instead of heading up to her apartment, she ran out onto the front lawn and let herself fall, pulling me down with her onto the thin dusting of snow. As we tumbled over each other I wrenched my back again, but Julie didn't notice.

"God," Julie said, coming to rest on her own back. "God, I am so drunk." Then she rolled towards me, coming up on one elbow, and asked: "You want to come upstairs for a while? It's still early."

"Um . . . OK," I said, and Julie, hearing the hesitancy in my voice, gave me a long look, as if she were making up her mind about something. She raised a hand to brush a snowflake from my eyelashes, then caught a lock of my hair, twirling it around her index finger.

"C'mon," she finally said, and stood up.

Upstairs in her kitchen, Julie poured two shot glasses of straight scotch. "Julie—" I began to protest, but she overrode me, saying: "Come on, Andrew, just one. One toast."

"Toast to what?"

"To new experiences," Julie said slyly.

So I gave in—I chose to give in—even though I knew I'd pay for it later. "To . . . to new experiences," I said, and drank. Julie tossed her shot down in one swallow; I tried to sip mine but ended up gulping it as well, nearly choking on the heat of it in my throat.

Julie refilled both our glasses and led me into her bedroom. Once again she left the overhead light off, plugging the Christmas tree in instead, illuminating the room in soft multicolor. She plopped down on the edge of her futon. I squatted, somewhat more delicately, on the floor a few feet away.

This time Julie saw me wincing. "Did you hurt your back?" she asked.

I nodded. "Twister," I said.

"Oh shit," said Julie. Then she patted the surface of the futon behind her. "Come on up here, I'll give you a backrub . . . Come on, Andrew. I won't bite."

I climbed on the futon and lay on my stomach as Julie directed. "God, you're tense," she observed, as she settled over me.

Yes, I was: tense with fear and excitement, in equal measure. I could sense Adam up in the pulpit and knew he'd be getting scared too, scared speechless in fact. Which was good—the last thing I wanted right now was to have him making wisecracks in the background.

Julie ran her hands lightly up and down my back a few times, checking out the lay of the land. I tried to relax—but then Julie yanked my shirttail out of my jeans.

"Jesus, Andrew, *calm down*," Julie said. "I promise I'm not going to hurt you. Now"—she gave my shirt another little yank—"is it OK if I take this off you?"

I wanted to say yes, but couldn't seem to get the word out of my mouth.

"OK," Julie said, after a moment. "We'll leave it on for now—but untucked." She shifted position above me; there was a sound of cloth sliding over skin—and then *Julie's* shirt came off, landing in a heap on the floor beside the futon. I let out a little gasp and jerked my head around . . . and was both relieved and disappointed to see that Julie was still wearing her bra.

"'Scuse me for being Dennis," she said, smiling down at me.

She wasn't Dennis. Take my word for it: Dennis without a shirt on and Julie without a shirt on were two totally different things.

When I'd climbed onto the futon I'd set my shot glass down in easy reach. I reached for it now, which seemed to amuse Julie, who waited patiently as I drank. Then she took the empty glass from me and set it aside, pushed me gently back down onto my stomach, and ran her cool soft hands up under the back of my shirt.

The next fifteen minutes were, without question, the happiest and most terrifying of my life up to that point—which admittedly is not saying quite as much as it would be for most twenty-six-year-olds. I don't know how good a backrub it was, objectively speaking—I had nothing to compare it to—but I enjoyed it immensely, even when Julie dug her fingers into one of my bruises hard enough to make me groan.

My eyelids had fluttered closed, and I was on the verge of letting go my anxiety, when Julie said: "So, Andrew . . . what are your goals for this coming year?"

My eyes snapped open again. "My . . . my goals?"

"Yeah, your goals," Julie said. Keeping one hand on my neck, she lowered the other to the small of my back, and brushed her fingertips across the skin just above the waistband of my jeans. "You know, like that toast we made. What *new experiences* are you hoping to have this year?"

"Ah . . . I . . . uh . . ."

"Don't think about it so hard." She brought her hand back up to my shoulders, and bent so low that she was practically lying on top of me, whispering in my ear: "Just pick something. One thing that you've never done before, that you'd like to do . . ."

My head was turned sideways on the futon now, and Julie must have seen how red my face was getting, because she backed off a little. "Andrew?"

"Julie . . ." I was petrified that I was about to make a terrible fool of myself, but I didn't know what else to do, and there was no one I could ask for help—Adam had left the pulpit when Julie took her shirt off. I forced myself to go on: "Julie, are you . . . are you making a pass at me?"

She laughed, but not as lightheartedly as before. "What if I am?" she said.

"*Are* you or *aren't* you?" The words came out much too loud. I tried to soften my voice: "Please . . . please don't tease me about this, Julie."

There was a long pause, and then I felt her rolling off me. "Shit."

"Julie?" I lifted my head up and looked at her. She was lying on her back staring up at the ceiling, pulling at her hair with both hands.

"Shit, shit, shit," Julie said. "What the fuck am I doing? What the fuck is *wrong* with me?"

"Wrong with you?" I said, though the question hadn't really been directed at me. "Julie, there's nothing wrong with . . . if you want to . . . you know. It's just, I don't understand—last week you said, I *thought* you said, that you wouldn't want to be lovers with me, because . . ."

"I know."

". . . because lovers don't last, and friends do, and you want me to stay in your life . . ."

"I know." Julie was nodding now. "I know. And you're right, Andrew."

I was right? "Wait a minute," I said. "Wait a minute, no, that was *your* argument. I don't think it's true—and if you don't really believe it either, that's fine with me . . . I just need to know what you're feeling, that's all."

"What I'm feeling . . ."

She took her hands out of her hair, and looked at me. It was a moment that would haunt me later: Julie looked so beautiful, lying there, and I had a definite sense of a window of opportunity opening, very briefly. If only I had done something then—leaned down and kissed her, touched her face, *something*—then maybe the evening would have ended differently. Maybe we could have been lovers after all. But I knew even less about seducing people than I knew about being seduced, so I hesitated, out of my depth.

And the moment passed. "No," Julie said, shaking her head. She sat up, giving me her back. "Could you hand me my shirt, Andrew?"

"Julie," I said, suddenly short of breath, as though ice water had been splashed on my chest. "Julie, it's OK, you don't have to . . . I mean . . . can't we just *talk*, or—"

"I really think I need to pass out, Andrew," Julie said, still not looking at me. "I'm sorry, I know it's still early, but . . . I really think that would be best. You should go home." Finally she turned towards me, offering me a brittle smile and patting my knee the way you'd pat a baby's head. "Now please, can you hand me my shirt?"

"OK . . ." I handed her the shirt. She turned all the way away from me to put it on, as if suddenly she were uncomfortable to have me looking at her in just her bra. Dressed, she hopped off the futon, scooped up both shot glasses and stumbled towards the door, flicking on the overhead light on her way out.

I got up too, blinking in the sudden brightness. I tucked my shirt in and went out to the kitchen, where Julie was making a big production out of washing the shot glasses. "Julie?" I said, keeping a respectful distance.

"Yes?" she said, bent over the sink, her back to me.

"I know you want me to leave now, but . . . tomorrow. Tomorrow, when you're more awake . . . can we talk about this?"

"Talk?" She shut off the water and reached for a dishtowel. "Sure." She dried the shot glasses and then her hands. "Sure," she repeated, hanging the towel up. My coat was on the kitchen table; she grabbed it and offered it to me. "Here you go."

"Julie—"

"Shh," Julie said, pressing the coat into my hands. She leaned forward to give me a quick kiss on the cheek; I started to turn my head, turn my lips towards hers, but she'd already stepped back. "Careful going down the stairs," she said, holding the apartment door open for me.

I slept badly that night. Although I was technically drunk—and you can be sure my father gave me nine shades of hell about that—I wasn't drunk enough to pass out. Besides, it really was still early—barely eight o'clock when I got home. By my normal bedtime, I'd sobered up enough to toss and turn for hours.

In the morning, Julie avoided me at first. I suppose the mature thing would have been to play along and pretend that nothing had happened, but I couldn't do that—and after Dennis made some suggestive comments about how I "must've been up pretty late last night," Julie noticed how haggard I looked and took pity on me. She came by my tent around noon.

"I'm *really* sorry, Andrew . . ." she said, standing contritely in front of my desk.

"You don't have to be sorry, Julie," I told her. "It's not like I mind you making a pass at me, if . . . if that's what happened. I just, I need you to explain it to me, that's all."

Julie let out a sigh. "There's nothing to *explain*, Andrew. I was drunk. You were drunk. We—"

"I drank what you gave me to drink," I said, and we both flinched at the edge in my voice.

"OK," said Julie. "OK, fine, I got drunk, I got you drunk, it's on me. There's still nothing to explain. People do stupid things when they're drunk, Andrew—that's all it was."

"But I thought you weren't even attracted to me—"

"Andrew, *of course* I'm attracted to you. You're a very attractive person. But—"

"Then *why* can't we be lovers? If you're attracted to me, and I'm attracted to you, and we *like* each other—"

Julie ended up giving me half a dozen reasons why we couldn't be lovers. Then there was the other reason, Adam's reason, which Julie herself never voiced but which I have come to believe is probably the real reason: that Julie, no matter what her behavior might occasionally have suggested to the contrary, just wasn't interested.

None of these reasons satisfied me—not even the ones I was willing to accept. What I really wanted to know was not "Why *can't* we be lovers?" but "How *can* we be lovers?" What did I have to do to open that window of opportunity again—that opportunity I was *sure* had been there—and this time not miss it? How do I seduce you, Julie?

I don't think Julie would have answered that question, even if I'd known enough to put it to her straight. And I didn't know enough; so I just kept asking her "Why not?" until eventually—pretty quickly—she got tired of making up reasons.

By the second week of January, Julie had stopped hanging out with me after work, and was doing a decent job of avoiding me inside the Factory as well; that month she made a record number of business-related trips to Seattle, often spending whole days in the city. One night I was waiting for her outside her apartment when she came home, well after dark, and she informed me tersely that I wasn't to come by uninvited anymore.

"Ever?" I gasped.

"For now," Julie said. She looked away from me, and tapped her foot impatiently.

"For now? For now until when?"

"Until you get over me," Julie snapped. "However long that takes." Softening: "I hope it won't be too long, Andrew. But . . ."

I thought that was as bad as it could get, the way I felt that night—and it was bad enough that I took the next day off work and went to see Dr. Grey on my own, without even asking my father's permission. But then a week later, I overheard Julie telling Dennis about the mechanic she'd met in Seattle and begun dating.

Adam and my father both warned me not to say anything—it would only cause more trouble, might even get me fired. I knew they were right, and managed to keep my feelings in check for almost twenty-four hours, but in the end I caved in. I went over to Julie's apartment uninvited, and climbed the stairs, and paused, trying to screw up the courage to knock, and heard a strange sound . . . and listened.

Dr. Grey doubted that my catharsis had been real. It was not an unreasonable conclusion for her to come to, but I didn't want to believe it. I remembered the relief I'd felt the next day, waking up, finding all that obsessive feeling about Julie just gone, taken away; it was distressing to think that that might have been some sort of sleight-of-mind trick. Still, if I wasn't willing to accept that the catharsis had been an illusion, I could maybe allow the possibility that it hadn't been totally successful. Maybe I was still carrying a *small* torch for Julie—just a little one, a tiny flame of unextinguished hope that that window of opportunity would open up again someday. Such a flame would have been easy enough to keep alive, I supposed: Julie's relationship with the mechanic hadn't lasted more than a month, and she hadn't dated anyone else since. So, maybe . . .

I thought it over—I thought all of this over—on the bus ride from Poulsbo to the ferry terminal and on the ferry back to Seattle. I could have gone inside the house to do my thinking, and let some of the other souls use the body while I was preoccupied, but I was tired and felt the beginnings of a headache, so I stayed out. This prompted complaints of unfairness from Angel and Rhea, who hadn't had any time outside yet today, and from Simon, who had had time outside but felt he deserved more. I told them all to leave me alone. My father, seeing the kind of mood I was in, supported my decision, and promised Simon and the others that he would make it up to them, if they behaved. That mollified Angel and Rhea, but not Simon, who was running a mood of his own.

When the ferry docked in Seattle, I made a dash for the Metro stop at Second and Madison, just missing the 3:20 bus to Autumn Creek. The next bus wasn't due until 4:10, which, Simon suggested, left time for a quick visit to Westlake Center mall. I warned him again to leave me alone. Then the 4:10 bus showed up late, with engine trouble, and had to be taken out of service. Simon began to whine. I lost my temper and yelled at him to shut up, which at least got me some real-world breathing space: when the replacement bus arrived, none of the other passengers would sit near me.

It was quarter to six by the time we got back to Autumn Creek. Trudging the last block up Temple Street towards home, I wanted nothing more than to get indoors, have a quick bite to eat, and take a long, hot bath . . .

. . . and that was when I saw Penny's Buick parked at the curb out front of the Victorian.

This was the last thing I wanted to deal with after such a long day. As it turned out, though, it may have been the perfect moment for Penny to catch up with me: I was simply too exhausted to panic again, and between my anger at Simon and my frustration with the Metro bus system, I had temporarily stopped thinking about Julie.

I walked up to the Buick. Out of the corner of my eye, I saw a seated figure jump to her feet on the porch of the Victorian, like a sentry leaping to attention.

"It's all right, Mrs. Winslow," I called out.

"Are you sure, Andrew?"

"Yes," I said—and realized, with no small amazement, that Mrs. Winslow was holding a shotgun. "It's OK, really, you can go inside. I'll be in for dinner in just a minute."

With an almost imperceptible nod, Mrs. Winslow retreated into the house. I got the feeling that she hadn't gone far—that she was waiting just inside the front door, gun in hand, ready to come charging back out if Penny showed the slightest sign of trying to abduct me in the Centurion. I didn't know whether to be reassured or worried by that.

Anyway, no more delaying: I opened the Buick's front passenger door, and climbed in. I recognized Foul Mouth in the driver's seat; she sat hunched forward over the steering wheel, her right hand drumming impatiently on the dashboard.

"Hello," I said. "I guess it's time we tal—"

"Close the fucking door," Foul Mouth said.

I sighed. Dr. Grey had warned me not to stand for any abuse, but I didn't want to start right off with a confrontation, so I did as I was told and pulled the door shut. "Now," I said, "can we—"

There was a tiny click from the dashboard: the cigarette lighter button, popping out. Foul Mouth turned towards me and pounced, snatching up the cigarette lighter as she leaned across the front seats.

"*Fucker!*" she hissed, her face suddenly just inches from my own, the hot coil of the lighter poised right above my cheek. "You *fucker!*"

In the pulpit, Adam cried an alarm. Instantly Seferis was there, ready to jump into the body and take over . . . but I wouldn't let him. I know I should have. I should have been terrified, too: the normal reaction when someone threatens to burn you with a piece of hot metal. Somehow, though, I just wasn't. There was a little thrill of fear, maybe, deep down in the pit of my stomach, but what I mostly felt was annoyed.

"Put that thing away," I said wearily.

The cigarette lighter trembled, as if Foul Mouth were steeling herself to plunge it into my face. I turned my head a fraction and looked her in the eye. "You're being very rude," I told her, "and I won't help Penny if you're rude to me."

She eased back, but only part way: the lighter coil remained pointed at me, her left arm cocked behind it. "You'll help her?"

I nodded. "*If* you're polite . . ."

"Polite!" Foul Mouth sneered.

"Civil, then," I said. "Look, I know I've been rude to you too, and I'm sorry. But if you agree to stop threatening me, and stop upsetting my land-lady, then I promise I'll try to help Penny like you wanted."

Foul Mouth regarded me thoughtfully a moment longer. Finally she low-ered her arm and reinserted the cigarette lighter in its slot. "Deal," she said.

". . . do you really mean it?" added another, friendlier voice. "You'll help us?"

"Yes, I mean it. Thread? It is Thread, isn't it?"

"Yes," she said, smiling. "Like Ariadne's thread, you know that story?"

"I think so . . . And what's the protector's name?"

"The protector?"

"The, um"—I glanced at the dashboard—"the one who swears."

Thread followed my glance to the cigarette lighter. "Oh," she said, "you mean the twins! Maledicta and Malefica. Maledicta does all of the talking—and the swearing—but they're always together."

"Are there others?" I asked.

"Oh, yes, lots of others." She eyed me curiously. "You have others too, don't you?" I nodded, and Thread nodded too, her smile widening. "I knew it!" she said. "I knew we weren't the only ones. And you know how to make it work, don't you? How to make it . . . less confusing."

"Yes."

It was as if she'd been holding her breath this whole time, and was now finally able to release it. "Oh, thank goodness! . . . So how do we start? What do we have to do?"

"It depends," I told her. "How much does Penny herself know?"

"Penny," Thread echoed. "You know, it's really kind of you to call her that."

"Instead of Mouse?"

Thread nodded. "Mouse is what Penny's mother always called her. And after Penny died—"

"After that fucking cunt killed her," Maledicta interjected.

"—Mouse is all that was left. She still thinks of herself as Penny, and I think she could still *be* Penny, if . . . well, with your help. And you calling her Penny, *knowing* to call her Penny, even after you'd been told otherwise—that was just a really good omen."

"I had some help figuring it out," I confessed.

"I did get a little worried when you wouldn't talk to us," Thread continued. "I'm sorry about the e-mail Maledicta sent you—she slipped that past me, so I didn't understand your reaction at first. It *was* very rude of her."

"It's all right. I know that—"

". . . and then when I got your e-mail back, I didn't know what to think. I—"

A sharp pain spiked at the center of my forehead, blurring my vision for a moment.

"—Mr. Gage?"

"I'm sorry," I said, massaging my temples. "I'm sorry, I . . . I'm kind of tired. Could we maybe pick this up again tomorrow, or Sunday? I promise I'm not trying to run away from you again, I just . . . right now I really need to get inside and rest."

"Of course," Thread said. She handed me a slip of notepaper. "That's Penny's home number. Call us anytime—if Penny answers, just say who you are, and one of us will take over."

"OK," I nodded. "I'll call you this weekend, for su—"

She was leaning across the seats towards me again. At first I thought she meant to hug me, but at the last second she tilted her head sideways and pressed her mouth against mine.

"Sweet thing," a new soul said, breaking the kiss. She traced a finger down the side of my face.

Outside the Buick, another car honked its horn. Penny's head snapped around towards the sound, eyes narrowing. "What the fuck is *she* doing here?" Maledicta said.

I was scrunched back against the passenger door, still trying to process the kiss. "I'm going to go inside now," I said.

"Sure," said Maledicta distractedly. "But hey! Don't lose that fucking number!"

"I won't . . ." I stumbled out of the car, and Maledicta took off, nearly sideswiping the Cadillac that had pulled up across the street. As the Centurion sped away, the Caddy honked its horn again.

"Julie?" I said.

"Andrew!" Julie called, frantically rolling her window down. "Andrew, *what the hell is going on?*"

I crossed the street to the Cadillac with a good deal more trepidation than I'd felt approaching the Buick. "What are you doing here, Julie?"

"What am I . . . Jesus Christ, Andrew, I'm looking for you! Where the hell have you been since yesterday?"

"Didn't you get my note?"

"Note? What note?"

"The one I left you at your apartment this morning."

Julie shook her head. "There wasn't any note at my apartment."

"Yes there was. Under—"

"*First* you cut out of work early yesterday, then you don't return my phone call last night, today you don't show up to work at all, and *now* . . ."—she looked over her shoulder, in the direction of the departed Buick—". . . now Penny gives me this look like I'm the Son of Sam and nearly takes my back fender off."

"I'm sorry about that. I'm sorry if you got a little worried, too, but I *did* leave you a note."

"Saying what?"

"Saying that the reason I wouldn't be in today is that I was going to see Dr. Grey, in Poulsbo, to ask about getting some help for Penny. Like you wanted."

"Oh," Julie said, instantly chastened. Then she said: "So how did it go?"

"It went . . . OK, I guess. But listen, Julie . . . I know you're anxious to hear about it, but I am *really* tired right now, so would it be OK if I held off telling you until Monday?"

"Monday!"

"First thing, I promise. I'll come into work early, and we can—"

"Come on, Andrew! You can't leave me hanging all weekend, not after—"

"Tomorrow, then," I said. "I'll call you tomorrow, and we'll talk."

I could tell she wanted to say no—wanted to insist on hearing the whole story right then and there—but I guess my exhaustion was obvious enough that she couldn't dismiss it. "All right, tomorrow," she conceded. "*Early* tomorrow."

"I'll call you as soon as I've finished breakfast," I promised. "Good night, Julie."

I started to turn away, but she reached out through the window and caught my arm. "Andrew?"

"Yes?"

"You're not mad at me, are you?"

"Mad at you? Why would you think I'm mad at you?"

"Well . . ." She glanced over her shoulder again. "Never mind. But listen: instead of calling me up after breakfast tomorrow, why don't you come over to my apartment and have breakfast with me?"

"Come over—"

"Yeah, like old times." She smiled, and her eyes shone. "You know, I really miss hanging out like we used to. I think about it, sometimes. I think about it a lot, actually." She let go of my arm and reached up to caress my cheek, the exact same gesture that that nameless soul of Penny's had made after kissing me. "What about you, Andrew?" Julie asked. "Do you ever think about that? . . . Andrew?"

FOURTH BOOK:
MOUSE

10

The envelope from the English Society of International Correspondents is sitting on Mouse's kitchen table when she wakes up on Sunday morning.

Sunday morning: Mouse is only sure of that after she's checked both of her date clocks, the plug-in one beside her bed and the backup battery-powered model on top of her dresser. Sunday, April 27th. Much of the preceding week has been lost time, especially Thursday and Friday, which she recalls only brief, confused flashes of. Friday night she must have been drinking again, because she woke up late on Saturday with a bad hangover (but alone, thank God, and in her own bed). She spent what was left of Saturday morning jittery and nervous, wanting badly to leave the apartment but unable to—every time she started to go out, she found herself turned around and coming back in again. Finally, on her fifth attempt, she discovered a piece of newsprint taped to the inside of her front door, with WAIT FOR THE FUCKING PHONE TO RING scrawled on it in black Magic Marker. So she gave up and stayed inside, and around one o'clock the phone rang, and then it was Saturday night.

And now it is Sunday morning. Mouse pads out to her kitchen in her bare feet, wiping sleep from her eyes, trying to decide if she is hung over again. Probably not—she has a headache, but not that kind of headache, and although her mouth is dry, there is none of the vile aftertaste that she woke up with yesterday.

She fills a glass with water at the kitchen sink. Raising the glass to her lips, she starts to turn around, spies the envelope out of the corner of her eye, turns further—and jumps.

It isn't the envelope that throws a fright into her. It is her mother, whose image she sees refracted through the bottom of the drinking glass. Her mother, sitting in a chair beside the kitchen table, hands folded primly in her lap, fingernails sharp.

"Little Mouse," her mother says, quite distinctly. *"You've got a letter."*

Mouse squeaks, hacking water out through her nose; the glass tumbles from her hand and smashes on the floor. On tiptoe now, coughing violently, Mouse sees that the chair is empty, that her mother is not really here—of course not, how could she be?

The envelope is real, though: a crisp white rectangle, propped up against the napkin holder. Mouse goes to pick it up, stepping gingerly. Despite her care, the ball of her left foot comes down on a sliver of broken glass, provoking another squeak, and she ends up limping to the table.

The envelope is cut from fine, thick parchment, the kind used for wedding invitations and royal summonses. It is an *expensive* envelope, or would be if it weren't stolen—shoplifted, most likely, from one of the stores in Pacific Place mall. There's no stamp. If Mouse were still living with her mother there would be one, a fancy UK stamp chosen more for its appearance than its denomination, but that pretense at least has been dropped; this envelope was not mailed from England, or indeed from anywhere.

Mouse studies the return address, written by hand in an elegant black script that manages to be graceful and mocking all at once:

English Society of International Correspondents
1234 Catchpenny Lane
Century Village, Dorset 91371
ENGLAND

Though she has seen it on dozens of occasions, Mouse is struck anew, each time, by the falsity—the *obvious* fakeness—of this address. Even as a teenager Mouse knew that British postal codes are not five-digit numbers. 91371 is an American zip code; more to the point, it's Mouse's birthdate: September 13th, 1971. Then there are the street and town names: Catch*penny* Lane; *Cent*ury Village. And the county, Dorset: a real place, sure (Mouse looked it up once), but also her mother's maiden name.

It's so blatant that even now Mouse can't help being disgusted by her mother's credulity, so impressed by the nice paper and pretty handwriting that she never even suspected the fraud. *Stupid woman,* Mouse thinks, or starts to think. *Stupid old—*

But sudden dread smothers the heretical thought before it is fully formed, the terror so intense that Mouse disappears for a moment, leaving Maledicta to observe, fearlessly: "Well, she *was* a stupid old cunt."

—and Mouse is back, clutching the envelope in her fist hard enough to wrinkle the expensive paper.

She's bleeding from the cut on her foot. She should see to that; she should clean up the broken glass, too. But first she needs to find out what secret message the "Society" has sent her. Risking further injury, she recrosses the kitchen floor to the silverware drawer beside the sink, and fishes for a knife to slit the envelope with.

She has always gotten strange mail. There are the lists, of course, the anonymously authored itineraries that allow her to maintain a semblance of order in her life. There are the graffiti, the surprise pop-up messages and harangues like the newsprint scrawl that appeared on her front door yesterday morning. And then there are the memoranda, detailed missives delivered sporadically from nowhere, that either warn Mouse of an unperceived danger or give her advice on how to overcome a problem she has been grappling with.

Now that her mother is dead and buried there is less to worry about, but when she was younger and still living in her mother's house, under her mother's power, Mouse was acutely aware that some kinds of mail were more dangerous than others. Lists were generally safe, unless they included a "to do" that violated her mother's ever-changing rules; Mouse's mother actually approved of the lists, thinking that Mouse herself wrote them. ("Good little Mouse," she recalls her mother crooning, "that's a good idea, keep that little scatter-brain of yours on track." This memory is entwined with another, of her mother pushing her down onto an unmade bed, shouting, "What did you forget? What did you forget?" and twisting Mouse's nipple until she screamed—the memory so vivid that just thinking of it makes Mouse gasp and cup her breast defensively.) Graffiti were slightly more dangerous, although they typically showed up in places where Mouse's mother couldn't see (in Mouse's locker in school, on the chalkboard of an empty classroom where she sometimes went to hide) or where they could be quickly disposed of (on a frosted windowpane, or a foggy bathroom mirror that could be cleared with one swipe of an arm).

Memoranda, though—those could be perilous. Mouse remembers one time in particular when she was in junior high school and a boy named Ben Deering had tried to pretend that he liked her. Ben had come over to her during lunch period one day—Mouse had been sitting alone, as usual, at a tiny table near the back of the cafeteria—and asked, "Hey, is it OK if I sit with you?" Mouse glanced up at the sound of his voice, looked back down just as quickly, and said nothing. Ben interpreted her silence as a yes, and sat down. "So," Ben said, poking at a congealed mass of refried beans on his lunch tray, "whaddya think of the food here?"

Mouse didn't respond to this, or to any of his other attempts at conversation. She didn't even look at him again. His acting friendly towards her was obviously a trick of some kind. Ben was a popular boy in the school, whereas Mouse was a nonentity, as good as invisible except when she was being picked on; it made no sense that Ben would *really* want to talk to her. So she ignored him, hoping that he would soon give up and go away.

But Ben didn't give up; he stayed the whole lunch period, in good spirits, too, as if getting the silent treatment from Mouse was one of the best things that had ever happened to him. When the bell rang for class, he got up, still smiling, and said, "Thanks. I'll see you tomorrow."

As promised, the next day he came and sat with her again, drawing stares and titters from some of the other kids in the lunchroom, who had belatedly noticed his odd behavior. Mortified by the laughter, Mouse sank deeper into herself, and once more refused to speak; Ben, in turn, continued to act as though he couldn't get enough of Mouse's deaf-and-dumb routine.

The next day Ben was absent from school. At first when he didn't show up for lunch Mouse was relieved, but halfway through the period she caught herself looking around the cafeteria, checking to see if Ben was really absent or if he'd just decided to sit with someone else. And the day after that, when Ben returned and once more came to sit at Mouse's table, she answered his cheery "Hello" with a barely audible "Hi."

Ben smiled broadly, acknowledging the milestone. "Sorry I wasn't here yesterday," he apologized. "My little sister was sick, so I had to stay home and take care of her."

"That's OK," Mouse mumbled.

Even then, they didn't exactly converse. Mostly Ben asked her questions—"How do you like school?" "What's your favorite band?"—which Mouse answered in a dull monotone, using as few words as possible. She didn't understand how he could possibly find this interesting, and behind her stunted replies she tried to screw up the courage to ask a question of her own: "Why do you care?" Of course she didn't come close to actually saying that—it took all the bravery she had just to tell Ben what kind of music she liked.

At the end of the lunch period, Ben thanked her again and wished her a nice weekend. Then he asked, as if the idea had just occurred to him: "Hey, you want to come hang out with me after school?" Mouse was startled back into speechlessness by this proposal; she not-quite shook her head, then half-nodded, then opened her mouth and let out a truncated squeak. "Tell you what," Ben said. "I'll be on the front steps after last bell. If you want to hang out, you come meet me there." With that, he collected his tray and marched off, leaving Mouse sitting mute at the table.

She spent the rest of the school day anxiously watching the clock, fearing the final bell and wondering what she would do when it rang. She still could not begin to fathom Ben's motive. If this were a trick of some kind, it was a very elaborate one: would Ben really waste three lunch periods just to set up a prank? On the other hand, if it wasn't a trick, and Ben really did want to be friends with her . . . *why?* Why, why, why?

What was she going to do? Mouse's one consolation as the minutes ticked away was a growing certainty that it wouldn't be *her* decision.

Her anxiety peaked at about three minutes to three. As the second hand on the classroom wall-clock made its last few circuits, Mouse began to feel dizzy, light-headed and light-bodied, too; there was a tapping at the back of her skull like someone knocking at a door for entry. The final bell, when it came, was like a gunshot going off in her head. Mouse convulsed, hands clutching the bottom of her seat to keep her from flying away into the stratosphere—

—and she was home in her own room, sitting at her little writing desk watching the sunset through the window. Her head pivoted automatically towards the clock-radio. It was 5:17 P.M.

Mouse was still dressed in the clothes she had worn to school that day, but her whole body was covered with a thin film of dust, and there was a smudge of mud on her right knee. A bramble had caught on one of her stockings, and there were scratches on her arms and the backs of her hands.

The memorandum lay on the desk in front of her, a three-paragraph note written in two scripts. The pen used to write it lay on top of it; when Mouse picked the pen up to move it aside, it was still warm from the hands of the writers.

The memorandum read:

Sorry Mouse but it's no good. After Ben Deering got tired of waiting for you on the school steps he went to South Woods Park and met up with two other boys, Chris Cheney (sp.?) and Scott Welch, and the three of them stood around joking about you. From what they said, Chris has bet Ben an old bicycle that Ben can't get you to hold hands with him. I don't know why, I guess Chris is just mean that way (although his girlfriend is Cindy Wheaton, the one who keeps tripping you in gym class, so maybe she's got something to do with it) and I guess Ben really wants the bike.

Anyway, it's no good. Ben doesn't really like you. It's just a mean trick.

Beneath this, a second, angrier hand had written:

*which you woud fucking KNOW already if you werent a COMPLETE
FUCKING MORON!!!*

As the import of the message sank in, Mouse's eyes began to fill with
tears. Her grief was bitter but strangely detached, as if it were causeless—if
asked, she could not have said whether she was crying out of disappointment, or hurt, or indignation. She just felt *bad*, that's all; bad, and certain in
her bones that whatever else was true, she had brought this on herself
somehow.

A tear spilled over and tracked down her cheek, and Mouse thought:
Worthless piece of shit.

"Little Mouse," her mother said, behind her.

Mouse squeaked and whirled around in her chair. She swiped desperately
at the water in her eyes, so unnerved at having been caught crying that she
forgot all about the memorandum lying in plain sight on the desk.

"Time to wash up for dinner," Mouse's mother told her, her own eyes
glittering with wicked amusement. She was always sneaking up on Mouse;
it was one of her favorite games. Sometimes she would announce her presence in a loud voice, to make Mouse jump; other times she would creep up
close and wait—long minutes, if that's what it took—for Mouse to notice
the breathing on the back of her neck.

Like most of her mother's games, Mouse hated this. That was why, when
she'd first gotten the writing desk, she'd wanted to set it up against the
other wall, facing the doorway. But her mother had insisted that it made
much more sense to put the desk by the window, so Mouse would have
"natural light" during the day. Of course, the desk went where her mother
thought it should go. And maybe it didn't make any real difference; as
Mouse had learned from years of sudden frights, there was really no place in
the entire house, no safe corner, where her mother could not get behind her
if she wanted to.

"Time to wash up, Mouse," her mother repeated, her vicious good
humor dimming by a fraction. Mouse took a last swipe at her eyes and
hopped out of the chair, moving quickly towards the hall.

Instead of stepping aside, Mouse's mother continued to stand in the
doorway. This was another game: to get out of the room, Mouse had to flat-
ten herself against the doorframe and edge past her mother's broad hips,
quietly accepting any pinches or slaps her mother chose to inflict as she did

so. This time, rather than lay a hand on her, Mouse's mother simply waited until she was halfway through the door and then leaned sideways, crushing Mouse into the doorframe with her full weight. Mouse gritted her teeth, knowing that to cry out was a violation of the rules. After a brief eternity the pressure eased off enough that she was able to finish squeezing through; she scampered up the hall to the bathroom.

Dinner that night was veal stew, served on the good china. There was no bad china in the Driver house; only good china, for ordinary meals, and very good china, for special occasions. Mouse knew the china was good because her mother never stopped commenting on it, or on her and Mouse's good fortune to live in such a nice home surrounded by such fine things.

"We're very lucky, aren't we," her mother said even now, "to live in such a nice home, with such fine things in it?"

"Yes," said Mouse, by rote, "we are."

"Yes, we are. And we're *very* lucky that your father was so careful to provide for us, so that we can afford those fine things."

"Yes," said Mouse.

A photograph of Mouse's father hung on the dining room wall. The photo showed Morgan Driver standing on a hill in front of a castle somewhere in the English countryside. His image was slightly fuzzy, as if the picture-taker couldn't decide whether to focus the camera on him or the grand edifice behind him, but by looking closely you could make out a solemn expression on his face—surprisingly solemn, for a man just married.

A honeymoon in England: that was among the first, and still one of the finest, of the fine things Mouse's father had provided. Mouse's mother had always had a passion for things British, "ever since I was a little girl, smaller even than you, little Mouse," and those weeks touring the British Isles remained one of the high points of her life. "So wonderful," she said whenever she mentioned it, which was often, "so fine, and with a fine gentleman to escort me."

A fine gentleman to escort me. Morgan Driver was not a rich man, though you'd never know that to hear Mouse's mother talk about him. He sold insurance for a living, and because his business required him to travel a lot, he knew how to get good deals on airfares and nice hotels. And he did have *some* money; but he wasn't rich.

What he was, though, was well-insured. Probably the single most important thing he'd ever done, as far as providing financially for Mouse and her mother, was to board a commuter jet plane with a faulty engine mount.

That had happened when Mouse was only two, so she never actually got to know her father as a real person. To her, he was a series of stories, some told by her mother, some by her grandmother, and a few more speculative tales delivered as memoranda. Mouse liked her grandmother's stories the best, but it was her mother's that loomed largest—stories of Morgan Driver the valiant knight, the gentleman who had died tragically, but not without first ensuring that his family would always have fine things.

"So good to have one's needs provided for," Mouse's mother said, spooning stew onto her plate. "So good to live in a nice house with fine things." Whenever she went on like this, her voice affected a phony aristocratic diction and lilt that Mouse secretly detested. But Mouse couldn't very well tell her mother to stop putting on airs, and besides, affected and irritating was better than plain-spoken and violent. Much better.

"So good . . ."

"Yes," said Mouse.

"Good to have fine food, and fine furniture, and fine clothes . . ."

Mouse, whose attention was beginning to drift, came alert again at the mention of clothes. Though she'd cleaned herself up as best she could in the bathroom, she knew her mother would not have failed to notice the dust on her blouse and skirt, or the rip in her stocking—and of course girls who were fortunate enough to be provided with fine clothes were not supposed to ruin them by crawling around in the mud.

Mouse gazed furtively across the table and wondered if she was about to be punished. Her mother was unpredictable that way: the same thing that made her horribly angry on one occasion might move her to laughter on another, and go totally unremarked on a third. And sometimes she seemed to overlook something only to bring it up later, in a totally unrelated context.

For now, Mouse decided, her mother wasn't going to make a fuss about the clothes—she'd already moved on in her litany of fine things, and her attention seemed to be focused on the food in front of her rather than on her daughter. Mouse allowed herself to relax a little.

"Ben Deering," her mother said suddenly, and Mouse felt a trapdoor open in the pit of her stomach. "Ben Deering, Ben Deering," her mother repeated, making it a singsong, "all the ladies love Ben Deering." She cocked her head, like an owl staring at something small that cowered at the bottom of a well. "Ben Deering, you know, I didn't think I knew that name—I certainly never heard it from *you*—but then I remembered, there's a Ben Deering *Senior* who manages a junkyard over in Trash Town."

Trash Town was Mouse's mother's name for Woods Basin, the part of town located below South Woods Park. It was a poor neighborhood of run-down one-bedroom houses and trailer lots, where only the worst sorts of people lived. Mouse's mother knew just how bad the Trash Towners were because, through an indignity of fate, she herself had been born in Woods Basin, and had languished there for thirty-two years until her superior character showed through and she was rescued by her marriage to Morgan Driver. Though she had finally escaped their clutches, the residents of Trash Town remained jealous of Mouse's mother and continued to conspire against her, seizing any opportunity to cause her grief. Whenever something went wrong in or around the Driver household—when a tree blew over in the yard, or the basement flooded, or a light bulb burned out ahead of schedule—Mouse's mother usually found some way to blame it on the Trash Town conspiracy.

Needless to say, Mouse was forbidden to go anywhere near Trash Town. And actually fraternizing with a Trash Town resident—even unintentionally—was a form of treason, a mortal sin against her mother. The trapdoor in Mouse's stomach swung wide as she realized just how much trouble she was in.

"A *junkyard* manager!" her mother exclaimed with mock cheerfulness. "And *you* know his *son*."

"No!" Mouse squeaked. "No, I—"

"No?"

"I don't," Mouse protested meekly, quailing under her mother's steady gaze, her voice falling almost to a whisper. "I don't . . ."

"Don't *what?*" her mother demanded. "Don't *know* him?" Her left hand dipped beneath the edge of the table and came up brandishing the memorandum. She lifted the piece of paper above her head, twisting her wrist as though she were shaking a tambourine. "You *don't know* him?"

And Mouse was lost, she knew she was lost, but still she managed to say, gesturing halfheartedly at the memorandum: "It was just a trick . . ."

"'It was just a trick,'" her mother mimicked her. "Why would someone try to trick you unless he thought you *could* be tricked? Hmm? What were you doing with this boy that made him think you'd hold hands with him?"

"Nothing."

"'Nothing.'"

"I never even *talked* to him before."

"I see. So I suppose he was just sitting around one day, wondering who he could get to hold hands with him, and suddenly a light went on and he said, 'What about Verna Driver's daughter? She's never even talked to me before, never shown any interest in me at all, but why make things easy on myself?'"

"I don't know why he picked on me," Mouse said sadly. "Maybe . . . maybe like it says, maybe Cindy Wheaton—"

"Who's your little friend, by the way?" When Mouse blinked uncomprehendingly at this, her mother gave the memorandum another shake. "Your *friend*. The one you sent to spy on Ben Deering, even though you weren't interested in him."

"I don't know," Mouse said, understanding even as the words left her mouth how crazy that must sound, and not just to her mother but to anyone who heard her say it.

"You don't know," her mother echoed. "Of course not, you don't even know Ben Deering, so how could you know who you sent to follow him?"

"I didn't—"

"You know what *I* don't know? I don't know if you're telling the truth when you say you understand how lucky you are. I don't know if you really appreciate all the fine things you've been given. I think maybe you're a worthless, ungrateful, lying piece of *shit* who wouldn't think twice about fucking up her life by fucking around with some gutter boy from Trash Town. I think—"

The cruel words hurt Mouse, and she began to tremble from the effort it took to keep from bursting into tears. There were places in the world where a display of tears would evoke pity, but this was not one of those places—there was no surer way to push her mother over the edge than by crying. Even as she fought to maintain her composure, she tried to think of some way to refute the terrible accusation her mother had just made. She hadn't even held hands with Ben, she'd barely even talked to him, and yet here her mother was suggesting that she . . . that she . . .

Mouse made the mistake of lowering her eyes for a moment; when she looked up again, her mother was no longer seated across from her.

Mouse screamed and tried to duck under the table, but her mother was too quick, catching her and tossing her back in her seat, then pitching the whole chair over backwards. The impact with the floor stunned Mouse, and by the time she recovered her mother had planted a foot in the center of her chest, pinning her.

Like a heavy stone weight, the foot on her chest made it difficult to breathe. "What's that?" Mouse's mother said, as Mouse struggled to fill her lungs. She reached back to the table, scooped up a handful of hot stew, and flung it into Mouse's gasping, upturned face. "Oh my goodness!" she exclaimed. "Who did that? *I don't know.*" Another handful. "What about that? *I don't know.*" Then she took her foot off Mouse's chest and—before Mouse could draw a full breath—swooped down, clamping one hand over Mouse's mouth and with the other pinching Mouse's nose shut. "Mommy, why can't I get any air?" she whispered in Mouse's ear. *"I don't know."*

After that, she pounded Mouse's head against the floor. Or maybe the pounding sensation was just lack of oxygen; it was hard to be sure, because by that point Mouse was leaving her body, sliding down into darkness. She curled up in the dark and went to sleep, and whatever else her mother did had nothing to do with her.

When she woke up nineteen hours later, she was sitting on the edge of her bed in her room. Even before checking the clock-radio, she sensed that no more than a day had passed: her nose was still tender from having been pinched so roughly, and she could feel a bruise where her mother had stood on her breastbone; the scratches on her arms, though faded, were still there too. (There were also some more mysterious aches and pains, in particular a raw soreness between her legs that made her want to dive straight down into the dark again—but she didn't let herself dwell on it.)

The first thing Mouse did after getting her bearings was make sure she was really alone. She looked in the closet three times and under the bed twice before accepting that her mother was not in the room. That led naturally to two more questions: where *was* her mother, and what mood was she in? One drawback to blacking out during her mother's rages was that Mouse could never be sure what sort of closure, if any, had been reached.

She checked around her room for a few more minutes, hoping to find a list that might offer her some clues, but her mother's reaction to the memorandum had apparently scared off the list-maker for the time being—either that, or her mother had gotten to the list first and destroyed it for spite. Whatever the reason, Mouse found nothing, and so she could only cross her fingers that her mother was not lying in wait for her as she slipped out into the upstairs hallway.

Her mother was not in the hall. Mouse moved quickly to the bathroom, shut the door (there was no lock), checked the corners, tub, and shower stall, and opened the hot-water tap in the sink. She sat on the toilet and peed, once more pointedly ignoring the soreness between her legs; by the time she was finished, the mirror over the sink had fogged up, and she stared into it for a long while in hopes that a graffito would appear. None did.

When she finally got up the nerve to go downstairs, she found her mother in the kitchen, chopping away at something on the cutting board by the sink. "Little Mouse," her mother said, without turning around. The words sounded neutral, her mother letting her know that she knew Mouse was there, but beyond that neither threatening nor welcoming. Mouse wanted to run and hide anyway, but she forced herself to loiter for a few minutes, to see if her mother would say or do anything else to her. She didn't, just went on chopping, and eventually Mouse slipped away, still uncertain whether the storm had passed.

On Sunday afternoon, Mouse's mother gave her a playful shove in passing that tumbled her down the stairs and sprained her wrist. That night at dinner, she served Mouse a side dish of frozen peas topped with a slab of unmelted butter, and pretended not to understand why Mouse didn't want to eat her vegetables (at first she played it like the joke that it was, but when Mouse wouldn't swallow even a spoonful of the gravel-like peas, she became genuinely angry, and ended up ordering Mouse from the table and sending her to bed hungry). These incidents were unpleasant, but they were also unexceptional—typical everyday fun and games—and thus not especially indicative of her mother's mood. It wasn't until Monday morning that Mouse got a clear sign that her mother was still upset about Ben Deering.

It happened as she was leaving for school. Mouse was on her way out the door when her mother—who up to that moment had appeared to be in the sweetest of humors—suddenly grabbed her by her bad wrist and pulled her up short, demanding: "Now what did we agree about that Trash Town boy?"

Mouse, who had no idea what they had agreed, had to think quickly: "I'm never going to speak to him again!"

"Goddamn right you're not," her mother snarled, though that seemed to be the correct answer. Smiling pleasantly again, she added: "Now when you come home today I may not be here, but I don't want you to worry. I have a little errand to run." Her head bobbed with a barely suppressed fit of giggles. "You just wait here for me to get back, and don't go answering the door to any strangers!"

That day at lunch Ben Deering tried to sit with her again. She saw him coming towards her table, braced herself to put him off—

—and found herself in class, shutting her notebook as last bell rang.

Ben Deering, Chris Cheney, Scott Welch, and Cindy Wheaton were standing in a group on the front steps of the school as Mouse left the building. They all stared at Mouse, openly hostile but nervous, too, as if they were afraid Mouse might attack them. Mouse, afraid they were planning to attack *her*, scurried past as quick as she could. "You're a fuckin' crazy girl, you know that?" Cindy Wheaton shouted at her back.

The house was empty when Mouse got home. At first this was a relief, but by dinnertime, when her mother had still not returned, Mouse began to worry. Maybe the house wasn't really empty after all; maybe her mother, instead of being out on an errand, was actually hiding somewhere, waiting for the perfect moment to pounce. The fact that Mouse was getting hungry did not help her nerves any.

Finally, about an hour after dark, her mother came home, in such a triumphant good mood that Mouse became even more worried. Her mother didn't say where she'd been, just pinched Mouse on the cheek and set about fixing a late supper. She made lamb chops with mashed potatoes and creamed spinach, one of Mouse's favorite meals: a very bad omen.

They were almost done eating when the doorbell rang. "Now I wonder who *that* could be," Mouse's mother chuckled, and ran to answer it. She'd been gone only a moment or two when she began yelling: "Penny! Penny, you get out here *right now!*"

Penny. Mouse's mother only called her by her true name in front of strangers—usually strangers she was trying to fool in some way. Wondering what new game was afoot, and how much it was going to hurt, Mouse slid down out of her chair and followed the sound of her mother's shouts.

Mouse was astonished to find Ben Deering at the front door—Ben Deering, and a tall man who she guessed was Ben's father. Ben looked both sullen and embarrassed, and he was trying hard not to make eye contact with anyone, especially Mouse; Ben's father and Mouse's mother were angry, though Mouse had an intimation that only Ben's father's anger was real.

"Is this her?" Ben's father asked, nodding at Mouse.

"Yes," Mouse's mother said, as if it pained her to admit it. "That's my daughter."

Mouse shied back a step, thinking that the tall man might be about to hit her, but instead he turned to his son and said, "Well?"

Ben sighed, and with an almost theatrical effort made himself look Mouse in the eye. "I'm sorry," he said.

Apparently this wasn't sufficient; no sooner were the words out of his mouth than his father smacked him hard on the back of his head. "You're sorry *what?*" Ben Senior said.

"I'm sorry about the bet I made," Ben recited grudgingly. "I'm sorry I tried to trick you. It was wrong." He glanced up at his father as if to add: *Is that enough?*

"All right," said Ben Senior. "You go wait in the car for me." Ben eagerly obeyed.

"Well," Ben Senior said, turning his attention to Mouse. He seemed to expect her to recite something now, but she only blinked at him, so he cleared his throat and went on: "As you can see, my son got your message. Or rather, we *all* got your message."

My message? thought Mouse, and Ben's father, noting her perplexity, growled: "Oh, for pity's sake!" Mouse shied back another step.

"For pity's sake . . ." Ben's father jammed a hand in his coat pocket. "The message I'm referring to, young lady—as if you didn't know—is the one you pitched through our living-room window earlier this evening." He brought out a chunk of brick with a tattered sheet of paper wrapped around it. Mouse had never seen the brick before, but when Ben's father smoothed the paper out she recognized it as her memorandum. For a horrified second she wondered what she had done. Then she remembered her mother's "errand."

"Penny!" Verna Driver's feigning of outrage was flawless. "Penny, my goodness, what's gotten into you? How could you *do* such a thing?" As she said this she turned, and when her back was to Ben's father she let the outrage-mask drop, revealing impish glee beneath; she stuck her tongue out at Mouse, and winked. "Oh, Mr. Deering," she continued, putting the mask back in place, "Mr. Deering, I'm so very sorry, I can't tell you how *shocked* I am by this."

"The boy acted badly," Ben's father said. "But"—he hefted the brick—"vandalism is not an appropriate response."

"Oh, of *course* not!" Mouse's mother said. "I don't know what Penny—"

"Neither is what you did at the school today, young lady," Ben's father added. "Yes, my son told me about that, too."

"At the school today?" The outrage-mask slipped a bit. "*She* did some-thing . . . at the school?"

"An uncontrolled temper is a dangerous thing," Ben's father said omi-nously. "I'll leave these with you," he continued, offering the memorandum and the chunk of brick to Mouse's mother, "and ask that you keep your daughter away from my son and away from my house."

"You can be sure of *that*," Mouse's mother said, the mask slipping a notch further, revealing an edge of malice. Then she caught herself, and went on soothingly: "Of course we'll pay for the damage to your window."

But Ben's father, perhaps sensing that something was not right here, said: "Never mind the damage. You just rein in your daughter before she hurts somebody. An uncontrolled temper . . ." he concluded, jabbing a warning finger at Mouse. He turned and left.

"'You just rein in your daughter before she hurts somebody,'" Mouse's mother mimicked to his back, discarding the mask. As the Deerings drove away, she asked: "What happened at the school?"

Mouse had just been wondering the same thing. Casting back over the events of the day, she recalled something that hadn't really registered at the time: when she'd passed Ben and his friends outside after class, Ben's hair was mussed, and his jacket and shirt were covered with splotches: dried food stains. "I think I dumped my lunch tray on Ben," Mouse said, in her smallest voice.

"You *think* you did?" Her mother shot her a sideways glance, and for a third time Mouse shied back. But then her mother burst out laughing, and threw an affectionate arm around her. "Well, I guess we showed those Trash Town bastards!" she crowed. "So, would my little Mouse like some ice cream?"

That was the end of the Ben Deering matter, at least as far as her mother was concerned. For Mouse herself it wasn't really over, of course; word of the brick-throwing and food-dumping incidents spread quickly at school, and Mouse, now a certified "crazy girl," became a magnet for taunts and abuse.

Then one morning about two weeks later, a school circular appeared mysteriously in Mouse's book bag. Mouse found it as she was packing away her homework, and her mother, who was hovering nearby, snatched it out of her hands before she could get a good look at it.

"What's this?" her mother said, scanning the circular. Her eyes widened, and she began to read more carefully, growing more and more excited. "Why, this is wonderful!" she exclaimed. "What a wonderful opportunity!" She turned, casually jabbing Mouse in the head with her elbow. "Why didn't you tell me about this last night?"

Mouse, wincing from the jab, could only shrug. When her mother was finished reading she took the circular back, and examined it herself. "Dear concerned parent," it began,

This is to inform you of an exciting new extracurricular program being made available to exceptional students such as your daughter. Through a special arrangement with the prestigious English Society of International Correspondents, we . . .

Right away Mouse noticed something peculiar. The paper was official school letterhead, but the text was typed, not mimeographed the way a regular circular would be, and the typewriter's tendency to drop its u's was oddly familiar. Some years ago Mouse's grandmother had given her an old Underwood manual typewriter that had dropped its u's that way; then Mouse's mother, irritated by the gift, had gone out and bought Mouse an expensive electric typewriter, and insisted she throw the Underwood away, which as far as she knew she had. But it seemed strange that the school's typewriter would have the exact same fault as the discarded Underwood, and the same typeface too—strange enough to make Mouse wonder why she couldn't remember actually putting the Underwood in the trash.

The "exciting new extracurricular program" described in the circular was pretty strange, too. What it was, once you got past the fancy language, was a pen-pal program. The English Society of International Correspondents set up letter exchanges between "exceptional" American high school students— Mouse had a very hard time applying that adjective to herself—and even more exceptional British boarding-school students, many of whom, the circular hinted, were members of the nobility. The apparent purpose of this, on the American side at least, was a sort of cultural osmosis—through long-distance exposure to the young lords and ladies of England, the American high schoolers would be elevated from exceptional to superexceptional status, thereby ensuring the brightest possible futures for themselves. What the British kids were supposed to get out of it the circular didn't say.

To Mouse, the whole thing seemed frankly ridiculous. It also seemed like a prank. There *was* a pen-pal program at school, but it involved sending postcards to poor village kids in Africa and Asia, an activity about as suitable for Verna Driver's daughter as volunteering at a soup kitchen in Trash Town.

"You're signing up for this," Mouse's mother said. "You're signing up for this *today*."

"OK," said Mouse.

And she tried to. She skipped out of lunch early and went to the after-school-program office, where the administrator Mr. Jacobs scratched his head and said he'd never heard of the English Society of International Correspondents.

"I'm sorry," Mr. Jacobs said. "I *could* sign you up for the Third World Postcard Buddies program, if you'd like . . ."

"No thank you," said Mouse.

"Well, then." He handed the circular back to her. "If I do hear something, I'll contact you, but it seems like this is probably a joke of some kind."

Of course it was a joke. But now Mouse had a problem, because she was going to have to go home and tell her mother that she hadn't done as she was told, that she *couldn't* do it. Thinking this, she felt a tickle in her left palm, and looked down to find a graffito written on her bare skin in ball-point pen: JUST PRETEND YOU DID.

And Mouse nodded to herself, and washed her hands, and after last bell she went home and told her mother she'd signed up for the letter-writing program. And a surprisingly short time after that the first of many envelopes from the English Society of International Correspondents appeared in the Drivers' mailbox. Mouse, who found it there, shook her head in disbelief at the return address, and also at the stamp: a colorful two-pence stamp, with a portrait of Queen Elizabeth and a smudged cancellation mark that did not extend onto the envelope itself. The stamp looked as though it had been glued in place with rubber cement.

Two pence, Mouse thought. *Two pennies*. Was that enough to mail a letter all the way from England to America? She very much doubted it, and her doubt churned up a memory of being in Bartleby's on Third Street with her mother not long ago. Bartleby's sold fine stationery, and also had a small section devoted to stamp and coin collecting. You could buy canceled foreign stamps there . . . or steal them, Mouse supposed.

The envelope was a prank, like the circular before it. Mouse would have destroyed it if she dared, but she didn't dare, and anyway by now her mother had seen it and grabbed it from her and was cooing over it, with none of Mouse's skepticism.

"Let's see what we've got here," Mouse's mother said. Too impatient to get a letter opener, she attacked the envelope like a grizzly bear ripping into a honeycomb. The simile was apt: having torn open the flap, she actually stuck her nose inside—and jerked back, as if stung. She tried again, reaching in more carefully with a pawlike hand—and jerked that back too. "Damn it!" she swore. "Damn it! Damn it! *Damn it! FUCK!*" The fit of fury vanished as quickly as it had come, and was replaced by a sullen petulance. "Here," she said, shoving the envelope at Mouse. "You do it."

When Mouse carefully spread the top of the envelope and peeped inside, she found neither honey nor stinging bees, but a second, smaller envelope, addressed simply "From Miss Penelope Ariadne Jones, To Miss Penny Driver." Mouse saw at once what had upset her mother: the inside envelope was purple.

Purple, her mother's unlucky color—a color that, like garlic to a vampire, produced an almost allergic reaction in Verna Driver. Mouse's head rocked back and forth on her neck, not-quite nodding. Her mother couldn't read the letter; the letter was for her eyes only.

"Well go on!" her mother snapped, raising a threatening hand. "Open it!"

Mouse opened the purple envelope. The two sheets of stationery inside were also purple, and covered in longhand, a longhand she knew. "My Dear Miss Driver," she read, "it is with the greatest pleasure that I begin what I hope will be a long correspondence with you . . ."

The letter's brief overview of life in "Century Village, Dorset" was as transparently fake as the return address on the outer envelope. Large portions of it appeared to have been plagiarized from a Jane Austen novel, or possibly a Harlequin romance. But it acted like a balm on Mouse's mother, the grizzly bear getting her honey at last; she ate it up, giving no sign that she suspected it was anything other than what it purported to be. Meanwhile Mouse had to fight to stay focused on what she was reading—she kept glancing ahead, looking for a hidden message, a letter-within-the-letter, meant only for her.

Eventually she found it: at the very end, beneath "Penelope Jones"'s signature, there was a line that said, "DO NOT READ THIS PART ALOUD," and beneath that, a postscript that turned out to be a memorandum, warning her about something that Cindy Wheaton was planning to do to her in gym class.

After she'd gotten over her initial surprise, Mouse decided she was angry with the memorandum-writer for choosing such a complicated and potentially risky subterfuge. What if her mother's enthusiasm for things British had overcome her phobia for purple? Then she would have read the letter herself, including the memorandum, and realized it was all a trick—and who knew what she might have done to Mouse then? Even if the trick were never exposed, this method of delivering memoranda created extra work for Mouse, because of course the first thing her mother did after Mouse finished reading was tell her that she must write back, immediately. She insisted on supervising, too: hanging over Mouse's shoulder as she crafted her reply, criticizing every sentence, every turn of phrase.

It was only later that Mouse realized that tricking her mother—and tricking her in as blatant a manner as possible—was not just a means to an end but was in fact one of the memorandum-writer's goals. The memorandum-writer was angry, too; this was made abundantly clear by Penelope Ariadne Jones's second letter to Mouse, which began:

My Dear Miss Driver,

Greetings to you and your family from enchanting Dorset. On behalf of myself and my fellow Englanders, please tell your mother that she is an ugly old CUNT, we woud love to take a big stinking SHIT on her and stick her fucking nice things up her motherfucking ASSHOLE . . .

Mouse, reading this aloud, stopped short on "please tell your mother that," and gaped in horror at the words that followed.

"Little Mouse?" her mother said, in the abrupt silence. "What is it? What does she want you to tell me?"

And Mouse looked up, choking on dread, and then she was folding the letter away as her mother said, "That was so beautiful, what a nice girl, why can't you be more like her?"

As soon as she was alone, Mouse tore that letter into shreds, not even checking it for a memorandum. "No more," she said—half commanding, half pleading—as she flushed the remnants of the letter down the toilet. "No more, no more, no more."

But there were more, of course. The envelopes from the English Society of International Correspondents continued to turn up in the months and years that followed. Mouse's mother never caught on to the trick, though she did destroy a number of the letters herself, during rages of frustration brought on by Penelope Jones's persistent refusal to switch to a more agreeable color of stationery. So some of the memoranda were lost, but most got through; and even after Mouse left home, even after her mother died and was put in the ground, the memorandum-writer continued to send important messages in care of the English Society, as a kind of inside joke.

And now here is another one. Mouse takes a butter knife from the silverware drawer and neatly slits the top of the envelope. She extracts the smaller envelope from inside it, secretly pleased by the rich purple hue, magic ward against her mother. "From Miss Penelope Ariadne Jones," she reads, "To Miss Penny Driver," and that pleases her too. Though the memoranda within typically refer to her as Mouse, on the outside of the envelope she is always Penny, and she likes that name. She wishes desperately that she could convince people to call her by it, but almost no one ever does.

She slits open the top of the purple envelope, too, and pulls out a single sheet of lavender stationery. On it is written:

THINGS TO DO TODAY (Sunday, 4/27/97):
1. SHOWER.

2. DRESS NICE.
3. MEET ANDY GAGE OUTSIDE HARVEST MOON
   DINER AT NOON.
4. *LISTEN TO HIM.*

Odd. It's not a memorandum at all, it's a list. For it to be delivered this way must mean it's important, but Mouse is puzzled. Meet Andy Gage? What for? And listen to him about what? What could he possibly have to tell her that would warrant such special notice?

Maybe it's not such a mystery. Maybe she's only pretending to be puzzled, to conceal the fact that she's been expecting something like this. Because the thing that comes immediately to mind, when she asks herself what this could be about, is that strange conversation she overheard at the Reality Factory on Monday. The conversation between Andrew and Julie, that Mouse eavesdropped on from between the tents. The conversation that seemed to be about her.

Yes, that's definitely it—Mouse is all at once sure, without knowing how she is sure. But she doesn't have time to mull it over further now. It's almost eleven o'clock, and if she is going to get herself cleaned up, dressed, and out to Autumn Creek by noon, she will have to move quickly.

She hobbles back through the apartment to the bathroom, trying not to track too much blood on the floor in the process. As she sits on the edge of the tub and pulls the glass sliver from the sole of her foot, her hands shake, but not from pain.

Mouse is excited.

Mouse is afraid.

11

When she first spots Andy Gage in front of the Harvest Moon Diner an hour later, Mouse flashes back on a photograph of her father. Not the solemn honeymoon photograph that brooded over her mother's dining table, but another, more congenial portrait that sat on the fireplace mantel in her grandmother's house.

The mantelpiece photo was taken on the morning after her father's high school prom. Morgan Driver and his friends had gone out cruising after the last dance, and ended up crashing their car into a ditch. Though no one was seriously hurt, they were far enough out in the countryside that it took them the rest of the night to get back to town. Around dawn, Mouse's father's date had snapped the picture: Morgan Driver, walking backwards along the side of the road, thumb outstretched to flag down a passing car. He had his jacket slung over his shoulder; his black tie hung loose around his collar, and his shirt was untucked. An unlit cigarette dangled from the corner of his mouth, and he was smiling, despite a nasty-looking gash above his left eye.

This photograph no longer exists. Mouse's mother burned it, along with several scrapbooks' worth of other photographs, shortly after Grandma Driver's death. *Those pictures were undignified,* she said when Mouse asked her why. By this she meant that the pictures did not fit the image of her husband that she wanted to perpetuate—like Grandma Driver's stories, they seemed to refer to a different person altogether, a Morgan Driver who smoked, and drank, and told dirty jokes, and, when he was eight, jumped into mud puddles with both feet.

Mouse is sorry that her mother destroyed them all, but the pictures remain sharp in her memory—it is almost as if she has actual copies of her grandmother's scrapbooks in her head, that she can leaf through whenever she wants to. And the after-prom photograph—that sits on a mantel in Mouse's mind now, as tangible as ever.

It's not immediately clear why Andy Gage should remind her of that photo. Standing on the sidewalk in front of the Harvest Moon, he is not trying to hitch a ride, or even paying attention to the traffic. His dress is casual but neat—jacket on, collar buttoned. He isn't bleeding from his fore-head. What it is, she decides, is something in his bearing. Andrew stands at ease, comfortable in the world, in a way that Mouse almost never is, in a way that she imagines her father always was, at least until he got married.

As she drives closer, she sees that Andrew is talking to himself. Telling himself jokes, maybe—he just burst out laughing. This is crazy behavior, but Andrew seems completely unself-conscious about it. When he notices Mouse in her Buick, instead of acting caught out—the way Mouse would, if someone had seen *her* talking to herself—he just smiles and waves. Comfortable in the world.

Mouse drives into the lot behind the diner, and parks in the corner far-thest from the entrance so that she will have as much time as possible to compose herself. She checks herself in the rearview mirror, then checks her list to see if any new instructions have been added to it. None have; there are still no clues about what Andrew has to tell her, no hints about what might be expected of her beyond listening.

She opens her door and gets out. Andrew is walking towards her across the lot, his hands in his pockets. Now he looks self-conscious. He is not as uneasy as he was last Monday, when they drove here together from the Reality Factory, but he is clearly thinking hard about some-thing.

"Hi," Mouse says, just to get things rolling, and to make it seem like she knows what she's doing.

Andrew, for his part, is content to appear confused. "Penny?" he inquires, as if they'd never met in person before. Mouse resists a powerful urge to reply, "Yes, it's me," and merely nods.

After that, there is an awkward pause. Mouse's instructions are to listen, not talk; besides, she needs Andrew to talk first, so she can follow his cues. But Andrew acts as if he's working off the same list, waiting for *her* to say something.

Finally, he breaks the silence: "You don't know why you're here, do you?"

Mouse blinks. She wonders whether she misheard, but Andrew follows up with an even more startling declaration: "When you got up this morn-ing, you didn't have any plans to come out to Autumn Creek today. But then you got a message—a note, or maybe a list—telling you to meet me here at—"

They're in a park, sitting on opposite ends of a long wooden bench. Mouse's cheeks are flushed, and she's a little out of breath; Andrew's cheeks are flushed, too. He's still got his hands in his pockets, and he's holding his arms close to the side of his body, occupying as little of the bench as possible, as if trying not to crowd her.

They don't appear to be in the middle of a conversation—Andrew's not even looking at her—so Mouse swivels her head, takes a quick look around. She doesn't recognize this park, or any of the houses in the adjoining street, but she assumes they are still in Autumn Creek. The Navigator points out that the sun has not changed position in the sky, so she can't have been gone long.

"Five minutes," Andrew says.

Mouse stares at him.

"We left the diner parking lot about five minutes ago," he tells her. "This is Maynard Park, four blocks south of Bridge Street. You were walking very fast." He stops to take a breath, and turns his head very slowly to face her. "Penny?"

Mouse gets it now: why he says her name as if it were a question: he knows. He knows about her blackouts, and he knows about her lists. What else does he know?

"I'm sorry if I spooked you back there," he continues, looking away again. "My father told me to be blunt. I hope that's right—I've never actually done this before."

How do you know about the lists? Mouse thinks, but doesn't say.

"You're wondering how I know about your lists," Andrew tells her. "And your b—"

Mouse is standing with her back up against a tree, and she is *very* out of breath now, hyperventilating. Her eyes are shut tight; she forces herself to open them, and sees more trees, all around her. She's in the woods, alone.

No, not alone: "Penny?" His voice, quiet but close, nearly frightens her away again. Mouse begins to fade but then rebounds, ejected from the darkness by the mental equivalent of a shove in the back.

"Penny, please don't be afraid of me," Andrew says. "I'm not trying to scare you; I just want to help. I know what you've been going through, and I need you to know that I know, so that we can talk about it . . ."

Mouse turns her head and he is there, about ten paces off to her left. He shuffles sideways into her field of view, keeping his hands in the air, like a bank robber trying to surrender. "I just want to help," he says again. He doesn't try to get any closer to her; instead he drops down where he is, and sits on the ground. "I'll just stay over here, OK?"

This act—plopping down casually in the dirt, like it's no big deal if his pants get muddy—makes Mouse think of her father again, her grandmother's version of her father. The thought doesn't completely calm her down, but it does distract her, momentarily, from the fact that she's frightened. She comes off the tree, and turns fully to face him.

"I'm sorry if this is upsetting to you, Penny," Andrew says. "But I do know about your blackouts, and about—"

"*How?*" The word comes out as a high squeak, but he understands.

"You aren't the only person in the world this has ever happened to. There are others."

Mouse raises a shaky hand, and points. "You?"

It's a yes-or-no question, but he frowns and says, "Not exactly." Then: "It's complicated . . . My father had blackouts like you do. He lost time—sometimes minutes, sometimes days—and he had to keep lists of things to do to keep himself oriented. Even with the lists, he was always getting in trouble, getting blamed for things he didn't remember doing. He couldn't keep his checkbook balanced. He was constantly losing things that belonged to him, and finding things that didn't belong to him—like clothes, for instance, not just individual pieces but whole wardrobes, clothes that fit him but that he hadn't bought, that he *wouldn't* have bought . . ."

Mouse, feeling faint, puts out a hand to the tree to steady herself.

"And the messages. He got anonymous notes, sometimes, or messages on his answering machine. Sometimes it was useful advice, but other times it was just meanness—insults, or even threats. Sometimes it was both at once, in the same message, like whoever was trying to help him was really fed up with him, too."

"The Society," says Mouse.

"What?" Andrew says.

"Oh," Andrew says. "Penny?"

"Yes," says Mouse, not standing by the tree anymore but squatting on her heels in front of him, with her arms wrapped around her shins and her chin on her knee. She's caught her breath now, and she feels at least a little calmer.

"The souls—the people—who sent messages to my father didn't have a special name for themselves," Andrew continues. "They weren't trying to fool anybody. I'm sure my father would have preferred it if they had been a little secretive—he couldn't afford to live alone, and when his apartment mates overheard some of the answering-machine messages he got . . . well, sometimes it was pretty embarrassing."

Was. Mouse hasn't overlooked Andrew's use of the past tense. She doesn't want to ask this next question, but she needs to know: "What happened to your father?" Then, before Andrew can answer, she answers for him: "He got locked up, didn't he? For being crazy?"

"What?" says Andrew, looking surprised. "No . . . I mean, no, he wasn't crazy. He did have some trouble with a few people *thinking* he was crazy, but . . ."

"He got locked up," Mouse says, nodding to herself.

"Not permanently," Andrew says. "For a little while, once—OK, twice. But he got out again, both times, because he wasn't really crazy. And eventually he got help: he found a way to stop the blackouts. Penny? *There's a way to stop the blackouts.*"

He is lying to her; he must be. It is a cruel trick, to get the Society to order her out here just so he can frighten her with his knowledge of her insanity, and then lie to her.

Mouse sighs deeply, to keep from crying. "How?" she asks. "How did he stop the blackouts?"

"He built a house," says Andrew.

This time she's sure she's misheard. "He . . ."

"He built a house," repeats Andrew. He frowns again. "Look, this is hard . . . I want to be totally straight with you, but I'm worried that if I don't explain this just right you're going to end up thinking *I'm* crazy. Either that, or you'll get scared and start running again. So will you do me a favor? Will you come with me right now and let me show you something? I don't know if it'll really help, but . . . it might. At least it might help me find the right words to say."

"Come with you where?" Mouse says guardedly.

"To where I live. It's not far—just a few blocks up, on the other side of Bridge Street."

"OK," Mouse says, thinking: *Maybe he is crazy.*

They stand up—Mouse's knees are sore from squatting—and he leads her out of the woods, which turn out to be a part of Maynard Park. As they leave the park and walk north, Mouse notices that Andrew is talking to himself again. It's mostly indistinct muttering, but Mouse catches her given name at least twice, and at one point Andrew exclaims "Cut it out!" loud enough to make her jump. Mouse is disturbed, not so much by the one-sided conversation itself as by the fear that, if it goes on much longer, she may start hearing a second voice.

Mouse thinks: *I'm not going to keep following him. When we get to Bridge Street, I'm going to turn off, go back to the diner, get in my car, and drive home. He can't stop me.*

She resolves herself to this, and takes another step, and then her hand is in her pocket, clenched around the Society's list. In her mind's eye, Mouse sees the last item, underscored:

4. *LISTEN TO HIM.*

They come to Bridge Street. Mouse does not turn off in the direction of the diner. Andrew crosses the street, and she follows him.

As they step onto the far curb, a voice calls to them: "Hey! Hey, Andrew! Mouse!"

It is Julie, waving frantically from down the block. When Andrew sees her he lets out a small hiss of annoyance. "Ah, Julie, not now," he mutters.

"—*means* well. And I, I really do care about her. A *lot.* But sometimes . . ."

Julie Sivik and Bridge Street are gone. Andrew and Mouse are walking along a quiet residential avenue.

"Anyway," Andrew concludes, as if winding up a lengthy oration. He gestures to a big house up ahead on the left. "It's this one."

A woman with white hair opens the front door of the house as they approach. "Hello, Mrs. Winslow!" Andrew calls to her. The woman waves, but her eyes are fixed on Mouse, and her expression is not altogether friendly. Mouse wonders if she and the woman have met before, and, if they have, what she might have done or said to make the woman look at her that way.

But then Andrew, bounding up the porch steps, says, "Mrs. Winslow, this is my friend Penny Driver," and the woman smiles warmly and says, "It's nice to meet you, Penny. Please come in and make yourself at home."

"—put some coffee on," Mrs. Winslow says, walking away down a hallway.

"Thank you, Mrs. Winslow," Andrew says. He opens a door off the middle of the hall and gestures inside. "This way."

But Mouse, instead of going in, turns nervously in place.

"Penny?" Andrew says.

"Yes," says Mouse, with a tremor in her voice.

Andrew tilts his head. "Oh," he says, and points. "The front door is right there, if you decide you want to leave. It's not locked," he adds.

"OK," says Mouse, not bothering to question how he knew she needed to know this. "Thank you."

She follows him through the door he just opened, into what he refers to as a sitting room. The room does have chairs in it—Mouse can see at least two, plus a short sofa—but it will take some reorganizing before anyone does any sitting. The room is fantastically cluttered, with the sofa, the chairs, the shelves that line the walls, and much of the available floor space piled with stuff: boxes, books, toys, clothes, diverse bric-a-brac, and junk. "Sorry," Andrew says, seeing the look on her face. "I have kind of a space-allocation problem."

One corner of the sitting room is taken up by a miniature house—not a dollhouse, but a professional-looking scale model, the kind an architect might build, complete with surrounding landscape. It sits on its own little table, and manages to stand out among the clutter. Mouse guesses that this is what Andrew has brought her here to see—he seems to be maneuvering towards it—but then he turns right, towards the sofa, gesturing at a large oil canvas that hangs on the wall above it.

It's a group portrait. A crowd of maybe twenty people stand in the foreground. They look like relatives; most of them look like Andrew. There are a lot of men, a few women, one little boy, and one giant. They are in a large, two-story room whose walls are paneled in bright glossy wood and lined with incandescent light sconces. These lights cast a cheery glow over the lower part of the room; but up above, on the long gallery that makes up the room's second level, the sconces are spaced farther apart and the bulbs burn less brightly. Along this shadowy overlook another group is gathered, larger than the first, its somber ranks composed almost entirely of sad-faced children. Their melancholy expressions unsettle Mouse; she is glad they are in the background, behind a railing.

The painting is signed "Samantha Gage."

Andrew points to a dark-haired figure in the foreground group. "This is my father," he says. The family resemblance is strong; Andrew and his father are practically twins.

Mouse indicates a fairer-haired figure at Andrew's father's side. "Is that you?"

"No." Andrew frowns. "That's Gideon." He speaks the name as if it were an evil charm. Then he points to another figure at the far left of the group, who stands a little apart from the others. "That one's me."

"Oh, I see," says Mouse, although the likeness isn't as good. The face is wrong.

"Forget about me," Andrew says, and puts his hand on the painting, covering the figure that is supposed to be him. "I'm a special case, anyway. But these others"—he gestures with his free hand— "these other people are my father's version of your Society. Things are much better with them now, because they can all see each other, communicate face-to-face, soul-to-soul. But before, when my father was like you are now, this room you see here was nothing but dark space, and most of the souls in the dark were asleep . . ."

Mouse would like to be able to say at this point that she doesn't know what he is talking about, but on some level she *does* know, and her understanding is coming clearer all the time. Staring at the painting as Andrew speaks, she feels a growing pressure in her temples, as if a mob of little people were assembling there, pushing at the inside of her skull like kids pressing their faces up against a plate-glass window.

". . . so he had to create a place where they could all be awake together at the same time. A meeting place, inside his head."

"Inside . . ."

"Right," says Andrew. "Because that's where they live. You do know that, don't you, Penny? Your Society—that's how they can always get messages to you, no matter where you are, and how they can take control of your body during your blackouts. They always know where you are, can always get to you, because they're always with you."

In a moment he is going to raise his arm, press the tip of his forefinger to the center of her forehead, and say, "The Society lives in here." He isn't doing it yet, but he is about to, she can feel it coming, and she knows that when he does do it her head is going to burst, and the members of the Society are going to come flying out of her skull like insects boiling out from under a stone. And then she *will* be crazy, stark raving mad, beyond all hope or question.

He is raising his arm.

"No," says Mouse, stepping back—

—and falling, face forward, into an icy stream.

She comes up screaming, staggering. The water isn't deep, but the current and the slippery rocks in the streambed keep her off balance. "Help!" she squeaks.

"Penelope!" a voice calls from behind her. "*Stamata! Perimene!*"

Mouse—

—runs through the trees, no little town park but true forest this time. The legs of her jeans are heavy with mud and leaves, but she keeps moving, sprinting for what seems like miles. Even the certainty that something terrible is gaining on her cannot keep her going forever, though; finally she has to stop, if only for a moment. She stumbles to a halt in a small clearing; she bends forward, hands on knees, and closes her eyes, listening for the sound of her pursuer.

When she opens her eyes again, words have been scratched in the ground at her feet: STOP THIS BULLSHIT. Mouse feels fresh dirt under her fingernails. There is a tingle on the back of her neck, the familiar sense of someone standing close behind her.

She doesn't turn around. She fakes like she is going to, then springs forward, *leaping* into a run, trying to accelerate fast enough to leave her body behind.

She slams full-speed into a tree.

"—bleeding," Andy Gage says, crouching beside her.

Mouse lies on her back, blinking up at the sky. She can feel a lump rising on her forehead, blood trickling down the side of her scalp; her neck hurts. She's calm now—in shock—but her heart is sick, and she is disgusted with herself: bloodied, muddied, laid out in the dirt. Insane.

"Penny?" Andrew says.

"I am *shit*," says Mouse, and then the tears start, dribbling out of the corners of her eyes, adding to the mess. "I'm a crazy, pathetic, worthless—"

"Penny . . ."

"—piece of *shit*."

"Penny, *stop it*," he commands, and she does. Stops saying it, that is. Inside her head, where the Society lives, she goes right on thinking it: *Worthless piece of shit.*

Then Andrew says: "Do you remember the little girl in the diner?"

Mouse, still crying, closes her eyes. *Go away*, she thinks. *Go away, I am a worthless piece of shit, leave me alone.*

"Last Monday," he persists. "The little girl whose father hit her, you remember? Penny?"

"Yes," Mouse says. Of course she remembers.

"Do you remember what he called her?"

"Yes."

"'This fucking kid,'" Andrew says. "'This fucking kid.' Do you think that was right, for him to say that?"

"No," says Mouse.

"No," Andrew agrees. "It was a terrible thing to say. An awful thing. Now what if he'd called her a worthless piece of shit, instead? Would *that* have been right?"

"No . . ."

"No. It would have been bad. Wrong, and not true. Just like it was wrong and not true when your mother said it to you."

She rolls her head sideways, feeling a sharp twinge from the back of her neck, and looks at him. "Who . . . who told you about my mother?"

"You told me," says Andrew.

"I never—"

"Not you personally. Your Society."

"They aren't *mine*," Mouse protests.

"Yes, they are. You called them out, to help you cope with something that was too terrible to handle all by yourself. And they're still there, still trying to help you, mostly, but they've got their own needs and wants now, and that complicates things."

"It's *crazy*."

"No," he says. "You *could* have gone crazy, with what your mother did to you. Or you could have turned mean, like the man at the diner. But you didn't. You did something creative. And that's great; only now you're going to have to be even more creative, if you want to get your life together."

Mouse sits up, slowly; Andrew helps her. She tries to turn her head to look around, but her neck and shoulders are really hurting now. "Where are we?" she asks, grimacing.

"In the woods behind the Reality Factory. About half a mile *past* the Reality Factory, actually; I almost lost you. I had to call out Seferis to keep up."

"Seferis?"

"It's complicated," Andrew says.

Mouse thinks: *Everything's going to be complicated now.*

"Tell me anyway," she says. "Tell me everything." Giving in: "Tell me what I have to do."

12

Three days later Mouse is in another cluttered sitting room—this one in Poulsbo, Washington, on the Kitsap Peninsula—wondering whether the doctor in the wheelchair is more like her mother or her grandmother.

Both Grandma and Verna Driver suffered crippling strokes. Grandma died very quickly from hers—one day she was fine, the next she was in intensive care, and the day after that she was gone. Grandma Driver's death was the saddest event in Mouse's early childhood, the loss so traumatic that, shortly after the funeral, Mouse retreated into the dark and went to sleep for a whole year, her longest blackout ever.

Mouse's mother's death was more protracted, and traumatic in a different way. Where Grandma had gone into a coma following her stroke, Verna Driver remained alert. Bedridden, too weak to move and unable or unwilling to speak, she tracked Mouse relentlessly with her eyes, glaring. The nurses who attended her told Mouse not to make too much of this; until they could establish definite communication (several attempts to get her to answer questions by blinking had proved unsuccessful) they couldn't know for sure how much awareness she had of her surroundings. But Mouse didn't need any additional communication beyond that ceaseless stare: her mother was aware, all right. Aware, and angry, and wishing with every last fiber of her being that she could force Mouse to change places with her.

The doctor in the wheelchair is angry too. She keeps it under control for the most part, but it gets away from her a couple times: once when the woman who cares for her is a little too aggressive in offering assistance, and then again when Andrew is slow to take the hint that the doctor wants to talk to Mouse alone. ("Why don't you go see if Meredith needs help in the kitchen," the doctor suggests, to which Andrew replies, "Help with what?" "With *whatever she may need*," the doctor tells him. But Andrew just sits there, still not getting it, and finally the doctor snaps: "Take a *walk*, Andrew! Come back in an hour.")

Andrew warned Mouse in advance that the doctor had a temper—"she's a little prickly sometimes," is how he put it. He assured her that it was nothing to be concerned about, but she's still nervous as he leaves the sitting room.

The doctor senses this, and immediately apologizes. "I'm sorry," she says. "That was very unprofessional of me. I'm supposed to set you at ease, not on edge. But I'm afraid I've always had an abrasive personality, and this"—she pats the side of her wheelchair—"hasn't helped. I hope you'll be patient with me."

This is a new experience for Mouse: someone asking her forbearance, and not even for getting mad *at* her, but for getting mad *around* her. "It's OK," she says.

"Good," says the doctor. "Now, getting down to business . . . I understand Andrew has told you about his own multiplicity. Is that correct?"

Mouse nods, wincing a little from her still-tender neck.

"And what was your reaction to what he told you?"

"My reaction?"

"What did you think? . . . It's OK, you can be honest. I won't repeat anything you say outside this room."

"It was . . . I thought it was very strange," Mouse says. Too strange, she doesn't say—her initial curiosity, her hope that some light was at long last about to be shed on her own condition, being gradually worn away as it dawned on her that the person Andrew referred to as his "father" was not, as Mouse had assumed, a biological parent, but a psychological one, an *earlier* Andy Gage. And he, the Andrew she spoke to, was not his father's biological son, but a member of his father's Society—a *special* member, maybe, but still essentially a figment of his, of the original Andy Gage's, imagination.

Too strange. Crazy. And Mouse would not be sitting here right now if not for the fact that her own Society had left her no choice in the matter. When her alarm clock went off this morning, she found identical to-do lists taped to every wall and door in her apartment. Her answering machine was blinking too, and though she erased the message without listening to it, she knows what she would have heard if she'd pressed Play: a voice, very like her own, warning her not to skip her appointment with Dr. Grey, and probably tossing in a few insults for good measure.

"'Strange,'" the doctor says, as if mulling over the possible implications of the word.

Mouse lowers her eyes. "I *know* I'm crazy. But at least I'm . . . I'm *real*."

"And you think Andrew isn't?"

Mouse hesitates, not wanting to say anything bad about Andrew, who has been nothing but nice to her. "He says his . . . his 'father' . . . made him up."

"Well," says the doctor, "all personalities are creations, after a fashion. People often speak of reinventing themselves, for instance; that doesn't mean those new selves are fakes."

"That's not the same thing."

"Maybe not exactly the same. But I'm confident Andrew is real. As for whether you're a multiple personality, that I don't know yet."

Mouse is suddenly hopeful. "You mean I might not be?"

The doctor shrugs. "Certainly it's possible. Although, from what Andrew has told me, you do seem to have many of the experiences that an untreated multiple personality would be expected to have. The blackouts; the things done, evidently by you, that you can't remember doing. Tell me, what do *you* think is going on?"

"What do I think . . ."

"How do you explain it? To yourself, I mean. When you wake up in a strange place, or get an anonymous message making reference to things that only you should know about. What do you tell yourself has happened?"

"I don't." Mouse spreads her hands in a gesture of helplessness. "It's not . . . I don't *explain* it. It just *happens*."

"But you'd like an explanation."

"I'd like it to *stop*."

"All right," says the doctor, nodding. "Let's see what we can do. What I'd like to try, if you're willing, is to induce one of your blackouts. Only this time—"

"I can't make them happen," Mouse objects. "I wish I could sometimes, but I don't control—"

"Oh, I don't think that'll be a problem," says the doctor. "But this time, I'd like to see if we can get you to remain conscious while the blackout is happening."

"Remain conscious . . . ?" Mouse shakes her head at the contradiction. "How?"

"Well answer me this," says the doctor, "and try not to think too hard about it before you do. Let's assume, for the sake of argument, that your blackouts involve more than you simply passing out. Let's suppose that they actually involve you being *transported* somewhere. What do you imagine that place is like?"

"I don't . . . I can't . . ."

"Don't think about it, just answer: where do you go when you're missing time?"

"Into the dark," Mouse says.

The doctor nods approvingly. "Good safe place, the dark. But what we've got to do is shed some light on it. Could you get that box over there, please?"

She points to a small white box on the mantel above the parlor fireplace. Mouse picks it up and attempts to hand it to the doctor, but the doctor says, "No, it's for you."

Mouse sits back down on the sofa with the box in her lap. She lifts the lid, and sees a gleaming hemisphere of yellow plastic. It's a safety helmet. A plastic hardhat, with a miner's light attached to the front.

"You want me to wear this?"

"If you would," says the doctor. "It may be a little big on you, but the inside headband is adjustable."

Mouse lifts up the helmet, and gently places it on top of her head. It is too big on her, and it's heavy. It hurts her neck. After a moment she takes it off again.

"No good?" says the doctor.

"It hurts my neck," Mouse says.

"That's all right," the doctor says. "Just hold onto it for now. It'll fit you better presently. And don't worry about the lamp—that'll come on by itself when you need it."

The doctor is leaning forward in her wheelchair, setting up another sort of lamp on top of the coffee table: a small strobe-light. She angles the strobe's reflector so that it is aimed at Mouse's face, and switches it on. "Focus on this, please, Penny," she says.

Mouse doesn't want to look in the light—its brilliance dazzles her, and it emits an ugly *tweet* with each flash—but she can't help herself; her eyes move of their own accord. As her gaze fixes on the center of the strobe's reflector, the quality of the light changes, cohering into waves, moving walls of luminance that slide over and through her. The *tweet*s draw out, dropping into a lower register, bass tremors synchronized to the waves of light.

The doctor speaks again, and her voice is changed, too, having become broader, all-encompassing, the voice of a preacher or a burning bush. "I want you to relax now, Penny," she says. "Relax, and stare at the light, and try not to be afraid. In a moment I'm going to ask a member of your Society to come forward and speak with me. Normally when this happens you go down deep inside yourself, into the dark place, and sleep until you're called out again. This time I want you to remain close to the surface, and awake— to make a place for yourself to stand, if you need to. The helmet you are holding in your hands will come inside with you; it will fit you properly there, and comfortably, and it will keep you safe from all harm. The head-lamp will come on automatically in the dark, so that you'll be able to look around and see the place that you've made. Do you understand?"

"Yes," says Mouse, not sure whether she does.

"Good. I'm going to count to three, and then I'd like to speak to the person called Thread. One . . . two . . . th—

—*ree.*"

The room telescopes, with the doctor, the coffee table, and the strobe-light going one way, and Mouse and the sofa flying back the other way.

No, that's not it. The sofa isn't moving; nothing is moving, except Mouse herself, being yanked back into . . . into . . .

Into where?

She is standing now, on a hard—or at least solid—surface. Looking straight ahead she can still see the sitting room, but smaller, and framed in jagged darkness, as if she were peering out through a hole in a wall, or the mouth of an unlit cave.

From just outside the cave mouth Mouse hears a voice—her own voice, but with a new cadence—echoing back to her: *"Hello, Dr. Grey."*

A hand comes into view from below the cave mouth. It's her hand; Penny Driver's hand. It reaches out, across the coffee table—dipping, briefly, to switch off the strobe—and shakes with the doctor.

"Nice to meet you," the doctor says. *"Are you Thread?"*

The sitting room bobs up and down in a way that ought to make Mouse seasick, but doesn't. *"Like Ariadne's thread,"* the voice, Penny Driver's voice, says. *"Do you know that story?"*

Mouse, unwilling to listen to this—someone else having a conversation using *her* voice—turns around. Behind her is only darkness. It frightens her, but she is still holding the helmet that the doctor gave her, and she remem-bers what the doctor said about the helmet's protective powers. She sets the helmet on her head again. This time it fits perfectly, with no discomfort. The pain in her neck is all gone.

The miner's light comes on, and she can see that she is in a tunnel, a cave tunnel. The tunnel narrows as it proceeds away from the cave mouth, becoming a single-file passage that slopes downwards. Even with the miner's light, Mouse cannot see far down this passageway, but she somehow senses that before long it widens out again, into a much larger space. A warm draft of air blows past her, up from the depths, and she has a sudden impression of a huge crowd of people asleep on the floor of a cavern, the sleepers arranged in rows and exhaling in unison.

"Hey, *Mouse*," a new voice hisses, somewhere very near. Mouse turns towards the sound; her miner's light illuminates a woman in a black leather jacket leaning against what was, just a moment ago, a blank section of tunnel wall. The woman is about Mouse's height, although the steel-toed boots she's wearing—black leather like her jacket, laced up to just below the knee—make her seem taller than she is. Her face, framed in an unkempt medusa tangle of raven locks, is badly scarred: her cheeks and forehead are covered with pockmarks, and even the unpitted portions of her skin are rough and chapped. Her eyes are a mean icy blue, frozen chips of disdain, and her cracked lips are drawn out in a permanent sneer.

"So," she says, "you finally decided to come inside with your fucking eyes open, eh?"

Mouse lowers her gaze and sees a second woman, crouched on the cave floor in a gargoyle posture. This woman is a twin of the first, with the same clothes and the same features, only even more hideous, if that is possible: her pockmarks deeper, her hair more tangled, her eyes colder.

Mouse, not saying a word, begins to back away from the evil-looking pair. Amazingly, she's not scared; just . . . *repulsed.*

"Little fucking Mouse," the first woman snarls. "What, you think we're here to fucking hurt you? Or are you just too fucking good for us? *Cunt.*"

Ugly and Uglier, Mouse thinks, trying to come up with names for the women. *Trashy, and Trashier.* Mouse doesn't know what their intentions are, but she wants nothing to do with them.

"Fucking Mouse," Ugly/Trashy repeats, actually sounding offended. "Fine then, cunt, you go fuck yourself . . ." She makes an obscene gesture, and she and her twin both vanish.

The doctor's voice echoes back from the cave mouth: "*—memory trace?*"

"*Well, I know a lot of what goes on,*" Penny Driver's voice says. "*I keep a journal—two of them. One is just a diary of day-to-day events, things that happen to us. The other is a historical record, things I know or suspect were done to us by Penny's mother. It's to help Mouse, when she's ready to start putting her life back in order.*"

"*Mouse is Penny?*"

"*Mouse was Penny.*"

Mouse enters the narrow passageway, descending. The voices from the cave mouth fade as she goes down; soon the only sound is the warm breath-wind, blowing past at regular intervals.

Then, right where she is expecting it to, the passage opens up again, into a space so large that its dimensions cannot even be guessed at. The miner's light is powerful, but as Mouse sweeps her head back and forth like a searchlamp, she sees only a rough stone floor stretching away into the gloom, perhaps to infinity. And yet despite its enormity, the space is some-how intimate, too; the draft has resolved itself into individual breath sounds, a harmony of snores. Mouse still can't see the sleepers, but—peering straight ahead into the darkness, now—she knows that they are close.

She takes a few steps forward and then stops, curious but nervous. What if she gets lost down here? Mouse looks for something to mark a path with, so that she will be able to find her way back to the exit passage. A pile of dis-tinctive white pebbles—exactly the sort of thing she is looking for—appears in the lamplight as she swings her head around. She stoops, and begins to gather up the stones.

As she is doing this, she hears a new sound below the breathing: foot-steps. Mouse looks up, expecting to see one or both of the Ugly twins com-ing back to harass her some more, but it isn't them. The footfalls are light, dainty slippers rather than hard-soled boots.

It is a young girl, about seven years old, dressed as if for a party. Her slip-pers are pink, and so is her dress, all silk and taffeta, festive. But her face is sad, and her eyes—brown, the same shade as Mouse's—are haunted.

She is carrying something: a small sack, velvet cloth cinched with a cord drawstring. She holds it in one hand, at waist level; the sack swings and twists as she comes forward.

Mouse drops the pebbles back onto the floor and stands up. She has a strong impulse to flee. As the girl comes nearer, Mouse can see that the dress is not as fine as it first appeared: its hem is tattered and dirty, and there is a thick brown stain running down one side. The stain looks like it could be oil, or dried blood, but Mouse knows suddenly that it is neither. It's chocolate syrup.

Mouse recognizes the dress now: it's *her* dress, or was once; a gift from her mother. A jealousy gift, the kind given not for its own sake, but to outdo somebody else's present, in this case a sundress that Mouse's grandmother had bought for her.

It happened in late summer. Mouse and Grandma Driver had gone to a matinee showing of *The Muppet Movie* at the Willow Grove Rialto. After-wards they'd stopped on Third Street to get ice cream, and Mouse had noticed the sundress in the window of the Little Misses clothing store. It was a simple dyed cotton dress, but something about it caught Mouse's eye. "Would you like to try it on?" her grandmother asked her, and Mouse said, "Yes, please," even though she wasn't really that interested; it was mostly an excuse to put off going home a little longer. But the dress fit her, and looked nice on her—at least Grandma Driver thought so—so Grandma bought it for her.

As soon as they got home and her mother saw the dress, Mouse knew she was in trouble. Verna Driver remained cordial in front of Grandma, saying only, "Oh Millicent, you really shouldn't have," but beneath her polite disapproval Mouse detected a much harsher emotion. As they stood in the front doorway watching Grandma drive away, Mouse felt her mother's hand grip her shoulder, her nails digging in so sharply that Mouse had to bite her lip to keep from shrieking. The moment Grandma's car was out of sight, Mouse's mother dragged her back into the house and slammed the door.

"What the fuck do you think you are," she demanded, "some kind of fucking charity case? You *have* clothes, *beautiful* clothes. Why would you need to go begging for more? What do you think that says about you? What do you think that says about *me?*"

"I didn't beg!" Mouse protested. "Grandma just asked me if I wanted it. She was being nice, she—"

"Nice!" Her mother's arm shot out in an open-handed blow that staggered Mouse and left her ear ringing. "It's *ugly!* No one who really cared about you would ever give you something so hideous. I can't believe you're that stupid!"

"I'm sorry!" Mouse squeaked, raising her own arms in a feeble attempt at self-defense. "I'll give it back, if you want! I'll throw it ou—"

"*Go to your room!*" Verna Driver roared, and then, before Mouse could obey, landed another blow that sent her crashing into the wall.

The next day, all smiles again, Mouse's mother came home carrying a gift-wrapped box. "Little Mouse!" she called from the front door. "I have a surprise for you!" Mouse, reading a book in her room, did not hear this as good news; she stayed quiet. But of course her mother came and found her anyway.

"This is an early birthday present," her mother said, shoving the box at her. "To show how much I love you." Mouse knew that was a lie. Not the part about her mother loving her—Mouse honestly believed that was true—just the idea that love was the motive for the present. It was a jealousy gift; Mouse could tell even before she opened the box and saw the dress inside.

"Oh, it . . . it's very pretty!" Mouse exclaimed, trying to sound as enthusiastic as possible.

"Yes, it's *beautiful*," her mother said. "And that's not all: we're going out for dinner tonight. We have reservations at Antoine's."

Antoine's Kitchen, which was attached to the Willow Grove Marriott, was the closest thing in town to a five-star restaurant. Mouse's mother liked to go there on special occasions. Mouse would have liked to like it too—Antoine's had wonderful desserts—but she was usually too busy pretending to have a great time to actually enjoy herself. And that was during a normal visit to Antoine's; dinner there as a jealousy gift was an event to dread.

Still, Mouse tried to be brave about it. She put on the dress and a pair of satin slippers that her mother had also bought for her, and remarked several more times how very pretty—how *beautiful*—the dress was. Her mother got dressed up too: white gloves, white high heels, big floppy white hat, and a low-cut navy blue dress with large white polka dots.

When they got to Antoine's, they were informed that the main dining room was closed, having been reserved for a wedding reception by the Hall-becks and the Burgesses, two prominent families in town (Carl Hallbeck published the *Willow Grove Reporter*, and the Burgesses owned the bottle factory that was Willow Grove's largest source of employment). Mouse would have expected her mother to be upset, but she took the news in stride, following along without complaint as the maître d' seated them in a smaller side dining room.

"Now, you order whatever you like," Mouse's mother said. Mouse pretended to struggle with the decision, asking her mother to describe a few of the more exotic dishes on the menu; then she chose the chicken croquettes, which she knew from experience were easy to eat even when she was too nervous to have an appetite.

Their table was close to the doorway that connected the two dining rooms, and they could hear the sounds of the wedding reception going on. Verna Driver, who sat facing the doorway, kept leaning sideways to get a better view; Mouse, only too happy to have her mother distracted, stared at her place setting until the croquettes arrived.

They ate dinner, or at least Mouse did; her mother, now totally focused on the wedding party, barely touched her plate, and she ignored Mouse completely. As a result, by the time the waitress asked if they cared for dessert, Mouse felt comfortable enough to order what she really wanted: an Antoine's triple-fudge sundae. Verna Driver ordered cheesecake, then announced, "I'm going to wash my hands," and disappeared into the main dining room.

Mouse's mother was gone a very long time. Mouse didn't mind. When her sundae came, she dug into it, wanting to savor as much of it as possible while she was alone.

She'd gone through two of the three scoops of ice cream, and was pouring extra chocolate syrup on the third, when she heard laughter coming from the main dining room. Something about it got her attention. She set the chocolate syrup down, slid out of her chair, and went over to the connecting doorway to have a look.

A bandstand had been set up at one end of the main dining room, and the tables rearranged to create a large open space in front of it. Mouse spotted her mother right in the middle of this makeshift dance floor—her hat, like a white signal flag, was hard to miss—dancing with the groom, Bennett Hallbeck. Judging from her smile, Mouse's mother was having a grand time, but Ben Hallbeck looked trapped; he kept throwing glances at the other couples around him as if pleading to be rescued. Finally, at a break in the music, he tried to disengage himself. But Verna Driver wouldn't let him go: she wrapped her arms around him, pulled him close, and started rubbing herself against him. This brought fresh laughter from some of the spectators at the tables, but was too much for the bride, who came storming onto the dance floor flanked by her bridesmaids.

Mouse didn't wait to see what happened next. She did a quick about-face and hurried back to the table. As she was climbing back up into her seat she knocked over the chocolate syrup; she felt it pour onto her dress and let out a cry of dismay.

There was a final explosion of laughter from the main dining room and then the band struck up again, loud. A moment later Mouse's mother reappeared at the table. She was still smiling, but the smile had become brittle; she had lost her hat, and her hair was disheveled. "We're leaving now," she said tonelessly.

"OK," said Mouse. With a fatalistic bow of her head, she stood up and let her mother see the chocolate syrup stain, which some frantic swabbing with a napkin had only made bigger. The dress was ruined; but Verna Driver didn't yell at Mouse, or hit her, only clucked her tongue once, the sound like the cocking of a gun. "We're leaving," she repeated.

They exited Antoine's through a back door, Mouse so frightened now that she barely noticed they'd left without paying. As they crossed the parking lot, she looked back forlornly at the restaurant, a receding oasis of laughter and light.

Then they were in the car. Mouse went to buckle up and realized that there was no way to fasten her seat belt without smearing chocolate syrup on it. This posed a dilemma: it was an ironclad rule of her mother's that she must always wear a seat belt in the car, but it was an equally ironclad rule that she must never dirty or soil the car; sticky messes, as from candy or melted ice cream, were especially taboo. Reasoning that it was best to go with the infraction that would leave no lingering trace and was thus most likely to be overlooked or forgotten, Mouse let the seat belt dangle, and arranged her dress carefully so that no part of the syrup stain touched the car's upholstery.

Her mother buckled her own seat belt and started the engine. She drove in silence for three or four blocks; then, without warning, she slammed on the brakes, hurling Mouse into the dashboard. Mouse wasn't badly hurt, but the sudden shock overcame her, and she burst into tears. Verna Driver smiled thinly and drove on.

The ride back seemed unusually long. Mouse was grateful at first; she was sure now that her mother had other punishments in store for her, and that they would begin in earnest as soon as the two of them were behind closed doors, so she was in no hurry to get home. But as her sobs tapered off, she became more aware of her surroundings, and realized that she didn't recognize the street they were on. They had detoured somewhere. Mouse looked ahead, and saw a sign at the next corner with the words SOUTH WOODS PARK above a right-turn arrow.

They didn't turn right; they turned left, going deeper into Trash Town. A series of further turns down shabbier and shabbier side streets brought them ultimately to a dead-end lane with no signpost or street lamps. Verna Driver hesitated at the head of the lane, as if she herself were reluctant to enter here, but she did, easing the car forward.

Only about half of the lots on the lane were occupied by real houses. Most of the rest held trailer homes; one was vacant, overgrown with weeds, and on one a burned-out log cabin rotted in the moonlight. A Doberman Pinscher chained up in front of the cabin barked ferociously as Mouse and her mother drove past.

They drove to the very end of the lane, to the last lot, where a dilapidated clapboard house stood dark and abandoned. It wasn't in quite as bad shape as the log cabin, but it was getting there: the roof sagged, and one of the side walls had started to buckle; every window Mouse could see was either broken out or boarded shut.

The house had no garage, just a pair of tire ruts that ran into the side yard. Verna Driver steered her car in there and killed the engine. Mouse, who knew something very bad was about to happen, sat frozen, breathing as lightly as possible, as if by being quiet she could somehow fool her mother into ignoring her.

A vain hope. There was a click as Verna Driver unbuckled her seat belt, and then she said, with a mournful sigh: "Little Mouse. You ruined your dress."

She sounded so sad that it was Mouse who ended up being fooled, thinking momentarily that she wasn't mad, just horribly disappointed. "I didn't mean to ruin it," Mouse told her. "It—"

"Oh," her mother said, looking at her, "but I think you *did* mean to."

And then Mouse was clawing at her door handle. She actually got her door open, got one foot out and on the ground, before her mother grabbed her by the hair and hauled her back in, across both front seats, and out the driver's side. As Mouse continued to struggle, her mother slung her over her shoulder and began carrying her around to the front of the house.

Mouse screamed as loud as she could; up the lane, the Pinscher answered with a fusillade of barks. But there was no response from any of the other houses or the trailers. Meanwhile, beneath Mouse's screams, beneath the barking, Mouse's mother continued to speak in level tones, as if they were still sitting in the car calmly discussing Mouse's shortcomings. "You know I try," she said. "I try so hard to get you to appreciate what you have. But you just keep taking it for granted, keep . . . throwing it away. Well, fine then— if you want to piss away what you have, if you want to end up a beggar, living in Trash Town, where no decent person will want anything to do with you, fine. Let's stop wasting time."

She kicked open the front door of the house. The interior was close and musty; Mouse smelled glue, saw torn wallpaper hanging in strips. Then the smells changed: they were in a kitchen, its floor littered with broken crockery, and her mother was opening another door. Mouse sensed a void behind her, and let out one last scream.

"There you go," Verna Driver said, and threw her down into the cellar.

It must have hurt, falling down the cellar stairs, but Mouse didn't feel anything. She was out of her body when it happened, or half out of it: she heard the bumps and thumps, heard them echoing, as though through a tunnel, but there was no pain. Then she was lying on her back on a cool dirt floor. The cellar door slammed, leaving her in total darkness.

She lay there for some time—maybe ten minutes, maybe an hour. Maybe three hours. The darkness itself didn't frighten Mouse. She found it peaceful, almost comforting. It was only when she thought about how she'd come to be there—what a bad person she was, had to be, for her mother to treat her this way—that she dissolved once more into tears.

The tears were drying on her cheeks, and she was beginning to think about getting up and trying to find a way out, when she heard a sound, the soft sly creak of a door being opened. It wasn't the door at the top of the stairs; it was another door, a door to a different part of the cellar or, maybe, a door that led directly outside. Mouse lay still, listening, and the creak came again—the same door, closing—and now her fear was back, because she wasn't alone in the cellar anymore.

Mouse sat up hurriedly. She was completely disoriented, but she thought she couldn't have fallen too far from the stairs, and she began groping around urgently in the dark. Her fingertips brushed a coarse wooden plank—the bottom step! She felt along the step until she found the banister support post, grabbed it, and pulled herself to her feet. Then she went to grip the banister, but instead of a wooden railing she felt the back of another hand, that had found the banister first. The hand flipped over, encircling her wrist in an iron grip.

And then . . .

. . . and then, she didn't know what happened. She blacked out in mid-scream; fell back, and found herself at home in her room, sitting on the edge of her bed in morning sunlight, while her mother called her down to breakfast. The pink party dress her mother had given her was gone, never to be seen again; so was the sundress Grandma had bought for her. And the memory of whatever had happened to her in the cellar after that hand grabbed her wrist, that was gone too—thank God.

Only now, standing in the cavern with the little girl, Mouse realizes: it's not true. Like the photographs of her father that her mother burned, the pink dress isn't gone; it's in here. Grandma's sundress might be in here too somewhere, if she knew where to look for it. And the knowledge of what happened in the cellar after she blacked out . . . that's in here too.

Yes. Mouse looks at the sack in the little girl's hand, twisting as though it were alive, and she thinks she knows what's in it now. As if to confirm her guess, the sack's drawstring loosens of its own accord. The opening puckers like a mouth, and Mouse hears the soft sly sound of a cellar door opening in darkness.

"No!" Mouse squeaks. She wants no part of this; she doesn't want to remember what happened. She takes a step back, and starts to turn and run, but even as she thinks to do it it is already happening: the cavern, the tunnel, the cave mouth, all go blurring past her in reverse.

—and she is back in the doctor's sitting room, reentering her body at such velocity that it is a wonder she doesn't go flying off the sofa. As it is, her torso jerks forward violently; the safety helmet slides off her lap and tumbles to the floor.

"Ohhh," Mouse groans. Her hands come up and go to the back of her neck, pressing hard; the pain has returned, and it's worse. "Oh God . . ."

"Penny?" says the doctor. "Penny, are you all right?"

Mouse doesn't answer. She tries massaging her neck for a moment, but that just sends the pain shooting up into her temples, so she stops, and then—when the pain has gone back a bit—she begins tracing her fingers up along the sides and top of her skull. Probing.

"Penny?" repeats the doctor. "What did you see?"

Her hands are on her forehead now, where she most expects to find it, but there's no hole, no cave mouth gaping above her eyebrows, just smooth skin.

"Penny."

Slowly Mouse lowers her hands. She eases back a little on the sofa, careful to keep her neck straight. "I'm not going back in there again," she says.

"What did you see? Did you meet someone?"

Mouse gets a furtive look on her face. To the doctor it must appear as though she is listening for something, but what she's really doing is *feeling* for something: concentrating on the space that she now knows is there inside her head, trying to sense if any of the members of the Society are lurking near the cave mouth, within earshot.

"Penny . . ."

She can't feel anyone, which doesn't necessarily mean they aren't there. But she decides to take a chance, speaking quickly in a low voice: "Can you take them out?"

"Take them . . . ?"

"The people in my head. Can you . . ."—Mouse wants to say "kill them," but that's too harsh, they'd hear that for sure even if she whispered it—". . . can you get rid of them?"

The doctor doesn't seem surprised by this request, but she also doesn't seem inclined to grant it. "Penny," she says, in that tone of voice used to deliver bad news, "do you understand why they're there in the first place? Did Andrew tell you—"

"I don't *care* why they're there! I just want them gone!" Mouse says, but then her courage crumbles. "Please," she begs. "I don't want anything to do with them. Not those awful twins, not that creepy little girl, not any of them. I just . . . can't you take them out?"

"I'm sorry," the doctor says.

"Can't you just hypnotize me? Or maybe . . . maybe there's a drug, some medicine I could take . . ."

But the doctor shakes her head. "Even if there were some magic pill that could suppress your alters, they'd eventually resurface—or you'd call out new ones."

"No," Mouse insists. "No, I wouldn't, I'd—"

"You would. It's what you do, Penny. It's how you handle stressful situations: by dissociating, devolving them on someone else. With the right therapy, you can learn less disruptive methods of coping with stress, but it's not going to happen overnight. I'm sorry."

"Andrew says," Mouse stammers, afraid that she is about to offend the doctor, "Andrew says that you . . . that your method of treating . . . our condition . . . is different than most psychiatrists'. Maybe . . . maybe if I talked to somebody else, maybe they would . . . well . . ." She fumbles to a halt.

The doctor frowns but doesn't get angry. "Some of my methods *are* unorthodox," she admits. "Andrew may not be in the best position to comment, since his own treatment, his father's treatment, was . . . interrupted . . . in an unfortunate fashion. But that's neither here nor there. Other psychiatrists may disagree with me about a great many things, it's true, but there's one thing they won't disagree about: an important step in treating your condition is coming to terms with the experiences that precipitated it. And for that, you're going to need your Society's help. Whether you choose to regard them as real people or psychological phantoms, you need access to information that they have. Later, after they've shared that information with you, there'll be plenty of opportunity to debate what their final disposition should be—whether you want to reintegrate them, or learn to live with them, or some combination of the two. It's an important question, but it's a question for the latter stages of treatment. You can't *start* by getting rid of them."

You need access to information that they have . . . Mouse thinks of the little girl with her bag. She thinks of the other people in the big cavern, too, the people she heard but didn't see. God! What if they are *all* children, all carrying bags? Take the terror she felt at the prospect of being reunited with that one memory, and multiply it by a hundred . . . no, worse, multiply it by every blackout she has ever had.

"No," says Mouse. "No, I don't think so. I can't do that." She looks at the doctor. "I *can't*."

"Only you can decide if and when you're ready," the doctor replies, with surprising patience. "Although the fact that you're here suggests to me that you're close to being ready. But we won't force it. What I'll do, I'll give you my number, and also the number of another doctor in Seattle—the one who'd actually be handling your treatment if you decided to go ahead with it. And then you can go home and think it over some more, as long as you need to.

"Just one suggestion," the doctor adds, raising a cautionary finger. "I think you are making a mistake by regarding your alters, your Society, in purely negative terms. I can understand why you might view them that way, given the degree to which they disrupt your life, but they aren't your enemies."

"They aren't my friends, either," says Mouse, remembering the way Ugly hissed at her.

"Not friends, perhaps, but . . . allies. People with common interests. Not *identical* interests: you may at times find yourself at cross-purposes with them, and even when you don't, you may not always like them, or they you. But in general, you are pulling towards the same ends, and I think you'll find it much more constructive to work with them than against them . . . and I can see now by your expression that you don't believe me, but that's all right. Just keep it in mind as you're deliberating."

"All right."

"All right. And now, if you would . . . please get Meredith in here . . ."

The doctor has her helpmate give Mouse a card with two phone numbers on it—the doctor's own, and one for a Dr. Eddington. Mouse tucks the card away in her wallet and tries to sound sincere as she says that she will carefully consider everything the doctor has told her.

A few minutes later Andrew comes back from his walk. He's clearly curious about what has happened in his absence, but—still smarting, maybe, from being yelled at before—he doesn't ask any questions. The doctor, who has suddenly become very sluggish, rouses herself enough to insist that Andrew call her again soon: "I want to talk to your father," she says, "and I want you to make that appointment to see Dr. Eddington." Andrew promises that he'll do as the doctor asks; Mouse thinks that his sincerity is only slightly more genuine than her own.

They are in the car, on their way out of Poulsbo, when Andrew finally breaks down and asks: "So, how did it go?"

Mouse shrugs. "All right," she says.

The inside of the car telescopes, the same way the doctor's sitting room did when the doctor counted to three. Mouse finds herself back in the cave mouth, without a helmet this time. She hears the voice of Ugly issuing from

Penny Driver's mouth: *"Bullshit. It wasn't all right. That little cunt took one look inside, saw us, and freaked out. Little fucking Mouse."*

"Maledicta," says Andrew. *"Were you . . . were you nice to her?"*

"She's afraid of her own fucking shadow. Why should I be fucking nice to her?"

"Maledicta . . ."

Mouse, in a sudden flare of anger, surges forward again. Ugly—Maledicta?—is caught by surprise; there is a brief struggle for control, during which Penny Driver's hands go slack on the steering wheel, and the Buick starts drifting to the left. Maledicta, realizing the danger, gives up the fight.

"Penny?" Andrew says, wide-eyed, as Mouse grips the steering wheel again and swerves the Centurion back into its proper lane. "Please don't talk to me right now," Mouse replies. "I need to concentrate."

"OK," Andrew says.

Mouse is furious. She wouldn't have thought it possible, but the visit with the doctor has made things worse. Bad enough to just lose consciousness, but to be tossed like a backseat driver into your own head and forced to listen and watch while someone else takes over your body and says terrible things about you . . .

She will have to be vigilant, now. She will have to stay alert, always alert, to attempts by the Society to seize control, and be ready to fight them off.

But vigilance, Mouse soon discovers, is hard work; by the time they get to the ferry landing, she is a wreck, trembling like someone who hasn't slept for days. As they wait for their turn to board, Mouse rests her head on the steering wheel—

—and lifts it again an hour and a half later. The Buick's engine is off; they are parked in front of the house in Autumn Creek where Andrew lives.

"Penny?" Andrew says softly.

Autumn Creek! Realizing what has just happened, Mouse jerks upright—and yelps, as pain stabs the back of her neck again.

"Oh, Penny," Andrew says, wincing sympathetically from the passenger's seat. "I thought you were going to have that checked out. Didn't you go to the hospital?"

Mouse looks at him, her eyes blurry with tears. "I don't know," she says. She *tried* to go to the hospital, on Sunday night; she knows that much. But as she approached the entrance to the emergency room, she saw a group of security guards wrestling a man in a straitjacket to the ground, and it occurred to her that if she told anyone how she bashed her head into a tree while trying to outrun herself, she might end up in a straitjacket too. So she froze up, and she doesn't know what happened after that. Maybe she went into the emergency room; maybe *somebody* did. But if so, it must not have done any good.

"Would you like me to go with you to the hospital now?" Andrew offers.

"No," says Mouse. "No, thank you." She swipes at her eyes with the back of her hand. Her vision clears, and she sees Andrew's landlady sitting on the front porch of the house, watching them. Watching *her*. "She doesn't like me, does she?"

"Who, Mrs. Winslow? She likes you just fine."

"She doesn't trust me. She thinks I might be dangerous to you."

"Mrs. Winslow does worry about my safety. But it's not personal, Penny. She—"

"She knows that I'm crazy. She's seen it."

"She's seen you acting out," Andrew concedes. "A couple times, now. But even if she hadn't, she'd still keep an eye out. Really, it's nothing against you in particular."

"Right," says Mouse. She closes her eyes and lowers her head towards the steering wheel again, wishing for another blackout, knowing she won't get one as long as she really wants it.

Andrew says: "Her family was murdered."

Mouse lifts her head again. "What?"

"Her husband and her two sons," Andrew says. "They were murdered. So, you know, if she seems a little overprotective of me, you shouldn't take it personally."

"Murdered how?" says Mouse, shocked.

Andrew thinks before answering, consulting with his own Society. "They were on a weekend trip to the San Juan Islands," he finally tells her. "This was years and years ago, before my father moved in here, before I was . . . before I took over. Anyway, they went on this trip, and Mrs. Winslow was supposed to go too, but she got sick at the last minute and had to stay home. And on the way up, on the ferry, they met"—here Andrew says something that sounds like "a cougar" but then corrects himself—"a very bad man, who convinced Mr. Winslow to give him a ride. Once they were off the ferry and away from people, the man pulled out a gun and made Mr. Winslow drive to a cliff overlooking the Sound. Then he shot Mr. Winslow, and made the two boys jump into the water."

"Did the police catch him?" Mouse asks, already knowing from the way Andrew has spoken that the answer is no.

Andrew shakes his head. "No, not for that. But my cousin Adam thinks he probably did get arrested for something in the end. At least we hope he did."

Mouse starts to shake her own head but then stops, wincing. "I don't understand."

"The police never caught him for the murders," Andrew explains, "but it wasn't the last they heard from him. They figure he must have gone through Mr. Winslow's wallet after he shot him, and found a picture of Mrs. Winslow, and something with a home address. And then later, after he made his getaway, he started writing to her . . ."

"*Writing* to her?"

"Notes, mostly," Andrew says. "*Awful* notes. Postcards, greeting cards, sometimes longer letters—all of it completely nasty, evil stuff, I mean a hundred times worse than the meanest message *you* ever got."

"But what . . . what did he write to her? Threats?"

"More like gloating. He would start out by reminding her who he was—he never gave his name, of course, but he'd remind her what he'd *done*—and then he'd go on and brag about what a great time he was having, traveling around, free. He really did travel a lot, too—the postmarks on the notes were from all over the country, never the same place twice.

"So this went on for about five years." Andrew pauses, cocks his head. "Five and a half years."

"Five . . ." The word chokes off in a squeak.

"Yeah," Andrew says. "And each new note that came, Mrs. Winslow would turn over to the police, so they could check it for clues. But they never got anything useful."

"But, but then . . . how can you say that he got caught in the end, if they didn't—"

"They didn't catch him for the murders, or for the notes," says Andrew, "but eventually the notes *stopped*—I mean they stopped all of a sudden, with no warning. And the police, and Adam too, they think that the kind of person who would keep up something like that for five and a half years, he wouldn't just decide to quit voluntarily. So something must have happened to him—most likely, he got arrested for some other crime. Or maybe, maybe he just died."

"But you can't know that for sure," says Mouse, horrified. "You—"

"No, but you can hope. The last note the man ever sent? It was postmarked from a town in northern Illinois. And this was in August of 1990, just a few days before a really big tornado touched down right near there. So who knows . . . maybe after he mailed that last note, maybe he got caught out in the open, with no storm cellar to run to. That's the way Adam wishes it ended. And sometimes . . . sometimes I wish it too.

"Anyway," concludes Andrew, "anyway, the reason I'm telling you this, I know it's a horrible story but I want you to understand, the things *you've* done? Switching souls, and running off to the woods last time you were here—that stuff is *nothing* to Mrs. Winslow. And when you say you're a bad person? Penny, seriously . . . I hear you say a thing like that, I want to say that you must not know what a bad person is. Except that you do know, don't you? You know very well."

Mouse doesn't answer, but she finds herself checking the rearview mirror to make sure her mother has not slipped into the Centurion's back seat somehow. She hasn't. Of course not.

"One other thing," Andrew says. "When my father first told me this, about what happened to Mrs. Winslow's family? He admitted to me that when *he* first heard about it, one of the things he wished he could do was take a look at the notes."

Mouse stares at him.

"Not for any morbid reason," Andrew explains hastily. "It's just—my father wanted to know what would motivate someone to do such an awful thing, what would make them *want* to do it . . . and he thought, if he could read what the killer actually wrote, maybe he could get a handle on it, see something between the lines." Andrew shrugs. "But of course, he didn't actually ask to see the notes. I mean, Mrs. Winslow didn't have them anymore, and besides, that's, that isn't something you can ask.

"So my father never figured out what the killer's motives were. But, he said, he knew what his *goal* was. That much was obvious: he wanted to destroy Mrs. Winslow's soul. Why, we don't know, but that's what he was after.

"And he failed."

And he failed: the words send a weird shudder up Mouse's spine, turning the pain in her neck to something else for a moment, something silvery and light that jangles in the back of her skull.

"He failed," Andrew repeats. "Oh, he hurt her, all right: made her into a different person than she would have been otherwise. And maybe he even made her a little crazy: she still waits for the mail every morning, and my father thinks she won't ever be able to move out of this house, not until she knows for sure that there aren't any more notes coming. She sleeps badly; and she worries about me. So there's that. But she survived. She got hurt, but she wasn't destroyed. And—Penny?—she's a good person. Still."

Mouse gets it—what he's really telling her—but she can't accept it. She shakes her head firmly, the pain settling back in hard, bringing fresh tears to her eyes. "I am *not* a good person."

"Why not? Because your mother tortured you?"

"Because," says Mouse, and stops, thinking: *Because I deserved it.*

Andrew reads her mind. "How could you have deserved it?" he demands evenly. "Remember the little girl in the diner, Penny. What could a little kid do to deserve that kind of treatment?"

"I don't know!" Mouse shouts. Crying, she bangs her fists on the steering wheel. "I don't remember! But I must have . . . must have . . ." She breaks off in sobs.

Andrew waits for her tears to subside and then asks, gently: "Penny? Would you like to come inside for a while?"

Still sniffling, Mouse shrugs noncommittally.

"You could," says Andrew, as if phrasing a delicate proposition, "you could meet my father. If you'd like."

"Your father?"

"I could call him out. You could talk to him."

"Your father," says Mouse. She wipes her nose on her sleeve. "Why . . ."

"The thing is," Andrew says, "what you're experiencing right now . . . it's not something that's ever happened to me. I've never had to come to terms with being multiple, because I always just have been. All of that, the part where you learn how to cope with it, that happened *before* me. Which is maybe why I'm not more help to you."

"Oh no," says Mouse automatically. "No, you're helping."

"I don't feel like I am," Andrew says. "Not enough. But maybe my father . . ." He shrugs. "So do you want to meet him?"

Not really, Mouse thinks. But then she thinks about driving home from here, alone—only not alone, oh God—and she decides that of the things that she *doesn't* want to do, meeting Andrew's "father" is probably the least worst option.

"OK," she relents. "All right."

"Great." Andrew smiles. "Come on inside then," he says, reaching for the door handle. "Mrs. Winslow will make you coffee, or tea if you like . . ."

He practically bounds out of the car, and Mouse thinks, *comfortable in the world.* A part of her is appalled that he can act so carefree just moments after describing a triple murder and the mental torture of an old woman, but another part of her is envious. Maybe Andrew, or Andrew's father, can teach her the trick of it: how to acknowledge evil without being consumed by it. Maybe if Mouse could do that, she wouldn't need to be terrified of the little girl in the cave.

Andrew trots up the front walk of the house, calling to Mrs. Winslow; as he mounts the porch steps she says something to him that breaks him up, and they laugh together, at ease.

Mouse gets out of her car and—moving slowly at first—goes to join them.

FIFTH BOOK: ANDREW

13

Julie was jealous of Penny.

That was what Adam thought, anyway; I wasn't sure what was going on. I'd expected Julie to be pleased about my decision to help Penny out, and she *seemed* pleased, especially at first . . . but she also started acting weird.

Like the invitation to have breakfast at her apartment on Saturday morning. That was nice, if unexpected. But when I showed up bright and early on Saturday, Julie was waiting for me outside her building.

"Let's go eat at the diner," she suggested.

"The diner?" I said. "But I thought . . . I thought you wanted to have breakfast here." I held up a grocery bag. "I brought frozen cinnamon rolls. The fun kind."

"The apartment's kind of a mess right now," Julie told me. "Besides, I've got no food in the fridge—I forgot. We can't just eat cinnamon rolls."

"OK," I said, disappointed.

"Here," Julie said, reaching for the bag. "I'll put those in the freezer so they won't thaw. Just wait down here for me . . ." She took the rolls and ran inside. She was gone a long time.

"Tell the truth," said Adam, while we were waiting. "The fact that you can't figure her out is part of the attraction."

"Be quiet. I'm not attracted to her anymore."

Adam wouldn't even dignify that with a laugh.

"So," Julie said, a little too cheerfully, when she finally reappeared, "let's go eat!" She hooked her arm in mine and started down the block at a brisk pace, practically dragging me along with her.

"Julie," I said, stumbling as I tried to keep up, "Julie, slow down a little!"

"I'm hungry!" Julie exclaimed, and kissed me on the side of the head, which temporarily scrambled my thoughts. By the time I got my equilibrium back we were on Bridge Street—moving at a more reasonable speed, now—and Julie was quizzing me about Penny.

"There isn't a whole lot to tell, so far," I said, which wasn't strictly true. But I'd already decided I wasn't going to mention the e-mails I'd gotten or the part about Maledicta chasing me into Thaw Canal, and if you left that stuff out, there *wasn't* a whole lot to tell.

"You've been hanging out with her though, right?"

"Not really, no."

"But yesterday, when I came by and saw you . . ."

"That wasn't hanging out," I explained. "Penny just showed up, just like you did. Or some of her people did, actually—Penny wasn't there."

Julie looked pleased. "So you've met the family."

"A few of them," I said, thinking of how Maledicta had threatened to burn me with the cigarette lighter.

"What did they want?"

"They want me to help Penny."

"So I was right."

"Maybe," I said. "I still don't know if Penny herself wants help, though. And—"

"Sure," Julie interrupted, "but if her people are trying to get her help, that's a good sign, isn't it?" Without waiting for an answer, she went on: "So what about Dr. Grey? What happened there?"

I shrugged. "Not much. She said she'd like to meet with Penny, if Penny's willing to meet with her. But I don't know if—"

"Good," Julie said. We were stopped on the corner across the street from the Harvest Moon Diner now; the crosswalk light had turned green, but Julie ignored it. "You and Penny will probably need to take another day off work for that, right?"

"I suppose. I hadn't actually thought about it. But . . . yes, I suppose we might. Or she might. It depends on—"

"Well whatever time off you need, that's no problem. Just try to give me a *little* advance warning this time, OK?"

"OK. But—"

"Also, if the two of you need a ride out to Poulsbo, I'd be happy to give you a lift. Assuming my car's running that day, of course . . ."

"Well thanks, Julie," I said politely, actually finding the offer a little strange, "but you know Penny's got her own car. And anyway, I think you're getting ahead of—"

"Just keep it in mind," Julie said. "Anything you need from me, I'll be happy to help out."

"OK," I said. "OK, thanks." I looked up at the light, which was green for the second time now. "So . . . are you still hungry?"

The Harvest Moon was crowded that morning. While we waited for a table to open up, I scanned the newspaper racks by the door. Warren Lodge's picture was on the front page of both the *Seattle Post-Intelligencer* and the *Autumn Creek Weekly Gazette*. MANHUNT CONTINUES, said the *P-I*'s headline; the caption beneath the *Gazette* photo read **"Cougar" Still at Large.**

Julie noticed my interest. "That's some story, isn't it?" she said. "You know what I want to know? Where was the mother?"

"The mother?"

"Yeah, you know: Mrs. Lodge."

"*Mrs.* Lodge? . . . I thought he was a widower."

Julie shook her head. "The papers said he was divorced, but I don't remember anything about the ex-wife being dead."

"But if she were still alive," I said, disturbed by the notion, "don't you think she would have known, or at least suspected, what her ex-husband was really like? And don't you think she would have tried to protect the girls?"

"Well yeah, I'd *think* so," said Julie. "Which is why I was wondering where she was."

A waitress came and seated us. After calling on my father to silence a few protests, I ordered a single breakfast, a shrimp-and-cheese omelet. While we ate, Julie continued to ask me questions about Penny, most of which I had no answers for. "Really, Julie," I said, "I haven't gotten to know her yet. At all. What little contact I've had has all been with other souls."

"Well what are they like, then? How many have you met?"

"A few. But—"

"So what are they like?"

Because she insisted, I gave her brief descriptions—the best I could do—of Thread and Maledicta.

"Maledicta." Julie grinned. "That's what, Bad Mouth?"

"Something like that."

Julie nodded. "I think I met her too. What is she, Penny's version of Adam?"

More like Penny's version of Gideon, I thought. Adam himself was not flattered by the comparison, but I'll omit his response. "Maledicta is Maledicta," I said diplomatically. "She's a protector, I know that much, but beyond that . . . I don't think it's fair to compare her to anyone in my house-hold."

"Of course," said Julie. "Is she the one who kissed you?"

I blinked in surprise. I'd wondered whether Julie had seen that . . . but of course she had. Julie was very observant when she wanted to be. "I don't know who that was . . . or, or *what* that was."

"Hmmph." Julie raised her eyebrows skeptically. "Well, if you can't say, you can't say."

After breakfast, as we were leaving the diner, a tow truck driving west on Bridge Street honked its horn as it went past us. This wouldn't have been noteworthy except for the way that Julie reacted: she caught me by the elbow and spun me around so that I was facing away from the street.

"So Andrew," Julie said brightly, "would you like to come back to my place and hang out for a while?"

"What?" I shook my arm loose and looked back over my shoulder at the tow truck, which was already a block away. "Who was that, Julie?"

"Who was who?" Julie said, all innocence, and I thought: Adam is wrong. I don't find this attractive at all.

But when Julie repeated her offer to come back to her apartment, of course I said yes. I didn't even bother to mention the obvious: that if her place had been too messy for visitors before breakfast, it ought to still be too messy now. I went back with her, and hung out for the rest of the morning, and actually had a really nice time, just like in the old days.

Then around noon I noticed that Julie was stretching and yawning for the third time in as many minutes. Figuring that might be a hint, I got up to go. "I should head back to Mrs. Winslow's," I said. "I promised Thread and Maledicta I'd call them this weekend, and I should probably do it this after-noon; Maledicta was kind of anxious about it."

"You can call from here if you'd like," Julie said, breaking her stretch.

"No, that's OK. It could be a long call."

"All right," Julie said. Then she smiled. "I knew you guys would hit it off."

I tried to keep my expression neutral. But what did she mean, *hit it off*? Hadn't she been listening before? With the exception of a few words exchanged at work, and at lunch that first day, I hadn't even spoken to Penny herself yet.

"Don't bother trying to explain it again," Adam counseled. "Just say see you later and get out of here."

"Right," I said, picking up my jacket. "See you later, Julie." I turned, started to walk out of the apartment . . . and stopped, my hand on the door. "Julie?"

"Yeah?"

"I think it's great, you wanting to be so helpful, but . . . you do understand, right? Even if Penny does decide to, to build her own house, you won't necessarily be a part of that process. I mean, *I* probably won't even be a part of it, beyond introducing her to Dr. Grey. And if Penny does come to me for advice, or whatever, I may not be able to tell you about it. Not because I don't want to, but because, well . . ."

"That stuff is private." Julie nodded. "Sure, of course, I understand. No problem."

"OK," I said, not totally convinced. "OK, good. Well anyway . . ."

"Call me later if you want."

I went home and dialed Penny's number. Thread answered on the first ring. "Hello, Mr. Gage."

"Hi." We spoke very briefly; Thread asked, right up front, if it would be all right if she and Maledicta came out to Autumn Creek to talk with me in person. I'd been halfway expecting this, and had decided that it would be OK so long as Maledicta and her twin behaved themselves. I told Thread they could come by Mrs. Winslow's anytime that afternoon. "Will Penny be coming too?"

"Oh no," said Thread, sounding surprised. "Penny still doesn't know anything about this."

At quarter to two the Buick Centurion pulled up to the curb in front of the Victorian. Mrs. Winslow had taken a seat on the porch a few minutes earlier, after I'd told her who was coming to visit; she watched my back as I went down the front walk to the car.

Maledicta was behind the wheel, puffing on a cigarette; Thread didn't know how to drive. "Would you like to come inside for some coffee or tea?" I asked.

Maledicta looked over at Mrs. Winslow sitting sentry on the porch. "No," she told me bluntly. Then: "Get in the fucking car. Let's go someplace else."

I frowned at her rudeness, but then turned, nodded reassuringly to Mrs. Winslow, and got in the car. "Where to?" I asked.

We ended up driving to a number of different places around town. While the car was in motion, Maledicta spoke to me; when we parked somewhere for a while, Thread took over. Between the two of them, I began to learn the answers to some of the questions Julie had been asking.

Thread gave me a broad outline of Penny's history: how she'd been born in Willow Grove, Ohio, in 1971; how her father, a traveling salesman, had died in a plane crash two years later; how over the next decade and a half her mother, a crazy woman named Verna Dorset Driver, had systematically broken Penny's soul apart; how Penny had finally escaped on a scholarship to the University of Washington; and how her mother's death the following year had freed her for good. Like a good reporter, Thread tried to keep her account as objective as possible; though she readily described Penny's emotions, she kept her own feelings to herself, and downplayed her own role in Penny's life.

Maledicta made no attempt at objectivity. She went out of her way to share her feelings, which consisted primarily of different flavors of hate, anger, and resentment. She bragged about her own actions, saying that she'd "saved Mouse's fucking ass" more times than she could remember, and that "without me and Malefica to look out for her, Mouse would be a fucking stain on the wall by now—and it's not that the little cunt doesn't deserve it, but it's our fucking neck, too."

In addition to telling me about Penny's life, Thread and Maledicta asked questions about mine. Thread was fascinated by the idea of the house, and wanted to hear all about the practical aspects of building and running it; Maledicta, more skeptical, wanted to know what problems to expect ("Do Malefica and I get our own fucking room?" she demanded. "What if someone acts up? How do you keep the assholes in line?"). I answered their questions as completely as I could, until finally—it was late afternoon by this time, and I was exhausted again—they were satisfied.

"All right," Maledicta said. "We'll do it. We'll build a fucking house."

"What about Penny?" I asked. "Will she cooperate?"

"Fucking Mouse," Maledicta sneered. "Yeah, she'll go along. She fucking well better."

"But does she even know that you—"

"She knows. Enough. She pretends to herself that she doesn't, but she knows. Mouse isn't stupid, she's just a fucking coward."

"OK. But—"

"What we'll do," said Maledicta, "we'll get Mouse to come out here tomorrow, and you'll tell her what's what. And we'll make sure she fucking pays attention."

"Tomorrow," I mused, not sure I wanted to give up my entire weekend, not without being *asked*, at least. But whatever objections I was thinking of making were put on hold as Maledicta thumbed the button on the car's cigarette lighter.

"Yeah," Maledicta said, pulling a pack of Winstons from her jacket pocket and shaking one loose. "Yeah, Mouse'll go along. We'll fucking see to it. And if she doesn't . . . if she doesn't, we'll get someone else to run the fucking show." She looked over at me. "We could do that, right?"

"I'll talk to Penny," I said, preoccupied now, waiting for the lighter button to pop back out. "You get her to meet with me, and I'll do my best to help her understand what's going on."

"Fucking right you will," said Maledicta.

And so the next day at noon I waited for Penny in front of the Harvest Moon Diner, trying not to laugh as Adam did Maledicta impressions: "How about this fucking weather? Pretty fuckingly clear fucking skies for fucking April, don't you fucking think?"

Then Penny arrived, and the laughs were over for a while.

There's a type of protector soul, called a runner, whose function is to remove the body from threatening situations. Penny had at least two runners, and it wasn't long before I'd met both of them.

The first runner came out only moments after Penny's arrival. I don't think it was my fault; when I'd asked my father's advice about how to speak to Penny, he recommended I be direct, but he also warned me that no matter what approach I used, Penny would probably switch several times in order to avoid hearing what I had to say. "It's a terrifying thing to find out about yourself. I remember."

"But Maledicta said Penny already knows . . ."

"I'm sure Penny *suspects* the truth, or part of it," my father said. "That's not the same as knowing for sure . . . or being told flat out."

Thread and Maledicta had told me that they would leave Penny a message instructing her to meet with me. I decided that would be a good opener: I'd say something about the message, and segue naturally into the question of who had sent it. It was a reasonable plan, but I never made it to the segue. As soon as I mentioned the message—something that, from Penny's perspective, I shouldn't have known about—Penny got scared, and out came the first runner.

This runner didn't actually run, just walked fast: ducked Penny's head down so that her chin nearly touched her chest, fixed her arms stiffly at her sides, clenched her fists, and shuffled off with surprising speed. Almost before I realized what was happening, she was out of the parking lot and scooting away up Bridge Street. I chased after her, calling Penny's name; she didn't look back, but as I came up behind her she started making a noise, a low caterwauling from deep in her throat, that caused the hairs on my arms to stand up. I wasn't the only person unnerved by that sound— other pedestrians, hearing that caterwaul come out of Penny's mouth, hurried to make way for her.

Then I was alongside her, putting a hand on her shoulder, and the caterwaul jumped octaves, rising up into a high keening—the sound a porcupine might make if it screamed. The keening froze me on the spot; the runner pulled free and kept moving, ducking out of sight around the next street corner.

"Don't lose her!" Adam warned.

So I took off again, following from a distance now, not wanting to hear that keening a second time. The runner was almost a block ahead of me when she went into Maynard Park, and for a moment I worried I had lost her; but when I entered the park myself, Penny's body was seated on a bench, waiting for me.

"Penny?" I said uncertainly. The runner was gone, that was obvious, but I wasn't sure what soul had taken its place.

Then Penny's face darkened in a scowl, and I knew.

"Sit down," Maledicta fumed. "We'll have her back out in a fucking minute."

I sat. The scowl disappeared, replaced by confusion, and Penny's shoulders hunched. I gave her a second to get her bearings, then started in again, commenting matter-of-factly that she'd just had a blackout, trying to make it sound like it was no big deal.

Out came another runner, this one a sprinter; it dashed off into the trees behind the bench.

"Oh boy," I sighed, getting up to follow. The direct approach wasn't working very well.

To make a long story short, I got my exercise that day. In the end, Penny did listen to everything I had to say, but only after I'd put several new miles on my sneakers, and only after Penny had nearly broken her own neck.

That evening, I called Dr. Grey's number to try to set up an appointment, but Dr. Grey wasn't available. "Danny's having a pretty bad weekend, Andrew," Meredith told me. "She hasn't been out of bed since yesterday."

"Oh no," I said. "Not . . . not because of my visit, I hope."

Rather than reassure me, Meredith simply asked: "Is there something I can help you with?" I explained why I'd called. "Uh-huh . . . well, she's definitely not going to be up to seeing anybody tomorrow. Maybe later in the week. You want to try back on Thursday or Friday?"

"OK," I said, wondering how Maledicta would feel about waiting.

On Monday morning I came into work early to talk to Julie—and to apologize. At one point on Sunday, in between flight responses, Penny and I had bumped into her on Bridge Street. It was bad timing, as Julie belatedly recognized—even as she came running up to us, she saw the look on my face, and slowed. "Hi," she said. "I hope I'm not interrupting anything . . ."

"You are," Maledicta piped up. "Fuck off."

I figured Julie might still be upset about that, and I was right. I found her in one of the storage tents, digging through a carton of old printouts, and at first she wouldn't look at me, though she grudgingly acknowledged my presence. "So," she said tersely. "What's up?"

"Well, Penny has agreed to go see Dr. Grey . . ."

"I know," Julie said.

"You do?"

"Sure. That's why she called in sick today, right?"

"Penny called in sick?"

Julie finally looked up, an expression of disgust on her face. She thought I was only pretending ignorance. "You're going to tell me you didn't know?"

"No," I said. "No, I didn't know. When did she call you?"

"This morning around five-thirty," Julie told me. "Not my best time of day."

"What did she say?"

"Just that she wouldn't be coming in. When I asked her what was wrong, she told me to mind my own fucking business."

"Maledicta," I said.

"Yeah, Maledicta. What does she have against me, exactly?"

"Against you?"

"She's been openly hostile to me every time we've met."

"I think Maledicta is hostile to everyone, Julie—even to Penny. It's her nature."

"No," Julie said, shaking her head. "With me it feels like it's personal, somehow." Her eyes narrowed. "Did you say something to her about me? Something to make her mad?"

"No," I said. "At least I don't think I did. Like what?"

"Did you tell her the only reason I hired Penny was so you could get her treatment for her MPD?"

"No! Why would I tell her that—it's not true, right? And besides, Male-dicta *wants* Penny to get treatment. She's more committed to the idea than Penny or even Thread at this point. So she wouldn't be mad at you for that."

"Hmmph," said Julie. "Hmmph, well . . . I suppose in one sense it's an improvement over last week, at least she called before not coming in this time . . . so she's *not* seeing Dr. Grey today?"

"I don't see how she could be. Dr. Grey is . . . she's not available today. If Penny called in sick, it's probably something to do with her neck."

"Her neck?"

"Penny got a pretty bad knock on the head yesterday," I explained. "I was worried that she might have given herself whiplash. And if her body is in pain, then whoever's in control of her body is in pain too, which could be why Maledicta seemed extra unfriendly."

"Oh," Julie said.

Seeing her soften a little, I took advantage of the opening: "About what happened yesterday, Julie, I'm *really* sorry . . . you just caught us at a bad moment."

"Saturday too I guess, huh?"

"Saturday?"

"Saturday afternoon, I saw the two of you driving in town. I waved, but you ignored me."

I shook my head, and Julie lost her temper again.

"Jesus Christ, Andrew!" she exclaimed. "I *saw* the two of you together, don't try to tell me I didn't!"

"No, Julie, I'm not saying we weren't together, I just, I don't remember seeing *you* on Saturday afternoon."

"You were looking right at me when I waved."

"Well that doesn't mean I saw you. If the car was moving, I was probably paying attention to Maledicta."

"Yeah, well, whatever," Julie said dismissively. "Never mind."

"Would you like me to call Penny and find out why she's not coming in?"

"No." Julie shook her head. "No, let's just try to get some work done today . . . however much we can get done with half the software team missing."

There were any number of tactless remarks I could have made at that point, but I wisely chose to keep my mouth shut. A little while later, though, Dennis, far less cautious than I, decided to crack wise about Penny's absence: "Gee, Commodore, that was a great idea you had about hiring a second programmer. It's only been a week and already I can't remember how we ever got by without her . . ."

Julie and Dennis were at each other's throats for the rest of the day, which at least kept Julie's attention off me. After work, though, as I was leaving the Factory, I spotted Penny's Buick idling just inside the gates, and got a sinking feeling in my stomach.

"Penny?" I called, walking up to the car.

Maledicta. "Fucking get in. Thread wants to ask you some more questions about the house."

"OK." I glanced back nervously towards the shed; Julie was still inside, but I knew she'd be out soon. "OK, but listen, I think we should go somewhere else. Julie's kind of upset that Penny skipped work today."

"Fuck Julie. Get in the car."

I got in. Rather than drive away immediately, Maledicta took the time to light a cigarette. I noticed she was still holding her neck a bit stiffly. "How are you feeling?" I asked.

"Fucking peachy," Maledicta replied. "But Mouse is being a fucking basket case. We decided she needed some time off."

"Oh. OK. Listen, can we please—"

"So did you make the appointment with the doctor yet?"

"No," I said. "I couldn't."

"Why the fuck not?"

"I'll tell you as soon as you start driving."

"Fine," Maledicta spat. She yanked the Buick out of neutral and stepped on the gas. But it was too late; as we passed through the Factory gates, I looked back and saw Julie standing out on the lot, her hands on her hips.

Tuesday was in many ways a repeat of Monday: I came in early, and Penny didn't come in at all. But Julie wasn't interested in hearing more explanations. "Whatever you two need to do, Andrew, you go ahead and do it. When Penny decides to come back to work, *if* she decides to come back to work, you just let me know."

"Julie . . . I did warn you that something like this might happen."

"That's right, you did. So there's no foul, no blame on you. Now can we drop it?"

That day after work, I again came out of the Factory to find a vehicle idling by the gates. But it wasn't Penny's Buick this time. It was a tow truck: the same tow truck that had honked its horn at Julie and me on Saturday morning. A man got out of the cab as I approached, and I recognized him too: he was the same Triple A mechanic that Julie had been dating over a year ago.

Julie came running past me, laughing, and jumped up on the mechanic, slinging her arms around his neck and her legs around his hips. I turned away as they kissed.

"Hey Andrew," Julie called, her feet back on the ground. "This is Reggie Beauchamps. I don't know if you two have ever actually met."

"No," said Adam from the pulpit, "but we sure have *heard* of him . . ."

"Be quiet," I muttered under my breath, at the same time raising my hand in a halfhearted wave.

"Well, we've got to go," said Julie. "Say hi to Penny for me if you see her, OK?"

It was then that Adam shared his insight that Julie was jealous of Penny.

"How can she be jealous?" I protested. "Penny and I aren't a couple! And Julie . . . Julie *is* part of a couple again, it looks like."

"Yeah," said Adam, "and even if she weren't part of a couple, she still wouldn't want to fuck you."

"Adam!"

"But even though she doesn't want to fuck you, she still thinks of you as a special friend. And now she sees you developing this friendship with Penny that seems like it's even *more* special, and she's cut out of it."

"But that's not what's happening!"

"Doesn't matter. It's what she sees: you spending a lot of time with Penny, both of you acting mysterious about it . . ."

"But we're not trying to be mysterious! And besides, all I'm doing is what Julie *wanted* me to do!"

"Yeah," said Adam. "I told you that was a bad idea."

Thinking that the sooner Penny started getting professional help, the sooner my relationship with Julie could return to normal, I gave Dr. Grey another call that evening. "Hello," I said, when Meredith picked up, "I know you said try back on Thursday, but I was hoping . . ."

"Andrew," Meredith said, in a flat tone I couldn't read. "Hi. Listen, Danny is still—"

I heard Dr. Grey's voice in the background. Then Meredith must have put her hand over the phone's mouthpiece, because everything got muffled. It sounded like she and Dr. Grey were yelling at each other.

Eventually Dr. Grey came on the line: "Andrew?"

"Dr. Grey," I said. "Is everything all right?"

"Yes, everything is *fine*." The connection got muffled again for a moment, and Dr. Grey shouted something that I couldn't make out. Then she came back on: "Andrew?"

"I'm still here."

"I assume you're calling about your friend?"

"Yes. She's ready to meet with you, if you're feeling—"

"Excellent. How does tomorrow sound?"

"It sounds great! I'll have to double-check with Penny, but I think—"

"Good. I'm looking forward to it."

But Penny, as it turned out, *wasn't* looking forward to it. When I first got her on the phone she seemed very disoriented; I had to explain twice why I was calling before I was sure she understood. "Tomorrow?" she finally said, sounding dismayed.

"Yes—tomorrow morning. I'm sorry it's such short notice, but you'll be glad you went. I promise."

"I don't know," Penny said. "I'm very sorry if you went out of your way to arrange this, but I've been thinking it over, and I—"

There was a loud clatter, as if Penny had dropped the phone. Then Maledicta came on the line: "Don't pay any fucking attention to her. Just say what time you want us to pick you up."

The Buick was out front of Mrs. Winslow's at 8:00 A.M. the next morning. My relief at discovering that Penny herself was driving faded as I realized how miserable she was. She looked like she hadn't slept much, and her neck was still troubling her; and though she didn't say so, it was obvious that she didn't really want to be doing this. I considered offering to cancel the appointment with Dr. Grey, but held off for what was, I admit, a very selfish reason: I didn't think Penny would be *allowed* to cancel, and I didn't want to have to spend the entire trip to Poulsbo in Maledicta's company.

At Dr. Grey's house, Meredith was in a bad mood too. I couldn't tell if she was mad at me specifically, but when Dr. Grey asked to be left alone with Penny, I decided to go for a walk outside rather than hang out in the kitchen.

I came back an hour later, curious to see how Penny was faring. My father warned me not to expect any miracles; it would take a lot longer than sixty minutes to put Penny's life in order. I knew that, but even so I was surprised to find Penny looking *more* miserable than when we'd first arrived. What had gone wrong?

During the drive back to the ferry, Maledicta popped out, furious, and blurted a profanity-laced explanation: with Dr. Grey's help, Penny had met some of her other souls in person for the first time. Evidently they hadn't hit it off too well. Maledicta seemed personally insulted, and she was revving up for a lengthy tirade against Penny when Penny forcefully retook control of the body, nearly wrecking the car in the process.

Penny stayed in control until we reached the ferry landing; then another soul took over. At first I thought Maledicta had come back, but when she didn't start cursing right away, I realized it was her twin.

Malefica reached across to the glove compartment and pulled out a fifth of vodka. "Hey!" I objected. "Hey, what are you doing?"

Ignoring my protest, Malefica spun the cap off the vodka flask and started guzzling the contents.

"Get out of this car right now," Adam said—a completely unnecessary piece of advice. I was already reaching down to unbuckle my seat belt.

But just then Malefica gasped, as if she'd been stabbed through the back of the driver's seat. She stiffened, and a new soul took charge of Penny's body.

The new soul was male—and sober, in all senses of the word. Glancing at the vodka bottle in his hand, he let out an irritated sigh and shook his head. He recapped the bottle, and instead of putting it back in the glove compartment slid it temporarily under his seat. Then he turned to me and apologized: "Sorry about that. Sometimes when they're very upset they get self-destructive—or just plain destructive. I try to keep things from getting out of hand."

His name was Duncan; he introduced himself as Penny's designated driver.

"Is Penny all right?" I asked.

"She's asleep right now," Duncan said. "I don't know how she'll be when she wakes up."

"What about Maledicta and Malefica?"

"They're awake. But"—and here he was speaking to a larger audience than just me—"they aren't getting out again until they settle down."

The ferry arrived and opened for boarding. After we were safely parked on the car deck, Duncan got out of the Centurion, taking the vodka bottle with him; when he came back a moment later he was empty-handed.

"I'm sorry about all the turmoil you're going through," I told him, after he'd settled back into the driver's seat. "I wish I could make it easier, but I'm not really sure what to do."

"You've been through this yourself, haven't you?"

"Not me personally. I have an idea what Penny's experiencing right now, but I don't really *know*, firsthand."

"Well then," said Duncan, "do you suppose you could let her talk to someone who does know?"

It was such an obvious suggestion that I was amazed I hadn't thought of it myself—and I knew just who Penny should talk to, too.

"I don't want to get involved in this," my father said.

"It wouldn't have to be a *long* conversation," I suggested. "You could just, I don't know, give her a sort of pep talk."

"A pep talk . . ."

"Yes! Just let her know, you know, that however frightened she is now, it all works out in the end. Like it did for you."

"You don't know what you're asking, Andrew."

He was right, I didn't know—but ultimately, my enthusiastic ignorance won out over his reluctant wisdom, and he agreed.

When we got back to Mrs. Winslow's, Duncan woke Penny up. As soon as she realized she'd blacked out most of the trip home, she got very upset, and it was a while before I could calm her down enough to suggest that she have a talk with my father. In the end, though, she also agreed. I called out my father, and while he and Penny talked, I went inside and took a long stroll around the lake, which was very misty that day.

When I came back out, nearly three hours had passed—so much for a quick conversation. My father was wiped out.

"Did it go all right?" I asked him. Penny had already gone home.

"She's better," my father said. "For now." Then: "I'm very unhappy that you put this on me, Andrew."

"Well," I said, "it's all over now anyway, right?"

"No," my father said. "I don't think it is."

The next morning, Penny returned to her job at the Reality Factory as if she'd never left. At first Dennis tried to tease her about her week-long "vacation," but she was so matter-of-fact about it that he soon gave up. And by midafternoon, having observed how easily Penny picked up the thread of her work, Julie seemed to have forgiven her her unexcused absence. "Say what you want about her," Julie remarked to me at one point, "but she sure can write code . . . So I take it things are better?"

"Better," I conceded.

"Good," said Julie, and patted me on the shoulder.

After work that day, Penny came up to me and asked, somewhat hesi-

tantly, if she could "talk to Aaron some more." The request caught me by
surprise, but my father seemed to be expecting it; he was already waiting in
the pulpit. "Tell her yes," he said. So I took another stroll around the lake,
and my father and Penny had another lengthy "pep talk."

. . . and the next day, another. Each succeeding conversation left my
father more drained, but by Friday night he reported what sounded like real
progress. "She's going to make an appointment with Dr. Eddington next
week," he told me. "She's going to start regular therapy."

"That's great!" I said. "So the worst is over, then—"

"No, Andrew, it's just starting."

"I'm sorry . . . I know she's still got a lot to go through, but—"

"You don't have the first inkling!" my father snapped. "This is . . . I know
this situation isn't entirely of your own making, Andrew, but I still really
resent being made a part of it. Certain things I just don't care to relive."

I apologized, of course, but secretly I was still gladdened by the thought
that, whatever hurdles lay ahead for Penny, my own life was starting to
return to normal.

On Saturday around noon I ran into Julie on Bridge Street, and after
some initial awkwardness, she invited me to lunch. While we ate I filled her
in on what had been happening—it was much easier now that I actually had
something to tell her—and when I finished, she told me she was sorry for
the way she'd been acting.

"I can see where this must have been a hard week for you," she said.

"It's all right, Julie," I told her. "I know it was hard for you too, feeling
left out . . ."

"Well . . ."

"Adam told me you were jealous."

Julie blinked. "Jealous," she said.

"In a special-friends kind of way," I added.

"Jealous. Huh." Julie tossed her head, in what might have been a sideways nod. "Oh-*kay*."

"So how are things with your mechanic?" I asked, trying to sound positive. "Reggie."

Julie made a seesawing gesture with her hand.

"Not so good?"

Julie shrugged. "He called me a couple weeks ago, after one of his friends
gave my car a tow. It was the first I'd heard from him since, well, since the
last time we were together. We've been having fun, but . . ." She shrugged
again. "It could still turn out to have been a mistake. Probably will, in fact."

After lunch, I went and hung out at Julie's apartment for several hours. It was the best, most relaxed visit I'd had there in over a year, and when I finally went home it was with a renewed sense that, yes, things were definitely looking up. I realize now that this was naive—that even if nothing else had happened, there would still have been plenty more problems with Julie and Penny both. But just then, and for the time being, I was blissfully, naively serene.

My serenity lasted about twenty hours, until Sunday afternoon, when I killed Warren Lodge.

After that, things started to get bad again in a hurry.

14

I was coming out of Magic Mouse Toys when I saw him, head down, hands jammed in his pockets, face buried deep in a blue jersey hood: a cougar in Pioneer Square.

After breakfast on Sunday I decided to take a day trip into Seattle. I wanted to get away from Autumn Creek for a while, to not be home if Penny or even Julie decided to call. I also thought it would be a good opportunity to make things up to those souls in the house who'd felt short-changed on time outside recently. So as I waited at the Metro bus stop on Bridge Street, I called Angel and Rhea out to the pulpit and asked them each to think of something they'd like to do in the city.

Predictably, before Angel and Rhea had even had time to start considering possibilities, Jake, Adam, Aunt Sam, Drew, Alexander, and Simon all came crowding onto the pulpit as well, each clamoring for their own time in the body. Pretending to be surprised, I reminded them all that they'd already had their special outside time, during that first trip to Poulsbo to visit Dr. Grey. "Angel and Rhea are the only ones who didn't get a turn. Fair is fair."

"Fair is *not* fair," Simon complained. "The only outside time *I* got on that trip was five minutes on a stupid ferryboat. I didn't get to *pick* what I wanted to do. What I *wanted* to do was go to the Westlake Center mall. What I *wanted* to do—"

As I say, this reaction was predictable, and I'd already discussed it with my father when I'd asked his permission for this special outing. Now, following my father's advice, I hushed Simon and laid down the law: "All right," I said, "these are the rules. Everybody gets to pick *one* thing that they want to do in Seattle. It has to be something within reason; it has to be in downtown, so we don't spend the whole day traveling around the city; and it can't take more than ten minutes or cost more than two dollars. Because they got skipped last time, Angel and Rhea's choices take precedence, and they get twenty minutes and four dollars each. Finally"—I focused in on Simon—"anyone who complains, gets impatient, or is rude not only forfeits their choice, they also spend the rest of the day in the house, locked in their room."

Drew still wanted to go to the aquarium, and Rhea decided that was a neat idea, so that was our first stop. The Seattle Aquarium, conveniently, is divided into two buildings; Rhea got to visit the seahorses, the tropical fish, and the giant octopus, while Drew checked out the salmon hatchery and the marine mammals. Next came rides on the waterfront streetcar: Angel rode from the Aquarium stop out to Pier 70; Alexander got the body for the return trip. We got off at Occidental Park, in Pioneer Square, where Aunt Sam found a café that served chocolate-covered croissants for $1.95.

It was a little after noon now. Simon still wanted to go to Westlake Center. Adam was the only soul who hadn't totally made up his mind, but he suggested that, if he couldn't just go into a bar and have a beer—and he couldn't—he might want to visit a "special" bookstore he knew of on Pike Street.

Both of those places were at the opposite end of downtown from where we now were, so it was Jake's choice that came next: a stop at Magic Mouse Toys. This is Jake's favorite Seattle toy store. It's smaller than FAO Schwarz, but the selection is good and includes a lot more items in Jake's typical price range.

Not that Jake really needed to spend any money. There's a trick most souls can do, that Jake has a special knack for: by holding an object in his hands, studying it from every angle, he can bring it inside, creating an imaginary copy of it in the house. This is a great way to acquire luxuries that you can't otherwise afford, and, if used more generally, it would probably cut down a lot on the real-world clutter that makes life as a multiple so cumbersome. But the trick has its limits. It works best with simple objects, or complex objects that can be *thought of* simply—a rocking horse or an electric train set being much easier to bring inside than, say, a jigsaw puzzle. Also, not all souls are equally skilled copiers—Aunt Sam and I are both pretty good at it, but my father is surprisingly bad (building the house and the geography, he says, is enough creation for one lifetime), and Adam, to his eternal chagrin, can't do it at all. Jake is a natural at it, but like most five-year-olds, he's also greedy: given a choice between real toys and imaginary ones, he wants both. So I knew that however many stuffed animals and tin soldiers he duplicated, he'd ultimately find something to spend his two dollars on.

I entered the store on the lower level, where most of the more expensive toys are kept, and turned Jake loose. He made a quick pass by the model trains; most of the locomotives and train cars were ones he already had copies of, but there were some new pieces of model scenery that he spent a moment absorbing. Then he moved on to the board games section.

To better entice passing children, Magic Mouse keeps open demonstration copies of many of the games it sells, and on a previous visit, Jake had become fascinated with one of these, a German import called The A-Maze-Ing Labyrinth. The price was twenty-five dollars, way beyond Jake's means, but he'd been trying—unsuccessfully so far—to copy it.

Board games are hard to duplicate inside. Even the most basic ones tend to have a lot of details to memorize, and chance elements, like die-rolling, raise thorny metaphysical problems. This particular game was especially detail-heavy: the labyrinth of the title was constructed from several dozen cardboard tiles, all different, which got shifted around during play. There were cards, too—just thinking about it makes my head hurt. But Jake was determined to possess the game, in installments if necessary. He squatted down by the demo copy, which was on a low shelf, picked up a handful of maze tiles, and concentrated.

"Now, you know," a voice boomed, "the required number of players is written on the side of the box."

Jake startled and dropped the tiles. A salesclerk, an older man with glasses and a goatee, had come up beside him. I'm sure the clerk was only intending to be helpful, but having an adult stand over him—tower over him, from his small soul's point of view—is inherently terrifying for Jake. "Wh-what?" he stammered.

"The required number of players," the salesclerk repeated. He tapped the side of the game box. "It's written right here, along with the recommended age range and other useful information."

"Oh-oh-*kay*," said Jake.

The clerk nodded and wandered away.

Jake picked up the tiles again.

"Have you been to the store before?" the clerk asked, reappearing. Jake let out a cry and, losing his balance, started to fall over; the clerk caught his arm to steady him.

"What is it you want?" I asked, standing up. Jake had left the body the moment the clerk touched him.

"I asked whether you'd been in the store before," the clerk said, smiling pleasantly, oblivious to the distress he'd just caused.

"Yes," I said, "we've been here before."

"Ah," said the clerk. "Then I don't have to tell you about Take Off."

"Take off?" I said, and for a dark moment wondered whether this pushy man really was a salesclerk after all. "Take off *what?*"

"Take Off, the airplane travel game," the clerk replied, indicating another, more prominent board-game display. "It's our most popular seller, by far."

"Oh," I said. "Well, that's nice, but . . . the fact is I'm interested in *this* game, over here, and I'd really prefer it if you left me alone."

"Of course," the clerk said, unperturbed. He nodded and wandered away again.

"Jake?" I said, turning back to the cardboard labyrinth. "Do you want to give it another try?" He didn't; his concentration was shattered, and he was so spooked that it was all I could do to coax him back out onto the pulpit. "It's all right, Jake; we'll go upstairs now."

Magic Mouse's upper floor is largely devoted to novelties, things like Silly Putty and Pez dispensers. I browsed, picking up various items and commenting on them in a leisurely tone of voice. Eventually Jake calmed down enough that I was able to pique his interest with something: a spotted yo-yo that made a mooing sound as it traveled up and down its string. It cost more than two dollars, but I bought it for him anyway.

With the yo-yo in my pocket, I stepped out of the store onto First Avenue. "My turn next," Simon said. "Your turn next," I agreed, trying to decide whether to catch a bus or just walk to Westlake Center.

It was then, as I stood distracted on the sidewalk, that a tall figure in a hooded blue jersey brushed past me, headed south along First Avenue. The man—I assumed it was a man—jostled me as he went by; ordinarily I might have ignored this, but coming so soon after the incident with the salesclerk it made me angry, and I called after him: "Hey!"

He didn't break stride or turn around; he gave no sign of having heard me at all, just kept walking, crossing Yesler Way against the light. Which might have been the end of it, except that on the far side of Yesler, two other men were loading an antique wardrobe into the back of a truck. As he stepped onto the far curb, the man in the blue jersey looked up, so that his face was momentarily reflected in the mirrors on the wardrobe doors. It was only a brief glimpse, and the man's face was still partially obscured by the jersey hood. But I recognized him.

Warren Lodge.

I didn't really believe it at first. He'd been on the run for ten days, and by now I would have expected him to have left the state, if not the country—the Canadian border is only a hundred miles away, after all. Then too, I'd only ever seen him on TV, and as a picture in the newspaper; to literally bump into him on the street, in the flesh, was like spotting the boogeyman on line at the post office.

But as the blue-jerseyed figure ducked past the men with the wardrobe, Adam, who'd gotten the same glimpse I had, spoke up from the pulpit. "It's him," he said.

You know that sensation when you're going along, not really paying attention to the weather, and all at once the sun goes under a cloud, and with the sudden dimming of the light you find yourself in a different landscape than the one you were walking through a second ago? This was like that: in an instant, the whole character of the day changed.

"You're sure?" I said.

"It's him," said Adam. "It's Warren Lodge."

Then Simon—who didn't know or care who Warren Lodge was, but was smart enough to guess that the afternoon's itinerary had just been revised—chimed in: "Hey! What's the holdup? It's *my turn* now!"

"Go to your room, Simon."

What do you do when you spot a cougar running loose on a city street? That's easy: get the police. But looking around me I couldn't see any, not even a traffic cop. There *were* some tough-looking civilians—the wardrobe-movers, for example—and I suppose I could have tried to enlist their help in detaining Warren Lodge, but even if that had occurred to me, it would have taken time to explain what I wanted . . . and meanwhile the figure in the blue jersey was getting away.

I started after him.

"Andrew," Adam said, "what the hell are you— Shit! Watch out!"

The light for the Yesler Way crossing was still red, and as I stepped out into the street, a car very nearly ran me down. Fortunately the driver was more attentive than I was and slammed on the brakes.

"Andrew," Adam tried again, when we were safely across the street, "what are you doing?"

"Following him," I said, "what do you think? That's Warren Lodge, we've got to catch him!"

"Catch him? Are you crazy? We've got to get the police. Let *them* catch him."

"I don't see any police here, do you?"

"So go to a pay phone—right there, there's one. *Call* the police."

"Not until I know where he's going."

Warren Lodge was half a block ahead of me now, still heading south. I made an amateurish attempt to hide the fact that I was tailing him, pausing every few yards to stare into the window of whatever building I was passing, whether or not there was anything to see. If Warren Lodge had looked behind him even once, it would have taken him all of three seconds to figure out what I was really up to.

But he never did look back; just kept plodding forward steadily, block after block. Then, as he neared the intersection of First Avenue and King, he suddenly pulled up short, seeing something that he didn't like. He darted across the Avenue and vanished around the corner.

I hurried to the end of the block. Off to the right, I saw what had frightened Warren Lodge: a police car sat parked by the curb. But it was empty, and there was no sign of the officers who'd left it there.

I turned left, looking down King Street in the direction Warren Lodge had run. The sidewalk was empty all the way to the Amtrak station, two and a half blocks away. I broke into a jog, checking side streets and alleyways as I went, but reached the train station without catching sight of him again. Intent on picking up the trail before it went completely cold, I ignored a side door that said SECURITY OFFICE and entered the main terminal on my own.

"This is *really* dumb, Andrew," Adam said. "I mean, he's not going to be in here, but it's really dumb anyway."

King Street Station is small, and it took me less than a minute to check the lobby and the passenger waiting area. I got excited when I spotted someone in a sports jersey standing at the ticket counter, but it turned out to be a woman with short hair.

By now my father had got wind that something was up. "What's going on out here?" he said, following Seferis onto the pulpit. "Simon is running all over the house complaining that he's been cheated."

"We saw Warren Lodge," I told him.

"You saw Warren Lodge? On the street?" He looked out, taking in our surroundings. "So what are we doing in a train station? Why aren't you talking to the police right now?"

"Andrew decided to make a citizen's arrest," Adam explained helpfully.

"He *what?*"

My father is a difficult soul to ignore even when he isn't hopping mad, but for just a moment, I pretended he didn't exist. "Adam," I said, "where do you suppose Warren Lodge was going on First Avenue?"

"I don't know," said Adam. "Maybe nowhere."

"What do you mean?"

"Well he's a fugitive now, right? The cops are watching his house, and they've probably frozen his bank and credit accounts. So if he can't go home, and he's got no money—"

"Homeless," I said. "So you think he might just be roaming around Pioneer Square?"

"Could be. Which is another reason why you don't need to chase after him personally, because sooner or later—"

"So if he got scared, and wanted to go somewhere around here where he could lose himself in a crowd for a while, where would that be?"

Adam didn't say anything, but he didn't need to; I already knew the answer. It was a place I'd been to once already today: Occidental Park.

"Andrew," my father said, as I raced up Occidental Avenue. "Andrew, are you *hearing* me?"

"I can hear you," I said, "and I know you're upset with me, but—"

"Do you understand how dangerous this is? You're putting the whole house at risk."

"I'm not going to confront him," I promised. "I just want to find him, and then—"

"Andrew . . ."

"Wait," I said.

Occidental Park stretches the length of two city blocks. Its southern half is lined with art galleries and antique furniture stores, but its northern half is seedier, bordered on one side by a parking lot, and with its many wooden benches it is a natural gathering spot for homeless people.

"Andrew . . ."

"There!"

He was sitting alone at the northernmost edge of the park. The hood of his jersey was still pulled up, and he was hunched over, as if sick or in pain, but it was him. Adam confirmed it.

"All right," I said. "*Now* we call the police."

There was a pay phone not far from where I was standing. I went to use it, but before I could dial 911 I noticed another of the park's occupants—a homeless man with a very long beard and even longer hair, like a desert island castaway—approaching the bench where Warren Lodge was sitting. The castaway, a true schizophrenic, came up shouting and waving his arms;

Warren Lodge jolted upright in alarm, slid sideways off the bench, and ran out of the park, fleeing along Washington Street.

"Damn it!" I said, setting the phone receiver back on its hook. By the time I got onto Washington Street myself, Warren Lodge was out of sight again. I ran east, uphill, for half a block . . . and found myself at a five-way intersection.

"All right, Andrew," my father said. "I want you to go back *now*, get to the phone—"

"But he can't have just disappeared!" I said, turning in place, searching in vain for a clue to which way he had gone.

I ended up facing south along the Second Avenue Extension. Most of the block on my side of the street was taken up by a furniture showroom; there was also a bus shelter at the curb about a third of the way down the block. Farther on, the Extension became an overpass that stretched above the railroad tracks, and there were steps leading down to King Street Station.

"The train station," I said. "Maybe he doubled back there . . ."

"That's not possible," said Adam.

"Why not?"

"Because," Adam said, obnoxiously, "to double back, he'd have to have gone there in the first place. But he didn't. You're the one who's running in circles."

"Adam—"

"Enough, Andrew," my father said. "Go back to the phone in the park; call the police."

"I will," I promised, heading towards the overpass instead. "I just want to check the train station one more time . . ."

Adam called out a warning then, but I was ignoring him and didn't listen. It took a few more seconds to realize my mistake: I'd thought the bus shelter was empty, but as I started to walk past it I saw that there was actually somebody inside, sitting hunched over . . .

"Just keep going," Adam said. "Pretend you don't see him." But I'd already stopped moving—and Warren Lodge had finally noticed me.

I was standing almost directly behind him, and the safety glass that formed the back of the bus shelter was between us, but he sensed me there anyway. He straightened up, and his head, still covered by the hood, turned sideways. I imagine he was wondering whether I was the castaway from the park, come to bother him some more.

He stood up.

My father and Adam both started yelling at me to run, and I felt Seferis straining forward, trying to take over the body. The funny thing was, though, I wasn't scared. I mean of course I was *scared*, I was fearful, but I wasn't *terrified*, the way you ought to be when a child-murderer turns his attention to you.

Maybe I wanted to get his attention; maybe that's why I wasn't terrified. I'd told my father I wasn't going to confront Warren Lodge, but I think now that subconsciously, that was really my intention all along. Not to make a citizen's arrest, as Adam had suggested, but to be there when he was arrested, and to look him in the eye before he was taken away and punished—to condemn him, and also just to see what there was to see, to satisfy my curiosity, the same curiosity that had made my father want to read Mrs. Winslow's letters.

Well, I was going to get my chance now: he was on his feet, and he was turning around. The fact that he wasn't in handcuffs yet didn't concern me nearly as much as it should have. I stood my ground. And then we were face to face, with only a thin panel of glass between us.

He was a sorry sight for a predator. His eyes were puffy with exhaustion, and his chin was covered with a patchy, uneven layer of stubble, as if he'd started shaving and then thought better of it. The scratch on his forehead— the one he'd supposedly gotten wrestling the big cat—was still there, and it had gone a fiery red. His nose was running.

Some cougar, I remember thinking. Then his lips moved, trying to frame a question—"Who . . . ?" or maybe "What . . . ?"—and I realized he was afraid, much more afraid than I was. For some reason this infuriated me; I wanted to slap him, but instead I shouted his name, "WARREN LODGE," and I raised my arm and pointed at him and said, "We know what you did."

Or at least I started to say it. I don't know if I got all the words out, because when I raised my arm to point, Warren Lodge began backing up. Maybe his eyes tricked him; maybe he saw my finger and thought I was aiming a gun at him. But whatever the reason, he took a step back, and another, and another, and another. The fourth step took him over the curb, into the street, and that's when the van hit him.

There was no warning, no horn or screech of brakes, just a green blur that came in from the side and swept up Warren Lodge with a loud bang. He never saw it coming; his attention was fixed on me right up until the moment he suddenly went away.

A period of confusion followed. I heard a squeal or a scream, and another bang, and a crash of glass, and some other sounds too, but it was difficult to place them all. My vision became choppy, as if I were watching a movie riddled with bad splices.

The next clear impression I had, I was looking south towards the overpass again. Someone had parked a green van in the middle of the overpass, angling it sideways across two lanes, at the end of a long trail of skid marks; the van's nose was caved in, and steam hissed from under its crumpled hood. Closer in, to my right, someone—maybe the same vandal who'd trashed the van—had smashed one of the plate-glass windows on the furniture showroom.

I managed to draw a connection between the van and the green blur, but the significance of the broken window eluded me. I kept expecting to see Warren Lodge in the street or on the sidewalk, and when I couldn't find him in either of those places I got worried that he'd run off again. Maybe he was hiding behind the van. I got down on my hands and knees to see if I could see under it, but I was too far away, so I stood up again and took a few steps forward, and then I heard a sound to my right.

I was in front of the broken showroom window now. Inside, a living-room furniture set had been arranged on a stage; for added realism, a mannequin in a blue jersey had been placed on the sofa in a sleeping posture. It was a nice display, but everything was covered in broken glass, and some of the furniture had gotten wet, so that the colors on the sofa fabric were starting to run.

No, wait, that wasn't right . . . I was missing something. "Adam, what am I missing?" I said, and the mannequin sat up, and I saw that it had the head of a cougar, and the cougar's face was cut up and bloody, and there was a big chunk of glass sticking out the side of its neck, piercing the fabric of the blue jersey. The cougar tried to leap at me, but it tripped over the coffee table, and as it stumbled it opened its mouth to growl, but no sound came out, only a red gush, and then the movie hit another splice.

There was a sound of lapping water that became the growl of a diesel engine. I found myself staring down at my hands, and became aware by slow degrees that my hands were in my lap, that I was sitting down, and that the seat was in motion.

I looked up and saw that I was on a Metro bus. Outside, a familiar stretch of I-90 rolled by; the bus had just passed Issaquah and was headed towards Autumn Creek. The sky, which had been mostly clear a moment ago in Seattle, was now overcast.

I turned my attention to the other passengers on the bus. None of them seemed surprised or even interested by my sudden appearance in their midst.

Maybe I hadn't suddenly appeared. Maybe I'd simply fallen asleep and was now waking up. Of course, in order to fall asleep on the bus, I would first have to have *boarded* the bus, something I couldn't remember doing. Still, the idea was strongly appealing: if I'd slept, I might have dreamed, which could mean that whole incident with Warren Lodge was nothing but a nightmare . . .

No good. Thinking of the accident I flashed back on it, vividly: I saw the van strike Warren Lodge, heard the showroom window shatter, felt broken glass crunch beneath my feet as I went to look—

I was staring at my hands again.

"Last stop," the bus driver called. "Autumn Creek, last stop."

I looked up; the bus was stopped on Bridge Street. I got to my feet and tottered outside. On the sidewalk a cool damp wind was blowing—no rain or drizzle yet, just little bits of moisture in the breeze, like phantom dewdrops—and it cleared some of the fuzziness out of my head. A dull throbbing replaced it.

I leaned against a lamppost and closed my eyes. "Adam?" I called.

My father answered: "Go home, Andrew."

"All right," I agreed, too tired to say anything more.

It was exactly the sort of day when I would have expected Mrs. Winslow to be waiting for me at the Victorian's front door, but she wasn't. I fumbled out my key and let myself in.

"Mrs. Winslow?" A television was on, its volume blaring. I followed the sound to the kitchen. Mrs. Winslow was standing in the middle of the room, staring at the TV, her hands gripping the back of one of the kitchen chairs for support. She was crying; but I couldn't tell from her expression whether they were sad tears or happy tears. "Mrs. Winslow, are you—"

"Ssssshhhh!" Mrs. Winslow hissed, with a fierceness I'd never seen in her before.

I turned to the TV, and saw a black-and-white image of the same downtown Seattle sidewalk where I'd just been. There was the bus shelter, and the shattered showroom window; farther down the street, slightly out of frame, was the van with the caved-in nose.

"—thorities believe that Lodge may have committed suicide," a voice on the TV was saying. The view switched to a close-up of the wrecked van. "Charles Daikos, the driver of the vehicle, has admitted to police that he was attempting to retrieve his cell phone from underneath his seat when the accident took place, and cannot confirm whether Lodge stepped in front of the van deliberately. Daikos suffered minor facial injuries in the collision but was otherwise unharmed . . ." The view switched back to the showroom window. Police officers were milling around out front of the jagged hole in the glass, while inside, a pair of paramedics lifted a long gray bag onto a gurney.

Then the TV was off, and I was sitting at the table, warming my hands on a mug of coffee. Mrs. Winslow, her tears wiped away, stirred a spoon in a cup of tea.

"So," I said, the question feeling strangely out of context as I uttered it, "Warren Lodge is dead, then? *Definitely* dead?"

"Yes," Mrs. Winslow said. "Are you hungry, Andrew?"

We ate a quiet dinner together, after which I retreated to my rooms. This was a time of day when I ordinarily would give up the body for a while, so that other souls could play or read or listen to music. But this evening I forgot all about that, and spent hours pacing aimlessly. No one complained about the change in routine, not even Simon.

It got dark out. Around nine o'clock the telephone rang; Mrs. Winslow knocked on the sitting-room door and told me it was Penny calling. "Tell her I'm not home," I said.

More time went by. At some point I realized that my father was calling my name from the pulpit. He seemed to have been calling it for quite a while without my hearing him, which was strange, because you can't not hear things said from the pulpit—that's not even a house rule, it's just the way things work. My puzzlement at this was displaced by horror as I suddenly remembered how the blood had gushed from Warren Lodge's mouth.

"Andrew! . . . Andrew!"

"So much blood," I murmured. Then: "I killed him, didn't I? *I* killed him."

"No, Andrew," my father said. "It was an accident."

"I was chasing him . . ."

"You were following him."

". . . I chased him into the street."

"You recognized him, and he got scared. You didn't push him in front of the van. He stepped back on his own."

"He stepped back because I scared him. He—"

"It was an accident, Andrew. The only thing you did wrong was to put your own safety at risk—*our* safety at risk—by confronting Warren Lodge yourself instead of getting a policeman like I told you. That was stupid. That was *very* stupid, and very dangerous. But it wasn't evil."

"I don't know," I said. I raked a hand through my hair. "God, the police . . . I'm going to have to call them, aren't I? Call them and tell them—"

"No," my father said, very firmly.

"But they don't know what really happened. On the news, they said they think Warren Lodge committed suicide . . ."

"They think he *might* have committed suicide."

"But that's not true!"

"It's OK, though. They don't need to know exactly what happened."

"But witnesses are supposed to come forward. They're not . . . they're not supposed to leave the scene of an accident without telling what they saw." I faltered, wondering: *how* did I leave the scene? How did I get on the bus? "It's a rule."

"It is a rule, but going back now and trying to unbreak it could cause more trouble than it's worth."

I frowned. "Trouble for us, you mean."

"Yes."

"So you want me to not tell the truth to keep from getting into trouble. But isn't that selfish?"

"It's the best choice, Andrew. What happened today was an accident. An *accident.*"

I shook my head, but didn't say anything.

"I think," said my father, "I think you should try to sleep now."

"No," I said. "No, I'm not tired yet." That was a lie—I was exhausted, the body was exhausted—but the thought of being unconscious frightened me.

"Andrew. You need to rest . . ."

How did I get on the bus? Why couldn't I remember?

I must have thought it aloud.

"You fell into the lake," my father said.

"What?"

"When Warren Lodge . . . when he got up and tried to climb out of the window, you left the body and fell into the lake. Seferis had to take over. He got us away from the accident, got the body safe onto the bus."

"I fell?"

". . . into the lake. It's why you don't remember what happened. You were asleep under the waters. I had to get Captain Marco to fish you out."

"Are you saying I *lost time?*"

"A little more than an hour. You weren't in the lake that long, but it took a while to wake you up, and to keep you awake." He sighed. "I'm sorry I didn't tell you this earlier, but I thought it would be better to wait until after you'd had a chance to rest."

"But it can't be. I *can't* lose time."

"You aren't meant to," my father corrected me. "But what happened to Warren Lodge . . . that was an awful thing to have to see, an awful shock."

"This is terrible," I said. "*Terrible.* If I start losing time—"

"I'm concerned," my father admitted. "But it wasn't your fault, Andrew. You've never seen anyone d—"

"It's my responsibility to run the body. You told me a thousand times: I'm not supposed to give up control, no matter what."

"I know, but—"

"No matter what. You *told* me."

There was a long pause then. When my father spoke again, he said: "Tomorrow, after you get home from work, I want you to call Dr. Eddington for an appointment."

"Dr. Eddington?"

"Dr. Grey was right," my father said, as if it cost him something to admit it. "You do need somebody to talk to, somebody professional I mean."

I thought about it. "Could I . . . could I tell him about Warren Lodge? About what happened today?"

"Yes," my father said. "And about anything else you wanted to . . . Penny, Julie, whatever."

"All right."

"You should try to sleep now, Andrew."

"No." I shook my head. "I don't think I can. It, it's too much like blacking out again . . ."

"Just try. Lie down. Don't worry, I'll stay with you."

"All right."

I put the lights out and lay down, thinking I'd never be able to sleep now—and, as often happens when you think that, I soon became very drowsy. My father stayed in the pulpit, talking softly with me as I began to drift off.

"Father?" I asked at one point, very near the edge of sleep.

"Yes?"

"It *was* an accident, wasn't it?"

"Yes, it was."

"OK," I said, finally believing it. But then another question came to me, why and from where I don't know, and even now I can't say whether I really asked it or only dreamed that I did: "Father? . . . Did Andy Gage's stepfather have an accident, too?"

And to that, no answer, only the lapping of the water on the shores of the lake, as I slid down imperceptibly into sleep.

15

I woke the next morning wondering for the second time whether I'd dreamed the whole thing, whether Warren Lodge's death had just been a nightmare; but an uncommon silence from the pulpit and the house told me that I hadn't, and it wasn't. When I went into the bathroom to start the morning ritual, Jake wouldn't come out to do the tooth-brushing; Seferis, running through his exercise routine, twice lost count of his sit-ups; and Adam and Aunt Sam, while still insisting on their shower privileges, didn't try to wheedle extra time the way they usually did.

Even Mrs. Winslow was acting out of sorts: I came out to breakfast to find she'd fixed us a single large helping of scrambled eggs and toast. "Oh goodness," she exclaimed, realizing her mistake even as she set the plate down in front of me.

"It's all right," I said. "I don't think the others are that hungry this morning."

"Are you sure, Andrew?"

"Yes." In fact Adam was already objecting, but when I ignored him he quickly gave up, and nobody else made a peep.

Mrs. Winslow sat down to her own breakfast. We chatted while we ate, same as we always did—about what, I honestly can't say, only that Warren Lodge was never mentioned—and after I cleaned my plate, my father came out for his usual mug of coffee. So that much at least was normal. But still there was something else missing, and as I was getting up to go I realized what it was: Mrs. Winslow had never turned on the morning news.

"Do you think she knows?" I asked Adam.

"About what really happened yesterday?" Adam snorted. "How could she?"

"I don't know. But—"

"She doesn't *always* listen to the news."

"But today of all days, not to—"

"Probably she just doesn't want to hear about how he killed his kids for the millionth time—you know they're going to rehash the whole story again."

"Well . . ." I had to admit, it made sense. "I suppose."

"I'll tell you something else, though," Adam added. "You owe me a breakfast."

"Adam . . ."

"Because *I'm* not upset about what happened."

I thought he probably was upset, though. Maybe it was only that my father had warned him not to, but it seemed to me that if Adam were really happy about how Warren Lodge had died, he'd have made a lot more jokes about it.

I said good-bye to Mrs. Winslow and set off for work. Coming onto Bridge Street, I had a bad scare: I saw a green van parked out front of the Autumn Creek Café. It was the wrong shade of green, and it had a roof rack and chrome trim where the van that had hit Warren Lodge had had neither, but still I stopped dead when I saw it. I waited; when the van didn't fade away like a mirage, I went up to it cautiously. I put out a hand, and touched one of its side panels.

There was a tremendous crash of glass. I whirled around: a deliveryman had just dropped several racks of bottled ice teas off the back of his truck. A passing group of kids on their way to school broke out in applause.

I bent over and vomited up most of my breakfast onto the sidewalk. This brought another wave of applause from the school kids; I half expected Adam to join in, but the pulpit was empty.

Penny was waiting in my tent when I arrived at the Factory. She looked like she wanted to have a long talk, and I tried to discourage her: I broke into a big yawn in the middle of saying hello, and pinched the bridge of my nose as if I had a headache.

"Are you all right?" Penny asked me.

"I didn't sleep very well," I told her. "Can I help you with something?"

She bit her lower lip nervously. "I'm going to call Dr. Eddington," she announced.

"I know. My father told me you'd decided to make an appointment. That's good news."

"No," Penny said. "I mean I'm going to call him this morning—right now. And I was wondering if . . . if you wanted to call him with me."

"With you?"

"Well . . . I remember Dr. Grey wanted you to make an appointment with Dr. Eddington too, so I thought maybe we could both—"

"Oh," I said. "Oh . . . no. No thank you." Of course I *did* intend to call Dr. Eddington, but right then, I didn't want to. "I'm not ready to call him yet."

"Oh . . ."

"Penny," I said. "You know it's all right. Dr. Eddington's a good person. You shouldn't be afraid to call him yourself."

"OK," she said. "All right." Her teeth came together again, not just biting her lower lip but worrying it, and I knew she was going to ask me if she could talk to my father. But neither he nor I was up for that, so I said hurriedly, "Is there anything else?" and gestured at my desk as if I had an important project to get to. Penny, taking the hint, shook her head no.

About an hour later, feeling guilty, I went by Penny's tent to see if she was OK. She was on the phone when I poked my head in; I listened, unnoticed, until I heard Dr. Eddington's name. *That's all taken care of, then,* I thought to myself as I ducked out again. *Penny will be in good hands now.* What I'd told her was true: Dr. Eddington *was* a good person, and a good doctor. I'd be calling him myself soon . . . only maybe not today. Today I didn't feel well.

In fact I felt so poorly that I decided to sneak out of work early. In the middle of the afternoon, as I returned from dumping a load of Honey Bucket waste out behind the shed, I saw Reggie Beauchamps's tow truck parked on the Factory lot. Reggie sat in the truck cab, alone, smoking a cigarette and listening to the radio, looking bored, and I thought . . . well, what I thought isn't really important. But I *knew* I didn't want to be there to see Julie go jumping up on him again. My head was aching for real now, and my stomach was an empty pit from throwing up breakfast and having forgotten to eat lunch, so I decided to get out of there. I snuck off the lot through a hole in the back fence so I wouldn't have to go by Reggie's truck.

Back at the Victorian, Mrs. Winslow was waiting with a freshly baked chocolate cake. As I sat in the kitchen and stuffed myself, I told Mrs. Winslow that I wasn't feeling well, and asked if she would please tell anybody who called that I wasn't available.

"I'll tell you what, Andrew," Mrs. Winslow said. "I'm a little under the weather myself. So I think I'm going to leave the phone off the hook this evening." And she did.

That night, I dreamed I was floating over the landscape in Andy Gage's head. Viewed from above, the dream-geography formed a series of concen-tric rings, from the outermost circle of dark forest-green to the rough gray bull's-eye of Coventry. I hovered over the island, expecting at any moment to see the face of Gideon leering up at me. But Gideon never appeared, and eventually I began to wonder why. In the dream, Coventry was a barren rock, with no buildings or caves for a soul to hide in. Where was he? I dropped lower, intending to make a careful search, but even as I did so, the mist sprang up, boiling off the lake; it obscured my view, and then I woke up to the sound of rain hissing against my bedroom windows.

By dawn the rain had stopped. It was still overcast as I walked to work, but the forecast promised sunshine by midmorning, and it did look as though the clouds were thinning. As for myself, I decided I felt better than yesterday; and I told myself I would definitely call Dr. Eddington today, by afternoon at the latest.

I came to the Factory and found Julie on the lot, sitting in her Cadillac, much as Reggie Beauchamps had been sitting in his truck the day before. Julie wasn't smoking or listening to the radio, though, just sitting. She looked like she'd been crying.

"Julie?" I said, approaching the car slowly so as not to startle her. She swung her head around lethargically and cranked her window down. Her eyes were bloodshot and red-rimmed: she *had* been crying. "Julie . . . what happened?"

Stupid question. Julie's cheeks colored, and her lips twisted in the way they did when she was about to say something really sarcastic. But she didn't say it. She took some deep breaths, and got her temper under con-trol. "Nothing," she finally told me. Then: "Reggie."

"Oh."

"As predicted."

"Oh."

There was an awkward pause, and then Julie said: "Do you feel like blowing off work today?"

I wasn't sure if this was a proposal or just a reference to my recent absen-teeism. "Um . . ."

"We could play hooky," said Julie. "Just go somewhere, take the whole day. What do you think?" I must have glanced over at the shed, because she added: "Don't worry about Dennis and Irwin; they don't really need us."

"I know," I replied, more readily than was tactful. "I mean . . . OK. Sure."

I climbed in the car. As I was pulling the door shut, Julie said: "Just one rule—we don't talk about Reggie." I was happy to agree to that. "So where should we go?" Julie asked me.

"I don't know," I said. "Did you have someplace in mind?"

She shook her head. "I don't want to go into Seattle, and I'd like to get away from here, but beyond that . . ."

"Mount St. Helens." The words just popped out. Mount St. Helens was one of those local tourist attractions I'd always thought of going to without necessarily *wanting* to go there, if you know what I mean. It was just something to say.

But Julie took the suggestion seriously. "OK," she said, and nodded. "Mount St. Helens it is." She leaned forward and keyed the ignition; the Cadillac started without a hitch. "Good omen," Julie said, smiling. "Next stop, Mount St. Helens . . ."

On Bridge Street, just before the west bridge, we passed Penny's Buick going the other way. I waved, and I think Penny saw me, but before she could wave back, Julie stepped on the gas.

"Uh, Julie," I said, as we sped across the bridge, "don't you think we should have stopped and told Penny where we're going?"

"Nah," said Julie. "This is *our* day out."

Because Julie had no road maps in her car—none for Washington state, anyway—we were forced to guess at our route: south on Interstate 5 until we saw a sign for Mount St. Helens National Park, then turn left, or possibly right (hopefully the sign would give a hint) onto the road that actually led to the volcano. It was a much longer drive than either of us anticipated, and we groaned aloud when, having finally reached the turn off, we discovered we still had another fifty miles to go. But it was good-natured groaning—we were still having fun, then.

We stopped for lunch at a visitor center high up on the mountain road. A scenic overlook offered panoramic glimpses of our goal: Mount St. Helens, swept by storm clouds, drifted in and out of view at the end of a long river valley. It was beautiful but not especially inviting, and rather than drive closer we decided to stay where we were, in the sunshine. We got a blanket out of the Cadillac's trunk and spread it on the grass, and sat down to watch the day go by.

"This is nice," Julie said, sighing contentedly. "Let's stay here forever, Andrew."

"OK," I replied. "I'll build us a cabin."

"Yeah . . ." With another sigh she lay down, resting her head in my lap. I tried not to move—I was sitting back, propped on my arms, not a comfortable position to maintain for long, but I thought if I could just keep still, Julie might fall asleep.

The weather betrayed me before my triceps could. The clouds obscured Mount St. Helens completely, and started heading our way; Julie sat up again, smelling a downpour in the wind. "We'd better head back," she said. "If it rains like last night, the car's not going to be happy."

It didn't rain; the clouds remained in the mountains as we returned to the highway. There was, however, plenty of traffic: I-5 was stop-and-go from Olympia northwards, so the car wasn't happy anyway, and soon neither were we. We were passing Tacoma when the Cadillac's engine coughed and died. Julie quickly got it restarted, but that was only the first of several stalls, each one requiring greater efforts of resuscitation. After the fifth or sixth—we were alongside Boeing Field now, almost within sight of Seattle's skyscrapers—we sat so long I thought for sure we were going to have to abandon the car and find a phone.

But Julie wouldn't hear of calling Triple A; with her luck, she knew which tow-truck driver they'd send to get us. "I will get out and *push* this car back to Autumn Creek if I have to," she said. The Caddy seemed to accept that; it started on the next try, and ran smoothly the rest of the way home.

We got back to Autumn Creek a little before five o'clock. I figured Julie would go straight to her apartment, or maybe swing by the Factory; instead, she found a parking space on Bridge Street outside her favorite bar.

"I could really use a drink," she said. "How about you?"

The correct answer to this question, of course, was "No thank you." Drinking was still against the rules of the house, and by this point in my life, experience argued against it as well: every other time I'd had alcohol—all three times with Julie—I'd ended up regretting it. Really, I knew better.

So I have no excuse for the bad choice I made then. I suppose I could try to blame it on lingering shock at having witnessed Warren Lodge's death; or on Adam, my father, and the other souls in the house, not one of whom spoke up to try to stop me—the pulpit was empty and had been all day, so that, sitting there in the car, I almost felt the way a singular person must feel, with no other selves to answer to. But these things don't even hold up as explanations, much less as justifications. The real reason—not excuse— was Julie herself: the way I felt about her; the way I'd felt when she laid her head in my lap on the mountain; and the way I still hoped, given the right combination of circumstances, she might come to feel about me.

"Sure," I said. "I'll have a drink with you."

We started with a pitcher of beer, then at Julie's recommendation moved on to depth charges, mugs of lager into which shot glasses of bourbon had been dropped like underwater mines. By the time we switched to straight scotch, Julie had broken her own taboo and started telling me all about her breakup with Reggie Beauchamps. It was difficult to listen to. Julie got really worked up, railing about what a bastard Reggie was . . . and against all logic, I felt myself getting jealous, envying the intensity of her feelings for him, even though it was a negative intensity.

Julie sensed my discomfort, and stopped. "Sorry," she apologized. "I wasn't supposed to talk about him."

"It's all right," I told her.

"No, it isn't. It upsets you."

"It doesn't upset me," I lied. "It's just . . . I don't understand. If he makes you as unhappy as you say, and you *knew* he was going to make you unhappy, after what happened the last time you were together . . . why did you hook up with him a second time? I mean isn't the whole idea of going out with somebody that you at least *think* you're going to enjoy it?"

Julie gave me a rueful smile. "Now you're being rational . . ."

"Seriously, Julie—"

"*Seriously*, Andrew . . . Look, I don't mean to make it sound like it was *all* bad. I mean we did have some fun, before Reggie reverted to being a shit . . ."

"OK, then," I said. "I still don't really get it, but OK."

Julie sighed. "You don't get it because you're more together than I am, Andrew. You're smarter than me." I made a face at that, but Julie insisted: "It's true. You are more together than me. And I'm not the only person who says so. Penny thinks you're really together . . . Penny thinks you're great."

I frowned. "Why do you keep doing that, Julie?"

"Doing what?"

"Talking about Penny like there's something romantic between us."

"Well, she does like you . . ."

I shook my head. "I don't think so, Julie. Not like that."

"Come on, Andrew. I saw the way she kissed you."

"And I told you, that wasn't her."

"Well it was *one* of her," Julie argued. Then: "Honestly, you don't think you'd make a good couple?"

"Based on what? The fact that we're both multiple?"

"Well . . ." Julie shrugged. "You have to admit . . ."

"Penny's an unstable multiple, Julie. It'd be like dating a mental patient. I don't know, maybe *you* should go out with her."

I was worried I'd crossed the line with that remark, but Julie responded with a grin, actually conceding the point. "Maybe," she acknowledged. "Penny's not my type, though."

"Well she's not my type, either. I mean I think she's basically a nice person, and once she gets through therapy I'm sure she'll make a good girlfriend for somebody, but . . . not me."

"OK," Julie said. She looked down at her glass, which was empty. "You want another round?"

"I shouldn't . . . Do you?"

"I've got a bottle back at my place," Julie suggested. "We could go there."

"OK."

We paid our tab and went outside. The sun was still out, which was very disorienting; I'd never been drunk in daylight before. I went to look at my watch to see how late it was, and stopped in surprise: my wrist was bare. Thinking I must have left the watch in the bar, I started to turn back.

Then I noticed Julie standing beside her Cadillac. "Hey," I called to her. "Julie, come on . . . you know you can't drive now."

"Hmm?" She glanced at me, then waved a hand dismissively. "Don't worry," she said, "the fucking thing probably wouldn't start, anyway." Her mouth set in an angry line. "The fucking thing . . . shit car, shit boyfriend, shit business plan. I really am a complete fuckup, aren't I?"

"If you are, Julie," I said, "it's not because you have to be." She didn't seem to hear that, which, upon reflection, was just as well.

"Fucking thing," Julie cursed her car once more. Then she said: "Come on, let's get out of here before I put some new dents in it."

We walked back to her building. Upstairs in her apartment, Julie made a beeline for the cupboard above her kitchen sink, taking down an unopened bottle of scotch. As she cracked the seal and filled two glasses, I thought about passing; I'd obviously already had my limit. But when she handed me a glass and said "Cheers," I drank.

Bringing the bottle with her, Julie went into her bedroom. I followed her.

"I'm going to take a shower," Julie announced.

"Huh?"

"I'm going to take a shower." Julie set the bottle and her glass on top of the dresser, and got a robe from her closet. "Just hang out," she told me. "I'll only be a few minutes."

She headed off to the bathroom, leaving me to wonder whether it was really strange, her deciding to take a shower right now, or if it only seemed strange because I was drunk. Pondering the matter, I took a sip of my scotch, which all of a sudden tasted terrible. "Gah," I exclaimed. "Enough." I set the glass down firmly on top of the dresser.

I sat on the futon and stared out the bedroom window. The sky outside was still bright, with just a hint of approaching nightfall. I checked Julie's alarm clock: 6:47 P.M. Mrs. Winslow would have started dinner by now, I thought, and then I remembered that I hadn't called to let her know where I was. She'd be worried.

I berated myself for the oversight. I'd better call, tell her that I was all right . . . or maybe I should just go home. Of course, if I went home now, Mrs. Winslow would know that I'd been drinking. She probably wouldn't say anything about it, but she'd be disappointed in me; she knew my father's rules as well as I did. So maybe I shouldn't go home. Maybe I should stay here awhile, sober up.

Absently, I raised my arm and took another sip of scotch. This time it didn't taste so bad—in fact, it didn't taste like anything—but even as I swallowed I found myself staring at the glass in my hand, confused. I thought: what's wrong with this picture?

I might have figured it out, but just then Julie returned from the shower, bringing her own logic puzzle. I distinctly remembered her taking a robe to the bathroom, but now coming back she was wrapped only in a towel. As a fashion choice it was beyond criticism—with the bare skin of her upper chest and shoulders still flushed from the heat of the shower, she was almost indescribably lovely—but the question remained: what happened to the robe?

Julie went to the dresser and picked up her glass. The arch of her neck as she drank had me mesmerized; I tried to think of a way to tell her how gorgeous she looked that wouldn't imply any inappropriate feelings on my part.

"So," Julie said, turning to face me, "you think I'm a fuckup."

I blinked. "What?"

"What you said outside the bar, when I asked if I was a complete fuckup . . ." Oh great. She had heard that. "'If you are, it's not because you have to be . . .' If you are. Meaning I am, right?"

"No! No, Julie, I—"

"It's all right," Julie said. "I'd rather you be honest with me, and if you think—"

"I *don't* think you're a fuckup, Julie. I think . . . you're impractical—"

"Impractical. Hmmph."

"—and sometimes it seems like you set out to frustrate yourself, and I don't *get* that, but I also know that you're really talented, and really smart, and, and beautiful, and if your life isn't everything you want it to be right now, it's not because you're *condemned* to that . . . you have all the qualities you need to make things better, you just . . . need to pick a different strategy, is all . . ."

"A different strategy. Uh-huh." Julie was smiling guardedly now, a sign that she'd only been teasing me, but I went on babbling, alternating apologies with further compliments, until she finally took pity on me.

"Andrew," Julie said at last, setting her glass back on the dresser and coming over to the futon. "It's OK . . ."

"No, it isn't . . . you were depressed, and I wanted to say something to make you feel better, and instead—"

"I knew what you were trying to say, Andrew . . . more or less."

"I'm sorry, Julie."

"Andrew, shh, stop apologizing." She sat beside me on the futon, put an arm across my shoulders. "You're my best fucking friend, you know you are . . ." She reached up with her other hand to stroke the side of my face, and then I couldn't help myself: I leaned over and kissed her.

Julie didn't pull away; she kissed back, softly. We broke from that, and then I, emboldened, bent my head down and brushed my lips against the tops of her breasts. Julie tensed. "Andrew," she said, starting to object. "Andrew, wait . . ." I didn't wait. I raised my head again halfway and kissed a spot in the hollow of Julie's throat, the right spot I guess; all at once she was tense in a different way. "Andrew," she repeated, her voice different too. "Ah, shit . . ."

We ended up lying side-by-side on the futon. My hand was on Julie's bare skin, tracing the curve of her shoulder.

"This is a *bad* idea, Andrew," Julie said. She said it like she believed it but might also be willing to overlook the fact, which was all the encouragement I needed. My wish had come true: the window of opportunity had opened again, and this time I was not going to be too shy or indecisive to go through it.

I propped myself up on one elbow and leaned over, kissing Julie on the mouth, on the face, on the chest. She accepted the kisses passively at first, but then I found that magic spot on her throat again, and she said "Ah, shit . . ." and started to reciprocate. She grabbed me by the collar, shoved me over onto my back, and rolled on top of me. She kissed the hollow of *my* throat, nibbled on it. Her fingers found the top button of my shirt and undid it, then groped for the second button; I reached for her towel, which was already slipping. We began to wrestle, fighting over who would get to undress who first. I had the advantage—in addition to the fact that towels have no fasteners, I had the better upper-body strength. But Julie was wilier; she slipped a hand free and reached down, meaning to throw me off balance by grabbing between my legs.

And that's where things started to go wrong. Julie grabbed my crotch . . . and paused. A puzzled expression came over her face—the look of mild bafflement you get when you reach for a set of keys that you know you just put down, only to find that they're not where you thought they were. Julie's hand resumed its groping, more urgently now, and her puzzlement increased . . . where were those keys?

"Andrew," Julie said, drawing back from me a little, even as her hand continued its groping, "you're not . . . you don't have . . ."

"What?"

She made herself say it.

"Oh," I replied casually, as if she'd expressed surprise over my choice of underwear. "Oh yeah. I don't have . . . one of those."

"You don't . . ." Julie blinked, struggling to keep a game face. "Is that . . . part of the abuse? Did your stepfather . . . ?"

"What?" Then I laughed, getting it. "Oh no! No, nothing like that. Nothing was . . . cut off. The body's female, that's all."

"*What?*"

"The body is female," I repeated. "What—"

"No," Julie protested. "No, that can't . . . you said 'he.' You always say 'he.'"

"What?"

"When you talk about Andy Gage . . . the original Andy Gage . . . you always say 'he,' not 'she.'"

"Well . . . yeah."

"But if Andy Gage was a girl, then—"

"Julie . . ." Of all the times to start talking about metaphysics . . . but it seemed important to her, so I curbed my impatience. "I call Andy Gage 'he' because, well, because my father always does . . . and Adam, and Aunt Sam, and everybody else in the house too."

"But if Andy Gage was female . . ."

"His body was female, but his soul was male." I didn't actually know this for a fact, but it made the most sense—and I wasn't about to call my father out for confirmation.

"You said that souls and bodies were twins, though. Reflections of each other."

"In people who are singular. But—"

"But Andy Gage *was* singular. I mean he was the original soul, right? He . . . she . . . existed before the split. So—"

"Julie," I interrupted, "Julie, I don't want to be rude, but . . . why does this matter? I mean I'd be happy to talk about it *later*, but—"

"*Why . . . ?*" She let out a crazy laugh, a half-strangled chuckle. "Oh my God . . ."

"I mean I'm sorry if the body is not . . . not everything you'd like it to be, but I'm sure I can make up for . . . anything that's missing." I smiled, still believing that this was a minor misunderstanding that would soon be put behind us. "Just tell me what you want." I reached for her but she wriggled away. She backed up to the far end of the futon, gathering her towel tightly around her.

"Julie?" I said, finally growing alarmed. "Julie, what is it?"

I sat up and reached for her again, but Julie shouted "*Don't!*" and slapped my hand away, hard. I couldn't have been more stunned.

"I'm sorry, Andrew," Julie said stiffly. "I'm sorry, but please don't . . . please don't touch me."

"Julie . . ." I felt a familiar dash of ice water on my heart, a dash that became a torrent. It had happened again: one moment we'd been intimates, open and loving, and now . . . now the window was closed again, nailed shut, shuttered and barricaded. And I didn't understand. "Does it really matter so much? I mean it's still *me*, even if I don't have—"

Julie laughed that crazy laugh again. "*Yes*, Andrew," she said. "It matters."

"But . . . but it was *me* you were going to, to make love to, right? And you knew the body isn't a perfect reflection of my soul, so—"

"Andrew . . ."

"—so it's really only a question of degree, right? It's still *me*, Julie . . ."

"I'm not a lesbian, Andrew."

This was such a non sequitur that for a moment I was completely lost. "What?"

"I'm not a lesbian. I—"

"But . . . *I'm not a lesbian, either.*" I felt a brief, irrational surge of hope, that died when I saw Julie's expression hadn't changed. She didn't care whether I was a lesbian; she cared that Andy Gage's body was female. Case closed.

And still I struggled, trying to come up with a new line of argument, some way of convincing her that it really didn't matter. At a loss for words, I started to reach for her again, but Julie evaded my touch, getting up off the futon with such incredible speed that she seemed to have evaporated.

"I'm sorry, Andrew," Julie said. She was standing over by the dresser, facing away from me, and I tried to figure out how she'd gotten all her clothes back on so quickly. "I'm sorry . . . I know it shouldn't make a difference, and I wish I could be more open to . . . to . . . but it matters. It *does* matter. It matters, and I, I just can't . . . And besides," she added, looking over her shoulder at me, "it's still true what I said, the two of us getting together would be a bad idea, I mean even if . . . it would be a mistake. So maybe this is a sign, huh? One more sign that we're meant to be just friends, *good* friends, forever . . ."

"Friends." The word was a dry croak in my throat. I raised my glass and took a big swallow of scotch, felt it warming me, numbing me. "Friends," I repeated, bitterly. "I *love* you, Julie . . . I love you, and you know I'd treat you well, but you still pick *him* . . . him, and all the ones before, who, who treat you like shit . . ."

"I didn't pick him, Andrew," Julie said, shaking her head. "I *slept* with him, OK, but now we're broken up, and he's out of my life—"

"Sure, until next time."

"Would you really rather be in Reggie's shoes, Andrew? Sleep with me, but then *not* be friends?"

"I want *both!*" I shouted. I felt my eyes start to get wet. "You're always flattering me, telling me how wonderful I am, how *together* I am . . . if all that's true, if you mean it, why can't you love me? Why?"

She didn't answer, and I raised the bottle to my lips, took a long pull. The scotch backed up in my throat and I choked. When my vision cleared, Julie was no longer standing by the dresser; she was sitting on the floor by the window. Her eyes were red, just like they had been this morning.

"Why, Julie?" I repeated hoarsely. "Why can't you love me?"

She wouldn't look at me. "Andrew," she sighed, sounding on the verge of total exhaustion, "I don't . . . I don't know what more you want from me. I mean I've tried—"

"I want to know *why*. I want you to tell me—"

"Andrew, *please* . . . I'm *sorry*, OK? I'm sorry I've hurt you so badly, I'm sorry if . . . if you think this is intentional cruelty. It's not, at least I don't think it is, but . . . I don't know anymore. But I'm *tired*, Andrew . . . I'm tired, and I feel like I've explained myself a million times already, but you still won't accept it, and I just don't have the energy to make it a million and one times . . . so can't we just stop? Please?"

"A million times?" I said. "You haven't explained *anything*, Julie . . ."

Julie covered her face with her hands.

I took another drink from the bottle.

"Julie . . ." I began again, and then paused, distracted by the glow of a street lamp shining through the window above Julie's head. When I finally shook my attention free and looked down again, Julie was gone.

"Julie?" I looked over at the dresser, but she hadn't moved back there; she wasn't in the room anymore. Where had she disappeared to? "Julie?"

I got up. Actually, I got up twice; my first attempt to stand failed when the floor pitched up suddenly, thwacking me in the side of the head with Julie's futon mattress. The second time I moved more slowly, concentrating on balance, and managed to gain my feet.

I searched the entire apartment, calling Julie's name repeatedly. She was nowhere to be found. Finally I noticed that the apartment's outer door was ajar.

"Julie?" I stumbled onto the landing at the top of the rickety staircase, imagining I heard footsteps descending just ahead of me. But there was no one on the stairs, and the street-level door, visible only as a faint outline far below, was closed. I started down, too fast, and after only a few steps my balance went out again; I tripped and fell, the walls of the staircase seeming to fall away too, so that I landed outside, face down on an asphalt surface.

"Ju-ulie," I gasped, sprawling. My shirt, untucked, caught beneath my hip; I heard a tiny *click-click-click* as a button popped off and bounced away. Something wet splashed my wrist.

I rolled onto my side. My hand was still holding the scotch bottle, I saw. The bottle had survived the fall intact, but the violence of the motion had caused some of the contents to slosh out of the neck; that was the wetness I'd felt. The scotch tingled on my wrist, making it seem more awake than the rest of me. I brought my wrist to my face, rubbed some of the wetness on my cheeks and forehead. I took another drink.

"Julie?" Somehow I got to my feet again. I was standing in the middle of a street, the street in front of Julie's apartment or maybe a different one, I couldn't tell. It was full dark now, and my vision had become grainy, so it was hard to resolve shapes, even those that were lit by street lamps. On the sidewalk to my left, I thought I saw a person—a woman? Julie?—but when I moved towards her she dissolved, like an eidolon morphing into a flock of doves.

"Julie . . ." Where was I? I needed to find a street sign, something I could focus on. Reasoning that a street corner would be a good place to look, I picked a direction and started walking.

Or lurching, is more like it. My soul swung loose in the body, as if it were attached to Andy Gage by a web of elastic tethers. Moving was like trying to operate a marionette from the inside—I swayed and pitched from side to side, using a line of parked cars as a combination handrail and crash barrier. Then I was at the corner, hugging a metal post and looking up at two narrow green bands set at right angles, one reading IRVINE ST, the other OSWEGO CT.

Irvine and Oswego, Irvine and Oswego, where was that? Above Bridge Street, or below it? I tried to place the intersection on a mental map of the town, then got sidetracked by another consideration: if I did figure out where I was, where did I want to go? Home to Mrs. Winslow's, or back to Julie's place? "Julie . . ." I sighed. My arm, the only part of me still capable of coordinated movement, started to come up; I caught it just in time, just as the bottle was about to touch my lips.

I decided on what, at the time, seemed like a practical strategy: I would just keep walking. Autumn Creek was small, after all; if I kept moving, kept trying new streets, and was careful not to cross any bridges, sooner or later I was bound to happen across Julie's building, or Mrs. Winslow's, or some other landmark that would allow me to orient myself. And Julie herself was still out on the streets somewhere, probably; with a little luck I might bump into her. That thought, more than any other, propelled me into motion again.

A step; a step; another step; and another. I don't know how long or how far I walked. I was losing time, of course: minutes and blocks were passing between each footfall that I was aware of. A step; a step; another step; and then suddenly I drew up short, feeling as though I was about to fall again. I pivoted, wheeled away from an unseen precipice; stumbled up over a curb; crossed an expanse of sidewalk; and staggered to a halt on a patch of mowed grass.

A voice called my name, and I came up into a state of relative sobriety. I was standing on the front lawn of Mrs. Winslow's Victorian. Mrs. Winslow was on the porch; it was she who had called to me. "Mrs. Winslow!" I cried, and my elation at finding myself home was eclipsed almost immediately by shame. I must look terrible . . . was I still carrying the scotch bottle? Yes, I was still carrying the scotch bottle. I thought seriously about walking away, ducking back out of sight before Mrs. Winslow could get a good look at me, but then she said "Andrew" again with such concern that it was obvious it was too late.

Mrs. Winslow wasn't alone on the porch. There was a man up there with her, a policeman I thought at first, and my shame intensified—she'd gotten so worried she'd reported me missing. But the policeman wasn't wearing a uniform. No suit, either, so he wasn't FBI . . .

It was Dr. Eddington, I realized. What was *he* doing in Autumn Creek?

On my own I never would have guessed it; I was still too drunk. But some other soul looked out from the pulpit then, and put it together. The thought came, not mine but clear just the same: *Something has happened to Dr. Grey. That's what brought him here the last time.*

I didn't want to hear it. It's my job to deal with the outside world, no matter how bad things get, but I didn't want to hear it. It was one blow too many. I'd killed Warren Lodge; I'd killed my friendship with Julie too, probably; if it turned out I'd killed Dr. Grey as well, tempting her back to work she no longer had the strength for, I didn't want to know. I refused to know.

"Andrew . . ." Dr. Eddington began, but I didn't stay to listen. I shook loose from the body, snapped the tethers. There was a sound of glass shattering, of house-timbers cracking; a chorus of souls crying out in anguish and alarm; and all of that swallowed up by the hissing roil of the mist as I fell back into the lake. I plunged down deep, down to the bottom where the water is black, and there is no bad news.

I fell into the lake; but somebody has to run the body. And somebody did: ran it, and ran with it: somebody who had been waiting a long time for just this chance. Even as the waters closed over me, Andy Gage's body was on the move again, running back into the street, back into the night; running far, far away.

SIXTH BOOK:
MOUSE

16

Mouse's first meeting with Dr. Eddington is scheduled for 7:30 P.M., which is pretty late in the day, but the only time he had available. When Mouse called to make the appointment, she was surprised that Dr. Eddington answered the phone himself; he explained that his regular secretary was getting married in two days, and her temporary replacement hadn't shown up, "so I'm running things by myself for the time being . . . What did you say your name was?" Mouse told him, and he replied cheerfully: "Oh, Penny! Danielle—Dr. Grey—told me you might be calling. And this is about treatment for multiple personality disorder, right?"

Mouse was taken aback by the matter-of-factness of the question; from his tone, he might have been asking whether she needed a cavity filled, or the tires checked on her car. "Y-yes," she said.

"OK, great," he said; there was a sound of shuffling papers in the background. "So for our first session, how does a week from Wednesday sound?"

"A *week* . . ." exclaimed Mouse.

"Sorry it can't be sooner," Dr. Eddington apologized. "I'm booked solid tomorrow, Wednesday is my secretary's wedding, and on Thursday I fly to San Francisco for a seminar that lasts through the weekend. So I really can't do anything until next week. Unless . . ."

"Unless?"

"Well, I'm just thinking . . . my last regular appointment tomorrow ends at five o'clock, and then I've got a karate class at 5:45. I *could* grab a quick dinner and come back to the office after that, say around half past seven. Would that work for you? . . . Penny? . . . Are you still there?"

"Yes," Mouse made herself say. Her disappointment at being told that she would have to wait had been replaced in the blink of an eye by a power-

ful reluctance, a last wish that she could forget about treatment and just go
back to the way things used to be—a miserable life, sure, but one she'd
grown accustomed to. But that wasn't an option now. "Yes, OK . . . half past
seven tomorrow, I'll be there."

"OK," said Dr. Eddington. "Let me give you directions."

Dr. Eddington's office is in Fremont, the hippie/Bohemian enclave on
the north bank of the Lake Washington Shipping Canal. Though not technically a slum, Fremont is still the sort of neighborhood Mouse's mother
would have turned her nose up at; it is also a neighborhood where, twice in
the past year, Mouse has awakened in strangers' beds after a lost night. She
will have to take care, coming and going from Dr. Eddington's, not to catch
the eye of anyone who "knows" her.

Mouse doesn't mind meeting with the doctor in the evening; the only
bad part about it is having to kill time between the end of her workday and
the start of the appointment. Ever since the hypnosis session at Dr. Grey's,
the Society have gotten bolder. They aren't content to just send written
memoranda anymore, or leave messages on her answering machine; Mouse
has begun to hear voices. Sometimes the voices are just whispers, like daydream thoughts that aren't her own. Other times they are loud and clear, as
though someone were talking over her shoulder. The voices can come at
any time, but they are most apt to speak up in moments of idleness, when
Mouse is alone with herself. For this reason, she had hoped to spend the
hours before her appointment with Andrew, or with Andrew's father. But
Andrew is off somewhere with Julie, and if he is unavailable, so is Aaron, by
definition.

It's amazing what a difference a week makes. When Andrew first offered
to introduce her to his "father," Mouse only agreed out of desperation; now
she actually wants to talk to him. It would still be going too far to say she
enjoys talking to him—Aaron Gage is not what you would call a pleasant
conversationalist—but she is grateful to have met him. In part it is simply a
relief to learn that once you get past the initial strangeness of somebody else
occupying Andy Gage's body, it's not *that* strange; and if having multiple
personalities doesn't make Andrew a complete freak, then maybe there's
hope for Mouse as well.

It's also true, what Andrew said: his father does understand what Mouse
is going through. "Of course you're scared to death at first. You've always
secretly believed that you're crazy, and now it's like the evidence is snow-
balling, so you're not going to be able to hide it anymore. People are going
to find out. And along with the fear, there's guilt, because you've also got

this idea that it's your fault, that you've brought this on yourself somehow, even if you can't remember what you did . . . so not only is the whole world going to know that you're nuts, they're going to know you're evil, too . . ."

"*Yes* . . . so what do you do?"

"If you're like me, you waste a lot of time being scared. Years, maybe. Then one day you decide you're sick of that, you don't want to be afraid or guilty anymore, and you try to get help. And if you're lucky, and you get the *right* help, and you don't get *betrayed* . . . eventually you work past it. When it stops being scary and starts being a pain in the ass, that's when you know you've made real progress."

Mouse looks forward to the day when hearing voices is only "a pain in the ass." For now it's still scary. But she tries to follow Aaron's advice: "Dr. Grey probably told you to think of your Society as allies. It's true, they are. But you can also think of them as rude houseguests. When they act up, instead of panicking or feeling ashamed, try being annoyed, the same way you would if a visitor left you with a sink full of dirty dishes. It's not a perfect solution, but it'll help keep you from jumping out a window until you can get some real therapy—which you should do, soon."

All right, she's doing it. But she still has a couple of hours to kill. Mouse doesn't go home after work; she goes to Seattle's University District and pokes around the shops on University Avenue. She loses some time while she's doing this—seven o'clock comes sooner than it should, and when she checks her wallet, she's short at least fifteen dollars—but she only hears voices once. That happens just before seven, at an all-but-deserted pizzeria where Mouse has stopped to get a bite before heading to Fremont. She only wants a cheese slice and a soda, but the counterman, deeply engrossed in a phone conversation, won't serve her, or even acknowledge her presence. Losing patience, Mouse finds herself thinking what a fat fucking slob the guy is . . . then realizes with a start that that's not her thought at all, it's Ugly, Maledicta, lurking in the cave mouth. "You cut that out!" Mouse says, which, to her acute embarrassment, finally gets the counterman's attention. "Hey, you *chill* out," he tells her, and the next thing she knows she's driving down Fremont Avenue with the remains of a McDonald's Extra-Value Meal scattered over the Buick's dashboard. *So much for getting annoyed*, she thinks.

Dr. Eddington's directions lead her to a three-story wood-frame building. There's a small garden out front, enclosed by a chain-link fence; as Mouse comes up on it—she parked her Centurion a block away and is on foot now—she sees a man hunched down in the dirt, patiently weeding a flower patch. He's dressed in khaki pants and a light cotton shirt with the sleeves rolled up; his bare forearms are tanned and muscular, and his hair—short, dark, and finger-combed—looks freshly washed.

"Dr. Eddington?" Mouse addresses him.

He looks up, and for the second time in two weeks Mouse is confronted by the ghost of her father. But this time the impression is much stronger than when she saw Andrew laughing in front of the diner. Dr. Eddington actually *looks* like Morgan Driver, physically resembles him: he has the same eyes, the same nose, the same jawline. He is older than Morgan Driver ever got to be—Mouse guesses Dr. Eddington is in his mid-forties—but if you smoothed away the early crow's-feet and put a drooping cigarette in the corner of his mouth, what you'd have would be a reasonable facsimile of the face in her father's morning-after-prom-night photo.

"Hello, Penny," Dr. Eddington says, and Mouse has to hook her fingers through the fence to keep from falling down. She doesn't know what her father's voice sounded like, but the way Dr. Eddington's voice sounds—that's the way it *should* have sounded. "It is Penny, right?"

Mouse manages a nod. Dr. Eddington stands up, starts to brush his hands on his pants, thinks better of it, and brushes them against each other instead. Then he reaches out and shakes Mouse's hand, and his grip, warm and friendly and firm, makes her feel two years old.

"So," he says, releasing her hand, "come on inside."

His office is on the second floor, in a converted two-bedroom apartment. He leads her down a hallway past a room whose desk and filing cabinets are piled with what look to be several hundred bridal magazines. At the end of the hall is another, larger room, with bookshelves on three walls and a desk off to one side. Like Dr. Grey, Dr. Eddington offers his patients a choice of seats: there is a fancy leather-upholstered executive swivel chair, and a decidedly less fancy chaise, covered in soft fabric over-printed with panels from the Dennis the Menace cartoon strip. "Garage sale," Dr. Eddington explains, grabbing a second swivel chair from behind the desk for himself. "Please, sit where you like." Mouse picks the executive chair, not because she doesn't like cartoons but because it is closer to Dr. Eddington.

"So," Dr. Eddington says, "tell me about yourself."

Mouse blinks, not sure what he's asking. "Didn't . . . didn't Dr. Grey already tell you . . ."

"She told me that you might be seeking treatment, and why," Dr.

Eddington says. "And that you're a friend of Andrew's. But I meant, tell me about yourself personally. What are you like?"

What is she like? "I'm . . ." Mouse begins, meaning to say "I'm no one special," but losing the last word: "I'm no one."

Dr. Eddington gives her a pained smile, like he can't believe that's true. "Where are you from?"

"Ohio."

"You still have family there?"

Mouse shakes her head. "They're all dead."

"I'm sorry to hear that," says Dr. Eddington. "Recently?"

"Recently . . . ?"

"When did they die?"

"Oh. My father died when I was very young, and my grandmother—my father's mother—died when I was nine. I never knew any of my other grandparents."

"Uh-huh," says Dr. Eddington. "And what about your mother?"

"She . . . died more recently," Mouse says. "Seven years ago." She looks away, worried that he's going to ask for specifics, but the next thing he says is: "So it's just you now."

"Yes," says Mouse. Then, remembering why she is here: "Well . . ."

"Right." Dr. Eddington smiles. "What about friends? You still have friends back in Ohio?"

"No. I never did, really . . ."

"What about here in Seattle?"

Mouse starts to answer no again, then reconsiders. "There's Andrew, I guess." She looks to the doctor for confirmation. "Dr. Grey did say that he was my friend, right?"

"Yes, she did."

"Right, so Andrew, and I guess . . . I guess maybe Julie Sivik, too. Although she's also my boss."

"What kind of work do you do?"

"It's a virtual reality company."

"Cool!" says the doctor. "So you're a computer programmer?"

"I guess so," says Mouse. "I mean yes, that's my job, I'm a programmer, only . . . I'm not really sure what I *do* at work. What happens, I go in in the morning, I come home at night, and in between, I go to lunch, I have conversations with the other people at the Factory, but I can never remember actually *working*. And it's always been that way, with every job I've ever had:

the work gets done, it gets done *well*, even, but I, I'm not aware of doing it. Which is OK, I guess, since most of the jobs I've had I'm not really qualified for—if I had to think about the work, consciously, I probably *couldn't* do it." She stops, amazed to be confessing this so openly.

Dr. Eddington accepts it all routinely. "You know," he says, "there are people who would really envy you . . . but I realize it's not so much fun from your perspective."

"It's not *not* fun," Mouse tells him. "It's just what happens."

"So you lose time at work," says Dr. Eddington. "And other times too, I take it?" Mouse nods. "And when this happens, do you just blank out, or do you sometimes find yourself watching, like you're a spectator to your own actions?"

"Well, it didn't used to be like that," says Mouse. "It used to be I'd just . . . go away. But since Dr. Grey hypnotized me—" She stops, catching the change in his expression. "What?"

"Dr. Grey hypnotized you?"

"Yes," says Mouse. "Why?"

"What happened when she hypnotized you?"

Mouse tells him: how the room stretched out, how she found herself in the cave mouth with the Ugly twins, and how, trying to escape the sound of her own voice, she went deeper down into the cavern. She mentions the sleepers, too, but omits the appearance of the little girl with the sack, saying only: "I didn't like it in there. I came back out, into the, into my, body, and told Dr. Grey I didn't want to go inside again. And she said I didn't have to, not until I was ready, but then, on the way home . . ." She describes Maledicta's brief takeover on the way to the ferry landing.

Dr. Eddington is frowning now. "Have there been other incidents since then?"

"Some," says Mouse. In fact she's only found herself back in the cave mouth a couple other times—most of her blackouts are still just that, blackouts—but she figures the voices also count as "incidents." "What is it?" she asks. "Did Dr. Grey make a mistake? Should she not have hypnotized me?"

"It's a judgment call," Dr. Eddington says, sounding more diplomatic than truthful. "My own preference is to reserve hypnosis for ongoing therapy; I don't think it's appropriate for a one-time visit. Especially not with a suspected MPD case."

"Why not?"

"Well, as a general rule, you don't risk stirring things up with a patient unless you know you're going to be there to help settle them down again. But Danny is . . . ambitious. *Over*ambitious, sometimes."

"Oh," says Mouse. It's disconcerting to think that Dr. Grey's eagerness might have gotten the better of her professional judgment, but Mouse cannot honestly bring herself to feel betrayed. She knows that Dr. Grey *was* trying to help her; and she also knows that even without the hypnotism session, the Society would still be making trouble for her now.

Still, she has to ask: "Can you undo it? Put me back the way I was?"

"Is that what you want?" Dr. Eddington asks.

A week ago the answer would have been yes. But thanks mostly to her discussions with Andrew's father, Mouse's attitude has changed. She still doesn't want to go through the *process* of therapy—doesn't want to face that little girl in the cave—but the result, if it works . . .

"No," says Mouse, "I guess not." Looking him in the eye: "You couldn't undo it anyway, could you?"

"No," Dr. Eddington admits. "Probably not."

"Then I want treatment," Mouse decides, with finality. "I want to . . . to build a house, or whatever it takes. If you'll help me."

"I'll help you," Dr. Eddington says. In another room, a phone begins to ring. "What we'll do, we'll set up regular sessions, starting next week." The phone continues to ring, and Dr. Eddington gets up. "Just a second," he says. "I think I left the answering machine off."

While Dr. Eddington is on the phone, Mouse sinks back in her chair, listening to the drone of the doctor's voice from the other room and swiveling back and forth contentedly. Drifting, she fantasizes an alternate life, one in which her mother died in the plane crash and her father survived. She imagines a man a lot like Dr. Eddington walking hand in hand with a girl a lot like herself. It's wicked, but it makes her happy.

In the other room, Dr. Eddington hangs up the phone. He comes back into his office looking distressed.

"What is it?" Mouse asks him, a part of her still lost in the daydream.

"That was Meredith Cantrell," he says.

"Dr. Grey's helper?"

Dr. Eddington nods. "Danny had another stroke this afternoon. She's dead."

It takes a moment for the news to penetrate, and when it does, Mouse finds she isn't all that surprised. "Oh no," she says, more for Dr. Eddington's sake than her own. Then she notices that Dr. Eddington is watching her—waiting to see if she's going to break down, or turn into somebody else. "I'm OK," she assures him. "I . . . it's sad that she's dead, but I wasn't that close to her. I didn't have time to be. Are you—"

"I was close to her," Dr. Eddington says, going off in his own head for a moment. Then he says: "Anyway, I don't mean to cut our meeting short, but I have to go out to Autumn Creek now, and break the news to Andrew."

"Andrew . . . oh God."

"Yes," Dr. Eddington says. "I have to see that he's all right . . . it's part of a commitment I made to Dr. Grey."

"Sure," says Mouse, starting to get up. "Of course. I'll just—"

"Would you like to come along?"

"Sure. If you think—"

"I think it would be good for Andrew to have a friend there," Dr. Eddington says. He smiles at her, and Mouse can't help but feel a rush of pleasure. He looks so much like her father.

"OK," she says.

"OK," says Dr. Eddington. "I'll just switch the answering machine on, and we'll go . . ."

17

Mouse was in her first semester at the University of Washington when her mother had her stroke. It took a while for the news to get to her, and there were times in the months that followed when she wished it had never reached her at all.

That she was in school in Washington state was due, she knew, to the Society. Of course Mouse's mother had wanted her to "attend university"— as all fine young ladies did these days—but the original plan was for Mouse to go to a college close to home, ideally within half a day's drive, so that her mother could keep an eye on her. With her mother's help, Mouse applied to Oberlin, Antioch, Notre Dame, and Northwestern; at the same time, applications in Mouse's name were sent to Oxford, Stanford, and the University of Washington . . . and those were just the schools Mouse later found out about.

Stanford rejected her, and she was never really sure what happened with Oxford. But the University of Washington not only accepted her, it offered her a modest scholarship, which, by means of a Society-authored cover letter, got inflated into a major honor—the kind only awarded to the most exceptional candidates. So Mouse went off to college at the UW. Her mother wasn't happy about the long distance, but she could hardly insist that Mouse refuse the "great honor," especially given her belief that the school had chosen Mouse without any prompting.

The joy Mouse felt at having escaped her mother's house (felt, but never openly expressed or acknowledged) was tempered by her instant dislike of her new college roommate, Alyssa Geller, who struck her as a slightly-grown-up version of Cindy Wheaton. Alyssa didn't like Mouse much, either. This was partly due to Maledicta's frequent outbursts, and partly due to Mouse's mother, who phoned the dormitory almost every day and became suspicious and abusive when Mouse wasn't available to take her calls. Relations between Mouse and Alyssa declined steadily over the first half of the semester, reaching a low point when Alyssa's bed and most of her possessions inexplicably ended up in the hall. Not long afterwards, Mouse found herself living in a basement apartment off campus.

The apartment, despite an inevitable tendency to dampness, was surprisingly nice, with brightly painted walls and a surfeit of lamps to drive away shadows. It was small but still larger than her dorm room, and it was all hers: after she got over the shock of the transition, Mouse was so pleased to be living alone that she went an entire week before wondering if her mother knew where she was. Several more days passed before it occurred to her that her new apartment had no telephone, so that even if her mother did know where she was, she couldn't call. At that point Mouse considered getting a phone, or at least calling home from a public booth, but instead of doing either she went to a florist's on University Avenue and bought a big wreath of dried purple flowers, which she hung on her apartment door like a NO TRESPASSING sign.

Another week went by. It was November now; one cold wet day Mouse was trudging across campus when Alyssa Geller tried to intercept her. Mouse could tell by the look on Alyssa's face what Alyssa wanted to talk to her about, but rather than hear how Verna Driver had been calling night and day demanding to know her daughter's whereabouts, Mouse ran away. An hour later, as she waited for a psychology lecture to begin in Kane Hall, a pair of university security guards entered the auditorium and called her name; Mouse, seated in the very last row, stayed quiet, and when the guards turned to confer with a teaching assistant, she slipped out the back.

She left campus immediately, ran home, and hid out like a fugitive for the next six days. Of course she understood that she was being ridiculous—she couldn't hide from her mother forever—but sitting alone in her apartment, with the door locked and no one creeping up behind her, Mouse decided she didn't care if she was being ridiculous.

In the early evening of the sixth day, there was a loud knock on Mouse's door. Mouse had to stop herself from rushing to put out the lights; that would only give her away.

The knock came again. A man's voice called through the door: "Ms. Driver? . . . This is the Seattle Police Department. Could you please open up? . . . Ms. Driver, are you there?"

Mouse held her breath. *Go away*, she thought, but after a third knock the voice, speaking to someone else outside, said, "Open it," and there was a rattle of a key in the lock. Mouse had a wild thought of toppling a bookshelf in front of the door to barricade it, but it was already swinging open. Four men entered: two policemen, one of the security guards from the lecture hall, and Mouse's landlord. Between them they took up most of the space in Mouse's little living room; one of the policemen was so tall that he had to duck his head below the low ceiling.

"Ms. Driver?" the tall policeman said. When Mouse only stared past him at the still-open door—she was waiting for her mother to come in—he turned to the landlord and asked, "Is this her?" The landlord nodded, and the policeman continued: "Ms. Driver, are you OK?"

"Where is she?" Mouse asked.

"Where is who, Ms. Driver?"

"My mother," said Mouse. "She sent you to find me, didn't she? Is she outside?"

"No," the tall policeman said uncomfortably, and hesitated.

The security guard cleared his throat. "As a matter of fact," he told Mouse, "your mother *was* pretty concerned that she couldn't get in touch with you. She was, um, very insistent that we track you down. She thought you might have gotten hurt."

"No," said Mouse. "No, I just moved . . ."

"That's what your roommate told us," the security guard said. "But, uh, I'm afraid your mother wasn't satisfied with that. In fact she suggested Miss Geller might have, well, done something to you."

"Oh God," said Mouse. It was even worse than she'd imagined; Alyssa must be furious. "Well you'll tell her that's not true, won't you? That I'm not . . ."

"Um . . ."

"Only," said Mouse, "only one thing, if you haven't told her where I am yet, could you maybe not? Tell her I'm OK, that I'm not hurt, but don't—"

The tall policeman took over again: "Ms. Driver," he said, "I'm afraid we can't tell your mother anything right now. The reason we're here—"

"Why not?" asked Mouse, thinking it must be some law-enforcement rule. Maybe they couldn't get involved, now that they knew Alyssa hadn't murdered her. "I'll pay for the call, if that's what the problem is. I—"

"Ms. Driver," the policeman said, "we can't tell your mother anything because she's in the hospital. She's had a stroke."

"A stroke?" said Mouse. "You mean she's *dead?*"

"No, no," said the security guard, holding up a hand reassuringly. "Not dead, just hospitalized."

"But . . ." Mouse shook her head, confused. "My grandmother had a stroke," she said. "*She* died."

The two policemen exchanged glances. Then the tall policeman said: "I don't know anything about your grandmother, Ms. Driver, but your mother is alive, at least for the time being."

"Well is she *going* to die?"

"Her condition was described to us as serious, but stable. Beyond that I really can't say. I'm sure the hospital staff could tell you more . . ."

"Which hospital is she in?"

"Blessed Family General Hospital," the tall policeman said, consulting a notepad. "In Spokane."

"Spokane, Washington?" More confusion. "What's she doing there?"

"She was on a plane," the policeman explained. "On her way here, I guess to look for you." A note of reproach crept into his voice as he said this. "The plane was over the Idaho-Washington border when it hit a patch of turbulence, and your mother had some sort of episode."

By "some sort of episode," Mouse assumed that the policeman was referring to her mother's stroke. In fact, as she would later learn, her mother's fear of flying (which was not as bad as her purple-phobia, but still severe), along with her anxiety about Mouse, plus whatever other dark currents moved in her brain, had combined to trigger a full-blown paranoid fit, to which the stroke was only a coda. As the plane rocked and bounced at 29,000 feet, Verna Driver had gotten out of her seat and begun loudly accusing her fellow passengers of conspiring against her; the flight attendants moved to restrain her, chasing her up and down the length of the plane twice before she finally collapsed, on her own, in the first-class galley.

"Spokane," Mouse repeated, trying to remember exactly where that was in relation to Seattle, how *far* it was.

"The plane had to make an emergency landing," the tall policeman concluded. "Your mother was taken to Blessed Family, and they eventually contacted us. Two days ago." Another note of reproach. "We had a devil of a time finding you." Mouse said nothing to this, and the policeman went on: "Ms. Driver, it's really none of our business, but were you and your mother having some sort of . . . difficulty?"

"Difficulty?" said Mouse.

—and the door clicked shut behind them as they left. Mouse, alone again, sat on her couch until a memorandum appeared with the address and telephone number of Blessed Family Hospital. The memorandum also contained scheduling information for the various planes, buses, and trains that

traveled from Seattle to Spokane, but, curiously, there was no accompany-
ing list, no "to do" specifying *when* Mouse should go.

Of course no list was necessary. Her mother was in the hospital, possibly—
but not definitely—dying. Mouse should go to her right away: that's what
any good daughter would do. But Mouse wasn't a good daughter, she was a
worthless piece of shit, and though the police had come to her apartment
on a Wednesday, it wasn't until Friday morning that she boarded an eastbound Amtrak train at King Street Station.

The train was scheduled to get into Spokane at 7:00 P.M., but as it made its
way over the Cascade Mountains, someone twice pulled the emergency brake.
After the second brake-pulling incident, the train sat for more than an hour as
a team of conductors interrogated everyone in Mouse's passenger car. No culprit was uncovered, and eventually the train started up again, reaching
Wenatchee at half past five and not getting to Spokane until almost midnight.
By then it was too late to go to the hospital, so Mouse found a hotel.

The next morning, she overslept, then got lost on the way to the hospital, and didn't actually set foot in Blessed Family until noon. Noon, Saturday: three days since she'd first heard of her mother's stroke, six days since it
had actually happened: more than enough time for her mother to have died,
if her stroke had been anywhere near as bad as Grandma Driver's.

But Verna Driver was still alive. "She's stable," the duty nurse said, as she
ushered Mouse down a long hallway.

Stable: the same word the tall policeman had used. Mouse guessed that it
meant her mother was as bad as she was likely to get for a while, without
getting any better, either. "But how bad is she? Can she talk?"

"Your mother isn't fully conscious," the nurse explained. "Since she was
admitted, she's opened her eyes a few times, but she doesn't seem aware of
where she is or what's happened to her. Also—and you should prepare yourself for this—she's suffered some paralysis, so even if she were wide awake,
she might not be able to speak."

"Paralysis," said Mouse. "And is that temporary, or . . ."

"You'd have to ask a doctor about that. After I show you to her room, I'll
see if I can find one to talk to you about her prognosis . . . Here we are."

The hospital room had two beds in it. The bed nearest the door was
unoccupied; in the other, beside a window that looked out on downtown
Spokane, Verna Driver lay still as a corpse.

Mouse had seen her grandmother in the hospital, after her stroke.
Mouse's mother hadn't wanted to take her, but Mouse had insisted, in a rare
show of defiance, and had actually gotten her way. The sight had torn her

heart: Grandma small and wasted in the bed, hooked up to a ventilator machine, with one whole side of her face gone slack. Mouse had begun to cry, and then her mother, seized by a fit of wickedness, had hooked a finger into the drooping corner of Grandma's mouth, pulled it up into a mock grin, and said brightly: "There you go! All better now!"

Well, time had come round, and now it was her mother's turn.

Verna Driver was breathing on her own, but the right side of her face had that same paralytic droop. Actually, *droop* might not be the best term. The word that really came to mind was *melted*: the slack folds of skin had an unnatural sheen that suggested wax or putty. Likewise her right arm, laid out above the bedsheet, seemed less a real limb than a damaged prosthesis, the fingers hooked halfway between a fist and a claw.

Remembering her grandmother, Mouse tried to be hard, to think of this as just deserts—an effort that lasted all of two seconds. "Momma," she said, and broke down sobbing. "Oh, Momma . . ."

"Poor girl," the duty nurse said. "I'll go find the doctor for you . . ."

"Hmmph?" Mouse sniffled, realizing belatedly that the nurse meant to leave her alone in the room. "No, please, wait—"

Too late. By the time Mouse turned around, the nurse had already stepped out. Mouse gave another sniffle, the tears drying up as her sorrow was displaced by sudden tension. With a nervous sigh, she turned back towards the bed.

Her mother's eyes were open.

—and Mouse was out in the hallway, balled up in a defensive crouch against the far wall. From the way people were clustered around her and the fact that she was gnawing on her fists she concluded that she must have been screaming.

"Dear?" said the duty nurse, gently touching Mouse's shoulder. "Dear, what's wrong?"

"Hey there," added a man in a white doctor's coat, squatting down on the other side of her. "Are you all right?"

Mouse managed to pull her hands away from her mouth long enough to say: "She's awake!"

The doctor and the nurse both looked around, as if they expected to see Verna Driver standing in the doorway of her room.

"In the bed," Mouse clarified. "She opened her eyes."

"Oh honey," said the nurse. "I told you, she's done that before. But—"

"No," said Mouse. "She looked at me. She *saw* me."

"Really?" said the doctor. "That's a good sign, then. Why don't we go in and have a look?" He stood up, and regarded the onlookers who were gathered around them. "I think the rest of you can move along now."

Back in the room, Verna Driver's eyes were still open, but her gaze had become unfocused, wandering and dull. "Mrs. Driver?" the doctor called to her, waving a hand in front of her face. "Verna, can you hear me?" She showed no sign of noticing him; her eyes rolled back and forth in their sockets, their movements synchronized but settling on nothing.

Mouse shook her head. "It was different before," she said. "She was looking *at* me." She shivered at the memory of it: her mother's eyes, alert, aware, and totally out of place in the slackness of her face—as if, for a joke, she'd donned a cheap rubber mask of her own features and was peeping out through the eyeholes.

The doctor took a penlight from his breast pocket and proceeded to shine it in each of Mouse's mother's eyes. Her pupils contracted as the light hit them, but her gaze continued to wander.

Growing frustrated, Mouse blurted out: "She's faking!"

The nurse frowned at this, but the doctor smiled. "You mean she's pulling our legs, pretending not to see me? That would be a good sign too, if it were true. But I don't think—"

Mouse stiffened. "There!" she said, pointing. The doctor turned back towards the bed.

Verna Driver's gaze, tracking haphazardly across the room, had fallen on Mouse . . . and stopped. Her eyes focused, regaining their awareness; it was obvious she knew who she was looking at.

At least it was obvious to Mouse. The doctor was still skeptical. "Mrs. Driver?" he called again. She was no more responsive than she had been the first time. But this time the lack of response was different; where before she might not have seen him at all, now (it was clear to Mouse) she was simply ignoring him, too intent on her daughter to pay any attention to waving hands or lights.

"She sees me," Mouse said, and took a half step to the right. Her mother's eyes followed her exactly.

As an experiment, the doctor had Mouse leave the room. Mouse's mother tracked her as far as she could without turning her head, and continued to stare out of the corners of her eyes for several minutes, as if waiting for Mouse to reappear. Finally her eyes lost focus, and resumed their aimless wandering. The doctor called Mouse back into the room. Another minute passed, and Mouse's mother's gaze happened across Mouse again . . . and locked on.

"All right," said the doctor, convinced at last. "Obviously she recognizes *something* about you . . . but until we can get her to respond positively to questions, we won't really know how much coherent thinking is going on in there. Still"—he nodded optimistically—"it's a good sign."

"So she's going to get better?"

"Well," the doctor hedged. "This is one improvement, and we'll hope for more in the days to come. But I have to be honest with you, given the severity of the stroke, to hope for anything like a full recovery would be unrealistic. She's going to be impaired for the rest of her life, and she'll very likely require full-time care."

"You mean," said Mouse, "you mean *I* have to take care of her?"

"Not if you don't want to," said the doctor, while the nurse's frown deepened. "Certainly not alone. Arrangements can be made for professional care, either in your home or at a facility."

"At a facility," Mouse said instantly. "Or maybe . . . maybe you could just keep her here?"

"We don't do long-term care at Blessed Family," the nurse informed her curtly.

"Besides," said the doctor, "I understand you're from . . . Kentucky, is that right?"

"Ohio," said Mouse. "That's where my mother is from, but I live in Seattle now."

The doctor nodded. "There are a number of suitable facilities in the Seattle area that your mother could eventually be transferred to. And I'm sure it would be more convenient for you, having your mother there . . ." There was a long pause, during which Mouse said nothing, and then the doctor continued: "Well, there'll be plenty of time to discuss options in the days ahead."

In the days ahead. They expected Mouse to stay in Spokane while her mother was in the hospital. The doctor suggested that her mother's recovery, however much or little it finally amounted to, would be helped by Mouse's presence. Mouse knew that he was probably right, and more, that it was her duty to stay . . . but notwithstanding her tears, she didn't *want* to. Not with her mother staring at her every second she was in the room—and especially not if her mother *did* recover. God, what if she started talking, saying terrible things? Or worse . . . what if, as a game, she only talked when she and Mouse were alone? The doctor and the nurse would think Mouse was crazy, and before long, she would be.

She stayed as long as she could bear to: five days. She only spent a small portion of each day actually in her mother's room. When the staring got to be too much—usually within a half hour, if she couldn't get someone from the hospital staff to stay in the room with her—Mouse would duck out and go for a walk around the city. On one of these walks, she happened upon a future construction site, a vacant lot near the riverfront where, according to posted signs, a new hotel was due to be erected the following spring. Mouse didn't think much of it at the time, but it must have stuck in her head.

On Mouse's fourth day at the hospital, the duty nurse asked her to stop by the accounting office on her way out, as there was a problem with her mother's medical insurance. The problem, it turned out, was that her mother's insurance had lapsed, and so long ago that it had taken the insurance company the better part of a week just to verify that she'd once had a policy; she hadn't paid a premium in over ten years. When Mouse was first told this, she wondered fleetingly if her mother had gone bankrupt without telling her. But that couldn't be it; Verna Driver had had plenty of money to pay for other things over the past decade. She must have just forgotten to pay her premiums—or chosen not to. Maybe, thought Mouse, she'd decided that health insurance was for poor people.

"Does this mean you're going to kick her out?" Mouse asked.

The accounts manager hastened to assure her that no, even completely indigent people were entitled to medical care. "We can work out a payment plan based on whatever she—and you—can afford. But this may create complications in trying to place her with a long-term care facility."

Mouse's embarrassment over the lack of insurance quickly gave way to anger. Back at her hotel room, anger escalated into rage, and she blacked out much of the night. The next day, coming into her mother's hospital room, into her mother's stare, she blacked out again . . . and found herself standing at her mother's bedside, one hand covering her mother's mouth. She wasn't pressing down hard—her mother could still breathe—but the implication so terrified her that she backed out of the room (her mother's eyes tracking her the whole way) and left the hospital without saying a word to anyone. The next thing she knew, she was back in Seattle.

The next several weeks were a blur. Between her time hiding out and her time in Spokane, Mouse had fallen hopelessly behind in her coursework, and she was completely unprepared for her upcoming finals. Yet somehow, without a single cram session—or, for that matter, a single exam session— that she could later recall, she passed all her classes. Sometime around

December 16th or 17th, after the exam period ended, her life became
coherent enough again that she was finally able to get a phone installed in
her apartment.

She called Blessed Family Hospital. Her mother was still alive, but had
not shown further improvement. In Mouse's absence, the hospital had
transferred her to a state-run nursing home. The transfer was only temporary; it was still up to Mouse, as her mother's next of kin, to see to a more
permanent arrangement.

Mouse procrastinated for another week, then headed back to Spokane,
by bus this time. She boarded a Greyhound a few hours before a blizzard
was due. The storm arrived ahead of schedule, and Mouse's bus, after only
just barely getting over the mountains, was forced to make an emergency
layover in Ellensburg. The full journey to Spokane took nearly two days.

The nursing home wasn't as nice as the hospital had been, but it was
cleaner than Mouse expected, and the staff seemed friendly, so from the
moment she arrived she began entertaining the notion that her mother
might be kept here indefinitely. Mouse knew that her mother would be
opposed to the idea—public facilities were definitely for poor people—but
in her current state, she probably wouldn't be able to tell the difference.
And if she could, well, it wasn't Mouse who'd let the health insurance lapse.

Her mother's new room had four beds in it rather than two, and a different view. All of the beds were occupied: two by older patients on ventilators,
a third by a young woman who, though she appeared outwardly healthy,
never moved a muscle in Mouse's presence.

Mouse's mother seemed unchanged: her eyes were open, and they immediately fixed on Mouse, that same baleful stare.

"Momma," Mouse heard herself saying. "Can you understand me? Do
you know where you are?"

Nothing: not a single blink, not even a quiver of an eyelash, just a focus
so intense that, very soon, Mouse had to go outside to get some air.

And yet something had changed. During Mouse's subsequent visits to
the room, it seemed to take her mother longer and longer to notice her—
once, her gaze swept over Mouse half a dozen times before stopping. So
maybe she was weakening; maybe she was even dying. But slowly.

Mouse arranged to have her mother permanently admitted to the nursing home. This took several days, as the nursing home administrator was
initially very resistant to the idea. But it got taken care of, somehow;
arrangements were made.

Mouse went to her mother's room one more time. For once, her mother was asleep, and in the absence of the stare Mouse relaxed enough that she was able to cry again. She cried, and promised her mother that she would visit often, and then she bent down, carefully, and kissed her mother on the cheek.

She never saw her mother alive again.

She didn't plan it that way, at least not consciously. Mouse honestly intended to return to Spokane once a month, or every two months at least. But once she was back in Seattle, caught up in the new school semester, those intentions were never quite realized. She was always *going* to visit her mother, soon. Soon, but never now.

She did call regularly. Every Friday evening without fail, Mouse rang the nursing home to check on her mother's condition. She told herself that she was showing her concern with these calls, but it was more complicated than that. The truth was that Mouse had begun having nightmares—guilt-induced, no doubt—in which her mother, having miraculously regained her mobility, would sneak out of the nursing home in the dead of night, intending to give her daughter one more good scare. Sometimes the nightmares ended with her mother still in transit, but closing the distance between Spokane and Seattle much faster than Mouse herself had ever done; other times she completed the trip, and found Mouse, and frightened her so severely that Mouse had a stroke and ended up paralyzed in bed, at her mother's mercy.

So Mouse's weekly calls to the nursing home were more than just an expression of daughterly devotion; they were also a way of looking over her shoulder.

Then one day—May 2nd, 1990, a little before nine in the morning, as Mouse was preparing to leave for class—the nursing home called to inform her that her mother was "in a bad way" and not expected to last much longer. Forty minutes later—Mouse was still in her apartment, trying to decide, or waiting to see, what she would do—the nursing home called again: her mother was dead.

This time Mouse didn't delay. Within two hours she was boarding a plane at Sea-Tac airport; a little over an hour after that, she was at an Avis counter in the Spokane terminal, asking if there were any station wagons for rent (one of the things Mouse had done over the last few months instead of visiting her mother was learn how to drive; it hadn't been easy—she'd had to take the driver's course three separate times—but as of April 12th, she had her license). A station wagon was, in fact, available; Mouse grabbed it and raced for the nursing home.

Not fast enough, though. "Your mother's gone already," the receptionist informed her when she got there.

"Yes, I know she passed away. But where—"

"No, I mean physically gone," the receptionist said. "She's not here any-more."

"What do you mean she's not here?" Mouse exclaimed. "She's *dead*, how can she not be here?"

The receptionist stared placidly at her computer screen. "According to this, the Archangel Funeral Home picked her up half an hour ago."

"How could they do that? Don't they need permission to do that?"

"I guess they thought they had it," the receptionist said. "If there's been a mistake, I can put you together with someone from administration . . ."

"Never mind," said Mouse, knowing it was pointless; for all she knew, she *had* given permission. "Could you just please tell me the address of the funeral home?"

The Archangel Funeral Home was located in a part of Spokane that reminded Mouse uncomfortably of Trash Town. Mr. Filchenko, the funeral director, was a squat hummock of a man in a rumpled black suit. When Mouse attempted, as discreetly as possible, to find out whether she had spoken to him before, Mr. Filchenko evaded her questions; he also tried to discourage her from viewing her mother's body.

"Why not let us make her a little more presentable first?" Mr. Filchenko suggested. "To lessen the shock . . ."

"No thank you," said Mouse. "I'd like to see her now, please."

"It's just that death, even the most peaceful death, can have an effect on the appearance that is . . . unkind. And when the deceased is someone we've been close to, a best friend or a parent—"

"I'd like to see my mother *now*, please," Mouse insisted, grateful that Mr. Filchenko was not much taller than she was.

Mr. Filchenko sighed. "If you're sure . . ."

He took her back into his mortician's workshop, which, like a police-movie morgue, had a double row of body lockers set into one wall. "I really think you'll be happier if you let us finish the cosmetic work first," Mr. Filchenko said, pausing in front of the lockers. "Let us make her up nice for the funeral, dress her properly, put her in a beautiful casket with some flow-ers . . . that way you'll have a lovely parting memory of her, not—"

"Oh," said Mouse, figuring it out. "You want to charge me lots of money."

Mr. Filchenko paused, mouth open at this impertinence, and then tried to go on as if Mouse hadn't spoken: "As I was saying—"

"I don't need her made up," Mouse told him. "There isn't going to be any funeral." She fingered the list in her pocket; it was quite specific about what was to be done. "I want her cremated."

"Cremated, very good, we can do that." Mr. Filchenko bowed his head graciously. "But"—looking up again—"perhaps a small memorial service first, just to—"

"No," said Mouse. "I just want to see her, once, and then I want her cremated. Nothing else."

"Oh-*kay* . . . we'll just have a look then"—Mr. Filchenko gestured at the lockers—"and then, back in my office, you can pick out a casket . . ."

"Why would she need a casket if she's going to be cremated?"

"My goodness!" Mr. Filchenko said, aghast. "My goodness, you don't . . . you wouldn't want us to just *toss* your mother into the furnace like a bag of *garbage*, now would you?"

Time broke up after that. Mouse had only one more solid chunk of memory, of a locker being opened, a slab rolling out, and a sheet being twitched back. She saw her mother's face, gone completely slack on both sides now. Verna Driver's lower incisors jutted shrewishly from her mouth; her eyes were open but fixed and unaware, finally emptied of all malice. "*All better now,*" Mouse heard a voice say.

—and then it was later, perhaps another day entirely, and Mouse was out behind the funeral home, watching as one of Mr. Filchenko's assistants loaded a covered plastic tub into the back of her rented station wagon. Mr. Filchenko was watching too; he stood just outside the rear door of what Mouse assumed must be the funeral home's crematorium, with a cross look on his face.

"This is really very improper," Mr. Filchenko complained. "State *laws* are being broken here."

Mouse looked at him, and was both gratified and startled to see him flinch. He recovered himself quickly, though, and said: "So, may I have it?"

"Have it?"

"My money," Mr. Filchenko said flatly. "No-frills or not, this isn't a free service."

Mouse reached without thinking into the pocket of the coat she was wearing, and brought out the plain envelope she found there. She handed the envelope to Mr. Filchenko, who immediately opened it, pulled out the packet of bills from inside, and began counting them. It looked like a lot of cash to Mouse, but Mr. Filchenko didn't appear to agree—he counted the bills four times, and rechecked the envelope to make sure he hadn't missed any. Finally he seemed to accept that he'd gotten all he was going to get, and tucked the money away again.

"I still say you should have gone with the urn," Mr. Filchenko groused. "I'd have given you an excellent deal."

Those were his last words to her. His assistant had already closed up the back of the station wagon and gone back inside the funeral parlor; now Mr. Filchenko followed, slamming the crematorium door behind him. Mouse got into the station wagon.

She looked into the rearview mirror, at the plastic tub containing her mother's ashes. She didn't like having it behind her, but at least she could keep an eye on it. To have it out of sight in a trunk—even a locked trunk—would have made her much more nervous.

She turned the key in the station wagon's ignition—

—and it was sometime later, definitely another day, just after sunrise. Mouse leaned up against the chain-link fence that surrounded the hotel construction site, the one she'd seen the signs for back in November. The site was active now. A convoy of cement trucks stretched in a line out the site's main entrance; they were pouring the hotel's foundation.

Mouse's back hurt, and she was very tired, as if she'd been up all the preceding night. She was filthy, too: her shoes were caked with mud, and there was dirt on her clothes, on her hands, and even in her hair. But though she was aware of all of this in a detached way, she ignored her own discomfort and focused on the work going on inside the fence. With each load of cement that was poured into the foundation pit, Mouse felt a corresponding lightening of her own spirits, all the anxiety of the last six months sloughing away.

Hours passed. At last—the sun was high in the sky now—the final truck emptied its mixer into the pit, and the construction workers hurried to finish smoothing the surface of the foundation before it set. Mouse turned away, satisfied. The Navigator helped her locate the station wagon; Mouse slid into the driver's seat and glanced up at the rearview mirror again. Her mother's ashes were gone.

Mouse drove to the airport, returned the rental car, and caught the next flight back to Seattle. Over the next few months, she tidied up her mother's remaining affairs. She never went back to Willow Grove; instead, she hired a lawyer to arrange the sale of her mother's house and its contents, and to close out her mother's bank accounts. Most of the money went to pay off her mother's hospital bills and other outstanding debts; the remainder went into a fund to help cover Mouse's college tuition.

A day came in September of that year when it dawned on Mouse that she had begun a whole new life. The last ties with her past had been cut; she had become, in effect, a blank slate, and could make of herself whatever she wanted to. This realization, though liberating, also marked the start of a new series of blackouts. Where before Mouse had most often lost time in the wake of traumatic events, now the blackouts started happening in moments of relative calm—when she was out walking, or at the library, or shopping in a store.

It was around that same time that Mouse first began finding things in her apartment—clothes, jewelry, children's toys—that she couldn't remember buying. Sometimes the things were in plain sight, but more often they were hidden away in drawers and cabinets, or at the back of shelves, where Mouse would happen across them by chance. There was one closet in particular, in the alcove that connected her kitchen and her bathroom, that she learned never to look into without a very good reason.

A third thing that happened around then was that Mouse's personal finances started to unravel. Over the course of her sophomore year, the money in her special college fund seemed to evaporate. By the start of her junior year, even with her scholarship, she had to request additional financial aid in order to make tuition. That was also when she started taking part-time jobs to help make ends meet—lots of part-time jobs.

In the years that followed, as she struggled to pull her new life together, Mouse tried to think of her mother as little as possible. Though she had no direct memory of it, she knew, on some level, what she had done with her mother's remains. She didn't like to dwell on that; it was a shameful act.

Shameful, and yet comforting, too. Occasionally Mouse would still have nightmares in which her mother, dead but not dead, would creep ever closer along back roads in the dark of night. And whenever Mouse woke, in terror, from one of these dreams, she had a ready antidote for the fear. She had memorized the phone number of the reservation desk at the Spokane Charter Hotel—long since completed—and any time day or night she could dial it, and as soon as the desk clerk picked up and said, "Spokane Charter. May I help you?" Mouse would know that the hotel was still standing—and still pressing down, with the weight of all fourteen of its floors, on everything buried beneath its foundation.

She was a bad daughter, a worthless piece of shit; she had treated her mother abominably in the last months of her life. But she knew where her mother was now—always—and to know that, to be sure of it, was worth all the shame in the world.

18

Now, driving towards Autumn Creek, a few car lengths behind Dr. Eddington's Volkswagen Jetta, Mouse wonders what sort of final arrangements Dr. Grey made for herself. It's not something Mouse should be concerned with—she should be thinking of Andrew—but she can't help speculating.

That the doctor planned her own funeral, if any, and arranged (and probably paid) in advance for the disposal of her body, is not even a question. Despite only having met her the one time, Mouse feels sure that Dr. Grey was not the sort of person who would trust such details to anyone but herself. And Mouse can almost pity—almost!—the poor funeral director who, like Mr. Filchenko, tried to sell her a service that she didn't want.

What services would she want? A small ceremony, Mouse guesses—just her helpmate, Dr. Eddington, a few other close friends and associates, maybe Andrew. Burial rather than cremation—Mouse has an intuition that the doctor would want to continue to *occupy space* in some way, not be scattered on the winds or compacted into an urn. So, burial: in a plain casket, in an inexpensive plot, but in a cemetery that allows actual headstones. The marker will be a simple one, no fancy etching or flowery epitaph, but still imposing somehow, maybe a darker-colored stone, something to catch the eye . . . or bark the shins of anyone who tries to walk by without paying the proper respect.

Mouse half-smiles, imagining this, until she realizes that the grave site she is mentally picturing is actually her grandmother's, and the thoughts she is imputing to Dr. Grey are based on statements her grandmother once made, when she talked about how *she* wanted to be buried.

The memory drives Mouse away for a few minutes, long enough for Malefica to tap the Buick's brakes and wake up the driver of a Toyota that has been riding their back bumper for the past few miles. The Toyota backs

off; Malefica grins and reaches into the glove compartment for a celebra-
tory shot of vodka. But the flask is gone, and Malefica gives way to Maledicta, who curses a blue streak at the meddling Duncan.

—and Mouse wakes up again, the Buick stopped behind Dr. Eddington's
Jetta at a Bridge Street traffic light.

Andrew's landlady is standing sentinel on the porch as they drive up to
the house. It's more than her usual watchfulness; she is pacing back and
forth as they come into view, and runs down to the sidewalk to meet them.

"Dr. Eddington," Mrs. Winslow says, as the doctor gets out of the Jetta.
She nods reflectively, as if his arrival is a clue to a puzzle she has been working on.

"Hello, Mrs. Winslow," Dr. Eddington greets her. "Is Andrew here?"

"No," she says, shaking her head now. "No, and I'm worried about him.
He never came home from work, and he hasn't called . . ."

Mouse says: "Maybe he's still with Julie."

Dr. Eddington and Mrs. Winslow both look at her.

"He and Julie drove off somewhere together this morning," Mouse
explains. "They never came back to work."

Mrs. Winslow gets a very complex expression on her face. "Well," she
says, after a moment, "I believe I have Julie's number. Please, come inside.
Both of you." As they are going back up the walk, she says to Dr. Eddington: "I gather you're here to deliver bad news."

"Yes, unfortunately . . ." He tells her about Dr. Grey.

"Poor woman," Mrs. Winslow says. "Andrew's going to take it very
badly, I'm afraid." She sighs. "I know there's never a good time for a thing
like this to happen, but I wish it needn't have happened just now."

"Is something else going on with Andrew?" Dr. Eddington asks.

"Yes, I think so." Mrs. Winslow is looking at Dr. Eddington as she says
this, but Mouse gets the feeling that the comment is really directed at her.

They go inside, to the kitchen at the back of the house, where Mrs.
Winslow puts on coffee and water for tea. While the coffee brews and the
water boils, Mrs. Winslow excuses herself and goes upstairs. She returns
just as the tea kettle starts to whistle.

"There's no answer at Julie's house," she tells them. She pours coffee for
Dr. Eddington, and tea for herself; Mouse politely declines both.

"So," says Dr. Eddington, "Andrew's been having problems?"

"Yes," Mrs. Winslow says, and Mouse braces herself, certain now that
Mrs. Winslow is going to start complaining about her. But instead, Mrs.
Winslow speaks a name that Mouse has never heard before: "It's got some-

thing to do with Warren Lodge, I think . . . have you been paying attention to the news reports about that?"

Dr. Eddington nods. "A number of my patients have been following the story. I take it Andrew was too?"

"We both were. I thought *I* was the most affected by it, and perhaps I was, at first. But on Sunday evening Andrew came home a few hours after Lodge had his accident, or killed himself, or whatever it was that really happened. Andrew had already heard about it, and he was in a state of . . . shock, I guess. I was pretty shaken up myself, so I didn't think much of it at first. But ever since then, he's been different. Distracted—more than usual, I mean. I'd been meaning to talk to him about it . . . and then today around five-thirty, when he hadn't come home yet and hadn't called, I started to get a bad feeling, and it occurred to me—Andrew was *in* Seattle when Warren Lodge died. So maybe he didn't just hear about it. Maybe he saw it."

"That could be," Dr. Eddington allowed. "But if he'd seen something, why wouldn't he tell you about it?"

"I don't know."

"Who is Warren Lodge?" asks Mouse. Mrs. Winslow looks at her like she'd forgotten that Mouse was at the table, and once again Mouse braces herself for a rebuke. But Mrs. Winslow only hunches her shoulders, and in a calm voice tells Mouse a terrible story.

"So you think Andrew saw Warren Lodge get hit by the van?" asks Mouse, when Mrs. Winslow is finished.

"More likely he came across the scene of the accident after it happened," Mrs. Winslow guesses. "Or maybe it was something else entirely, I don't know. *Something* happened to him on Sunday. I—" She breaks off in mid-sentence. There is a pause as she cocks her head, and then she is flying up out of her seat. "Andrew?" she calls. She dashes up the hall towards the front of the house. Dr. Eddington flashes Mouse a quizzical look—*he* didn't hear anything—and the two of them go after Mrs. Winslow.

When they catch up to her she is on the edge of the porch, peering up the darkened street like a sailor scanning the horizon for landfall. For a moment Mouse thinks Mrs. Winslow is imagining things, but then she sees him: Andrew, still about a block away, walking in the middle of the street.

As he comes closer Mouse can see that he is disheveled, his shirt misbuttoned, his hair sticking up on one side. His appearance might almost be perceived as comical, but something about it gives Mouse the creeps. In one hand Andrew grips a bottle, but he doesn't move like he's drunk; he moves like he's on autopilot, sleepwalking. He swings the bottle absently in his fist, as if unaware that he's holding it. His expression is blank.

It looks as if he's going to go right past the house without stopping, but as he comes in line with the Victorian's front door, he jerks up short, hitting the end of an invisible leash, and executes a neat quarter-pirouette— another comic touch that isn't funny. Still blank-faced, he threads the gap between Mouse's Buick and Dr. Eddington's Volkswagen and hops up on the curb.

Missing the walk, he stumbles onto the lawn and stops short again. His eyelids flutter, and behind them, some higher level of awareness sparks to life. Mouse, thoroughly unnerved now, finds herself hiding behind Dr. Eddington.

"Andrew?" Mrs. Winslow says. Andrew looks at her, befuddled, still not all there yet. "Mrs. Winslow?" he says, slurring the words.

Mouse shifts her weight from one foot to the other, causing the porch to creak. It is a small sound, but Andrew hears it; his head pivots in Mouse's direction.

He sees Dr. Eddington.

"Andrew . . ." Dr. Eddington begins, but Andrew is already backing up, shaking his head. He stumbles over a crack in the sidewalk, and lets go of the bottle in his hand; the crash of glass, like the firing of a starter pistol, throws him into full motion. He turns and bolts back out into the street.

Mrs. Winslow leaps off the porch and chases after him, but by the time she reaches the street, Andrew has already got a substantial lead. She calls his name one more time, her voice cracking, then hurries to an old Dodge sedan that is parked in front of Dr. Eddington's Jetta. There is a jingle, then a clatter, of keys; Mrs. Winslow curses and bends down to the ground.

While Mrs. Winslow is retrieving her keys, Dr. Eddington turns to Mouse and says: "I'd better go with her. Can you stay here in case Andrew comes back on his own?"

"OK."

Mrs. Winslow has managed to unlock the sedan and is behind the wheel now, trying to start the engine. Dr. Eddington runs up on the passenger side and raps urgently on the window; the sedan's engine roars to life, and for a moment there is some question as to whether Mrs. Winslow is going to let Dr. Eddington in or drive off without him. Then the front passenger door pops open, Dr. Eddington slips inside, and, before he can shut the door again, Mrs. Winslow backs up, ramming the rear end of the Dodge into the front of the Jetta. She reverses, hits the gas, and roars off in pursuit of Andrew, the Dodge's passenger door still flapping like an unlatched gate.

"Well, *fuck!*" a voice exclaims. Mouse doesn't acknowledge it. She takes a seat in Mrs. Winslow's porch swing.

Andrew never does return to the Victorian, but over the next half hour, the sedan comes back twice. Each time, Mrs. Winslow slows down just long enough for Mouse to stand up and shake her head; then the Dodge peels out again, heads off on another search. Finally—it's getting late, after nine-thirty now—the Dodge comes back a third time and parks haphazardly. Mrs. Winslow gets out, and marches into the house with barely a glance at Mouse; Dr. Eddington, looking a bit haggard from the ride, comes up the walk more slowly.

"You didn't find him," says Mouse, more observation than question.

"We thought we spotted him out by the elementary school," Dr. Eddington says. "But by the time we got the car turned around"—he looks back at the Dodge, which has a brand-new dent in the right front fender—"he'd disappeared again. Still no sign of him here?"

Mouse shakes her head.

Dr. Eddington climbs the steps and leans heavily against the porch railing. "So," he says, "how are you holding out?"

"Fine," says Mouse. "Do you think . . . will Andrew be OK?"

"He should be, once he has a chance to calm down." Dr. Eddington inclines his head towards the front door. "Mrs. Winslow is calling the police right now, so they'll be looking for him . . . though quite frankly, I think it might be best if he comes back on his own, once he's himself again."

"This isn't supposed to happen to Andrew, is it?" asks Mouse. "I mean I know he's like . . . like me . . . but he told me he doesn't have blackouts. He's supposed to be . . . more stable."

"He's supposed to be. But the thing about Andrew is . . ." Dr. Eddington hesitates, choosing his next words with care. "He, his people, should really still be in therapy."

"He seems OK to me," observes Mouse. "Except for tonight."

"There are some important aspects of Andrew's own history that I don't believe Andrew is aware of," Dr. Eddington says. He shakes his head at the question in Mouse's eyes. "Sorry, I can't get into details. Let's just say the initial course of treatment with Dr. Grey . . . didn't reach the intended outcome."

"Oh, I know about Dr. Grey having her first stroke while Aaron was still building the house. He told me about it himself: how he had to finish it on his own, with some help from you . . ." But Dr. Eddington only looks at her, tight-lipped, and Mouse realizes there's more to the story than she's heard. "Well," she continues, "maybe after tonight Andrew will make an appointment with you, like Dr. Grey wanted him to."

"I hope so," Dr. Eddington says. "Tonight *could* be a blessing in disguise, if Andrew doesn't get into too much trouble before we find him . . ."

"The way Andrew was acting tonight," says Mouse. "Is that . . . is that what *I'm* like, when the Society takes over?"

"It frightened you."

Mouse nods.

Dr. Eddington smiles warmly at her. "I'll tell you what," he says. "I'm forty-three years old, I don't smoke, I'm not overweight, and there's no history of cardiovascular disease in my family. So the odds are I'm *not* going to have a stroke while you're in my care." He looks out at the dented Dodge, parked catty-corner by the curb. "About car accidents I can't be so sure," he adds, "but after tonight I think I'm going to stick to doing my own driving."

Mouse smiles too, moved more by his concern for her than by his sense of humor.

"Wow, almost ten," Dr. Eddington says next, checking his watch. "You have work tomorrow?"

"Yes," says Mouse. "I guess."

"You may want to think about going home, then."

"Oh no. I should stay . . ."

"If Andrew does come back tonight, it may not be for several hours yet. I'll probably stay a while myself, but—"

"Mrs. Winslow doesn't want me here, does she?"

Dr. Eddington laughs politely at this notion. "At the moment I'd say Mrs. Winslow is too focused on Andrew to even notice other people"—he glances at the Dodge again—"much less want them gone. You're welcome to stick around; there's just not a lot for you to do here, especially if Andrew stays out all night . . ."

"Maybe I should take a turn looking for him," Mouse suggests.

"If you'd like. We pretty much covered the town, but maybe you'll have better luck." Dr. Eddington smiles encouragingly. "You know the number here, if you do find him?" Mouse nods. "Here's my home number, too," Dr. Eddington says, handing her a card. "Ordinarily I have a rule about patients not calling me after eleven, but tonight I don't think I'm going to sleep much, so even if you don't find Andrew, if you feel like you need to talk to someone later on . . ."

"Thank you," says Mouse. She hops down the steps, then turns around, unable to help herself, and tells him: "You remind me of my father." Dr. Eddington blinks, looking surprised but flattered too, and before he can say anything Mouse runs to her car.

She doesn't know Autumn Creek well enough to conduct any sort of systematic search. If she does find Andrew, it will be by blind luck. Still—and maybe it is only Dr. Eddington's parting smile to her that makes her feel this way—Mouse is unusually optimistic. She has an idea where she might look first: Maynard Park, the same park where she ran to hide on the day Andrew broke the news about her multiplicity. There's no particular reason why Andrew would hide there himself, but Mouse is moved to give it a try.

The intuition does not pan out. The park—at least the open, lit part that Mouse feels comfortable walking around in at night—is deserted. Andrew might be hiding back in the trees, but Mouse cannot quite bring herself to go poking around in there in the dark. Feeling a bit cowardly, she returns to her car and drives back up to Bridge Street.

And that is where she spots him: on Bridge Street, at the Metro bus stop, hiding in plain sight. Mouse can hardly believe it. He must have just gotten here: the bus shelter is bracketed by street lamps, and Andrew is visible from a block away. There's no way Mrs. Winslow could have missed him.

Mouse worries that Andrew will run when he sees her car coming, but in fact he pays no attention as she drives by, turns the Buick around, and pulls it up to the curb just beyond the bus stop. Even after she gets out and starts walking towards the bus shelter he ignores her, not in a calculated way, but in the casual way you do when a stranger joins you in a waiting area and you don't feel like talking.

Still concerned about spooking him, she stops outside the shelter and calls his name: "Andrew?"

No reaction. Andrew is looking the other way, staring into the distance, as if trying to summon a bus through sheer concentration; his hands beat an impatient rhythm against his thighs.

Mouse moves closer. "Andrew?" she repeats.

His hands stop in midpatter; his head jerks around.

"Hey," Andrew asks her. "Do you know what time the next bus is due?"

His voice is different: higher in pitch, quicker in tempo.

"The next bus?" says Mouse. "No, I—"

"There's *supposed* to be a schedule," he complains, indicating an empty rectangular frame fastened to one of the bus shelter's support posts. "It's really very irresponsible that there's supposed to be a schedule but there isn't one."

He's not slurring his words anymore. Mouse can still smell alcohol on his breath—a *lot* of alcohol—but his fast-forward diction is crisp and distinct. He's neatened himself up, too: his shirt has been rebuttoned and the tail tucked in, his hair smoothed back down.

"Where are you going?" Mouse asks him.

He regards her suspiciously for a moment. Then he shrugs, and says: "Michigan."

"What are you going to Michigan for?"

He sighs and looks away. "So you don't know when the next bus is due?"

"Actually, I don't think there are any more buses tonight."

"No more buses?" He jerks his head back around, outraged. "Why not?"

"Well . . . it's late," says Mouse. That doesn't satisfy him, so she stumbles on: "It's late, and these buses are mostly for commuting back and forth to the city . . ."

"And? So?"

"So . . . most people don't commute this time of night."

"Oh," he says. "Oh, right." He slaps out a quick percussion riff on his stomach, then asks, with forced casualness: "What city?"

"Seattle," says Mouse. Just in case: "Seattle, Washington."

"Right." He nods, like he knew it all along. "How far is that from Michigan?"

"A long way. About two thousand miles."

His reaction to this news is difficult to interpret. He seems to go blank for a second, and then, just as abruptly, he's nodding, frowning, and drumming his hands again. "So . . . I guess that's too far to walk, huh?"

"Uh . . . yes," says Mouse. "Yes, it would be."

"A plane ride, though," he says slyly. "A plane ride could take you that far . . . right?"

"Sure."

Frowning: "But plane rides are expensive."

"Yes, they are," says Mouse. "Why do you want to go to Michigan?"

He pats his back pockets, looks momentarily confused, then nods, reaches into one of his front pockets, and pulls out a wallet. He opens the wallet and takes out a small wad of bills: a few twenties, some tens, and some singles. "Is this enough for a plane ride to Michigan?"

"No," says Mouse. "Even a discount ticket would be more than that."

"I have this, too," he tells her, and produces a credit card. "It was hidden," he adds proudly, showing her a secret fold in the wallet, "but I found it." His pride deflates. "But I don't know how much credit is on it . . . If I tried to buy a plane ticket and I went over the limit, do you think I'd get in trouble?"

"I don't know," says Mouse. "Probably not, if . . . if it's your credit card."

He doesn't respond to that, just stuffs the money and the credit card back in the wallet.

"You know what, though," Mouse continues, "if you need some more cash, I bet I know where you could get some. There's a house, just a few blocks from here, and if you came with me I'm sure the lady who lives there would—"

"I should try to get a taxi, I guess," he says, putting the wallet away. "If there are no more buses tonight."

"I could give you a ride," Mouse offers.

His brows knit in suspicion again: "How much?"

"For free . . . and like I was saying, if you need more cash, we can stop at this house . . ."

But he shakes his head. "I shouldn't make any detours. I really need to get to Michigan as soon as possible."

"Why?" Mouse asks, for the third time. By this point she's not expecting an answer, but her persistence pays off.

"I have to collect the inheritance, OK?" He sighs impatiently. "The money I was *supposed* to get from the stepfather."

"The stepfather . . . Andrew's stepfather?"

"Of course Andy's stepfather." He seems amazed by the question. "What other stepfather would I get money from?"

"So he died?"

In the same tone of voice used to complain about the missing bus schedule: "He *should* have. He *looked* like he was dying. He was on the floor in the living room, and there was blood all over the carpet . . ." Unhappily: "But I didn't stick around. I was cold, and I just wanted to get away." He hugs himself. "So you don't think I'd get in trouble if I used the credit card?"

"I-I don't know," says Mouse, struggling to maintain her composure. "But, but listen, why don't we—"

He steps out over the curb, glancing up and down the street. "Where would I go to get a taxi?"

"I don't know. I don't know if you can, here."

"No taxis, either? What kind of place is this?"

"It's a small town," Mouse says.

There's a pause, and then his head starts bobbing. "Where I'm going in Michigan is like that too," he tells her. "They don't even have *buses* there." He frowns again. "How far is the airport?"

"Pretty far," says Mouse. "Too far to walk. But I could drive you."

He looks at her: "No detours?"

"No detours," Mouse lies. She is thinking: if he needs to ask what part of the country he's in, he probably won't be able to tell that she's driving him back to Mrs. Winslow's before they actually get there. She can drive right up on the lawn if need be, right up to the porch, where Mrs. Winslow, with her psychic powers and her bionic ear, will surely be waiting—and between her, Mouse, and Dr. Eddington, they should be able to keep Andrew from running away again.

"Free of charge?" he says, still uncertain.

"Sure," says Mouse. She gestures towards her Buick. "Come on."

The offer of a free ride quickly overcomes his suspicions; within moments they are seated in the Centurion. "Nice car," he says, checking over the interior.

"Thank you," says Mouse.

"If you need to get gas," he adds magnanimously, "I could probably chip in for that. If it's a long drive to the airport, I mean."

"OK," says Mouse. Half a block from the bus stop, she has to stop for a red light. She tries to appear nonchalant as she flicks on her blinker.

The light goes green. Mouse depresses the accelerator and starts to turn right . . . and a third hand grabs the steering wheel, fighting the turn. Mouse has to hit the brakes to keep from plowing into the curb at the far side of the intersection.

"Wh—" Mouse starts to say, her voice rising to a squeak as she sees what has become of her passenger.

He's changed again. He seems bigger, somehow, and the spirit that animates him has transformed from the flighty, manic individual Mouse bantered with at the bus stop into someone far more sinister. Mouse recognizes the dark soul she got a glimpse of on her first day at the Reality Factory: the one who called Julie Sivik a meddling cunt.

He tells her: "*That's* not the way to Michigan . . . *Mouse.*"

Mouse disappears in a cascade of fright. Maledicta comes out, teeth bared . . . but she's scared too. This fucker in the passenger's seat has the same gleam in his eye that Mouse's mother used to get, just before she really went off. So Maledicta is scared, but she doesn't show that she's scared: "Get your motherfucking hand off my steering wheel," she snarls.

"Pardon me," he says, smirking, and lets go of the wheel. Good thing for him: Malefica is up next, and she's *not* scared, she's pissed. But Andrew—whoever the fuck he is right now—isn't interested in pushing his luck. Quicker than Malefica can make a fist, he opens his door and steps out. "Thanks for the lift," he says, "but I'll make my own way from here." With mock courtesy, he eases the door shut, waves good-bye, and trots off into the night.

"Yeah," says Maledicta, resurfacing. "You'd *better* fucking run."

—and Mouse is staring at the empty passenger's seat, while a car horn blares beside her. She puts out a hand to confirm that Andrew is really gone; she checks the back seat, too. Only then does she look outside to see who's honking.

Her car is still in the middle of the intersection, stalled out. The late-night Bridge Street traffic has been detouring around her, but now a minivan wants to get by on the cross street. Mouse restarts the Centurion and backs it up; with a last blast of the horn, the minivan rolls by.

Mouse parks the Centurion at the corner. She sits for a moment, gathering her wits, then checks the rearview mirror and sees that, half a block behind her, the bus shelter is empty now. She gets out of the car and takes a longer look up and down Bridge Street, and up and down the cross street as well; she doesn't see Andrew anywhere. She feels relief, and damns herself for it; Andrew has gone out of his way to help her, and now, in return, she's failed him. She gets back in the car.

What to do? She didn't black out for long—a couple minutes at most, she thinks—so Andrew, if he is still on foot, can't have gone far. With a bit of luck, Mouse could probably find him again. But then what?

Another option, probably the best one, would be to go back to the house and let Mrs. Winslow and Dr. Eddington know what just happened. But that would mean telling them how she actually had Andrew in her car, only to let him get away a second time. Besides, last week, when the shoe was on the other foot and it was Mouse who was on the run, Andrew didn't waste time getting help, he came after her himself; if he hadn't, she might still be stumbling around in the woods behind the Factory.

Maybe she can strike a compromise: she will look for Andrew on her own for the next ten or fifteen minutes. If she doesn't find him, she will go and tell the doctor and Mrs. Winslow what happened. If she *does* find him, she won't try to confront him, she'll just track him, follow him until he stops somewhere; then she will find a phone and call Dr. Eddington.

It's a plan. But before she can put it into practice, there's a piece of information she needs, and to get it she will have to pass a test of courage.

Mouse rests her hands lightly on the rim of the steering wheel, takes a breath, and looks up into the rearview mirror. *Into* it, not just at it. Catching her own eye in the glass, she imagines the mirror is large enough to show her whole face, her entire body; imagines that it reflects, behind her, not the back seat of the Buick, but the mouth of a darkened cave.

"All right," Mouse addresses the figures who gather there, the Society members responding to her summons, "you tell me, whoever saw it . . . which way did he go?"

II

CHAOS

SEVENTH BOOK:
TO THE BADLANDS

19

I was rocking back and forth in the dark.

I had fallen into the lake; I knew that. It had happened in a blur, I'd only been semiconscious, but it seemed like only moments ago so I knew that it had happened, and that I must still be down there, down in the black waters at the bottom of the lake, my soul curled in a fetal position, rocked by the dark currents.

The water was freezing. It flowed around me like a cold wind, caressing my skin, ruffling my hair. It tugged at my whole soul, trying to sweep it away, but my hands had caught in the weeds that grow from the lake bed, each hand grasping a ropy strand, and a third strand of lakeweed had wrapped itself around my left forearm, cinching tight. The weeds stretched but didn't break, and with the ebb and flow of the currents pulling at me I was rocked back and forth, back and forth, back and forth.

I opened my eyes.

I wasn't at the bottom of the lake. I was outside, in the body, in the open air, in daylight. I was sitting in some sort of swing or sling, and a dinosaur was smiling at me.

I blinked.

A dinosaur *was* smiling at me: a green and purple brontosaurus. A ladder was fixed to its side, and a slide ran down the length of its back and tail.

I looked left and right, and saw more dinosaurs: a bright red pteranodon whose wings formed a seesaw; a trio of baby triceratops, yellow, orange, and blue, each one set on a thick, coiled spring, their backs saddled, handholds jutting out from behind the armored ruffs of their collars.

And standing right beside me, arcing over me: a tyrannosaurus. A goofy, smiling, kid-friendly tyrannosaurus, its arms outstretched, its fists holding the ends of the chains that suspended the swing I was sitting in. To keep little fingers from getting pinched in the links, the chains had been sheathed in plastic tubing, flexible and slick to the touch.

I lowered my legs to stop the swing. I slid my hands up the plastic-covered chains and pulled myself to my feet, feeling a sharp pain in my left forearm as I did so. I looked past the brontosaur, past the chain-link fence that surrounded the playground (I was in a playground; I was outside, in the body, in a playground—but *where?*), and saw a rough grassy plain extending towards a line of jagged hills. The hills were barren, almost lunar, their stark weathered faces striped in dull horizontal bands of gray and brown.

Strata, I told myself: *Those bands are called strata.* The word, till now no more than a dictionary definition to me, took on new meaning, and I was frightened. This was an alien landscape I was looking at: I didn't know where it was, but I knew it wasn't anywhere in Autumn Creek, or anywhere *near* Autumn Creek, either.

Something small and white came fluttering down out of the sky, danced for a moment on the air currents in front of my face, lit briefly on my nose, and blew away again.

A snowflake, I thought. A snowflake? It was—it had been—the first week in May. *It doesn't snow in May . . .* no, wait, that wasn't true, it *can* snow in May, it's just not that common, not in Autumn Creek anyway. So OK, I wasn't in Autumn Creek, that much was already established. Maybe I was somewhere farther north, or at a higher elevation; maybe it was a freak spring cold front; maybe the "snowflake" was just a piece of windblown lint.

Maybe. Or *maybe it wasn't May anymore.* I knew I'd lost time, but what if I'd lost *lots* of time? What if it was November now? What if I'd lost *six months . . .* or worse, worse still, what if I'd lost *years*? How old was the body now?

My legs got rubbery, and I had to grab the swing chains to steady myself. I felt the pain in my arm again; this time, seeking a distraction, I looked to see what was causing it. My arm had been bandaged; almost the whole length of my forearm had been wrapped in gauze. It looked like whoever had done it had used an entire roll of the stuff: the gauze was so thickly layered that my shirt sleeve had had to be left rolled up above my elbow.

My shirt sleeve!

"Oh thank God," I exclaimed, collapsing into the swing seat.

My shirt sleeve: it was the *same shirt* I'd been wearing when I blacked out!

Wait. Wait. Was it the same shirt? I remembered falling down drunk in the middle of the street, remembered the tick of a button bouncing away. I checked . . . yes! The shirt was missing a button. I bent my head, sniffed the fabric . . . yes! It stank of scotch. And my pants, socks, and shoes were all the same ones I'd been wearing that night, too.

OK. OK. So it *hadn't* been years or months. A few days maybe, probably, but no more than that. I hadn't blacked out a huge chunk of my lifetime.

I rocked in the swing, laughing with relief.

Of course, this didn't mean that everything was fine. I was still a long way from home, in space if not in time. I still didn't know *where* I was. I also didn't know what the body had been doing, what acts I'd have to take responsibility for; though I did know that before blacking out completely, I'd willfully broken the house rules, and embarrassed myself in front of both Mrs. Winslow and Julie.

Julie . . . oh my God.

No. Don't think about her now. Get oriented first.

"Where am I?" I said, aloud, and then inside: "Where are we? Hello?"

No reply. But it wasn't like there was no one in the pulpit to answer; it was like the pulpit itself wasn't there. That scared me. I wanted to go inside and investigate, but I couldn't leave the body unattended in this playground.

I stood up again.

All this time I'd been facing more or less in one direction. Now I made myself turn around and see what was behind me.

A motel rotated into view. The playground was situated at the narrow end of a V-shaped parking lot; two single-level rows of guest rooms extended diagonally left and right along the lot's outside edges, while a triangular island in the center held the motel office. A slowly turning neon sign on the office roof said BADLANDS MOTOR LODGE.

I took a few steps out into the parking lot, moving cautiously, as if it were paved in black ice rather than asphalt. The lot opened out onto a four-lane road. Directly across the road was a pair of fast-food restaurants, but beyond them I saw what looked like private houses, and more buildings and rooftops beyond them, though nothing taller than two or three stories. A small town, then; I was on the edge of a small town, a town in the Badlands . . . wherever that was.

I tried to imagine the chain of events that had brought me to this place—not the whole story, just the last ten or fifteen minutes. Was I staying at the motel, or had I just been passing by, seen the playground, and decided to have a swing? The latter was the kind of thing Jake would have done—like most little kids, he loves dinosaurs—but on the other hand, he's not much for wandering around strange places on his own, and I couldn't picture him just walking aimlessly down that road. Of course if house discipline had broken down completely, somebody else could have been doing the walking, only to have Jake pop out at the sight of the dinosaurs.

I thought about going into the office to see if the motel manager recognized me. That might work, unless I'd signed in when a different manager was on duty. Then again, if the manager *didn't* recognize me, I could try asking straight out whether I was registered at the motel—but what name should I ask for?

Then it hit me: a key. If I was registered at the motel, I should have a key.

I started checking my pockets. In one of them, a different one than I usually kept it in, I found my wallet. It was light; the last time I'd taken it out, at the bar in Autumn Creek, I'd had almost a hundred dollars in cash, and now I had less than half that. It looked like someone had been using my credit card, too; there's a "secret" compartment where it's supposed to be hidden, but the card had been moved to the center billfold, next to the remaining cash. The wallet's other contents—my library and video rental cards, my father's expired driver's license, and a picture of Andy Gage's mother—appeared untouched.

I searched the rest of my pockets. I found my house key but no motel-room key. It occurred to me that that still didn't settle the question—I might have left the key in the room when whoever-it-was decided to visit the playground. I scanned the rooms on both sides of the parking lot, looking for one with an open door. All the doors were closed.

For the first time, I began to get a real sense of the chaos my father had lived with before the house was built—the chaos Penny Driver *still* lived with.

Penny . . . wait a minute. In a parking space off to my left was a familiar-looking black sedan: a black Buick Centurion, with—yes!—Washington state license plates. I moved up for a closer look, and as I did so, the door of the nearest motel room swung open, and Penny herself came running out. She was barefoot, wrapped in a fuzzy green bathrobe with dinosaurs on it, her hair wet and plastered to her skull. When she saw me standing by the car, she pulled up short and let out a squeak.

"Penny?" I said.

At the mention of her name, Penny looked freshly startled . . . and suddenly hopeful. "Andrew?" she said. I nodded. "Oh thank God! . . . Andrew! . . . *Finally!*"

"Finally," I repeated, wondering just how much lost time that word represented. "What day is it, Penny?"

"May 8th," she told me. "Around ten o'clock in the morning, local time. It's OK, it's only been two days. You left Autumn Creek the night before last."

I nodded again, thinking that it wasn't OK at all but that at least it wasn't as bad as it could have been. I looked back at the playground, at the landscape beyond it. "Where are we?"

"South Dakota," Penny said. "I don't know the name of this town, but it's close to Rapid City." She frowned. "Or at least that's what I was told."

"South Dakota . . ." I went off for a moment, trying to picture where in the country that was—east of the Rocky Mountains, I recalled vaguely, and at least two or three states over from Washington. But this was procrastination, a way of delaying the big question: "How did we get here?"

"That . . ." said Penny, and sighed. "It's complicated."

20

As they follow the truck across Washington state, Maledicta and Malefica take turns at the wheel; Mouse is relegated to backseat driver status, stuck in the cave mouth. This is not what Mouse had in mind when she asked the Society for help. But she's learning there's a price to be paid for requesting the Society's assistance—and for voluntarily giving up control.

"Which way did Andrew go?" she had asked, back in Autumn Creek. It was a simple question, and the answer, when it came, was one that Mouse could have guessed on her own: west. He was headed towards the highway, probably intending to hitch a ride to the airport.

"But what the fuck are you going to do when you catch up to him?" Maledicta inquired, as Mouse started up the Centurion and got rolling. "Run him down? Punch his fucking lights out?"

"No," said Mouse coolly, not interested in talking to herself now that she had what she needed. "Leave me alone now, please."

"Cunt."

Mouse reached the Interstate junction without catching sight of Andrew. Crossing her fingers that he had not already been picked up by someone, she drove up the westbound on-ramp. At the top of the ramp, as she paused to scan the road shoulder in both directions, she saw brake lights flaring on the other side of the median—an eighteen-wheeler was pulling into the eastbound breakdown lane.

"Oh God," said Mouse, as a figure came running up behind the truck and was briefly illuminated by its taillights. It was Andrew. Mouse was on the wrong side of the highway. "He said he wanted to go to the airport!"

"He said he wanted to go to Michigan," someone corrected her. "And you told him he couldn't afford a plane ticket."

Mouse glanced at the broken, rocky strip that separated the two sides of the Interstate. She recalled how, coming to work the first day at the Reality Factory, she'd missed the Autumn Creek exit and had to go miles out of her way before she could turn around.

"Let me drive," Maledicta suggested from the cave mouth. "I'll get you over there in no time."

Andrew had boarded the truck. The eighteen-wheeler's brake lights went off and it started moving again. At the same moment, there was a surge in westbound traffic, vehicles whizzing by so close together that now even getting on the highway going the wrong way was going to be a challenge. Mouse started to panic.

"Come on!" Maledicta pressed her. "Let me fucking drive. He's going to get away!"

The truck was out of the breakdown lane now, picking up speed, about to disappear around a curve.

"You're going to fucking lose him!"

"All *right*," Mouse said, and let go. Reality telescoped; Mouse flew back into the cave mouth. She braced herself there, expecting Maledicta to tromp the accelerator and cut right into traffic. She wondered what a car crash would feel like from inside the cave.

But instead of going onto the highway, Maledicta threw the Buick into reverse and started backing down the on-ramp. "Oh God," Mouse said, cringing, as another car appeared behind them. "Ah, you cocksucker," Maledicta exclaimed. Steering one-handed, she swerved around the other car; the Centurion's fender scraped a guard rail, but there was no collision. Maledicta repeated the maneuver a few seconds later, dodging around another car. And then they were at the bottom of the ramp, coasting backwards onto West Bridge Street. "*Fuck* but I'm good," Maledicta praised herself.

She braked and shifted into drive. She should have gone straight forward, taking the underpass to the eastbound side of the Interstate, but once again she behaved unexpectedly, pulling a U-turn and driving back towards Autumn Creek.

"Hey," cried Mouse, "what are you doing? You're going the wrong way!"

She tried to step forward and take the body back, but found that she couldn't. It wasn't even a question of a struggle, like the last time Maledicta had tried to keep the body from her; Mouse simply couldn't get beyond the cave mouth.

"You're going the wrong way!" Mouse repeated, frustrated. "We're going to lose Andrew!"

"The fuck we are," said Maledicta. "That's a long-haul truck he's on; it'll stay on the fucking Interstate, and we'll fucking catch up to it, no problem. But"—she flicked a finger at the gauges on the Buick's dashboard—"before we drive over the fucking Cascades, we need gas. Gas and supplies."

"Oh," said Mouse. "Oh, OK, that's fine then . . . but let me drive . . ."

Maledicta laughed. "Fuck you."

There was a gas station and convenience store right next to the west bridge; Maledicta drove in there and pulled up to the self-service pumps. She started one of the pumps running, using a Shell credit card that Mouse had never seen before (come to think of it, Mouse couldn't specifically recall ever buying gas before). While the Buick's tank filled, she went into the convenience store to get junk food and cigarettes.

As Maledicta pawed through a Hostess display rack, Mouse made another attempt to retake control of the body. No use: it was as though an invisible barrier had been stretched across the cave mouth, a force field that only got stronger the harder she fought against it.

"*Give it up, fucking give it up, baby* . . ." Maledicta sang. She went to the register and tossed two packages of Ding Dongs on the counter. "Winstons," she told the clerk. "Unfiltered."

The clerk reached up to a rack above his head. Mouse, still pushing futilely against the barrier, tried calling to him: "Help! . . . Help!" The clerk dropped Maledicta's Winstons next to the Ding Dongs and began ringing up the purchase.

"Hey," Maledicta asked him, "do you hear something?"

The clerk gave her a blank look. "Like what?"

"Sounded like a fucking mouse squeaking."

"Probably just my new shoes," the clerk said. He demonstrated by squeaking a heel against the floor behind the counter.

"Yeah," Maledicta laughed, "that must be it."

Maledicta paid and returned to the car. Mouse, defeated, tried to resign herself to captivity inside her own head. But when Maledicta *still* didn't head for the Interstate, Mouse lost her composure again: "What are you *doing?*"

"Jesus fucking Christ," Maledicta said, puffing on one of her new Winstons. "Get off my ass."

"We're supposed to be following Andrew! We—"

"I want to get a fucking drink first."

"There's no time for that!"

"If you don't get off my fucking ass," Maledicta warned, "I'm going to stop the fucking car and not go another mile until I smoke every fucking cigarette in this pack. And then I'm *still* going to get a drink. You can't fucking handle that, then go back down in the cave and sleep—it's what you're fucking best at anyway."

There was a liquor store on Bridge Street, but it had closed at nine o'clock, so Maledicta went to a bar instead. As they swung around to park, Mouse recognized Julie Sivik's Cadillac among the other cars along the curb. She thought she might have seen Julie sitting in the Cadillac, too, but because Maledicta controlled the view, Mouse couldn't look around to make sure.

"Hey," said Mouse, as Maledicta lit a fresh cigarette and hopped out of the Buick. "Hey wait, turn right, is that Julie over there?"

"Who the fuck cares?" Maledicta said, and entered the bar.

This late on a weeknight, the bar was almost empty—just a few couples in booths (including a raucous pair of drunks near the back), and no one at all at the bar counter except the woman tending it.

The bartender was a vampire: white skin, black hair, black eye shadow, black lipstick, black nail polish, and stainless-steel piercings in her nose, eyebrows, and both cheeks. Mouse thought she looked hideous. Maledicta thought she looked hideous, too, and for that very reason warmed to her—briefly.

"Popov," Maledicta said, stepping up to the bar. "No ice."

"Ah," said the vampire, sourly. "The good stuff."

As the vampire poured her a shot of cheap vodka, Maledicta asked: "How much for the whole fucking bottle, to go?"

"We don't do carry-out," the vampire informed her. "Liquor store's down the street."

"Liquor store's closed," Maledicta said.

"Well, that's too bad then, huh?"

"I'll give you forty fucking dollars," Maledicta offered, holding up Mouse's wallet.

"Wow!" exclaimed the vampire sarcastically. "Forty *fucking* dollars! Let me think about it . . . no!"

"Lousy cunt," Maledicta muttered, as the vampire replaced the bottle on its shelf. She picked up the shot and downed it in one angry gulp. Up in the cave mouth, Mouse heard a soft scraping sound and saw Malefica come crawling forward, panther-like.

Then someone behind them said: "Mouse?"

Maledicta looked around. It was Julie Sivik. "Fuck off," Maledicta greeted her, and turned back to the bar.

"Maledicta," said Julie.

Maledicta turned around again. "Well," she said, "I see somebody's got a big fucking mouth." Then she shrugged, and held up her shot glass. "You drinking?"

"What?" said Julie, as if she hadn't noticed they were in a bar. "Oh . . . oh God, no, no more for me tonight. The past couple hours I've been, well, *hiding*, I guess . . . but I'm on my way home now, so I just thought I'd stop and get my car, and then I saw you coming in here . . ."

"Uh-huh," Maledicta said, already bored with this story.

"Anyway, listen, have you seen Andrew? I *don't* want to see him," Julie added hastily, "but I'm a little worried about him, and I wanted to make sure he made it home OK. And I thought, if *you're* still here in town this time of night—"

"You're the one who got him shitfaced," Maledicta guessed. "Good fucking job."

"Shitfaced," Julie echoed. "So you have seen him, then . . ."

"Fuck yeah," said Maledicta, grinning. "We saw him."

"Is he OK? Did he get home?"

"For about ten seconds," Maledicta told her. "Then he fucking took off again."

"Took off?"

"He said he was leaving town . . . what the fuck did you do to him, anyway? I've never seen anyone so fucking upset before."

"Don't do this," Mouse spoke up, from the cave mouth. "This is *mean*."

"He told you he was leaving town?" said Julie. "What does that—you don't mean leaving for good, do you?"

Maledicta crooked a finger, gesturing for Julie to lean in close. When Julie did, Maledicta whispered in her ear: "I need you to do me a fucking favor. You see this fucking cunt behind me? I need you to get her away from the bar for a minute."

"What?" Julie said.

"Just go back to the bathroom for a few seconds, then come back up here and tell her there's no fucking toilet paper. Or no, wait, that might not be fucking good enough, she might not give a shit . . . I know! Tell her the fucking sink is broken, that it's flooding back there . . ."

"Mouse—Maledicta!" Julie said. "*What did Andrew say to you?*"

"Ah!" Maledicta dismissed her, annoyed. She turned back to the bar, and rapped her shot glass on the wood counter to get the vampire's attention. "Hit me."

"Love to," said the vampire. She started to pour another shot of vodka, but suddenly there was a loud crash from the rear of the barroom, followed by roars of laughter. It was the two noisy drunks, who had somehow contrived to smash the light fixture above their booth. "Goddamnit!" the vampire spat. Leaving the vodka bottle on the counter, she went to yell at the drunks. Maledicta was delighted; as soon as the vampire's back was to her, she snatched the bottle and ran out of the bar.

"Hey!" Mouse squeaked impotently from the cave mouth. "You can't do that! That's stealing!"

"Fucking-A," said Maledicta. "The stupid cunt should've taken the forty bucks when she had the chance."

"But . . . *I'm* going to be blamed for that!"

"Yeah." Maledicta laughed. "It wouldn't be the first time."

They were at the car now. Julie Sivik came running after them: "Maledicta! . . . Maledicta, wait! You have to tell me what happened with Andrew!"

"Don't fucking stress about it," Maledicta said, fishing for her keys. "We're going to bring him back."

"Bring him back? You mean you know where he is?"

"We know how to fucking find him."

"I'm coming with you . . ."

"The fuck you are."

"Maledicta—"

The front door of the bar banged open; the vampire came out. "Hey!" she yelled.

"Gotta go," Maledicta said, ducking down into the driver's seat. As she sped away, she looked back to see Julie making a dash for her own car, only to be body-checked by the vampire. No doubt they would have an interesting conversation.

"Ha ha ha—*fuck!*" Maledicta hooted joyously. She tipped up the vodka bottle, which was still capped by a speed server, and poured a perfectly measured shot into her open mouth. "Aaaahhh . . . that was pretty fucking exciting, huh?"

"You're *horrible*," said Mouse.

"Yeah, I'm a worthless piece of shit, all right," Maledicta said, and laughed again.

That was two and a half hours ago. Once they were on the Interstate, it took them less than an hour to catch up to the truck (or what Maledicta says is the truck; Mouse hopes they've got the right one). Since then they've been tailing it in a relatively low-speed pursuit that, after the previous excitement, has already become tedious.

For the past hour Maledicta and Malefica have been spelling each other at the wheel, switching off every ten minutes or so; Mouse suspects she could probably cut in during one of these switches, but she doesn't want to risk a car wreck, so she stays in the cave mouth and waits for a safer opportunity. It doesn't look like they will be stopping anytime soon, however, and as the miles drag on, it gets harder and harder for her to stay alert—

—and then she is back in the body.

It's dawn, the sky brightening to a gray overcast. The Buick is parked in a rest area off the highway, outside an International House of Pancakes. A memorandum tucked into the sun visor above Mouse's head reads: I-90 REST STOP, 10 MI. PAST IDAHO BORDER.

Mouse yawns and stretches, rubs her face. She checks the dashboard clock: 5:31. Strange. In one sense, she's been asleep for the last few hours; in another sense, she hasn't slept at all. Her soul is rested—sort of—but her body has been up all night. This is not a new experience for her, but it's the first time it's happened that she's fully understood it, and the understanding leaves her feeling disjointed, punch-drunk.

Or maybe she's just drunk. She sniffs. Her breath, her clothes, her car, all reek of vodka and cigarettes. The pack of Winstons Maledicta bought in Autumn Creek lies crumpled on the dash, empty. The Popov bottle, on the floor beneath her feet, is empty too, but on closer inspection most of its contents appear to have been spilled, not consumed—the floor mat is soaked.

Mouse pulls down the memorandum from the sun visor and reads the whole message: I-90 REST STOP, 10 MI. PAST IDAHO BORDER. 4-CAR PILEUP ON ROAD = SHIT TRAFFIC LAST HOUR, SHOUDVE LET YOU FUCKING DRIVE AFTER ALL. TRUCK DROPPED ANDWHO OFF HERE & LEFT WITHOUT HIM SO YOUR UP DONT FUCK UP.

Mouse is grimly amused by Maledicta's gripe about the traffic—*serves her right*, she thinks, *for stinking up my car*. And Andrew . . . Andrew is on foot again, it seems. But where exactly is he? The memorandum doesn't say.

"Where's Andrew?" Mouse asks, aloud. "Did he go into the IHOP?"

No answer. Maledicta and Malefica must be back in the cavern, sleeping off the drive; and whatever other Society members are awake either don't know or aren't talking.

Mouse gathers the empty cigarette pack and the Ding Dong wrappers, and picks up the vodka bottle, holding it by the neck between two fingers. She gets out of the car. The air outside is bracing, but she doesn't mind; after disposing of the trash, she just stands there for a while, leaning into the wind with her arms outstretched, letting the cold deodorize her. It's not especially effective; what she really needs is a hot shower and a change of clothes. A good tooth-brushing wouldn't hurt, either. But first things first.

She goes over to the IHOP and peers in one of the windows. Sure enough, Andrew is inside: he's got a big table all to himself, and is skimming a newspaper as he works his way through two separate stacks of pancakes—one swimming in butter and syrup, one dry.

There's a pay phone right outside the restaurant. Mouse doesn't have enough change for a long-distance call, so she dials Dr. Eddington's number collect. She gets his answering machine, and the operator won't let her leave a message. Next she tries Mrs. Winslow's number; her phone is busy. Mouse hangs up. Now what? She could dial 911, but she's not sure the police would believe her story, particularly in her current condition; they might decide to lock her up for drunk driving and send Andrew on his way. She also doesn't want to get Andrew in trouble: what if the police question him, and he starts talking about his stepfather?

Still trying to come up with a plan, Mouse returns to the window. Inside, Andrew has finished one stack of pancakes and pushed the other aside. He sips coffee and reads his newspaper. Now he sets the coffee cup down, picks up a teaspoon, and begins beating on the tabletop with it.

No, not beating—he's *drumming* on it, tapping out a rhythm . . .

"Hi," Mouse says, as she slips into an empty chair at Andrew's table.

"Hello," he says, looking curious but not all that surprised to see her. "What are you doing here?"

A high-pitched, quick-tempoed voice . . . Mouse guessed correctly: this is the person she met at the bus stop last night, the one who accepted her offer of a ride. Now if she can just finesse this next part without bringing out that *other* guy . . .

"Just passing through," Mouse says simply, in answer to his question, and he nods, like it's no big coincidence that she'd just happen to drive three hundred miles and show up at the same rest stop he's at. "But what about you? I thought you were going to fly to Michigan last night."

"Oh," he says, missing a beat. "Oh, it, uh, turned out I couldn't get a flight."

"Oh," says Mouse. "Well that's too bad."

"Yeah . . . after you, after you dropped me off at the airport, I, there must not have been, there were no flights available." He gets lost for a moment, then continues: "It's OK, though, I got a ride on a truck."

"Oh." Mouse makes a point of looking around. "Is the driver—"

"Well actually, it's not *totally* OK," he interrupts her. "The way I understand it, the truck was *supposed* to take me all the way to Chicago—that's near Michigan, right?—but then the truck driver and I had a, I guess you'd call it a personality conflict, and he made me get off here. Which is not a very responsible thing to do, going back on a promise you made, even if you decide you don't *like* a person . . . So do you think it'll be hard for me to get another ride?"

Mouse hesitates, trying to gauge how much subtlety is required here. Probably not much. "I could give you a ride," she says.

"Yeah?" He hesitates too, and Mouse can tell he's debating whether to ask if this ride will cost money.

"No charge," Mouse says, sparing him the question. "I feel bad that your plane ride didn't work out."

"Oh, well . . . that's not your fault, I'm sure. So you're driving to Michigan now?"

Mouse nods. "I'm hoping to see a friend there."

"Well, OK then . . . let's go!" Ready to leave that instant, he starts to get up from the table, notices that Mouse isn't doing the same, and pauses, confused. "Oh," he says, after a moment's thought, "are you . . . did you want to eat something first?" He gestures at his leftover pancake stack. "The waitress brought me two orders by mistake. So if you'd like . . ."

"No thank you," says Mouse. The cigarettes Maledicta smoked have temporarily suppressed her appetite, and when it comes back she's afraid she's going to be sick to her stomach, so eating someone else's leftovers is probably not a good idea. "But there is one thing," she says. "I know you don't want to make any detours, but I am going to have to stop and rest for a few hours."

"What?"

"I've been driving all night. I need sleep, or at least a nap. Not right away—I could go another hour yet, probably—but then I'm going to need to stop at a motel for a while."

He frowns. "A motel?"

Mouse nods, thinking: *Someplace off the Interstate, where you'll be stranded while I call Dr. Eddington.*

"And how long would you want to stop?"

"Not long," Mouse promises. "A few hours."

"A few hours . . . well . . ."

"I understand you don't want to delay, but I'd be worried that if you stay here, you might not get a ride at all . . . at least, not a *free* ride . . ."

It doesn't take much of this to persuade him. Once he's agreed, Mouse asks: "By the way, what's your name?"

"Xavier," he tells her. "Xavier Reyes."

"Hello, Xavier, I'm Penny." Mouse shakes his hand, then adds: "Now you just wait here a second while I go use the bathroom, OK? I'll be right back."

Mouse intends to freshen up quickly and then duck outside to the pay phone to try Mrs. Winslow's number again, but when she comes out of the bathroom, Xavier is waiting by the door for her. He jerks his head impatiently, indicating that they should go, and Mouse has little choice but to follow him.

Outside, he walks straight to her car without bothering to ask where she's parked—and instead of standing aside and waiting for her to unlock the doors, he steps up to the driver's side and holds out his hand for the keys. "I think I'll drive for a while," he says. "Since you're so tired."

"You'll—"

". . . *Mouse*," he adds, grinning savagely.

Him. Mouse draws back fearfully and very nearly disappears; only the all-too-recent memory of being trapped in the cave mouth stops her from giving up control. Instead she gathers herself to run away physically. But he doesn't pounce, or try to grab her; in fact he makes no threatening overtures at all, except for that nasty grin.

"Now you listen," he says. "I'm not stealing your car, all right? If you want to tag along with me, that's fine—but I'm *not* going back to Autumn Creek, and I'm not going to tap my toes at some motel while you call for the men in the white coats."

"Who are you?" Mouse asks.

He ignores the question, and gestures impatiently with his outstretched hand. "Give me the keys."

She shakes her head.

"Fine," he says, and shrugs. "I'll just get another ride, then. Feel free to follow me if you think you can stay awake . . ." He starts to walk away.

"Wait!"

He turns back.

"I don't," Mouse stammers, "I don't trust you."

"I don't trust you either," he says, "and I've got better cause not to. But I'm not going to hurt you, if that's what you're afraid of—not unless you try to hurt me first." He holds out his hand again. "Keys."

Mouse takes her keys out of her pocket but doesn't hand them over. "You . . . you're sure you can drive?"

"I might be out of practice," he allows, "but I won't fall asleep at the wheel."

"What about your head? You were awfully drunk last night . . ."

"That wasn't me."

"It was your body."

"Yours too, by the smell of things." He shrugs. "Maybe I am a little hung over this morning—I'm tough, I can cope with that. It's not *my* hangover. And I did get some sleep in that truck, once I got the driver to shut the hell up . . ." Losing patience again: "So are we doing this, or not?"

Still full of misgivings, but with no idea of what else to do, Mouse gives him the keys. As he snatches them out of her hand, the panic comes welling up again: she's a fool, he's tricked her, he *is* going to steal the car, just drive off and leave her here . . .

He reads the fear in her eyes, and laughs. "I *could* leave you behind," he says, "but I won't. I'm going to need you to drive when I get tired." He unlocks the Centurion's back door for her, and opens it. "Go on, lie down—I'll wake you when it's your turn."

She gets in, but she doesn't lie down. Though no less tired than she was five minutes ago, she can't imagine sleeping now. Instead she sits up straight, her hands worrying at the Buick's rear seatbelts, which are tangled and frayed and have never buckled properly anyway.

"God," he says, sliding in behind the wheel, "what a stench!" He looks over his shoulder at her. "Not your fault, I suppose."

"I," Mouse begins, and then gives up. He doesn't really care whose fault it is that the car smells; he's just taunting her.

Moving slowly, like a pilot at the controls of an unfamiliar plane, he gets the Buick's engine started, then spends a long moment studying the dashboard gauges and indicators, the blinker switches, and the gearshift. Mouse expects him to be reckless behind the wheel, like Maledicta, but just the opposite is true—when he finally releases the parking brake and gets moving, he turns out to be even more cautious a driver than Mouse herself. On the way out of the rest stop, he yields to every vehicle that crosses his path, and at the top of the highway on-ramp hesitates so long before merging, waiting for the perfect gap in traffic, that other cars and trucks stacked up behind him start to honk. Once on the Interstate, he keeps to the right-hand lane and holds the speedometer at fifty, twenty-five miles per hour below the posted speed limit.

"So," says Mouse, thinking to make small talk, maybe learn his name and something about him, but he cuts her off.

"Don't distract me while I'm driving," he says.

"Sorry," Mouse apologizes. Chagrined, she slides down in her seat a little—

—and the car is stopped again, and she's being shaken awake. When Mouse opens her eyes and sees him leaning over her, a hand on her leg, she lets out a sharp squeak, and he starts, thumping his head hard against the roof of the car.

"OW!" he roars, stumbling backwards out of the Centurion, hand pressed to the back of his skull. "Damn it, you stupid bitch! . . . I wasn't try-ing to hurt you, it's just your turn to drive . . ."

Mouse sits up. They're parked at another rest stop. It's smaller than the last one, set in a broad green valley among snow-capped mountains, the Rockies most likely. Mouse checks the dashboard clock: 11:25. "Where are we?"

"Montana," he tells her, wincing. "Past Missoula, coming up on Butte. I just got us gas . . . Ow!"

"Sorry," says Mouse, though she isn't, really. She gently fingers the back of her own neck; she's mostly recovered from her run-in with the tree, but there's still some residual tenderness, and she's going to have to watch that it doesn't flare up again. For now, though, she feels OK.

She's also starving. She climbs out of the car, and looks around to see what the rest stop has to offer in the way of food.

"I've got you covered," he says.

"What?"

"You're hungry, right?" He points to a white paper sack on the roof of the car. "I got you a hamburger and fries. There's a Pepsi in there, too."

"Oh . . . thank you." Of course he's not really being considerate; he just doesn't want to have to worry about her sneaking off to use the phone. Mouse thinks about going into a restaurant anyway, just to defy him—now that she's seen him bump his head, he's not so scary anymore. But scary or not, he's still got the car keys, and if he gets mad he might drive off without her.

Despite the snowy peaks, it's actually warmer here than at the Idaho rest stop. The sky is clear and the sun is almost directly overhead; the midday wind is gentle and not so cold. Mouse eats standing up beside the car. He leans against the front hood and smokes a cigarette—a Winston, Male-dicta's brand.

"Are you going to tell me your name?" Mouse asks between bites.

He shakes his head, exhaling smoke.

"What do I call you, then?"

"Try 'Andrew.'"

"No," says Mouse. "I don't think so."

He scowls at her. "I *am* Andy Gage, you know," he says. "More than any of those others. They aren't even real, they're just . . . delusions with egos."

"What about Xavier?"

"What about him?"

"Well, it seems like the two of you are . . . working together, sort of. Is *he* a delusion?"

"Xavier is a tool," he says. "A *useless* tool," he adds, annoyed. "I mean, you've met him: he was supposed to be clever, but it turns out he's got about as much guile as a hubcap. A housefly could outwit him. And he's also a coward . . ."

"A coward?" says Mouse.

He puffs on his cigarette.

"Did you," Mouse tries a different tack, "did you *make* Xavier? Call him out, the way Aaron called out Andrew?"

He chuckles, as if she's just said something amusing, but he doesn't answer the question.

"Finish up," he tells her a moment later, dropping his cigarette butt on the ground and stepping on it. "I want to keep moving."

"All right . . ." Mouse pops a last french fry into her mouth and looks around for a place to dump her garbage . . . but he takes the bag and the half-empty soda can from her and tosses them on the ground beside his cigarette butt. "Come on," he says.

He hands her the car keys and climbs in the back. Mouse gets into the driver's seat. She doesn't like having him behind her, but it's more discomfort than fear now; she's all but certain he has no intention of harming her. And even if something happened where he did try to hurt her, she can sense Maledicta and Malefica lounging near the cave mouth, ready to step forward to defend her.

A realization hits her then, and she can't help laughing.

"What?" he says. "What's funny?"

"Nothing," says Mouse. She uses the sound of the engine start to mask another snort of laughter. No, nothing's funny, except that against all expectation, and without meaning to, she's taken Dr. Grey's advice and started thinking of her Society as *allies.*

The realization leads to another: she may have allies, but evidently *he* doesn't. He called Xavier "useless"; and it doesn't sound like there are any other souls he can call on in a crisis. So maybe if Mouse could precipitate a crisis, create a situation that he couldn't handle on his own, maybe that would cause someone else, a *non-ally,* to come out—Andrew, or Andrew's father, or at least someone who could put her in touch with them.

It's something to think about while she's driving. She does think about it, even going so far as to discuss the idea, silently, with Maledicta. But Maledicta's not much help; when Mouse asks what would be a good way to shock their passenger into giving up control of Andrew's body, Maledicta replies: "Why don't you let Malefica tie him to the back bumper and drag him for a few miles?" She says this like she's not kidding.

"I don't want to hurt him," Mouse says. "At least, I don't want to hurt Andrew."

"What you need to do," another Society member speaks up, "is get him talking about himself. Find out what he's afraid of."

It's a good idea, but he's not interested in talking, particularly not about his fears. "Just keep driving," he tells her.

She keeps driving; she talks to herself. The Society keeps its collective eyes peeled for an opportunity to fool or force him into switching.

By 2:45 on the dashboard clock they're in Billings, where Mouse stops for more gas. Rather than hunt up Maledicta's Shell card, she insists that *he* pay for it. After the gas station they go to an Arby's to eat—he pays for that too, with one of Andrew's twenty-dollar bills—and use the bathrooms. Once more Mouse tries to hurry her business, but when she comes out of the ladies' he's right there waiting for her. They go back out to the car. He's ready to drive again, but Mouse, unwilling to give up control, says she's good for another few hours.

They cross the state line into Wyoming at 4:52. At 6:39 Mouse notices the sun starting to go down, which seems early, until she remembers: traveling east, almost a thousand miles from Seattle already, they're in a new time zone. She thinks about resetting the dashboard clock, but Maledicta, up in the cave mouth, argues against it: "You *want* it set to the wrong time, to headfuck that fucker in the back seat. If you're going to fucking change it, you should make it *more* wrong. Set it to fucking Tokyo time." In the end, Mouse leaves the clock as it is.

The Rockies are well behind them now; they are crossing a broad swath of grassland that stretches between the Bighorn Mountains and the Black Hills. Traffic is very sparse here, and the rolling sameness of the scenery makes for dull driving. Mouse, who has maintained a conservative sixty-five miles an hour for most of the afternoon, lets the Buick's speed creep up to the posted maximum of seventy-five. Then Malefica, bored and in a mood for mischief, slips out in a moment of distraction and puts some real lead in Penny Driver's right foot.

—and so just as the sun dips below the horizon, flashing lights appear behind them, a siren wails, and Mouse looks to find the speedometer needle edging towards one hundred.

"Oh God," Mouse says.

"—slow down, you idiot!" he yells from the back seat, has been yelling. "Slow down, slow down, slow down—"

She is slowing down—her foot is off the gas, and the needle swings back, to ninety, eighty, sixty, forty. The patrol car is right on her tail now, its lights still flashing, signaling her to pull over. Mouse steers the Centurion obediently onto the soft shoulder.

In the back seat he's having a meltdown.

"You stupid, stupid . . ." he sputters, at a loss for an epithet to use on her. "What were you driving so *fast* for?"

"It . . ." Mouse sputters in turn, "I don't think it was me."

"Oh great."

"*I'm* the one who's going to get in trouble, you know," Mouse points out. "I don't see what you're getting so upset about."

"You'd just better not try anything," he warns. "You'd better not say anything, about . . ."

"Don't worry about it." In fact Mouse has already considered the possibility, and rejected it. If she was unwilling to dial 911 from the Idaho rest stop, there's no way she's going to try explaining her situation to a cop who's just pulled her over for speeding.

The Wyoming state trooper is out of his car, one hand holding a flashlight, the other resting on the butt of his gun. He walks up, raps a knuckle on Mouse's window. She rolls it down.

"Good evening," the trooper says. He bends his face down to the window and shines his flashlight around the Centurion's interior. Mouse waits patiently and surprisingly calmly to be asked for her license and registration, but her passenger rocks anxiously in the back seat, sucking in his breath as the light flicks over him.

The trooper's nose twitches.

Oh God, Mouse thinks, remembering. The car's been aired out some since this morning—she had the front windows cracked through most of Montana—but it still smells like a distillery.

The trooper shines his flashlight in Mouse's face, in her eyes. "Have you consumed any alcohol this evening, ma'am?" he asks.

"No," Mouse replies, hearing another nervous inhalation behind her. "No, I'm sorry, I know how it smells, but . . . no, I haven't been drinking."

The trooper waits, still shining the light on her.

"We . . . I was at a party last night," Mouse continues.

"You had a party in your car last night?"

"No!" says Mouse, her voice cracking a little now. "No, I was *at* a party, parked, and there was . . . an accident. A bottle of vodka got spilled, and I just haven't had a chance to get it cleaned up. I, we, we've been driving all day."

"I see," the trooper says. He steps back from her door. "Could you get out of the car please, ma'am?"

"OK," Mouse says, and does. "I'm sorry, I know I was going pretty fast—"

"Yes ma'am, you were. Could you step over here to the back of your car, please? . . . That's fine, now what I'm going to ask you to do is hold your arm straight out from your shoulder like this, close your eyes, and touch your nose."

Mouse does as she's told. Finger on the tip of her nose, eyes still closed, she waits for the next instruction. But when the trooper speaks again, the words are not directed at her: "Sir!" he calls, his voice moving away from Mouse, "Sir, would you stay in the car, please? *Sir!*"

Mouse opens her eyes. In the back seat of the Buick, her anonymous passenger has panicked and wants to get out. But the trooper steps up to the car door and blocks it with his body. Mouse's passenger makes a frightened mewling sound and shoves hard against the door; the trooper, dropping his flashlight, shoves back. "Sir!" he says, his voice straining with the effort it takes to keep the door closed. "I need you to stay in the car, sir!"

"Oh God," says Mouse. "Please, he's . . . he's claustrophobic! Please, don't—" She takes a step towards the car; the trooper draws his gun.

—and all is quiet again. Mouse is back in the driver's seat. The Centurion is still parked on the road shoulder, but the patrol car is gone. The dashboard clock reads 7:48.

With a shaking hand, Mouse turns on the Centurion's inside lights. A speeding ticket is tucked into the sun visor; Mouse pulls it down, glances at it unseeingly, and sets it aside.

"Andrew?" she says, looking behind her. The back seat appears to be empty—but then a head rises into view.

"Why are we stopped?" he asks. "Are we in Michigan yet?"

"*Xavier?*"

"I'm sorry, I must have fallen asleep." Xavier looks out the windows at the darkened landscape. "Where are we? Is this Michigan?"

"N-no," says Mouse, heart hammering in her chest. "No, it's . . . we're about halfway there."

"Only halfway? Why are we stopped, then?"

"Uh . . . car trouble," Mouse tells him. "I, I think it's OK now, but I'm going to have to make a stop at a garage to get it checked . . ."

"*Another* stop?" Xavier says.

"It's OK, really," says Mouse. "We're making great time." She turns around and reaches for the ignition.

"*Mouse,*" he says. "Don't."

Mouse stops, her hand on the ignition key. She feels like crying.

"Get out," he tells her. "I'm driving."

Mouse fights back the tears. "You *can't,*" she says.

"No? You don't think so?"

"What if we get stopped by the police again?"

"*I'm* not going to drive like it's the Indy 500."

"What if we get stopped again anyway?" Mouse says. "Do you even have a driver's license?"

"Do I—" He pauses. Mouse hears him pull out his wallet and flip through it. "Ah-hah!" he cries triumphantly, but the cry cuts off too soon. "Wait," he says. "What year is this?"

"1997," says Mouse.

"Goddamnit! . . ."

"So you don't have a driver's license," Mouse says. "And if we do get stopped again, especially with the car smelling like this, you'll probably be arrested."

"Fine," he says. He reaches for the door handle. "I'll just get out here, then, and—"

"We're in the middle of nowhere," Mouse reminds him. "It's getting cold out. You might freeze before you get another ride."

The look he gives her is withering. "All right," he says. "You want to drive, then drive—to the next big town. Then I am getting out."

Mouse hesitates. "Look," she says, softening her voice, "I really wasn't trying to get us pulled over. If you want to go on traveling together, I promise, I won't—"

He cuts her off. "Just drive . . . or else."

She drives.

The next big town is Rapid City, South Dakota—no more than an hour and a half away, even if Mouse keeps the car's speed down. She has ninety minutes to think of something. At first it seems hopeless: every time she checks the rearview mirror he's staring at her, as if he can hear her plotting against him.

But as Mouse herself has learned firsthand, vigilance can be exhausting. Not long after they cross the state border, she looks in the mirror for the umpteenth time and finds him asleep.

Most of him, anyway: his body has slumped down in the seat, and his head is lolling back. But as Mouse continues to watch him, dividing her attention between the mirror and the road ahead, his right arm comes up, like a cobra rising out of a basket, until the back of his hand brushes the roof of the car. His hand recoils from the contact, tenses, and begins striking the roof deliberately, alternating between soft and hard blows.

Thump-THWACK-THWACK-thump . . . thump . . . THWACK-thump . . . THWACK-thump . . . THWACK-thump-THWACK-THWACK . . .

"Xavier?" says Mouse. But this isn't one of Xavier's drum solos; it's something else.

. . . thump-THWACK-THWACK . . . thump-thump-thump-thump . . . thump . . . thump-THWACK-thump . . . thump . . .

Code, Mouse realizes. It's a message in code.

"I don't understand," she says.

The rapping hand pauses, then starts over again: *Thump-THWACK-THWACK . . . thump-thump-thump-thump . . .*

"No," says Mouse, "I mean I don't know Morse code. Unless . . . Maledicta? Do you—"

Suddenly *he* snaps awake, his head jerking forward. "What . . . ?" he exclaims, staring at his upraised arm. He glowers at Mouse. "What the hell just happened?"

"Nothing," Mouse says, not very convincingly. "You were just stretching in your sleep."

"Right." They are passing a road sign: RAPID CITY—42. "Drive faster," he says.

"I've got it at fifty," says Mouse. "I thought you didn't want me to—"

"Drive faster. I want this ride over with."

He settles back in the seat, his left hand gripping his right forearm as if to restrain it. Mouse can see that he is scared now. The encounter with the state trooper must really have shaken him up; he is starting to lose control. But barring a second police stop, Mouse still doesn't know how she is going to push him over the edge in the short time she has left.

In the end, the South Dakota state tourist bureau does the job for her.

Besides the mile markers, they are passing a lot of billboards touting various tourist attractions: Mount Rushmore, the Crazy Horse Monument, Wounded Knee, Petrified Gardens, and something called Wall Drug, which Mouse has never heard of, but which is apparently a very big deal around here. FILL UP YOUR JUG . . . AT WALL DRUG, one billboard invites, somewhat cryptically. Another, showing a display case overflowing with merchandise, reads: WALL DRUG STORE—ALL THIS AND *FREE ICE WATER*, TOO!

"My goodness," he says from the back seat. "Is that *the* Wall Drug Store?"

It's a new voice. "I-I don't know," says Mouse. "I guess so. What is it, some kind of mall?"

"It's supposed to be one of the most amazing malls in the country," he says. "It's *much* better than Westlake Center, I bet."

"Oh. Well—"

"I got cheated out of my last mall visit," he adds confidentially. "Do you suppose we could stop at Wall Drug for just a few minutes? No one else would have to know."

"Sure," says Mouse. "Sure, I'd be glad to stop there, only—do you think I could talk to Andrew first?"

Andrew's body convulses, and *he* comes back out. "Stop the car!" he shouts. "Stop—"

Another billboard goes by. "Ooh!" he cries, in a little-boy falsetto. "Wooly mammoths!"

Mouse says nothing, only waits. They pass another billboard, this one advertising Camel cigarettes.

He leans forward, blinking rapidly. "Dear," he says, in a woman's voice, "could I get a smoke to clear my hea—"

"*NO!*" He convulses again. "Stop the car! Stop the car!"

Mouse keeps driving.

"Stop the car!" he bellows, and kicks the back of her seat. "Stop it, stop it, *stop it*—"

A sliver of time drops out, and then they are pulled over at a curve in the highway. Mouse, turned halfway around in her seat, gets just a glimpse of her passenger as he bails out of the car, leaving the door open behind him.

"Andrew!" Mouse calls—

—and then she is out of the car too, standing at the edge of a big ditch that runs alongside the road shoulder. She hears him screaming.

"Andrew?" Mouse calls. "Andrew?"

The ditch is about eight feet deep, and by the glow of the Buick's tail-lights, Mouse can just make out Andrew's body thrashing around at the bottom of it. He's caught in something; from the violence of his motions, and the bloodcurdling shrieks coming out of his mouth, Mouse is afraid it's a bear trap, or something equally gruesome. Then another car drives by on the highway, and as its headlights sweep the ditch, Mouse sees what he has blundered into: barbed wire.

Someone has dumped a length of barbed-wire fence in the ditch, and he has gotten tangled in the coils. Instead of holding still and trying to pick himself out carefully, he has panicked and is fighting. Mouse can see the whole heap of wire and fence posts shaking.

"Oh God, Andrew!" Mouse says. "Andrew, don't, you'll really hurt yourself . . ." She wants to go down and help him, but she's afraid that the way he's flailing around, he'll end up knocking her into the wire too. She hovers at the top of the ditch, pleading with him to stop thrashing.

He lets out one last piercing scream and falls still. Mouse waits another ten seconds, then scrambles down to him.

It's not as bad as she thought. She'd gotten the impression that Andrew's whole body was wrapped in barbed wire, but it turns out only his left arm is caught. Still, it's bad: the wire is looped around his forearm at least twice, and his struggling has pulled it taut, digging the barbs in deep. When Mouse touches his sleeve, she finds it tacky with blood.

"Andrew . . ." It looks like he's fainted, which is just as well, although she doesn't know how she's going to get him back into the car. First she needs to untangle him. Feeling carefully in the dark, Mouse traces the barbed wire where it loops around his arm, trying to determine if there is any slack to work with. It feels like there might be; but when Mouse gives an experimental tug on the wire, Andrew comes alive again.

His free hand comes up and seizes her roughly by the shoulder. *"Pou eimaste?"* he demands of her. *"Ti symbainei?"*

Mouse squeaks.

21

"—and that's the last thing I remember," Penny concluded. "The next thing I knew, we were here."

We'd gone back inside the motel room while she told her story; now she retrieved a sheet of dinosaur-themed stationery from the top of the television set. "The Society left me a note," she said, and handed it to me.

The note read:

Penny,

We are in a town on the edge of the Badlands National Park, southeast of Rapid City; I didn't think it would be smart to stop in the city itself, or to continue on towards Wall, so I left the main highway and came here (see map on reverse side). Andrew was unconscious for most of the drive, and hopefully he will continue to sleep for a while yet. I cleaned and bandaged his arm as best I could, but he'll need to see a doctor for a tetanus shot. Call Dr. Eddington.

Duncan

"Duncan," Penny said, as I finished reading. "I don't know who that is."

"I do. I met him once. He's—" I paused, seeing how she was looking at me. "It's OK, Penny," I said. "Duncan is one of your protectors. He's good." I glanced down at the note again. "So did you call Dr. Eddington?"

"I *tried*," Penny said. "But the phone was out of order"—she gestured at the nightstand—"and I was afraid if I left the room to call from somewhere else, you'd run away again. So I slept in the chair, and when I woke up you were still out cold, so I thought I could sneak a shower, but—"

She was on the verge of tears. "Penny," I said. "It's all right. You did fine. I—"

"I *didn't* do fine!" Penny said, pounding her fist against her thigh. "I almost lost you again! I wanted to take a shower, but I didn't want to leave the bathroom door open, in case *he* woke up—"

"It's OK, Penny. I didn't run away. And I'm certainly not going to begrudge you a shower, after all that . . . really, I don't know how I'm even going to *begin* to thank you for following me all this way . . . I mean, when I think about the last couple weeks, I'm not sure I deserve it."

She shook her head, dismissing the notion. "You came after me when I ran away."

"What, you mean when you ran into the woods? That was a couple miles, Penny. But this . . . What I did for you doesn't compare."

"You helped me," Penny insisted, "so I helped you. But I shouldn't have left you alone, not for a moment, not until I was sure . . ."

"Penny, come on . . . you know if one of us is going to beat themselves up, it really ought to be me. This is all my fault."

"No. You couldn't help—"

"Oh yes I could," I said. "I should never have gotten drunk. It's against my father's rules—I don't think I ever really appreciated *why* it's against the rules, but now I know. I let myself lose control." I sighed, feeling all sorts of guilt-thoughts and self-recriminations—about the drinking, about Julie, about Dr. Grey (Dr. Grey! . . . could she really be dead?)—just waiting for a chance to surge forward and swamp me. But I couldn't afford that right now.

"Do you know," Penny asked, "who the nasty one is? The one who wouldn't tell me his name?"

"No. I don't know either of the souls you met. I've never heard of Xavier before. And the other one . . . he *sounds* like Gideon, but he can't be."

"Gideon," said Penny. "He's bad?"

"He's selfish." I fingered the bandage on my arm. "He's also really afraid of sharp things with points—knives, nails, thorns—I mean *really* afraid, like he can't deal with them at all. But the thing is, he's not supposed to be able to come out anymore, so if it *was* him running the body . . ."

"So what happens now?" asked Penny. "You're back in control now, right?"

"I hope so . . . I guess the first thing, we have to find a phone that works, and call Dr. Eddington and Mrs. Winslow. God, Mrs. Winslow! She's got to be so worried by now."

"Well," Penny said, "Maledicta did tell Julie that we were going after you. So maybe if Julie talked to Mrs. Winslow . . ."

"Maybe," I said, doubtful. Somehow, I didn't think hearing about Julie's encounter with Maledicta would have put Mrs. Winslow's mind at ease. "I'd still better go call her. And then, afterwards, I'm going to need to go inside to talk to my father, and see what kind of shape the house is in. Maybe you could watch the body for me while I do that."

"Um . . . OK," said Penny. She pinched the collar of her bathrobe. "Just let me get dressed, and I'll come with you to make the phone call."

As I waited for Penny outside the motel room, I tried to call out my father. At first there was no response—the pulpit still wasn't there—but then I heard my name, from what sounded like a long way off: ". . . drew? . . ."

"Father?" I said.

The motel-room door opened and Penny came out in a rush, hopping on one foot as she struggled to pull on her shoe. She saw the distant expression on my face and got scared. "Andrew?" she said.

"It's all right," I told her, abandoning my attempt to make contact with the house. "It's still me."

We went to the motel office and told the manager that the phone in our room was out of order. He shrugged, as if unclear why this should be his concern; but when I pressed him, he reluctantly agreed to let me use the office phone.

I dialed Mrs. Winslow's number, and was surprised to get an answering machine: "This is Mrs. Winslow speaking. If this is Andrew, Aaron, or another member of their family, please leave a message telling me where you are. If you don't know where you are, you need to dial 911 immediately; tell whoever answers that you're lost, and give them my phone num—"

The recording cut off with a beep in midsentence. "Mrs. Winslow?" I said. "It's all right, Mrs. Winslow, I'm—" There was another beep, a crackle of static, and then the connection was broken.

"What?" Penny said.

"I got an answering machine," I told her. "I didn't know Mrs. Winslow had one of those . . . I mean I guess it makes sense that she would, but she's almost always home."

"You didn't leave a message?"

I shook my head. "Something was wrong with it . . ." I dialed the number again, and got a busy signal. Frustrated, I hung up, and started to dial Dr. Eddington's number.

"Ahem." The motel manager cleared his throat. "Just how many calls are you planning to make, exactly?"

"Just one more," I said. The phone rang twice, and then Dr. Eddington's answering machine picked up. But at least it seemed to be working properly. I left a lengthy message.

"All right," I said to Penny after I hung up. "Let's go back to the room, and—"

The manager cleared his throat again. "That'll be fifteen dollars."

"Fifteen—. . . for what?"

"Three long-distance calls," the manager said. "I figure five bucks per."

"The first call was only thirty seconds long," I pointed out. "And the second was a busy signal."

The manager shrugged. "I didn't hear any busy signal."

"You . . ." I gave up; I didn't have the energy to argue.

"Sorry," Penny apologized as we walked back to the room. "I guess Duncan picked the wrong motel."

"He had more important things to worry about— you both did. Anyway, the money doesn't concern me so much as not being able to talk to Mrs. Winslow."

Back in the room, I thought about taking a quick shower, but reluctantly decided against it. First things first. I explained to Penny what I was going to do.

"So you'll be unconscious again?" she said.

I nodded. "It'll look like I'm sleeping," I said. "And you can shake me awake, if there's an emergency, but it may take me a few seconds to wake up."

"What if somebody else wakes up instead?" Penny asked. "What if *he* wakes up?"

"That shouldn't happen."

She just looked at me.

"Right," I said. "Right . . ." I searched the room for something pointy and sharp, but not too sharp; in the drawer of the nightstand, alongside a Bible and a Book of Mormon, I found a letter opener. "Here," I said, offering it to her. "If Gideon does show up, just wave this at him . . ."

Penny blinked. "Are you fucking kidding me?" Maledicta said. "You want me to fucking stab you?"

"Not *stab*," I said. "You wouldn't actually have to use it, just show it to him. Threaten to, to poke him with it . . ."

"Poke him with it," said Maledicta. "Tell you what, why don't I bust out the fucking window and threaten to poke him with a piece of *that*?"

"Oh-*kay*," I said, "maybe this isn't such a good idea . . ."

She blinked again. "No," Penny said, "no, I'm sorry, it's all right. I'll do it."

I wasn't sure I wanted her to, now. "You don't have to, Penny. If you're not comfortable staying in here while I—"

"It's all right. Give me the letter opener."

I gave it to her, not without a trace of reluctance. "Just . . . be careful," I said. "Maybe, if Gideon does show up, maybe the best thing would be to step back and let him go."

Penny didn't say anything to that, just sat in the chair, holding the letter opener awkwardly in her fist.

I lay down on the bed and closed my eyes.

Going inside was much harder than it usually is. When I went to step out of the body, I encountered resistance; it was like trying to back through a tunnel that had been packed with cotton. But I concentrated, and pushed, until finally something gave; and then I was down, in a landscape so changed that I thought I'd stumbled into the wrong geography.

The mist which ordinarily shrouded Coventry had thickened into fog and boiled over, obliterating the lake and much of the lakebank; a thinner but still substantial haze extended as far as the encircling forest, turning the trees into shadowy silhouettes. Standing on the hill where the column of light touches down, I couldn't see the house.

"Father?" I called, the haze swallowing my words. "Adam? . . . Anybody?"

There was no answer, but I heard a sound like muffled hammering in the distance. I moved towards it, and found myself at the house.

It was in shambles. It was still standing, but it looked like it had been picked up and dropped from a height: the grounds around were littered with sprung boards, broken glass, and cracked shingles. The pulpit, as I'd expected, was totally gone, torn away; the door that had connected it to the second-floor gallery was boarded over with heavy planks.

My father stood on the front lawn, surveying the damage. When he noticed me standing beside him, his reaction was surprisingly subdued. "Andrew," he said. "So you're awake, finally."

"Yes," I said, thrown by his demeanor. "Since just a little while ago. I . . . I'm back in control of the body, too."

"And where is the body?" he asked, in a tone of voice that suggested he wasn't all that interested. "A long way from Autumn Creek, I'm guessing."

"Yes," I said. "We're in South Dakota. It's Thursday." I waited for him to react; when he didn't, I blurted out: "I'm really sorry about getting drunk."

"Yes, you should be." His brow contracted, and I thought he was going to let me have it; but then his anger just dissipated. "Well, I suppose it's my failure too."

"Aren't you . . . don't you want to yell at me?"

He shook his head, smiling his disappointment. "There's not much point. You know it was wrong; you knew it was wrong before you did it; and it's not the first time it's happened. But you did it anyway."

"Well I didn't think *this* would happen, or—"

Still smiling: "Why did you imagine I forbade it, Andrew? Did you think I was just trying to keep you from having a good time?"

"I don't know what I thought. I guess I *didn't* think, at all." I hung my head, but after a moment, when he still didn't yell at me, I looked back up at the house. "What happened here?"

"It was a lot like an earthquake," my father said, "only the sky shook, too. And then the mist on the lake . . . well, you can see what happened with the mist."

"Is everyone else OK? Where are they?"

"The Witnesses are inside, in the nursery. The others . . . are around. I've been trying to get them together for a meeting, but they keep scattering, wandering off into the fog." He was silent for a few seconds. Then he said: "South Dakota?"

"Yes. Near Rapid City."

"And Penny Driver is with you?"

"Yes. How did you know? Have you been—"

"Watching? No. Since the pulpit blew away, I haven't been able to get more than vague impressions from outside; I knew we were traveling, but not much more. I haven't been able to get out, either, except once, and even then only partway. The body was in the back seat of Penny's car, and we were driving on a highway at night."

"The Morse code message. That was you."

He nodded. "Stupid of me, really—I should have tried signaling for a pen or a pencil instead. Not that there would have been time for that . . . I'd barely made contact when *somebody* kicked me out. Who was that, by the way? Who's been controlling the body? Do you know?"

"Not really." I gave him a very abbreviated summary of what Penny had told me about the journey from Autumn Creek to the Badlands.

"I don't know any soul named Xavier," my father said when I was finished. He gazed off into the mist, in the direction of the lake. "I suppose he could be new . . ."

"I don't think he is new. From what Penny told me, it sounded like he'd been to Michigan before, and that he'd . . . seen the stepfather." I paused, realizing something. "But wait a minute—if that's true, then you'd *have* to know him, wouldn't you? I mean, wasn't part of the whole process of building the house that you took an inventory of all the souls?"

My father was gazing into the mist very intently now. "He said his last name was Reyes?"

"Yes . . . I think so."

"That's interesting," my father said. "We knew a man named *Oscar* Reyes back in Michigan, when we were little. He ran a pest-control service in Seven Lakes."

"Pest control . . . you mean he was an exterminator?"

My father nodded. "He'd come out to the house once a year to fumigate the kitchen. Also one time, our mother was having trouble with rabbits attacking her vegetable garden . . ." He trailed off, which was just as well; I didn't think I wanted to hear about the rabbits.

"What about the other soul?" I asked. "The one who wouldn't give his name. Could it be Gideon?"

"Gideon's stuck on Coventry."

"I know he's supposed to be," I said, "but . . ." But if there were souls running loose in the geography that my father didn't even know about, all bets were off.

"Yes, but . . ." My father sighed. "I suppose we'd better go check on him."

"We?" I said.

"This is your responsibility too. Come on."

We descended the path to the boat dock. Captain Marco waited there, keeping an eye on the ferryboat that was—or was supposed to be—the only means of passage to or from Coventry. Of course I knew even then that that wasn't really true. The lake may appear to be a formidable obstacle, but what really kept Gideon confined was my father's dominance of the geography; if that had slipped, a soul as willful as Gideon would have little trouble engineering an escape.

The ferry, a flat-bottomed skiff, steadied itself in the water as we stepped aboard. My father rode up front, I sat in the middle, and Captain Marco stood in the stern, holding a long pole. The crossing was brief: Captain Marco pushed us away from the dock, which vanished almost instantly into the fog, and dipped the pole in the lake three times; then there was a shift, and the prow of the ferry bumped up against Coventry's gray shore.

Coventry Island, if it were real, would measure just an eighth of a mile from end to end, with a surface area of about ten acres. Within these small confines, my father had granted Gideon a modicum of autonomy, allowing him to build his own house. And so he did, continually: the last time my father had visited the island, Gideon's home had been a wooden fishing lodge; the time before that, a lighthouse; and the time before that, a medieval keep. I'd only been to Coventry once before, myself, shortly after I was born, and on that occasion Gideon had gone all out, covering the whole island with a sprawling prison complex; after my father and I had patiently threaded our way through the maze of walls and security gates, he'd refused to speak with us, other than to call us both names.

"What do you think it'll be this time?" I asked, as we stepped out of the boat.

My father wasn't in a mood to guess. "We'll see soon enough," he said. We set off uphill towards the center of the island, where Gideon was most likely to be found.

Here on the island the fog had thinned to mist again. It got thinner still with every step we took, until something amazing happened: the mist parted completely, revealing a tiny patch of blue sky—the only clear sky in the entire geography, as far as I could tell.

From the open sky a soft light shone down on a meticulously crafted scene of ruin. Burned and broken stones were scattered in a ring around a circular foundation, as though a round tower had exploded from inside; I was reminded of my dream, in which Coventry had appeared as a bull's-eye. At the center of the wreckage, seemingly unscathed by whatever force had destroyed the tower, a lone soul sat at a table, playing a game of checkers solitaire. The light glinted theatrically in his hair.

"Gideon," my father called, picking his way through the rubble ring. About halfway across he stopped, bent down, and pulled something from among the jumbled stones: a barred metal grille, like the kind you find in a jail cell window. The symbolism wasn't hard to decipher. "Gideon!"

Gideon bent forward over the checkerboard, and made a series of jumps—*bang, bang, bang, bang, BANG!*—that captured every remaining enemy piece. Grinning, he removed the opposition from the board, and kinged his own man.

"Gideon."

"Good *morning*," Gideon said, with a glance at the sky. "Something I can help you with?" As he turned to face us, I couldn't help but stare; the resemblance between Gideon's soul and Andy Gage's body is so striking it's scary. It's no wonder, really, that he thinks he deserves to be in charge.

Gideon's grin widened when he noticed my reaction. "Well," he said to my father, "I see you brought the little figment with you."

In response, my father tossed the metal grille on the table. It landed in the middle of the checkerboard, scattering Gideon's pieces and decapitating his new king. Gideon started to laugh, but then my father snapped his fingers and the grille sprouted foot-long spikes in all directions, punching holes in the tabletop. Gideon cursed and jerked back, falling out of his chair.

"Now that I've got your attention . . ." my father said. The spikes retracted; the grille disappeared.

Gideon stood up slowly; he held his left hand in his right, rubbing at a sore spot just above the ball of his thumb. "Get out," he seethed. "I don't have anything to say to either of you."

My father made no move to leave. "Long sleeves," he said, noting the billowy shirt that Gideon's soul was clothed in. "That's unusual."

"Get out," Gideon repeated. "This is my island."

"It's yours if you stay on it," my father said. "I gave you a choice two years ago: this, or the pumpkin field. If you've changed your mind, I want to know now."

I shifted uncomfortably at this ugly threat. Gideon's eyes flicked briefly in my direction, and the corner of his mouth twitched. But then my father said, "Well?" and Gideon's attention switched back where it belonged.

"I haven't changed my mind about anything," he said. "I know you're having problems running your little playhouse, but that's got nothing to do with me."

"It had better not. What do you know about a soul named Xavier?"

"Who?"

"Gideon . . ."

"You're the one in charge of the census. If you don't know who he is, how am I supposed to?"

"Gideon, I swear to you—"

"I don't know any soul named Xavier."

He *did* know who Xavier was; it was written all over his face. I was pretty sure too that he had been off the island, in the body, and that if he were to roll up his left sleeve we would see the wounds from the barbed wire. But my father didn't force the issue. "All right," he said. "But there had better not be any more trouble with Xavier . . . or with any other *nameless* souls." He gave this warning a moment to sink in, then turned to go.

"Has it occurred to you," Gideon said, "that this may be a problem with honesty?"

My father stopped.

"I mean," said Gideon, "a house built on a foundation of lies can't be all that stable, can it?" He looked at me and smiled. "Aaron never has told you, has he?"

"Told me what?"

My father turned back around. "Gideon," he warned.

"Told me what?" I said.

"Oh, come on," Gideon chided my father. "You wouldn't try to punish me for telling the *truth*, would you?"

"What truth?" I said. "What's he talking about?"

"I'm talking about the big master plan," Gideon said. "The one Aaron here cooked up with old Greyface. You still think you were a part of it, don't you? But you weren't."

"I don't understand . . . 'Greyface'? You mean Dr. Grey?"

"The one who just *died*. She and Aaron had it all worked out: tame the multitudes, put up the house, create a new front man—except that last bit wasn't part of the original plan."

I shook my head, still not following.

"*He* was supposed to run the body," Gideon said, pointing at my father. "*That* was the plan."

"No." I shook my head again. "No, that was supposed to be my job. My father was tired—"

"We were all *tired*. But Aaron wanted to be in charge. And hey!"— Gideon held up his scarred left hand—"he proved he was tougher than I was . . . or at least more ruthless. But he was supposed to take charge of *everything* . . . only at the last minute, he decided he wasn't really up to it. So he improvised, and called out a little helper . . ."

I turned to my father. "Is that—that's not true, is it?" My father didn't answer; but from the way he looked at Gideon, and from the fact that Gideon did not spontaneously shrivel up and die, I realized that it might be true. "Father?"

"Let's go back to the house," my father said.

"Wait. Does that mean it *is* true?"

"We're not going to discuss this in front of *him*," my father said. "Let's go back to the house." And he turned and walked off into the mist.

"That's right," said Gideon, "go back to your playhouse!" Then, seeing that I was still there, he decided to sow one more seed of mischief. "Speaking of the house," he said, "there's something you can help me with. Do you happen to remember how many doors there are on the first floor?"

"What?"

"The first floor of Aaron's playhouse. How many doors does it have?"

"Three," I said. "Front door and back door."

Gideon nodded. "Front door and back door . . . and that makes three, does it?"

"Andrew!" my father called.

"I . . . I've got to go," I said, and started backing away. Gideon smirked at me.

"That's right, little figment," he said, "you go on back to the playhouse with your father. But we'll see each other again soon maybe, huh?" All at once he lunged forward, stamping his foot and throwing his arms wide as if to grab me. I fled, Gideon's mocking laughter chasing me all the way back down to the shore.

I rejoined my father aboard the ferryboat, and Captain Marco pushed off again. This time he didn't take us straight across. Instead, sensing that my father and I had private matters to discuss, he took us out on the water, out of sight and earshot of both Coventry and the mainland, and stopped poling. We drifted in the fog.

"It's true, isn't it?" I said.

"It's not *all* true," my father replied.

"Not all . . . then what part is true?"

"Let's start with the part that's false," my father said. "I didn't 'improvise.' I didn't call you out on the spur of the moment."

"Then what—"

"There was more than one plan. Always. In therapy, Dr. Grey and I discussed a number of options for the final disposition. One plan, the one I personally favored, is the one you know about: I would run things inside, and create someone new—you—to run the body."

"The plan *you* favored," I said. "But Dr. Grey didn't?"

"Dr. Grey felt . . . given the problems I'd had with Gideon trying to take over, she thought it would be better if I didn't share authority with anyone. She wanted me to at least try running the body on my own. She always stressed that it was ultimately my decision, but that was what she recommended. And it is true," he added, "that at the last session we ever had together, I did agree to try her plan. But then after she had her stroke, I rethought it, and changed my mind again."

"Did Dr. Eddington agree with you about changing your mind?"

"No," my father admitted. "He thought I was making a mistake."

Which would technically make my whole existence a mistake—but I didn't care to dwell on the implications of that. Instead I asked: "How come you never told me this before?"

"I didn't think you needed to know it."

"Was there anything else I didn't need to know?"

No answer. I took that as a yes.

"Gideon asked me a funny question right before we left," I said, a few moments later.

"What question?"

"He wanted to know how many doors there are on the ground floor of the house."

"Three," my father said. "Front door and back door."

"Yes, that's what I told him. Only . . . that doesn't really add up, does it?"

My father looked at me curiously. I had to count it out, holding up fingers: "Front door is one . . . back door is two . . ."

"Right."

"Right, but then what's three?"

"Three is the front—. . . no. No, three is . . . it's . . ."

"I don't know either," I said. "I know there *are* three, but—"

"Wait," my father said. "Wait. Three is . . . the door under the stairs! Right, that's it!"

"The door under the stairs." I struggled to picture it, and finally it came to me: a small wooden door, in the shadows beneath the staircase that ran up from the common room to the second-floor gallery. "Right, OK . . . and where does that door lead to, again?"

"Where . . . ? It leads . . . it leads to . . ." He blinked, and fell silent.

"By any chance," I asked next, "does the house have a basement?"

EIGHTH BOOK:
LAKE VIEW

22

Andrew said that while he was inside, it would look like he was sleeping, but to Mouse it seems more like he's comatose: his breathing is so slow it's almost undetectable, and he doesn't move at all. When Mouse tiptoes up to the side of the bed to take a closer look at him, she notices that beneath their closed lids, even his eyeballs are still, with none of the rapid motion that signals a dream in progress.

As she waits for Andrew to come back from where he's gone, she becomes increasingly fidgety. She tries sitting in the chair but can't get comfortable. She stands up, goes to the window, and looks out at the parking lot for a while; gets bored with that, wanders over to the door, and does a Xavier impersonation, using the handle of the letter opener to whap out a rhythm against the side of the doorframe; gets bored with that, and goes back to the window. Except for the one check to make sure Andrew is really still breathing, she stays clear of the bed.

Time passes. Mouse thinks it's been at least half an hour, but when she checks the clock on the nightstand, only ten minutes have gone by. Mouse decides she needs to pee.

She goes into the bathroom. She leaves the door open a crack, enough to hear through but not enough to see in or out. She sits.

While she goes about her business, she reflects on what will happen after Andrew wakes up. He has said nothing about his intentions—whether he means to return to Washington, or continue on to Michigan, or do some other thing. Probably he doesn't know himself yet what he wants to do.

Mouse tells herself that she would like to go home, but as she continues to think about it, she finds that she isn't so sure. For one thing, Maledicta's behavior in the bar on Tuesday night has left her with a mess to take care of, if and when she returns. Mouse supposes that Julie may understand and not fire her for Maledicta's rudeness, but if Mouse intends to keep working in Autumn Creek, she is also going to have to make restitution for the stolen vodka bottle, and she doubts that the vampire bartender will be as forgiving.

Even if she didn't have that hanging over her head, it's no secret that Mouse doesn't particularly like her life in Seattle. So maybe she shouldn't go back to it: maybe, after Andrew has been safely delivered to wherever it is he decides to go, she should just keep driving, to . . . well, she can just keep driving, and see where she ends up.

No.

No, that's a ridiculous idea; of course she has to go back. She doesn't have the money to just uproot herself and run away. And besides, Dr. Eddington—Mouse's flagging spirits rally at the thought of him—has promised to help her. She can't disappoint him. She—

From the other room, she hears the sound of the television being turned on.

"Andrew?" Mouse starts to call out, but then she remembers that she is sitting on a toilet with her pants down. She pulls a wad of paper from the roll and quickly wipes herself. She gets up. She doesn't flush, but steps quietly to the door, and opens it just wide enough to look out.

Andrew is sitting up on the bed, punching buttons on the TV remote control. He has a frustrated look on his face.

"Andrew?" Mouse calls softly.

Either he doesn't hear her or he ignores her. He goes on punching buttons until suddenly his frustration turns to satisfaction. "Ah!" he exclaims, and the television switches to a new channel.

Mouse opens the door a little wider. "Andrew?"

"Sorry," he says. He looks at her, a smirk playing on his lips, and Mouse thinks: *him!* But then he says: "Don't worry, I'm not Gideon. He's with Aaron and Andrew right now, playing King of the Mountain . . . but since they're all busy, I thought it'd be a waste to leave a perfectly good body just lying around. By the way"—he glances around the room—"is there a minibar in here by any chance?"

"Minibar? . . . No!" says Mouse. "You can't get drunk again!"

He arches an eyebrow, as if to say *Oh yeah?*, but fortunately the point is moot; there is no minibar in the room. "Well, that sucks," he says. Then he shrugs and turns his attention back to the TV.

Mouse looks at the TV too—and is appalled. The scene on the screen is a motel room, not all that different from this one . . . except that there are naked women on the bed.

"The Indian whacking off in the background is Hyapatia Lee," he informs her helpfully. "And the two actually getting it on, that one is Summer Knight, and the little one is Flame." He leans forward, as if noticing something. "You know," he says, "she kind of looks like you . . . if you had red hair, I mean." He grins. "And were really flexible."

"I can be flexible," says Loins, stepping forward past Mouse's horror. "I don't look that good in cowboy boots, though." The scene on the screen shifts, showing a fourth woman, who for some reason is not taking part in the action on the bed. "Wow," says Loins. "I wish I looked like *her.*"

"Mmm, Christy Canyon," he says. "I bet a lot of people wish they looked like—" He stops. "Wait a minute," he says, turning to look her in the eye.

He's not smirking anymore; all at once he's wary. Loins kind of likes that. She goes and sits beside him on the bed, giggling as he shies away. "What's the matter?" Loins purrs. "Don't tell me you only like to watch." She puts her hand on his thigh; he gasps, tenses up . . . and just as quickly relaxes.

He pats the back of her hand, affectionately but with no passion. "The thing is, dear," he says, his voice gone feminine, "you're just not my type." He plucks Loins's hand off his leg, and deposits it in her own lap. "Now that we've got that straight, would you happen to have a cigarette?"

"No," says Maledicta. "That cocksucker Duncan wouldn't stop to get any last night. You sure you still don't have some? You were smoking Winstons yesterday."

"Winstons." He—she—makes a face. "Not my favorite brand." She frisks herself anyway, but comes up empty. "Well, if I did have them, I don't know what I did with them."

"Could be you dropped them in that fucking ditch. You want to go get some more?"

"Yes, that would be lovely." Offering a hand: "I'm Samantha, by the way. Sam to my friends."

"Maledicta," Maledicta says. "I don't have friends." But then she grins and shakes hands. "All right, Sam, let's go get some fucking smokes before the grown-ups come back."

They go outside. As they cross the parking lot, Sam spins around, taking in the view. "What a beautiful landscape," she says.

"You're fucking joking, right?" Maledicta says. "Desolate fucking dinosaur country . . ."

"I don't mind desolate," Sam tells her. "I've always wanted to live in a desert. If I had a choice, I'd go to New Mexico, and open an art gallery in Taos or Santa Fe."

"Yeah? So what, the others voted you down on that?"

Sam laughs. "No vote. We're not a democracy. Aaron and Andrew make all the important decisions; the rest of us just try to fit in." A sigh. "I *do* understand why it has to be that way, but still, sometimes I wish . . . well . . ."

"Hmmph," says Maledicta, troubled. "Mouse had better not start expecting *me* to just fucking fit in." She shakes her head for emphasis. "Fuck that."

They find a cigarette machine outside the motel office. Maledicta goes first, feeding in dollar bills and pulling the selection knob for Winstons. There's a click, but no cigarettes come out. "What the fuck . . . ?" Maledicta says. She pulls the Winstons knob a second time, then tries the one for Camels. Nothing happens. She kicks the machine; still nothing.

"Wait," says Sam. "Try Kools."

The machine isn't dispensing menthol cigarettes either. Maledicta looks for a knob or button that will give her her money back, but instead finds a handwritten note taped above the bill slot: THIS MACHINE DOES NOT GIVE CHANGE; ABSOLUTELY NO REFUNDS.—MGMT.

"*Fucker.*" Maledicta starts towards the office door with blood in her eye, but Sam catches her by the arm. "Wait," Sam says. "Don't make trouble."

"Get the fuck off me!" Maledicta says. "I'm not going to let this fucker rip me off!"

"Please," says Sam, hanging on. "If there's trouble I might not be able to stay outside. And if Andrew comes back, he's not going to want to smoke with you."

Maledicta hesitates, still fuming.

"Please, dear," Sam says. "Can't we just drive to a convenience store? I'll pay for your cigarettes, I promise."

"Yeah?" says Maledicta. "With whose money?"

"Don't worry about that. I'll just . . . borrow the money from Andrew, and settle with him later."

"If he even notices, you mean . . . All right," Maledicta relents, "we'll go to a fucking convenience store. But when we get back, I *am* going to kick somebody's ass."

They get into the car, where the smell of vodka, faded but still potent, brings Malefica forward for a moment. She checks the glove compartment to see if a new flask has by any chance materialized there, but none has.

"Motherfucking Duncan," Maledicta complains. "Hey Sam, as long as we're going for smokes, what do you say we hit a fucking liquor store, too?"

"I don't think that would be very wise," Sam says. "Considering."

"Fuck wisdom. We could get ripped, and make a run for New Mexico."

"*Where* are we now?"

"Brontosaur Cock, South Dakota. It's a long fucking drive from Santa Fe, but . . ."

Sam laughs. "We'd never make it," she says, her eyes shining with the possibility.

"No, but we could fucking try."

But Sam shakes her head. "It's tempting, dear, but I think I'd better content myself with simpler pleasures. Just a cigarette, maybe two if there's time." She pauses, concentrating. "We're going to have to hurry, though—they'll be back soon."

"No fucking problem," Maledicta says, and gets the car moving.

Now of course she wasn't being serious, offering to light out for New Mexico; Maledicta knows they can't *really* do that, although it would be fun to see Mouse's reaction when she woke up in Georgia O'Keeffe country. But the part about getting shitfaced—that was for real. Maledicta could use a drink; Malefica could definitely use a drink; and as for Sam, Maledicta kind of likes her—underneath the "please"s and the "dear"s, she senses a kindred spirit—but thinks she could stand to loosen up a little.

There's a mom-and-pop convenience store just up the road, but right next to it is a bar called The Pink Mammoth. *Stupid fucking name*, Maledicta thinks; on the other hand, it does appear to be open for business. She drives into the Mammoth's parking lot. Sam frowns but doesn't otherwise object.

"Come on," Maledicta coaxes her. "One fucking drink. What do you say?"

"Do you think they serve tea?"

"The Long Island kind, maybe."

They go inside. The Mammoth turns out to be a complete dive: Wild West decor, fucking *sawdust* on the floor, and an underscent of petrified vomit, like a pack of saber-toothed tigers threw up in here back before the last ice age and it was allowed to just fossilize. On the plus side, the bar's cigarette machine works, and despite the early hour, booze is being served. Sam and Maledicta have the place almost entirely to themselves: the only other customer is an old drunk watching cartoons on the TV above the bar.

They buy cigarettes. While Sam lights up, Maledicta orders a couple of beers. "Not for me, dear," Sam says, but Maledicta says, "Ah, come on," and repeats the order. The bartender draws them two Budweisers. Maledicta gives one to Sam, who accepts it but won't drink, even when Maledicta proposes a toast. Maledicta starts to get pissed, but cools down again when

Sam, without being asked, takes out Andrew's wallet and pays for both beers.

Maledicta jerks her thumb towards a pool table at the other end of the barroom. "Feel like a game?"

Sam smiles. "That would be lovely."

They go over to the table and Maledicta grabs a rack off the wall. "You any fucking good at this?" she asks.

"I used to be. My old sweetheart taught me to play, years ago. He said I had a knack for it." Her smile falters. "Of course he said a lot of things, but I think that one was true."

"Sweetheart, huh? This was before Andrew got put in charge?"

"Long before. We were still in Seven Lakes then, in the house where we grew up."

The rack's full. Maledicta slides it back and forth a couple times to get the balls grouped tightly. "Can I ask you a fucking personal question, Sam?"

"All right."

"Do you have a cock, or a cunt?"

Sam rears her head back, like she's really put out, but she recovers quickly. "A cunt," she says primly, "if you must know."

"I fucking thought so." Maledicta hangs the rack back on the wall and grabs a cue stick for herself. "You can't really tell, you know, when Andrew or Aaron are in the fucking driver's seat, but with you in the body, it's just fucking obvious. You sure you shouldn't be running the show instead of them?"

Sam shakes her head. "I might dream about it, but I'm not strong enough to cope with reality full-time. I proved that."

"Yeah? You seem strong enough to me. Not that I'm the world's best fucking judge of character . . . OK if I break?"

Sam nods her assent. Then, as Maledicta is chalking her cue, Sam says: "I tried to kill myself. Twice."

"Yeah? What for?"

"Jimmy Cahill—my sweetheart—joined the army. We were supposed to run away together, but he decided to run away on his own. He sent me a Dear John letter from basic training camp . . . so I tried to kill myself. Pills, the first time. I swallowed a bottle of prescription sleeping pills, and a pint of scotch—"

"—and woke up in the fucking hospital?"

"No, actually; I woke up at home, with a hangover. I've never figured out who, but I'm pretty sure one of the others sabotaged me, emptied out the pill capsules and refilled them with flour. I was constipated for days afterwards, but I didn't die. So next I tried hanging myself, but the knots kept slipping—and then before I could come up with a third alternative, I went to sleep, for a very long time. I didn't get out again until we were in Seattle, in therapy with Dr. Grey."

"Hmmph," Maledicta grunts, not sure what to say. She leans down over the pool table, and breaks; a few balls bounce around the edge of the pockets, but nothing goes in. "Fuck."

"So what about you?" Sam asks. "Did you ever have a sweetheart?"

"Me?" Maledicta laughs. "Nah. Fucking's not my department." Sam starts to look put out again, so Maledicta adds: "Or romance, either . . . in case you haven't noticed, I'm a fucking antisocial." She nods at the table. "Your shot."

They play two games. Sam's not kidding about having a knack; in the first game, she kicks Maledicta's ass. For the second game, Maledicta lets Malefica handle all the hard shots, and ekes out a narrow victory.

While they are playing, Maledicta drinks her beer, and Sam's too; she also splits a double vodka with Malefica. By the time she sinks the eight ball in the second game, she needs to pee again. She tells Sam to hang out for a minute and heads back to the john.

When Maledicta returns to the barroom, Sam isn't at the pool table anymore. She's sitting at the bar, watching TV with the old drunk. She's laughing.

Or *somebody's* laughing—Maledicta has heard Sam's laugh, and this isn't it. Sam's laugh is low and raspy, almost a wheeze; this laugh—actually more of a cackle—is high-pitched, clear, and very loud. A little kid's laugh, in other words. The body language is a little kid's too: rocking dangerously on the bar stool, clutching her (or his) stomach, pointing, knee-slapping.

Maledicta looks up at the TV. Cartoon time's over; the show now playing is *Young Frankenstein*, that stupid fucking Mel Brooks monster-movie parody. Gene Wilder as Frankenstein has just been met at the Transylvania train station by Marty Feldman's Igor. "Walk this way," Feldman says; when Wilder imitates his hunchbacked limp, Andrew's inner child nearly shits himself with glee.

Then Wilder looks into the back of Igor's hay wagon and discovers Terri Garr, playing Inge, the lab assistant with big tits. "Would you like to have a roll in the hay?" she asks. Andrew's laugh shifts to a more adolescent register; keeping his eyes fixed on Garr's cleavage, he picks up a mug from the counter in front of him and starts to drink out of it, only to gag when he realizes the mug contains milk, not beer. "Bartender!" he calls.

But before he can place a new order, another moronic pun, this one concerning werewolves—"Where wolf? Where wolf?"—brings out the little kid again. "*There* wolf!" he hoots. He slaps his knee, leans over a little too far on the stool, and goes crashing to the floor.

"Hey," Maledicta says, as he's picking himself up. "Hey Sam, are you still in there?"

"*Pou eimaste? Ti—*"

"Speak fucking English. And get Sam back out here—we've still got a fucking tiebreaker to play."

He blinks, and switches—to Andrew. "Penny?" Andrew says, confused.

"Fuck." Party's over. Maledicta is so annoyed that she jumps back down in the cave, drags Mouse out of storage, and kicks her out front without bothering to bring her up to speed on what's happened. Mouse comes out gasping. Her last memory is of the TV in the motel room, and now, as she reawakens, her eyes naturally gravitate to the set above the bar; she wonders how it ended up hanging from the ceiling, and what new perversion is on display that can only be shown in black-and-white.

"Maledicta?" Andrew says, still a step behind.

"Andrew?" says Mouse.

"Penny," says Andrew.

And then, in unison: "Where are we?"

"You're on the planet Mongo," says the old drunk. "I'm Flash Gordon, and this ugly fellow"—he gestures towards the bartender—"is Ming the Merciless."

The bartender, playing along, grabs an empty beer mug and holds it up in a mock salute.

"Welcome to our galaxy," he says. "Would you like some more milk?"

23

We couldn't get the door open.

Upon landing at the boat dock, my father and I went straight back to the house (although we walked back rather than just *being* there). My recollection of the door beneath the stairs got clearer the closer we got; but at the same time I wondered whether this wasn't some trick of Gideon's, a false memory that he'd somehow infected us with, so that even up to the last second I wasn't sure the door would actually be there.

It was there, though. And it was in plain view: not hidden in shadow but set prominently into the side of the staircase, impossible to miss.

"The earthquake must have affected it," I mused. "I mean, if it was always this obvious I can't see how we overlooked it . . . but we must have known it was here in order to count it . . ." I looked at my father, troubled that he wasn't saying anything. "You're *sure* you never put in a basement, or maybe just a big storage closet?"

"I think I'd know if I did, Andrew."

"I'd think you'd know, too," I replied. "But you didn't know about Xavier . . ."

Having confirmed the door's existence, we stood in front of it for a long time before trying to go through it. I surprised myself by being the first to actually touch it—I expected my father to take the initiative, but a paralysis seemed to have gripped him, and as the minutes passed I realized that we could be standing here all day if I waited for him to make the first move. So I steeled myself for a possible shock, reached out, and closed my hand around the knob.

It wouldn't move. I don't just mean that it wouldn't turn—I couldn't even rattle it. And the door itself was equally immovable, as though it were not a door at all but a marble statue of a door, cleverly painted to resemble the real thing. "I can't budge it," I said, stepping back. "You try."

At first I thought he wasn't going to, but then he roused himself. The knob wouldn't turn for him either, and the door remained solidly closed.

I fell back to musing. "Could it be that there's *nothing* behind it?" I said. "Could it just be some kind of a trick, that Gideon—"

The house's front door banged open, and Aunt Sam came in. She had an expression on her face that usually signifies she's been squabbling with Adam or Jake, but instead of complaining to my father and I, she avoided us, heading upstairs without a word. In her wake I caught the faintest suggestion of cigarette smoke—less a smell than a thought. That should have been a clue that something was up, but I was too preoccupied to pay attention.

"So what do you think?" I said, turning back to the mystery door. "*Is* it a trick?"

Before my father could answer I felt a gust of air from below, and heard a crackle of paper. I looked down and saw the corner of a page sticking out from under the door, fluttering in a draft.

This time my father acted first, stooping and grabbing up the paper—it was actually two sheets, folded in half and stapled along the seam to form a slim pamphlet—while I was still puzzling over what it could be. He held the pamphlet in a way that made it hard for me to see, but I could make out the image of a cross on the cover, and the words IN MEMORIAM.

"What is it?" I tried to reach for the pamphlet, to tilt it down so I could see what was written inside, but my father held it away from me. As he leafed through it, I got the impression that he wasn't reading the pamphlet so much as examining it, as though he'd seen it before and was just verifying that it was what he remembered it to be.

"Father," I said. "What is it?"

"In the boat," my father said, "you asked if there was anything else that I hadn't told you. And there is something—"

The front door banged open again. Adam stumbled in. Jake was right behind him, moving like the devil was at his heels; he sprang past Adam and charged up the stairs to his room.

"What—?" I started to say. Then from outside there came a warning cry.

"Seferis," my father said. "Trouble with the body."

I was already moving. I flew out the front door and up the column of light, emerging into a scene that was more mystifying than threatening. Somehow the body had been transported from the motel room to a saloon. Penny was in the saloon too, looking confused. There were also two strange men, who were no help at all getting us reoriented.

Penny and I got out of there as quickly as we could (one of the men, the one behind the saloon's bar counter, insisted I owed him a dollar for "moo juice," and I paid, even though I had no idea what he was talking about). Fortunately it turned out we hadn't traveled far from the motel; as soon as we stepped outside I saw the Motor Lodge's neon sign just up the road.

"I'm sorry," Penny said, after we'd located her car.

"Sorry for what? Do you know what just happened?"

She told me what she remembered: she'd been watching over my body, and had just stepped into the bathroom to wash her hands when somebody woke up and turned on the television. "To an X-rated channel," she said, her cheeks coloring. "And then you, whoever it was, said that I looked like . . . like one of the people in the movie that was playing. And after that . . . I don't really know how we got here."

Adam, I thought, inwardly furious. "Well then," I told Penny, "I'm the one who should apologize to you."

"What happened inside?" Penny asked, eager to change the subject. "Did you find out what you needed to?"

"Not enough," I said. "I'm going to have to go back in—don't worry, not right away. Later. And next time, I won't ask you to body-sit."

"No, it's all right," Penny said. "Just . . . maybe next time, we can unplug the TV."

The smell of vodka in the Centurion reminded me of something; I cupped a hand over my mouth and sniffed my own breath to see whether I'd been drinking. My breath smelled like . . . milk.

"Moo juice," I said.

"What?" said Penny.

"Nothing," I said. Then: "Do you ever get used to it? Waking up in weird situations, not knowing what the heck is going on?"

"I don't know," said Penny. "I mean, that's normal for me. I never had to get used to it."

I looked over at her. "You know I really am sorry, Penny."

"For what?"

"When Julie first suggested I help you . . . when you asked me for help . . . I almost said no. I *tried* to say no."

"That's all right. I tried to say no too, remember? Anyway, you did say yes."

"Yes, but . . ." But only because Julie wanted me to; I guessed I could be honest with myself about that now. "I'm sorry I didn't say yes sooner."

We were back in the motel parking lot now. We didn't go into the room right away, but stayed sitting in the car, too tired to move. Actually, I think Penny was more than just tired; her breath *didn't* smell like milk.

"So are we going back home now?" Penny said. She was asking out of curiosity, but I heard it as something more than that.

"You should go back, definitely," I told her, trying to sound encouraging.

"No." Penny shook her head. "It's not that I'm in a *hurry* to go back, I just wanted to know. If you still want to go on to Michigan, to see . . . to find out . . ."

To see what had happened to the stepfather. To find out whether Xavier Reyes had exterminated him.

". . . or maybe somewhere else," Penny continued. "If that's what you want to do, I don't mind taking you."

"I think," I said, rubbing my eyes, "I think I want to take a hot shower. And then maybe get some food, and try calling Mrs. Winslow again. And then, then I'll decide . . . is that OK?"

Penny nodded. "I think I'll wait out here while you take your shower, though," she said.

"Sure." I smiled. "I'll take care of the TV, too, while I'm in there."

The door to the motel room was unlocked, and inside the television was still on, still tuned to the sex channel. "Adam," I said, exasperated. I didn't actually unplug the TV, but I did turn it off, and I also hid the remote control. Then I got undressed and went into the shower. I stood under the hot spray a long time, barely moving.

I found myself thinking about Billy Milligan.

Probably you've at least heard his name; though not quite as famous as Sybil or Eve White, he's one of the better-known MPD cases. Billy Milligan was a small-time drug dealer and thief who was arrested in 1977 for the kidnapping, robbery, and rape of three women. He pled not guilty by reason of insanity, claiming that the crimes had been committed by other souls over whom he, Billy, had no control. After four different psychiatrists—including Cornelia Wilbur, Sybil's doctor—testified on his behalf, the court accepted the insanity defense.

He spent the next thirteen years in a succession of state mental hospitals. In 1991 he was pronounced "cured" and released. Then in 1996 he was arrested again, this time for allegedly threatening a judge. That story made the news in Seattle, and piqued Julie's curiosity. She wound up borrowing my father's copy of *The Minds of Billy Milligan*.

"Wow," Julie said, a few days later. "This is a really fascinating case."

"I suppose," I replied, without much enthusiasm.

"What?" said Julie. "You're not impressed?"

"Impressed? That's a funny word to use. He raped three people, Julie."

"Well, yes and no."

"Mostly yes—especially from the point of view of the women who got raped."

"You think he faked being multiple?"

"No," I said. "I mean it's hard to know for sure just from reading a book, but I believe he probably was—is—a multiple personality. The court thought so. But he was also a rapist."

"Only part of him, though. Billy Milligan—the *soul* called Billy—was innocent."

"Well just because he's innocent doesn't mean he's not responsible," I said. I quoted my father: "When you're in charge of a household, you're accountable for the actions of every soul in that household, even if they do things you would never do yourself."

"But at the time the rapes took place," Julie argued, "Billy Milligan wasn't in charge. It sounds like nobody was—his household was in chaos."

"Which is not very impressive."

"Jesus, Andrew. I didn't mean—why are you being so weird about this?"

"I'm not being weird," I said. "I just don't think Billy Milligan is a credit to multiples everywhere. He's like . . . the O.J. Simpson of the MPD community."

Julie laughed at that. "Still," she said, "it's not like he got off scot-free. And don't you think a hospital was really a better place for him than jail?"

"I think wherever they lock you up, thirteen years isn't enough time for raping somebody . . . or for allowing somebody to be raped."

Julie looked thoughtful. "What would you have done?"

"If I was in charge of Billy Milligan's case?"

"No," Julie said, "if you *were* Billy Milligan."

"Excuse me?"

"Suppose you found out that one of your other souls had . . . well, let's not say raped somebody, something less vile, like bank robbery . . ."

"Bank robbery?"

"Yeah. Suppose—"

"I'm not going to rob a bank, Julie."

"Not *you*. Another soul."

"Nobody else in the house is going to rob a bank either. If anybody even tried something like that, my father would send them to the pumpkin field."

"Well let's say it happened back before the house was built," Julie persisted, "and you only just found out about it. Let's say you come across an, I don't know, a storage locker that belonged to some other soul before you were even born. You open it up, and inside you find a sack of money labeled 'Property of the First National Bank.' And there's also a gun, and a Ronald Reagan mask . . ."

"A Ronald Reagan mask?"

". . . or whatever kind of mask fashionable bank robbers were wearing ten years ago. You find all this, plus conclusive evidence that it was you—your body—that originally stashed the stuff in the locker. What would you do?"

"This is not something that would ever happen, Julie."

"I'm not saying that it is—it's a hypothetical. But what would you do?"

I shrugged. "Call the police, I guess. Tell them what I'd found."

"Just like that?"

"What else could I do?"

"You'd just turn yourself in . . ."

"Well, I wouldn't necessarily be turning myself in. I mean, there *might* be another explanation . . . but of course I'd have to tell the police about it, if I really thought the money was stolen."

"So you'd just throw yourself on the mercy of the cops. No hesitation."

"I'd accept responsibility for the body's actions. I might not want to—maybe I *would* hesitate, a little—but ultimately I'd have no choice. It's my job."

Julie was skeptical. "I don't know," she said. "That sounds very noble, but I think it's also pretty naive, expecting the police to treat you fairly just because you're straight with them. And if you were really facing prosecution for bank robbery—"

"But I'm not really facing it," I said, annoyed. "It's a hypothetical. And if you can hypothesize guns and Ronald Reagan masks, I can hypothesize living up to my obligations."

"Well that's another interesting question. How can you ever be certain it is just a hypothetical?"

"Julie—" I was starting to get mad now.

"I don't think you *did* rob a bank. I'd be very, very surprised if that were really true. But how can you be a hundred percent sure that, back before the house was built—"

"Adam did some shoplifting, back then," I told her. "And Seferis broke a man's finger in a bar fight once, although that was self-defense. And there were some other incidents—petty crimes, and some misunderstandings—

involving various other souls. But no felonies, and definitely no unprovoked attacks on strangers."

"That you know of . . . but you've told me that there are still gaps in your information about those years, so—"

"No bank robbery–sized gaps."

"But how can you be *sure?*"

"Because if anything like that *had* happened, my father would know about it. He'd have found out. That's *his* job, Julie."

"But—"

"Can we change the subject now, please?"

My father would know about it . . . That's his *job, Julie.* And it was. But it was also my father's job to know all the souls, to maintain order in the geography . . . and to be honest with me.

What if Xavier—or Gideon—*had* done something bad to the stepfather, something that my father either didn't know about or had chosen not to tell me?

In one sense, it was an easy question. What I'd told Julie was true: as the soul in charge of Andy Gage's body, I stood accountable for all the body's actions, past and present, even those I wasn't technically guilty of. It had to be that way, for reasons of both house discipline and simple good citizenship. You can't have crimes being committed and no one owning up to them.

Easy. But also hard, because this was no longer just a hypothetical case. As I considered the consequences I might have to accept if the worst proved true, I realized that at least one thing I'd told Julie was wrong: I wasn't just a *little* hesitant to take responsibility.

Suppose the worst *was* true: suppose Andy Gage had killed his stepfather, murdered him, and not in self-defense or in the heat of the moment, but in cold blood. How bad was that? Ordinarily, of course, I'd say that murder is one of the few acts that is worse than rape. But what about murdering a rapist? What about murdering *your* rapist? Is *that* worse? Revenge is not supposed to justify violence—but couldn't it, if the thing being revenged was horrible enough?

It's not, I thought, like what Billy Milligan did. He became a predator in his own right, and hurt strangers, people who had never done anything to him. He made a habit of it. Andy Gage killing his stepfather would have been a one-time thing, a provoked, singular act, not part of a pattern.

Unless you counted what happened to Warren Lodge.

No. No. Don't think about him now. Focus on one killing—one *death*—at a time.

Come to that, I wasn't even sure the stepfather *was* dead. I thought he was—it *felt* true—but I couldn't recall ever specifically having been told it was so. I should really check on that, before I got too worked up about this. I should also find out *how* he died—if he'd had a heart attack, or cancer, I'd obviously be off the hook.

Or maybe I shouldn't find out.

What I didn't know, I couldn't take responsibility for: a flawed but attractive piece of reasoning. If Xavier had done something to the stepfather, it would have to have been several years ago, probably at least five. After that much time, it was unlikely the truth would come looking for me unless I went looking for it first. What if I decided to just let it be?

It wouldn't even have to be a permanent decision. I could just go back to Autumn Creek for the time being, and defer all questions about Michigan, and what might or might not have happened there, until after I got the house restabilized . . . however long that took. If the stepfather was dead he wasn't going anywhere; I could always take responsibility later.

Tempting. Tempting.

But.

Before getting into the shower, I'd unwrapped the gauze from around my arm. The wounds from the barbed wire had scabbed over, but they still stung beneath the hot spray. I studied them, then turned my hand over and looked at the old puncture-mark scar on Andy Gage's palm. My father had done that, during his last fight with Gideon.

It had happened at a diner—not the Harvest Moon, but another one, closer to Bit Warehouse. My father had just finished lunch and was settling the bill when Gideon tried to seize control. This was no ordinary takeover attempt: Gideon meant to put my father down permanently, and my father, recognizing the seriousness of Gideon's intent, was forced to take drastic action. He lifted up his arm and—to the horror of the diner cashier—impaled his hand on the receipt spike beside the cash register. It won him the battle.

Maybe you don't understand that (although, by now, maybe you do). Dominance, in a multiple household, is all about being able to endure more trauma than anybody else. The more a particular soul can resist the impulse to switch, the more it gains power over those that can't. By spiking his hand, my father demonstrated not only that he was able to withstand great pain, but that he had the courage to inflict it on himself if need be. Gideon, meanwhile, couldn't even take the pain; and while it may seem like cheating that my father had chosen a source of pain that Gideon was especially sensitive to, this was not a contest where fairness mattered.

So my father won the struggle for control, and, in winning, gained enough power over Gideon to confine him to Coventry. Then later, when he called me out of the lake and gave up running the body, my father's power was weakened; that, plus my own show of weakness two nights ago, was probably what had given Gideon the latitude he needed to sneak off the island.

Which was my dilemma: any further demonstration of weakness could be an invitation to a full-fledged takeover. If Gideon was willing to go on to Michigan, while I tried to turn back out of fear of the possible consequences . . . well, just because I started back towards Autumn Creek didn't mean I'd *get* there.

I didn't want to lose the body to Gideon—that would be the ultimate failure. But I also really, really didn't want to go to prison for murdering someone I'd never even met.

I imagined Billy Milligan, wherever he was now, laughing at my predicament: *Ha ha ha. That'll teach you to judge other people!*

"Go to hell," I said, and thrust my fists against the wall beneath the showerhead. "I *will* live up to my obligations. I *will* accept my responsibilities." I grabbed my wounded forearm and squeezed hard enough to start it bleeding again; the pain made me grit my teeth, but it also made me feel better. Billy Milligan had nothing further to say.

I got out of the shower and dried myself off. When I went to get dressed I realized I had no clean clothes to change into, just the same shirt and pants that I'd been wearing the past two days. There was no extra gauze, either, so I had to rewrap my arm in the same bandage.

Feeling less refreshed than I'd hoped, I went back out to the car. "All right, Penny," I said, getting in, "I think I know what I want to do. Or what I *need* to do, anyway."

"Yeah?" she said, and I noticed she was smoking a cigarette.

"Maledicta."

"Fucking swift, as always."

"Maledicta," I said, "I need to talk to Penny. I've decided to go on to Michigan, and—"

"I want concessions," Maledicta said.

"What?"

"I want fucking concessions. Mouse may have agreed to chauffeur you cross-country, but I fucking didn't. You want to go to Michigan, I want some things in return."

"Like what?"

She lifted one shoulder in a half-shrug. "Sam and I have another game of pool coming."

"Sam . . . Aunt Sam? You and Aunt Sam played pool?"

"Like I said, you're fucking swift."

"What else do you want?"

"Well you know I'm going to end up doing a lot of the fucking driving, right? I want Sam riding shotgun for part of that."

I shook my head. "If I do that, the others are going to want time out, too. I can't afford to start a fight about that now."

"What fucking bullshit," Maledicta said. "Look, you fucking told Mouse that you were going to have to go back inside again, right? And it's pretty fucking obvious that somebody's going to have to be outside keeping an eye on things while you're gone. So why not give Sam the fucking duty?"

I thought about it, and it actually made sense. Until order could be fully reestablished in the house, somebody probably would have to occupy the body when I was out of it, and Aunt Sam was a much better choice than Adam—although Seferis would be a better choice than either of them. But Seferis wasn't much of a traveling companion. Still, it struck me funny that Aunt Sam would have hit it off with Maledicta.

"All right," I finally said. "Maybe we could do that. But then I want a concession too."

Maledicta shot me an impatient look. "What?"

"Can Penny hear us right now?"

"No. She's asleep in the fucking cave."

"Did you put her to sleep?"

"I wanted another fucking smoke. It's not like she was fucking doing anything except sitting out here."

I nodded. "From now on, when you want a cigarette, or anything else that requires the body, I don't want you to just take over. I want you to ask permission."

"Fuck you."

"Maledicta, I'm serious."

"No fucking chance," Maledicta said. "One, I don't have to ask for fucking permission, and two, if I did, and Mouse said no, I couldn't—"

"Exactly. Another thing, I don't want you knocking Penny unconscious against her will anymore. It's one thing if she gets upset and goes to sleep on her own; but if you're just coming out for a cigarette break, there's no reason she can't keep watching over your shoulder."

Maledicta looked away, muttering disgustedly under her breath. "What bullshit . . ."

"It's not bullshit," I said. "You came to me for help managing your MPD. Discipline is a big part of it."

"Discipline!" Maledicta turned back with a sneer on her face. "Like you should fucking talk!"

"I am having problems with that right now," I admitted. "Which is another reason why I'm asking you for this. If you and I both start switching uncontrollably at the same time, God knows where we'll end up. But if you focus really hard on keeping things orderly, and I do the same, then hopefully at least one of us will be stable at any given moment."

"Ehhh . . ." Maledicta drew her arm back, as if to sweep the suggestion away, but I could tell I'd scored a point with her.

"So is it a deal?" I asked.

"Ehhh, fuck." She rolled down her window and pitched her cigarette butt onto the parking lot. "I'm not going to make any fucking promises," she told me. "If Mouse doesn't give me the time I want, or if she starts putting on fucking airs just because I say please—"

"I'm sure Penny will be gracious about it." I offered her my hand. "Deal?"

Maledicta regarded my hand with disdain. "What are you, Jimmy fucking Stewart? I'm not going to shake on this. I told you, no fucking promises. I'll just . . . I'll fucking try, all right?"

"All right," I said. "Good enough."

"Yeah, yeah, fuck, all right," Maledicta said. "So can we get some fucking food now?"

24

After checking out of the motel and getting some lunch, they take stock of their resources. Mouse has about sixty dollars in cash left; Andrew is down to fifteen dollars. Neither of them has an ATM card. Andrew does have his credit card, which has a limit of a thousand dollars, but he's going to have to call the 800 number to find out how much of that has been used up already (at least two hundred dollars' worth; because they missed the official noon checkout time by ten minutes, the manager of the Badlands Motor Lodge charged them for an extra night).

They have half a tank of gas in the Centurion, and at least one gas card. They have two partially smoked packs of cigarettes. They don't have any spare clothes or any toiletries.

They go back to Rapid City and find a Wal-Mart. Andrew and Mouse stick together in the store and keep up a running conversation, the better to resist unauthorized switches. They each pick out a couple of tops, underwear, socks, and blue jeans; they get gauze and disinfectant for Andrew, some aspirin for Mouse, and toothbrushes and toothpaste for both of them. At one point Maledicta, lurking in the cave mouth, spies a kerchief that she likes—a red, white, and black bandanna with a motif of flaming skulls—and asks if Mouse would "please" buy it for her. Mouse is surprised both by the request and by the unprecedented (if sarcastic-sounding) courteousness of its phrasing. Since the kerchief is only $4.99, she agrees to get it, although she will pay for it separately, in cash.

At checkout there's a moment's suspense as the main purchase is rung up, but the charge on Andrew's credit card is accepted. They change clothes at a gas station on the outskirts of the city, and are about to get back on the Interstate when Maledicta speaks up again from the cave mouth: "Could I *please* drive for a while?"

"What?" says Andrew, noticing Mouse's reaction. Mouse tells him what Maledicta has just asked her. "Oh," he says. "She wants to hang out with Aunt Sam. I told her she could if she was polite—and if it was OK with you."

"You did?" says Mouse; she doesn't like the position this puts her in.

Andrew comes to her rescue: "Tell Maledicta I said not today. It's too soon after what happened this morning. Maybe tomorrow, if I feel stronger."

"All right . . ." Mouse starts to repeat Andrew's refusal, but Maledicta cuts her off: "I heard the fucker! Tell him he's a lying cocksucker! He fucking promised!" Mouse does not relay this message.

By evening they are in Sioux Falls. It's still light out when they finish eating dinner, but Mouse is very tired. "Do you want to stop here for the night?" she asks Andrew.

Andrew is conflicted. He would like to stop here, but as he tries to explain to Mouse, he is concerned that he not appear to be procrastinating. "Maybe we could go just a little farther?"

"I don't know," says Mouse, consulting the road atlas. "I'm not sure that we can go just a *little* farther, on this highway . . . it looks like the next big town is all the way on the other side of Minnesota."

Andrew frowns, not wanting to pressure her, but not wanting to give up yet, either.

"Maybe . . ." Mouse muses. "Would *you* like to drive?"

He shakes his head. "I can't."

"You know you don't really need a license," Mouse tells him. "I mean, as long as you're careful, and don't speed or crash the car."

"It's not just the license; I don't know how to drive."

"I can show you how. It's not hard. There won't be much traffic, either, so it's mostly just keeping it between the lines."

Mouse isn't trying to challenge Andrew—she's just worried that if she keeps driving, she'll fall asleep behind the wheel—but that's how he seems to take it. He takes a deep breath, lets it out, and says: "OK. I can do this."

"You don't *have* to," Mouse tells him. "Maybe, if I just took a nap—"

"No, I can do it."

They get in the Centurion, and Mouse explains the rudiments: gas, brakes, shifting, turn signals. When Andrew looks like he's got it all down, Mouse has him switch seats with her again. "I'll drive until we're out of the city," she says.

She gets them out of Sioux Falls, to a rest stop near the state line. Then

Andrew takes the wheel. He's nervous at first—and Mouse is too, wondering if this is a mistake—but he gains confidence quickly. Too much confidence: soon Mouse has to remind him to watch his speed.

"Sorry," he says, easing off on the accelerator. "You were right, though. This isn't hard."

"I'm surprised you never learned," says Mouse. "It's very convenient."

"*Too* convenient," he says. "Like having a cash card. My father used to love driving, but having access to a car could also be a bad thing, when he lost time. Eventually he decided it wasn't worth it. When I came along I suppose we could have taken it up again, but the truth is I never really felt like I needed a car. It's not like I get out of Autumn Creek all that often." He looks out at the roadside. "This is actually the farthest I've ever traveled."

"Do you know where we're going?" says Mouse.

He nods. "The town in Michigan where Andy Gage was born is called Seven Lakes. It's on the west side of the mitten, near Muskegon and Grand Rapids."

"But you've never been there before?"

"Not personally. But I have looked it up on a map a couple times, so I know about where it is, and my father can give us directions when we need them."

Mouse studies him. "Are you scared?"

"Of going there? Yes," Andrew says. "But I'm curious, too. I'd like to see the house where Andy Gage grew up, if it's still standing. As for the stepfather—I guess in my gut I still don't quite believe I could have killed him, unless . . . unless it was an accident." He looks at her. "What do you think? Do you think that I, that one of me, could have—"

"I tried to kill my mother once," Mouse says.

"You did?" says Andrew, sounding surprised but not shocked. "How?"

"In the hospital. I put my hand over her mouth . . ." She tells him about it, summarizing at first but then adding more and more detail until she's pretty much covered the whole story of her mother's death—everything except what she did with her mother's ashes.

"It doesn't sound to me like you were really trying to kill her," Andrew says, when she's finished. "It sounds like you were fantasizing about killing her. Which it seems like you'd have to be superhuman *not* to do, under the circumstances."

"It wasn't just a fantasy. I had my hand over her mouth."

"But not pressing down hard enough to stop her breathing, you said. And you stopped right away when you realized what you were doing."

"I shouldn't have been doing it at all. It was wicked."

"Well I'll tell you what, Penny," Andrew says. "If we get to Seven Lakes and I find out that the worst I ever did was pinch the stepfather's nose shut one time when he was sleeping, I'll be happy to live with the guilt for that."

"What did he do to you?" Mouse asks. "Do you know?"

"My father didn't tell you?"

Mouse shakes her head. "We talked mostly about what happened after he left home—how he figured out he was multiple, and dealt with that. I got the feeling he didn't want to talk about it before."

"It's true, he doesn't like to," Andrew agrees. Then he tells her: "I know in general what the stepfather did. For one thing, it was a lot more sexual than what happened between you and your mom. I mean, there was violence, too—he had a bad temper—but mostly it was about using Andy Gage as his toy. As his, his fuck doll." Andrew winces at his own choice of words, and Mouse, remembering Loins's tank top, feels her ears redden. "It started really early, too—just how early exactly I can't say, but my father thinks it was early enough that, that it's beyond the point where you could even call it obscenity. And then the whole time Andy Gage was growing up . . ." He pauses, his teeth gritting involuntarily, then continues on a different tack: "We, they, were pretty isolated too. Seven Lakes is about the size of Autumn Creek, but the Gage house was out beyond the edge of town. It'd be the equivalent of living on East Bridge Street, four or five miles past the Reality Factory."

"And it was just you and the stepfather?"

"Yes."

"What about your mother? Did she die?"

He starts to say yes, then hesitates. "I . . . yes, I assume so," he says. Mouse tilts her head in an unspoken question. "I mean," Andrew continues, "I don't remember ever talking about that, but I do know my father loved her. He loved her a lot . . . and I can't see him feeling that way if she'd just run off, and left him with the stepfather. So yes, she must have died . . ." But he frowns, unsatisfied with his own logic. "I'll have to ask about that."

They talk a while longer. Then, about a half hour after sunset, Mouse lays her head back, and the next thing she knows they are pulled over by the side of the highway again.

"What?" she says, sitting up straight. "Where are we?"

"Coming up on the Wisconsin border," Andrew tells her. "There's a city up ahead, so I thought you should probably take the wheel again. I'm ready to stop for the night."

Wisconsin . . . Mouse checks the dashboard clock, which reads 10:29. She tries to remember whether she reset it to the correct time before leaving the motel this morning; even if she did, they've probably crossed another time zone by now. So it's really after eleven, maybe after twelve.

It's late. Mouse takes the wheel, and drives across the Mississippi River into La Crosse, Wisconsin. They find a motel. Mouse, ready to nod off again, pays scant attention as Andrew negotiates the check-in.

Loins isn't so sleepy.

"Twin or queen-size?" the girl at the check-in counter asks.

"Huh?" says Andrew.

"One bed, or two?"

"Oh . . . Two *rooms*, please."

"No, that's all right," Loins interrupts, deftly putting Mouse under. "We can share a room. *I* don't mind."

"You're sure?" Andrew says.

"I'm very sure," Loins tells him, trying hard not to give herself away. "There's no need to waste money on a second room."

"All right . . ." He turns back to the check-in clerk. "Two beds, then."

"Excuse me." Loins leans across the counter and whispers something in the clerk's ear that starts them both laughing.

"What?" says Andrew.

"Oh, nothing," the clerk giggles. "Here you go, room 230."

They go up to the room, which only has one bed. Andrew frowns when he sees it. "Sorry," he says, like it's his fault. "Let's go back down and fix th—"

"It's all right," Loins says, stepping past him into the room. "It's a big bed." She sits on a corner of the mattress and bounces up and down a few times to test it. "We'll both fit."

"Uh, Penny . . ."

"I'm *really* tired, Andrew," she says. "I don't want to go through the hassle of changing rooms. I'll just curl up small on one side, and you won't even know I'm here."

"Penny . . ." He knows something's off, but not what. "Maledicta?"

Loins laughs. "Do I sound like Maledicta? It's *me*, Andrew." She gets up quickly, and goes into the bathroom to wash her face and hands. When she comes back out, Andrew is still standing by the open door. "What's the matter?" Loins asks him. "You're not going to stand there all night, are you?"

"Penny . . ."

"At least close the door."

"Penny, what—"

"You know what you need?" Loins says. "A good shower."

"A shower?"

"Yeah." She nods. "To relax you. Wash the day off." She tosses her head and smiles in a way that she knows is seductive. "Or maybe a nice hot bath . . . I'm going out to get a soda, anyway, so while I'm gone, feel free . . ."

"You're going for a soda? I thought you were really tired."

"Oh, I am," says Loins. "But I'm really thirsty, too." She steps past him again, unable to resist stroking his cheek with her finger in passing. "See you when I get back . . ."

Five minutes, Loins tells herself, as she makes her way to the ground level. She finds a soda machine in an open breezeway that runs between two sections of the motel. There's a cigarette machine, too, but Loins barely glances at it; she doesn't actually like to smoke, and only does it for effect. But Andrew, her intuition tells her, isn't someone who finds smoking sexy.

But speaking of sexy smokers . . . as Loins is making her selection, a cigarette coal flares in the shadows farther down the breezeway. The cigarette's owner is a shaven-headed man in a jogging suit. He's cute enough to make Loins forget about Andrew momentarily.

"Hi there," she says, making her voice a purr. "Looking for some company?"

The smoker smiles at the come on, but then holds up his left hand and waggles the digits; a wedding band glints on his ring finger.

"Your loss," Loins informs him. She takes a can of 7-Up from the soda machine, and—although the night air is cool—presses it to the side of her neck as if she is very, very hot. "Sleep well . . ."

When Loins gets back upstairs, the bathroom door is closed and the water is running in the shower. She drops the soda can on the bed, primps briefly in the mirror above the dresser, and goes to join Andrew.

"Hi there," she says, pushing the bathroom door open without knocking. "Want some comp—"

The bathroom is empty. The shower-sounds Loins heard are coming from the room next door.

"What are you doing?" Andrew says from behind her.

She whirls around. Andrew is sitting in a chair by the door with his arms crossed. Coming in, Loins must have walked right by him.

"What are you doing?" Andrew asks again.

Loins smiles and gives a little shrug. "Just checking to see if you needed any help . . ."

"You aren't Penny."

"You caught me." Loins raises her arms in a fetching display of surrender, but Andrew's not fetched.

"Do you think it's right, you pretending to be someone you're not?" he asks her.

"Right . . . ?" says Loins, her tone implying: *What a concept!* "I think it's fun."

"I think it's rude. Rude to me, and rude to Penny, too. Did you even think to ask her permission before popping out like this?"

"Ask *permission?*" Loins laughs. "She doesn't even know me. She's too boring to know me."

"I don't think she's boring. I think she's a nice person, and a good friend—and I'd like to talk to her. Could you bring her back out, please?"

"No, I couldn't. *I* want to have some fun. If you're not interested, fine, I'll find someone else . . ."

She exits the room in a huff. Descending once more to the breezeway, Loins thinks: *All right, we'll see what that wedding ring is worth. Five minutes, max.* But when she gets there the smoker has departed—finished his cigarette and jogged back to his wife. Loins walks to the far end of the breezeway just to be sure, but she can find no sign of him, nor does she see any other prospects.

Then she hears a whirring noise behind her—someone feeding money into one of the vending machines. She pastes on a sexy smile and turns around. "Hi there . . ."

Her smile falters; it's only Andrew. On the other hand, what the hell? "Changed your mind?" Loins purrs, approaching him.

"No," Andrew says. He retrieves a pack of cigarettes from the machine and holds it up so she can read the label: Winstons. "Catch," he says, and tosses it at her.

". . . fucker!" Maledicta snarls, snatching the pack out of the air. She brandishes the smokes: "You think you can fucking bribe me with this?"

"No," says Andrew, "but I thought it would get your attention. And I trust you more with Penny's body than that other girl."

"Trust!" sneers Maledicta. "Don't get me started on fucking trust." Then: "Fucking Loins . . . I swear, that fucking slut . . ."

"I'm sorry you didn't get to hang out with Aunt Sam this afternoon . . ."

"You should be fucking sorry!"

". . . but I never promised it would be today. Now maybe tomorrow—"

"Maybe? That's what 'please' gets me, a fucking maybe?"

"I'm tired, Maledicta. If I swear to let you spend time with Aunt Sam tomorrow—no maybes—will you go back up to the room and stay there? Make sure Penny stays there?"

"Where are you going to fucking sleep?" Maledicta demands. "Not with me."

"No, not with you," Andrew agrees. "I'll get another room, I guess. Or maybe I'll just sleep in the car . . ."

"You're not sleeping in my fucking car."

"Then I'll get another room." He holds out the key to room 230. "OK?"

"Fucker . . ."

"I noticed there's a minibar in this one," Andrew adds, parenthetically, as she takes the key. "Don't go crazy."

—and so about seven hours later Mouse wakes up alone with cigarette breath and a mild hangover. There's a note on the pillow beside her, in Maledicta's hand: HES FUCKING AROUND. It takes all the concentration Mouse can muster to figure out that this is a reference to Andrew's physical location.

Mouse gets out of bed, showers, and brushes her teeth. She swallows three aspirin. She gets dressed and goes out to the motel parking lot, and finds Andrew waiting for her by the car.

"Something happened last night," she says, walking up to him.

"You switched," he tells her. "I had to call out Maledicta to make sure you didn't . . . wander off."

"Who was in control before," Mouse wants to know, "that you thought Maledicta would be *better?*"

"Well," says Andrew hesitantly, "I'm not sure, but I think her name is Loins . . ."

"Oh God," says Mouse, when she hears what Loins did, or tried to do.

"It's all right, Penny."

"All *right?*"

"I mean it wasn't aggressive. She backed off as soon as I made it clear I wasn't going to play along. I got the feeling she was used to dealing with men who didn't resist."

"Great," says Mouse. Then: "It's *not* all right. You don't know, but this . . . Loins . . . has caused me a lot of trouble. The night before I came to work at the Reality Factory . . ." But she can't tell him that story.

"Well, Penny," Andrew offers, "if you don't like the way she acts, you can always tell her to stop."

"Tell her?"

He nods. "Track her down, inside, and let her know you're not happy. Lay down the law."

"Would that work?"

"Probably not the first few dozen times, but if you keep after her . . ." He shrugs. "It's your household, Penny—or it can be, if you take charge of it.

"I'm going to have to go inside myself today," he adds, "to get some directions from my father, and finish a conversation he and I were having. And since I did kind of promise Maledicta that she could hang out with Aunt Sam, maybe we could coordinate: I'll go inside to see my father, you go inside to talk to Loins, and we let Maledicta and Aunt Sam handle the next leg of the trip."

"Maledicta . . ." Mouse blinks with bloodshot eyes. "You think that's a good idea?"

"I can talk to Aunt Sam beforehand, impress on her that they're not to take any side trips. And Maledicta, if you ask her nicely . . ."

Mouse is skeptical, but she realizes that the real source of her reluctance is not concern over what Maledicta may do with the body, but fear about what she herself may encounter in the cavern. She thinks of the little girl in the party dress. "What if Loins and I don't get along?" she asks. "Or what if I meet somebody else inside, who I don't want to talk to at all?"

"Tell them you don't want to talk to them." He thinks a moment. "When you had your meeting with Dr. Grey, did she do the thing where she has you wear a miner's helmet?"

"Yes."

"She had my father do that too," Andrew says. "He said it really helped, before he got the sun going inside. Bring the helmet with you when you go to talk to Loins—it'll keep you safe."

They check out of the motel. After breakfast, they go to a Shell station to get gas for the Centurion (Andrew, in his determination to go "just a little farther," nearly ran the tank dry last night). Since gassing up the car is Maledicta's self-appointed task, they do the switch right there—first Andrew calls out Sam, and then Mouse, more reluctantly, calls Maledicta forward.

The miner's hard hat is lying on the ground just inside the cave mouth. Mouse picks it up and places it on her head—the fit is as perfect as last time—and the lamp comes on.

"*I got it fucking figured, Sam,*" Maledicta says, outside, talking around the cigarette in her mouth. "*We stay on this road till the Illinois border, just to fucking make it look good, then we cut straight south and make a right turn at St.*

Louis. If we fucking floor it, and don't stop to piss, we could be in fucking Santa Fe by dawn tomorrow . . ."

That had better be a joke, Mouse thinks. On the other hand, if Maledicta and Sam do get up to mischief, it will provide a good excuse for cutting this exploration short.

Mouse descends to the big cavern, pausing at its entrance to listen for the sound of footsteps. She hears none, just the steady inhale-exhale of the sleepers. Still she's nervous, and it occurs to her to wonder whether the lamp in the miner's helmet can be made brighter. She reaches up, and sure enough, there's a knob set into the side of the lamp. Mouse gives it an experimental twist, and the light blazes up, bright enough to blind any approaching memories.

Good. Mouse dials the knob back again, not wanting to see too much herself unless she has to.

The pile of white pebbles is right where Mouse dropped them last time she was down here. She begins gathering them up again, then hesitates, thinking that it will be awkward, carrying a bunch of pebbles around; she'd rather have at least one hand free, in case she needs to turn up the lamp-light. She looks around her immediate vicinity some more and finds a coil of heavy white twine, conveniently wound on a reel.

Now, to anchor it somewhere . . . a handy stalagmite presents itself. Mouse ties one end of the twine around it, and gives a few hard tugs. The knots hold.

"OK." As an added precaution in case the twine breaks, Mouse decides to follow the cavern wall. She does eenie-meenie-meinic-moe to choose a direction, and strikes off to the left, unwinding the twine behind her as she goes.

She hasn't gone far when she hears a familiar sound—*slap slap*—and freezes. This time, though, it's not approaching footsteps; it's water. Splashing. There's a smell, too, a salty musky smell, like warm brine. Suddenly sure she's on the right track, Mouse continues, and comes to an opening in the cavern wall. The space beyond is awash in soft pink light.

Mouse goes inside. It's a grotto, like a sea cave or a desert mountain lair; at its center is a shining pool, lit from below, as if whatever force gouged it out of the grotto floor struck neon beneath the rock. Mouse steps forward to the lip of the pool, and sees herself floating in the gently steaming waters.

No, it's not her: the soul in the pool may be similar in form—not an exact twin, but close—but in *essence* she and Mouse are light-years apart.

Loins.

She is naked, of course. She floats on her back, arms and legs moving languidly in the water, stirring up little waves that lap at her upturned breasts, at her . . . oh God that's disgusting. Mouse stares, repelled yet fascinated, too.

It's the outward likeness that gets to her. Mouse—she doesn't ever spend time thinking about this, but she knows it's true—is no more sexually attractive than dirt; she's *never* been sexy, not once in her whole life. But Loins is. It's hard to say exactly why or how—she's not actually *doing* anything, just floating there—but it's undeniable, she just exudes it somehow, other people viewing this same scene would see it too. And if Loins can be sexy, and Loins resembles Mouse, then that would seem to imply that Mouse could be sexy too, that she's got potential.

This is not information Mouse wants. It's shameful, another strike against her already tainted character. And yet for an instant—the barest millisecond, you could say—she feels an astonishment that is not entirely unpleasant.

Then the shame comes welling up, and Mouse hears her mother's voice condemning her, cursing her for wanting to throw away her good fortune, wanting to *fuck* it all away on some Trash Town boy. It is almost too much—Mouse has to fight to keep from blacking out.

Loins notices her then. She splashes upright in the pool, and her hands come up to smooth back her wet hair, a gesture that has the side effect, probably intentional, of thrusting her nipples forward. Her mouth twists in a grin.

"Well," she says, "I didn't ever expect to see *you* down here. Come for a swim?"

Mouse makes a gagging noise.

"I guess not," Loins says, and giggles. She starts to get out of the pool; Mouse backs up in a hurry. "So what is your pleasure? Is this about last night?" Loins steps out of the water, and reaches for a towel that's been draped over a boulder. She dries herself—hair, face, neck, arms, back, breasts, belly—always managing to hold the towel in a way that leaves the maximum amount of skin exposed to Mouse's view. "Nothing happened, you know. I *tried* to fuck Andrew, but he wouldn't play along at all . . ." Dry above the waist, Loins places one foot up on the boulder, flips the towel between her legs and rubs vigorously, much more vigorously than necessary. Her head tilts back and she stops talking for a moment.

Mouse shuts her eyes.

"Oh, *my!*" Loins exclaims, her tone conveying much of what Mouse can't see. "Hoo! . . . Excuse me. What were we talking about? Oh right, Andrew—he was a perfect gentleman." She laughs. "Perfectly boring . . . although I suppose he was a sweet thing after all, trying to protect your virtue." More laughter. "You know he really chewed me out . . . figuratively, that is."

Stop it, Mouse thinks.

"Yeah, he read me the riot act. Pissed me off a little. He said some nice things about you, though . . . I don't know, maybe you should try fucking him."

"Stop it," Mouse says, her eyes open now but averted, which is no way to lay down the law. She forces herself to look at Loins directly: "Don't say that."

Loins, done drying herself, has slung the towel around her neck—but it's shrunk to the size of a washcloth, so it doesn't cover anything. She's still naked. "Don't say what, 'fucking?' I'd think you'd be used to hearing that by now, hanging out with Maledicta. But then I guess it's more of an adjective when she uses it." She sits down on the boulder. "You want me to stop saying it, or you want me to stop doing it?"

"Doing it." Pushing the words out: "I'm tired of . . . of waking up with strangers."

"So you want me to stop picking up guys in bars."

"Yes."

"Yes," Loins echoes, for a moment sounding reasonable and accommodating, like it's no problem, Mouse should have said something a long time ago. Then her smile turns wicked again: "Well, I guess we all want *something*, huh? Me, I want a good time."

"A good time." Mouse loads the words with all the scorn she can muster. "Is that why you have to get drunk? Is that why you leave me to deal with them in the morning?"

"Mornings are boring," says Loins, unruffled. "And the drinking, half the time that's not even me, and even when it is, it's just part of the play. It *is* a good time—you'd know that if you had the courage to do it yourself once. You want to know what the best part of it is?"

"No, I don't, I want you to—"

"It's not the actual fucking—oh, I won't lie, that can be fun too, if the guy knows what he's doing. But the absolute *best* part is right at the beginning, hooking them, getting them to want you. The moment when you know you have them, when you know they'd do *anything* to be with you . . . mmm, there's no other satisfaction like it." Loins closes her eyes, as if savoring a memory. "Oh, *my* . . ." She leans back over the boulder. "Just thinking about it gets me . . . right . . . *here*." Her feet come off the ground, tucking up under her behind, and her knees splay apart, and Mouse stands there, gaping, the miner's lamp shining like a spotlight on—

Too much. Mouse retreats, stumbles from the grotto into the big cavern. The miner's lamp switches off, she *wills* it off, and she blunders on, in darkness, out into the middle of the cavern, and throws herself down among the sleepers, letting the shame roll over her.

Time passes. Mouse lies in the dark, fading in and out of consciousness, until she feels a tug on the twine that is still wrapped around her fist—

—and then it is afternoon, and Mouse and Andrew are sitting in a restaurant booth. Judging by the empty plates on the table between them—and the bloated feeling in Mouse's stomach—Maledicta and Sam have just finished gorging on pastry and cheesecake. "Sam!" Andrew exclaims, as he examines the bill.

"H-how did your meeting go?" Mouse asks. About as well as her encounter with Loins, if his demeanor is any indication.

"I have a new place I need to stop, before we go to Seven Lakes," Andrew tells her. "If I'm lucky, Seven Lakes may not matter so much."

"OK," says Mouse. She looks out the window at the restaurant parking lot, and sees little to distinguish it from the other roadside parking lots of the past three days. "Where are we now?"

"Gary, Indiana," Andrew says. "Almost there."

He pays the bill, and they go outside and find the car; Mouse drives. Half an hour later they are in Michigan. They follow the coast of the great Lake; by late afternoon they are in Muskegon. Andy Gage's hometown is inland from here, but Andrew has Mouse keep driving north.

Eventually they leave the highway for a narrow two-lane road that runs right along Lake Michigan's shore. After a few miles the road forks, with one branch going down to a sandy beach, and the other curving up to a wooded bluff. They take the high branch.

The cemetery is called Lake View: a half-acre wedge of grassy plots set right at the edge of the bluff, bounded by a low stone wall and flanked by stands of maples. The ground slopes up from the drop-off, giving the rows of headstones the appearance of seats in an amphitheater. "'Lake View,'" Maledicta observes derisively from the cave mouth. "Boy, it must have taken some fucking inspiration to come up with *that* name."

"Be quiet," says Mouse, still nauseous from one too many slices of pie, not to mention one too many cigarettes.

"What? What did you fucking say?"

"You heard me." Loins may be more than Mouse can handle, but Maledicta doesn't scare her anymore.

Andrew has already gotten out of the car. He walks as far as the cemetery gate and then stops; Mouse can't tell if he's afraid or just thinking. She carefully sets the Centurion's parking brake—the cemetery visitors' lot is on a slope, too—and goes to join him.

"Andrew?" says Mouse.

"It reminds me of the pumpkin field," he says. "It's not exactly the same—we don't have so many graves—but still . . ." He turns to her. "Hold my hand?"

She nods, and slips her hand in his. Andrew lifts the latch on the gate. They go in.

"They won't be buried out here," Andrew says, as they walk among the rows of the amphitheater. "This is only part of the cemetery—the oldest part—and my father says it filled up a long time ago." Mouse examines some of the headstones in passing and sure enough, the most recent dates are from the late 1950s.

Andrew heads for an opening in the stone wall; beyond it, a path winds uphill through the trees to another graveyard. This one is much larger than the amphitheater, but lacks the view of the lake, unless you want to climb one of the taller monuments.

"OK," Andrew says, pausing to confer with a member of his household. "OK." He points. "That way."

They cross the graveyard on a diagonal. Andrew counts rows under his breath; around row twenty-five, he slows down and starts checking individual headstones.

"What name are we looking for?" Mouse asks.

"The stepfather's," Andrew says. "There."

It's a huge standing slab of polished granite, the kind normally used to memorialize entire families. The chiseled inscription reads:

HORACE GARFIELD ROLLINS
FEBRUARY 3, 1932—MAY 24, 1991
Here I sleep but for a while
Until I am called up again
Into my Father's house

Andrew's face betrays a welter of emotional states. Whatever else he is feeling, though, he is angry; his hands clench into fists, and Mouse's own hand gets squeezed so hard that she cries out. "Sorry," Andrew says absently, releasing her.

He shakes his head at Horace Rollins's gravestone. "May 24th. That's the wrong date."

"The wrong date?"

"Not the date I was hoping for," Andrew clarifies—though for Mouse, this doesn't actually clear up anything.

Andrew stares at the headstone a while longer. Then he says "OK," steps back, and turns to the grave to the immediate right, which, according to its marker, belongs to Joshua Green, who died on June 5th, 1996.

Andrew's brow creases. He checks the space to Horace Rollins's left, but that's an empty plot.

"Where is she?" Andrew asks; the question is not addressed to Mouse. "Is it possible that she isn't really—. . . Well, she's not where she's supposed to be, father."

Andrew begins a systematic search of the surrounding graves. Three rows up and half a dozen plots over, he finds what he's looking for.

This marker is much more delicate, a slender tablet of rose-veined white marble. It reads:

Althea Gage
December 8, 1944—December 16, 1994
Beloved

"1994," Andrew says, and this time his face reveals no conflict of feeling, just pure sadness. "It's true, then."

Mouse doesn't have to ask what he means. Obviously, Andy Gage's mother didn't die when he was young; and the fact that she is buried here, so close to Andy Gage's stepfather, suggests that she didn't run away, either . . . although it's interesting that she's not buried right next to the stepfather, as she was apparently meant to be.

Andrew's eyes well up with tears, slowly at first; then all at once his whole body sags and is consumed by weeping. "Momma," he says, the voice not Andrew's now but Aaron's.

Mouse steps up beside him, wanting to comfort him but not sure how. He looks at her sidelong, and smiles bitterly through his tears. "You see?" he says. "You thought *you* were worthless. But at least your mother felt *something* for you, even if it was wicked. Our mother, though . . ." He turns back to the stone, his bitterness beginning to ferment into anger. "Why couldn't you love us?" he demands. "How could you love *him*, and not us? How?"

Without warning he whirls around and charges across the rows at Horace Rollins's marker, as though meaning to tackle it. The sheer mass of the stone defeats him; his fists glance harmlessly off its polished surface, and when he hurls his whole body against it, it barely shudders, while he is thrown back off his feet.

"Aaron!" Mouse calls, running over to see if he is all right. When she reaches him he is weeping again. He raises an arm and grasps her hand as she bends over him; his knuckles are skinned and bloody.

"Why didn't she love us?" he asks, through sobs; Mouse isn't sure who is speaking now. "What could we have done that was so wrong, that she would reject us so totally . . ."

"I don't know," is all Mouse can think to say. "I'm sorry, Aaron . . . Andrew . . . I don't have an answer."

Letting go of her hand again, he rolls over on his side and curls into a ball.

"Why didn't she love us?" Andy Gage wails. "Why?"

NINTH BOOK:
HOMECOMING

25

"You thought our mother died when Andy Gage was very young, didn't you?" my father said.

"I never really thought about it at all," I told him. "I mean yes, I guess I assumed she'd died a long time ago—that's how it always sounded when you talked about her—but I never dwelled on the question. Why would I? It's not my job to look back."

We were sitting on the front steps of the house. Sitting in daylight: the mist had receded overnight, though it still shrouded the entire lake. Early this morning my father had managed to rebuild the pulpit (a definite patch-job, but functional), and Seferis was up there now, keeping an eye on the body—or rather, keeping an eye on Aunt Sam, who was in the body, riding across Wisconsin with Maledicta.

"This is the program from our mother's funeral," my father said. He held up the pamphlet that he'd pulled from under the mystery door yesterday. "I threw the original away, but I guess somebody brought a copy inside when I wasn't paying attention . . . either that, or the memory persisted on its own somehow."

He handed it to me. The cover bore Althea Gage's name, and a date.

"December 1994," I said, surprised. "Is that right? Only three years ago?"

"Two and a half."

"That recently?" Then it hit me: "This would have been just two months before I was born."

He nodded. "I got the news about our mother the same week Dr. Grey had her stroke."

"And did that have anything to do with your decision—"

He started crying.

I'd seen my father angry before, many times, but I'd never seen him cry. I hadn't known he was capable of it. But now his eyes flooded with tears, and his soul was wracked by horrible sobs. It hurt me to see, but it scared me, too; I found myself checking the sky repeatedly, to see if the sun would darken in sympathy. It didn't; but I could swear that the mist on the lake got thicker again.

"I loved her, you know," my father said, when he was able to speak again. "I loved her, and for years I waited for a sign, any sign, that she loved me too. Of all the hopes I ever had, that was the one I held the longest, and the strongest. I wanted her love more than anything, even more than, than to get away from *him*."

"The stepfather," I said, as another realization fell into place. "She was there, living in the same house, the whole time he . . ."

"Yes."

"Did she know?"

"Don't be stupid, Andrew. Of course she knew. She *never* abused us herself," he added forcefully. "Not once. And when it was just the two of us, when *he* wasn't home, it was fine. It was wonderful, in fact. But when he was home . . . she knew."

"Then she was as evil as he was," I said.

He exploded at me: "Don't you say that! You weren't there! Don't you *ever* say that about her!"

"I'm sorry, father, but you know it's true. If she knew what was going on, and did nothing to stop it—"

He disappeared. His face got very red, until I thought he was going to lash out at me, and then he vanished. A few seconds later, in the forest behind the house, a series of loud crashes began—whole stands of trees being uprooted and hurled in anger. This went on for some time, and once again I checked the sky, this time for incoming meteors.

The crashes subsided. My father, calmer now, reappeared beside me.

I didn't try to pick up where we'd left off. "Why did she do it?" I asked instead. "Could she really have loved the stepfather that much, to let him—"

"I don't know what motivated her," my father said. "What moved her. I never knew that. All I can say . . . it must have suited her to be married to him, suited her enough that she was willing to overlook . . . to allow . . ." His composure faltered. "I guess she must have loved him, if she loved anyone. More than she loved me.

"But still," he continued, "I held out hope, and watched for a sign. And I thought I had it, once. It was near the end of high school, when the time came to start applying to colleges. The stepfather didn't want me leaving home, but she argued in favor of it. It was the only time I'd ever seen her argue with him about anything. And I thought, this is it, this is the proof. Maybe she can't stop him from, from doing that to me, not while we're under the same roof, but she is trying to help me escape. She *does* care. She does love me . . ."

He shook his head. "I should have let it go at that; I should have just believed what I wanted to believe, and been content. But it wasn't enough; I had to try to confirm it. And so after it was settled that I *was* going away to college, I got her alone, and tried to thank her. I told her how grateful I was, and I told her that I understood what it *really* meant, her sticking up for me like that.

"She cut me off before I could finish. She told me I shouldn't make assumptions. She said that it wasn't anything she'd done *for* me, it was just . . . she was tired of competing with me for his attention." He paused, and I thought he might cry again, but instead he smiled, a ghastly smile. "So that . . . that was not the response I'd been hoping for."

"And after that you gave up hoping . . ."

He actually laughed. "Come on now, Andrew," my father said. "Vain hopes don't die that easily. *You* should know that."

"But how could you still think, after she said such a horrible thing to you, that she might—"

"You never met the stepfather. He had . . . power. He was a monster, but he could be charming, too, and where he couldn't charm he could persuade. He could get you to say things, or not say them. It was a long time after we got away from him before I could tell anyone about what he'd done; and if he could have that kind of control over me when he wasn't even there, it wasn't hard to believe that he had control over our mother, too, and that when she said what she said, that wasn't really *her* talking, just . . . his power.

"But he was older than she was. And he drank; he drank more as time went on. It seemed very likely that she'd outlive him, and that there would come a day—maybe in ten or twenty years, but still—when she wouldn't be under his influence anymore, and then, then finally, her true feelings could come out . . ."

"That's . . ."

"Ridiculous?" my father said. "I suppose. But not too ridiculous to hang a hope on."

"And you were willing to wait for that?" I asked. "For him to die of natural causes?"

"It wasn't a question of being willing. I couldn't have killed him. I couldn't even stop him from fucking me; to actually stop him from living . . ." He shook his head. "There would be no way. My only chance of beating him was to get beyond his reach; my revenge was to survive him, and maybe one day shit on his grave—*after* he'd gone there on his own."

"About that," I said. "*Is* the stepfather—"

"Oh yes," said my father. "He's dead. But for a long time I didn't know it.

"Going away to school was only the first step in my escape," he told me. "MSU, where I started college, wasn't really far enough. It was only a two-hour drive from Seven Lakes. During the first semester, he tried to, to *visit* me, on campus. He tried twice. The first time, I knew he was coming, so I hid for three days. The second time, there was no advance warning, and I ended up jumping out a window to get away from him.

"There wasn't any third time. After that surprise visit I dropped out of school, and left no forwarding address . . ." He paused, then corrected himself: "I say 'I,' but really it was Gideon who did that. Gideon and probably Adam. All I did, I closed my eyes in East Lansing one afternoon, and when I opened them again it was nine months later and I was living in Ann Arbor.

"I never went back to Seven Lakes. Never called either, not even from a pay phone—I would have liked to hear our mother's voice again, but I was always afraid he'd trace the call somehow, or maybe just come crawling through the line. So I didn't call, or write, but I did come up with what I thought was a clever way of keeping tabs: every so often I would dial directory assistance and give them the stepfather's name. I figured as long as he was listed he was still alive; it didn't occur to me that our mother might keep the phone in his name even *after* he died.

"So anyway there I was, in Ann Arbor. And this part of the story you mostly know: I, we, slowly started putting things together, understanding our multiplicity. Eventually we met Dr. Kroft, and worked with him until our falling out. And then we moved to Seattle, and found Dr. Grey.

"That part you know. But what I never told you, because I didn't think it mattered, is that I finally did try to contact our mother again. This was after we'd been in therapy with Dr. Grey for a while. The therapy was going really well, and I had what was either a fresh burst of optimism or a perverse impulse to screw things up. I decided to try and get in touch with our mother and let her know that we were alive, and see if she missed us. If she was ready to love us yet."

"Oh boy," I said.

"Yes," said my father. "Dr. Grey didn't think it was such a hot idea, either. But Mrs. Winslow was more supportive. I decided to write rather than call—I was still afraid of the stepfather tracking us down—and Mrs. Winslow had a suggestion for how I could make the letter harder to trace. I rented a post office box in Seattle, one that I could stop and check on my trips to Poulsbo, and wrote to our mother care of that PO box. Mrs. Winslow also promised me that if the stepfather did find out where we were living somehow, *she* would deal with him." He smiled. "I think I would have paid to see that. He had power, but Mrs. Winslow could have taken him."

"He *didn't* show up, though, right?"

"No. He was already dead by then. But our mother didn't write back, either. I waited a few months, and then wrote another letter, and then another . . . five in all. The last one, I didn't even bother with the PO box— I included our home address and phone number in Autumn Creek." He shook his head. "Stupid . . . but still she never got in touch.

"In January of 1995, though, right after Dr. Grey went into the hospital, I got a call from a Police Chief Bradley in Seven Lakes. I remembered him from when we were little, when he was still just Officer Bradley—he'd been a friend of our father, our *real* father, and he would come by the house once in a while to see how our mother was doing."

"Did you ever tell him about the stepfather?"

"I tried to," my father said. "Once. But I was so scared I botched it—he had no clue what I was talking about—and then afterwards, the stepfather just *knew* somehow, knew that I'd been bad . . . and from then on, believe me, I knew better than to even think about telling.

"Anyway, it was Chief Bradley who called to tell me about our mother's death. He said he regretted not getting in touch sooner—they'd already had the funeral—but he'd only just found our last letter to her."

"She did receive it, then," I said. "And she kept it."

"I think she just forgot to throw it away," my father replied. "It came out during the conversation that the stepfather was dead, too, for going on four years. *Four years*—that just killed my heart. I mean I'm sorry, he had power, I know he did, but four years was more than enough time for her to, to get past that.

"And then the final straw: Chief Bradley said that the other reason he was calling, besides just to let us know—in her will, our mother had left everything to her sister, only it turned out *she* was dead too, and had no heirs. So Chief Bradley thought that it was only right that we should get the property, and the house. 'I'm sure that's what your mother would have wanted,' he said.

"But it wasn't true." My father looked at me. "It wasn't true, and I couldn't pretend any longer. I don't know what we did wrong, what we lacked, but she didn't love us. She didn't love us.

"And that *is* why I decided to call you out," he concluded. "What happened to Dr. Grey, that was hard, but I could have coped with it. But our mother . . . finding out that our mother . . ." His eyes brimmed with tears again.

"How did the stepfather die?" I asked next.

"He had an accident of some kind."

"An accident."

"That's what Chief Bradley told me. He wasn't more specific, and I didn't care enough to ask questions."

"Well that," I said, "that isn't the response I was hoping for."

"I really doubt we could have had anything to do with it, Andrew," my father said.

"Just because you don't think *you* could have killed him—"

"Not just me. I don't think any of us who knew him could have done it. Including Gideon. Besides, Gideon wasn't desperate for our mother's love. The only love Gideon ever needed was Gideon's."

"There are other reasons for killing someone."

"Like revenge?" My father shook his head. "Gideon has the same problem hating people as he does loving them—in order to feel that strongly about someone you first have to think of them, and Gideon would rather think of himself."

"He seems to do a pretty good job of hating you."

"Only because he can't ignore me. If we weren't trapped in the same head together . . ."

"What about money?" I said. "Xavier told Penny he was going to Michigan to collect an inheritance."

"Well," my father admitted, "it's true that Gideon wanted me to take the house in Seven Lakes. That was the catalyst for our last fight." He looked at the scar on his palm. "I'd thought I had Gideon settled down, ready to accept his place in the geography, but then we got that phone call. When Gideon found out I'd told Chief Bradley I didn't want our mother's property, he was furious. He said that the property was rightfully his, and I had no business refusing it."

"And that's when he tried to take over?" My father nodded. "And what about before then?" I asked. "Is it possible that sometime earlier on, while the stepfather was still alive, that Gideon might have gone to him and tried to demand, I don't know, some kind of *advance* on his inheritance?"

". . . and then killed him when he said no?" My father was skeptical. "That's hard to imagine. I told you—"

"Maybe he didn't do it personally. Maybe he called out somebody else, somebody new, to do it for him. That could be what Xavier was for."

"I don't know. I don't know anything about Xavier, and I'm embarrassed that I don't, but—"

"Do you know where we were, the day the stepfather had his accident? I mean, is it even possible that we were in Seven Lakes that day?"

"I don't even know the exact date he died. I never asked."

"Father!"

"I didn't care about that, Andrew! I was glad to hear he was gone, but the questions I had for Chief Bradley were all about our mother."

"Do you know *approximately* when—"

"Late spring of 1991. Which was a pretty chaotic period for us. That was when I had my big blowup with Dr. Kroft."

"Dr. Kroft . . . so there's a chance we were locked up in Ann Arbor when the stepfather had his accident."

He nodded. "It depends on the date. For most of April that year things were pretty stable; I lost some time, a couple hours here and there, but no really big chunks. Then on April . . . 29th, I think . . . I had a session with Dr. Kroft where we tried a forced fusion, and the next five days are all lost time, although the last three of those days we were in lockdown in the Psychiatric Center. They let us out on May 6th, and then the next day I went back to the Center for what turned out to be my last session with Dr. Kroft. That was the session where I lost my temper—and then for the next two weeks, more or less, we were back in lockdown."

"More or less?"

"The last two weeks of May are a complete blank," he told me. "When I blacked out on the 18th—or maybe it was the 19th—I was still on the ward. When I woke up on June 2nd I was on a Greyhound bus, on my way to Seattle."

This was a version of events I hadn't heard before. "You woke up on a bus? But I thought . . . you always told me you *decided* to leave Michigan."

"Well I did," my father said. "I mean I could have gotten off the bus in Chicago and turned back. But when I checked my wallet, I found a cashier's check for what looked like my entire savings, and a number to call to have my possessions forwarded . . . so I had a pretty good idea that if I went back to Ann Arbor, I wouldn't still have an apartment waiting for me, or a bank account—and I was *sure* I didn't have a job anymore. And besides, there just didn't seem to be any reason to go back. I was done with Dr. Kroft, done with that whole chapter of my life; it was time to try something new. So I decided—*I* decided—to stay on the bus and keep going."

"But . . ." I stopped myself. This was definitely a topic to be explored in more detail later, but for now it was a side issue. "So two whole weeks are missing. May 18th or 19th through June 2nd."

"Right."

"Which is not good."

"Well, that depends on what day the stepfather died . . . You could look it up on his tombstone, I suppose. The cemetery's just outside Muskegon, so it's practically on the way."

"You know where the stepfather is buried?"

"I know where our mother is buried. They had adjacent plots." He gazed out at the mist on the lake. "If you do stop there . . ."

"You really want to say good-bye to her?"

"She was our mother," he said.

We talked a while longer, then sat, not talking, longer still. Eventually my father stood up and said he was going for a walk in the forest. I offered him back the funeral program, but he didn't want it. "Keep it yourself," he said, "or throw it in the lake."

"Keep it where? I can't just leave it lying out, and I'd rather not bury it . . ."

"If you really want to hang on to it," my father said wearily, "you can put it up in my room."

He turned away and disappeared; I went into the house. As I climbed the steps to the second floor I was struck by how quiet it was. Usually there are at least four or five souls in the common room, or up in the gallery. Today there were none. It felt as if the house were empty, though I doubted everyone could be outside; probably a lot of them were just hiding in their rooms.

A soul's own room is an intensely private space—as private, in its way, as a singular person's whole mind—and ordinarily permission to go inside, especially unaccompanied, is a sign of great trust. In this case, however, I think my father was just too tired to worry about me poking around. Not that there was much for me to poke around *in*. My father's room is the definition of Spartan: four walls and a bed pretty much describes it.

It was this very simplicity that inadvertently led to me being nosy. I had to find a place to put the funeral program. It was obvious that my father didn't want to have to look at it, so just dropping it on the floor or on top of the bed was out. If he'd had shelves or trunks or a filing cabinet I could have stuck the pamphlet in there, but he didn't, so that left only one place: *under* the bed. When I reached beneath the box spring, though, there was already something else down there. I grabbed onto it, meaning only to shift it aside a little—I swear—but ended up pulling it out to look at it.

The something was a painting. Oil on canvas, like the kind Aunt Sam did, but in a very different style than hers. The painting showed a woman hugging a little girl. There was no background, no sense of location; just the two figures. The girl's face was hidden, pressed to the woman's breast, but the woman's face—the most detailed part of the portrait—was aglow with love, and even if I hadn't recognized her from the photograph in my wallet, her identity wouldn't have been hard to guess.

I slid the painting back beneath the bed, and the pamphlet along with it. Resisting the temptation to hunt around under there some more, I got up to go . . . and that's when I saw the Witness standing out on the gallery, staring in at me. She was one of the older Witnesses, a girl of eleven or twelve.

"What do you want?" I asked her brusquely, embarrassed to be caught snooping.

She didn't answer, only turned and walked out of my field of view. I stepped to the doorway, but by the time I got there she was all the way across the gallery. She disappeared into the nursery.

I didn't try to follow her. Instead, I went downstairs and gave the mystery door another try. It still wouldn't open. On a whim I tried knocking; that didn't work either, and the echo of my knocks in the empty common room spooked me so much that I quickly stopped. Finally—feeling the draft again—I got down on my hands and knees and listened at the crack under the door. I heard a faint irregular sigh that might have been muffled snoring.

I stood up, and felt eyes on me again: the Witness was back, watching me from the gallery. This time, I didn't ask what she wanted; I left the house. "Sam!" I called, hurrying across the geography to the column of light. "Time's up, Sam."

We were in Indiana already; Aunt Sam and Maledicta had made good time. They'd *been* good, too, except for a twenty-dollar dessert orgy that I caught the tail end of. I didn't make a big fuss about that; it was midafternoon, and I was anxious to get to Horace Rollins's grave before dark, to see if he'd been cooperative enough to die in April, early May, or June.

No such luck. The death date on the gravestone was May 24th, which put it right in the middle of the two-week blackout period. So we weren't in the clear.

It was going on six o'clock by the time we left the cemetery. We could still have made it to Seven Lakes before nightfall, but while I didn't want to show fear or hesitation, I also didn't want to push it; next morning, I decided, would be soon enough.

We went back to Muskegon and found a motel. To avoid a repeat of the previous night's events, I asked for two widely separated rooms. But when we had our respective keys and it was time to part company, Penny was suddenly reluctant. "Wait," she said.

"What?" I replied, instantly on guard.

"It's still me," she promised. "Not . . . not Loins. But I don't want to *become* Loins tonight, or anybody else either, so do you think you could just sit with me until I start to fall asleep?"

"Ah . . . Penny . . ."

"Please? I know it's awkward, after . . . but I don't want to wake up in some stranger's room tomorrow morning. Or with another hangover."

"You know if you do switch, I might not be able to do anything about it."

"I know. But . . . please?"

We went to her room. Penny lay down on the bed, and I sat in a chair.

"How far is it to Seven Lakes from here?" Penny asked. "I know we're close—"

"Very close. Less than an hour away."

"What will you do when we get there?"

"Go up to the house first, I guess, and see if . . . if there's anything to see. Then maybe the town library." She flashed me a quizzical look. "Old newspapers," I said.

"Oh right."

"Hopefully there'll be a story about his . . . how he died. With enough details so that I don't have to bother the police about it. The police, I guess they'd be our third stop. There's a Police Chief Bradley who might be able to help."

"You're brave," Penny said.

"I don't feel brave. It's just my job."

"You know," she said, "this is as close as I've been to *my* hometown since my mother died."

"That's right," I said, "Ohio. Would you want to go there, after—"

"No!" Penny said firmly. "There's nothing in Willow Grove I need to check on. Ever."

"Nothing about your father, even?"

"I know what I need to know about him." A small smile attached itself to her face. "My grandmother told me lots of stories."

"That must have been nice," I said. "To have at least one good parent. Even if he died."

"What about your biological father?" Penny asked. "Was he a bad person?"

"I don't know. I don't know much about him. I know he served in the army, and that he drowned a few months before Andy Gage was born, but as for what kind of person he was—if we have any stories about that, I haven't heard them."

"Well maybe you'll hear some tomorrow. Maybe we'll meet someone in town who knew him."

"I don't know, Penny. I'd rather not talk to anyone in Seven Lakes if I can help it. I'd like to just go in, find out what I need to about the stepfather, and then go home."

Which reminded me: I picked up the phone and tried to call Mrs. Winslow again. "Still no answer?" Penny said, after I'd let it ring two dozen times.

"No." I hung up. "I don't understand. Where could she be?"

"Remember it's earlier there. She could still be out . . . well . . ."

"Out looking for me," I finished for her. I grabbed the phone again and dialed Dr. Eddington's number. His answering machine picked up, and I left another message, talking until the machine cut me off.

I replaced the receiver in its cradle and started to sit down on the bed. "Sorry," I said, catching myself. "I guess I should go to my room now."

"You don't have to," said Penny, looking uncomfortable. "I mean . . . if you want to stay, I won't—"

It was probably a bad idea, and if I'd seen even a trace of a smile on her face I'd have left immediately. But this wasn't Loins being coy; it was Penny, still frightened of what she might do if she were left alone. And when I thought about being alone myself, with all the things I had to worry or feel guilty about . . .

I lay down carefully, staying as close to the edge of the bed as I could without falling off; Penny likewise scootched as far over on her side as possible. We remained like that, talking quietly, until at some point, drowsing, I reached out an arm, and Penny did too, and we clasped hands long-distance, and in that way fell asleep.

In the morning I slipped out quietly while Penny was still snoring and went to my own room to shower. As I stepped into the shower stall, Adam surprised me by appearing on the rebuilt pulpit and asking for his customary two minutes. "What's the matter?" he said. "It's only been a few days. Don't tell me you've forgotten what it's like to hear voices."

"I *was* getting used to the peace and quiet, now that you mention it," I said. Then: "I'm not sure you deserve any time out, after what you pulled in South Dakota."

"All I did in South Dakota was turn on the TV—it was Sam who went to the bar. And even so, you gave her half a day in the body yesterday . . . but I'm not going to harp on that."

I let him have his two minutes, which were actually more like ten. When he finished, I tried to see if any of the others wanted their usual morning time, but Aunt Sam and Jake wouldn't even answer my call. "They're hiding in their rooms," Adam informed me. "A lot of the other souls, too. They're scared; they know where we're going today."

Seferis wasn't scared, though. When we got out of the shower, he ran through a modified workout, mindful of the body's still-sore hands and arm; and after he finished, I got back in the shower and rinsed off a second time. By the time all that was done, Penny was awake. She knocked on the motel-room door just as I finished dressing.

We ate a quick breakfast and then set out. The drive was no more than forty miles, but it seemed to take forever; I passed the time by digging my fingers into the seat upholstery. "We could still turn around," Penny said, when she saw how white my knuckles were.

"No." I shook my head. "I have to do this."

Seven Lakes sits right on the edge of the Manistee National Forest. The lakes that it is named for are more like big ponds, and according to my father their exact number varies from year to year, depending on the amount of rainfall. We saw the first one just moments later: a kidney bean–shaped body of water that lapped up against a bend in the road. It hardly seemed large enough to support more than a token fish or two, but there was a man in hip-waders standing out in the middle of it just the same, making a lazy cast with a fishing pole. The man looked around as we drove by, but between the big straw hat he had jammed down on his head and the glare of the morning sun off the water's surface, I couldn't see his face.

A few hundred feet past this "lake," there was another bend in the road, and a sign that said ENTERING SEVEN LAKES. We rounded the curve, and found ourselves on the main street of Andy Gage's hometown.

My father and Adam had been out on the pulpit the whole way from Muskegon; now, despite their apprehension—in some cases, terror—other souls began to come forward. Many of them only stepped onto the pulpit long enough for a quick peek before darting back inside the house; the sounds of their coming and going formed a constant shuffle at the back of my mind.

Penny slowed the car to a crawl, and I examined each building and store-front we passed in turn, waiting on a glimmer of recognition that never came: there was a one-engine firehouse with a sleepy bulldog lazing in the driveway; an Exxon station; a bakery; a diner named Winchell's; a CD, record, and book exchange; a tiny post office; a barber shop; a clothing store, a tailor's, and a Laundromat, all in a row in the same brick building; the Seven Lakes police station; a video rental shop; a grocery store; a hardware store; a beauty salon; a couple of shabby-looking antique stores; and a boarded-up, partially dismantled fast-food restaurant that, judging by the outline and the color scheme, had probably been a Kentucky Fried Chicken. All this on the main street; and looking down the cross streets as we passed them, I also saw a pair of churches, a bar, a school, and what was either a library or the town hall.

I didn't recognize any of it. Of course there was no reason why I should, but still I'd been expecting something, some sense of familiarity. It seemed like I should know this town, although I'd never been here. But the only recollections I had were secondhand, from the pulpit, where the shuffling of the souls was punctuated by whispers and exclamations about this or that landmark.

"Which way now?" asked Penny, after we passed the defunct KFC.

"I'm not sure," I said. "Why don't we—wait! Stop here!"

The Centurion jerked to a halt in front of what looked like a private house. A wooden shingle hung from the eaves above the front porch; it read "Oscar Reyes, Esq.—Attorney At Law."

"A lawyer?" I said, speaking to my father. "I thought you told me he was an exterminator."

"He was both," my father replied. "A lot of people in Seven Lakes have more than one job. His law practice must have picked up a lot since we left, though—this house is new."

I turned to Penny: "Can you park here and come inside with me?"

"You want to hire a lawyer?"

"No," I said. "At least, not yet. This may sound a little strange, but I'd like to see if this man reminds you of Xavier at all."

"All right . . ."

When we got up on the porch, though, there was a note on the front door that said Mr. Reyes was vacationing in Canada and wouldn't be back until June 1st. Frustrated, I tried to look in through the front windows—looking for what, I can't say—but the curtains and shades were drawn.

As Penny and I returned to the car, I noticed a couple of passersby casting glances in our direction from across the street. At first I assumed they were curious because they'd seen us nosing around Mr. Reyes's house; then I realized that it could be because they thought they knew me. I wasn't ready to deal with that, so I climbed hurriedly into the car and asked my father for directions to the Gage house.

I relayed his instructions to Penny: "Straight down this road another three miles. Then we turn left onto a dirt trail, and go another mile and a half through the woods." The first part went smoothly enough, but when we got to the trail it had been widened and blacktopped, and Penny drove right by it. After my father caught the mistake and we made a U-turn, we discovered that large sections of the woods had been cut down and cleared to make room for new houses. "Huh," I said; not having seen what it was like before, I couldn't fully appreciate the extent of the changes, but I got a general sense from my father's reaction. "Not so isolated anymore."

For the final half mile the trail reverted to dirt and the woods came back, pressing in close on both sides. And then, without fanfare, we were there, pulling into the front yard of the house where Andy Gage had lived and died. Penny set the Buick's parking brake and switched off the engine; we sat there in the sudden stillness—the pulpit had gone dead quiet, too—staring at the house as though it were the bones of a dragon, or some other thing out of myth.

It was smaller than I'd expected. Not that I'd given it much thought, but I guess, extrapolating from the two houses I was most familiar with—the house in Andy Gage's head, and Mrs. Winslow's Victorian—I'd been picturing something fairly substantial, with two or even three floors, and lots of rooms. Instead, the Gage house was what a realtor would optimistically describe as "cozy": a cottage, basically, with just one story, plus a low-ceilinged attic tucked beneath a shallow-peaked roof.

The outside walls of the cottage were white, and looked to have been painted since Andy Gage's mother's death. And though it was immediately obvious—for a reason I will get to in a moment—that the cottage was not currently occupied, there were other signs of at least intermittent maintenance: the front yard had been mowed recently, and the narrow beds on either side of the front door had been planted with new spring flowers.

"Do you want to go inside?" Penny asked.

"No," I said, meaning: I have to.

"It might not be safe," Penny suggested.

"No," I agreed.

One other important fact about the cottage: it *leaned.* Soil erosion had undermined the foundation on one side, to the point where the house was visibly tilting, like a ship beginning to capsize. Someone—probably the same someone who'd been tending the grounds—had shored it up with a bunch of long wooden planks and a cut-down telephone pole. This emergency bracing appeared to have worked, for the moment, but it was only a temporary solution: most of the planks were bowing under the strain, and the telephone pole had developed a spiral crack around its midsection. While I had no general objections to the cottage collapsing, I didn't want it to happen while Penny and I were inside.

Best to get it over with quickly, then: I went up to the front door to see if the maintenance man had left it unlocked. He hadn't. But then at Adam's suggestion I checked around the threshold, and found a loose flagstone.

The canting of the house had begun to warp the front doorframe, not enough to jam the door completely, but enough to make it stick; after wrestling the lock open, I had to shove hard to gain entry. The door swung in to a small vestibule. Beyond the vestibule was a living room full of ghosts.

Not real ghosts. Not emotional ghosts, either—I still didn't recognize any of the things I was seeing. The ghosts in the living room were furniture ghosts: a loveseat, a rocking chair, a coffee table, a tall skinny thing that turned out to be a grandfather clock, all of them draped in white sheets like dusty trick-or-treaters. Through an open doorway on the opposite wall I could see a kitchen where more ghosts were gathered.

"Does it look safe to go in?" Penny asked, coming up behind me.

"I guess so," I said. I started to step forward into the living room, but then from outside came the sound of another car entering the yard. "Who's that . . . ?"

My first thought, seeing the police car pull up beside Penny's Buick, was that I'd walked into a trap. It was true: I had killed the stepfather, the Seven Lakes police knew it, and they'd had the house staked out all this time, just waiting for me to come back . . .

"Don't panic yet," said Adam. "We passed this guy on the main road, right after we made the U-turn. He must have seen us turning onto the trail and gotten curious."

The driver had gotten out of the patrol car and was walking towards us. He had thick blond hair and a pencil moustache; I guessed he was about my age. "Hey there, folks," he greeted us. "You have business on this property?"

"Not official business," I told him. "I used to live here."

Either because of what I'd just said, or because he was close enough to get a good look at me, the patrol-car driver's eyes suddenly widened in recognition. "Who is this man?" I asked urgently. "Do we know him?"

"Yes," my father said from the pulpit. "This is going to be awkward. He's . . ."

The patrol-car driver continued to walk towards us. As he came within conversational distance, I saw that the nameplate on his uniform read OFFICER CAHILL. His first name was James, although his friends—and his girlfriends—knew him as Jimmy.

"Hey there, Sam," he said.

26

Officer Cahill doesn't get it.

"Sam . . ." he says, in a wounded, wheedling tone.

"I'm not Sam," Andrew tells him, for the third time.

"Look, I know you're mad—"

"I'm not mad; I'm just not who you think I am. My name's not Sam, it's Andrew . . ."

"Sam . . . Andrea . . . please. I can understand you wanting to cut me dead after what I did, but—"

"You don't understand at all," says Andrew, and Maledicta weighs in from the cave mouth: "That's for fucking sure." Andrew continues: "I'm not pretending to not know you to punish you for whatever it is you did to Sam; I *really* don't know you. I'm not the person you think I am."

"I'm not the same person either, Sam," the officer replies. "When I think about that selfish young kid who ran out on you—"

"Officer Cahill—"

"Sam—"

"Is Gordon Bradley still in Seven Lakes?"

Officer Cahill pauses, thrown off track by the question. "Chief Bradley? Yes, he's still here."

"I need to talk to him."

Starting up again: "Sam—"

"I need to talk to him," Andrew interrupts, "because I think I may have killed someone."

Another pause, longer this time. "What?"

"I think I may have killed someone. I'm not sure I did, I hope not, but I need to talk to Chief Bradley about it."

"Killed *who*?" Officer Cahill says, incredulous.

"Officer—"

"Sam, if you're in trouble—"

"I'm *not* Sam," Andrew says, losing his temper. "Maybe Sam will agree to talk to you later, but not until *I* talk to Chief Bradley. So could you take us to him? Please?"

"All right," Officer Cahill says, still with a look of disbelief on his face. "You want to ride back with me in the cruiser?"

"No," says Andrew. "We'll follow you in our car."

"All right . . ." He starts to walk away, stops, turns back, says "Sam . . ." and then gives up. For the moment.

Meanwhile Andrew tilts his head, and says angrily to someone inside: "What did you want me to tell him? I'm going to have to talk about it if I want to find out . . . *You* be quiet!"

"Your Aunt Sam," says Mouse, a few moments later in the car. "She and Officer Cahill had a . . . relationship?"

"I don't really know," says Andrew. "Aunt Sam always talked about having a 'sweetheart,' and I guess this might be the guy. But I don't know the story, and Sam's not talking right now."

"He called you Andrea, too."

"Andrea Samantha Gage. That's my legal name."

"Your mother named you Andrea?"

"Yes," Andrew tells her, his voice sullen. "The body is female." He looks at her expectantly, but all Mouse can think to say is: "Oh . . . OK."

"OK?" says Andrew. "You're not freaked out?"

Mouse shakes her head. "I'm . . . surprised, I guess. But freaked out? No." She waves an arm, trying to encompass, in a gesture, everything that has happened since she started work at the Reality Factory three weeks ago. "You know, at this point . . ."

"Right!" Andrew says, as if he's been waiting for someone to see things this way. "Right, exactly, it's *not* that big a deal. *I* never thought it was. But Julie . . ." He stops and thrusts his hands out, as if pushing something away. "No . . . I'm not going to get going on that again."

The inside of the Seven Lakes police station looks more like a real estate office than a bastion of law enforcement. The front door opens into a veneer-paneled reception area, one wall of which is covered by an enormous surveyor's map of the town, marked off into individual property lots. At the rear of the room, past a pair of messy desks, the barred door of the station's main holding cell has been propped open, and partially concealed, by a big potted fern; the cell itself is being used to store stacks of brown-

and-white file-folder boxes. Mouse deduces they do not see many felons in here; she wonders whether that bodes well or ill for Andrew's situation.

"Mortimer," Officer Cahill says to a man sitting at one of the desks. "Is the chief around?"

Mortimer shakes his head. "He should be in soon, though. He radioed a while ago and said he was just going to grab a slice of pie at Winchell's."

"All right," Officer Cahill says. "When he gets in, tell him I need to see him." He looks around at Andrew and Mouse. "We'll wait for him in the break room. This way."

Officer Cahill leads them to a kitchenette in a back corner of the building. Shutting the door, he starts in on Andrew again: "All right, Sam, what's going on?"

"I'm not—"

"Listen, Sam: you may want to pretend that you don't know me, but I do still care about you, and if this business about killing someone isn't just a joke, you're going to need someone who cares about you. So before the chief gets here and things go too far, why don't you tell me what happened. Did you and"— he shoots a suspicious glance at Mouse—"your friend here get into some kind of trouble on the road?"

"No." Andrew shakes his head. "Penny had nothing to do with it. This is an old murder, if it was a murder. It's the stepfather—*my* stepfather."

"Horace?"

"Yes, Horace Rollins. Did he—"

"Horace wasn't murdered, Sam," Officer Cahill says, sounding confused. "He killed himself."

"The stepfather *committed suicide?*"

"Well, it was an accident . . . but everybody knows it was his own damn fault."

"What kind of accident?"

"You really don't know?" the officer says, and then shrugs. "He was drunk. He tripped and fell on some kind of glass table. Cut himself really bad . . . You didn't know this?"

Andrew ignores the question. "Are you sure he tripped?"

"Am I—"

"You say everybody knows it was his fault. But did you investigate the accident personally?"

"No," Officer Cahill says. "No, I wasn't on the force then . . . I was in West Virginia." There's a heavy note of shame in his voice as he makes the latter admission, as though living in West Virginia were some kind of sin.

"What is it?" Andrew says.

"I was married," the officer blurts out. "Till just last year . . . After I got out of the service, I got married." He gives Andrew the same expectant look that Andrew gave Mouse in the car.

Andrew's reaction is the same as Mouse's was: he couldn't care less. "Oh," he says. "OK."

Then the room telescopes unexpectedly, as Maledicta yanks Mouse back into the cave mouth and storms forward to take her place. "You *fucker!*" she explodes. "After that line of bullshit you fed Sam about not wanting to be fucking tied down, you went and fucking got *married?* How long was this after you fucking dumped her, two days?"

Officer Cahill flinches—he'd been braced for a rebuke, but not from this direction. He defends himself, speaking to Andrew but keeping his eyes on Maledicta: "Sam, it wasn't like that—what I wrote you in that last letter, it was wrong of me, but I meant it at the time."

"I'm sorry, Officer Cahill," Andrew says, "but I really don't care about that. I—"

"Well *Sam's* going to fucking care," Maledicta interrupts. "Let her out for a minute, I bet she takes a fucking *bat* to this cocksucker . . ."

"Maledicta!" says Andrew. "This isn't helpful." Ignoring him, Maledicta opens her mouth to say something else, and that's when Mouse cuts back in, wrestles the body away from her.

"Sorry," Mouse apologizes. "This is none of my business, of course."

Officer Cahill just stands there, perplexed into speechlessness.

"Getting back to the stepfather," Andrew says. "Are you sure his death was an accident, or is it possible that someone else—"

"Sam," the officer sputters, "Sam, I don't know what the *heck* is going on here, but—"

The door opens, and another officer—an older man, with graying temples—enters the room. He is carrying a fishing pole, and has a wide-brimmed straw hat tucked under his arm. His ruddy face is fixed in a scowl. "What's this now?" he demands of them, his voice loud enough to make Mouse jump.

"Chief!" exclaims Officer Cahill. "Uh . . . this is"—he points to Andrew—"this is . . ."

"Althea Gage's daughter Andrea," Chief Bradley says. "I know." He glances at Mouse. "You I haven't met." Mouse can't tell whether this is a simple statement of fact or a solicitation for an introduction; but before she can say anything, the chief shifts his gaze back to Officer Cahill. "Why are they here?"

"Sam—Andrea—has some, uh, questions about her stepfather's death."

"Does she." Chief Bradley purses his lips. Then he says to Officer Cahill: "Coming in, I saw Dave Brierson had his truck blocking the hydrant out front of his store again. Why don't you go talk to him about it—tell him if I have to warn him one more time I'm impounding the vehicle."

"Sure, I can go talk to Dave," Officer Cahill says. "But if you don't mind, I'd like to stay here while Andrea—"

"Now would be a good time to get on it, actually," the chief interrupts him. "Before Dave moves the truck on his own and tries to pretend I was just seeing things."

"Right," Officer Cahill says. "Right, well . . ." He looks at Andrew. "Hope to see you later, Sam . . ."

Chief Bradley waits until he is gone and then says: "Let's go to my office."

Mouse doesn't think the invitation extends to her, but Andrew takes her by the hand and pulls her along with him. They all go into Chief Bradley's office. Once there, the chief takes his time about putting away the fishing pole and hanging up his straw hat and his jacket.

"Well, Andrea," he finally says. "I didn't expect to ever see you back here, after our last conversation. I thought you were out of this town for good."

"I thought I was too," Andrew says. "But the thing is, Chief Bradley," he continues haltingly, probably worried that the chief isn't going to get it any more than Officer Cahill did, "the thing is, it's complicated, but the person you spoke to on the phone after my mother died, that wasn't me exactly. I mean it was, but it wasn't . . ."

"Uh-huh," says Chief Bradley. "And this would be your multiple personality disorder, I suppose?"

Andrew blinks. "You *know*? Did my father—did I—tell you about that when . . . no, I didn't."

"Your doctor told me."

"Dr. Eddington called you?" Andrew gets excited. "What about Mrs. Winslow? Does she know I'm—"

"Slow down, Andrea." Chief Bradley raises a hand. "I don't know any Mrs. Winslow. And the doctor I spoke to was named Kroft, not Eddington."

"Dr. Kroft . . . but why would he be calling? There's no way he'd know I was coming here. We haven't been in touch with him since—"

"This was six years ago," the chief explains. "May of '91, I got a call from this Kroft fellow saying that Andrea Gage had escaped from a psychiatric ward in Ann Arbor, and she might be coming back home to do some mischief. He also said that you'd probably be dressed as a man, and going by the name Aaron or Gideon . . . and that wasn't the strangest part of the conversation. I'll tell you honestly, I thought the man was a crank at first, either a mental patient himself or a prankster with a grudge against you. But I did some checking, and found out that at least he wasn't crazy. The Ann Arbor police had a report filed on your escape from the Psychiatric Center.

"So I called the doctor back, and we spoke some more—and at the end, I was still left with the impression that he was a man with a grudge. I was almost glad when you didn't show up; I was concerned for your safety, of course, but for that very reason I would have been reluctant to return you to that doctor's care."

"So you're saying I didn't come back here?" Andrew says.

"Is that what this is about?" asks the chief. "You're worried *you* killed Horace?"

"Yes . . . I know everyone thinks he had an accident, but—"

"I don't just think it, I know it. I was there when it happened."

"You *saw* it?"

Chief Bradley nods. "During my follow-up conversation with Dr. Kroft, he made some . . . allegations about your stepfather." His eyes flick briefly to Mouse and then back to Andrew. "I assume I don't have to spell out what those allegations were?"

"No," Andrew says. "Penny already knows, but no, you don't have to say it."

"All right then . . . the doctor made these allegations, and my first thought was, more craziness . . . but then after I'd hung up the phone I remembered another odd conversation I'd had, with you, back when you were ten or eleven. You'd been trying to tell me something about Horace, but you were so vague that at the time I had no idea what you were getting at. But suddenly, in light of what the doctor had alleged, the conversation made sense.

"And then I started recalling some other things. You remember a girl named Kristin Williams?"

Andrew starts to shake his head, stops, concentrates, then says: "She baby-sat me a few times when I was in grade school."

"I arrested her for a DUI on her sixteenth birthday," Chief Bradley says.

"She drove her father's Plymouth into Greenwater Lake. When I tried to take her statement at the lakeside, she made a crack about Horace."

"What kind of crack? Did she say he'd done something to her?"

"It was nothing that made any sense at the time—she was half out of her head. And after she sobered up, she wouldn't explain herself, so I wrote it off as drunken rambling . . . until I had that talk with your doctor.

"I mulled all this over for a day or so, and decided I'd better go talk to Horace about it. Your mother was out of town at the time, visiting her sister, so it seemed like a good opportunity. But when I got up to the house, Horace was drunk. He didn't want to talk—and when I insisted he let me in, and explained what I'd come about, he got very agitated. He started pacing, all up and down the house, and that's when he had his accident. He was crossing the living room, and he tripped over your mother's glass coffee table." Chief Bradley points to the scar above Andrew's eye. "The same table you got that on, as I recall . . . only in Horace's case, being a two-hundred-fifty-pound man, and falling square on it, he shattered the glass, and cut himself in a dozen places. I did what I could to help him, but by the time the ambulance arrived he'd bled to death."

As the chief finishes his account, Andrew's shoulders slump in relief. "So it wasn't me," he says.

"No," Chief Bradley confirms. "You've been carrying that around with you?" Andrew nods. "Well," says the chief, "I'm glad to finally set your mind at ease."

All this time they've been standing. Now the chief sits down behind his desk, and indicates that Andrew and Mouse should help themselves to a pair of folding chairs that are leaning against the wall. But Andrew stays on his feet, and Mouse, still feeling like an outsider here, does the same.

After he's had a minute to consider all that he's just been told, Andrew asks: "Why didn't you mention any of this when we spoke to you on the phone two years ago?"

"Well, I did *try* to talk to you about what had happened to Horace, but you were pretty determined to avoid the subject."

"I know we didn't want to talk about him," Andrew says, "but—the part about Dr. Kroft, and our having escaped from the Psychiatric Center—you didn't bring that up at all." He pauses. "Is that . . . am I a fugitive, because of that?"

"Well," Chief Bradley says, "I wouldn't recommend you getting pulled over for a traffic stop in Ann Arbor—or anywhere else in the state, for that matter. But no one's actively searching for you, and I'm not going to make any calls. I *did* check with the Washington state police two years ago, to see whether you'd gotten into any more trouble out there. But you hadn't, and you sounded sane enough to me on the phone, so I decided to let that matter rest. You had enough to concern you, I thought, with your mother passing. As for your 'multiple personality disorder'—I won't pretend to believe in that, but if you feel a need to playact at being someone else, I guess that's understandable." His expression becomes grave. "I am very sorry, you know, not to have caught on to Horace's nature a whole lot sooner. Not seeing the truth in time to protect you—that's got to be one of my biggest failures. I can't tell you how much I regret it." This apology sounds heartfelt, but somehow it also strikes Mouse as perfunctory. Maybe it's just the speed with which the chief, having uttered it, moves on to another topic: "So . . . have you been up to your old house yet?"

"Yes," Andrew says. "Briefly."

"That's another thing I have to apologize for. I've tried to keep the condition of the property up since your mother died, on the chance you'd change your mind about wanting it, but there's a limit to what I could do. That foundation was in trouble for years, and during the big rains we had last fall . . ."

"You should have just let it fall over."

"Don't talk that way," Chief Bradley says, chagrined. "Your mother loved that house."

"Well I *don't* love it," Andrew replies. "I appreciate you trying to keep it for me, Chief Bradley, but I still don't want it. I never will."

"Well that's fine, Andrea, but in that case you should sell it, not just abandon it . . ." Andrew starts to shake his head and the chief adds: "Hey, *I'd* buy it if the price was right."

"Why would you want to buy a house that's falling down?"

"Parts of it are still salvageable. And the land is worth something." Chief Bradley shrugs, as if it's not that big a deal to him, but Mouse gets the feeling that it actually is a big deal, and the chief just doesn't want Andrew jacking up the price. "Something for you to think about, maybe," he says. "Now that you've had your questions answered, do you plan on staying in town for a while?"

"I don't know," Andrew says. "I don't really have a plan."

"Constance McCloy just opened a bed-and-breakfast up on Two Seasons Lake. The rates are very reasonable."

Andrew shakes his head. "If we do stay in the area, I won't be sleeping here in town. Muskegon is close enough."

"Suit yourself," says the chief. "Maybe . . . if you like, you could come to dinner at my house one night. We could discuss a fair price for the property. You remember Oscar Reyes?"

"I . . . know who he is."

"He's on vacation right now, but he owes me a few favors. He could help arrange the title transfer."

"I'll think about it," Andrew says. "I guess I know where to reach you."

Chief Bradley smiles for the first time in the entire conversation. "The job has its privileges." He stands up and offers his hand. Andrew shakes with him. The chief doesn't bother to say good-bye to Mouse.

"I didn't like him," Mouse says, when they are back in the Centurion.

"Oh, I don't know," says Andrew. "He seemed like a nice enough person."

"He was sorrier about the condition of the house than he was about what your stepfather did to you."

"Maybe he's afraid to feel too sorry about that. If he admits to himself how bad it really was, it makes it harder to live with not having put a stop to it."

"Maybe," says Mouse. "I still think it was rude, asking to buy the house from you that way. And the way he was acting, pretending like he wasn't *really* interested—is it possible the house has some hidden value that you don't know about?"

"You mean like gold deposits under the backyard?" Andrew is politely skeptical. "I doubt it, Penny."

"Are you going to sell it to him?"

"I might. I definitely don't want to keep it."

"Well you shouldn't just give it away," Mouse argues. "Don't sell it too cheaply."

"I'm not going to sell it at all, just yet . . . what I'd like to do now, if you're up for it, is go back out to the property and finish looking around."

"You still have questions?"

"Nothing specific," Andrew says. "I'm off the hook for the stepfather's death, and that's the most important thing, but . . . something still feels unsettled. Whatever it is, I want to figure it out, and set it right, so I don't ever have to come back to Seven Lakes again."

"I understand," says Mouse, and starts the car.

27

The replacement coffee table that Andy Gage's mother had bought after the stepfather's death had a top made of wood, not glass. That's no big surprise, I guess, although when I first lifted up the sheet that covered it, there was a part of me that was expecting to find, not just *a* glass coffee table, but *the* glass coffee table, either painstakingly pieced back together or magically restored. Even after recognizing that the table was new, I still had to run my hand over its surface, checking for cracks and bloodstains. Of course I found nothing, and the rug underneath the coffee table was likewise unblemished; I resisted an urge to examine the floorboards.

"Well . . ." I said, dropping the dust cover back in place. "Let's look around."

The living room took up roughly a quarter of the cottage's ground floor, its inside corner dominated by a big brick fireplace. As I've already mentioned, the wall opposite the vestibule had an open doorway that led into the kitchen; but if you turned right from the vestibule, you encountered another door, one that was held closed by the cottage's leftward tilt.

"That was their bedroom," my father told me. The way he said it didn't make me anxious to look inside, but I was still determined to be bold, or at least *act* bold, so I stepped to the door and opened it before I had a chance to get scared.

The air in the bedroom was close and musty, though not as much as I would have expected after two and a half years. I wondered if Chief Bradley, as part of his effort to keep the place up, had aired it out occasionally. The bed was only a full-size, which bothered me for some reason; maybe it was the thought of anyone, even a bad mother, being forced to lie in such close proximity to a monster like the stepfather. Besides the bed, there was a dresser, a small vanity table, a nightstand supporting a lamp with a dented shade, and a TV set balanced precariously on a wicker pedestal. Beneath the sheets that covered them, I could make out the shapes of standing photo frames and other personal effects on both the dresser top and the vanity; those would probably warrant further investigation later, but for now I turned left and crossed to another pair of doors. One door opened on a closet, the other on a bathroom. The bathroom was cramped but managed to contain both a toilet and a tub.

"Is this . . . ?" I started to ask, and my father finished for me: "The only bathroom in the house? Yes."

So any time Andy Gage had wanted to take a bath or use the toilet, he'd have had to come through Horace Rollins's bedroom. And—I checked— the door had no lock. All at once Adam's and Aunt Sam's fanaticism about shower privileges—not to mention my father's great pleasure at being able to take a private shit in his own bathroom—made perfect sense.

"Andrew?" Penny called. Hanging back, she'd only come a few steps into the bedroom. "What is it?"

"Just another reason not to like this house."

We went back out to the living room and moved on into the kitchen. This was the brightest and technically the cheeriest room in the cottage, although I found it cold. It was an eat-in kitchen, with a round table and four chairs. The table and three of the chairs had been draped in a sheet, but the fourth chair had been pulled out into the middle of the room and left uncovered. Curious, I ran a finger over the seat; it was clean, not dusty.

I went over to the back door, and looked out into the yard behind the cottage. Like the front yard, it had been mowed. There were more garden plots, roughly outlined with borders of flagstone, but unlike the flower beds out front, these plots had not been planted recently, and contained only weeds.

My father drew my attention to the line of thornbushes that ran all around the edges of the backyard, forming a natural barrier between it and the woods. "Blackberry bushes, mostly," he said. "There were some roses, too, along the sides of the house, but they never did well." The barrier was unbroken except in one place, where a gated footpath led off into the woods. A small shed stood just inside and to the right of this gate; it had probably been used for storing garden tools, but its size and location suggested a tollbooth.

"What's out that way?" I asked my father.

"Quarry Lake," my father said, and I sensed there was a story there, maybe a lot of stories. "It's about half a mile, if you stick to the path. Longer if you're sneaking through the trees."

I noticed Penny was staring at the path as well. "What is it?"

Penny just shook her head, but then Maledicta came out: "That fucking toolshed. Verna would have fucking loved it—perfect spot for an ambush, coming or going. And fucking *woods* to creep around in, like the big bad wolf . . ."

She turned away from the yard and went to inspect the pantry that branched off the kitchen. It doubled as a laundry room; a niche held a washer and dryer. Maledicta looked this over, then examined the pantry shelves, which were still well-stocked with spider-webbed cans and jars. "Thousand-fucking-year-old preserves," she said. "Yum." She stepped back out into the kitchen proper, patted herself down in search of cigarettes, got frustrated, and gave way to Penny again.

"Andrew," Penny wanted to know, "where did you sleep? If there's only one bedroom . . ."

I'd been wondering that myself, but the answer was right in front of us: between the back door and the pantry, there was one other door, that opened on a narrow flight of stairs leading up.

"God," said Penny. The attic staircase looked like it would have been treacherous even when the cottage was perfectly level. Now, with the risers on a backward tilt, it was a positive hazard.

"You can wait down here," I told Penny. "I'll just go up for a really quick look around."

"No," Penny said unhappily. "I'll come up with you."

I led the way, holding tight to the stairway railing—a series of unfinished two-by-fours secured to the inside wall with metal brackets. Partway up the stairs turned right, then right again, coming out under a low ceiling.

As I reached the top, I heard Penny stumble behind me; Maledicta cursed. "Are you all right?" I said. I looked back; Penny was down on one knee at the last turn in the stairway. I thought of the stepfather, drunk, going up and down these same stairs, and it occurred to me that my father had been right: we must have been too intimidated to kill him, or he would never have survived as long as he had.

"I'm OK," Penny said, getting back to her feet.

The attic reminded me of the Reality Factory. The space was smaller, of course, but it was a single large room beneath a questionable roof, with a crumbling brick column—the fireplace chimney—rising up like a support post in the middle. There wasn't much light; the attic had windows at either end, but they were small and the glass was grimy, Chief Bradley's maintenance efforts having apparently overlooked this part of the cottage. And he wasn't the only one who'd neglected it—as I walked across the attic floor, my feet kicked up clouds of dust, long years' worth. Althea Gage hadn't done much cleaning up here either after her only child left home. But then, I thought bitterly, why would she? It's not like you'd expect her to be nostalgic or anything.

The half of the attic closest to the stairs had been Andy Gage's bedroom. The actual furnishings weren't familiar to me, but something in their configuration was; I could imagine my father, Adam, Aunt Sam, and the others— at best only vaguely aware of each other then—arranging and rearranging the layout in a never-ending roommates' squabble. There by the window was the folding cot—not a real bed, a cot—where they had slept, maybe looking out at the back garden as they drifted off each night; there by the chimney column was a desk, set up defensively with a clear view of the stairs; there and there, along the sides of the room where the roof sloped down towards the attic floor, were low shelves of the cinderblock-and-plank variety, filled with books and toys and general clutter. I was amazed by how much had been left behind, but I suppose there had been a limit to how much junk my father could take with him to college. The last days of packing must have been especially chaotic, with every half-aware soul trying to steal time to make sure their favorite possessions were included.

The other half of the attic, the part on the far side of the chimney, was given over to storage. Actually, the division wasn't as clear-cut as that; as my eyes adjusted to the dimness, I realized that a lot of the "storage" was really just more clutter. It looked like we'd always had a space-allocation problem.

I hunched down by one of the shelves, brushing dust and dead silverfish from a line of books. I didn't recognize all the titles, but once again there was a more general sense of familiarity: these books had belonged to someone—a collection of someones—whose tastes I knew. One volume in particular caught my eye: *Tales of the Greek Heroes*, by William Seferis. I picked it up; on the cover, a princess cowered behind Hercules as he prepared to lop the heads off a menacing hydra.

I turned to show the book to Penny and found her staring again, this time at the piles of stuff in the storage end of the attic.

"Too many shadows, huh?" I said.

"Thank God," replied Penny, "thank God our house in Willow Grove didn't have an attic. My mother . . . I would have gone crazy in a room like this."

I thought of joking that I *had* gone crazy in a room like this, but decided my father might not appreciate the humor. Instead I said: "Do you really think your mother would have put you in an attic room, even if she had one? I mean, from what you've told me about her, it seems like that'd be too much like—"

"Poverty?" Penny shrugged. "Maybe." Trying for a joke of her own: "She would have insisted on better stairs, at least."

"Let me guess: marble steps?"

Penny nodded. "With gold banisters. And velvet carpeting, so you couldn't hear her coming." She smiled, more at her own daring than at the joke itself, I think. I smiled too, and then the dust, which had been tickling my nose since we'd gotten up here, made me sneeze. Something jumped in the shadows on the other side of the chimney column; a box fell off a stack and crashed to the floor. Penny let out a terrified squeak.

"It's all right," I said, fighting back another sneeze, "it's OK, I think—it's too small to be a ghost . . ." I saw a pair of eyes glittering in the darkness, and a bushy tail that swished indignantly. "It's a squirrel! It's all right, Penny, it's just a squirrel . . ." The squirrel chittered at me, working its jaw like a little old man whose dentures had slipped; then it bolted, exiting the attic through whatever hole it had come in by.

I went to the box that the squirrel had knocked over. It was full of wind-up alarm clocks. I took one out and held it up to look at it. "Were these yours?" I started to ask my father, but before I could finish the question I saw, reflected in the crystal, the face of someone standing behind me, peering over my shoulder. Not Penny; it was a young girl.

A Witness. *The* Witness, I should say: the same one who'd come up behind me in the house when I was searching under the bed in my father's room.

Of course, she wasn't really looking over my shoulder. The reflection was only an illusion, that faded even as I noticed it—but even after it had faded, I could still feel the Witness's presence.

A funny idea popped into my head. I turned around.

"Penny," I said, "could you step aside for a second?"

"W-what?" Penny said, still reacting to the squirrel.

"Just move over a little." I gestured with one hand. "I want to try something."

Penny stepped aside, and I tossed the alarm clock underhand towards the stairs. The clock dropped out of sight into the stairwell, and went banging down the steps, caroming off the walls, all the way down into the kitchen, where it finally came apart. We could hear the crystal breaking, and individual gears and springs scattering across the linoleum.

We could hear it very clearly. It wasn't just that the door at the bottom of the stairs was open; the sound carried easily through the attic floor itself. If I arranged to have another alarm clock smashed in the living room or the bedroom, I thought, it would come through almost as clearly.

"What do you think, Penny? If a little kid yelled for help up here, would you be able to hear it downstairs?"

Penny blinked nervously, as if wondering whether I was still myself. "I guess so," she said.

"I guess so too," I agreed, and felt the Witness again, like a phantom tugging at my shirtsleeve for attention.

I went over to the cot. A couple of dresses in my size had been laid out on the mattress as if for comparison and then left to gather dust. Holes had been chewed in the dress fabric, and when I moved the dresses aside I saw that something had been at the blanket, sheets, and mattress ticking too; and all of it was filthy. The cot's frame still seemed sturdy, though. I tested it with my hands, then sat down carefully.

"Penny," I said, "can you do me a favor?"

"Oh God . . . you want to go inside again? *Here?*"

"I think somebody wants to show me something. I'll try not to be gone long."

Penny's jaw moved, in a fair imitation of the squirrel—but unlike the squirrel, she didn't run away. "All right," she said. "Only please hurry. I don't like it up here."

The Witness was waiting for me as I appeared on the hilltop beside the column of light. She didn't greet me or wave hello; her sole acknowledgment of my arrival was the look she gave me.

My father, who was also there, was a bit more expressive.

"What the hell are you doing, Andrew?"

The question was rhetorical, but I answered it anyway, my reply edged with an irony that I didn't fully intend: "I'm learning."

"You shouldn't be doing this *here*," my father said. "Not in this house. Back in Seattle maybe, under Dr. Eddington's supervision—"

"Well unfortunately we aren't *in* Seattle just now," I said, my sarcasm growing more deliberate. "Maybe we would be, if you'd been more honest with me."

"I'm sorry I kept things from you, Andrew. It was bad judgment; I see that now. But this"—he waved a hand at the Witness—"this is dangerous."

"She has something to show me."

"You won't learn anything you don't already know. It'll just hurt more."

I sensed that he was telling the truth, or at least believed what he was saying, but it didn't matter; I was committed. "Go back to the pulpit, father," I said. "Keep an eye on the body."

"Andrew . . ."

"Go back to the pulpit. If this is as dangerous as you say, and Gideon tries to take advantage . . . well, I don't want Penny to have to deal with him again. We've put her through enough already."

He hesitated, wanting to order me not to do this. But the balance of power had shifted between us, and in the end, it was my will that carried. My father went back to the pulpit.

I turned to the Witness, who still stood by patiently. "All right," I told her.

When a Witness shares its secrets with you, it swallows your head. I'd never actually experienced this, but I understood what was involved well enough to regard the Witness in the same way I imagine a circus tamer does the lion whose jaws he is about to pry open.

I made myself kneel down beside her, bringing my ear level with her mouth, just as I would if she were going to whisper something to me. And at first it seemed as if that was exactly what she was doing: she gripped my shoulder with one hand, cupped the other around her lips, and leaned in close. I heard her mouth open, felt her breath tickling my ear, but what came rolling off her tongue was not words but a much broader collection of sounds, background noise from another time and place. The force of her breath increased—too late, I lost my nerve and tried to pull away, but the hand on my shoulder held on implacably—and her mouth gaped wider, impossibly wide, less a human mouth now than the mouth of a bag or the neck of a hood that slipped, *flowed*, over the top of my head, covering my eyes. There was a moment of suffocating darkness, of terrible pressure—my soul's skull in a vise—and then—*fusion*—the Witness and I were one, we are one, we am—

—I am standing on a lakebank, watching a stone skip across the surface of the water. My weight is on my left foot and my left arm is extended in front of me; I can feel tension in my wrist and shoulder, and the fading impression of a hard, flat object recently grasped in my upturned palm.

I stagger, off-balance. The stone skips, and skips, and finally sinks, just a skip or two shy of a big mound of sand and gravel that forms an island in the middle of the lake. As I steady myself, ripples spread out from the skipping-stone's splash points, forming a chain of expanding concentric rings.

These are some of the things that I know: This body of water in front of me is called Quarry Lake. It is fed by a trio of creeks that trickle down from Mount Idyll to the northeast, and it feeds, in turn, a larger stream—Hansen's Brook—that flows west for several miles to Two Seasons Lake. The sand-and-gravel pile has no official name, but I think of it as Devil's Island. Right now, in bright sunlight, it doesn't look very devilish—just barren—but I know that under moonlight or in morning fog it is a different story. Also, though it doesn't seem that far to swim, I know that getting to or from the island is actually quite difficult: the waters of Quarry Lake are deeper than they first appear, and shockingly cold even in summer.

Besides my detailed knowledge of the lake and the geography surrounding it, I know that I am eleven years old, that my given name is Andrea Gage, and that I live in a cottage set back in the woods behind me. I know that I am very unhappy there, and I know why.

These are some of the things that I *don't* know: What day it is. What time it is. What I was doing two minutes ago. What I was doing an hour ago. What I did yesterday, or the day before that.

Why I am scared.

Actually, I do know why I'm scared: because something very bad is about to happen. But the exact nature of the something, how I came to be aware of it, and what, if anything, I've done to deserve it—all of that is missing information.

I scan the lakebank and the line of trees that border it for some clue to what's coming. There's nothing obvious, but when my eyes light on a particular stand of tall flowering shrubs—shrubs that mark the beginning of the path that leads back to the cottage where I live—my whole nervous system jumps. I stare at the shrubs, searching for someone hiding among them, a face peering out through splayed branches. I see nothing. But I know what I'm afraid of now.

It's when I turn away and resume scanning the tree-line that the call comes, a singsong cry that echoes on the lake:

Yoooooooooo-hoooooooooo . . .

My gaze snaps back to the shrubs in time to see a branch rustling. I still can't see *him*, but I'm sure he's there now. I wait, half-paralyzed with fright, for him to step out and show himself. He doesn't, and the cry is not repeated.

Time passes. I can feel him watching me, waiting for me to make a move. I start to get mad, hating being toyed with this way, but my anger dissipates in the knowledge of my own helplessness. Next my knees get weak; I want to fall down, to beg him to come out and get it over with, do whatever he's going to do. This feeling also fades, although it takes longer. What I am left with, finally, is a kind of stubborn fatalism, a sense that I must try to escape, even though it's not going to do any good.

There are, I know, three ways out of here: the path that leads back to the cottage where I live; the trail that goes up and around Mount Idyll; and the path that runs beside Hansen's Brook all the way to Two Seasons Lake. Of these, the Mount Idyll trail is the best choice for an escape route. Steep and rugged, it favors small spry people over big lumbering ones. It also forks and doubles back a lot, offering numerous opportunities to outwit as well as outrun a pursuer. If I can make it as far as the first split in the trail, I should have no trouble getting lost; and while I cannot *stay* lost forever, still a reprieve is better than nothing. Maybe he will get bored, waiting for me to come back, and decide he doesn't want to do it anymore. Or maybe tonight will be one of those rare nights when there are guests over at the cottage, everyone on their best behavior; maybe he'll drink too much at dinner and fall asleep right after.

There's just one problem with the mountain trail: to get to it I will have to walk east along the lakebank, going right past his hiding place. It's not really possible to go the other way around, and even if it were, by the time I waded across the mouth of Hansen's Brook and beat my way through the thick undergrowth that renders much of Quarry Lake's north bank impassable, he would have strolled over to the trailhead himself and be laying for me, laughing at my feeble attempt to evade him.

I stare at the shrubs and try to calculate my chances of dashing past them without getting grabbed.

I decide that I'll never make it. The Mount Idyll trail is not an option; I'll have to try the brookside path instead—a mostly level track on which long legs will have the advantage.

I start walking backwards, slowly, as if by not running I can somehow conceal my intentions. I know he is not truly deceived by this, but if I am lucky he will play along, and let me have at least a small head start before chasing after me. Then, if I am *very* lucky, his stamina will give out before my lead does. So I back up—a step; a step; another step—until suddenly a new sound comes, a disembodied giggle that rises and falls as it echoes across the lake. Something lands in the water beside me with a big splash.

I break and run. The hem of my skirt flaps between my knees, threatening to tangle my legs and trip me; I stub my toe on a rock, stumble, and keep going. I follow the lakebank to the mouth of Hansen's Brook. I turn left, onto the path that leads to Two Seasons Lake.

. . . and pull up short, my way blocked by thorns.

My first confused thought is of *Sleeping Beauty*, where the evil fairy conjures a forest of brambles to stop the prince from reaching the castle. But these brambles are dead: dead dried-up rosebushes, their branches tied in bales, dragged down here and heaped with a bunch of old tree limbs into a big thorny deadfall. Some part of me is amazed by the effort it must have taken to construct, the work that went into it.

It completely blocks the path. There's no question of climbing over it, and as for going around . . . when I look to my right, into the brook's rocky bed, I see something sparkling among the mud-slicked stones, something gleaming and sharp: broken glass. Smashed liquor bottles.

No escape. The thought comes with such clarity it might have been spoken aloud. I wait to hear that giggle again, to feel his hand on the back of my neck. It doesn't happen. Of course not, I think: he knows it's not necessary to chase after me. All he has to do is wait, wait for me to see that I can't get away, wait for me to give up and come back. Even this deadfall—(how long must he have worked on it? Hours? Days?)—isn't *really* necessary. So what if I did outrun him? What if I made it all the way to Two Seasons Lake without getting caught? In the end, no matter how fast or how far I go, I've still got to come home.

No escape. All right then, I give up. I surrender. I'm a little surprised, when I come back out onto the lakebank, not to find him waiting out in the open for me. No matter, though: I know where he is. Head down, I walk towards his hiding place, preparing myself for the moment when he will leap out and grab me.

It doesn't come. I'm there now, I'm at the shrubs, and still he hasn't pounced. I lift my head up, confused: where is he?

I know he was here—the call, that giggle, I *heard* them—but somehow now he's not. My mind scrambles for an explanation: is it possible he forgot about building the deadfall? That he saw how fast I was running and decided he couldn't catch me, and gave up the chase?

It's an absurd notion, but before I can knock it down an irrational hope sweeps over me. The Mount Idyll trail, I think: I can get to it now. I can go, and lose myself, and maybe I *won't* come back, maybe I'll just stay out there in the woods forever.

Quick, I think, quick, before he realizes his mistake and comes back—
No. Wait.

The Mount Idyll trail: of course. He hasn't given up. He hasn't gone away. He's still toying with me, letting me think he's given up, letting me run a little farther before he finally pounces. The Mount Idyll trail: that's where he's hiding.

Is that where he's hiding? Uncertain, I look towards the trailhead.

I see a shadow move among the trees there. It's him!

Wait. Wait. Is it him?

My head's still in doubt but my feet have decided: I am moving again, through the shrubbery, up the path to the cottage. I run, the woods blurring past me. My toe catches on another rock and this time I do fall down, but it's OK, I'm back up again in a heartbeat, and the cottage is just ahead now, I can see the backyard gate standing open, invitingly.

I go charging through the open gate—stupid—and that, of course, is when he grabs me, stepping out from behind the toolshed and scooping me up as neat as you please. I let out a shriek that is as much frustration as fear—stupid, *stupid*—and flail my arms and legs uselessly. He laughs, holding onto me effortlessly—one hand on my breastbone, splayed across my chest, the other up underneath my skirt, fingering between my legs—and lets me struggle as long as I want.

Resignation comes soon enough. My strength is no match for his, and we both know it. I stop kicking, and my arms fall limp at my sides. He pulls me in closer, an intimate embrace; the movements of his hands become more insistent, and I feel his lips pressing on the side of my neck, on the hollow of my throat. I try to make myself go dead inside. I'd leave my body if I could, but I can't, I am charged to endure this, so I try to go dead, let it happen without feeling it. In one of the garden plots that dot the yard, pumpkins are growing in profusion; I imagine myself buried among them, covered in soft earth.

The sun goes under a cloud. The light in the yard changes.

And suddenly I come alive again. With the sun's glare dimmed, I can see a face in the kitchen window. It's my mother. She's not looking out—it looks like she's washing dishes, her eyes are on the sink—but if she lifts her head for even a second, she'll see me. She'll see *us*.

Hope fills me up again before I can stop it. It's a vain hope—some part of me knows this perfectly well—but it electrifies me anyway, animates me. Have to get her to look up, have to: she'll see, she'll save me, she'll put a stop to this!

I open my mouth. I scream.

And maybe the scream is very loud, loud enough to rattle the kitchen window in its frame.

And maybe the scream is soundless, stifled by my own terror, by the rude hand on my chest.

Deafening or silent, my mother hears it. She looks up. She sees us. Her eyes go wide.

The joy I feel in that moment is indescribable. She's going to save me. She's going to save me. In another second she's going to come bursting out the back door, dishwater streaming from her hands, and she will yell, she will yell at him to stop it, she will scream at him and hit him to make him let me go. I stretch out my arms in anticipation of rescue.

And then her brow creases. Her expression turns cross, not outraged but annoyed. She takes a breath, lets out a sigh of . . . exasperation? Her hands come into view; she's drying them with a dishtowel, making brisk, impatient movements. Finished, she tosses the dishtowel aside.

She turns her back.

She turns her back, and I can see the back of her head receding, moving away from the window, deeper into the house. I don't understand, and then I do: she's going to her bedroom, *their* bedroom. She's going to close her eyes and take a nap. She does this often. I know this.

She's gone.

She's gone, and then it is just him and me, I and the stepfather. He shifts his grip, holding me with one arm while the other reaches back behind him. I hear the creak of the toolshed door opening. He whirls me around, carries me inside—

—"Andrew!"—

—and the door bangs shut behind us—

—my foot slammed down, smashing through the plank.

"Stop it, Andrew! Andrew, *please*, stop it, you're going to"—

—and he sets me down, on the floor, facing the back wall of the toolshed. His hands are all over me now, but I no longer care. No need to deaden my feelings anymore; I am dead, I—

—"want to get yourself fucking killed, you stupid fucking cocksucker? *Knock it off!*"—

—and as his weight pushes against me from behind, my face is shoved up against the toolshed wall, but what I see is not the wall but the kitchen window, and my mother, frozen in the act of turning away, always turning away.

And then there is a sound of wood cracking, and the wall gives way beneath my hands, curves back in on itself—

—and my arms were wrapped around the telephone pole, muscles straining as I pulled at it. Maledicta yelled "Knock it off!" one more time and then Malefica grappled me from behind. She punched me in the back of the head, broke my grip on the pole and flung me to the ground. She kicked me in the ribs, once to make me stay down, twice to make sure I'd stay down, and a third time just because she was angry. The kicks were painful, but I didn't cry out or try to defend myself, just lay there where she'd dropped me.

My fusion with the Witness had only been temporary. But I guess the Witness had been hoping for permanence: inside somewhere, on the lake-bank or in the forest, I could hear her wailing, lamenting her own continued existence. I would have felt sorry for her, except I was too busy being glad, so glad to have the vision fade, its vitality leaching away, and the memory that had briefly been mine becoming someone else's again, becoming to me just a memory of a memory, a story I'd been told but hadn't lived through.

My head hurt. My heart hurt worse. *But you were wrong, father,* I thought. *I did learn something.*

"I did learn something," I said. I said it again, inside, but there was no answer from the pulpit.

I sat up—slowly, so Malefica wouldn't kick me again. We were outside the cottage, and I could see that all of the bracing planks had been pulled down or broken. It looked like someone had taken a sledgehammer to them, but a fresh set of aches in Andy Gage's feet, legs, hands, and arms told a different story: my knuckles were bloody, and full of splinters.

"What happened?" I said.

"What *happened?*" Maledicta was livid. "What the fuck do you think happened, asshole?"

"I tried to pull the house down?"

"*Yes,* you fucking tried to pull the fucking house down! With *us* still inside it!"

"With you . . . no. No, Maledicta, I would never—" I stopped, noticing a bruise on her cheek and a bubble of blood in her nostril. "What happened to your face?"

In answer, she aimed another kick at my side, but caught herself, spun on one heel, and stomped off into the backyard. A moment later I heard a rhythmic banging start—Malefica pretending the toolshed was my rib cage. As the banging went on, I found myself staring at the telephone pole that was the cottage's sole remaining prop, and realized a part of me was still itching to bring it down. I crossed my arms over my chest and shoved my hands up under my armpits, ignoring the scratch of the splinters. I was very cold.

TENTH BOOK:
CHIEF BRADLEY'S TEARS

28

"My father was wrong," Andrew tells her. "He said I wouldn't learn any-thing that I didn't already know, that it would just hurt more. But feeling that pain firsthand did teach me something, after all."

They are sitting in a booth in Winchell's Diner, untouched cups of coffee growing cold on the table between them. Mouse holds a piece of ice wrapped in a napkin against the bruise on her cheek.

"She hurt us more than he did," Andrew says. "Not in terms of the actual amount of damage done—the stepfather is still the one responsible, I think he's the one responsible, for breaking Andy Gage's soul into pieces. In terms of, of *quantity*, he's still the worst by far. But the *way* she hurt us . . . there was a quality to it, a depth, that nothing the stepfather did came close to, not even when he . . ."

She hurt us more than he did. Andrew has been trying to articulate this point for a while now, and though on an intellectual level Mouse grasps what he is saying readily enough, emotionally it's just not clicking. Andrew's story of the cat-and-mouse game the stepfather played with him around the shore of Quarry Lake—*that* she can relate to. It's the same sort of entertain-ment her own mother specialized in. But when Andrew starts describing how his mother's failure to protect him was somehow more hurtful than the stepfather's assault . . . well, Mouse gets it, but not really. She can't help thinking that she would have traded everything she had, and then some, for a mother whose worst sin was that she did nothing.

"It just felt like such a violation," Andrew says.

"Violation? But it was the stepfather who—"

"I don't mean physical violation. I mean violation of, of *order*, of the way things are naturally supposed to be . . . The stepfather, he was always a monster, and that's all he ever was. He was never a *real* father to us; he was just this awful person who lived in our house. And it's like, if a wild animal bites you, it hurts, it's traumatic, but it's not as if it's any kind of big surprise. Wild animals bite; it's what they do; you may not like it but you know to expect it.

"But what we felt, when our mother turned her back and walked away—it was like, like watching water flow uphill. And I know, you know, that she must have done that all the time, turned her back on us, and so I don't really understand how it is we came to expect anything different from her, but I know—I felt it—that we did. There was this incredible sense of disappointment, of betrayal, and it must have been like that every time, whenever she just stood by and let him do that to us . . .

"And so what I *really* don't understand," he says, taking a deep breath, "is how I could go for so long without having even a clue about this. I mean you remember: two nights ago you asked me about my mother and I couldn't even tell you whether she'd survived giving birth to us. And even after my father told me the truth, even after I saw him cry, *break down* over her, still . . . I never, ever would have guessed. All my life, whenever my father, Adam, or any of the others talked about the abuse they'd suffered, it was always the stepfather they talked about—*his* wickedness, what *he* did to them. Never a single word about *her*."

Andrew looks at Mouse as if expecting her to have an answer to this riddle, but the best response she can manage is a shrug—a gesture that makes her face hurt.

"How's your cheek?" Andrew asks, seeing her wince.

"It hurts."

"Oh."

This is of course another reason she's having a hard time commiserating: she's still in shock over what happened at the cottage.

Andrew had lain unmoving on the dusty cot while Mouse, standing guard, got more and more spooked by a furtive scuttling noise in the shadows at the far end of the attic. Maledicta, up in the cave mouth, kept telling Mouse to stop being such a jumpy cunt, it was just the fucking squirrel again—but Maledicta sounded as if she were spooked too, and her vulgar admonitions only served to make Mouse even more jumpy. She sidled closer and closer to the cot, until finally she was standing right over Andrew, nudging the edge of the filthy mattress with her leg. The nudges got stronger and more insistent until the whole cot was shaking, but still Andrew just lay there; and then something *galloped* across the far end of the attic, and Mouse began to shake Andrew's body directly, saying, "Wake up! Wake up!"

At which point Andrew had opened his eyes and leapt up screaming. Mouse was knocked aside, tossed face-first onto the attic floor. The impact left her dazed, and by the time she recovered Andrew was gone: down the stairs, out the back door, and around to the side of the house. As Mouse got back to her feet, she heard boards breaking somewhere below her. Her first thought was that Andrew was trying to tear the cottage apart; then she remembered the bracing planks and realized that was exactly what he was doing.

Which is the part that's still got her weak-kneed. Andrew knocking her down in a moment of panic is no big deal—that's something Mouse could see doing herself, something she's already done *to* herself. But Andrew nearly bringing a house down on her is something else again. Not that he was trying to hurt her—he, whoever he was at that moment, wasn't thinking of her at all probably, but still . . . if she'd landed a little differently, hit her head a little harder, she could have been lying in the attic unconscious until the cottage fell over. She could be dead now. For that matter so could Andrew: when Mouse came running downstairs to stop him demolishing the place, he hadn't seemed too concerned about his own safety.

"I think," Mouse says, "that I'm ready to go back to Seattle now. I know you have things to figure out, and I still want to be helpful, but . . . I don't want to go to the cottage again, or anywhere else that's going to make you react that way." She looks at him. "Can we be done here? Please?"

Before Andrew can answer, the bell above the diner's front door jingles, and a voice calls out breathlessly: "Sam!"

Oh God. Mouse, who has been sitting with her back to the door, turns to see Officer Cahill striding towards them. The officer is red-faced from exertion, and Mouse guesses it's no coincidence that he's come in here; he must have seen the Centurion parked a block and a half away and come running down the street, looking in every window until he found them.

Mouse braces herself for another round of Mistaken Identities, but when she turns back to Andrew his posture has changed, gone poised and feminine. Either Aunt Sam has successfully petitioned for some time out, or—more likely, Mouse thinks—she's taken advantage of Andrew's disrupted mental state and seized the moment.

"Sam . . ." As Officer Cahill arrives at the booth he visibly gathers himself, preparing to launch into a speech. But Sam heads him off, smiling sweetly and saying: "Hello, Jimmy. How are you?"

Officer Cahill blinks, stunned by the welcome. Then he smiles, too. "Sam," he says warmly. "Can I . . . is it all right if I join you?" Not waiting for an answer, he starts to slide into the booth on Mouse's side; Mouse realizes she's about to get sat on, scoots over hastily, and loses control to Malefica, who snatches up a teaspoon and prepares to jam it into Officer Cahill's buttocks.

"Wait, Jimmy," Sam says, and Officer Cahill halts obediently, half-in and half-out of the booth. "Before you sit down, could you get me a slice of pie?"

"Pie?" For a moment he's at a loss, like he's never heard the word before. Then he smiles again. "Sure. What kind?"

"Cherry, please." Sam returns his smile, her eyes shining. "With whipped cream. *Extra* whipped cream."

"Cherry with extra whipped cream. You got it." He hurries off to the counter.

"Sam?" Maledicta says.

"Dear." Still smiling, but sadly now. "Do you have a cigarette?" Her hands are trembling.

"No. Sorry." Maledicta drops the spoon back on the table. "What the fuck was that, Sam? You're not going to give this cocksucker the time of day, are you?"

Sam doesn't answer, just stares at her hands. By the time Officer Cahill returns with the cherry pie, she's got them to stop shaking.

"Here you go, Sam . . ." He lays a fork and a fresh napkin on the table in front of her and starts to set the pie plate down too, but she catches his wrist. "Sam?"

"Jimmy . . ." She tilts her head like she wants to whisper something to him, so he leans forward, and Sam slips her other hand up underneath the pie plate and shoves it, extra whipped cream and all, into his face. Officer Cahill lets out a muffled squawk—"Urk!"—and steps back sputtering. Sam gets up and runs out of the diner, in her rush very nearly making the day's knockdown score two for two.

"Yeah, *Sam!*" hoots Maledicta, pounding the table hard enough to upset both coffee cups. She slides out of the booth and makes her own exit, pausing at the door to holler to a startled waitress: "Don't worry about the fucking check—lover boy there's got it!"

She catches up to Sam on the block where they parked the Centurion. Sam's standing in front of a Laundromat, staring blankly in the window. Maledicta comes up and gives her a good hearty clap on the back.

"That was fucking *excellent*, Sam." She gestures to a nearby cross street, where she remembers seeing a bar. "Come on, let's go get a drink. I'm fucking buying."

"No thanks. A drink is the last thing I need right now."

Andrew. Maledicta's expression of glee turns to a scowl. "Fuck!"

"Sorry to disappoint you," Andrew says.

"Disappoint my fucking ass, you fucker. Get Sam back out here."

"Sam's gone to her room. She won't be coming out again today." He glances down the street towards the diner. "That was really . . . unfortunate, what just happened back there."

"'Unfortunate,'" Maledicta mocks him. "It was fucking great!"

"Well I'm glad you enjoyed it, Maledicta. But I think we'd better leave town now. Could you get Penny for me, please?"

"No, I could not get fucking Mouse for you. And I'm not leaving town until I get a fucking drink."

"Maledicta . . . in case you didn't notice, I just attacked a policeman."

"Oh, bullshit! That was no fucking policeman, that was an asshole ex-boyfriend who got what he fucking had coming."

"Well even so, I think we should go. I'm done here, at least for—"

"Well I'm *not* fucking done here. I want a fucking drink." Glaring: "I need to calm my fucking nerves after *someone* nearly collapsed a house on me."

"Maledicta, I'm really, really sorry about that, but—"

Enough of this bullshit. "You fucking coming?" she says, and starts walking.

"Maledicta . . ."

She doesn't even look back, just gives him the finger over her shoulder and keeps going.

"Maledicta!"

"Maledicta!" I called, but she just made a rude gesture and kept walking away. I stood there indecisively for a moment and then, hoping it might startle her into switching, yelled out: "Penny!"

No good. Maledicta continued on to the corner, then started to cross the street, cursing out a driver who had assumed that a green light gave him the right of way. Frustrated, not knowing what else to do but follow her, I stepped sideways into the street myself, my back to the flow of traffic.

The blare of a horn sent me leaping back to the curb. I turned as a patrol car pulled up alongside me. I thought it was Officer Cahill again, but the face that leaned over from the driver's seat was Gordon Bradley's.

"Good way to get yourself killed there, Andrea," he admonished me.

"Chief Bradley. I'm sorry, I—" I started to point to Maledicta, then lowered my arm. "I was distracted."

"Yeah, that's generally how it happens. Did Jimmy find you?"

"Officer Cahill? Um . . ."

"I sent him to look for you. We just got a call from that woman you were asking about."

"What woman?"

"Your landlady. Mrs. Winslow, is it?"

"Mrs. Winslow called? How is she? Did you tell her I'm OK?"

"I did," Chief Bradley said, "but she was determined to come see for herself. She's on her way to the airport right now."

"Oh my God." I didn't know whether to be excited or embarrassed. "She's flying all the way out from Seattle?"

"Rapid City, actually. I believe."

"Rapid City? Why would she be . . . oh no."

"She said she was calling from a motel in the South Dakota Badlands. Apparently she'd gotten word from some doctor that you'd been there—I didn't really follow that part too clearly. Anyway, she knows you're here now, and she asked me to make sure you stayed put until she arrived. Now I'm not going to detain you officially, but—"

"It's OK," I told him. "I'm not going anywhere."

"All right then . . ." The chief looked over his shoulder at a couple of cars that had come up behind him. "Listen, I can't keep blocking traffic here, but would you want to come back to my house and get some lunch? We could talk some more about me buying that property off you."

"Um, actually . . ." I looked up the street the way Maledicta had gone; she was out of sight now. Then I looked back the other way, and saw Officer Cahill coming out of the diner. He had a fistful of napkins and was still wiping whipped cream off his face.

". . . actually, yes," I said.

The patrol car's front passenger seat was already taken by a big box of fishing tackle, so I climbed in back, sliding down as low as I could in the seat. Chief Bradley observed me curiously but didn't say anything; he drove on, taking a left at the next corner. This took us right past the bar where Maledicta had gone to have her drink, and I thought about asking the chief to stop so I could try and talk her into coming with us. But I doubted I could convince her, and didn't think it would be a good idea to bring her to Chief Bradley's house anyway. Penny, yes; but not Maledicta.

We turned left at the next corner, too, and then left again, and finally right, coming back onto Main Street on the same block as Winchell's Diner. I crossed my fingers that Chief Bradley wouldn't stop to tell Officer Cahill he'd found me. He didn't, and when I finally sat up to take a look around, we were already past the firehouse and headed out of town.

"Uh, Chief Bradley," I said, "where exactly is your house? Don't you live in Seven Lakes?"

"Just outside the town limits, actually. I have a couple acres next to Sportsman's Lake." That would, I guessed, be the kidney bean–shaped pond where he'd been fishing this morning.

I thought of Maledicta again, and realized I should at least have stopped to let her know where I was going. "Listen, it just occurred to me, my friend's still back in town, uh, doing some shopping, and if she finishes and can't find me, she might get worried."

"We won't be gone long," Chief Bradley said. "And I can always radio Jimmy and have him let your friend know where you are."

"Well, to be honest, Chief Bradley, I'd rather Officer Cahill didn't know where I was."

He looked at me in the rearview mirror. "You and Jimmy having a problem of some kind?"

"Of some kind," I agreed.

"He's still sweet on you, isn't he?" Chief Bradley shook his head, then said "Men," as if he wasn't one himself. "Men are fools for love, Andrea . . ."

Chief Bradley's house had a raised deck that faced Sportsman's Lake, although it was set back a very long way from the water. The chief pointed this out himself as we were coming up the drive. "I wanted to build right up on the bank, but the problem with that damn pond is that it has a habit of changing size. Those same rains that undercut the foundation at your mother's place? They nearly flooded me out. It's one of the reasons I'm in the market for a new property."

"Well, but that's not very practical," I observed. "If the same rain nearly destroyed my mother's cottage, wouldn't you just be trading one property for another with the same problems?"

He chuckled, as if I'd caught him out at something. "You have a point there, Andrea. I guess I'm not a very practical person."

He parked, got out, and came back to open my door for me. I took the hand he offered, but instead of stepping back and helping me to my feet he just stood there, staring at my hand like he was going to kiss it.

"Chief Bradley?"

"My Lord, Andrea," he said, "what did you do to yourself?"

Oh. He was looking at my knuckles. In the washroom at Winchell's Diner I'd gotten out most of the splinters and run cold water over my hands until they stopped bleeding, but I hadn't got around to bandaging them yet—the gauze was still in the Centurion.

"It's nothing," I said. I wasn't going to explain to him how I'd tried to knock down the house he wanted to buy from me. "It's all right, really—it looks much worse than it is."

"You should get some disinfectant on this, Andrea. You don't want—"

"It's all right," I repeated. "Could I, could you let me get out now, please?"

"Of course." He moved back, and I got out. "Well," Chief Bradley said, gently shutting the car door as I stepped away, "are you hungry?"

I wasn't, and all at once I very much didn't want to be here. I wanted to run back into town, get Penny, and get as far away from Seven Lakes as possible. But I couldn't leave yet; Mrs. Winslow was coming.

"All right," I said, and forced myself to smile. "Sure. Let's eat something."

Maledicta is just finishing her second vodka when Officer Cahill comes into the bar. She's expecting Andrew—with no one to drive him, where the fuck else is he going to go?—but then she sees who it really is and breaks into a fresh scowl.

Fuck. Not *this* cocksucker again. Maledicta thinks about hiding, but there's not much chance of that: the bar is small and mostly empty right now, the only occupants besides Maledicta and the bartender being a handful of gray-haired alcoholics, clones of the old geezer from the Pink Mammoth. She could duck into the ladies' room but decides it's not worth the bother.

The bartender and the geezer-clones all raise their hands, greeting the officer the way you do a regular. He starts to high-five them back, then spots Maledicta and does a double-take. This tells Maledicta that the officer hasn't followed her here; he's come into the bar on his own to drown his sorrows. That's one of the problems with a pissant town like this: too few places to get drunk. And of course, even though the officer wasn't looking for Maledicta, now that he's found her he's going to have to interrupt her happy hour. He can't help himself.

Sure enough, he walks straight over to her. "Is Sam here?" he asks, demanding and pleading at the same time.

It's dangerous to curse out a policeman—even Maledicta understands that—but this guy just pushes all her buttons. "Go fuck yourself," she tells him.

He bristles. "Look here," he says, starting to lean into her, "I don't know who you are, but—"

"That's right," Maledicta cuts him off, "you *don't* know who the fuck I am." She rises up on the barstool until she's eye to eye with him, right in his face. "You don't know who I am because all day you've been fucking ignoring me, acting like I'm fucking invisible. Fifteen minutes ago you nearly fucking *sat* on me. So you don't know who the fuck I am, but you know who I'm *not*? I'm not the one who fucked things up between you and Sam. You fucking did that yourself, you stupid cocksucker, and you'd better not even fucking *think* about giving me a hard time over it!"

Dead silence in the bar following this. The bartender and the geezer-clones pretend to be statues, although real statues' ears don't turn crimson. As for Officer Cahill, his color scheme goes in the opposite direction: his ears, cheeks, and forehead take on a cheesecloth hue as the blood drains out of them.

Satisfied, Maledicta turns back to the bar and raps her shot glass on the counter to reanimate the bartender. He pours her another vodka, while Officer Cahill struggles to restore circulation to those portions of his brain required for speech. "Listen," he stammers, "I didn't mean to . . . I'm sorry if I . . ." He hits a block, stops, shuts his eyes for a second, sighs, and goes on: "Can you tell me where Sam *is*, please?"

Maledicta holds her shot glass up under her nose, letting the fumes curl the hairs of her nostrils. "Sam's gone home," she says.

"Home? You mean back up to the cottage, or—"

"*Home* home," Maledicta says. She grins in sudden inspiration. "Back to New Mexico."

"New Mexico?"

Maledicta tilts her head back, downs the shot. "Ye-a-h," she gasps. "Yeah, New Mexico. Santa Fe. That's where we fucking live. Sam and I, we've got our own fucking art gallery there."

"So you're both . . . artists."

"Nah, not me. I mean, I fuck around—performance art, that kind of shit—but Sam's the real fucking talent. I'm more like the business end of it. She paints, I take care of the fucking money."

"And you live together."

"Yeah," she says, then realizes what he's really asking. "Oh, Christ, not like *that!* We're not *dykes*, for fuck's sake."

"OK," says Officer Cahill, trying to come off like that wasn't what he meant at all.

"We're fucking *friends*," Maledicta emphasizes. "Good friends, *best* friends, but not—"

"OK, OK . . ." He's clearly relieved, despite his effort to hide it. "So Sam, she's not involved with anybody right now?"

Up in the cave mouth, Mouse is making an enormous fuss, shouting that this is wrong, that Maledicta mustn't do this. But it's Maledicta's happy hour, so of course she's going to do it. "Not involved? Oh, I didn't say *that* . . . the truth is, she's married . . ."

The *look* on his face when he hears this—it's fucking priceless! "Married . . ." The blood starts to drain from his cheeks again. "But you said she lives with you . . . so you live with Sam *and* her husband?"

"Well, it's a complicated fucking situation . . ." Just then she has another inspiration. She holds out her shot glass. "Get me another vodka."

He just stares, blinking.

"Don't worry, I'm not going to fucking throw it at you," Maledicta says. "But I came in here to drink and unwind, and if you're going to make me answer fucking questions then you're fucking well buying, too."

Officer Cahill hesitates. He's not a complete idiot, and some part of him must suspect that he's being fucked with. But at the end of the day, unrequited love swings more weight than good sense: he sits down on the stool to Maledicta's right, and signals the bartender. "Two more vodkas."

"And cigarettes," Maledicta adds. "I need some fucking smokes."

"How spicy do you like your chili?" Chief Bradley asked.

"I'm not sure," I told him. "I don't think I've ever eaten chili."

"Never?"

"Not that I remember."

"Not too spicy, then," Chief Bradley said, and went back to banging pots. What was supposed to be a simple, quick lunch was turning into a major cooking operation, at least judging by the noise level.

The front of Chief Bradley's house was built on an open plan. Coming off the deck through the sliding glass doors, you entered a high-ceilinged, U-shaped space. The left arm of the U was the kitchen; the right arm, the living room; and connecting them, a dining room with a view. At first I sat at the dining table looking out over the deck towards the distant pond, but as Chief Bradley went on banging pots and it became clear that the chili was going to take a while, I got up and wandered into the living room.

The room was a mix of sparseness and clutter: there wasn't much furniture, but the walls were crowded. There was a lot of artwork—mostly paint-by-numbers but also some cross-stitch—and a couple of hanging shelves that held old sports trophies; there were also lots and lots of photographs. One wall in particular was covered with them, as if the contents of two or three photo albums had been hung up for easy viewing. At first glance this photo array seemed totally chaotic, but on closer inspection I saw that the photos were grouped by subject into rough constellations or clusters.

One cluster featured a young Gordon Bradley and a friend who, it slowly dawned on me, was Andy Gage's biological father, Silas Gage. It took time for me to recognize him because I'd only ever seen one picture of him before—a wedding portrait that my own father had managed to preserve—and in many of these pictures he was still in his teens: here he and Chief Bradley were posing in front of an old car that looked a lot like Julie Sivik's Cadillac; here they were in a high school band (Chief Bradley with a trombone, Silas Gage with a saxophone); here they were on a football field, half-covered in mud; here—getting a little older—they were standing at attention with a dozen other men, all in uniform; here they were in uniform again, but clowning now, Chief Bradley covering his ears while Silas Gage aimed a hammer at the nose of an artillery shell.

And here they were at a wedding, standing beside a woman in a bridal gown whose face I knew well: Althea Gage. That was the last picture in which Silas Gage appeared, but there were a couple of other snapshots of Althea: one with her and Chief Bradley together at a party, and another of her in front of the cottage—still level, then—gesturing at it with obvious pride. That picture made me wish I could borrow the artillery shell from the army photo.

"Chili's on simmer," Chief Bradley said, coming to join me. "Should be ready in about twenty minutes. You thirsty? I know it's a little early, but . . ." He held out a bottle of beer.

"No thank you," I said. I nodded at the pictures: "I didn't know that you and . . . my father, were so close."

"Close as brothers, from the day we met. Well . . . second day, actually."

I shook my head, not knowing what he meant.

"I'm from Peoria, originally," Chief Bradley explained. "But my momma ran out when I was thirteen, and my dad wasn't up to raising me on his own, so he sent me up here to live with his sister and her husband." He indicated some photos of an older couple I'd assumed were his parents. "Coming here, I was the new kid in a small school, and on my first day, your father got it into his head to pick a fight with me—and since I was angry about all kinds of things right then, I was more than happy to oblige him . . ." He hooked a finger in the corner of his mouth and pulled his lip up, exposing a gap in the line of his molars.

"My father knocked your tooth out?" I said.

"Nope," he replied, letting his mouth snap back into shape. "I knocked one of *his* teeth out. He knocked one of mine loose, but it didn't fall out till later." He chuckled. "Next day, we both came into school wondering whether there was going to be a rematch, but he took one look at me, and I took one look at him, and we both saw . . . I don't know, something." He shrugged, looking mildly embarrassed. "From that moment on, we were the best of friends."

"Huh," I said, not understanding how best friendship would follow from a fistfight. I turned back to the photos and pointed to another group that showed Chief Bradley with a pretty but mostly unsmiling blond woman. "Is this your wife?"

"It was." I couldn't tell if that meant he was widowed or divorced, but then he added: "She left me."

"Oh. I'm sorry."

"Don't be. Ellen was a decent woman but the two of us tying the knot was a mistake. Not the marriage I wanted." He took a swig of beer. "What about yourself?"

"Myself?"

"You're an attractive young lady. Are you married?"

I'd begun to get used to him referring to me as "Andrea," but being called an "attractive young lady" threw me—all the more so because he wasn't just being kind, but actually seemed to mean it.

"I-I . . . no," I said. "I'm not married."

He smiled. "But with prospects, surely."

"No, not even that. I mean there was one person who I . . . but sh— they didn't feel the same way about me."

"That can be hard," Chief Bradley said. He glanced up at the photo array. Then he asked: "Did you ever get that program I sent you?"

"What program?"

"From your mother's funeral. I know you said you didn't want it, but I thought you should have it."

"Oh," I said. "That was from you? . . . I mean yes, we got it." I started to add a perfunctory "thank you," but just then my mouth went dry. Without thinking, I raised the bottle—the bottle that was, after all and somehow, in my hand—and took a swallow of beer.

"I'm only sorry you couldn't attend the ceremony," Chief Bradley said. "It was sad, but it was beautiful . . . she was a good woman, your mother . . ."

"If you say so," I muttered. I took another swallow of beer, and another. The bottle was nearly empty by the time I noticed what I was doing—and by then, it was already too late.

". . . so the two kids are living with her husband now, in Seattle," Maledicta says. "Which is where we were visiting just before we came here."

"So Sam and her husband," says Officer Cahill, "her husband . . ."

"Dennis," Maledicta says, and has to pinch the inside of her wrist to keep from laughing. She's been doing this almost constantly, but it's becoming less effective—the more she drinks, the less she can feel the pinches. She's on her seventh vodka now.

"Dennis, right—they're separated?"

"Not legally. And don't get your fucking hopes up. It's just fucking temporary—he'll come to his fucking senses one of these days, move down to Santa Fe to be with her. No fucking doubt about it."

Officer Cahill sips his own vodka as if it were castor oil or some other foul-tasting medicine. It's his third glass, though, and that as much as anything tells Maledicta that he's buying her story. Officer Cahill is still on duty, and meant to limit himself to one drink—he said as much earlier—but when Maledicta told him that Sam had kids (twins!), that limit went out the fucking window.

"So if all this is going on with her husband," he wants to know next, "what's Sam doing back in Seven Lakes? And what the heck was that about this morning, with Sam saying she thought she might have killed Horace?"

"Oh that." Maledicta waves a hand and sways a little on her barstool. "Well, you know, a lot of Sam's problems, like with her fucking husband and all, that all goes back to, to what her fucking stepfather did to her. *You* know."

"No, I don't. What—"

"Oh give me a fucking break. You're the fucking ex, the guy she was going to fucking run away with. Don't tell me you didn't fucking know about it."

"I know Sam and Horace didn't get on well—"

With a snort: "'Didn't get on well.'"

"All right, Sam hated him. But—"

"She hated him because he was *fucking* her, asshole!" At the other end of the bar, one of the geezer-clones twitches, and Maledicta feels a flash of embarrassment. She'd meant to tell only lies here, and now she's gone and blurted out the truth.

Well, fuck it.

"He was *what?*" Officer Cahill says. "Excuse me?"

"You fucking heard me." Maledicta raps her shot glass on the bar to signal for another refill, but Officer Cahill grabs her arm. "Hey!" Maledicta objects. "What the fuck?"

"Is this a *joke?*" Officer Cahill demands. "Are you making this up to, to I don't know what . . ."

"No, it's not a fucking joke! Fuck you! You don't believe me, go ask your fucking boss."

"Chief Bradley knows about this?"

"Yeah, he fucking knows about it. A day late, but . . ." She jerks her arm free and draws back, pissed off but curious. "You really didn't know? Sam never told you?"

"No! No, Sam never said any—" He stops suddenly, and Maledicta can almost hear the memory falling into place, like a dropped brick. "No, that couldn't have been what she meant . . ."

"Right," says Maledicta. "So she did fucking tell you—you just didn't fucking get it. Par for the fucking course."

"Oh God. Oh Sam . . ."

"Oh please. Fucking spare me." Maledicta knocks a cigarette loose from the pack in front of her and lights it.

"So Chief Bradley knew about it?" Officer Cahill says. "He found out?"

"Not in time to do any fucking good, but yeah."

"God. That must have nearly killed him."

"Oh yeah," says Maledicta. "He was really fucking dying when we talked to him."

The officer looks at her coldly. "I'm sure Chief Bradley was mortified when he found out about that. God, and not just for Sam's sake—for himself, too."

"For himself? Why? Because he fucked up?"

"For not stopping it, sure. And also . . ."

"What?"

"Nothing."

"Bullshit, nothing. Why else would he feel bad for himself?"

Now it's Officer Cahill who looks embarrassed, like he's the one about to reveal a confidence. But Maledicta stares at him until he tells her.

"It's just," he says, "that it must be bad enough to lose out to a good man, let alone one who's . . . like that."

"What do you mean, lose out? Lose out at what?" A light goes on: "Oh, fuck."

"Sam's mother," Officer Cahill says. "The chief and Sam's father—her real father, Silas—both courted the same woman. Silas won: he married her. But then not long afterwards he died, and Chief Bradley—"

"Oh fucking nice," says Maledicta. "What'd he do, propose to her at the fucking funeral?"

Officer Cahill gives her another frosty look. "I'm sure it wasn't like that. But Althea was fond of him, and she had a new baby to think of, and I guess she gave indications that she might be interested—but then before anything really happened, she turned around and took up with Horace."

"And how the fuck do you know about this? You must have been a fucking baby yourself at the time, right?"

"Chief Bradley told me." Officer Cahill taps a finger against the rim of his shot glass. "We were drinking up at the cottage one time about a year ago—"

"What, is that your private fucking clubhouse now?"

"No, but—the chief, you know, he's been trying to keep the place in shape since Althea died. One evening I found him up there, not doing any work, just sitting in the kitchen with a bottle. So I sat down with him, and he started talking about how he'd been in love all those years . . ."

"So that would have been hard enough," the officer concludes, "feeling that way and being rejected, not just once but twice. But to find out on top of that that you'd lost out to a, a child molester . . . I can't imagine." He adds hastily: "Not that that compares to what Sam went through, of course . . ."

Maledicta would like to hit Officer Cahill now, but instead she looks at the bartender—who's hovering right on top of them, pretending not to listen—and holds up her empty glass. "One more for the road."

"Don't you think you've had enough?" Officer Cahill says.

"Don't you think you should mind your own fucking business?" Maledicta retorts.

Officer Cahill sighs. "All right," he says, "it's your liver—it's my *tab*, but it's your liver." He pulls out his wallet and checks to make sure he actually has the money to pay for all these drinks. "Just tell me one last thing. When you said Sam was on her way home to Santa Fe already, that wasn't true, was it? She's still here in town."

"Only for as long as it takes me to crawl back to the fucking car," Maledicta says. "But . . ."—her glass is full again; she tosses it back—"A-a-a-ah! . . . you're *not* going to fucking bother her anymore. And you're definitely not going to tell her what I fucking told you about her stepfather."

"No, of course not, I wouldn't . . . at least not unless she . . . but I *would* like to talk to her one more time before you go. Not to bother her, just . . . hey, are you all right?"

"Fucking fine," Maledicta says, but she's not. The last shot of vodka hits her brainstem hard—she drops the glass, and has to grab the edge of the bar to steady herself.

"You don't look fine," Officer Cahill observes. "You look green."

Maledicta doesn't answer; her stomach's rolling over.

". . . ten thousand dollars," Chief Bradley was saying, his voice slightly muffled by the closed door between us. "I know that may not sound like much, but you understand, the cottage is almost surely a loss. I would love to save it if I could, if there were some way to fix the foundation, but my sense is I'm going to have to tear the whole place down and build new. And there's also the matter of the maintenance work I've done over the past two years— I know you didn't ask for that, but I did pay for it out of my own pocket and I believe it deserves some consideration . . . So what are your thoughts, Andrea?"

"I think it sounds . . . fair." I kept my head raised as I spoke, so he'd be able to hear me. "It's just, I'm still not really ready to make a decision about this."

"Well, and I don't want to rush you," Chief Bradley said, "but from what you've told me it sounds like you're pretty set against staying on in Seven Lakes yourself."

"That's true. But—"

"Right, and I don't imagine you'd be visiting much either . . ."

"That's true, too."

"Right! So there you go—it seems like a waste to leave a perfectly good property abandoned, if you have no intention of using it yourself. And you know . . ."

But the rest of his words were lost as another wave of nausea gripped me, and I bent my head once more to the bowl.

I was tempted to blame my current distress on Chief Bradley's chili: a mostly bland hamburger stew spiked here and there with chunks of incredibly hot pepper. But I'd eaten very little of it—I could see, gazing into the toilet, that I'd eaten very little of it—maybe five or six spoonfuls in all.

The beer was a more likely culprit. I wasn't sure how much I'd drunk. I'd only become aware that I was drinking at all when we were about to sit down at the table, and Chief Bradley, pointing to the bottle in my hand, asked if I wanted another. Startled, I told him no, and yet only moments later, as I hurried to wash down a bite of chili, I found myself tipping up a fresh Budweiser, still cold from the fridge. And then a little while after that, when a sliver of jalapeño got stuck on the way down and started spot-welding the back of my throat, I reached coughing for what I thought was a water glass, only to taste still more beer as I swallowed.

That was when I'd started to feel ill. The jalapeño, though safely extinguished, left an after-impression that was like a finger pressing down on my gag reflex. As the feeling rapidly grew worse, I stood up and asked where the bathroom was. I barely made it in time.

At least Chief Bradley didn't seem offended that I'd lost his lunch. Indeed, he hardly seemed to have noticed at all.

". . . and if you'd like to get a better sense of the local property values before you make up your mind, of course I understand. I want you to be comfortable about this, Andrea. But what I think you'll find . . ."

My nausea seemed to have run its course. I waited another minute just to be sure, then got up to use the sink. I was dizzy from being hunched over so long, so after rinsing my mouth out, I plugged the drain and let the basin fill with water. As I splashed my cheeks and forehead, I heard a creak of hinges and felt someone come up behind me. "I'm OK, Chief Bradley," I said, but when I looked up into the mirror the bathroom door was still closed, and the face peering over my shoulder wasn't the chief's.

"Hello again, figment," Gideon said.

A plastic cup on the back corner of the sink held a toothbrush and a steel-pointed dental pick. I made a grab for the pick, but my left hand got there first and knocked the cup away. Then the hand was at my throat, and the bathroom walls faded into open sky as I was dragged from the body. I looked down and saw the lake far below me, its dark waters swirling around the gray dot of Coventry.

"Andrea?" Chief Bradley called, his voice echoing with distance. "What just fell? . . . Andrea, are you all right in there?"

"I'm fine," Gideon replied. "I'll be right out."

• • •

There's a soda machine outside the grocery store on Main Street. Mouse is hoping it's the kind of soda machine that offers bottled spring water as a selection—that's what she really needs right now, fresh water—but this is Seven Lakes, not Seattle, and the machine is stocked only with pop. She could go into the store to buy water, but the idea of waiting in a long check-out line, trying not to pass out or faint from shame as the cashier and the other customers catch a whiff of her, is more than she thinks she can stand.

Soda pop it is. She puts coins in the machine and punches the button for ginger ale. The can comes out of the machine warm, and the ginger ale tastes like something you'd clean dentures with, but Mouse forces herself to drink it anyway. She needs the fluid.

She looks across the street to where the Centurion is parked. Andrew has still not reappeared. Mouse tells herself that she can't blame him for wandering off, but the truth is she does blame him. He should have waited. He should have come after her. All right, no, he shouldn't have come after her—Maledicta was being abusive, and if he'd followed her to the bar it would have just made a bad situation worse—but he *should* have waited.

Mouse leans back against the soda machine and slides down until she is sitting on the sidewalk with her knees up under her chin. She drinks warm ginger ale and feels wretched. People coming in and out of the grocery store give her funny looks, as if she were a homeless person.

She *feels* homeless. She's got no motel room, no safe place in this town where she can go to sleep for a few hours. And she can't go somewhere else, because even if she were willing to abandon Andrew—the way *he* abandoned *her*, she thinks petulantly—she can't drive. A lot of the vodka that Maledicta drank got left behind in the bar, but enough of it is still in Mouse's system that she doesn't dare get behind the wheel.

The only remotely good thing about her current circumstance is that she's pretty sure Officer Cahill won't be bothering her again. When Mouse ran out of the bar he was still in the men's room, cleaning himself up, but that was just a temporary measure—he's going to have to go home and change, and probably take a long hot shower. Mouse knows she shouldn't be happy about this—she should be disgusted with herself, and furious with Maledicta—and she is—but at this point anything that cuts down the number of obstacles between her and a clean getaway from this town is a welcome occurrence.

"Come on Andrew," she says. "Come back. Let's get out of here."

But it's a while yet before Andrew comes back. The sound of his voice rouses Mouse from a drunken doze; she wakes confused, needing a swallow of warm ginger ale—it's gone flat now too, yuck—to remind her where she is.

Andrew is across the street, shaking hands with Chief Bradley through the window of the chief's police car. "Seven-thirty tonight," Mouse hears Andrew say; then he steps back, and the chief drives off.

Mouse gets up from the sidewalk. "Andrew!" she calls.

He turns towards her, caught off guard, in his surprise looking almost hostile . . . but then he smiles. "Hey there, Penny!" he greets her. "How's it going?"

Mouse waits for another car to pass and crosses the street. "Andrew," she says, drawing near him. "Where were you?"

"Chief Bradley's house." Belatedly picking up on her mood: "Gosh, Penny, I hope you weren't worried."

"I *was*," says Mouse. "But never mind that now. Are you ready to go?"

"Well, actually," he says, "that's kind of what I came back to tell you: I can't leave yet."

"What?"

"I've decided to sell the cottage to Chief Bradley," Andrew explains. "It won't be official until I can establish clear title to it myself, of course, but we've agreed to do the deal, and he's even going to give me a down payment. I'm going back to his house tonight to pick up the money."

"Tonight? So we have to stay here?" Please, no.

"*We* don't have to stay," Andrew says. "I have to, but there's no reason for you to hang around. In fact, if you wanted to head back to Seattle on your own . . ."

"No," says Mouse. "I can't do that."

"Sure you can. Don't worry about me, I—"

"No, I mean I *can't* do that. Maledicta got us drunk, got *me* drunk. I can't drive."

"Oh." He leans forward, sniffs. "Wow! Gee, Penny . . ."

"So I need you to do it." Mouse shoves her car keys into his hands before he can refuse. "Please . . . just take me somewhere, anywhere I can rest. And then if you want to borrow the car and come back and see Chief Bradley tonight, I guess that's OK, I'll just wait for you wherever."

Andrew bounces the keys in his palm and looks thoughtful. "Hmm, OK, I suppose that could work . . ."

"Only let's *go*," Mouse stresses. "I can't stand up much longer."

"Sure." He's smiling again. "You just lie down in back, I'll take care of the rest."

Before stretching out on the Centurion's back seat, Mouse rolls down the windows, hoping that fresh air will counteract any lingering urge to vomit. It works: her stomach lurches a little while Andrew is pulling out of the parking space, but once they are on the move the cool breeze is very soothing. "Just one other thing . . ." she says, her eyes drifting closed.

"Hmm? What's that?"

"I could really use a drink of water. Could you run in somewhere, and get me . . ."

"Sure thing, Mouse," he says. "You relax, I'll get right on that."

"Thanks . . ." She settles down, lulled by the smooth forward motion of the car, and—

—something is tickling her eyelid. A breeze is still blowing through the windows, but less steadily now; the Centurion is stopped somewhere. Mouse lifts a hand to her face, bats sleepily at the thing tickling her. A leaf.

She sits up, blinking away sleep. She tries to call Andrew's name, but her mouth and throat are totally dry. She glances at the driver's seat and sees that it's empty.

Mouse assumes they are at a rest stop off the highway somewhere. Andrew must have gone to get her water. She yawns deeply, and is surprised by how much better she feels: she's parched and she has a headache, but she's sobered up quite a bit, and if she didn't know any better, she'd almost think she'd been asleep all afternoon.

Huh. That's funny. According to the dashboard clock, Mouse *has* been asleep all afternoon. And—taking a good look outside, now—this is a very unusual rest stop: the parking lot is covered in grass, and there are no gas pumps or fast-food restaurants, just a single white cottage-like structure, tilted to one side . . .

Oh God.

Mouse twists around to look out the back window, hoping that this will turn out to be some sort of mirage. But there's no rest stop behind the car, either, just a dirt road that is becoming all too familiar.

Why would Andrew have come back here?

On second thought, never mind—Mouse doesn't care why. She just wants to get out of here. She leans over the seat back and honks the Buick's horn. Short honks, first, and then a sustained blast that causes birds to take flight from the surrounding trees. But Andrew does not come running.

Damn it. If the keys were in the ignition, Mouse would be tempted to drive away—she's sober enough, now—but they aren't, and anyway she knows it would be wrong to just leave. Whatever is going on here, it's at least partly her own fault. If she hadn't been too drunk to drive in the first place . . .

Mouse gets out of the car and goes up to the cottage. There's no answer to her knock on the front door, and she can't remember which stone the key is hidden under. She walks around the side of the cottage. Here she finds a clue to what Andrew may have come back for: the broken bracing planks have all been cleared away, and those planks that are still intact have been set back up, spaced evenly to conceal the fact that there are fewer of them now. Chief Bradley will probably still notice, but without the debris lying around he'll have a hard time figuring out what happened.

Mouse continues around to the back door, which is unlocked. Inside, the cottage is dead quiet—strong circumstantial evidence that nobody's home. She takes a look around anyway. Andrew is not in the kitchen, the pantry, the living room, or anywhere in the ground-floor bedroom that can be seen from the doorway. Mouse goes to the attic door next. She pokes her head in the stairwell and listens; there's no sound, not even the chittering of squirrels. Andrew could still be up there, lying comatose on the cot again, but if he is, he's on his own; not even a promise of fresh water could get Mouse to climb these stairs alone.

Water. The kitchen sink is right behind her; she opens both taps, but not a drop comes out. She makes a second check of the pantry, searching for beverages this time. Many of the glass jars contain vegetables or fruits preserved in liquid, but Mouse isn't desperate enough to drink vinegar or heavy syrup. As for the canned goods, it's obvious from the selection that Andrew's mother made a lot of soups and stews: there's an entire shelf stocked with nothing but salted beef broth, salted chicken broth, and condensed clam chowder.

She returns to the sink and looks out the window at the backyard, just in case someone's come by and installed a fountain in the last two minutes. No one has, but there is something else that's different: the footpath gate is hanging open.

The gate was closed when she and Andrew were here earlier today. Mouse tries to remember whether it was still closed when she came around the side of the cottage just now, but she can't recall.

Mouse stares at the footpath, and envisions the lake at the other end of it. About half a mile, Andrew said. She does not really want to go down there, but her options are limited. It's a much longer hike back to Seven Lakes, and she's not going to find Andrew or her car keys in town.

The woods beyond the gate are dense and shadowy; Mouse walks quickly. Soon enough she glimpses the lake through the trees up ahead. Even from a distance the water looks inviting; Mouse speeds up to a jog, and nearly goes tumbling when the path takes a final unexpected dip.

Quarry Lake is pretty much the way Andrew described it from his—or the Witness's—memory. A few things are different: there are no big shrubs at the end of the footpath, and the "island" at the Lake's center is even smaller than Andrew made it sound, really just a tip of rubble sticking up above the surface of the water.

The lake is certainly deep and cold—and the water is delicious. Mouse cups her hands and scoops up mouthful after mouthful, until her stomach starts to cramp in protest. She pauses then, breathing hard, and becomes aware of a figure standing in the periphery of her vision.

"Hello, Penny," Andrew says.

Mouse, her voice restored, lets out a healthy squeak and falls over.

"Penny . . ." Andrew says. He holds up his hands reassuringly . . .

. . . and right in the middle of the gesture changes his mind, deciding not to bother.

"Forget it," he says. "You aren't worth the effort."

Mouse looks up at him and blinks. "Andrew?" she says.

He doesn't bother to correct her, just stares at her contemptuously until she figures it out.

"No," Mouse says. She rises slowly to her feet. "Not you. You can't—"

"Can't *what*?" says Gideon. "Can't be out? And why's that, exactly? Because Andrew's brave and true? Because he doesn't run away from his responsibilities?" He laughs. "Andrew's not even real, *Mouse*."

"He *is* real!" Mouse protests. "He, he is brave."

"Compared to you, maybe. But it doesn't matter how brave he acts; he was born out of fear and weakness, and in the end that's all he really is: fear and weakness. Aaron's fear." Gideon is grinning as he says this, showing teeth, but his hands make little trembling movements of suppressed rage. "Aaron! Bad enough he steals my life, gives away my property, and tries to keep me bottled up like a goddamn genie! But after all that, to turn around and just . . . *abdicate*, like he didn't even want it himself . . . Ah!" For a moment he's so mad he can't speak. "You have no idea, the frustration . . . but weakness is weakness. It was just a matter of biding my time, waiting for the right moment."

Mouse doesn't say anything to this, but Gideon suddenly glares at her as if she'd contradicted him. "I know what you're thinking," he says. "You're thinking I already got out once before and couldn't hold it. You're thinking

I may keep the body for a day or even a week, but eventually Andrew will rally."

"I didn't—"

"Well *fuck you*, Mouse!" He stoops and snatches up a rock; Mouse flinches, but rather than throw it at her he skims it out over the lake. It's a weak toss, and the rock only skips a couple of times before sinking; Gideon, seeming pleased rather than dissatisfied by this, watches as the splash-ripples spread across the lake's surface and begin to fade. Then he says: "Andrew won't be back. I wasn't really ready, before. But this time I put him down properly."

"So what . . . what happens now?" says Mouse.

"I told you what happens now: I'm selling the cottage to Chief Bradley. Once I've got my money—all of it—I'm going to get the hell out of here. Go somewhere new, and start living the life I was meant to live."

"You know I'm not going to help you."

Gideon laughs at her. "You think I *need* your help? Here . . ." He fishes her car keys out of his pocket and tosses them at her feet. "Go ahead, take off. Go back to Seattle. Get yourself some therapy. Hah!"

Surprised, Mouse picks up the keys.

"What?" says Gideon. "Were you expecting me to hold you prisoner or something?"

Actually, yes, she was expecting something like that.

"Why would I want to?" he says. "I'm not afraid of you, if that's what you're thinking. There's nothing you can do to stop me."

Mouse isn't so sure about that—she seems to recall doing a pretty good job of stopping Gideon the last time he was out—but her look of skepticism gets him laughing again.

"What?" he challenges her. "What do you think you can do? Report me to the police for stealing Andrew's body? I'd love to see you try to explain that one to Jimmy Cahill. Or Chief Bradley—try telling him he can't have the cottage after all, because he's dealing with the wrong Andy Gage now. Even if you could get him to believe that, do you think he'd care?"

Mouse closes her hand around the keys. "You still need a ride to Chief Bradley's house tonight."

"Not really. I could walk there if I had to—I used to go for long hikes around here all the time. But I won't have to walk. You'll take me."

"No, I won't."

"I think you will. You don't believe me when I tell you Andrew isn't coming back. You think he is, and until you think otherwise, you're going to want to stay close to me. And that means when it's time to go to Chief Bradley's, you're either going to have to drive me there, or follow me in your car at four miles an hour—if I'm nice enough to hike along the road-side." He shrugs. "I think you'll give me the lift."

Mouse would like to walk away now, to prove him wrong. Unfortunately he's not wrong.

"Still here?" Gideon says smugly, scanning the ground for another skip-ping stone.

Mouse decides to change the subject: "Tell me about Xavier," she says.

Gideon smiles, like he's been expecting this, too. "What about him?"

"The first time I asked you about Xavier you said he was a tool. But you never said what for."

"You want to know if I called him out to kill the stepfather?" He laughs. "'Xavier the Exterminator': is that what he seems like to you?"

"No," says Mouse. "But he doesn't seem like much of a lawyer, either."

"He *isn't* much of one. Real lawyers cost money, and I didn't have any to waste. That was the whole point."

"You wanted money from the stepfather."

"I wanted money," Gideon says. "The stepfather seemed like an easy person to get it from."

"So you made a lawyer, to sue him. To blackmail him."

"Xavier was going to give him a choice. Paying me was one of the choices."

"Only Xavier came too late. Chief Bradley was already there."

"That wasn't *my* fault," Gideon says, irked. "If Mr. Useless hadn't gotten lost in the woods, we'd have been there first."

"So it's true, then. It was that same night. What Xavier said about the blood on the living-room floor—that was the accident. He saw it."

"It was the night the stepfather died, yeah. Talk about the world's worst timing. I don't know about any *accident*, though."

"What do you mean?"

Gideon plunks another stone in the lake, not even trying to skip it this time. "You understand," he says, "I wasn't exactly there. Xavier's the one who went up to the cottage; I wasn't looking when he looked in the window. But I did overhear some things, before he panicked and ran off. What's the official story? The stepfather tripped over a coffee table?"

". . . and cut himself." Mouse blinks. "That's not what happened?"

"Well I don't know," says Gideon, enjoying her reaction. "Could be he was just delirious from all that blood loss. But it seems kind of strange to beg a *coffee table* for mercy, don't you think?"

I was dead.

That in itself didn't concern me much. I'd never been afraid of death. Of *dying*, yes; of a painful end, or a premature one—important things left undone—definitely. But the thought of actually *being* dead held no particular terror for me. I remembered the moment of my birth, and having come out of the dark, it seemed only right that I should eventually return there. The scary parts were all in-between.

So being dead didn't bother me. What bothered me was the *way* it didn't bother me. In the no-place of oblivion, there aren't supposed to be emotions; the time to be comfortable with your death is before it happens, not after. How was it I still had feelings on the subject?

And as long as I was asking questions: how come I could still see? In the dark there is, by definition, nothing to look at. But here—wherever here was—there was something: though what the something was, exactly, was hard to say.

A labyrinth, maybe: a symmetrical maze of raised and tightly winding pathways, divided down the middle by an especially deep trench. It was gray, which made me think of Coventry, but the layout seemed far too convoluted, unless Gideon was once again trying to discourage visitors.

I was suspended above it, looking down, unable to move. That last part at least seemed appropriate: when you're dead, you shouldn't be able to move. As for the rest, though . . .

I thought back over my death, trying to work out where and how the process might have gone wrong. Gideon had dropped me into the lake from a great height, and I'd struck the surface with tremendous force—I could only hope the house hadn't been swept away by the tsunami that surely resulted. The impact alone had nearly killed me; I was already deep underwater by the time I came to my senses, and then there was nothing I could do but drown, my soul twirling like a bent propeller in the cold currents, spiraling downwards.

It wasn't physical, or metaphysical, damage that kept me from saving myself (though I thought I had a good idea now what it would feel like to break my back jumping off a bridge). It was despair: the certain knowledge that I had failed. Not just this latest failure, this sneak attack that I should have seen coming. *All* my failures: every inadequacy, misstep, and fuckup of my short life, all concentrated into a single self-revelation, like a weighted chain that bound me. *You'll learn*, my father was always saying, and I had, one last lesson: I was useless. Useless.

And so I drowned. It was a relief to finally reach the lake bottom, to slide down past the weeds and sink into the muck that is not muck, last light going out as my soul was sucked back into the void to be unmade. All over now, all finished. Nothing left to do but disappear.

Wait. Wait.

Yes, that was it: that was where the death scene had started to unravel: right at the point where I did. For my soul didn't just dissolve uniformly into nothing; it came apart in stages, layers of identity peeling away, paring me down towards nonexistence. Only it never got that far, because the part of Andrew that was feeling sorry for himself, that welcomed dissolution, was among the first bits to be discarded. Once that distraction had been sloughed off, the Andrew that remained—the core Andrew who was thinking these thoughts even now—was no longer willing to give up so easily. Couldn't give up: because his job wasn't finished yet. *That* Andrew clung stubbornly to his Purpose, and held what was left of his soul together even as it continued to sink, down into . . .

Oh.

Oh, of course.

The gray labyrinth: I wasn't above it, looking down; I was *below it*, looking *up*. It was a geography, *the* geography, only seen from the other side. I hadn't drowned in the lake bottom; I'd just passed through, and come out underneath, in—

"The antipodes," a voice said.

Antipodes, right, of course that's what you'd call it; although, like the strata in the Badlands hill faces, I'd never actually seen an antipodes before. Not what I would have expected from the name. I wondered about the plural: what portion of what I was looking at constituted a single antipode?

"I really shouldn't be wasting time on word games."

Who was that speaking? I tried to turn towards the voice but still couldn't move, which was frustrating now that I knew I wasn't dead. Thinking that a little more substance might help, I gathered back some of the layers I'd shed on the way down here, and sure enough, as my soul recoalesced, I started to regain my mobility. But then the sense of failure came back too, threatening to paralyze me all over again.

Fortunately, there was a solution for that: I reached up to the geography and smoothed out a rough spot on one of the gray ridges. As though an emotional volume control had been turned way down, the bad feeling diminished to a level where I could handle it.

It was still there, though. I really had made some bad mistakes, and some very bad decisions, and I knew it. It would be a lot nicer *not* to know it. What if I were to grab hold of that gray ridge and pull it clean off?

"I'd better not," the voice said. "That's exactly the sort of thing that got me into this mess in the first place."

I could turn around now, so I did. But there was nobody else there.

Talking to myself. Typical.

"Typical," the voice agreed good-naturedly, as I turned back to the geography. "So now what?"

"Simple," I said. "I've got to get back up there."

"And how do I plan to do that? This isn't like walking around the house, or even like trying to escape from Coventry. To come back from *here*, I need someone to call me out."

"My father . . ."

". . . probably thinks I'm gone for good. If Captain Marco tried to fish my soul out of the lake and couldn't find anything—"

"Well then, I'll just have to do it myself."

Skeptically: "Call myself out? Is that even possible?"

"I don't know," I admitted. "But if there's no one else to do it for me . . ." I reached up again, and taking hold of the whole geography for leverage, said: "My name is Andrew Gage."

—and then cold, *cold* shock as I burst once more from the lake bed, the weeds and dark water parting violently as I drew myself up.

The surface of the lake as I broached it was wild with storm. The mist was all gone, blown away by the same wind that was whipping the water into a frenzy. The sky above was black with clouds, and it was raining, thundering too. I treaded water and bobbed among the whitecaps until a lightning flash revealed the nearest stretch of shore. It seemed a long way off, but I knew that was an illusion: I'd already come a lot farther. I started swimming.

There was no one waiting for me on the lakebank this time. The boat dock and the pumpkin field were both deserted; Captain Marco's ferryboat rode unattended in its moorings, and Silent Joe's shovel leaned mutely against the pumpkin-field gate. At first glance it looked like the house might be deserted too: the pulpit was empty, and all the windows facing the lake had been shuttered. But looking more carefully, I could see light shining under the front door. I marched up the path, and without stopping to knock, let myself in.

The house wasn't empty; it was full. A meeting had been called: the long table was set up in the common room, and every chair but mine was occupied; above, in the gallery, the full complement of Witnesses was gathered behind the railing.

All heads turned my way as I came in. Adam greeted my arrival with his usual insolent smirk, but every other soul at the table seemed stunned to see me. "Andrew!" my father cried, jumping to his feet.

I should have said something—"Hi," at least—but a sense of mission drove me now, and I went straight for the door under the stairs. The knob rattled beneath my grasp but still wouldn't turn.

I decided that wouldn't do.

"This door is not locked," I said.

The knob turned. The door opened, swinging inwards, and I stepped through onto a narrow landing. The landing and the flight of stairs that descended from it were festooned with cobwebs, and there was a layer of dust as thick as the one in the cottage attic. Visible in the dust were two distinct sets of footprints.

The basement below was pitch black.

I decided that wouldn't do, either.

"Lights!" I called, and a string of bulbs materialized above the stairs. In the basement proper, there was a bright white flicker of fluorescents coming on.

I descended, leaving my own set of footprints in the dust.

Imagine the cellar of an overstocked art museum, and you'll have a pretty good idea what I found. The house basement was square, about the same size as the common room above it, with a cement floor and cinderblock walls. Arranged within this space, in a not-quite-chaotic pattern that reminded me of Chief Bradley's picture wall, were scores of artworks in many diverse styles.

The range of media was impressive, but in every case that I could see the subject matter was identical, the same subject matter as the painting I'd found under the bed in my father's room: a woman—a mother—embracing her young daughter.

"Andrew?" my father said. He'd come down the stairs after me, and looked around bewildered at the assembled artworks, the many faces of Althea. "What is this?"

In answer I gestured to a section of wall where a hole had been broken through the cinderblock. Beyond it a rough-hewn tunnel sloped down out of sight. A steady draft blew from it, bringing a smell of lake water.

"This is Gideon's escape route," I said. "That tunnel must go all the way to Coventry. My guess is he's been using it to steal little bits of time for a while now, but he had to wait for a crisis to really exploit it."

"But . . ." After glancing briefly at the tunnel, my father went back to staring at the oils and watercolors, the charcoal sketches and crayon scrawls, the marble, bronze, and papier-mâché statuary. "What *is* this?"

"A storeroom. This is where you put all the feelings about our mother that you couldn't deal with, that *none* of you could deal with—except for Gideon, because he didn't care. This is your blind spot, father."

"No." He shook his head. "I didn't make this room."

"Yes, you did. You kept it hidden, even from yourself, but you built it. I'm surprised Dr. Grey didn't find out. I'm sure she would have gotten it out of you eventually. But after she had her stroke, you were able to keep the secret . . . from everyone but Gideon."

"Gideon," my father said darkly.

"You shouldn't feel too bad about him escaping. In a way he's done us a favor. And it's not that he's stronger than you are, emotionally. It's just, like you said, he's so self-centered, he never needed our mother's love in the first place. Which I guess is one way to cope with not getting it."

"I'll give Gideon something to cope with. When I get my hands on him—"

"No, father."

"No?"

"Gideon isn't your responsibility anymore. He's mine."

"Wrong, Andrew—house discipline is my job."

"It *was* your job," I said. "But that's one of the things that's going to have to change. If we really want lasting order, we can't go on treating the body and the house as if they're separate—we need one soul in charge of both. And that soul has to be me."

"Andrew—"

"It can't be you, father. You've done your part: you brought us out of the dark room, you built the house. But you're tired now. And Gideon can't run things, as much as he wants to—he's *too* selfish, he'll try to deny the rest of us, and that'll never work.

"So that leaves me. I think I'm ready to take charge now. All these feelings that you shut away down here, I think I could bear them. I'm not like Gideon; I *do* care, it hurts me that our mother didn't love us, but not so much that I couldn't learn to live with it. I can live with our history, father—all of it. And that, in the end, isn't that really what you called me out for?"

"I . . ." my father said, and stopped, looking suddenly very old. He sat down on the stairs. From the landing up above I could hear shuffling noises: other souls, growing curious.

"Getting the body back from Gideon won't be easy," my father said. "He's determined to hold on this time."

"We'll see about that. But first . . ." I started moving around the basement, searching for something.

"What is it, Andrew?"

"I just remembered, there were *two* sets of footsteps on those stairs . . . and Gideon wasn't the only one missing from the meeting. Here!" On the floor between two sculptures, I found a soul-shaped lump covered by a drop cloth. I bent down and drew the cloth aside.

Xavier Reyes opened his eyes and sat up. "Hello," he said. "Is it time for me to go to work again?"

"No work today," I told him. "But I do have a few questions . . ."

"Mind the bones," Chief Bradley says, and sets a steaming platter on the table.

The chief has gone all-out for dinner: fresh-baked cornbread, long-grain and wild rice, boiled asparagus, and for the main course, some kind of white fish that has been dredged in cornmeal and pan-fried. It all looks remarkably unappetizing. Well, maybe not *all*—the rice looks OK. But as for the rest: the asparagus is limp, the cornbread is sweating lard on top and burned on the bottom, and the fish looks . . . crispy.

Mouse is hungry, but after looking over the fare decides to pretend that she isn't. Maybe she can fake an upset stomach—not such a stretch, after what happened this afternoon.

But Gideon beats her to it: "Actually," he says, looking warily at the fish platter, "my gut is still pretty shaky from that chili . . ."

"Oh, the fish isn't spicy," Chief Bradley assures him. "Just a little pepper in the coating is all."

"Even so," says Gideon. "I think I'll just have some rice . . ."

Maledicta, watching from the cave mouth, makes an observation. Mouse listens carefully, then speaks up in a loud voice: "No, Andrea, you can't do that!"

Gideon glances at her sharply. "Excuse me?"

"You, you can't just have rice," Mouse says, faltering a bit. "Not after Chief Bradley went to so much trouble, catching these fish for us . . ."

Chief Bradley chuckles. "To be honest, I caught them at the Main Street market," he says. "I don't think I'd serve the kind of fish that come out of Sportsman's Lake to guests."

"Well these look delicious!" Mouse says. Picking up the spatula from the platter, she lifts two pieces of the fish onto her own plate. She tries to serve Gideon as well, but he blocks her arm.

"No thank you," he says.

"Come on, Andrea," says Mouse. "You don't want to be rude . . ." She lunges with the spatula but he grabs her wrist. Squeezing hard, he forces her arm back, then twists it until the fish drops back into the serving platter.

"Really," Gideon says, giving her wrist another painful squeeze before releasing it. "I don't want any."

"No one's going to force you to eat it, of course," Chief Bradley says, sounding put out. Then, turning his head and smiling: "That just leaves more for you and me, right . . . Penny, is it?"

"Actually," says Gideon, "she likes to be called *Mouse*."

"Mouse, then . . . how about some asparagus to go with that?"

Chief Bradley sees to it that Mouse has generous helpings of asparagus and cornbread, then sets to work serving himself. Gideon hogs the long-grain and wild rice, heaping it on his plate so there is no room for anything else.

Mouse takes a bite of fish. It's dreadful—sand-coated rubber, with a hint of Tabasco—but rather than gulp it down, she holds it on her tongue as if savoring it.

"Mmmph!" she says suddenly. She reaches into her mouth and pulls out something long and slender. "You weren't kidding about the bones." She holds it up so Gideon can see it. "Like a little spear."

"Yeah, you want to be careful about swallowing any of those," Chief Bradley says.

"I certainly wouldn't want to get one stuck in my throat," says Mouse. She sets the bone on the edge of her plate, sticking out over the rim, pointed at Gideon.

"So what do you do for a living, Mouse?" Chief Bradley asks.

"I'm a computer programmer," Mouse replies. She pauses to spit out another bone, then adds: "Andrea is a janitor for the same company."

"A janitor?" says Chief Bradley. "I thought you said you were an office manager, Andrea."

"I am," says Gideon. "That is, I was, and I will be again soon." Glaring at Mouse: "The janitor's job was just temporary. I've already given my notice. I won't be going back."

"It's nothing to be ashamed of, you know," Chief Bradley says. "My aunt was a cleaning woman for many years."

"I'm not *ashamed* of it," Gideon says. "It's just not something I'd choose to spend *my* life on."

Mouse takes another bite of fish and arranges another pair of bones on the rim of her plate. By now the pepper in the fish coating has begun to sting, and she has to drink something. Chief Bradley has poured them all glasses of water and glasses of white wine. Maledicta recommends the wine, but more alcohol is the last thing Mouse needs right now and she decides to stick to water. Then she notices Gideon is only drinking water, too.

"What about a toast?" she says, picking up her wineglass after all. "To the sale of the property."

"I'll drink to that," says Chief Bradley. He raises his wineglass, and Gideon is forced to do the same. They toast, and drink.

Chief Bradley drinks, anyway. Mouse only pretends to, and Gideon takes no more than a perfunctory sip . . . at first. When Gideon goes to return his glass to the table, however, instead of setting it down he transfers it from his left hand to his right, brings it back up to his lips, and drains it in one quick swallow. Then he sets the glass down for real, and—seemingly unaware of what has just transpired—picks up his spoon in his left hand and resumes eating rice.

Mouse, watching this out of the corner of her eye, feels a thrill of elation. She considers proposing a second toast but decides that would be too obvious. Then Maledicta offers another suggestion.

"So Chief Bradley," Mouse says, "what are you going to do with the cottage? I guess you'll have to tear it down."

"Probably," Chief Bradley says. "As I was telling Andrea at lunch, if I could find a way of fixing the foundation without knocking the cottage down, I would, but—"

"What about taking the cottage apart deliberately? You can do that, can't you? Disassemble it, and then rebuild it on a new foundation?"

"I'd thought about that," the chief says, nodding. "I think it would be difficult, and expensive . . . but then so is building a whole new house. And I'd really like to preserve the cottage if I could, for sentimental reasons . . ."

"Of course," says Mouse, "if you were going to do that, you'd have to do it soon, before the cottage falls over on its own."

"Well, hopefully there's still some time before that happens."

"Oh, I don't know about that." Mouse touches a finger to the bruise on her cheek. "When Andrea and I were out there this morning, I thought for sure it was going to collapse on top of us."

There's a clink as Gideon drops his spoon.

"What do you mean?" Chief Bradley says. "What happened?"

"Well—" says Mouse.

"Nothing happened," Gideon overrides her. "*Mouse* is exaggerating." His voice is controlled and pleasant, but his eyes flash a warning. Mouse almost loses her nerve, but then she sees that while Gideon is focusing on her, his right hand is reaching out independently for the wine bottle.

"Exaggerating about what?" Chief Bradley wants to know. "How did you hurt yourself, Mouse?"

"Penny," Mouse corrects him, with renewed confidence. "I really actually prefer Penny."

"*Penny* . . . how did you get hurt? What happened?"

"We were up in the attic. Andrea was . . . looking through some old things, and all at once I got thrown off my feet. I thought the cottage was going to fall down right there."

"You went up in the *attic?* Andrea, are you crazy?"

"I told her it was dangerous," says Mouse, "but she really wanted to see her old room."

"When you say you got thrown off your feet," the chief asks her, "do you mean that the floor moved?"

"I'm not really sure—it happened so suddenly." Mouse turns to Gideon, who is drinking from his refilled wineglass. "What do you remember, Andrea? Did the floor move?"

Gideon smiles nastily at her. "You know, *Mouse,*" he says, "I don't even remember you falling down—I guess I was in my head at the time. But are you sure it wasn't just a case of you being clumsy? You know how careless you are."

"I suppose it could have been clumsiness," says Mouse, matching his smile, "but don't forget about the bracing planks—"

"How did you hurt your hands, Andrea?" Chief Bradley interrupts.

"My hands?" says Gideon. "I—" He stops; in glancing at the scabs on his knuckles, he suddenly notices the wineglass. "My *hands,*" he repeats, and throws Mouse a look of what might almost be grudging admiration. "Well," he says, "I guess I've been careless too . . ." And he stares at his traitorous right hand until the hand lowers itself to the table and sets down the wineglass.

"Andrea?" Chief Bradley says.

Gideon raises his right hand again, flexing the fingers to test his control over them. Satisfied, he turns his attention back to the chief: "I'm sorry, Chief Bradley, it's been an emotional day. *You* understand: all the memories about what my stepfather did to me . . ."

"Of course," says Chief Bradley, cheeks coloring.

"And of course you're right that it was stupid of us to go up in the attic," Gideon continues. "I don't know what possessed me, to do something so idiotic. But despite what *Mouse* says, I really don't think there was any harm done. Besides," he adds, "I seem to recall, when we were dickering about a fair price for the property, you told me several times that you expected the cottage to be a total loss."

"Well that's true, Andrea, but obviously if I can keep the cottage intact I'd prefer it."

"Well, it *is* intact—at least it was still standing the last time *I* saw it, and I have no intention of going back to it again, so what happens to it now is up to you . . . Did you get the money?"

"For the down payment?" Chief Bradley nods. "Yes, that was no problem."

"In cash?"

"Yes. I was going to give it to you after we ate—"

"Why don't you give it to me now?" Gideon says. "I'd like to get our business out of the way, and then we can . . . enjoy the rest of the meal."

"All right," says Chief Bradley. He pushes his chair back. "Come with me."

He gets up and heads through the living room towards the back of the house. Gideon goes to follow him, but as he's leaving the table he whispers in Mouse's ear: "If you've fucked up this deal for me, you'll be sorry."

Gideon catches up to the chief at the door to the back hallway, and Mouse hears Chief Bradley ask: "What was that she was saying about the bracing planks?"

They are gone for several minutes. By the time they come back, Mouse has finished her fish and has slipped both her asparagus and her cornbread back onto their respective serving plates.

"So you think it could be done by the end of June?" Gideon is saying, as he and Chief Bradley return to their seats.

"Possibly," Chief Bradley tells him. "We'll have to see what Oscar says, when he gets back from his vacation. He's pretty well-connected in the county, and I've seen him work miracles cutting through red tape before, so I imagine it could all be settled that quickly."

"Good," says Gideon. "With the money you've given me tonight, plus whatever other savings I have, I should be fine through July. And *you*"—he looks at Mouse—"you can go back to Washington now. Say good-bye to everybody for me." He picks up his spoon, and takes a big mouthful of rice.

"You do understand, Andrea," Chief Bradley says, "I can't guarantee it will happen that fast. I'm as anxious as you are to get this done quickly, but until we talk to Oscar . . . Andrea?"

Gideon's jaw has frozen in midchew. For a moment he just looks confused, but then his cheeks puff out, and his eyes begin to dart around in alarm.

"What's the matter, Andrea?" says Mouse. "Is something wrong with your food?"

He looks at her, then down at the rim of her plate, and finally at his own plate. His eyes go wide as he spies at least a dozen fish bones mixed in with the long-grain and wild rice.

Retching, Gideon opens his mouth and lets the half-chewed mass of rice fall out. He makes a grab for his water glass, only to spot another fish bone floating in the water.

"You *cunt!*" he says, rice and saliva spraying from his lips. "You *CUNT!*" He half-turns in his seat, arm cocked to fling the water glass into Mouse's face, but before he can make good on his intention something catches in his windpipe. He gasps, then whoops in terror; the glass slips harmlessly from his grasp, and his hand claps to his throat.

"Jesus Christ," Chief Bradley says, "she's choking," and starts to get up. But Gideon grunts "No!" and the chief, thinking this is addressed to him, pauses halfway out of his seat.

"No . . . you . . . don't!" Gideon says. The cords of his neck stand out, and his face turns red; while his left hand continues to clutch at his throat, his right hand, turning traitor again, reaches across his plate. "*No!*" Gideon hisses at it, but the hand, trembling with exertion, keeps reaching, until its fingers close once more around the wineglass. This time, though, the hand doesn't try to lift the glass; it just clenches.

"Oh God," says Mouse, guessing what comes next. The bowl of the wineglass cracks with a dry-stick snapping sound, then shatters; the hand continues to close, making a bloody fist.

Gideon screams. He screams, but still he hangs on, not giving up the body, until the traitor hand comes up in front of his face and opens to show a palm studded with broken glass. The sight is too much for him; he shrinks back, trying to escape his own hand, and then his chair tips over backwards.

"Jesus Christ . . ." Chief Bradley knocks his own chair over as he dashes around the table to Gideon's aid. "Andrea!" he calls, bending down over the body, which is thrashing violently now, eyelids fluttering. "Andrea, can you understand me?" Getting no response, the chief turns to Mouse and asks: "What is this? Is she an epileptic?" Mouse, who has balled both of her own hands into fists now and is trying to bite the knuckles off them, doesn't answer. "Hey!" the chief yells at her. "Is Andrea an epileptic?" Mouse manages to shake her head no. "Well," says Chief Bradley, "she's having some kind of seizure . . . I'm going to go call EMS, but I need you to get down here and watch that she doesn't choke to death. Can you do that? . . . Hey! Girl! Can you do that?" Mouse makes another head movement that Chief Bradley chooses to interpret as a nod; he gets up and runs into the back of the house.

Andy Gage's body continues to thrash on the floor, but Mouse does not get down to take Chief Bradley's place. She remains in her chair, thinking that this is how it must have looked when her mother had her stroke aboard the airplane. That was Mouse's fault, that stroke, and now she's done it again. She thought she was being so clever, outwitting Gideon, but instead she's gone and given him a seizure, and Andrew will probably die as a result, and—

But even as Mouse imagines the worst, the "seizure" begins to subside: the thrashing stops, and the unconscious eyelid flutter becomes controlled blinking. Andy Gage lifts his head and looks at Mouse. Then he turns to regard his bloody right hand, and says wearily: "Why couldn't he be afraid of the dark?"

"*Andrew?*"

"The janitor," Andrew confirms.

"Oh thank God . . ." Mouse gets out of her chair finally, practically falling on top of him; one of her knees ends up crushing his thigh. "Sorry," she says, "sorry . . ."

"'S'all right," Andrew grunts. Mouse rolls off him, and he sits up slowly. "That was a good idea, with the fish bones . . ."

"Maledicta suggested it. But I thought you were choking for real."

"Yeah," he says, with a touch of pride, "Gideon thought so too. He really didn't want to give up, though, so I had to do something more drastic." He looks at his hand again. "I just hope that's the last round—I'm running out of room for new scars." He lifts his head and looks around curiously. "Where did Chief Bradley go? To call an ambulance?"

"Yes," says Mouse. Then she lowers her voice and adds: "Listen, Andrew, we have to be careful. Gideon told me he thought Chief Bradley might have killed your stepfather."

"I know," says Andrew. "I talked to Xavier, inside. He said the stepfather didn't trip over the coffee table; Chief Bradley knocked him down, and let him bleed to death."

"Oh God. We have to get out of here, then. We have to—"

"Hello, Chief Bradley," Andrew says, looking over Mouse's shoulder.

"Andrea," says Chief Bradley, his voice flat. "I see you're doing better."

"Yes," Andrew says. Mouse is amazed at how calm he sounds. "Better, but not perfect." He holds up his wounded hand, and a line of blood runs down the inside of his forearm. "Is the ambulance coming?"

"No," Chief Bradley says. "I'm afraid not. I called Seven Lakes EMS, and they said the ambulance is already out on call. The dispatcher was going to try to get another paramedic team out here, but since you're better, I think I'll just run you over to the emergency clinic myself."

"That's OK. You don't have to bother. Penny can drive me."

"No, I'll take you. I'll take both of you. Just wait here a moment . . ."

He stalks off through the living room again. Mouse scrambles to her feet the moment he's out of sight; she gets Andrew up, too, and together they move towards the sliding glass porch doors. But before they can get out, Chief Bradley reappears, coming through the kitchen this time, heading them off. Mouse sees that he is wearing his gunbelt now.

"Wrap your hand in this," Chief Bradley says brusquely, grabbing a dish-towel off the kitchen counter and tossing it at Andrew. Then he stands back, indicating that they should walk in front of him. "Let's go."

And so they do, out onto the porch and down into the open yard where the cars are parked. Mouse, feeling like she's floating, starts to drift towards her Buick, but Chief Bradley calls out sternly: "No!" Mouse stops and turns around; the chief steps to the back of his cruiser, opens the door, and gestures for both Andrew and Mouse to get in.

Andrew starts to comply, but Mouse balks. "No," she says, in a barely audible refusal, "no, I, I'll take my car—"

The chief doesn't contradict her, just shifts his stance, giving her a clearer view of the gun on his hip. Then Andrew, perhaps fearing what could happen if Mouse tries to run, says: "Come on, Penny. We'll ride in the chief's car."

"Andrew . . ."

"Come on," he says, taking her hand. "It'll be fine."

Mouse shakes her head: *Oh no it won't.* Andrew, smiling—how does he stay so calm?—leans in close enough to whisper.

"Don't be afraid," he tells her. "We have him outnumbered."

After shutting us in the back of the patrol car, Chief Bradley grabbed a radio from the front seat and stood outside talking into it. I couldn't hear what he was saying, but I could guess: he was calling the paramedics back, telling them his previous call had been a false alarm, and probably telling his own dispatcher not to try contacting him for a while, that he had some private business to take care of.

I waited impassively for whatever that business might be. Penny was terrified, which was understandable: unlike me, she hadn't just returned from the dead, and didn't have the feeling of invulnerability such an experience confers. That she also hadn't had as much wine with dinner, that she wasn't bleeding, and that her assessment of our situation might therefore be more clearheaded than my own—that didn't occur to me.

Chief Bradley finished talking on the radio. He got in the patrol car, glancing at us in the rearview mirror without saying anything, and started the engine. He drove towards town. As we came around the bend onto Main Street a few moments later, I saw another patrol car up ahead, in front of the police station. I wondered if it was Officer Cahill, and what, if anything, Chief Bradley would say to him.

But Chief Bradley didn't go that way. He turned off Main Street almost immediately, taking a left just past the firehouse. Three blocks along this cross street, we came to the Seven Lakes Emergency Clinic. It was a small but brightly lit building, with a glowing red cross on the front lawn. Chief Bradley slowed the car as we neared the entrance to the parking lot, and I sat up in surprise, thinking I'd had him wrong after all; but then he stepped on the gas again. Penny watched the red cross go by and made an abortive squeak of protest.

"I think you missed a turn, Chief Bradley," I said.

He kept on driving. The street ended in a T-junction, and Chief Bradley turned right, onto a gently curving road that followed the shoreline of yet another lake. Between the bungalows and cabins that clustered along the lakebank, I could see dark water glinting red with the last of the sunset.

From its name, you would think Two Seasons Lake was only full for part of the year, like Thaw Canal back in Autumn Creek. In fact, it is one of the largest and most permanent bodies of water in Seven Lakes; only Greenwater Lake is bigger. The shore around the west end of the lake is well-settled, but the east end, where Hansen's Brook flows in, remains mostly undeveloped except for a few isolated cabins and some hiking trails.

This was where Chief Bradley was taking us. As we continued along the shore road, the houses got fewer and fewer and then disappeared; the road got rougher, and not long after that it appeared to dead-end. But Chief Bradley made a final turn onto an overgrown track; it led straight down to the lake and right on into it. As a warning to drivers of non-amphibious vehicles, a chain with a reflectorized stop sign had been strung across the track just a few yards from the water's edge.

The police car didn't want to obey the sign. When we were still some distance from the chain, Chief Bradley took his foot off the gas, but the car continued to roll forward. The chief let it roll, as if curious to see how far it would go; he let go of the steering wheel too. It looked like we were going to go swimming, but at the last moment Chief Bradley dropped his hand and engaged the parking brake. The police car shuddered to a halt.

Chief Bradley killed the engine but left the headlights on; they shone out over the murky waters. I almost asked the chief what he'd brought us here for, not because I needed to be told, but because I thought the question might shame him into reconsidering. In the end I decided to let him speak first. Several times he seemed about to say something, only to sigh as if the words had escaped him at the last second.

"Do you know," he finally said, "this is where your father drowned." Penny let out a gasp at the blunt mention of drowning, while I had to think a moment which father he was referring to. "Not *here*," Chief Bradley added. "Out there, in the deep water. There used to be a wooden raft anchored out there, for diving. Kids would go out there sometimes, night-swimming, sometimes drunk, and occasionally there would be accidents."

"Silas Gage had an accident," I said, managing to bite off the last word: *too?*

"Not like *that*." He turned around, facing me through the cage that separated the front and back seats, and I was surprised to see what looked like tears starting in his eyes. "How could you even *think* . . ." He trailed off, started to face forward again, then turned back, demanding: "What *are* you thinking, Andrea? What do you want from me? This morning, when I came into work and found you talking with Jimmy, I thought . . . and then that crazy story you told, how you were worried maybe *you* killed Horace . . ." He shook his head. "What is it you're after? Is it blackmail? I've already said

I'll give you money for the property, and if you want more . . . Or do you just want to punish me for some reason? If that's it, you're too late. Life has already punished me."

"I don't want to punish you." I fingered the steel cage-mesh, and wondered how long it would take Seferis to break through it. "Tell me what happened to Silas Gage."

"I didn't drown your father, Andrea. He did that on his own."

"You were jealous of him."

Chief Bradley sighed. "Jimmy told you."

"No," I said, "you did. Wanting my mother's house so bad, and before that, arranging her funeral . . . and her burial. That was you, wasn't it, who had her plot changed?"

"That was just simple decency. I couldn't leave her lying forever next to that man."

"Or with his name. The tombstone said Althea Gage, not Althea Rollins."

He chuckled bitterly. "You have sharp eyes, Andrea."

"I saw the epitaph, too. So it's kind of obvious that you were in love with her."

"Yes," Chief Bradley said. "Yes, I was, and more fool me . . . but I loved your father, too. I could have put your mother's maiden name on that stone, if I'd wanted—or my own. There was no one to object. I was the last, the only person who still cared about her at the end. Even if she never . . .

"I suppose I was jealous of your father," he went on. "But more than that, I was frustrated by him. I don't know if you can appreciate this, Andrea, but the one thing that is worse than not getting what you want, is seeing someone else get it who doesn't value it the way you do. When we were both courting Althea, Silas worked hard to win her love; but once he had her, in particular once they'd married, it was as if he'd decided he didn't have to try anymore. *I* would have doted on her . . . and even if I hadn't, even if she weren't special, a woman *worth* doting on, still . . . when a man takes a wife, starts a family, he's supposed to change. Grow up, for God's sake! It's what's done. But Silas wouldn't. He was fond of her, and I believe he was faithful, but in other ways he failed to give her the consideration that a wife—that *she*, especially—deserved. And who knows"—he shrugged—"who the hell knows, maybe she was attracted to that. Maybe that was part of it, maybe she *liked* being taken for granted. But it made me see red.

"The night he died, I was working, out on patrol; I met up with your father on the road. Eleven-thirty on a Tuesday night and he's out driving, with a six-pack on the seat right next to him—and he's *not* headed for home.

"I asked him where he was going. He told me he'd had a fight with Althea, and she needed some time to cool down, so he'd decided to come out and have some fun. 'Fun?' I said. 'She's five months pregnant, you mean to say you just left her alone? What if something happens?' He told me she'd be fine—she'd fume for a while, then be asleep by the time he got back. He asked me if I wanted to go swimming with him. I blew up: told him he needed to start acting like an adult, told him, if she was my wife . . . but he laughed. 'She's *not* your wife,' he said. 'She picked me, remember? Anyway, you should be happy—if she divorces me for neglect, you'll get another shot at her.'

"I came close to hauling him out of the car for that. If I had, if I'd beaten the hell out of him, like he deserved . . . but I didn't. I told him to get out of my sight before I arrested him. I told him, I told him I hoped he drowned his stupid self . . .

"What happened," Chief Bradley continued, "what we eventually decided happened, Silas drank most of the six-pack sitting in his car, here, and then he took the last can with him and swam out to the raft. He made a bad dive, hit his head, and lost consciousness. By morning his body had drifted down to the west end of the lake. I got the call around nine A.M."

"So he had an accident," I said. "And then, what, did you and my mother—"

"*She* came to *me*, Andrea. I don't know what you must think of me, but I did not see your father's death—my best friend's death—as some sort of golden opportunity. No matter what *he* said, that night. But she came to me. Asking for help. And then how could I say no?

"Do you know I was there, the day you were born? It's true: I drove your mother to the clinic, and stayed at her side. And the cottage, too: I helped her with that. Silas's death benefit, it didn't amount to much, but I helped out, I traded some favors to get her a deal, so you wouldn't have to grow up in a trailer . . ."

"But you didn't do any of this," I said, "for *selfish* reasons."

His shoulders moved in what might have been a shrug. "Of course I still wanted her," he said. "A man dreams . . . and she seemed to want me too, for a time, though I guess I was wrong about that. But what you have to understand, Andrea, what happened, it wasn't just about wanting—it was about *making sense*.

"I suffered terrible guilt over your father's death. No, I wasn't responsible, but I was haunted by the thought of how easily I could have prevented it. If I'd stopped him that night, or if I'd just gone with him . . . I used to have dreams about that, nightmares that I *did* go with him, that I was there on the raft when he hit his head, and just stood there doing nothing while he drowned.

"So when Althea came to me, when she *needed* me, that wasn't just a second chance with the woman I loved. It was a chance to justify what happened to Silas. If a man simply dies, that's a senseless tragedy. But if, because he dies, a woman—a good woman, and her daughter—end up in the care of another man, one who's not necessarily better than the first, but better *for them*, then the tragedy acquires meaning, an underlying order, however terrible . . .

"I *know* that's a self-serving way to think," he said, looking at me in the rearview mirror as if expecting an argument. "I know it, and I have paid for it. But I truly believed it at the time. It's *because* I believed it that I suffered so badly, snared by my own logic, when the second man, the supposedly better man, turned out not to be me."

"How did the stepfather come into it?" I asked. "Was he another friend of yours?"

"No!" Chief Bradley said, appalled by the suggestion. "No, he was a stranger, an outsider. She met him at her sister's house . . . I'd asked her to marry me. It was too soon, I knew it was, but I'd worked it out in my head by then that this was fate, we were meant to be together. So I proposed, and Althea asked for time to think it over. She was going to visit her sister in Mount Pleasant, and she told me she'd give me her answer when she returned. Of course I agreed—I thought it was just a formality at that point. She was gone eleven days. She was supposed to be gone for three, but she was gone eleven, and when she came back, the engagement ring she was wearing wasn't mine.

"I got angry with her, of course. I accused her of leading me on, and worse. I was not a happy or a pleasant man. And I *never* liked Horace, not even after I came to know him—after I *thought* I knew him. But when Althea told me straight out that he was the man she really needed, what argument could I raise against that?

"Snared by my own logic. It all had to make sense: but it didn't have to make sense in a way that I *liked*. And so in time—not before I'd made a complete ass out of myself in front of Althea—I was forced to accept it: Horace was the better man. If I couldn't see how, still it had to be so. Reason demanded it.

"For more than twenty-five years I made myself believe that. And then in one day, in one phone call, I found out it wasn't so, after all. Couldn't be so. A drunkard, a violent man, even a cruel man—he could still, conceivably, in some unfathomable way, be a better husband than, than . . . but a man like *that* . . . there could be no sense to it. There was no goddamned sense to it. It was like some horrible practical joke."

"So you killed him," I said.

"It was an accident," said Chief Bradley. "I just got so mad, when he denied it. I could see he was lying. And when I thought of him lying to her all those years, about what he was . . ."

"She knew what he was."

"I almost didn't tell her about him," the chief went on, not hearing me. "I shouldn't have. But Althea was so sad for so long after Horace died, that finally I couldn't help myself—I had to let her know what she was mourning. She didn't believe me, of course. She said I'd made it up, that *you* had made it up. She told me never to speak to her again. And she never, she never forgave me."

"Chief Bradley," I said.

He looked up, wet-eyed, into the rearview mirror. "What, Andrea?"

"My mother lied to you. She knew all about the stepfather. If she pretended not to believe you, it was only so no one would hold *her* responsible. But she knew."

"No." He shook his head, slowly at first, then more emphatically. "No, you are mistaken, Andrea. Your mother would never have condoned that."

"She did."

"No. I understand you being bitter, but if you're going to blame someone for not protecting you, blame me. If I'd listened to you more carefully that time—"

"You know you can't do that, Chief Bradley. You can't say you killed the stepfather by accident and then apologize for not murdering him sooner. Besides, you didn't do it for my sake—or for hers."

"Maybe not," the chief said hotly. "Maybe not. But—"

"And another thing. I can't claim to understand my mother's motivations any better than you did, but one thing I've figured out about her is that she didn't give her love to anyone who really needed it. So even if you'd gotten rid of the stepfather years earlier, it still wouldn't have gotten you what you wanted. She never would have picked you. Not if you'd killed a hundred stepfathers."

"Well . . ." Chief Bradley said. "I suppose that's a moot point, now."

"It is," I agreed. "So there's no reason to talk about it anymore. I appreciate you telling me the story, but my hand hurts, and I'd like to go to the emergency clinic now."

"Andrea . . ."

"You can drive us there if you want, or you can just unlock these doors. I'm sure Penny wouldn't mind walking."

He stared out the front windshield at the lake, both hands gripping the steering wheel. "You still haven't answered my question, Andrea," he said. "About why you came back here."

"It wasn't to hurt you, or get you in trouble," I told him. "But it's not my place to excuse what you did, either. Now if you want to tell your story to a judge, maybe—"

"A *judge?*" He laughed, a high bleak sound. "A judge . . . so you did come back to punish me."

"No, Chief Bradley."

"You know no one would believe you, if you told them. A troubled girl who's spent time in a mental institution." He shook his head. "You probably make up all kinds of stories . . . but no one would believe it, without proof."

"Then there's nothing for you to be afraid of. You can let us go."

There was a long silence. When he spoke again, his tone was regretful but resolved, and though he addressed me by name, I could tell he was really talking to himself. "I'm sorry, Andrea. I never intended to harm anyone. I only ever meant to be a good and just man . . ."

"You still can be, Chief Bradley."

". . . but I loused up almost everything. I lost my best friend, and the woman I loved . . . even the woman I didn't love. My name and reputation in this town, they are all I have left now, and if I were to lose them too, that would be the end. I can't risk that. I'm sorry, I'm very sorry, but I can't." His left hand came off the steering wheel and dropped out of view. Adam cried an urgent warning from the pulpit, but there was no need.

"I'm sorry too, Chief Bradley," I said. Then, preparing myself: "Seferis. Get us out of here."

When the moment comes, Mouse is on the verge of blacking out. Ever since Chief Bradley drove past the medical clinic without stopping, she has been trying, unsuccessfully, to melt through the floorboards of the car and escape. Unable to bend the laws of physics, she's been forced to listen with steadily mounting terror to the dialogue between Chief Bradley and Andrew. Chief Bradley's every statement—even the most self-pitying—is freighted with menace, but it's Andrew's side of the conversation that really sets her on edge. Rather than watch what he says, the way you do when someone has you at their mercy, Andrew is recklessly free-spoken, and at points seems almost to be trying to goad Chief Bradley into losing his temper. *Shut up*, Mouse wants to yell at him, *shut up*, and Maledicta, in the cave mouth, does more than just think about yelling it.

Finally they reach a critical juncture, the dialogue becoming a monologue as Chief Bradley readies himself to do something very bad. Up in the cave mouth, Maledicta is chanting "Oh fuck, oh fuck, oh fuck, oh *fuck*," and Mouse feels her grip on time begin to give, blackness looming, and she welcomes it, not wanting to be present at her own murder.

And then Andrew beside her says "I'm sorry too, Chief Bradley," in a loud clear voice that makes her turn her head. She sees him change, his posture shifting in a way that makes him seem to bulk up in his seat, as if he were physically expanding. He raises his right arm and places his elbow against his car-door window; his arm jerks, and the window bursts outward. Before Mouse can even gape at this feat, he dives through the opening.

"Andrea!" Chief Bradley bellows. From outside, Mouse hears footsteps pounding, circling the car; they reach the driver's side just as the chief gets his door open and steps out. There is a loud grunt, and sounds of a scuffle; something heavy clatters across the front hood.

Then Mouse's door is wrenched open and Andrew leans in. "Come on, Penny," he says—

—and they are outside. Andrew tugs at Mouse's arm, trying to get her to keep moving, but she hesitates, seeing Chief Bradley staggering dazed in the glow of the police car's headlights. The chief appears to stumble and drops out of sight, but just as quickly he pops back up, clutching his gun. Andrew tugs at Mouse's arm again—

—and they are crashing through dense underbrush in the dark. Invisible branches smack Mouse repeatedly in the face, but Andrew's arm is around her waist, bearing her up and carrying her along.

"Andrea!" Chief Bradley calls, blundering through the brush not far behind them. "Andrea, stop! Andrea, I *see* you—"

—and there is a flat *crack!*, like a big branch breaking—

—and Mouse and Andrew stand with their backs up against the bole of a tree. Andrew has a hand over Mouse's mouth to keep her from squeaking, which is a good thing, because Chief Bradley is *directly* in front of them, almost close enough to reach out and touch. He stands with his back to them, poised, listening; to Mouse, the sound of her own breath in her nostrils seems suddenly as loud as a jet engine.

Chief Bradley looks left, then right, then left again. It's full dark now, but this close, if he turns all the way around, he can't help but see them.

He doesn't turn around. He takes a step backwards. This brings him within arm's length, and Mouse feels Andrew tense up, preparing to push her aside and grapple the chief from behind.

Then something else moves, out in the dark; some animal. Chief Bradley fixes on the sound, starts moving towards it. The animal, whatever it is, hears him coming and bounds away; Chief Bradley gives chase. He vanishes in the gloom.

Andrew relaxes again. He removes his hand from Mouse's mouth.

Mouse slumps—

—and she is crouching in a thicket of weeds alongside a footpath that is just barely visible in the moonlight. She can hear water somewhere close by; the lake, maybe, although it sounds more like the burbling of a river or a brook. Farther off, in the opposite direction, something is crashing around in the brush again. Chief Bradley, Mouse guesses, still chasing after wildlife; he's making a lot of noise but he doesn't seem to be getting any closer.

But where is Andrew? Keeping her voice below a whisper, Mouse speaks his name. A shadow on the other side of the footpath responds with a soft "Shhhh . . ."

Andrew crawls over to her. Cupping a hand to her ear, he murmurs, "Are you hurt?"

Actually, Mouse realizes, what he said was, "Are you *hit?*" as in shot.

"I don't think so," she murmurs back.

"Good," Andrew says, and raises his head for a moment. "I think Chief Bradley's far enough away now. We're going to go along this path—stay low until it turns by the side of the brook, then stand up and start running."

"Where does the path go?" Mouse starts to ask, but Andrew puts a finger to her lips. The sound of crashing underbrush has suddenly gotten louder again.

"Move fast," Andrew whispers, and—

—Mouse *runs.*

There was a moment's sting as I dipped my hand into Hansen's Brook. Then the cold water went to work, rinsing out and anesthetizing the cuts. I knelt at an angle on the edge of the bank, gripping a branch with my other hand so that I wouldn't fall in.

We'd come about a mile up the path. It probably wasn't smart to stop here, but Penny was out of breath, and I was starting to feel dangerously lightheaded; my hand was throbbing in time with my heartbeat, and I was worried I might be losing too much blood. Before kneeling beside the brook I'd listened carefully for sounds of pursuit, and because his hearing is better than mine, I'd called Seferis back out and had him listen too. Neither of us had heard anything.

After a couple of minutes I pulled my hand out of the water. I tried to examine it, but it was too dark to make out much detail; in starlight, blood and shadow are the same color. Shivering a little, I wrapped my hand up tight again in the dishcloth.

Penny was shivering too. She hugged herself, twisting back and forth in an attempt to stay warm.

"Hey," I said softly, "how are you doing?"

"Cold," came her answer. "Scared."

"Me too," I told her. "But I think we'll be all right . . ."

"All *right?*" Penny said, and had to struggle to keep her voice low. "Andrew, the chief of police is after us. You *hit* him—I'm glad you hit him, but now if he doesn't just kill us, he'll probably put us in jail."

"No," I objected. "It isn't going to happen that way. He's the one who did wrong, not us!"

"That doesn't matter. He's the chief of police. He can *do* wrong, if he wants to."

"He *confessed.* To both of us! If we tell people—"

"They won't believe us. It's true, what he said: you're officially crazy in the state of Michigan, and I, I'm traveling with you. Both our words together won't measure up to his."

"Officer Cahill will believe us. Or at least he'll want to give me the benefit of the doubt. And when Mrs. Winslow gets here . . ."

"Mrs. Winslow?"

"Yes," I said, "she's coming here. Chief Bradley spoke to her this morning. She could be here already."

"Well even if that's helpful," Penny said, "how is she going to find us?"

"Well . . ." I had to think about that for a moment. "Well, this path we're on, it goes all the way to Quarry Lake, and from there, you know, we can get up to the cottage, and then . . ."

"Oh God," said Penny, making it clear that that was the last place she wanted to go back to.

"I know," I said, "I don't want to go there either, but . . . what else can we do? I mean you're right, if we stay out here Mrs. Winslow will never find us.

What we really need to do is sneak back into town, and from the cottage I think we have some choices how to go."

"But won't Chief Bradley find us, if we go to the cottage? He must know where this path leads to." As the thought took hold, she looked away fearfully up the path in the direction of Quarry Lake, as if expecting the chief to already have outflanked us.

She had a point: Chief Bradley was sure to be familiar with the hiking trails in the area, especially one that led up the back way to a house he coveted. But Adam, chiming in from the pulpit, argued that the chief didn't necessarily know we'd gone this way, and that even if he suspected, he would resist the conclusion as long as possible. "He *wants* to find us by the lake," Adam said, "so even if he guesses we aren't there anymore, he'll keep beating the bushes a while anyway, hoping he's wrong."

"But why . . . ?"

"Chief Bradley doesn't want to shoot us. He wants us to have an accident—something that even he can think of as an accident. The cottage doesn't have a swimming pool."

"Quarry Lake," I pointed out.

"He can't roll his car into Quarry Lake . . . Look, I'm not saying he won't go to the cottage, but we've probably got some time before he does. Don't waste it."

Penny, following her own internal discussion, had come to a similar conclusion. Saying, "Oh God, let's just get it over with," she started walking again. I went with her.

I thought of Xavier, coming along this same path six years ago. Gideon had left him a map and written instructions specifying that he was to sneak up on the cottage from behind, slip through the back gate around sunset, and bang on the kitchen door after first making sure that there were no visitors in the house. The rest of the plan, which involved threatening to expose Horace Rollins as a child molester unless he wrote out a check for ten thousand dollars, struck me as improbable on a number of levels, but the stepfather never got a chance to laugh in Xavier's face. Reaching Quarry Lake at dusk, Xavier had missed the path to the cottage and gone up the Mount Idyll trail instead. By the time he realized his error—by the time Gideon got him turned around—the sun had set completely, and if not for the almost-full moon that night, he might never have found the right way. And then it was too late: coming through the gate at last, he heard shouts from inside the cottage . . .

I stopped short; the brookside path had just come to an abrupt end, and

Quarry Lake was before us. Caught by surprise, I turned to look back the way we'd come.

"What is it?" Penny whispered, misinterpreting the gesture. "Do you hear something?"

"No," I said. "It's just . . ." Hadn't there been a forest of brambles here, only this morning? No, I thought, that was twenty years ago . . . and the evil conjurer was dead now, having met up with the wrong prince. "It's nothing," I told her, shaking my head. "Ghosts."

"Come on," Penny said. She took my hand, and led me along the lake-bank to the start of the cottage path. Then, huddling close together, we stepped into the woods.

It's pitch-black beneath the trees. They climb slowly, stopping often to make sure they have not left the path. They listen for suspicious sounds ahead, and the woods oblige them with all manner of strange noises: at one point they hear a weird scraping that reminds Mouse of a manhole cover being dragged open. They wait to see if the scraping will be repeated, but it isn't, and so they continue on.

The ground levels out, and the quality of the darkness changes, becoming less total; up ahead, Mouse sees an irregular line of shadow interrupted by a gate.

The gate is closed; it does not beckon them inside. Mouse takes this as a good sign. Still, they don't rush through it. They stand just outside, looking for monsters. After the dark of the woods, the faint moonlight shining down on the cottage's backyard is like a searchlamp; Mouse doesn't see Chief Bradley, or anything that looks like it might turn into Chief Bradley. No sound or sign of movement comes from the cottage itself, and while they can't see the front yard from here, if a car came up the drive right now, they'd know it.

Mouse, afraid to speak even in a whisper, gives a light tug on Andrew's hand to see if he's ready to proceed. He isn't; Mouse, thinking he's noticed something she hasn't, makes another scan of the backyard.

"It's the fucking toolshed," Maledicta advises, from the cave mouth. "He's petrified of it."

The toolshed: Chief Bradley *could* be hiding behind it, or inside it, but Mouse doesn't think so; this close, listening this hard, she thinks she'd hear him. Andrew has more experience here, though. Still holding his hand, she makes a sideways gesture: does he want to avoid the backyard entirely, and go around?

He hesitates long enough that she knows he is tempted, but finally he shakes his head. If they go around, they will probably blunder into a thorn-bush; and they will make noise. Bracing himself, Andrew reaches out; he lifts the latch and pulls the gate open.

The latch clanks. The gate hinges shriek.

Nothing jumps out at them.

"All right," Andrew whispers, "straight through here, on tiptoe around the side of the cottage, and as soon as we see there's no one in the front yard we start running. Adam says there's another footpath that starts about two hundred yards down the road; it should take us most of the way back to town."

They pass through the gate, Andrew jigging sideways to give the tool-shed a wide berth, pivoting to keep it in sight. Chief Bradley is not hiding behind it, and he does not come bursting out from inside. They cross the backyard without incident.

Then, as they reach the rear of the cottage and start to go round the side, Mouse is suddenly wary. She senses that something is wrong, something is *different*, but she can't figure out what it is until her foot strikes a hard object, and then it comes to her.

The bracing planks: they have all been taken down again. The telephone pole is still in place, but the planks that Gideon rearranged this afternoon have been pulled down and laid flat on the ground. Mouse is tripping over one of them.

She hits the ground and a flashlight comes on, pinning both her and Andrew in its beam. Mouse looks up into it and is blinded.

From behind the blinding light, Chief Bradley's voice: "Stop right there, Andrea."

And Andrew's voice, once more unbelievably calm, answering: "Hello, Chief Bradley."

Chief Bradley's right hand moves into the light beam, holding the gun, pointing it. "*Right* there, Andrea," he says. "Now listen carefully. You and your friend are going to turn around, and you're going to walk slowly to the back door of the cottage. And then we're all going to go inside."

"Why?" says Andrew. "So we can have an accident?"

"Andrea . . ."

"I'm surprised you're willing to sacrifice the cottage. But I guess Adam was right, you have no choice: there's no swimming pool."

"Andrea, I'm serious." Chief Bradley's thumb cocks the hammer of the gun back. Mouse, hearing the click, lets out a squeak and starts to crawl backwards. The gun's aim shifts, Chief Bradley saying: "Don't."

Andrew sidesteps, interposing himself between Mouse and the gun. "Do you think my mother would be impressed by this?" he says. "Do you think it would make her fall in love with you?"

"Andrea, goddamnit . . ."

"You're being very selfish, Chief Bradley," Andrew says. "I'm sorry you didn't get what you wanted; I'm sorry too you're afraid to face the consequences of the things you've done. But if you put that gun down, then whatever else happens, you'll have the consolation of knowing that you made at least one right decision . . ."

"Andrea . . ." Chief Bradley's tone is unreadable. He might be wavering, or he might be preparing to pull the trigger.

"But if you won't put the gun down," Andrew continues, "if you aren't going to let us go, then I'm not going to help you pretend that you aren't doing a *really* bad thing. You're going to have to shoot me; and when you do, I'm going to scream my mother's name, so that for the rest of your life, whenever you think of her, you're going to remember this moment, remember *choosing* to do what you know is wrong . . ."

"Andrea . . . Andrea, goddamnit . . ."

"Althea," Andrew says. "Althea. *Beloved* Althea . . ."

"God*damn*it . . ." The chief's voice cracks, and Mouse claps her hands to her head, anticipating the shot, but even as she goes to bury her face in the grass, she sees the light move.

Chief Bradley has lowered his arms. The gun and the flashlight are pointed at the ground now, and the chief's shoulders are shaking. He is sobbing: Mouse sees Chief Bradley's tears gleaming on his cheeks.

Gleaming . . . but it isn't the moon or the stars, or the reflected light of the flash, that makes his tears shine like that. A new glow fills the air, and with it a new sound: the roar of an engine.

A car is coming. Chief Bradley realizes it at the same time Mouse does. He turns towards the front yard, even as headlights sweep around the last curve in the road.

There is a squeal of brakes: the car is coming too fast, the driver not expecting the cottage so soon. The light damps down again, and then goes out completely, as the new car slams into the back of Chief Bradley's cruiser. The cruiser leaps forward in chain reaction, and smashes into the front of the cottage.

The whole cottage shudders with the shock of the impact. Timbers groan and windows shatter; there is a shriek of tearing wood.

And Mouse, rearing up, feels Andrew's hand on her shoulder, dragging her backwards out of harm's way. Chief Bradley tries to get clear too, but his heel catches on one of the bracing planks, and with no one to steady him he stumbles over backwards.

"Oh hell," Chief Bradley says, flinging his arms up over his face.

The cottage falls on him.

III

ORDER

LAST BOOK:
EPILOGUE

29

Later that night, after the rescue team had dug him out from under the cottage, Chief Bradley confessed.

He wasn't too badly hurt, though that wasn't obvious at first. He'd broken his arm and a few ribs, and a four-inch wooden splinter had pierced the shoulder of his broken arm; he was bruised and in shock. The doctor who examined him at the Seven Lakes clinic didn't find any evidence of a head injury or damage to his internal organs, but just to be safe, it was decided to transfer him to a hospital in Muskegon. Officer Jimmy Cahill rode along in the ambulance, and on the way asked Chief Bradley questions about some disturbing things we had told him. Chief Bradley, his tongue loosened by painkillers (and maybe by the fear of dying with a guilty conscience), told Officer Cahill everything: what he had done to Horace Rollins, and what he had thought of doing to us.

Then the next day, when the painkillers wore off and it became clear that he wasn't going to die of a broken arm, he recanted his confession. He told the detectives who came to see him that he had been confused the night before, and that Officer Cahill had twisted his words. He said that he was the victim of a conspiracy, orchestrated by a mentally disturbed young woman who for some reason had decided to blame him for her stepfather's accidental death. He suggested that Officer Cahill's affection for this mentally disturbed young woman was being used to manipulate him.

Things might have gone badly from there, but at this point, Mrs. Winslow intervened. Hobbling on crutches—she'd broken her foot when her airport rental car rammed into the back of Chief Bradley's police cruiser—she paid a visit to the chief in his hospital room. She was alone with him for more than an hour. What passed between them remains their secret, but when they were done, Chief Bradley called the detectives back in, admitted he'd been lying, and reaffirmed his original confession.

That wasn't quite the end of it. We still had to stay in Michigan while an official inquiry was held. We spent most of the time at a motel in Muskegon, keeping our fingers crossed that Dr. Kroft wouldn't show up with a team of men in white coats. But neither he nor anyone else from the state psychiatric bureau ever appeared, and finally we were told we were free to go home.

On the same day that Chief Bradley was due to be officially charged with the killing of Horace Rollins, we took a last drive up to Seven Lakes. Officer Cahill—who'd been temporarily appointed acting chief of police—was waiting for us on the Gage property with a demolition crew.

The cottage had only partially collapsed, which was one reason why Chief Bradley hadn't been more badly hurt. One wall had come down, and about half of the roof, but the majority of the structure, its frame still propped by that telephone pole, remained intact. It probably wouldn't have lasted much longer in any event, but Officer Cahill had decided to declare it a public-safety hazard and bulldoze it into the ground; and he'd invited us to come watch.

"Does anyone want to say anything?" Officer Cahill asked, when we were all gathered in the front yard. He looked at Andrew, who seemed lost in thought, and Andrew roused himself and said, "No, I don't want to say anything, but . . . give me a minute, OK?" Officer Cahill nodded, and Andrew faced the cottage, his expression going through a whole series of changes as a parade of souls came forward for a final look at the place. I recognized some of them—Aaron, Jake, Samantha, Seferis—but there were others I don't think I'd met before.

Then Andrew was back, and he turned to Officer Cahill and said, "Go ahead." Officer Cahill signaled the bulldozer.

The cottage was down in just a few minutes, but Officer Cahill had the bulldozer operator drive back and forth over the wreckage for a while, mashing it flat. Finally Officer Cahill turned to Andrew again and said, "Enough?" Andrew nodded.

Officer Cahill gave another signal, and the bulldozer rolled off into the backyard. Meanwhile Andrew's face changed again, taking on a mischievous expression: Adam. He walked up to where the cottage's front door had been, and took out a salt shaker that he'd stolen from Winchell's Diner that morning. He unscrewed the top, poured the salt into his hand, and sowed it over the ruins.

When Adam was done he tossed the shaker away and gave the body to

Aunt Sam. Sam went over to Officer Cahill, surprising him by giving him a big kiss on the cheek, and surprising him again by saying: "You're still a bastard, Jimmy, but thank you for this." Then Sam gave way to Andrew, who stepped back red-faced and muttered, "Sorry."

"It's OK," Officer Cahill said, "I understand. Or actually, I don't, but . . . I'll live."

There was one more crash as the bulldozer knocked down the toolshed. The bulldozer operator leaned out of his cab and called to Officer Cahill: "Anything else?"

"No," the officer told him. "No, that's good!"

And then Andrew, looking tired, turned to me and said: "What do you think, Penny? Are you ready to go home now?"

"Yes," I said. "I'm ready. Let's go home."

30

Surprised?

I couldn't resist including that, but at the same time, I don't want you to get the wrong idea; Penny did not undergo any sort of miraculous transformation as a result of our adventures. It would take almost a year of weekly therapy with Dr. Eddington before she came to honestly regard herself as Penny rather than Mouse, and another year and a half for her case to reach its final disposition. As part of her therapy, Penny would eventually read through Thread's electronic diaries—the same diaries I have drawn on in recounting her side of this story—and rewrite portions of them in the first person; but that came very late in the course of her treatment. In the nearer term, the fact that she was now in direct communication with her other selves did represent a major breakthrough, but it was only the first step in a lengthy process.

So we went home to Washington and resumed the course of our lives there, a return to order that went much more smoothly than I, at least, had any right to expect. Not only did we still have our jobs at the Reality Factory, but Julie, in an incredible act of generosity, insisted on paying us full wages for the time we'd been away. "Medical leave," she said. "All the best companies offer it."

Julie. One of the first things I did after getting back to Autumn Creek was write Julie a long letter of apology, which I delivered to her in person. After she read it, we went out to dinner (by unspoken agreement, we chose a restaurant with no liquor license) and had a long heart-to-heart talk. I won't claim that we worked out all our issues, but by the end of the evening I felt like we'd repaired most of the damage to our friendship.

Of course, Julie being Julie (and—let's be fair—me being me), there were always new challenges. My second week back I started my own course of therapy with Dr. Eddington. My appointments were on Friday afternoons at four. Penny drove me; we'd leave the Reality Factory around three and head into the city. Coming back I'd take the bus sometimes, but most often Penny would drive me home, too—or Maledicta would drive Aunt Sam, if they'd both been good. Penny's own sessions with Dr. Eddington were on Wednesdays, and I took to riding along on those, as well; I'd let Adam, Jake, and the others explore Fremont while Penny was with the doctor, and afterwards, depending on Penny's mood, we'd go see a movie, or take a walk along Lake Union, or—if the session had been an especially bad one—just sit in Gas Works Park and talk.

All of which was nice, but it did mean that we were both leaving work early twice a week. At first Julie was perfectly fine about this—anything to keep us from running off to Michigan again—but by midsummer she began to grouse about the lost work hours, saying it was "hurting productivity." I don't think it was hurting productivity; I think Julie was just jealous of all the time Penny and I were spending together. Penny got her therapy sessions rescheduled to Friday, directly after mine, to cut down on the lost worktime, but Julie continued to complain anyway, and I surprised myself by not caring all that much.

As it turned out, the Reality Factory's days were numbered. In September, a big venture capital deal that Julie had been working on for months fell through. She called a meeting and informed us that unless she could find a new source of funding, the Factory would soon be bankrupt. Then Dennis dropped his own bombshell: bankruptcy or no bankruptcy, he said, he had decided to move back to Alaska.

"What are you talking about?" said Julie. "You can't just *leave!* How are we supposed to finish the project without—"

"Come on, Grand Poobah," Dennis said, fanning himself with his open shirtfront. "You know as well as I do that it's never gonna be finished. I'm sick of it."

Penny and I slipped out during the ensuing bloodbath. Irwin was right behind us. "I'm *not* going back to Alaska," he announced fiercely, and fell to silent brooding until Julie came to tell us it was all over: we were out of business.

By the middle of October, Dennis had gone. Irwin, true to his word, and much to his brother's surprise, chose to remain in Washington, though he left Autumn Creek. He moved to Renton, and got a job with a fantasy card-game company that was headquartered there; Jake was pretty envious when he heard.

Penny and I both landed jobs at Bit Warehouse. Yes, that same one. I know what you're thinking, but it turned out Adam's joke was true: enough time had passed for them to forget about my "drug problem." Actually, high employee turnover had produced a conveniently selective memory loss. Mr. Weeks was long gone, as were all my father's closest coworkers. But my father's mostly positive work record was still on file, so I had very little trouble getting rehired, as a cashier rather than a restocker this time. Penny went to work in the Technical Services Department, fixing and upgrading computers.

As for Julie, I'm not altogether sure what she did for work in the months following the Reality Factory's closure. I know she did a number of odd jobs for her uncle, and she spent a lot of time in Seattle, probably temping. But she didn't like to talk about it. Much of her time was taken up by a lawsuit: when she tried to break the lease on the Factory lot, the landlord sued her for unpaid rent and for her failure to complete the promised improvements to the property. The case was eventually settled out of court, with Julie paying the landlord a couple thousand dollars (don't ask me where she got it) and letting him keep all the gear inside the shed, or at least that portion of it that hadn't already been seized by the Factory's other creditors. The computer equipment was sold for cash, and the Honey Bucket, I hope, was taken out and burned, but as far as I know the tents are still there, gathering dust and mildew and waiting for the next visionary entrepreneur to come along.

One day near the end of the following summer, Julie took me out to lunch and announced that she too would be leaving Autumn Creek. "And you'll never guess where I'm going: Alaska."

"Alaska?" I said. "What, are you planning to track down Dennis and get even with him?"

"No, I've already forgotten all about Dennis . . . I mean, OK, if I do come across him, and if he happens to be standing at the edge of a cliff with his back turned to me, who knows, but no, I'm not *planning* to kill him." What she was planning to do, she said, was get work aboard a fish processor, which is a kind of big factory ship that goes to sea for months at a time, catching thousands of pounds of cod and haddock and processing them right on board into frozen fillets and fish sticks. From Julie's description, it sounded like the worst job in the world—sixteen-hour shifts, hazardous work conditions, crews composed largely of male ex-convicts, etc.—but Julie insisted that, if she survived, it would be well worth it: "They pay you a percentage of the proceeds, which if the catch is big can be a huge amount of money."

"What if the catch isn't so big?"

"Well, that's why you've got to pick the right ship . . . don't worry, it'll work out. I'll spend a few months in hell, make my fortune, and then I'll come back here and we'll start a new company."

She had a couple of going-away presents for me, even though she was the one who was leaving. The first was her Cadillac. "I can't take it with me," she said. "It wouldn't survive the drive up, and even if it did, three months in an Anchorage parking garage would kill it for sure."

"Well I'll be happy to watch it for you, Julie, but you know I still don't have a driver's license."

"You'll get one," Julie said. "*Penny* tells me you're a really good driver . . ."

Which brought us to her other going-away gift. Julie's apartment lease ran through next February, and after all the hassle over the Reality Factory's lease she didn't want to risk breaking it. So she'd arranged to sublet the place to Penny, whose current apartment in Queen Anne rented on a month-to-month basis. "Lose one neighbor, gain another," Julie said. "Now I know you won't be lonely."

I had no objection—I thought it would be great to have Penny living in Autumn Creek—but I said: "It's still not going to happen, Julie."

"What's not going to happen?"

"You know perfectly well what. You're matchmaking again. But Penny and I are just friends."

"Matchmaking? Me?" She smiled the fake-innocent smile I knew so well. "You're imagining things, Andrew. Still . . . the two of you *would* make a cute couple . . ."

She left for Alaska in September. In December I received a letter from her saying that the fish-processing job hadn't panned out, and she was working a concession stand at the Anchorage Zoo. "Big joke, really. We're only open during daylight hours—ten to four this time of year—and half the exhibits are hibernating right now. Still it's a living. P.S. I need you to sell my car and send me the money."

I sold the Cadillac, for a sum far smaller than Julie had once hoped to realize, and sent her a cashier's check padded with a little extra money from my own savings. Since then I have received occasional letters and e-mails from her, providing sketchy details of her life in various Alaskan cities and towns—she seems to be moving closer to the North Pole as time goes on. Her last postcard read: "Wedding plans canceled. I am in Fairbanks taking flying lessons & by spring should be a licensed bush pilot. XXX, Julie."

That was seven months ago. I haven't heard another word since, though I would be willing to bet that Julie has not, in fact, become a bush pilot. Beyond that, your guess is as good as mine. I hope that whatever she is doing, she is happy. I still love her, of course, and while I accept now that it was not meant to be, I will never wish her anything other than the best.

And no, I have no idea what wedding plans she was referring to.

If this were a made-up story, Julie's matchmaking efforts would ultimately have succeeded: Penny and I would have fallen in love and lived happily ever after. Reality has (so far) fallen well short of that, though not as short of it as I would once have predicted.

For a long while after we came back from Michigan, we really were just friends, albeit several times over: I was friends with Penny, and Aunt Sam was friends with Maledicta; Adam was friends—poker buddies—with Malefica; and Jake, strangest of all, was friends with Loins, who had an unexpected soft spot for *The Little Mermaid* and other Disney videos. We discovered other affinities between our households as well, though there weren't enough hours in the day to cultivate them all.

After Julie left Autumn Creek and Penny moved into her apartment, our friendship(s) naturally intensified. Penny was already driving me to and from work every day. Now we started having breakfast together too (sometimes she'd come over to Mrs. Winslow's, sometimes we'd go out to the Harvest Moon Diner), and spending a lot of our evenings and weekends together, I mean even more than we had before.

At first I thought it would feel strange, hanging out with Penny in Julie's old apartment. But Penny completely redecorated: she threw out all the furniture Julie had left behind, repainted the rooms, and got the landlord's permission to put new tile on the bathroom floor and new linoleum in the kitchen; she strung lights in the outside staircase, and finally replaced the knob on the downstairs door. By the time she was done, it looked like a whole new place, and though I still experienced occasional flashes of déjà vu—most often going up or down the stairs—it wasn't anything like what I'd been expecting.

It wasn't just the new paint job and furnishings that made the difference, of course; it was Penny herself. Although our friendship had its rough spots, Penny never mystified me the way Julie had. If there was something about her behavior that I didn't understand, I could ask her to explain it to me, and her explanations made sense. If she got mad at me it was usually for a good reason; an apology meant that a fight was over, rather than signaling a new phase of discord. Most of all, I never had the feeling, so common with Julie, that I was dealing with someone whose perspective on reality was bent ninety degrees from my own. Penny and I might reach different conclusions sometimes, but we saw the same things. We got each other.

"This is too easy," Adam complained one time after Penny and I had, without rancor, agreed to disagree about something. "Where's the passive-aggressive behavior? Where are the mixed signals and the hidden messages? Where's the pain?"

"You can keep all that," I told him. "I *like* this."

Penny seemed to like it too, and so I guess it's not all that surprising, given how close we became, that we would eventually explore the possibility of moving beyond friendship. It started one night in February of 1999, when in honor of my birthday we went into the city to attend a Lyle Lovett concert. It was snowing when the show let out, and Penny and I decided to go for a ride on the Seattle monorail and watch the snow fall. Somehow during the ride we ended up kissing. That's all we did that night, kiss, but from then on things were different between us, and later—not very much later—we did other stuff.

We did stuff, and it was fun, but it also caused problems with the other souls in our households, some of whom weren't happy with this new development. More crucially, a couple of the more intimate things we did dredged up memories about Penny's mother, very dark memories that Penny had, until then, been successfully avoiding. In March she started having blackouts again, her first in more than a year. In April she disappeared for three whole days, and woke up in the basement of the Charter Hotel in Spokane. After that incident, we decided to go back to being just friends, at least until Penny worked through a few issues.

She began going to therapy two and then three times a week. I saw less of her, which was hard; but when I did see her, I could still ask questions, so I always knew where we stood. And she was getting better: as though a last barrier had been knocked down, her therapy progressed with great rapidity, until by midsummer she was talking about a final resolution.

But before she could conclude her treatment, Penny had a decision to make; and her choice, when it came, left me stunned.

"Reintegration?" I said, not sure I'd heard right. "Penny, that's . . ."

". . . a shock, I know," she said.

Crazy, I was going to say; like opting for a lobotomy. I tried for a more tactful phrasing: "Reintegration doesn't work, Penny. It doesn't work, and if it did, it'd be like dying. You wouldn't be *you* anymore."

She bit her lip, unhappy that I was reacting this way. "Dr. Eddington thinks it could work," she told me. "He thinks—"

"He's wrong," I interrupted her. "If Dr. Grey were here—"

"Dr. Grey never said reintegration couldn't work, Andrew. I've read her book: she said reintegration was optional, not impossible."

"It's a *bad* option," I insisted. "What about the others? They can't all agree to this."

"They do," said Penny. "At least, none of them disagrees. And anyway it's my decision. I don't want to go on living my life as a time-share; I want to be one person. You can understand that, can't you?"

I could understand it. I just couldn't accept it. I continued to argue against the idea, and the next time I saw Dr. Eddington, I really lit into him.

"You know I can't discuss Penny's therapy with you, Andrew," he said. "If you feel this raises a question with regard to your own treatment . . ."

"My treatment? It's got nothing to do with me. *I'm* never going to reintegrate."

"Which I believe is the right decision—for you. But you aren't Penny." He sighed. "Look, Andrew . . . I know you think you and Penny have a lot in common, but there are some important differences between your two cases. With Penny, the basic personality split, as profound as it seems, just isn't as severe: the original Penny Driver still exists, and still *wants* to exist. Now"—he held up a hand—"that doesn't guarantee that reintegration will work, but it means there's a chance. And since this is what Penny wants, I would hope that you, as her friend, would choose to be supportive."

I did *try* to be supportive, but Penny and I still argued regularly about her decision to reintegrate. My father, usually a good peacemaker, was no help either—he was even more opposed to Penny's decision than I was. But nothing we said or did could get her to reconsider.

In August, Penny left for a monthlong retreat at The Orpheus Center in Port Townsend, a sort of multiples' halfway house that specialized in reintegration. She went without saying good-bye (we'd fought the night before), though she did leave a note and the key to her apartment. For the next four weeks, I dutifully collected her mail, all the while wondering if the person I was collecting it for would still exist when September rolled around.

The day she came back, I was in Fremont for my own weekly therapy session; when our fifty minutes were up, Dr. Eddington asked if I'd like to go say hi to an old friend. Penny was waiting for us at a café a few blocks from the doctor's office. She was sitting at an outside table, and I was relieved to see I could still recognize her without help. Her hair was longer—she'd been growing it out all summer, and now it had finally reached her shoulders—but other than that she looked like the same Penny.

Her body language confused me, though. As we approached, she was smoking a cigarette, ordinarily a sign that Maledicta had control. But when she looked up and saw us coming, her reaction—the look on her face, the slightly tentative way she waved hello—said "Penny" to me . . . and then, without changing expression, she took a last draw on the cigarette and stubbed it out with an impatient gesture that was pure Maledicta.

I spent the first few minutes of our reunion imitating a fencepost. I think I did manage to say hi, but after that, Dr. Eddington had to handle the opening round of small talk on his own. He didn't stay long; after getting me settled in a chair and verifying that I wasn't actually catatonic, he excused himself, saying that he'd be in his office for a while yet if either of us needed him.

In the silence that followed his departure, Penny reached for the pack of Winstons on the table in front of her. I watched her knock out a cigarette and light it, her hand gestures once again suggesting Maledicta. But after taking her first puff, she exhaled over her shoulder rather than directly at me, and when the smoke started to drift back over the table, she waved it away.

"I'm sorry," I said finally, lowering my eyes. "I don't mean to stare . . ."

"No, it's OK," said Penny. Her voice seemed fuller, or at least louder; and also—but this had to be my imagination working overtime—I thought I detected a trace of harmony. "I know this must be weird for you. It is for me too, still, and I've had some time to get used to it."

"What's it like?" I asked.

"Hard to describe." She laughed, a laugh I associated with Loins. "Like this . . ."—she held up her cigarette—"I don't actually *enjoy* smoking, but at the same time, I really do. I mean, I want to quit, but I don't."

"Maledicta and the others," I said. "Are they . . . ?"

"Still alive?" Penny nodded. "It isn't like I thought it would be—they, we, we're all still here, just, less separate than we used to be. We don't have to occupy the body one at a time now; we coexist in it."

"*Co*exist? So you're still multiple?"

"Yes and no." She laughed again. "This is the hardest part to put into words. It's like, right now, I'm looking at you, and I'm seeing you, feeling about you, the way Penny does, and at the same time, I'm seeing you and feeling about you the way Maledicta does. And I can sort out, if I want to, the Penny-feelings from the Maledicta-feelings, but I can also just let them flow together . . ."

"And the others, too? All of them?"

"Everybody at once is hard. I *can* bring them all up at the same time, but it gets confusing."

"And that's . . . this is better, you think, than the way things used to be?"

"Yes." Having finished her cigarette, Penny started to draw another from the pack, then shook her head and shoved it back. "Yes, it's better—*most* of the time. The doctors at Orpheus, they said it would get easier with practice, that as we shared more experiences we'd start to mesh better. I'm not sure if that's really true, though, or if the doctors just thought it ought to be true. I guess I'll find out."

"Well," I said. "As long as you're happy . . ."

"We're . . . content," said Penny. "I'm sorry if I don't explain it very well. But that reminds me: I have something for you." She brought out a small gift-wrapped package. "I meant to give you this before I went to Orpheus, but, well . . ."

I was suddenly uneasy, for no reason I could put my finger on, but I took the package from her and opened it. Inside was a gold-colored CD with "Thread.doc" written on it in Magic Marker.

"It's a copy of my Thread diaries," Penny said.

"What are you giving it to me for?"

"To read . . . if you want. It's to help you understand why I felt I had to do this. And also—"

"Oh, Penny," I said, "you don't owe me any explanations. I'm sorry if I—"

"No, Andrew, I want you to understand. And there's more: there are things in there about you, from when we first met . . . well, it's not *all* flattering, but I wanted you to know, to have a record, of how important you've been to me."

I got it then, what was troubling me: this was a going-away present. "Penny," I said. "You are coming back to Autumn Creek, right?"

She bit her lip. "For a while," she said.

"A while," I said. "And then what? You're moving away? This . . . this isn't because of the way I was acting, is it? You're not—"

"No! No, Andrew, this is something I have to do for me, kind of the last step in my therapy: starting over in a new place, as a new me."

"What new place?"

"California," she said. "I'm not sure what city yet, but . . . maybe San Diego. One of the other residents at Orpheus had some really good things to say about it."

San Diego: southernmost California, over a thousand miles from Seattle. I felt hollow. "When would you go?"

"I was thinking after Thanksgiving."

"Three months." My voice got husky, and my eyelids started blinking. "Wow . . . wow."

"Andrew?" Penny said. "You are going to be OK, aren't you?"

I wanted to say no, but after all the grief I'd given her over the reintegration, I thought I'd pretty much used up my selfishness quota for the year. "It'll be . . . hard," I told her. "But if this is what you need to do . . ."

She reached out and took my hand, and that gesture, the feel of her small palm in mine, was all Penny. "It's still three months," she said. "We'll spend lots of time together until then. And I will come back to visit."

"Good," I said, tears tracking down both cheeks now. "OK, that's good . . ."

Penny drove me back to Autumn Creek that night, and from then on until she left, we spent pretty much every free moment we had together—but of course, it wasn't enough. To make three months go by faster, you'd have to lose time.

It *was* long enough for me to get a better sense of how Penny's reintegration had changed her, although in trying to describe it I find myself drawn to the same contradictory locutions that she used: Penny was different, but she also wasn't. I eventually got used to the "new" Penny, the one who exhibited characteristics of as many as half a dozen souls simultaneously, but she wasn't always like that: there were times, most often in moments of stress or great emotion, but occasionally in calmer moments too, when a single soul seemed to predominate, so that I would have sworn I was in the presence of Maledicta—the "old" Maledicta—or Loins, or Duncan. Or Mouse. I said nothing about this—if they were content, I wasn't going to spoil it for them—but I did take comfort in the thought that reintegration wasn't so scary after all. My best friend, all of her, still existed.

And then it was the end of November. We said good-bye in the parking lot of the Harvest Moon Diner, following a last breakfast together. It was a drawn-out farewell, with pretty much everyone insisting on coming out to wish Penny a safe trip, and I got worried she wouldn't have anything left for me. But she did. We hugged each other a very long time, and then Penny got in the car.

"You'd better write," I told her, hanging on the driver's door. "And call."

"I will," Penny promised. She drew my head down and kissed me on the lips. "Sweet thing," she said, and winked. "Don't take any shit from anybody." Then, with one hand on the steering wheel and the other reaching over to thumb the button on the cigarette lighter, she drove away.

• • •

A month later, I stayed up with Mrs. Winslow to welcome in the year 2000. We moved my TV out to the kitchen so we could watch the fireworks in color, and when midnight came we opened a bottle of nonalcoholic sparkling grape juice. I was happier than I'd been for a long while, but my happiness was still tinged with a melancholy I couldn't conceal.

"You miss her, don't you?" Mrs. Winslow said.

"Every day." Then, not wanting to spoil the evening: "It's OK, though. I still have you."

"Well . . . it's funny you should mention that . . ."

"Why funny?" I said. "You're not . . . oh my God, Mrs. Winslow! You're not *dying*, are you?"

She laughed. "No, not dying. Just the opposite, I hope. I don't suppose you've noticed, but lately I haven't been waiting on the mail as much."

I had noticed, actually—or Adam had. For the past several weeks, after seeing me off on my way to work in the morning, Mrs. Winslow had been going back inside the Victorian instead of taking up sentry on the porch. "But I thought, I don't know, maybe you were just cold . . ."

"My creaky old bones not able to handle the winter anymore?" She smiled. "I'm not that old yet—but I will be. This spring will be fifteen years since Jacob and the boys died; almost a decade since the last note came. It's time I moved on."

Oh no, I thought, *not you too.* "That's great!" I said. "That's wonderful!"

"You're a lousy liar, Andrew," Mrs. Winslow said, not unkindly. "I *know* this is going to be hard for you, and if I thought it was more than you could handle . . . but it isn't. You've had some difficult times this past year, but you've held up well. I think you're ready to go on without me."

"Sure," I said, not sure at all.

"Good. Because I'm going to need your help."

"Sure," I said, more certainly. "Anything. What do you need me to do?"

"I should probably make a clean break with the past, but I don't think I'm strong enough to do that—not all at once. So if I do leave this house, I'm going to want somebody I can trust to stay behind and keep an eye on the mailbox for me. Just in case. It wouldn't be forever. A year at most—if I didn't come back—and then I'll be ready to let it go for good."

"I can do that. I mean, it'll save me having to look for a new apartment, so that works fine."

"You'd have the run of the whole house, too," Mrs. Winslow said. "And of course I wouldn't charge you rent anymore."

"Oh no, Mrs. Winslow, you don't have to do that."

"It's all right, Andrew. I'd prefer you put the money into savings, and start thinking about what *you* want to do next. As I say, this won't be forever—in a year, maybe two, I'll want to sell this house."

"All right then," I said. "I'll keep it for you until you're ready to get rid of it."

Like Julie, Mrs. Winslow also left me her car, but it was a true gift and not just a temporary loan. She insisted I get a license, too, so when she left town on the first day in May, I was able to drive her to the airport. She was headed to Galveston, Texas; she had people there, old college friends who'd been trying to get her to move down for years. "Mostly it's to get me moving *some-where*," Mrs. Winslow said. "If I don't like Texas, there are other places."

After Mrs. Winslow's plane took off, I got back in the car and went for a very long, aimless drive around Puget Sound. It was well after dark by the time I returned to Autumn Creek. My plan had been to go straight to bed, so I wouldn't have to think about how empty the Victorian was, but I couldn't get to sleep. I went into the kitchen and made both tea and warm milk. I fixed the tea the way Mrs. Winslow liked it, and set the mug at her place at the table. Then I sat in my own seat, drank warm milk, and cried.

I survived the night, though. And in the morning I made my own breakfast. Adam's bacon strip was a little crispy, and my scrambled eggs had too much salt, but I knew that I'd get better with practice.

A week later I got a letter from Mrs. Winslow. Galveston was very hot, but she'd found a nice place, an air-conditioned bungalow right on the beach by the Gulf of Mexico. "Swam all afternoon yesterday," she wrote, "& last night, for the first time in memory, I slept until dawn . . . I believe I may stay here awhile." And so she has.

Which just leaves me to account for.

It is now the middle of June, 2001. I am thirty-two years old—or six years old, depending on how you want to count it. I still live in the Victorian in Autumn Creek; I have spread out a bit since Mrs. Winslow left—the kitchen is more cluttered than she would ever have tolerated—but I have refrained from taking over any of the upstairs rooms. In my mind that is still Mrs. Winslow's domain, and besides, with more space comes the temptation to get more stuff, and I am trying to save money.

I still get up every day at the same time, and still go through the same morning ritual. I drive myself to and from my job at Bit Warehouse, and in the evenings, if I'm not out somewhere with friends from work, I come home and dole out time to those souls who want it (contingent, as always, on good behavior).

My therapy with Dr. Eddington concluded—successfully, we both think—late last year. I still see him about once a month for the mental-health equivalent of a check-up, but these sessions are extremely informal: usually we'll meet at his office and then go out to eat somewhere. Last time we got together we took the ferry to Bainbridge Island for Sunday brunch at the Streamliner Diner, and then went up to Poulsbo to put flowers on Dr. Grey's grave. We also stopped in to see Meredith; she's living in a new house, with a new partner. She seems happy.

Inside Andy Gage's head, there have of course been some changes. I am in charge of the house now; I still go to my father for advice, but the final say on all official matters is mine. I sit at the head of the table during house meetings. I handle house discipline. It isn't always easy, but on balance I would say the responsibility has been good for me.

The house is emptier than it once was. Over the course of my therapy, I absorbed all but a handful of the Witnesses, making their memories my own, and in the process learning more than I ever wanted to about Horace Rollins and Althea Gage. Like taking charge of the house, this was hard but ultimately beneficial; if I am somewhat less carefree than I used to be, I am also more mature, closer to my nominal age. And for better or worse, I know my own history.

Perhaps the most surprising change is that Gideon now has the run of the geography. After what happened in Seven Lakes, my father wanted to send him to the pumpkin field; one of my first acts as new head of the household was to issue a stay of execution. I did keep Gideon confined to Coventry for several months, but after talking it over with Dr. Eddington, I decided I wanted to take another shot at socializing him. I reopened the escape tunnel between Coventry and the house basement, and later on, after I'd cleaned out some of the junk down there, turned the basement itself into a sort of guest bedroom for Gideon to stay in when he wanted to.

This attempt at rehabilitation has proved a mixed success. Gideon remains the single most disruptive force in the house. On his worst days, he continues to deny that the rest of us are real; on his best days, he is still a huge pain, constantly making trouble. He and my father refuse to speak to one another at all; on the rare occasions when Gideon attends house meetings, the two of them will only communicate through third parties.

It can be very difficult sometimes, but Gideon has made no further attempts to seize control of the body. I doubt I will ever be able to trust him enough to allow him out voluntarily, but the fact that I have "reintegrated" him into the household even this much is a source of some pride to me; and as good a proof as any that the house is, finally, in order.

Three letters came this week.

The first was from Mrs. Winslow, letting me know that she was finally ready to sell the Victorian. "It won't happen right away," she hastened to make clear. "My plan would be to come back to A. Creek around Labor Day, look the house over & see what repairs need to be made, contact a realtor, pack up my remaining things, &c. With the downturn in the economy it will probably not sell quickly, in fact I probably should not try to sell it right now at all—but that becomes a temptation to keep hanging on forever . . . in any case, you still have plenty of time to decide where you are going next."

The second letter was from Gordon Bradley, the now ex–police chief of Seven Lakes, Michigan. No, he did not write to me from prison; despite his confession, Chief Bradley never served a day in jail for the murder of Horace Rollins. He'd been allowed to plead guilty to involuntary manslaughter, and was sentenced to eighteen months' probation. As for what he'd tried to do to me and Penny, that was written off as temporary insanity and/or a huge misunderstanding, and he was never even charged.

I knew he was a free man, but I was still surprised to get a letter from him. After a largely incoherent opening paragraph—which, I eventually figured out, was an attempt to apologize for almost drowning me in Two Seasons Lake—Chief Bradley said that he'd heard from Oscar Reyes that I had finally established my ownership of the old Gage property. (This is true. A year ago, as a peace offering to Gideon, I contacted Oscar Reyes—who else?—and asked if it was still possible for me to inherit Althea Gage's land. He arranged it for a small fee.) "While I can well understand that you might not want to deal with me," Chief Bradley went on to say, "I am still interested in purchasing the property. Please let Oscar know if you would be willing to hear my offer."

Adam suggested I write back and tell Chief Bradley I'd sell the property to anybody *but* him, but the truth is, even after what happened, I don't feel

especially vindictive towards him. I don't know what I feel towards him,
frankly. I think what I am going to do is ask Oscar Reyes to sell the property
for the best price he can get, and just not tell me who the buyer is. If Chief
Bradley really wants to pay to own the ruins of my mother's house, so be it.

The third letter I got this week, actually an e-mail, was from Penny in
San Diego.

Subject: July 15th OK?
Date: Thu, 21 Jun 2001 8:08:51
From: Penny Driver <pdriver@catchpennylane.org>
To: housekeeper@pacbell.net

Andrew,
Finally got a commitment for some time off so I can come
visit. How does eight days starting on the 15th of July
sound? Let me know so I can book the ticket.
Love,
Penny

Following this there was a break of about ten lines, and then:

PS teLl Sam I fucking said hi . . . M

"Well," said Adam from the pulpit, "this should be an interesting little
get-together."

Sunday, June 24th, 2001, 7:35 A.M. (give or take a couple minutes): I am sitting in the Victorian's porch swing, drinking my morning coffee. I am not
waiting for anything—there's no mail today, and Penny isn't due for
another three weeks—I'm just watching the day get started, and thinking,
not too urgently, about what I want to do next with my life.

I have my fantasies, of course, about what may happen when Penny
finally does get here. I am grown up enough now to know that they are
only fantasies, however, and thus cannot be relied on. The truth is it's been
over a year and a half since I've seen Penny face to face, and while we have
tried to keep in touch during that time, I don't have that good a sense of
what she is like now (and if that P.S. from Maledicta isn't just a joke, it may
be that Penny doesn't know herself that well these days). So while I may
dream of her inviting me to come join her in San Diego, I am not going to
count on it.

Maybe we can do some fun things together while she is here, though.

As for farther in the future, after Mrs. Winslow sells the Victorian, I think I might travel for a while—deliberately, this time. I'd like to see some more of the country, see if there's anywhere else I might enjoy living, maybe someplace where land is cheap enough that I wouldn't have to rent.

I find myself thinking about New Mexico. I know that's Aunt Sam's dream, and so maybe she's just found some way of sneaking her desires into my subconscious—although Aunt Sam wants to live in Santa Fe, and I don't think I could afford to buy property there. Outside the city, though, out in the desert—maybe there I could have a few acres. Build my own house out of adobe: why not?

"Oh yeah," says Adam, "and if you grow straw you can make your own bricks. You could get Julie Sivik to fly down from Alaska and help you."

OK, so maybe it's not a practical idea.

Still, I can picture what the house might look like: small—one story would do, I think—but with a big porch or a patio facing east, a place to take my breakfasts in the morning sun. Some space around it, enough to plant a few trees, and a long open driveway that always lets me see who's coming. A garden out back. And inside, protected but not hidden, lots of shelves and cabinets and closets, so that everything I own, and everything I have yet to acquire, can find its rightful place.

ACKNOWLEDGMENTS

As always, I owe a lot of people, but by far my greatest debt is to my wife, Lisa Gold, who helped so constantly and in so many ways that she really deserves her own acknowledgments page. She acted variously as muse, sounding-board, critic, editor, proofreader, research assistant, best friend, cheerleader, business counselor, and general handler of things practical. Thanks, Lisa.

Thanks also to Michael B., whose questionable taste in women provided the initial inspiration for this story.

Thanks to my agent and second-greatest supporter, Melanie Jackson.

Thanks to my three editors: Dan Conaway, who got me going, Jennifer Hershey, who liked where I went, and Alison Callahan, who did a great job finishing up after Jennifer was lured away by a strange house.

Thanks to Brenda Cavender, for providing me with a truly amazing home to live in while I finished this book.

Thanks to Josh Spin, Greg Delaney, Neal Stephenson, Ellen Lackermann, Harold and Rita Gold, Susan Weinberg, Lydia Weaver, Elliott Beard, Olga Gardner Galvin, Michael McKenzie, Andrea Schaefer, Cynthia Geno, Lee Drake, Michael Alexander, Noah Price, Karen Carr, Lisa Fogelman, Jonathan Jacobs, George Coulouris, and Christodoulos Litharis. Thanks finally to the librarians, Web authors, and Usenet posters who helped answer my many research questions.

Visit Matt Ruff on the Web at www.bymattruff.com.

ABOUT THE AUTHOR

MATT RUFF is not a multiple personality, but he is an obsessive personality, a condition for which he self-medicates with marriage to a patient woman. He is the author of two previous novels, *Fool on the Hill* and *Sewer, Gas & Electric: The Public Works Trilogy*. He lives in Seattle, Washington, in what is arguably the most beautiful apartment house in the city.